The Norton Anthology of Contemporary Fiction

The Norton Anthology of Contemporary Fiction

R. V. Cassill
Brown University

W • W • NORTON & COMPANY • INC •
NEW YORK

Printed in the United States of America.

First Edition

Library of Congress Cataloging-in-Publication Data

The Norton anthology of contemporary fiction.

1. Short stories, American. 2. American fiction—20th century.
I. Cassill, R. V. (Ronald Verlin), 1919-
PS648.S5N67 1988 813'.01'08 87-20380

ISBN 0-393-95619-9

W. W. Norton & Company, Inc., 500 Fifth Avenue, New York, N.Y. 10110
W. W. Norton & Company Ltd., 37 Great Russell Street, London WC1B 3NU

1 2 3 4 5 6 7 8 9 0

ACKNOWLEDGMENTS

Alice Adams: "Barcelona" from *Return Trips* by Alice Adams. Copyright © 1984 by Alice Adams. Reprinted by permission of Alfred A. Knopf, Inc.

Woody Allen: "The Kugelmass Episode" Copyright © 1977 by Woody Allen. Reprinted from *Side Effects* by Woody Allen, by permission of Random House, Inc.

Margaret Atwood: "Rape Fantasies" from *Bluebeard's Egg*, published by McClelland & Stewart, 1983 and Houghton Mifflin, 1986. Used by permission of the author and the Canadian publishers, McClelland and Stewart Limited, Toronto.

John Barth: "Life Story" by John Barth from *Lost in the Funhouse*. Copyright © 1963, 1966, 1968, 1969 by John Barth. Reprinted by permission of Doubleday & Company, Inc.

Donald Barthelme: "The Indian Uprising" from *Unspeakable Practices, Unnatural Acts* by Donald Barthelme. Copyright © 1975 by Donald Barthelme. Reprinted by permission of Farrar, Straus and Giroux, Inc.

Ann Beattie: "The Burning House," Copyright © 1979 by Irony and Pity, Inc. Reprinted from *The Burning House: Short Stories* by Ann Beattie, by permission of Random House, Inc.

T. Coraghessan Boyle: "Decent of Man," Reprinted by permission of Georges Borchardt, Inc. and the author. Copyright © 1979 by T. Coraghessan Boyle. Originally published in *The Paris Review*.

Raymond Carver: "Where I'm Calling From" from *Cathedral* by Raymond Carver. Copyright © 1981, 1982, 1983 by Raymond Carver. Reprinted by permission of Alfred A. Knopf, Inc.

Robert Coover: "The Babysitter" from *Pricksongs & Descants* by Robert Coover. Copyright © 1969 by Robert Coover. Reprinted by permission of the publisher, E. P. Dutton, a division of New American Library.

Mark Costello: "Murphy's Christmas" from *The Murphy Stories* by Mark Costello. © 1967 by Mark Costello. Reprinted by permission of the University of Illinois Press.

Andre Dubus: "A Father's Story" from *The Times Are Never So Bad* by Andre Dubus. Copyright © 1983 by Andre Dubus. Reprinted by permission of David R. Godine, Publisher, Boston.

Louise Erdrich: "Saint Marie" from *Love Medicine* by Louise Erdrich. Copyright © 1984 by Louise Erdrich. Reprinted by permission of Henry Holt and Company.

Irvin Faust: "Roar Lion Roar" from *Roar Lion Roar and Other Stories* by Irvin Faust, published by Random House, Inc. Copyright © 1963 by Irvin Faust.

Ernest Gaines: "Just Like a Tree" by Ernest Gaines from *Bloodline*. Copyright © 1963 by Ernest J. Gaines. Reprinted by permission of Doubleday & Company, Inc.

Eugene Garber: "The Poets" reprinted from *Metaphysical Tales: Stories* by Eugene K. Garber by permission of the University of Missouri Press. Copyright © 1981 by Eugene K. Garber.

Gabriel Garcia Marquez: "The Handsomest Drowned Man in the World" from *Leaf Storm and Other Stories* by Gabriel Garcia Marquez. Translated from the Spanish by Gregory Rabassa. English translation copyright © 1971 by Gabriel Garcia Marquez.

George Garrett: "An Evening Performance" by George Garrett from *An Evening Performance*. Copyright © 1985 by George Garrett. Reprinted by permission of Doubleday & Company, Inc.

William Gass: "In the Heart of the Heart of the Country" reprinted by permission of International Creative Management. Copyright © 1968 by William Gass.

Oakley Hall: "Horseman" from *The Coming of the Kid* by Oakley Hall. Copyright © 1985 by Oakley Hall. Reprinted by permission of Harper & Row Publishers, Inc.

Amy Hempel: "In the Cemetery Where Al Jolson Is Buried" from *Reasons to Live* by Amy Hempel. Copyright © 1985 by Amy Hempel. Reprinted by permission of Alfred A. Knopf, Inc.

Jincy Kornhauser: "Melinda Falling" by Jincy Kornhauser. Reprinted by permission of Jincy Kornhauser.

William Kotzwinkle: "Follow the Eagle" from *Elephant Bangs Train*. Reprinted by permission of William Kotzwinkle. Copyright © 1969 William Kotzwinkle.

Ursula Le Guin: "The New Atlantis." Copyright © 1975 by Ursula K. Le Guin; reprinted by permission of the author and her agent, Virginia Kidd.

David Madden: "No Trace" from *The Shadow Knows*, copyright © by Louisiana State University Press, 1970. "No Trace" originally appeared in *The Southern Review*. Reprinted by permission of David Madden.

Susan Minot: "Lust," reprinted by permission of the author. Copyright © 1984 by Susan Minot. First published in *The Paris Review*.

Alice Munro: "The Beggar Maid" from *The Beggar Maid* by Alice Munro. Copyright © 1977, 1978 by Alice Munro. Reprinted by permission of Alfred A. Knopf, Inc.

Beth Nugent: "City of Boys" by Beth Nugent. First appeared in *The North American Review*, copyright © 1984 by the University of Northern Iowa.

Joyce Carol Oates: "How I Contemplated the World from the Detroit House of Correction and Began My Life Over Again" reprinted from *The Wheel of Love*

CONTENTS

INTRODUCTION

SWIFT and profound changes have marked the paths of all the arts in our century. It seems that no sooner have we acknowledged some trend to be contemporary than it shows signs of withering and yielding place to newer modes of experience and expression. In trying to decipher the meaning of the changes, we give abundant credit to historic events, evolutions in technology, the merchandising of fashions, and the continuing spread of popular education.

Obviously the short story changes with the pressures of changing times. But even as we grant this general truth, we must make the important qualification that this particular form has flourished and undergone mutations notably different from the courses of poetry, drama, or the novel. In a word, the story has been responsive to unique conditions in publishing and has maintained interest because it appealed to special expectations. Its persistence on the scene has been both humble and proud. Individual stories rarely become the bywords of an epoch as some novels do. In our time an almost uncountable number of stories are issued every year in magazines of minuscule circulation, yet somehow leave their collective traces on the sensibilities of the reading public. In their protean multiplication, they explore areas of contemporary existence that no other art would illumine. An anthology like this therefore celebrates not only the survival of a hardy literary form but its continuing energy and diversity.

In concentrating on what is contemporary we have to skimp historical lines of development. But, in doing so, we should acknowledge in a general way that the short story has a vivid history. It is a relatively new manifestation among the major literary forms. The niche it currently occupies in public consciousness is very different from what it was when O. Henry delighted a large audience of readers with the surprise endings of his stories published in popular magazines, or—to come a bit closer to the present—when Anderson, Hemingway, Fitzgerald, Lawrence, Mansfield, and Faulkner achieved a different sort of fame among readers of serious literature.

Certainly our contemporary fiction has debts to the master works—and to some of the more frivolous—written in times that have become history for us. The stories in this collection show that what is old, venerable, and sometimes faded can be given a new blush of life. It is a song sung in a new voice with fresh vigor. It is *ours* in a sense that need not be precisely defined because it will be felt.

Since our definition of what is contemporary must remain tentative, we must take some care not to assume it is the production of a particular generation. Old as well as young create the forms and images that are most emphatically present to our interests and most incisively address our concerns. Also to be avoided is the facile assumption which identifies the contemporary with the *avant garde*. By now, we have watched enough new experiments with form and language wither into musty quaintness after a brief period of celebrity that we should realize all of them are merely fractions of the art of any time, not the peak achievements they were proclaimed.

In recent times there has been a widespread interest in "post modernism" and the "new fiction." Part of this was inspired by a feeling that fiction ought to march at the pace of contemporary innovations in painting, music, and film. There was a groundswell of feeling that new "versions of reality" ought to be created in modern stories since conventional perceptions had become too dull and predictable to excite the imagination. As against these impulses to "depart from reality," there was a period when the "new journalism" was much in vogue because it borrowed devices from fiction (not the "new" variety) in order to stir the reader's sensuous imagination more forcibly than conventional journalism could.

What happened to fiiction as these counterforces pulled and hauled at it? Quite a lot, actually, and in many stories in this volume you will find alterations, tints, and shadings that probably would not have evolved without the more extreme programs advocated by critics and writers. Barth and Barthelme were activists and examples of the trend to resume the experimentation of "modern" writing early in the century. And in Beth Nugent or Oakley Hall can be seen the intent to skip from reality into the realm of fable. Nevertheless there is a certain inertia—something in the nature of the relation between words and the world of conscious experience —that exerts a continual drag against major departures from reality. As soon as a character is named and set in action, the old demands of the story and its actuality begin to exert themselves. The most imaginative program of experiment is domesticated to a degree, though not without leaving traces that often enrich the reading experience. Reality is given sublter colors.

It may be that the state of publishing itself has conditioned the short story as mightily as manifestoes or aesthetic theory. Short fiction is surely as popular now as it was fifty or a hundred years ago, but it reaches a different audience by different channels.

Time was when the circulation of stories was accomplished mainly by a wide spectrum of magazines, many of which have vanished with the advent of television or have changed their makeup to exclude fiction. Among the popular magazines only *The New*

Yorker has continued for more than half a century to blend a generous portion of fine fiction with articles, reviews, and topical commentary. In the days when family magazines were the main outlet for short stories, their concern with moral values exercised some constraints on the form, content, and attitudes to be included.

This is not to say that the writers who observed the constraints of that epoch were thereby emasculated. After all, most of Fitzgerald's stories were featured in "establishment" magazines, and Faulkner was, for several years, a regular contributor to *The Saturday Evening Post,* which was the very citadel of Middle American tastes in the Thirties. But yet in the same period it was in the novel that sexual candor, political extremism, and formal innovation advanced boldly. For examples, note: Joyce's *Ulysses,* Lawrence's *Lady Chatterley's Lover,* the aberrant sexuality in Djuna Barnes's *Nightwood,* or the experimental *montage* of Dos Passos's *USA* trilogy or Faulkner's *The Sound and The Fury.* And even in the little magazines before World War II, fiction was markedly conservative, as if in respect to the standards set by the Big Slicks.

Though it is by no means as simple as this, one can generalize that short fiction was liberated by losing its once lucrative market. It was never in the cards that stories would become extinct. Too many writers and readers of every period feel that what is dear, salty, melancholy, personal, and inescapable has to be delivered up to judgment in this form of writing. It carries the baggage that might be lost in more majestic vessels. So with the passage of a certain style of dissemination came a period when a whole new and differently conditioned population of readers perceived the still unrealized potential of the story. More people were writing it, and the expedients of writers and readers together wrought the means to make the art burgeon as never before. In a way it was being democratized, but standards were not swept away in the process. The new standard bearers became an army in their own right. In fact, there has been an expansion of accomplishment—going on to this day—that has outrun criticism of all sorts, so the critics can account for only a fraction of what has been created in the last decades.

Surely the expanded vitality of the short story had a good bit to do with the multiplying numbers of students enrolled in college. In higher education they were encouraged not only by examples of historic literature but with the idea that imaginative writing is a commitment available to anyone with the inclination to make it. No longer was it being argued that journalism is the proper apprenticeship for a writer. Courses in creative writing—with short stories as their main product—go on proliferating at an astonishing rate. This melding of creative work with general literary education has educated readers of fiction as well as writers. Under such combinations of stimuli, the short story has been enhanced to do the poetic work of journalism and the yeoman work of poetry.

The swelling success of stories in our time is due in part, also, to the role of anthologies of all sorts. We often think of anthologies as merely a form of packaging, a convenience for academic usage or readers for pleasure—a gathering of many goodies in one basket—to dip into on a leisurely cruise, perhaps. Yet, just as large and small magazines have influenced the quality of fiction over the decades, so have the kinds of collections to be found in anthologies. Those with a special bias have advertised new trends. Others have brought together the best quality of work being done without regard to program, manner, or topic.

To be sure anthologies are gathered from other initial forms of publication—from magazines most often, or sometimes from a book collection by a single author. The initial printing is often makeshift, ephemeral, or merely inadequate to reach the audience particular stories deserve. Every anthology is a reconsideration and a resifting, giving a degree of permanence to stories that might have blown away in the breeze without this second incarnation. The anthology makes an individual story public not merely by offering it to a more substantial audience but also by setting it among other stories that will enrich it with their reflected tones and lights. Sometimes an anthology rescues a deservedly famous story from the fog of boredom that can dull even an ardent reader when he sets out to wade through the collected works of a master. I would hardly suggest that a story by Ernest Hemingway, Flannery O'Connor, or John Cheever is in better company in an anthology than in the collections of these authors, but only that the anthologized piece may show off different facets of excellence when it appears in the multicolored company of an anthology. And who can guess how many readers go on to the collected works from an enthusiasm generated by a first acquaintance made in an anthology?

Such serial anthologies as the annual *Best American Stories*, the *O. Henry Prize Stories*, and the *New Directions* anthology have offered serious and substantial publication to first rate writers through all the times I can remember. In keeping with recent shifts in the publishing base, *The Pushcart Prize* annually gathers what its editors consider the best from the offerings of small presses subsidized by universities or, more often, kept afloat by the commitment of devoted individuals with no commercial incentive. *Intro* gathers the best from the college writing programs banded together as the Associated Writing Program. *The New Yorker* and *Esquire*—and at the other extreme such small ventures as *Accent* and *Epoch*—have occasionally gathered into anthology form the best fiction printed over a period of years.

But on a much larger scale, and with a more definitive impact on the taste of readers, and thereby on the shape and quality of the art, publishers of college texts have made available since the early Fifties a very large number of fiction anthologies. It is not too much to say that this ongoing tide has provided the luckiest of forums where maturing generations of writers were exposed to maturing generations of readers to the profit of both.

In choosing stories for this anthology, I somewhat arbitrarily took only those published since 1960. Who is to say that such a cut-off date guarantees that they are—in a satisfying sense—contemporary? All such categories blur almost before we can mark them. It must suffice to insist that I have meant to show the present state of the art and, as far as subject matter is concerned, to show the mutant rainbow of circumstances that have engaged our best witnesses in the decades just past.

Most of the fears, quandaries, and exaltations that have preoccupied literature from its beginnings are here. The celebrated circumstances of the Sixties, Seventies, and Eighties are polished by the subtleties of the fictive imagination. If—as Dryden said of a much earlier epoch—the wars brought nothing about and the loves were all untrue, yet our loves and our wars are what our writers reclaim and build from. Stories like David Madden's "No Trace" and Tim O'Brien's "Going After Cacciato" may help us reclaim the tragedy of the Vietnam War. Janet Beeler Shaw and Jincy Kornhauser do not find love to be "the same old story," as the popular song puts it. There are new masquerades for the timeless passions. This is the way we are, in the ranks of our time, with the quick and the experimental dancing to the same drums of fate as the backward-looking and the reluctant.

ALICE ADAMS

Barcelona

IN the darkened, uneven cobbled square, in the old quarter of Barcelona, the Barrio Gótico, the middle-aged American couple who walk by appear to be just that: American, middle-aged. The man is tall and bald; his head shines dimly as he and his wife cross the shaft of light from an open doorway. She is smaller, with pale hair; she walks fast to keep up with her husband. She is wearing gold chains, and they, too, shine in the light. She carries a small bag in which there could be—more gold? money? some interesting pills? They pass a young Spaniard lounging in a corner whose face the man for no reason takes note of.

Persis Fox, the woman, is a fairly successful illustrator, beginning to be sought after by New York publishers, but she sees herself as being in most ways a coward, a very fearful person; she is afraid of planes, of high bridges, she is overly worried by the illnesses of children—a rather boring list, as she thinks of it. Some years ago she was afraid that Thad, her husband, who teaches at Harvard, would take off with some student, some dark, sexily athletic type from Texas, possibly. More recently she has been frightened by accounts everywhere of muggings, robberies, rapes. She entirely believes in the likelihood of nuclear war. She can and does lie awake at night with such thoughts, for frozen hours.

However, walking across these darkened cobbles, in the old quarter of Barcelona, toward a restaurant that Cambridge friends have recommended, she is not afraid at all, only interested in what she is seeing: just before the square, an arched and windowed walk up above the alley, now crenellated silhouettes, everywhere blackened old stones. Also, she is hungry, looking forward to the seafood for which this restaurant is famous. And she wishes that Thad would not walk so fast; by now he is about five feet ahead of her, in an alley.

In the next instant, though, before she has seen or heard any person approaching, someone is running past her in the dark—but not past; he is beside her, a tall dark boy, grabbing at her purse, pulling its short strap. Persis' first instinct is to let him have it, not because she is afraid—she is not, still not, afraid—but from a conditioned reflex, instructing her to give people what they want: children, her husband.

In the following second a more primitive response sets in, and she cries out, "No!"—as she thinks, Kindergarten, some little boy pulling something away. And next thinks, Not kindergarten. Spain. A thief.

He is stronger, and with a sudden sharp tug he wins; he has pulled the bag from her and run off, as Persis still yells, "No!"—and as (amazingly!) she remembers the word for thief. "LADRÓN!" she cries out. "*Ladrón!*"

Then suddenly Thad is back (Persis has not exactly thought of him in those seconds), and almost before she has finished saying "He took my bag!" Thad is running toward the square, where the thief went. Thad is running, running—so tall and fast, such a sprint, as though this were a marathon, or Memorial Drive, where he usually runs. He is off into the night, as Persis yells again, "*Ladrón!*" and she starts out after him.

Persis is wearing low boots (thank God), not heels, and she can hear Thad's whistle, something he does with two fingers in his mouth, intensely shrill, useful for summoning children from ski slopes or beaches as night comes on. Persis, also running, follows the sound. She comes at last to a fairly wide, dimly lit street where Thad is standing, breathing hard.

She touches his arm. "Thad—"

Still intent on the chase, he hardly looks at her. He is not doing this for her; it is something between men. He says, "I think he went that way."

"But Thad—"

The street down which he is pointing, and into which he now begins to stride, with Persis just following—this street's darkness is broken at intervals by the steamy yellow windows of shabby restaurants, the narrow open door of a bar. Here and there a few people stand in doorways, watching the progress of the Americans. Thad sticks his head into the restaurants, the bar. "I don't see him," he reports back each time.

Well, of course not. And of course each time Persis is glad—glad that the boy is hidden somewhere. Gone. Safe, as she and Thad are safe.

They reach the end of the block, when from behind them a voice calls out, in English, not loudly, "Lady, this your bag?"

Thad and Persis turn to see a dark, contemptuous young face, a tall boy standing in a doorway. Not, Thad later assures Persis, and later still their friends—not the thief, whom he saw as they first crossed the square, and would recognize. But a friend of his?

The boy kicks his foot at something on the cobbles, which Thad walks over to pick up, and which is Persis' bag.

"I can't believe it!" she cries out, aware of triteness, as Thad hands over the bag to her. But by now, now that everything is over, she is seriously frightened; inwardly she trembles.

"Well, we got it." Thad speaks calmly, but Persis can hear the pride in his voice, along with some nervousness. He is still breathing hard, but he has begun to walk with his purposeful stride again. "The restaurant must be down here," he tells her.

Astoundingly, it is; after a couple of turns they see the name on a red neon sign, the name of the place they have been told about, where they have made a reservation.

The kitchen seems to be in the front room, next to the bar: all steam and steel, noisy clanging. Smoke and people, glasses rattling, crashing. "I really need a drink," Persis tells Thad, as instead they are led back to a room full of tables, people—many Americans, tourists, all loud and chattering.

At their small table, waiting for wine, with his tight New England smile Thad asks, "Aren't you going to check it? See what's still there?"

Curiously, this has not yet occurred to Persis as something to be done; she has simply clutched the bag. Now, as she looks down at the bag on her lap, it seems shabbier, a battered survivor. Obediently she unsnaps the flap. "Oh good, my passport's here," she tells Thad.

"That's great." He is genuinely pleased with himself—and why should he not be, having behaved with such courage? Then he frowns. "He got all your money?"

"Well no, actually there wasn't any money. I keep it in my pocket. Always, when I go to New York, that's what I do."

Why does Thad look so confused just then? A confusion of emotions is spread across his fair, lined face. He is disappointed, somehow? Upset that he ran after a thief who had stolen a bag containing so little? Upset that Persis, who now goes down to New York on publishing business by herself, has tricks for self-preservation?

Sipping wine, and almost instantly dizzy, light in her head, Persis tries to explain herself. "Men are such dopes," she heedlessly starts. "They always think that women carry everything they own in their bags. Thieves think that, I mean. So I just shove money and credit cards into some pocket. There's only makeup in my bags."

"And your passport." Stern, judicious Thad.

"Oh yes, of course," Persis babbles. "That would have been terrible. We could have spent days in offices."

Gratified, sipping at his wine, Thad says, "I wonder why he didn't take it, actually."

Persis does not say, "Because it's hidden inside my address book"—although quite possibly that was the case. Instead, she says what is also surely true: "Because you scared him. The last thing he expected was someone running after him, and that *whistle*."

Thad smiles, and his face settles into a familiar expression: that of a generally secure, intelligent man, a lucky person, for whom things happen more or less as he would expect them to.

Persis is thinking, and not for the first time, how terrible it must be to be a man, how terrifying. Men are always running, chasing something. And if you are rich and successful, like Thad, you have to hunt down anyone who wants to take away your possessions. Or if you're poor, down on your luck, you might be tempted to chase after a shabby bag that holds nothing of any real value, to snatch such a bag from a foreign woman who is wearing false gold chains that shine and glimmer in the dark.

WOODY ALLEN

The Kugelmass Episode

KUGELMASS, a professor of humanities at City College, was unhappily married for the second time. Daphne Kugelmass was an oaf. He also had two dull sons by his first wife, Flo, and was up to his neck in alimony and child support.

"Did I know it would turn out so badly?" Kugelmass whined to his analyst one day. "Daphne had promise. Who suspected she'd let herself go and swell up like a beach ball? Plus she had a few bucks, which is not in itself a healthy reason to marry a person, but it doesn't hurt, with the kind of operating nut[1] I have. You see my point?"

Kugelmass was bald and as hairy as a bear, but he had soul.

"I need to meet a new woman," he went on. "I need to have an affair. I may not look the part, but I'm a man who needs romance. I need softness, I need flirtation. I'm not getting younger, so before it's too late I want to make love in Venice, trade quips at '21,'[2] and exchange coy glances over red wine and candlelight. You see what I'm saying?"

Dr. Mandel shifted in his chair and said, "An affair will solve nothing. You're so unrealistic. Your problems run much deeper."

"And also this affair must be discreet," Kugelmass continued. "I can't afford a second divorce. Daphne would really sock it to me."

"Mr. Kugelmass—"

"But it can't be anyone at City College, because Daphne also works there. Not that anyone on the faculty at C.C.N.Y. is any great shakes, but some of those coeds . . ."

"Mr. Kugelmass—"

"Help me. I had a dream last night. I was skipping through a meadow holding a picnic basket and the basket was marked 'Options.' And then I saw there was a hole in the basket."

"Mr. Kugelmass, the worst thing you could do is act out. You must simply express your feelings here, and together we'll analyze

1. Budget, expenses. 2. Celebrity nightclub and restaurant.

them. You have been in treatment long enough to know there is no overnight cure. After all, I'm an analyst, not a magician."

"Then perhaps what I need is a magician," Kugelmass said, rising from his chair. And with that he terminated his therapy.

A couple of weeks later, while Kugelmass and Daphne were moping around in their apartment one night like two pieces of old furniture, the phone rang.

"I'll get it," Kugelmass said. "Hello."

"Kugelmass?" a voice said. "Kugelmass, this is Persky."

"Who?"

"Persky. Or should I say The Great Persky?"

"Pardon me?"

"I hear you're looking all over town for a magician to bring a little exotica into your life? Yes or no?"

"S-h-h," Kugelmass whispered. "Don't hang up. Where are you calling from, Persky?"

Early the following afternoon, Kugelmass climbed three flights of stairs in a broken-down apartment house in the Bushwick section of Brooklyn. Peering through the darkness of the hall, he found the door he was looking for and pressed the bell. I'm going to regret this, he thought to himself.

Seconds later, he was greeted by a short, thin, waxy-looking man.

"*You're* Persky the Great?" Kugelmass said.

"The Great Persky. You want a tea?"

"No, I want romance. I want music. I want love and beauty."

"But not tea, eh? Amazing. O.K., sit down."

Persky went to the back room, and Kugelmass heard the sounds of boxes and furniture being moved around. Persky reappeared, pushing before him a large object on squeaky roller-skate wheels. He removed some old silk handkerchiefs that were lying on its top and blew away a bit of dust. It was a cheap-looking Chinese cabinet, badly lacquered.

"Persky," Kugelmass said, "what's your scam?"[3]

"Pay attention," Persky said. "This is some beautiful effect. I developed it for a Knights of Pythias[4] date last year, but the booking fell through. Get into the cabinet."

"Why, so you can stick it full of swords or something?"

"You see any swords?"

Kugelmass made a face and, grunting, climbed into the cabinet. He couldn't help noticing a couple of ugly rhinestones glued onto the raw plywood just in front of his face. "If this is a joke," he said.

"Some joke. Now, here's the point. If I throw any novel into this cabinet with you, shut the doors, and tap it three times, you will find yourself projected into that book."

Kugelmass made a grimace of disbelief.

3. Scheme, confidence trick. **4. Secret fraternal society.**

"It's the emess,"[5] Persky said. "My hand to God. Not just a novel, either. A short story, a play, a poem. You can meet any of the women created by the world's best writers. Whoever you dreamed of. You could carry on all you like with a real winner. Then when you've had enough you give a yell, and I'll see you're back here in a split second."

"Persky, are you some kind of outpatient?"

"I'm telling you it's on the level," Persky said.

Kugelmass remained skeptical. "What are you telling me—that this cheesy homemade box can take me on a ride like you're describing?"

"For a double sawbuck."[6]

Kugelmass reached for his wallet. "I'll believe this when I see it," he said.

Persky tucked the bills in his pants pocket and turned toward his bookcase. "So who do you want to meet? Sister Carrie? Hester Prynne? Ophelia? Maybe someone by Saul Bellow? Hey, what about Temple Drake?[7] Although for a man your age she'd be a workout."

"French. I want to have an affair with a French lover."

"Nana"[8]

"I don't want to have to pay for it."

"What about Natasha in 'War and Peace'?"[9]

"I said French. I know! What about Emma Bovary? That sounds to me perfect."

"You got it, Kugelmass. Give me a holler when you've had enough." Persky tossed in a paperback copy of Flaubert's novel.

"You sure this is safe?" Kugelmass asked as Persky began shutting the cabinet doors.

"Safe. Is anything safe in this crazy world?" Persky rapped three times on the cabinet and then flung open the doors.

Kugelmass was gone. At the same moment, he appeared in the bedroom of Charles and Emma Bovary's house at Yonville.[1] Before him was a beautiful woman, standing alone with her back turned to him as she folded some linen. I can't believe this, thought Kugelmass, staring at the doctor's ravishing wife. This is uncanny. I'm here. It's her.

Emma turned in surprise. "Goodness, you startled me," she said. "Who are you?" She spoke in the same fine English translation as the paperback.

5. Truth. **6.** Twenty dollars. **7.** Respectively, the fallen heroine of Theodore Dreiser's *Sister Carrie* (1900); the adulterous heroine of Nathaniel Hawthorne's *The Scarlet Letter* (1850); Hamlet's fiancée, who drowns herself; Bellow's heroines are intensely neurotic, sexual, and vindictive; the victim of a bizarre rape in Faulkner's *Sanctuary* (1931), who is also the heroine of his *Requiem for a Nun* (1950). **8.** Prostitute-heroine of Émile Zola's *Nana* (1880). **9.** Saucy heroine of the novel, 1865–69, by Tolstoy. **1.** Fictional town in Normandy, where much of Flaubert's novel *Madame Bovary* (1857) is set.

It's simply devastating, he thought. Then, realizing that it was he whom she had addressed, he said, "Excuse me. I'm Sidney Kugelmass. I'm from City College. A professor of humanities. C.C.N.Y.? Uptown. I—oh, boy!"

Emma Bovary smiled flirtatiously and said, "Would you like a drink? A glass of wine, perhaps?"

She is beautiful, Kugelmass thought. What a contrast with the troglodyte who shared his bed! He felt a sudden impulse to take this vision into his arms and tell her she was the kind of woman he had dreamed of all his life.

"Yes, some wine," he said hoarsely. "White. No, red. No, white. Make it white."

"Charles is out for the day," Emma said, her voice full of playful implication.

After the wine, they went for a stroll in the lovely French countryside. "I've always dreamed that some mysterious stranger would appear and rescue me from the monotony of this crass rural existence," Emma said, clasping his hand. They passed a small church. "I love what you have on," she murmured. "I've never seen anything like it around here. It's so . . . so modern."

"It's called a leisure suit," he said romantically. "It was marked down." Suddenly he kissed her. For the next hour they reclined under a tree and whispered together and told each other deeply meaningful things with their eyes. Then Kugelmass sat up. He had just remembered he had to meet Daphne at Bloomingdale's. "I must go," he told her, "But don't worry, I'll be back."

"I hope so," Emma said.

He embraced her passionately, and the two walked back to the house. He held Emma's face cupped in his palms, kissed her again, and yelled, "O.K., Persky! I got to be at Bloomingdale's by three-thirty."

There was an audible pop, and Kugelmass was back in Brooklyn.

"So? Did I lie?" Persky asked triumphantly.

"Look, Persky, I'm right now late to meet the ball and chain at Lexington Avenue, but when can I go again? Tomorrow?"

"My pleasure. Just bring a twenty. And don't mention this to anybody."

"Yeah. I'm going to call Rupert Murdoch."[2]

Kugelmass hailed a cab and sped off to the city. His heart danced on point. I am in love, he thought, I am the possessor of a wonderful secret. What he didn't realize was that at this very moment students in various classrooms across the country were saying to their teachers, "Who is this character on page 100? A bald Jew is

2. Australian newspaper baron, who, in addition to several British papers, owns the New York *Post*, the *Village Voice*, and *New York* magazine.

kissing Madame Bovary?" A teacher in Sioux Falls, South Dakota, sighed and thought, Jesus, these kids, with their pot and acid. What goes through their minds!

Daphne Kugelmass was in the bathroom-accessories department at Bloomingdale's when Kugelmass arrived breathlessly. "Where've you been?" she snapped. "It's four-thirty."

"I got held up in traffic," Kugelmass said.

Kugelmass visited Persky the next day, and in a few minutes was again passed magically to Yonville. Emma couldn't hide her excitement at seeing him. The two spent hours together, laughing and talking about their different backgrounds. Before Kugelmass left, they made love. "My God, I'm doing it with Madame Bovary!" Kugelmass whispered to himself. "Me, who failed freshman English."

As the months passed, Kugelmass saw Persky many times and developed a close and passionate relationship with Emma Bovary. "Make sure and always get me into the book before page 120," Kugelmass said to the magician one day. "I always have to meet her before she hooks up with this Rodolphe character."[3]

"Why?" Persky asked. "You can't beat his time?"

"Beat his time. He's landed gentry. Those guys have nothing better to do than flirt and ride horses. To me, he's one of those faces you see in the pages of *Women's Wear Daily*. With the Helmut Berger[4] hairdo. But to her he's hot stuff."

"And her husband suspects nothing?"

"He's out of his depth. He's a lackluster little paramedic who's thrown in his lot with a jitterbug. He's ready to go to sleep by ten, and she's putting on her dancing shoes. Oh, well . . . See you later."

And once again Kugelmass entered the cabinet and passed instantly to the Bovary estate at Yonville. "How you doing, cupcake?" he said to Emma.

"Oh, Kugelmass," Emma sighed. "What I have to put up with. Last night at dinner, Mr. Personality dropped off to sleep in the middle of the dessert course. I'm pouring my heart out about Maxim's[5] and the ballet, and out of the blue I hear snoring."

"It's O.K., darling. I'm here now," Kugelmass said, embracing her. I've earned this, he thought, smelling Emma's French perfume and burying his nose in her hair. I've suffered enough. I've paid enough analysts. I've searched till I'm weary. She's young and nubile, and I'm here a few pages after Léon and just before

3. The provincial aristocratic womanizer who seduces Emma, after she has a first romantic, idealistic flirtation with the mooning young Léon (who is mentioned below). The Abbé Bournisien and Binet, mentioned later, are minor characters in the novel.
4. Handsome German actor (b. 1942). *Women's Wear Daily* is a gossipy New York fashion newspaper. **5.** Fashionable Paris restaurant.

Rodolphe. By showing up during the correct chapters, I've got the situation knocked.

Emma, to be sure, was just as happy as Kugelmass. She had been starved for excitement, and his tales of Broadway night life, of fast cars and Hollywood and TV stars, enthralled the young French beauty.

"Tell me again about O.J. Simpson."[6] she implored that evening, as she and Kugelmass strolled past Abbé Bournisien's church.

"What can I say? The man is great. He sets all kinds of rushing records. Such moves. They can't touch him."

"And the Academy Awards?" Emma said wistfully. "I'd give anything to win one."

"First you've got to be nominated."

"I know. You explained it. But I'm convinced I can act. Of course, I'd want to take a class or two. With Strasberg[7] maybe. Then, if I had the right agent—"

"We'll see, we'll see. I'll speak to Persky."

That night, safely returned to Persky's flat, Kugelmass brought up the idea of having Emma visit him in the big city.

"Let me think about it," Persky said. "Maybe I could work it. Stranger things have happened." Of course, neither of them could think of one.

"Where the hell do you go all the time?" Daphne Kugelmass barked at her husband as he returned home late that evening. "You got a chippie stashed somewhere?"

"Yeah, sure, I'm just the type," Kugelmass said wearily. "I was with Leonard Popkin. We were discussing Socialist agriculture in Poland. You know Popkin. He's a freak on the subject."

"Well, you've been very odd lately," Daphne said. "Distant. Just don't forget about my father's birthday. On Saturday?"

"Oh, sure, sure," Kugelmass said, heading for the bathroom.

"My whole family will be there. We can see the twins. And Cousin Hamish. You should be more polite to Cousin Hamish—he likes you."

"Right, the twins," Kugelmass said, closing the bathroom door and shutting out the sound of his wife's voice. He leaned against it and took a deep breath. In a few hours, he told himself, he would be back in Yonville again, back with his beloved. And this time, if all went well, he would bring Emma back with him.

At three-fifteen the following afternoon, Persky worked his wizardry again. Kugelmass appeared before Emma, smiling and eager. The two spent a few hours at Yonville with Binet and then re-

6. Famous football running back. **7.** Lee Strasberg's acting school teaches the natural acting style known as "The Method."

mounted the Bovary carriage. Following Persky's instructions, they held each other tightly, closed their eyes, and counted to ten. When they opened them, the carriage was just drawing up at the side door of the Plaza Hotel, where Kugelmass had optimistically reserved a suite earlier in the day.

"I love it! It's everything I dreamed it would be," Emma said as she swirled joyously around the bedroom, surveying the city from their window. "There's F.A.O. Schwarz.[8] And there's Central Park, and the Sherry[9] is which one? Oh, there—I see. It's too divine."

On the bed there were boxes from Halston and Saint Laurent.[1] Emma unwrapped a package and held up a pair of black velvet pants against her perfect body.

"The slacks suit is by Ralph Lauren," Kugelmass said. "You'll look like a million bucks in it. Come on, sugar, give us a kiss."

"I've never been so happy!" Emma squealed as she stood before the mirror. "Let's go out on the town. I want to see 'Chorus Line' and the Guggenheim[2] and this Jack Nicholson character you always talk about. Are any of his flicks showing?"

"I cannot get my mind around this," a Stanford professor said. "First a strange character named Kugelmass, and now she's gone from the book. Well, I guess the mark of a classic is that you can reread it a thousand times and always find something new."

The lovers passed a blissful weekend. Kugelmass had told Daphne he would be away at a symposium in Boston and would return Monday. Savoring each moment, he and Emma went to the movies, had dinner in Chinatown, passed two hours at a discothèque, and went to bed with a TV movie. They slept till noon on Sunday, visited SoHo, and ogled celebrities at Elaine's.[3] They had caviar and champagne in their suite on Sunday night and talked until dawn. That morning, in the cab taking them to Persky's apartment, Kugelmass thought, It was hectic, but worth it. I can't bring her here too often, but now and then it will be a charming contrast with Yonville.

At Persky's, Emma climbed into the cabinet, arranged her new boxes of clothes neatly around her, and kissed Kugelmass fondly. "My place next time," she said with a wink. Persky rapped three times on the cabinet. Nothing happened.

"Hmm," Persky said, scratching his head. He rapped again, but still no magic. "Something must be wrong," he mumbled.

"Persky, you're joking!" Kugelmass cried. "How can it not work?"

"Relax, relax. Are you still in the box, Emma?"

"Yes."

8. Well-known toy store. **9.** Sherry-Netherland Hotel. **1.** Famous and expensive fashion designers and couturiers, as is Ralph Lauren, below. **2.** The Solomon R. Guggenheim Museum. **3.** Restaurant frequented by publishing and newspaper notables. SoHo is the center of the contemporary art scene, south of Greenwich Village.

Persky rapped again—harder this time.

"I'm still here, Persky."

"I know, darling. Sit tight."

"Persky, we *have* to get her back," Kugelmass whispered. "I'm a married man, and I have a class in three hours. I'm not prepared for anything more than a cautious affair at this point."

"I can't understand it," Persky muttered. "It's such a reliable little trick."

But he could do nothing. "It's going to take a little while," he said to Kugelmass. "I'm going to have to strip it down. I'll call you later."

Kugelmass bundled Emma into a cab and took her back to the Plaza. He barely made it to his class on time. He was on the phone all day, to Persky and to his mistress. The magician told him it might be several days before he got to the bottom of the trouble.

"How was the symposium?" Daphne asked him that night.

"Fine, fine," he said, lighting the filter end of a cigarette.

"What's wrong? You're as tense as a cat."

"Me? Ha, that's a laugh. I'm as calm as a summer night. I'm just going to take a walk." He eased out the door, hailed a cab, and flew to the Plaza.

"This is no good," Emma said. "Charles will miss me."

"Bear with me, sugar," Kugelmass said. He was pale and sweaty. He kissed her again, raced to the elevators, yelled at Persky over a pay phone in the Plaza lobby, and just made it home before midnight.

"According to Popkin, barley prices in Kraków have not been this stable since 1971, he said to Daphne, and smiled wanly as he climbed into bed.

The whole week went by like that. On Friday night, Kugelmass told Daphne there was another symposium he had to catch, this one in Syracuse. He hurried back to the Plaza, but the second weekend there was nothing like the first. "Get me back into the novel or marry me," Emma told Kugelmass. "Meanwhile, I want to get a job or go to class, because watching TV all day is the pits."

"Fine. We can use the money," Kugelmass said. "You consume twice your weight in room service."

"I met an Off Broadway producer in Central Park yesterday, and he said I might be right for a project he's doing," Emma said.

"Who is this clown?" Kugelmass asked.

"He's not a clown. He's sensitive and kind and cute. His name's Jeff Something-or-Other, and he's up for a Tony."[4]

Later that afternoon, Kugelmass showed up at Persky's drunk.

"Relax," Persky told him. "You'll get a coronary."

4. Broadway Drama Critics' Award comparable to Oscar.

"Relax. The man says relax. I've got a fictional character stashed in a hotel room, and I think my wife is having me tailed by a private shamus."

"O.K., O.K. We know there's a problem." Persky crawled under the cabinet and started banging on something with a large wrench.

"I'm like a wild animal," Kugelmass went on. "I'm sneaking around town, and Emma and I have had it up to here with each other. Not to mention a hotel tab that reads like the defense budget."

"So what should I do? This is the world of magic," Persky said. "It's all nuance."

"Nuance, my foot. I'm pouring Dom Pérignon and black eggs[5] into this little mouse, plus her wardrobe, plus she's enrolled at the Neighborhood Playhouse[6] and suddenly needs professional photos. Also, Persky, Professor Fivish Kopkind, who teaches Comp Lit and who has always been jealous of me, has identified me as the sporadically appearing character in the Flaubert book. He's threatened to go to Daphne. I see ruin and alimony jail. For adultery with Madame Bovary, my wife will reduce me to beggary."

"What do you want me to say? I'm working on it night and day. As far as your personal anxiety goes, that I can't help you with. I'm a magician, not an analyst."

By Sunday afternoon, Emma had locked herself in the bathroom and refused to respond to Kugelmass's entreaties. Kugelmass stared out the window at the Wollman Rink[7] and contemplated suicide. Too bad this is a low floor, he thought, or I'd do it right now. Maybe if I ran away to Europe and started life over . . . Maybe I could sell the *International Herald Tribune*, like those young girls used to.

The phone rang. Kugelmass lifted it to his ear mechanically.

"Bring her over," Persky said. "I think I got the bugs out of it."

Kugelmass's heart leaped. "You're serious?" he said. "You got it licked?"

"It was something in the transmission. Go figure."

"Persky, you're a genius. We'll be there in a minute. Less than a minute."

Again the lovers hurried to the magician's apartment, and again Emma Bovary climbed into the cabinet with her boxes. This time there was no kiss. Persky shut the doors, took a deep breath, and tapped the box three times. There was the reassuring popping noise, and when Persky peered inside, the box was empty. Madame Bovary was back in her novel. Kugelmass heaved a great sigh of relief and pumped the magician's hand.

"It's over," he said. "I learned my lesson. I'll never cheat again, I

5. An especially fine champagne and caviar. **6.** Famous acting school. **7.** Skating rink in Central Park.

swear it." He pumped Persky's hand again and made a mental note to send him a necktie.

Three weeks later, at the end of a beautiful spring afternoon, Persky answered his doorbell. It was Kugelmass, with a sheepish expression on his face.

"O.K., Kugelmass," the magician said. "Where to this time?"

"It's just this once," Kugelmass said. "The weather is so lovely, and I'm not getting any younger. Listen, you've read 'Portnoy's Complaint'? Remember The Monkey?"[8]

"The price is now twenty-five dollars, because the cost of living is up, but I'll start you with one freebie, due to all the trouble I caused you."

"You're good people," Kugelmass said, combing his few remaining hairs as he climbed into the cabinet again. "This'll work all right?"

"I hope. But I haven't tried it much since all that unpleasantness."

"Sex and romance," Kugelmass said from inside the box. "What we go through for a pretty face."

Persky tossed in a copy of "Portnoy's Complaint" and rapped three times on the box. This time, instead of a popping noise there was a dull explosion, followed by a series of crackling noises and a shower of sparks. Persky leaped back, was seized by a heart attack, and dropped dead. The cabinet burst into flames, and eventually the entire house burned down.

Kugelmass, unaware of this catastrophe, had his own problems. He had not been thrust into "Portnoy's Complaint," or into any other novel, for that matter. He had been projected into an old textbook, "Remedial Spanish," and was running for his life over a barren, rocky terrain as the word "*tener*" ("to have")—a large and hairy irregular verb—raced after him on its spindly legs.

8. The leading character in Philip Roth's 1969 novel.

MARGARET ATWOOD

Rape Fantasies

THE way they're going on about it in the magazines you'd think it was just invented, and not only that but it's something terrific, like a vaccine for cancer. They put it in capital letters on the front cover, and inside they have these questionnaires like the ones they used to have about whether you were a good enough wife or an endomorph or an ectomorph,[1] remember that? with the scoring upside

1. Popularized terms for types of body structure.

down on page 73, and then these numbered do-it-yourself dealies, you know? RAPE, TEN THINGS TO DO ABOUT IT, like it was ten new hairdos or something. I mean, what's so new about it?

So at work they all have to talk about it because no matter what magazine you open, there it is, staring you right between the eyes, and they're beginning to have it on the television, too. Personally I'd prefer a June Allyson movie[2] anytime but they don't make them any more and they don't even have them that much on the Late Show. For instance, day before yesterday, that would be Wednesday, thank god it's Friday as they say, we were sitting around in the women's lunch room—the *lunch* room, I mean you'd think you could get some peace and quiet in there—and Chrissy closes up the magazine she's been reading and says, "How about it, girls, do you have rape fantasies?"

The four of us were having our game of bridge the way we always do, and I had a bare twelve points counting the singleton with not that much of a bid in anything. So I said one club, hoping Sondra would remember about the one club convention, because the time before when I used that she thought I really meant clubs and she bid us up to three, and all I had was four little ones with nothing higher than a six, and we went down two and on top of that we were vulnerable. She is not the world's best bridge player. I mean, neither am I but there's a limit.

Darlene passed but the damage was done, Sondra's head went round like it was on ball bearings and she said, "*What* fantasies?"

"Rape fantasies," Chrissy said. She's a receptionist and she looks like one; she's pretty but cool as a cucumber, like she's been painted all over with nail polish, if you know what I mean. Varnished. "It says here all women have rape fantasies."

"For Chrissake, I'm eating an egg sandwich," I said, "and I bid one club and Darlene passed."

"You mean, like some guy jumping you in an alley or something," Sondra said. She was eating her lunch, we all eat our lunches during the game, and she bit into a piece of that celery she always brings and started to chew away on it with this thoughtful expression in her eyes and I knew we might as well pack it in as far as the game was concerned.

"Yeah, sort of like that," Chrissy said. She was blushing a little, you could see it even under her makeup.

"I don't think you should go out alone at night," Darlene said, "you put yourself in a position," and I may have been mistaken but she was looking at me. She's the oldest, she's forty-one though you wouldn't know it and neither does she, but I looked it up in the employees' file. I like to guess a person's age and then look it up to see if I'm right. I let myself have an extra pack of cigarettes if I am, though I'm trying to cut down. I figure it's harmless as long as you don't tell. I mean, not every-

2. Sentimentalized love story.

one has access to that file, it's more or less confidential. But it's all right if I tell you, I don't expect you'll ever meet her, though you never know, it's a small world. Anyway.

"For *heaven's* sake, it's only *Toronto*," Greta said. She worked in Detroit for three years and she never lets you forget it, it's like she thinks she's a war hero or something, we should all admire her just for the fact that she's still walking this earth, though she was really living in Windsor the whole time, she just worked in Detroit. Which for me doesn't really count. It's where you sleep, right?

"Well, do you?" Chrissy said. She was obviously trying to tell us about hers but she wasn't about to go first, she's cautious, that one.

"I certainly don't," Darlene said, and she wrinkled up her nose, like this, and I had to laugh. "I think it's disgusting." She's divorced, I read that in the file too, she never talks about it. It must've been years ago anyway. She got up and went over to the coffee machine and turned her back on us as though she wasn't going to have anything more to do with it.

"Well," Greta said. I could see it was going to be between her and Chrissy. They're both blondes, I don't mean that in a bitchy way but they do try to outdress each other. Greta would like to get out of Filing, she'd like to be a receptionist too so she could meet more people. You don't meet much of anyone in Filing except other people in Filing. Me, I don't mind it so much, I have outside interests.

"Well," Greta said, "I sometimes think about, you know my apartment? It's got this little balcony, I like to sit out there in the summer and I have a few plants out there. I never bother that much about locking the door to the balcony, it's one of those sliding glass ones, I'm on the eighteenth floor for heaven's sake, I've got a good view of the lake and the CN Tower and all. But I'm sitting around one night in my housecoat, watching TV with my shoes off, you know how you do, and I see this guy's feet, coming down past the window, and the next thing you know he's standing on the balcony, he's let himself down by a rope with a hook on the end of it from the floor above, that's the nineteenth, and before I can even get up off the chesterfield he's inside the apartment. He's all dressed in black with black gloves on"—I knew right away what show she got the black gloves off because I saw the same one—"and then he, well, you know."

"You know what?" Chrissy said, but Greta said, "And afterwards he tells me that he goes all over the outside of the apartment building like that, from one floor to another, with his rope and his hook . . . and then he goes out to the balcony and tosses his rope, and he climbs up it and disappears."

"Just like Tarzan," I said, but nobody laughed.

"Is that all?" Chrissy said. "Don't you ever think about, well, I think about being in the bathtub, with no clothes on . . . "

"So who takes a bath in their clothes?" I said, you have to admit it's stupid when you come to think of it, but she just went on, " . . . with lots of bubbles, what I use is Vitabath, it's more expensive but it's so relaxing, and my hair pinned up, and the door opens and this fellow's standing there. . . ."

"How'd he get in?" Greta said.

"Oh, I don't know, through a window or something. Well, I can't very well get out of the bathtub, the bathroom's too small and besides he's blocking the doorway, so I just *lie* there, and he starts to very slowly take his own clothes off, and then he gets into the bathtub with me."

"Don't you scream or anything?" said Darlene. She'd come back with her cup of coffee, she was getting really interested. "I'd scream like bloody murder."

"Who'd hear me?" Chrissy said. "Besides, all the articles say it's better not to resist, that way you don't get hurt."

"Anyway you might get bubbles up your nose," I said, "from the deep breathing," and I swear all four of them looked at me like I was in bad taste, like I'd insulted the Virgin Mary or something. I mean, I don't see what's wrong with a little joke now and then. Life's too short, right?

"Listen," I said, "those aren't *rape* fantasies. I mean, you aren't getting *raped*, it's just some guy you haven't met formally who happens to be more attractive than Derek Cummins"—he's the Assistant Manager, he wears elevator shoes or at any rate they have these thick soles and he has this funny way of talking, we call him Derek Duck—"and you have a good time. Rape is when they've got a knife or something and you don't want to."

"So what about you, Estelle," Chrissy said, she was miffed because I laughed at her fantasy, she thought I was putting her down. Sondra was miffed too, by this time she'd finished her celery and she wanted to tell about hers, but she hadn't got in fast enough.

"All right, let me tell you one," I said. "I'm walking down this dark street at night and this fellow comes up and grabs my arm. Now it so happens that I have a plastic lemon in my purse, you know how it always says you should carry a plastic lemon in your purse? I don't really do it, I tried it once but the darn thing leaked all over my chequebook, but in this fantasy I have one, and I say to him, "You're intending to rape me, right?" and he nods, so I open my purse to get the plastic lemon, and I can't find it! My purse is full of all this junk, Kleenex and cigarettes and my change purse and my lipstick and my driver's licence, you know the kind of stuff; so I ask him to hold out his hands, like this, and I pile all this junk into them and down at the bottom there's the plastic lemon, and I can't get the top off. So I hand it to him and he's very obliging, he twists the top off and hands it back to me, and I squirt him in the eye."

I hope you don't think that's too vicious. Come to think of it, it is a bit mean, especially when he was so polite and all.

"*That's* your rape fantasy?" Chrissy says. "I don't believe it."

"She's a card," Darlene says, she and I are the ones that've been here the longest and she never will forget the time I got drunk at the office party and insisted I was going to dance under the table instead of on top of it, I did a sort of Cossack number[3] but then I hit my head on the bottom of the table—actually it was a desk—when I went to get up, and I knocked myself out cold. She's decided that's the mark of an original mind and she tells everyone new about it and I'm not sure that's fair. Though I did do it.

"I'm being totally honest," I say. I always am and they know it. There's no point in being anything else, is the way I look at it, and sooner or later the truth will out so you might as well not waste the time, right? "You should hear the one about the Easy-Off Oven Cleaner."

But that was the end of the lunch hour, with one bridge game shot to hell, and the next day we spent most of the time arguing over whether to start a new game or play out the hands we had left over from the day before, so Sondra never did get a chance to tell about her rape fantasy.

It started me thinking though, about my own rape fantasies. Maybe I'm abnormal or something, I mean I have fantasies about handsome strangers coming in through the window too, like Mr. Clean,[4] I wish one would, please god somebody without flat feet and big sweat marks on his shirt, and over five feet five, believe me being tall is a handicap though it's getting better, tall guys are starting to like someone whose nose reaches higher than their belly button. But if you're being totally honest you can't count those as rape fantasies. In a real rape fantasy, what you should feel is this anxiety, like when you think about your apartment building catching on fire and whether you should use the elevator or the stairs or maybe just stick your head under a wet towel, and you try to remember everything you've read about what to do but you can't decide.

For instance, I'm walking along this dark street at night and this short, ugly fellow comes up and grabs my arm, and not only is he ugly, you know, with a sort of puffy nothing face, like those fellows you have to talk to in the bank when your account's overdrawn—of course I don't mean they're all like that—but he's absolutely covered in pimples. So he gets me pinned against the wall, he's short but he's heavy, and he starts to undo himself and the zipper gets stuck. I mean, one of the most significant moments in a girl's life, it's almost like getting married or having a baby or something, and he sticks the zipper.

So I say, kind of disgusted, "Oh for Chrissake," and he starts to cry. He tells me he's never been able to get anything right in his entire life,

3. Russian folk dance called the *kazatzka*. 4. Character featured in detergent ads.

and this is the last straw, he's going to go jump off a bridge.

"Look," I say, I feel so sorry for him, in my rape fantasies I always end up feeling sorry for the guy, I mean there has to be something *wrong* with them, if it was Clint Eastwood it'd be different but worse luck it never is. I was the kind of little girl who buried dead robins, know what I mean? It used to drive my mother nuts, she didn't like me touching them, because of the germs I guess. So I say, "Listen, I know how you feel. You really should do something about those pimples, if you got rid of them you'd be quite good looking, honest; then you wouldn't have to go around doing stuff like this. I had them myself once," I say, to comfort him, but in fact I did, and it ends up I give him the name of my old dermatologist, the one I had in high school, that was back in Leamington, except I used to go to St. Catharine's for the dermatologist. I'm telling you, I was really lonely when I first came here; I thought it was going to be such a big adventure and all, but it's a lot harder to meet people in a city. But I guess it's different for a guy.

Or I'm lying in bed with this terrible cold, my face is all swollen up, my eyes are red and my nose is dripping like a leaky tap, and this fellow comes in through the window and *he* has a terrible cold too, it's a new kind of flu that's been going around. So he says, "I'b goig do rabe you" —I hope you don't mind me holding my nose like this but that's the way I imagine it—and he lets out this terrific sneeze, which slows him down a bit, also I'm no object of beauty myself, you'd have to be some kind of pervert to want to rape someone with a cold like mine, it'd be like raping a bottle of LePage's mucilage the way my nose is running. He's looking wildly around the room, and I realize it's because he doesn't have a piece of Kleenex! "Id's ride here," I say, and I pass him the Kleenex, god knows why he even bothered to get out of bed, you'd think if you were going to go around climbing in windows you'd wait till you were healthier, right? I mean, that takes a certain amount of energy. So I ask him why doesn't he let me fix him a NeoCitran[5] and scotch, that's what I always take, you still have the cold but you don't feel it, so I do and we end up watching the Late Show together. I mean, they aren't all sex maniacs, the rest of the time they must lead a normal life. I figure they enjoy watching the Late Show just like anybody else.

I do have a scarier one though . . . where the fellow says he's hearing angel voices that're telling him he's got to kill me, you know, you read about things like that all the time in the papers. In this one I'm not in the apartment where I live now, I'm back in my mother's house in Leamington and the fellow's been hiding in the cellar, he grabs my arm when I go downstairs to get a jar of jam and he's got hold of the axe too, out of the garage, that one is really scary. I mean, what do you say to a nut like that?

5. Patented cold medicine.

So I start to shake but after a minute I get control of myself and I say, is he sure the angel voices have got the right person, because I hear the same angel voices and they've been telling me for some time that I'm going to give birth to the reincarnation of St. Anne who in turn has the Virgin Mary and right after that comes Jesus Christ and the end of the world, and he wouldn't want to interfere with that, would he? So he gets confused and listens some more, and then he asks for a sign and I show him my vaccination mark, you can see it's sort of an odd-shaped one, it got infected because I scratched the top off, and that does it, he apologizes and climbs out the coal chute again, which is how he got in in the first place, and I say to myself there's some advantage in having been brought up a Catholic even though I haven't been to church since they changed the service into English, it just isn't the same, you might as well be a Protestant. I must write to Mother and tell her to nail up that coal chute, it always has bothered me. Funny, I couldn't tell you at all what this man looks like but I know exactly what kind of shoes he's wearing, because that's the last I see of him, his shoes going up the coal chute, and they're the old-fashioned kind that lace up the ankles, even though he's a young fellow. That's strange, isn't it?

Let me tell you though I really sweat until I see him safely out of there and I go upstairs right away and make myself a cup of tea. I don't think about that one much. My mother always said you shouldn't dwell on unpleasant things and I generally agree with that, I mean, dwelling on them doesn't make them go away. Though not dwelling on them doesn't make them go away either, when you come to think of it.

Sometimes I have these short ones where the fellow grabs my arm but I'm really a Kung-Fu expert, can you believe it, in real life I'm sure it would just be a conk on the head and that's that, like getting your tonsils out, you'd wake up and it would be all over except for the sore places, and you'd be lucky if your neck wasn't broken or something, I could never even hit the volleyball in gym and a volleyball is fairly large, you know?—and I just go *zap* with my fingers into his eyes and that's it, he falls over, or I flip him against a wall or something. But I could never really stick my fingers in anyone's eyes, could you? It would feel like hot jello and I don't even like cold jello, just thinking about it gives me the creeps. I feel a bit guilty about that one, I mean how would you like walking around knowing someone's been blinded for life because of you?

But maybe it's different for a guy.

The most touching one I have is when the fellow grabs my arm and I say, sad and kind of dignified, "You'd be raping a corpse." That pulls him up short and I explain that I've just found out I have leukaemia and the doctors have only given me a few months to live. That's why I'm out pacing the streets alone at night, I need to think, you know, come to terms with myself. I don't really have leukaemia but in the fantasy I do,

I guess I chose that particular disease because a girl in my grade four class died of it, the whole class sent her flowers when she was in the hospital. I didn't understand then that she was going to die and I wanted to have leukaemia too so I could get flowers. Kids are funny, aren't they? Well, it turns out that he has leukaemia himself, and *he* only has a few months to live, that's why he's going around raping people, he's very bitter because he's so young and his life is being taken from him before he's really lived it. So we walk along gently under the street lights, it's spring and sort of misty, and we end up going for coffee, we're happy we've found the only other person in the world who can understand what we're going through, it's almost like fate, and after a while we just sort of look at each other and our hands touch, and he comes back with me and moves into my apartment and we spend our last months together before we die, we just sort of don't wake up in the morning, though I've never decided which one of us gets to die first. If it's him I have to go on and fantasize about the funeral, if it's me I don't have to worry about that, so it just about depends on how tired I am at the time. You may not believe this but sometimes I even start crying. I cry at the ends of movies, even the ones that aren't all that sad, so I guess it's the same thing. My mother's like that too.

The funny thing about these fantasies is that the man is always someone I don't know, and the statistics in the magazines, well, most of them anyway, they say it's often someone you do know, at least a little bit, like your boss or something—I mean, it wouldn't be *my* boss, he's over sixty and I'm sure he couldn't rape his way out of a paper bag, poor old thing, but it might be someone like Derek Duck, in his elevator shoes, perish the thought—or someone you just met, who invites you up for a drink, it's getting so you can hardly be sociable any more, and how are you supposed to meet people if you can't trust them even that basic amount? You can't spend your whole life in the Filing Department or cooped up in your own apartment with all the doors and windows locked and the shades down. I'm not what you would call a drinker but I like to go out now and then for a drink or two in a nice place, even if I am by myself, I'm with Women's Lib on that even though I can't agree with a lot of the other things they say. Like here for instance, the waiters all know me and if anyone, you know, bothers me . . . I don't know why I'm telling you all this, except I think it helps you get to know a person, especially at first, hearing some of the things they think about. At work they call me the office worry wart, but it isn't so much like worrying, it's more like figuring out what you should do in an emergency, like I said before.

Anyway, another thing about it is that there's a lot of conversation, in fact I spend most of my time, in the fantasy that is, wondering what I'm going to say and what he's going to say, I think it would be better if you could get a conversation going. Like, how could a fellow do that to a person he's just had a long conversation with, once you let them know you're human, you have a life too, I don't see how they could go ahead with it, right? I mean, I know it happens but I just don't understand it, that's the part I really don't understand.

JOHN BARTH

Life-Story[1]

I

WITHOUT discarding what he'd already written he began his story afresh in a somewhat different manner. Whereas his earlier version had opened in a straight-forward documentary fashion and then degenerated or at least modulated intentionally into irrealism and dissonance he decided this time to tell his tale from start to finish in a conservative "realistic," unself-conscious way. He being by vocation an author of novels and stories it was perhaps inevitable that one afternoon the possibility would occur to the writer of these lines that his own life might be a fiction, in which he was the leading or an accessory character. He happened at the time* to be in his study attempting to draft the opening pages of a new short story; its general idea had preoccupied him for some months along with other general ideas, but certain elements of the conceit, without which he could scarcely proceed, remained unclear. More specifically: narrative plots may be imagined as consisting of a "ground-situation" (Scheherazade desires not to die) focused and dramatized by a "vehicle-situation" (Scheherazade beguiles the King with endless stories), the several incidents of which have their final value in terms of their bearing upon the "ground-situation." In our author's case it was the "vehicle" that had vouchsafed itself, first as a germinal proposition in his commonplace book—D comes to suspect that the world is a novel, himself a fictional personage—subsequently as an articulated conceit explored over several pages of the workbook in which he elaborated more systematically his casual inspirations: since D is writing a fictional account of his conviction he has indisputably a fictional existence in his account replicating what he suspects to be his own situation. Moreover E, hero of D's account, is said to be writing a similar account, and so the replication is in both ontological directions, et cetera. But the "ground-situation"—some state of affairs on D's part which would give dramatic resonance to his attempts to prove himself factual, assuming he made such attempts—obstinately withheld itself from his imagination. As is commonly the

* 9:00 A.M., Monday, June 20, 1966.

1. The author has attached a few footnotes that must be considered an integral part of his story and read as such. These are marked with asterisks and printed above a line at the bottom of the page. Editor's footnotes appear below the line.

case the question reduced to one of stakes: what were to be the consequences of D's—and finally E's—disproving or verifying his suspicion and why should a reader be interested?

What a dreary way to begin a story he said to himself upon reviewing his long introduction. Not only is there no "ground-situation," but the prose style is heavy and somewhat old-fashioned, like an English translation of Thomas Mann,[2] and the so-called "vehicle" itself is at least questionable: self-conscious, vertiginously arch, fashionably solipsistic, unoriginal—in fact a convention of twentieth-century literature. Another story about a writer writing a story! Another regressus in infinitum![3] Who doesn't prefer art that at least overtly imitates something other than its own processes? That doesn't continually proclaim "Don't forget I'm an artifice!"? That takes for granted its mimetic nature instead of asserting it in order (not so slyly after all) to deny it, or vice-versa? Though his critics sympathetic and otherwise described his own work as avant-garde, in his heart of hearts he disliked literature of an experimental, self-despising, or overtly metaphysical character, like Samuel Beckett's, Marian Cutler's, Jorge Borges's. The logical fantasies of Lewis Carroll[4] pleased him less than straight-forward tales of adventure, subtly sentimental romances, even densely circumstantial realisms like Tolstoy's. His favorite contemporary authors were John Updike, Georges Simenon, Nicole Riboud.[5] He had no use for the theater of absurdity, for "black humor," for allegory in any form, for apocalyptic preachments meretriciously tricked out in dramatic garb.

Neither had his wife and adolescent daughters, who for that matter preferred life to literature and read fiction when at all for entertainment. Their kind of story (his too, finally) would begin if not once upon a time at least with arresting circumstance, bold character, trenchant action. C flung away the whining manuscript and pushed impatiently through the french doors leading to the terrace from his oak-wainscoted study. Pausing at the stone balustrade to light his briar he remarked through a lavender cascade of wisteria that lithe-limbed Gloria, Gloria of timorous eye and militant breast, had once again chosen his boat-wharf as her basking-place.

By Jove he exclaimed to himself. It's particularly disquieting to suspect not only that one is a fictional character but that the fiction one's in—the fiction one is—is quite the sort one least prefers. His wife entered the study with coffee and an apple-pastry, set them at

2. German novelist (1875–1955) who lived in the United States after 1938. **3.** Infinite regression. **4.** Beckett is an Irish author and playwright (b. 1906); Borges is an Argentinian author (b. 1899); Lewis Carroll is the pseudonym of Charles Lutwidge Dodgson (1832–1898), British mathematician and author of *Alice's Adventures in Wonderland* and *Through the Looking-Glass*; Marian Cutler unidentified, perhaps fictitious. **5.** John Updike is an American author, poet, and essayist (b. 1932); George Simenon is the Belgian-born master of the detective story (b. 1903); Nicole Riboud is not identified.

his elbow on his work table, returned to the living room. Ed' pelut' kondo nedode; nyoing nyang.[6] One manifestation of schizophrenia as everyone knows is the movement from reality toward fantasy, a progress which not infrequently takes the form of distorted and fragmented representation, abstract formalism, an increasing pre occupation, even obsession, with pattern and design for their own sakes—especially patterns of a baroque, enormously detailed character—to the (virtual) exclusion of representative "content." There are other manifestations. Ironically, in the case of graphic and plastic artists for example the work produced in the advanced stages of their affliction may be more powerful and interesting than the realistic productions of their earlier "sanity." Whether the artists themselves are gratified by this possibility is not reported.

B called upon a literary acquaintance, B——, summering with Mrs. B and children on the Eastern Shore of Maryland. "You say you lack a ground-situation. Has it occurred to you that that circumstance may be your ground-situation? What occurs to me is that if it is it isn't. And conversely. The case being thus, what's really wanting after all is a well-articulated vehicle, a foreground or upstage situation to dramatize the narrator's or author's grundlage. His what. To write merely C comes to suspect that the world is a novel, himself a fictional personage is but to introduce the vehicle; the next step must be to initiate its uphill motion by establishing and complicating some conflict. I would advise in addition the eschewal of overt and self-conscious discussion of the narrative process. I would advise in addition the eschewal of overt and self-conscious discussion of the narrative process. The via negativa and its positive counterpart are it is to be remembered poles after all of the same cell. Returning to his study.

If I'm going to be a fictional character G declared to himself I want to be in a rousing good yarn as they say, not some piece of avant-garde preciousness. I want passion and bravura action in my plot, heroes I can admire, heroines I can love, memorable speeches, colorful accessory characters, poetical language. It doesn't matter to me how naively linear the anecdote is; never mind modernity! How reactionary J appears to be. How will such nonsense sound thirty-six years from now?* As if. If he can only get K through his story I reflected grimly; if he can only retain his self-possession to the end of this sentence; not go mad; not destroy himself and/or others. Then what I wondered grimly. Another sentence fast, another story. Scheherazade my only love! All those nights you kept your secret from the King my rival, that after your defloration he was unnecessary, you'd have killed yourself in any case when your invention failed.

* 10:00 A.M., Monday, June 20, 1966.

6. Nonsense syllables, a parody of language itself.

Why could he not begin his story afresh X wondered, for example with the words why could he not begin his story afresh et cetera? Y's wife came into the study as he was about to throw out the baby with the bathwater. "Not for an instant to throw out the baby while every instant discarding the bathwater is perhaps a chief task of civilized people at this hour of the world."* I used to tell B—— that without success. What makes you so sure it's not a film he's in or a theater-piece?

Because U responded while he certainly felt rather often that he was merely acting his own role or roles he had no idea who the actor was, whereas even the most Stanislavsky methodist would presumably if questioned closely recollect his offstage identity even onstage in mid-act. Moreover a great part of T's "drama," most of his life in fact, was non-visual, consisting entirely in introspection, which the visual dramatic media couldn't manage easily. He had for example mentioned to no one his growing conviction that he was a fictional character, and since he was not given to audible soliloquizing a "spectator" would take him for a cheerful, conventional fellow, little suspecting that et cetera. It was of course imaginable that much goes on in the mind of King Oedipus in addition to his spoken sentiments; any number of interior dramas might be being played out in the actors' or characters' minds, dramas of which the audience is as unaware as are V's wife and friends of his growing conviction that he's a fictional character. But everything suggested that the medium of his life was prose fiction—moreover a fiction narrated from either the first-person or the third-person-omniscient point of view.

Why is it L wondered with mild disgust that both K and M for example choose to write such stuff when life is so sweet and painful and full of such a variety of people, places, situations, and activities other than self-conscious and after all rather blank introspection? Why is it N wondered et cetera that both M and O et cetera when the world is in such parlous explosive case? Why et cetera et cetera et cetera when the word, which was in the beginning, is now evidently nearing the end of its road? Am I being strung out in this ad libitum fashion I wondered merely to keep my author from the pistol? What sort of story is it whose drama lies always in the next frame out? If Sinbad sinks it's Scheherazade who drowns; whose neck one wonders is on her line?

II

Discarding what he'd already written as he could wish to discard the mumbling pages of his life he began his story afresh, resolved this time to eschew overt and self-conscious discussion of his narrative process and to recount instead in the straight-forwardest manner possible the several complications of his character's conviction

* 11:00 A.M., Monday, June 20, 1966.

that he was a character in a work of fiction, arranging them into dramatically ascending stages if he could for his readers' sake and leading them (the stages) to an exciting climax and denouement if he could.

He rather suspected that the medium and genre in which he worked—the only ones for which he felt any vocation—were moribund if not already dead. The idea pleased him. One of the successfullest men he knew was a blacksmith of the old school who et cetera. He meditated upon the grandest sailing-vessel ever built, the *France II*,[7] constructed in Bordeaux in 1911 not only when but because the age of sail had passed. Other phenomena that consoled and inspired him were the great flying-boat *Hercules*, the zeppelin *Hindenburg*, the *Tsar Pushka* cannon,[8] the then-record Dow-Jones industrial average of 381.17 attained on September 3, 1929.

He rather suspected that the society in which he persisted—the only one with which he felt any degree of identification—was moribund if not et cetera. He knew beyond any doubt that the body which he inhabited—the only one et cetera—was et cetera. The idea et cetera. He had for thirty-six years lacking a few hours been one of our dustmote's three billion tenants give or take five hundred million, and happening to be as well a white male citizen of the United States of America he had thirty-six years plus a few hours more to cope with one way or another unless the actuarial tables were mistaken, not bloody likely, or his term was unexpectedly reduced.

Had he written for his readers' sake? The phrase implied a thitherto-unappreciated metaphysical dimension. Suspense. If his life was a fictional narrative it consisted of three terms—teller, tale, told—each dependent on the other two but not in the same ways. His author could as well tell some other character's tale or some other tale of the same character as the one being told as he himself could in his own character as author; his "reader" could as easily read some other story, would be well advised to; but his own "life" depended absolutely on a particular author's original persistence, thereafter upon some reader's. From this consideration any number of things followed, some less tiresome than others. No use appealing to his author, of whom he'd come to dislike even to think. The idea of his playing with his characters' and his own self-consciousness! He himself tended in that direction and despised the tendency. The idea of his or her smiling smugly to himself as the "words" flowed

7. One of seven five-masted barques ever built. Its masts stood 210 feet high, it was 422 feet in length, carried 60,000 square feet of canvas, and was manned by a crew of 45. **8.** The *Hercules* was a flying boat built in the 1940's by the Hughes Aircraft Corporation. It weighed 200 tons, had wings 13 feet thick at the roots, and was powered by eight engines. The Hindenburg was a German-manufactured dirigible built in 1936. On May 6, 1937, while landing at Lakehurst, N.J., it burst into flames, killing 36 persons. The highly ornamented *Tsar Pushka* cannon was cast in 1586. It stands in a line of cannon in front of the Kremlin Arsenal.

from his "pen" in which his protagonist's unhappy inner life was exposed! Ah he had mistaken the nature of his narrative; he had thought it very long, longer than Proust's, longer than any German's, longer than *The Thousand Nights and a Night* in ten quarto volumes. Moreover he'd thought it the most prolix and pedestrian *tranche-de-vie*[9] realism, unredeemed by even the limited virtues of colorful squalor, solid specification, an engaging variety of scenes and characters—in a word a bore, of the sort he himself not only would not write but would not read either. Now he understood that his author might as probably resemble himself and the protagonist of his own story-in-progress. Like himself, like his character aforementioned, his author not impossibly deplored the obsolescence of humanism, the passing of *savoir-vivre*,[1] et cetera; admired the outmoded values of fidelity, courage, tact, restraint, amiability, self-discipline, et cetera; preferred fictions in which were to be found stirring actions, characters to love as well as ditto to despise, speeches and deeds to affect us strongly, et cetera. He too might wish to make some final effort to put by his fictional character and achieve factuality or at least to figure in if not be hero of a more attractive fiction, but be caught like the writer of these lines in some more or less desperate tour de force. For him to attempt to come to an understanding with such an author were as futile as for one of his own creations to et cetera.

But the reader! Even if his author were his only reader as was he himself of his work-in-progress as of the sentence-in-progress and his protagonist of his, et cetera, his character as reader was not the same as his character as author, a fact which might be turned to account. What suspense.

As he prepared to explore this possibility one of his mistresses whereof he had none entered his brown study unannounced. "The passion of love," she announced, "which I regard as no less essential to a satisfying life than those values itemized above and which I infer from my presence here that you too esteem highly, does not in fact play in your life a role of sufficient importance to sustain my presence here. It plays in fact little role at all outside your imaginative and/or ary life. I tell you this not in a criticizing spirit, for I judge you to be as capable of the sentiment aforementioned as any other imagin[ative], deep-feeling man in good physical health more or less precisely in the middle of the road of our life. What hampers, even cripples you in this regard is your final preference, which I refrain from analyzing, for the sedater, more responsible pleasures of monogamous fidelity and the serener affections of domesticity, notwithstanding the fact that your enjoyment of these is correspondingly inhibited though not altogether spoiled by an essentially romantical, unstable, irresponsible, death-wishing fancy. V. S.

9. Slice of life. 1. Knowing how to live.

Pritchett, English critic and author, will put the matter succinctly in a soon-to-be written essay on Flaubert, whose work he'll say depicts the course of ardent longings and violent desires that rise from the horrible, the sensual, and the sadistic. They turn into the virginal and mystical, only to become numb by satiety. At this point pathological boredom leads to a final desire for death and nothingness—the Romantic syndrome. If, not to be unfair, we qualify somewhat the terms horrible and sadistic and understand satiety to include a large measure of vicariousness, this description undeniably applies to one aspect of yourself and your work; and while your ditto has other, even contrary aspects, the net fact is that you have elected familial responsibilities and rewards—indeed, straight-laced middle-classness in general—over the higher expenses of spirit and wastes of shame attendant upon a less regular, more glamorous style of life. So to elect is surely admirable for the layman, even essential if the social fabric, without which there can be no culture, is to be preserved. For the artist, however, and in particular the writer, whose traditional material has been the passions of men and women, the choice is fatal. You having made it I bid you goodnight probably forever."

Even as she left he reached for the sleeping pills cached conveniently in his writing desk and was restrained from their administration only by his being in the process of completing a sentence, which he cravenly strung out at some sacrifice of rhetorical effect upon realizing that he was et cetera. Moreover he added hastily he had not described the intruder for his readers' vicarious satiety: a lovely woman she was, whom he did not after all describe for his readers' et cetera inasmuch as her appearance and character were inconstant. Her interruption of his work inspired a few sentences about the extent to which his fiction inevitably made public his private life, though the trespasses in this particular were as nothing beside those of most of his profession. That is to say, while he did not draw his characters and situations directly from life nor permit his author-protagonist to do so, any moderately attentive reader of his oeuvre,[2] his what, could infer for example that its author feared for example schizophrenia, impotence creative and sexual, suicide—in short living and dying. His fictions were preoccupied with these fears among their other, more serious preoccupations. Hot dog. As of the sentence-in-progress he was not in fact unmanageably schizophrenic, impotent in either respect, or dead by his own hand, but there was always the next sentence to worry about. But there was always the next sentence to worry about. In sum he concluded hastily such limited self-exposure did not constitute a misdemeanor, representing or mis as it did so small an aspect of his total self, negligible a portion of his total life—even which totalities were they

2. Complete works.

made public would be found remarkable only for their being so unremarkable. Well shall he continue.

Bearing in mind that he had not developed what he'd mentioned earlier about turning to advantage his situation vis-à-vis his "reader" (in fact he deliberately now postponed his return to that subject, sensing that it might well constitute the climax of his story) he elaborated one or two ancillary questions, perfectly aware that he was trying, even exhausting, whatever patience might remain to whatever readers might remain to whoever elaborated yet another ancillary question. Was the novel of his life for example a *roman à clef?*[3] Of that genre he was as contemptuous as of the others aforementioned; but while in the introductory adverbial clause it seemed obvious to him that he didn't "stand for" anyone else, any more than he was an actor playing the role of himself, by the time he reached the main clause he had to admit that the question was unanswerable, since the "real" man to whom he'd correspond in a *roman à clef* would not be also in the *roman à clef* and the characters in such works were not themselves aware of their irritating correspondences.

Similarly unanswerable were such questions as when "his" story (so he regarded it for convenience and consolement though for all he knew he might be not the central character; it might be his wife's story, one of his daughter's, his imaginary mistress's, the man-who-once-cleaned-his-chimney's) began. Not impossibly at his birth or even generations earlier: a *Bildungsroman*, an *Erziehungsroman*, a *roman fleuve!*[4] More likely at the moment he became convinced of his fictional nature: that's where he'd have begun it, as he'd begun the piece currently under his pen. If so it followed that the years of his childhood and younger manhood weren't "real," he'd suspected as much, in the first-order sense, but a mere "background" consisting of a few well-placed expository insinuations, perhaps misleading, or inferences, perhaps unwarranted, from strategic hints in his present reflections. God so to speak spare his readers from heavy-footed forced expositions of the sort that begin in the countryside near —— in May of the year —— it occurred to the novelist —— that his own life might be a ——, in which he was the leading or an accessory character. He happened at the time to be in the oak-wainscoted study of the old family summer residence; through a lavender cascade of hysteria he observed that his wife had once again chosen to be the subject of this clause, itself the direct object of his observation. A lovely woman she was, whom he did not describe in keeping with his policy against drawing characters from life as who should draw a condemnee to the gallows. Begging his pardon. Flinging his tiresome tale away he pushed impatiently

3. A novel introducing real characters under fictitious names. **4.** A form of novel in which the members of a family or social group are chronicled in a long and leisurely narrative; the other two terms apply to novels of educational development.

through the French windows leading from his study to a sheer drop from the then-record high into a nearly fatal depression.

He clung onto his narrative depressed by the disproportion of its ratiocination to its dramatization, reflection to action. One had heard *Hamlet* criticized as a collection of soliloquies for which the implausible plot was a mere excuse; witnessed Italian operas whose dramatic portions were no more than interstitial relief and arbitrary continuity between the arias. If it was true that he didn't take his "real" life seriously enough even when it had him by the throat, the fact didn't lead him to consider whether the fact was a cause or a consequence of his tale's tedium or both.

Concluding these reflections he concluded these reflections: that there was at this advancèd page still apparently no ground-situation suggested that his story was dramatically meaningless. If one regarded the absence and his vain endeavors to supply the defect, as itself a sort of ground-situation, did his life-story thereby take on a kind of meaning? A "dramatic" sort he supposed, though of so sophistical a character as more likely to annoy than to engage.

III

The reader! You, dogged, uninsultable, print-oriented bastard, it's you I'm addressing, who else, from inside this monstrous fiction. You've read me this far, then? Even this far? For what discreditable motive? How is it you don't go to a movie, watch TV, stare at a wall, play tennis with a friend, make amorous advances to the person who comes to your mind when I speak of amorous advances? Can nothing surfeit, saturate you, turn you off? Where's your shame?

Having let go this barrage of rhetorical or at least unanswered questions and observing himself nevertheless in midst of yet another sentence he concluded and caused the "hero" of his story to conclude that one or more of three things must be true: 1) his author was his sole and indefatigable reader; 2) he was in a sense his own author, telling his story to himself, in which case in which case; and/or 3) his reader was not only tireless and shameless but sadistic, masochistic if he was himself.

For why do you suppose—you! you!—he's gone on so, so relentlessly refusing to entertain you as he might have at a less desperate than this hour of the world* with felicitous language, exciting situation, unforgettable character and image? Why has he as it were ruthlessly set about not to win you over but to turn you away? Because your own author bless and damn you his life is in your hands! He writes and reads himself; don't you think he knows who gives his creatures their lives and deaths? Do they exist except as he or others read their words? Age except we turn their pages? And can he die until you have no more of him? Time was obviously

* 11:00 P.M.; Monday, June 20, 1966.

when his author could have turned the trick; his pen had once to left-to-right it through these words as does your kindless eye and might have ceased at any one. This. This. And did not as you see but went on like an Oriental torturemaster to the end.

But you needn't! He exclaimed to you. In vain. Had he petitioned you instead to read slowly in the happy parts, what happy parts, swiftly in the painful no doubt you'd have done the contrary or cut him off entirely. But as he longs to die and can't without your help you force him on, force him on. Will you deny you've read this sentence? This? To get away with murder doesn't appeal to you, is that it? As if your hands weren't inky with other dyings! As if he'd know you'd killed him! Come on. He dares you.

In vain. You haven't: the burden of his knowledge. That he continues means that he continues, a fortiori you too. Suicide's impossible: he can't kill himself without your help. Those petitions aforementioned, even his silly plea for death—don't you think he understands their sophistry, having authored their like for the wretches he's authored? Read him fast or slow, intermittently, continuously, repeatedly, backward, not at all, he won't know it; he only guesses someone's reading or composing sentences such as this one; the net effect is that there's a net effect, of continuity and an apparently consistent flow of time, though his pages do seem to pass more swiftly as they near his end.

To what conclusion will he come? He'd been about to append to his own tale inasmuch as the old analogy between Author and God, novel and world, can no longer be employed unless deliberately as a false analogy, certain things follow: 1) fiction must acknowledge its fictitiousness and metaphoric invalidity or 2) choose to ignore the question or deny its relevance or 3) establish some other, acceptable relation between itself, its author, its reader. Just as he finished doing so however his real wife and imaginary mistresses entered his study; "It's a little past midnight" she announced with a smile; "do you know what that means?"

Though she'd come into his story unannounced at a critical moment he did not describe her, for even as he recollected that he'd seen his first light just thirty-six years before the night incumbent he saw his last: that he could not after all be a character in a work of fiction inasmuch as such a fiction would be of an entirely different character from what he thought of as fiction. Fiction consisted of such monuments of the imagination as Cutler's *Morganfield,* Riboud's *Tales Within Tales,* his own creations; fact of such as for example read those fictions. More, he could demonstrate by syllogism that the story of his life was a work of fact: though assaults upon the boundary between life and art, reality and dream, were undeniably a staple of his own and his century's literature as they'd been of Shakespeare's and Cervantes's, yet it was a fact that in the corpus of fiction as far as he knew no fictional character had become convinced as had he that he was a character in a work of fiction. This being the case and he having in fact become thus convinced it followed that his conviction was false. "Happy birthday," said his wife et cetera, kissing him et cetera to obstruct his view of the end of the sentence he was nearing the end of, playfully refusing to be nay-said so that in fact he did at last as did his fictional character end his ending story endless by interruption cap his pen.

DONALD BARTHELME

The Indian Uprising

WE defended the city as best we could. The arrows of the Comanches came in clouds. The war clubs of the Comanches clattered on the soft, yellow pavements. There were earthworks along the Boulevard Mark Clark[1] and the hedges had been laced with sparkling wire. People were trying to understand. I spoke to Sylvia. "Do you think this is a good life?" The table held apples, books, long-playing records. She looked up. "No."

Patrols of paras[2] and volunteers with armbands guarded the tall, flat buildings. We interrogated the captured Comanche. Two of us forced his head back while another poured water into his nostrils. His body jerked, he choked and wept. Not believing a hurried, careless, and exaggerated report of the number of casualties in the outer districts where trees, lamps, swans had been reduced to clear fields of fire we issued entrenching tools to those who seemed trustworthy and turned the heavy-weapons companies so that we could not be surprised from that direction. And I sat there getting drunker and drunker and more in love and more in love. We talked.

"Do you know Fauré's 'Dolly'?"

"Would that be Gabriel Fauré?"[3]

"It would."

"Then I know it," she said. "May I say that I play it at certain times, when I am sad, or happy, although it requires four hands."

"How is that managed?"

"I accelerate," she said, "ignoring the time signature."

And when they shot the scene in the bed I wondered how you felt under the eyes of the cameramen, grips, juicers, men in the mixing booth:[4] excited? stimulated? And when they shot the scene in the

1. Mark Wayne Clark (b. 1896), American general in charge of allied armies in Italy in World War II. The fictitious squares and streets in this story are named after famous American military officers of that war. **2.** Paratroops. **3.** Gabriel Urbain Fauré (1845–1924), French organist and composer. **4.** Film technicians: grips are stagehands; juicers are electricians; the mixing booth is where images from various cameras are edited and coordinated.

shower I sanded a hollow-core door working carefully against the illustrations in texts and whispered instructions from one who had already solved the problem. I had made after all other tables, one while living with Alice, one while living with Eunice, one while living with Marianne.

Red men in waves like people scattering in a square startled by something tragic or a sudden, loud noise accumulated against the barricades we had made of window dummies, silk, thoughtfully planned job descriptions (including scales for the orderly progress of other colors), wine in demijohns, and robes. I analyzed the composition of the barricade nearest me and found two ashtrays, ceramic, one dark brown and one dark brown with an orange blur at the lip; a tin frying pan; two-litre bottles of red wine; three-quarter-litre bottles of Black & White, aquavit, cognac, vodka, gin, Fad #6 sherry; a hollow-core door in birch veneer on black wrought-iron legs; a blanket, red-orange with faint blue stripes; a red pillow and a blue pillow; a woven straw wastebasket; two glass jars for flowers; corkscrews and can openers; two plates and two cups, ceramic, dark brown; a yellow-and-purple poster; a Yugoslavian carved flute, wood, dark brown; and other items. I decided I knew nothing.

The hospitals dusted wounds with powder the worth of which was not quite established, other supplies having been exhausted early in the first day. I decided I knew nothing. Friends put me in touch with a Miss R., a teacher, unorthodox they said, excellent they said, successful with difficult cases, steel shutters on the windows made the house safe. I had just learned via an International Distress Coupon that Jane had been beaten up by a dwarf in a bar on Tenerife[5] but Miss R. did not allow me to speak of it. "You know nothing," she said, "you feel nothing, you are locked in a most savage and terrible ignorance, I despise you, my boy, *mon cher*,[6] my heart. You may attend but you must not attend now, you must attend later, a day or a week or an hour, you are making me ill. . . ." I nonevaluated these remarks as Korzybski[7] instructed. But it was difficult. Then they pulled back in a feint near the river and we rushed into that sector with a reinforced battalion hastily formed among the Zouaves[8] and cabdrivers. This unit was crushed in the afternoon of a day that began with spoons and letters in hallways and under windows where men tasted the history of the heart, cone-shaped muscular organ that maintains *circulation of the blood*.

But it is you I want now, here in the middle of this Uprising, with the streets yellow and threatening, short, ugly lances with fur at the throat and inexplicable shell money lying in the grass. It is when I

5. Largest of the Canary Islands, located in the Atlantic. **6.** My dear. **7.** Alfred Korzybski (1879–1950), American writer on semantics. **8.** Units of French infantry distinguished by their Algerian uniforms.

am with you that I am happiest, and it is for you that I am making this hollow-core door table with black wrought-iron legs. I held Sylvia by her bear-claw necklace. "Call off your braves," I said. "We have many years left to live." There was a sort of muck running in the gutters, yellowish, filthy stream suggesting excrement, or nervousness, a city that does not know what it has done to deserve baldness, errors, infidelity. "With luck you will survive until matins," Sylvia said. She ran off down the Rue Chester Nimitz,[9] uttering shrill cries.

Then it was learned that they had infiltrated our ghetto and that the people of the ghetto instead of resisting had joined the smooth, well-coördinated attack with zipguns, telegrams, lockets, causing that portion of the line held by the I.R.A.[1] to swell and collapse. We sent more heroin into the ghetto, and hyacinths, ordering another hundred thousand of the pale, delicate flowers. On the map we considered the situation with its strung-out inhabitants and merely personal emotions. Our parts were blue and their parts were green. I showed the blue-and-green map to Sylvia. "Your parts are green," I said. "You gave me heroin first a year ago,"[2] Sylvia said. She ran off down George C. Marshall Allée,[3] uttering shrill cries. Miss R. pushed me into a large room painted white (jolting and dancing in the soft light, and I was excited! and there were people watching!) in which there were two chairs. I sat in one chair and Miss R. sat in the other. She wore a blue dress containing a red figure. There was nothing exceptional about her. I was disappointed by her plainness, by the bareness of the room, by the absence of books.

The girls of my quarter wore long blue mufflers that reached to their knees. Sometimes the girls hid Comanches in their rooms, the blue mufflers together in a room creating a great blue fog. Block opened the door. He was carrying weapons, flowers, loaves of bread. And he was friendly, kind, enthusiastic, so I related a little of the history of torture, reviewing the technical literature quoting the best modern sources, French, German, and American, and pointing out the flies which had gathered in anticipation of some new, cool color.

"What is the situation?" I asked.

"The situation is liquid," he said. "We hold the south quarter and they hold the north quarter. The rest is silence."[4]

"And Kenneth?"

"That girl is not in love with Kenneth," Block said frankly. "She is in love with his coat. When she is not wearing it she is huddling

9. Chester William Nimitz (1885–1966), commander-in-chief of the U.S. Pacific Fleet during World War II. **1.** Irish Republican Army. **2.** Parody of line 35 of *The Waste Land* by T. S. Eliot (1888–1965): "You gave me hyacinths first a year ago." **3.** George Catlett Marshall (1880–1959), U.S. Army Chief of Staff and designer of the Marshall Plan. **4.** Hamlet's dying words, *Hamlet*, V. ii.

under it. Once I caught it going down the stairs by itself. I looked inside. Sylvia."

Once I caught Kenneth's coat going down the stairs by itself but the coat was a trap and inside a Comanche who made a thrust with his short, ugly knife at my leg which buckled and tossed me over the balustrade through a window and into another situation. Not believing that your body brilliant as it was and your fat, liquid spirit distinguished and angry as it was were stable quantities to which one could return on wires more than once, twice, or another number of times I said: "See the table?"

In Skinny Wainwright[5] Square the forces of green and blue swayed and struggled. The referees ran out on the field trailing chains. And then the blue part would be enlarged, the green diminished. Miss R. began to speak. "A former king of Spain, a Bonaparte, lived for a time in Bordentown, New Jersey. But that's no good." She paused. "The ardor aroused in men by the beauty of women can only be satisfied by God. That is *very* good (it is Valéry)[6] but it is not what I have to teach you, goat, muck, filth, heart of my heart." I showed the table to Nancy. "See the table?" She stuck out her tongue red as a cardinal's hat. "I made such a table once," Block said frankly. "People all over America have made such tables. I doubt very much whether one can enter an American home without finding at least one such table, or traces of its having been there, such as faded places in the carpet." And afterward in the garden the men of the 7th Cavalry played Gabrieli, Albinoni, Marcello, Vivaldi, Boccherini.[7] I saw Sylvia. She wore a yellow ribbon,[8] under a long blue muffler. "Which side are you on," I cried, "after all?"

"The only form of discourse of which I approve," Miss R. said in her dry, tense voice, "is the litany. I believe our masters and teachers as well as plain citizens should confine themselves to what can safely be said. Thus when I hear the words pewter, snake, tea, Fad #6 sherry, serviette, fenestration, crown, blue coming from the mouth of some public official, or some raw youth, I am not disappointed. Vertical organization is also possible," Miss R. said, "as in

pewter
snake
tea
Fad #6 sherry
serviette
fenestration
crown
blue.

5. Jonathan Mayhew ("Skinny") Wainwright (1883–1953), U.S. Army general. 6. Paul Valéry (1871–1945), French poet and philosopher. 7. Italian composers of the seventeenth and eighteenth centuries. The Seventh Cavalry, commanded by General Custer, was defeated by the Indians at the Little Big Horn. 8. Worn, according to tradition, by the sweethearts of cavalry men in the U.S. Army.

I run to liquids and colors," she said, "but you, you may run to something else, my virgin, my darling, my thistle, my poppet, my own. Young people," Miss R. said, "run to more and more unpleasant combinations as they sense the nature of our society. Some people," Miss R. said, "run to conceits or wisdom but I hold to the hard, brown, nutlike word. I might point out that there is enough aesthetic excitement here to satisfy anyone but a damned fool." I sat in solemn silence.

Fire arrows lit my way to the post office in Patton Place[9] where members of the Abraham Lincoln Brigade[1] offered their last, exhausted letters, postcards, calendars. I opened a letter but inside was a Comanche flint arrowhead played by Frank Wedekind[2] in an elegant gold chain and congratulations. Your earring rattled against my spectacles when I leaned forward to touch the soft, ruined place where the hearing aid had been. "Pack it in! Pack it in!" I urged, but the men in charge of the Uprising refused to listen to reason or to understand that it was real and that our water supply had evaporated and that our credit was no longer what it had been, once.

We attached wires to the testicles of the captured Comanche. And I sat there getting drunker and drunker and more in love and more in love. When we threw the switch he spoke. His name, he said, was Gustave Aschenbach.[3] He was born at L——, a country town in the province of Silesia. He was the son of an upper official in the judicature, and his forebears had all been officers, judges, departmental functionaries. . . . And you can never touch a girl in the same way more than once, twice, or another number of times however much you may wish to hold, wrap, or otherwise fix her hand, or look, or some other quality, or incident, known to you previously. In Sweden the little Swedish children cheered when we managed nothing more remarkable than getting off a bus burdened with packages, bread and liver-paste and beer. We went to an old church and sat in the royal box. The organist was practicing. And then into the graveyard next to the church. *Here lies Anna Pedersen, a good woman.* I threw a mushroom on the grave. The officer commanding the garbage dump reported by radio that the garbage had begun to move.

Jane! I heard via an International Distress Coupon that you were beaten up by a dwarf in a bar on Tenerife. That doesn't sound like you, Jane. Mostly you kick the dwarf in his little dwarf groin before he can get his teeth into your tasty and nice-looking leg, don't you, Jane? Your affair with Harold is reprehensible, you know that, don't you, Jane? Harold is married to Nancy. And there is Paula to

9. George Smith Patton, Jr. (1885–1945), American tank commander in World War II. **1.** American contingent of the International Brigade, which fought on the Republican side in the Spanish Civil War, 1936–1939. **2.** Frank Wedekind (1864–1918), German dramatist and expressionist writer. **3.** Fictitious protagonist of *Death in Venice* by Thomas Mann (1875–1955).

think about (Harold's kid), and Billy (Harold's other kid). I think your values are peculiar, Jane! Strings of language extend in every direction to bind the world into a rushing, ribald whole.

And you can never return to felicities in the same way, the brilliant body, the distinguished spirit recapitulating moments that occur once, twice, or another number of times in rebellions, or water. The rolling consensus of the Comanche nation smashed our inner defenses on three sides. Block was firing a greasegun[4] from the upper floor of a building designed by Emery Roth & Sons. "See the table?" "Oh, pack it in with your bloody table!" The city officials were tied to trees. Dusky warriors padded with their forest tread into the mouth of the mayor. "Who do you want to be?" I asked Kenneth and he said he wanted to be Jean-Luc Godard[5] but later when time permitted conversations in large, lighted rooms, whispering galleries with black-and-white Spanish rugs and problematic sculpture on calm, red catafalques. The sickness of the quarrel lay thick in the bed. I touched your back, the white, raised scars.

We killed a great many in the south suddenly with helicopters and rockets but we found that those we had killed were children and more came from the north and from the east and from other places where there are children preparing to live. "Skin," Miss R. said softly in the white, yellow room. "This is the Clemency Committee. And would you remove your belt and shoelaces." I removed my belt and shoelaces and looked (rain shattering from a great height the prospects of silence and clear, neat rows of houses in the subdivisions) into their savage black eyes, paint, feathers, beads.

4. Slang for a rapid-firing automatic pistol. 5. French New Wave film director (b. 1930).

ANN BEATTIE

The Burning House

FREDDY Fox is in the kitchen with me. He has just washed and dried an avocado seed I don't want, and he is leaning against the wall, rolling a joint. In five minutes, I will not be able to count on him. However: he started late in the day, and he has already brought in wood for the fire, gone to the store down the road for matches, and set the table. "You mean you'd know this stuff was Limoges[1] even if you didn't turn the plate over?" he called from the dining room. He pretended to be about to throw one of the plates into the kitchen, like a Frisbee. Sam, the dog, believed him

1. Fine porcelain.

and shot up, kicking the rug out behind him and skidding forward before he realized his error; it was like the Road Runner tricking Wile E. Coyote into going over the cliff for the millionth time. His jowls sank in disappointment.

"I see there's a full moon," Freddy says. "There's just nothing that can hold a candle to nature. The moon and the stars, the tides and the sunshine—and we just don't stop for long enough to wonder at it all. We're so engrossed in ourselves." He takes a very long drag on the joint. "We stand and stir the sauce in the pot instead of going to the window and gazing at the moon."

"You don't mean anything personal by that, I assume."

"I love the way you pour cream in a pan. I like to come up behind you and watch the sauce bubble."

"No, thank you," I say. "You're starting late in the day."

"My responsibilities have ended. You don't trust me to help with the cooking, and I've already brought in firewood and run an errand, and this very morning I exhausted myself by taking Mr. Sam jogging with me, down at Putnam Park. You're sure you won't?"

"No, thanks," I say. "Not now, anyway."

"I love it when you stand over the steam coming out of a pan and the hairs around your forehead curl into damp little curls."

My husband, Frank Wayne, is Freddy's half brother. Frank is an accountant. Freddy is closer to me than to Frank. Since Frank talks to Freddy more than he talks to me, however, and since Freddy is totally loyal, Freddy always knows more than I know. It pleases me that he does not know how to stir sauce; he will start talking, his mind will drift, and when next you look the sauce will be lumpy, or boiling away.

Freddy's criticism of Frank is only implied. "What a gracious gesture to entertain his friends on the weekend," he says.

"Male friends," I say.

"I didn't mean that you're the sort of lady who doesn't draw the line. I most certainly did not mean that," Freddy says. "I would even have been surprised if you had taken a toke of this deadly stuff while you were at the stove."

"O.K.," I say, and take the joint from him. Half of it is left when I take it. Half an inch is left after I've taken two drags and given it back.

"More surprised still if you'd shaken the ashes into the saucepan."

"You'd tell people I'd done it when they'd finished eating, and I'd be embarrassed. You can do it, though. I wouldn't be embarrassed if it was a story you told on yourself."

"You really understand me," Freddy says. "It's moon-madness, but I have to shake just this little bit in the sauce. I have to do it."

He does it.

Frank and Tucker are in the living room. Just a few minutes ago, Frank returned from getting Tucker at the train. Tucker loves to visit. To him, Fairfield County[2] is as mysterious as Alaska. He brought with him from New York a crock of mustard, a jeroboam of champagne, cocktail napkins with a picture of a plane flying over a building on them, twenty egret feathers ("You cannot get them anymore—strictly illegal," Tucker whispered to me), and, under his black cowboy hat with the rhinestone-studded chin strap, a toy frog that hopped when wound. Tucker owns a gallery in SoHo,[3] and Frank keeps his books. Tucker is now stretched out in the living room, visiting with Frank, and Freddy and I are both listening.

" . . . so everything I've been told indicates that he lives a purely Jekyll-and-Hyde existence. He's twenty years old, and I can see that since he's still living at home he might not want to flaunt his gayness. When he came into the gallery, he had his hair slicked back—just with water; I got close enough to sniff—and his mother was all but holding his hand. So fresh-scrubbed. The stories I'd heard. Anyway, when I called, his father started looking for the number where he could be reached in the Vineyard[4]—very irritated, because I didn't know James, and if I'd just phoned James I could have found him in a flash. He's talking to himself, looking for the number, and I say, 'Oh, did he go to visit friends or—' and his father interrupts and says, 'He was going to a gay pig roast. He's been gone since Monday.' *Just like that.*"

Freddy helps me carry the food out to the table. When we are all at the table, I mention the young artist Tucker was talking about. "Frank says his paintings are really incredible," I say to Tucker.

Makes Estes look like an Abstract Expressionist," Tucker says. "I want that boy. I really want that boy."

"You'll get him," Frank says. "You get everybody you go after."

Tucker cuts a small piece of meat. He cuts it small so that he can talk while chewing. "Do I?" he says.

Freddy is smoking at the table, gazing dazedly at the moon centered in the window. "After dinner," he says, putting the back of his hand against his forehead when he sees that I am looking at him, "we must all go to the lighthouse."

"If only *you* painted," Tucker says. "I'd want you."

"You couldn't have me," Freddy snaps. He reconsiders. "That sounded halfhearted, didn't it? Anybody who wants me can have me. This is the only place I can be on Saturday night where somebody isn't hustling me."

2. In Connecticut, close to New York City. **3.** Center of the contemporary art scene in New York. **4.** Martha's Vineyard, an island off the Massachusetts coast.

"Wear looser pants," Frank says to Freddy.

"This is so much better than some bar that stinks of cigarette smoke and leather. Why do I do it?" Freddy says. "Seriously—do you think I'll ever stop?"

"Let's not be serious," Tucker says.

"I keep thinking of this table as a big boat, with dishes and glasses rocking on it," Freddy says.

He takes the bone from his plate and walks out to the kitchen, dripping sauce on the floor. He walks as though he's on the deck of a wave-tossed ship. "Mr. Sam!" he calls, and the dog springs up from the living-room floor, where he had been sleeping; his toenails on the bare wood floor sound like a wheel spinning in gravel. "You don't have to beg," Freddy says. "Jesus, Sammy—I'm just giving it to you."

"I hope there's a bone involved," Tucker says, rolling his eyes to Frank. He cuts another tiny piece of meat. "I hope your brother does understand why I couldn't keep him on. He was good at what he did, but he also might say just *anything* to a customer. You have to believe me that if I hadn't been extremely embarrassed more than once I never would have let him go."

"He should have finished school," Frank says, sopping up sauce on his bread. "He'll knock around a while longer, then get tired of it and settle down to something."

"You think I died out here?" Freddy calls. "You think I can't hear you?"

"I'm not saying anything I wouldn't say to your face," Frank says.

"I'll tell you what I wouldn't say to your face," Freddy says. "You've got a swell wife and kid and dog, and you're a snob, and you take it all for granted."

Frank puts down his fork, completely exasperated. He looks at me.

"He came to work once this stoned," Tucker says. "*Comprenez-vous?*"[5]

"You like me because you feel sorry for me," Freddy says.

He is sitting on the concrete bench outdoors, in the area that's a garden in the springtime. It is early April now—not quite spring. It's very foggy out. It rained while we were eating, and now it has turned mild. I'm leaning against a tree, across from him, glad it's so dark and misty that I can't look down and see the damage the mud is doing to my boots.

"Who's his girlfriend?" Freddy says.

"If I told you her name, you'd tell him I told you."

5. "Do you understand?"

"Slow down. What?"

"I won't tell you, because you'll tell him that I know."

"He knows you know."

"I don't think so."

"How did you find out?"

"He talked about her. I kept hearing her name for months, and then we went to a party at Andy's, and she was there, and when I said something about her later he said, 'Natalie who?' It was much too casual. It gave the whole thing away."

He sighs. "I just did something very optimistic," he says. "I came out here with Mr. Sam and he dug up a rock and I put the avocado seed in the hole and packed dirt on top of it. Don't say it—I know: can't grow outside, we'll still have another snow, even if it grew, the next year's frost would kill it."

"He's embarrassed," I say. "When he's home, he avoids me. But it's rotten to avoid Mark, too. Six years old, and he calls up his friend Neal to hint that he wants to go over there. He doesn't do that when we're here alone."

Freddy picks up a stick and pokes around in the mud with it. "I'll bet Tucker's after that painter personally, not because he's the hottest thing since pancakes. That expression of his—it's always the same. Maybe Nixon really loved his mother, but with that expression who could believe him? It's a curse to have a face that won't express what you mean."

"Amy!" Tucker calls. "Telephone."

Freddy waves goodbye to me with the muddy stick. " 'I am not a crook,' " Freddy says. "Jesus Christ."

Sam bounds halfway toward the house with me; then turns and goes back to Freddy.

It's Marilyn, Neal's mother, on the phone.

"Hi," Marilyn says. "He's afraid to spend the night."

"Oh, no," I say. "He said he wouldn't be."

She lowers her voice. "We can try it out, but I think he'll start crying."

"I'll come get him."

"I can bring him home. You're having a dinner party, aren't you?"

I lowered my voice. "Some party. Tucker's here. J.D. never showed up."

"Well," she says. "I'm sure that what you cooked was good."

"It's so foggy out, Marilyn. I'll come get Mark."

"He can stay. I'll be a martyr," she says, and hangs up before I can object.

Freddy comes into the house, tracking in mud. Sam lies in the kitchen, waiting for his paws to be cleaned. "Come on," Freddy says, hitting his hand against his thigh, having no idea what Sam is doing. Sam gets up and runs after him. They go into the small downstairs bathroom together. Sam loves to watch people urinate. Sometimes he sings, to harmonize with the sound of the urine going into the water. There are footprints and pawprints everywhere. Tucker is shrieking with laughter in the living room. " . . . he says, he says to the other one, 'Then, dearie, have you ever played *spin* the bottle?' " Frank's and Tucker's laughter drowns out the sound of Freddy peeing in the bathroom. I turn on the water in the kitchen sink, and it drowns out all the noise. I begin to scrape the dishes. Tucker is telling another story when I turn off the water: " . . . that it was Onassis in the Anvil,[6] and nothing would talk him out of it. They told him Onassis was dead, and he thought they were trying to make him think he was crazy. There was nothing to do but go along with him, but, God—he was trying to goad this poor old fag into fighting about Stavros Niarchos. You know—Onassis's *enemy*. He thought it was Onassis. In the *Anvil*." There is a sound of a glass breaking. Frank or Tucker puts "John Coltrane Live in Seattle" on the stereo and turns the volume down low. The bathroom door opens. Sam runs into the kitchen and begins to lap water from his dish. Freddy takes his little silver case and his rolling papers out of his shirt pocket. He puts a piece of paper on the kitchen table and is about to sprinkle grass on it, but realizes just in time that the paper has absorbed water from a puddle. He balls it up with his thumb, flicks it to the floor, puts a piece of rolling paper where the table's dry and shakes a line of grass down it. "You smoke this," he says to me. "I'll do the dishes."

"We'll both smoke it. I'll wash and you can wipe."

"I forgot to tell them I put ashes in the sauce," he says.

"I wouldn't interrupt."

"At least he pays Frank ten times what any other accountant for an art gallery would make," Freddy says.

Tucker is beating his hand on the arm of the sofa as he talks, stomping his feet. " . . . so he's trying to feel him out, to see if this old guy with the dyed hair knew *Maria Callas*. Jesus! And he's so out of it he's trying to think what opera singers are called, and instead of coming up with '*diva*' he comes up with '*duenna*.' At this point, Larry Betwell went up to him and tried to calm him down, and he breaks into song—some aria or something that Maria Callas was famous for. Larry told him he was going to lose his *teeth* if he didn't get it together, and . . ."

"He spends a lot of time in gay hangouts, for not being gay," Freddy says.

6. Raunchy gay bar in New York. Onassis and Niarchos: extremely wealthy Greek shipping magnates. Onassis, before his highly publicized marriage to Jacqueline Kennedy, was involved with the opera star Maria Callas, mentioned below.

I scream and jump back from the sink, hitting the glass I'm rinsing against the faucet, shattering green glass everywhere.

"What?" Freddy says. "Jesus Christ, what is it?"

Too late, I realize what it must have been that I saw: J.D. in a goat mask, the puckered pink plastic lips against the window beside the kitchen sink.

"I'm sorry," J.D. says, coming through the door and nearly colliding with Frank, who has rushed into the kitchen. Tucker is right behind him.

"Ooh," Tucker says, feigning disappointment, "I thought Freddy smooched her."

"I'm sorry," J.D. says again. "I thought you'd know it was me."

The rain must have started again, because J.D. is soaking wet. He has turned the mask around so that the goat's head stares out from the back of his head. "I got lost," J.D. says. He has a farmhouse upstate. "I missed the turn. I went miles. I missed the whole dinner, didn't I?"

"What did you do wrong?" Frank asks.

"I didn't turn left onto 58. I don't know why I didn't realize my mistake, but I went *miles*. It was raining so hard I couldn't go over twenty-five miles an hour. Your driveway is all mud. You're going to have to push me out."

"There's some roast left over. And salad, if you want it," I say.

"Bring it in the living room," Frank says to J.D. Freddy is holding out a plate to him. J.D. reaches for the plate. Freddy pulls it back. J.D. reaches again, and Freddy is so stoned, that he isn't quick enough this time—J.D. grabs it.

"I thought you'd know it was me," J.D. says. "I apologize." He dishes salad onto the plate. "You'll be rid of me for six months, in the morning."

"Where does your plane leave from?" Freddy says.

"Kennedy."

"Come in here!" Tucker calls. "I've got a story for you about Perry Dwyer down at the Anvil last week, when he thought he saw Aristotle Onassis."

"Who's Perry Dwyer?" J.D. says.

"That is not the point of the story, dear man. And when you're in Cassis, I want you to look up an American painter over there. Will you? He doesn't have a phone. Anyway—I've been tracking him, and I know where he is now, and I am *very* interested, if you would stress that with him, to do a show in June that will be *only* him. He doesn't answer my letters."

"Your hand is cut," J.D. says to me.

"Forget it," I say. "Go ahead."

"I'm sorry," he says. "Did I make you do that?"

"Yes, you did."

"Don't keep your finger under the water. Put pressure on it to stop the bleeding."

He puts the plate on the table. Freddy is leaning against the counter, staring at the blood swirling in the sink, and smoking the joint all by himself. I can feel the little curls on my forehead that Freddy was talking about. They feel heavy on my skin. I hate to see my own blood. I'm sweating. I let J.D. do what he does; he turns off the water and wraps his hand around my second finger, squeezing. Water runs down our wrists.

Freddy jumps to answer the phone when it rings, as though a siren just went off behind him. He calls me to the phone, but J.D. steps in front of me, shakes his head no, and takes the dish towel and wraps it around my hand before he lets me go.

"Well," Marilyn says. "I had the best of intentions, but my battery's dead."

J.D. is standing behind me, with his hand on my shoulder.

"I'll be right over," I say. "He's not upset now, is he?"

"No, but he's dropped enough hints that he doesn't think he can make it through the night."

"O.K.," I say. "I'm sorry about all of this."

"Six years old," Marilyn says. "Wait till he grows up and gets that feeling."

I hang up.

"Let me see your hand," J.D. says.

"I don't want to look at it. Just go get me a Band-Aid, please."

He turns and goes upstairs. I unwrap the towel and look at it. It's pretty deep, but no glass is in my finger. I feel funny; the outlines of things are turning yellow. I sit in the chair by the phone. Sam comes and lies beside me, and I stare at his black-and-yellow tail, beating. I reach down with my good hand and pat him, breathing deeply in time with every second pat.

"*Rothko?*" Tucker says bitterly, in the living room. "Nothing is great that can appear on greeting cards. Wyeth[7] is that way. Would "Christina's World" look bad on a cocktail napkin? You know it wouldn't."

I jump as the phone rings again. "Hello?" I say, wedging the phone against my shoulder with my ear, wrapping the dish towel tighter around my hand.

"Tell them it's a crank call. Tell them anything," Johnny says. "I miss you. How's Saturday night at your house?"

"All right," I say. I catch my breath.

"Everything's all right here, too. Yes indeed. Roast rack of lamb. Friend of Nicole's who's going to Key West tomorrow had too

7. Mark Rothko (1903–1970) and Andrew Wyeth (1917–   ), both famous painters. "Christina's World" is a well-known Wyeth painting.

much to drink and got depressed because he thought it was raining in Key West, and I said I'd go in my study and call the National Weather Service. Hello, Weather Service. How are you?"

J.D. comes down from upstairs with two Band-Aids and stands beside me, unwrapping one. I want to say to Johnny, "I'm cut. I'm bleeding. It's no joke."

It's all right to talk in front of J.D., but I don't know who else might overhear me.

"I'd say they made the delivery about four this afternoon," I say.

"This is the church, this is the steeple. Open the door, and see all the people," Johnny says. "Take care of yourself. I'll hang up and find out if it's raining in Key West."

"Late in the afternoon," I say. "Everything is fine."

"Nothing is fine," Johnny says. "Take care of yourself."

He hangs up. I put the phone down, and realize that I'm still having trouble focusing, the sight of my cut finger made me so light-headed. I don't look at the finger again as J.D. undoes the towel and wraps the Band-Aids around my finger.

"What's going on in here?" Frank says, coming into the dining room.

"I cut my finger," I say. "It's O.K."

"You did?" he says. He looks woozy—a little drunk. "Who keeps calling?"

"Marilyn. Mark changed his mind about staying all night. She was going to bring him home, but her battery's dead. You'll have to get him. Or I will."

"Who called the second time?" he says.

"The oil company. They wanted to know if we got our delivery today."

He nods. "I'll go get him, if you want," he says. He lowers his voice. "Tucker's probably going to whirl himself into a tornado for an encore," he says, nodding toward the living room. "I'll take him with me."

"Do you want me to go get him?" J.D. says.

"I don't mind getting some air," Frank says. "Thanks, though. Why don't you go in the living room and eat your dinner?"

"You forgive me?" J.D. says.

"Sure," I say. "It wasn't your fault. Where did you get that mask?"

"I found it on top of a Goodwill box in Manchester. There was also a beautiful old birdcage—solid brass."

The phone rings again. I pick it up. "Wouldn't I love to be in Key West with you," Johnny says. He makes a sound as though he's kissing me and hangs up.

"Wrong number," I say.

Frank feels in his pants pocket for the car keys.

J.D. knows about Johnny. He introduced me, in the faculty lounge, where J.D. and I had gone to get a cup of coffee after I registered for classes. After being gone for nearly two years, J.D. still gets mail at the department—he said he had to stop by for the mail anyway, so he'd drive me to campus and point me toward the registrar's. J.D. taught English; now he does nothing. J.D. is glad that I've gone back to college to study art again, now that Mark is in school. I'm six credits away from an M.A. in art history. He wants me to think about myself, instead of thinking about Mark all the time. He talks as though I could roll Mark out on a string and let him fly off, high above me. J.D.'s wife and son died in a car crash. His son was Mark's age. "I wasn't prepared," J.D. said when we were driving over that day. He always says this when he talks about it. "How could you be prepared for such a thing?" I asked him. "I am now," he said. Then, realizing he was acting very hardboiled, made fun of himself. "Go on," he said, "punch me in the stomach. Hit me as hard as you can." We both knew he isn't prepared for anything. When he couldn't find a parking place that day, his hands were wrapped around the wheel so tightly that his knuckles turned white.

Johnny came in as we were drinking coffee. J.D. was looking at his junk mail—publishers wanting him to order anthologies, ways to get free dictionaries.

"You are so lucky to be out of it," Johnny said, by way of greeting. "What do you do when you've spent two weeks on 'Hamlet' and the student writes about Hamlet's good friend Horchow?"

He threw a blue book into J.D.'s lap. J.D. sailed it back.

"Johnny," he said, "this is Amy."

"Hi, Amy," Johnny said.

"You remember when Frank Wayne was in graduate school here? Amy's Frank's wife."

"Hi, Amy," Johnny said.

J.D. told me he knew it the instant Johnny walked into the room—he knew that second that he should introduce me as somebody's wife. He could have predicted it all from the way Johnny looked at me.

For a long time J.D. gloated that he had been prepared for what happened next—that Johnny and I were going to get together. It took me to disturb his pleasure in himself—me, crying hysterically on the phone last month, not knowing what to do, what move to make next.

"Don't do anything for a while. I guess that's my advice," J.D. said. "But you probably shouldn't listen to me. All I can do myself is run away, hide out. I'm not the learned professor. You know what I believe. I believe all that wicked fairy-tale crap: your heart will break, your house will burn."

Tonight, because he doesn't have a garage at his farm, J.D. has come to leave his car in the empty half of our two-car garage while he's in France. I look out the window and see his old Saab, glowing in the moonlight. J.D. has brought his favorite book, "A Vision,"[8] to read on the plane. He says his suitcase contains only a spare pair of jeans, cigarettes, and underwear. He is going to buy a leather jacket in France, at a store where he almost bought a leather jacket two years ago.

In our bedroom there are about twenty small glass prisms hung with fishing line from one of the exposed beams; they catch the morning light, and we stare at them like a cat eyeing catnip held above its head. Just now, it is 2 A.M. At six-thirty, they will be filled with dazzling color. At four or five, Mark will come into the bedroom and get in bed with us. Sam will wake up, stretch, and shake, and the tags on his collar will clink, and he will yawn and shake again and go downstairs, where J.D. is asleep in his sleeping bag and Tucker is asleep on the sofa, and get a drink of water from his dish. Mark has been coming into our bedroom for about a year. He gets onto the bed by climbing up on a footstool that horrified me when I first saw it—a gift from Frank's mother: a footstool that says "Today Is the First Day of the Rest of Your Life" in needlepoint. I kept it in a closet for years, but it occurred to me that it would help Mark get up into the bed, so he would not have to make a little leap and possibly skin his shin again. Now Mark does not disturb us when he comes into the bedroom, except that it bothers me that he has reverted to sucking his thumb. Sometimes he lies in bed with his cold feet against my leg. Sometimes, small as he is, he snores.

Somebody is playing a record downstairs. It's the Velvet Underground—Nico, in a dream or swoon, singing "Sunday Morning." I can barely hear the whispering and tinkling of the record. I can only follow it because I've heard it a hundred times.

I am lying in bed, waiting for Frank to get out of the bathroom. My cut finger throbs. Things are going on in the house even though I have gone to bed; water runs, the record plays, Sam is still downstairs, so there must be some action.

I have known everybody in this house for years; and as time goes by I know them all less and less. J.D. was Frank's adviser in college. Frank was his best student, and they started to see each other outside of class. They played handball. J.D. and his family came to dinner. We went there. That summer—the summer Frank decided to go to graduate school in business instead of English—J.D.'s wife and son deserted him in a more horrible way, in that car crash.

8. A prose work by William Butler Yeats (1856–1939), Irish poet.

J.D. has quit his job. He has been to Las Vegas, to Colorado, New Orleans, Los Angeles, Paris twice; he tapes postcards to the walls of his living room. A lot of the time, on the weekends, he shows up at our house with his sleeping bag. Sometimes he brings a girl. Lately, not. Years ago, Tucker was in Frank's therapy group in New York and ended up hiring Frank to work as the accountant for his gallery. Tucker was in therapy at the time because he was obsessed with foreigners. Now he is also obsessed with homosexuals. Before the parties he does TM and yoga, and during the parties he does Seconals and isometrics. When I first met him, he was living for the summer in his sister's house in Vermont while she was in Europe, and he called us one night, in New York, in a real panic because there were wasps all over. They were "hatching," he said—big, sleepy wasps that were everywhere. We said we'd come; we drove all through the night to get to Brattleboro. It was true: there were wasps on the undersides of plates, in the plants, in the folds of curtains. Tucker was so upset that he was out behind the house, in the cold Vermont morning, wrapped like an Indian in a blanket, with only his pajamas on underneath. He was sitting in a lawn chair, hiding behind a bush, waiting for us to come.

And Freddy—"Reddy Fox," when Frank is feeling affectionate toward him. When we first met, I taught him to ice-skate and he taught me to waltz; in the summer, at Atlantic City, he'd go with me on a roller coaster that curved high over the waves. I was the one—not Frank—who would get out of bed in the middle of the night and meet him at an all-night deli and put my arm around his shoulders, the way he put his arm around my shoulders on the roller coaster, and talk quietly to him until he got over his latest anxiety attack. Now he tests me, and I retreat: this man he picked up, this man who picked him up, how it feels to have forgotten somebody's name when your hand is in the back pocket of his jeans and you're not even halfway to your apartment. Reddy Fox—admiring my new red silk blouse, stroking his fingertips down the front, and my eyes wide, because I could feel his fingers on my chest, even though I was holding the blouse in front of me on a hanger to be admired. All those moments, and all they meant was that I was fooled into thinking I knew these people because I knew the small things, the personal things.

Freddy will always be more stoned than I am, because he feels comfortable getting stoned with me and I'll always be reminded that he's more lost. Tucker knows he can come to the house and be the center of attention; he can tell all the stories he knows, and we'll never tell the story we know about him hiding in the bushes like a frightened dog. J.D. comes back from his trips with boxes full of postcards, and I look at all of them as though they're photographs taken by him, and I know, and he knows, that what he likes about them is their flatness—the unreality of them, the unreality of what he does.

Last summer, I read "The Metamorphosis" and said to J.D., "Why did Gregor Samsa wake up a cockroach?" His answer (which he would have toyed over with his students forever) was "Because that's what people expected of him."

They make the illogical logical. I don't do anything, because I'm waiting, I'm on hold (J.D.); I stay stoned because I know it's better to be out of it (Freddy); I love art because I myself am a work of art (Tucker).

Frank is harder to understand. One night a week or so ago, I thought we were really attuned to each other, communicating by telepathic waves, and as I lay in bed about to speak I realized that the vibrations really existed: they were him, snoring.

Now he's coming into the bedroom, and I'm trying again to think what to say. Or ask. Or do.

"Be glad you're not in Key West," he says. He climbs into bed.

I raise myself up on one elbow and stare at him.

"There's a hurricane about to hit," he says.

"What?" I say. "Where did you hear that?"

"When Reddy Fox and I were putting the dishes away. We had the radio on." He doubles up his pillow, pushes it under his neck. "Boom goes everything," he says. "Bam. Crash. Poof." He looks at me. "You look shocked." He closes his eyes. Then, after a minute or two, he murmurs, "Hurricanes upset you? I'll try to think of something nice."

He is quiet for so long that I think he has fallen asleep. Then he says, "Cars that run on water. A field of flowers, none alike. A shooting star that goes slow enough for you to watch. Your life to do over again." He has been whispering in my ear, and when he takes his mouth away I shiver. He slides lower in the bed for sleep. "I'll tell you something really amazing," he says. "Tucker told me he went into a travel agency on Park Avenue last week and asked the travel agent where he should go to pan for gold, and she told him."

"Where did she tell him to go?"

"I think somewhere in Peru. The banks of some river in Peru."

"Did you decide what you're going to do after Mark's birthday?" I say.

He doesn't answer me. I touch him on the side, finally.

"It's two o'clock in the morning. Let's talk about it another time."

"You picked the house, Frank. They're your friends downstairs. I used to be what you wanted me to be."

"They're your friends, too," he says. "Don't be paranoid."

"I want to know if you're staying or going."

He takes a deep breath, lets it out, and continues to lie very still. "Everything you've done is commendable," he says. "You did the right thing to go back to school. You tried to do the right thing by finding yourself a normal friend like Marilyn. But your whole life you've made one mistake—you've surrounded yourself with men. Let me tell you something. All men—if they're crazy, like Tucker, if they're gay as the Queen of the May, like Reddy Fox, even if they're just six years old—I'm going to tell you something about them. Men think they're Spider-Man and Buck Rogers and Superman. You know what we all feel inside that you don't feel? That we're going to the stars."

He takes my hand. "I'm looking down on all of this from space," he whispers. "I'm already gone."

T. CORAGHESSAN BOYLE

Descent of Man

I WAS living with a woman who suddenly began to stink. It was very difficult. The first time I confronted her she merely smiled. "Occupational hazard," she said. The next time she curled her lip. There were other problems too. Hairs, for instance. Hairs that began to appear on her clothing, sharp and black and brutal. Invariably I would awake to find these hairs in my mouth, or I would glance into the mirror to see them slashing like razor edges across the collars of my white shirts. Then too there was the fruit. I began to discover moldering bits of it about the house—apple and banana most characteristically—but plum and tangelo or even passion fruit and yim-yim were not at all anomalous. These fruit fragments occurred principally in the bedroom, on the pillow, surrounded by darkening spots. It was not long before I located their source: they lay hidden like gems in the long wild hanks of her hair. Another occupational hazard.

Jane was in the habit of sitting before the air conditioner when she came home from work, fingering out her hair, drying the sweat from her face and neck in the cool hum of the machine, fruit bits sifting silently to the carpet, black hairs drifting like feathers. On these occasions the room would fill with the stink of her, bestial and fetid. And I would find my eyes watering, my mind imaging the dark rotting trunks of the rain forest, stained sienna and mandalay and Hooker's green with the excrements dropped from above. My ears would keen with the whistling and crawking of the jungle birds, the screechings of the snot-nosed apes in the branches. And then, slack-faced and tight-boweled, I would step into the bathroom and retch, the sweetness of my own intestinal secrets a balm against the potent hairy stench of her.

One evening, just after her bath (the faintest odor lingered, yet still it was so trenchant I had to fight the impulse to get up and urinate on a tree or a post or something), I lay my hand casually across her belly and was suddenly startled to see an insect flit from its cover, skate up the swell of her abdomen, and bury itself in her navel. "Good Christ," I said.

"Hm?" she returned, peering over the cover of her Yerkish[1] reader.

"That," I said. "That bug, that insect, that vermin."

She sat up, plucked the thing from its cachette, raised it to her lips and popped it between her front teeth. "Louse," she said, sucking. "Went down to the old-age home on Thirteenth Street to pick them up."

I anticipated her: "Not for—?"

"Why certainly, potpie—so Konrad can experience a tangible gratification of his social impulses during the grooming ritual. You know: you scratch my back, I scratch yours."

I lay in bed that night sweating, thinking about Jane and those slippery-fingered monkeys poking away at her, and listening for the lice crawling across her scalp or nestling their bloody little siphons in the tufts under her arms. Finally, about four, I got up and took three Doriden. I woke at two in the afternoon, an insect in my ear. It was only an earwig. I had missed my train, failed to call in at the office. There was a note from Jane: Pick me up at four. Konrad sends love.

The Primate Center stood in the midst of a macadamized acre or two, looking very much like a school building: faded brick, fluted columns, high mesh fences. Finger paintings and mobiles hung in the windows, misshapen ceramics crouched along the sills. A flag raggled at the top of a whitewashed flagpole. I found myself bending to examine the cornerstone: Asa Priff Grammar School, 1939. Inside it was dark and cool, the halls were lined with lockers and curling watercolors, the linoleum gleamed like a shy smile. I stepped into the BOYS' ROOM. The urinals were a foot and a half from the floor. Designed for little people, I mused. Youngsters. Hardly big enough to hold their little peters without the teacher's help. I smiled, and situated myself over one of the urinals, the strong honest scent of Pine-Sol in my nostrils. At that moment the door wheezed open and a chimpanzee shuffled in. He was dressed in shorts, shirt and bow tie. He nodded to me, it seemed, and made

1. From work of Robert Hearns Yerkes (1875–1956), American psychologist who founded Yale Labs of primate biology.

a few odd gestures with his hands as he moved up to the urinal beside mine. Then he opened his fly and pulled out an enormous slick red organ like a peeled banana. I looked away, embarrassed, but could hear him urinating mightily. The stream hissed against the porcelain like a thunderstorm, rattled the drain as it went down. My own water wouldn't come. I began to feel foolish. The chimp shook himself daintily, zippered up, pulled the plunger, crossed to the sink, washed and dried his hands, and left. I found I no longer had to go.

Out in the hallway the janitor was leaning on his flathead broom. The chimp stood before him gesticulating with manic dexterity: brushing his forehead and tugging his chin, slapping his hands under his armpits, tapping his wrists, his tongue, his ear, his lip. The janitor watched intently. Suddenly—after a particularly virulent flurry—the man burst into laughter, rich braying globes of it. The chimp folded his lip and joined in, adding his weird nasal snickering to the janitor's barrel-laugh. I stood by the door to the BOYS' ROOM in a quandary. I began to feel that it might be wiser to wait in the car—but then I didn't want to call attention to myself, darting in and out like that. The janitor might think I was stealing paper towels or something. So I stood there, thinking to have a word with him after the chimp moved on—with the expectation that he could give me some grassroots insight into the nature of Jane's job. But the chimp didn't move on. The two continued laughing, now harder than ever. The janitor's face was tear-streaked. Each time he looked up the chimp produced a gesticular flurry that would stagger him again. Finally the janitor wound down a bit, and still chuckling, held out his hands, palms up. The chimp flung his arms up over his head and then heaved them down again, rhythmically slapping the big palms with his own. "Right on! Mastuh Konrad," the janitor said, "Right on!" The chimp grinned, then hitched up his shorts and sauntered off down the hall. The janitor turned back to his broom, still chuckling.

I cleared my throat. The broom began a geometrically precise course up the hall toward me. It stopped at my toes, the ridge of detritus flush with the pinions of my wingtips. The janitor looked up. The pupil of his right eye was fixed in the corner, beneath the lid, and the white was red. There was an ironic gap between his front teeth. "Kin ah do sumfin fo yo, mah good man?" he said.

"I'm waiting for Miss Good."

"Ohhh, Miz *Good*," he said, nodding his head. "Fust ah tought yo was thievin paypuh tow-els outen de Boys' Room but den when ah sees yo standin dere rigid as de Venus de Milo ah thinks to mahsef: he is some kinda new sculpture de stoodents done made is what he is." He was squinting up at me and grinning like we'd just come back from sailing around the world together.

"That's a nice broom," I said.

He looked at me steadily, grinning still. "Yo's wonderin what me and Mastuh Konrad was jivin bout up dere, isn't yo? Well, ah tells yo: he was relatin a hoomerous anecdote, de punch line ob which has deep cosmic implications in dat it establishes a common groun between monks and Ho-mo sapiens despite dere divergent ancestries." He shook his head, chortled. "Yes in-deed, dat Mastuh Konrad is quite de wit."

"You mean to tell me you actually understand all that lip-pulling and finger-waving?" I was beginning to feel a nameless sense of outrage.

"Oh sartinly, mah good man. Dat ASL."

"What?"

"ASL is what we was talkin. A-merican Sign Language. Developed for de deef n dumb. Yo sees, Mastuh Konrad is sumfin ob a genius round here. He can commoonicate de mos esoteric i-deas in bof ASL and Yerkish, re-spond to and translate English, French, German and Chinese. Fack, it was Miz Good was tellin me dat Konrad is workin right now on a Yerkish translation ob Darwin's *De-scent o Man*. He is mainly into anthro-pology, yo knows, but he has cultivated a in-teress in udder fields too. Dis lass fall he done undertook a Yerkish translation ob Chomsky's *Language and Mind* and Nietzsche's *Jenseits von Gut und Böse*.[2] And dat's some pretty heavy shit, Jackson."

I was hot with outrage. "Stuff," I said. "Stuff and nonsense."

"No sense in feelin personally treatened by Mastuh Konrad's chievements, mah good fellow—yo's got to ree-lize dat he is a genius."

A word came to me: "Bullhonk," I said. And turned to leave.

The janitor caught me by the shirtsleeve. "He is now scorin his turd opera," he whispered. I tore away from him and stamped out of the building.

Jane was waiting in the car. I climbed in, cranked down the sunroof and opened the air vents.

At home I poured a water glass of gin, held it to my nostrils and inhaled. Jane sat before the air conditioner, her hair like a urinal mop, stinking. Black hairs cut the atmosphere, fruit bits whispered to the carpet. Occasionally the tip of my tongue entered the gin. I sniffed and tasted, thinking of plastic factories and turpentine distilleries and rich sulfurous smoke. On my way to the bedroom I poured a second glass.

In the bedroom I sniffed gin and dressed for dinner. "Jane?" I called, "shouldn't you be getting ready?" She appeared in the doorway. She was dressed in her work clothes: jeans and sweatshirt.

2. "Beyond good and evil."

The sweatshirt was gray and hooded. There were yellow stains on the sleeves. I thought of the lower depths of animal cages, beneath the floor meshing. "I figured I'd go like this," she said. I was knotting my tie. "And I wish you'd stop insisting on baths every night—I'm getting tired of smelling like a coupon in a detergent box. It's unnatural. Unhealthy."

In the car on the way to the restaurant I lit a cigar, a cheap twisted black thing like half a pepperoni. Jane sat hunched against her door, unwashed. I had never before smoked a cigar. I tried to start a conversation but Jane said she didn't feel like talking: talk seemed so useless, such an anachronism. We drove on in silence. And I reflected that this was not the Jane I knew and loved. Where, I wondered, was the girl who changed wigs three or four times a day and sported nails like a Chinese emperor?—and where was the girl who dressed like an Arabian bazaar and smelled like the trade winds?

She was committed. The project, the study, grants. I could read the signs: she was growing away from me.

The restaurant was dark, a maze of rocky gardens, pancake-leafed vegetation, black fountains. We stood squinting just inside the door. Birds whistled, carp hissed through the pools. Somewhere a monkey screeched. Jane put her hand on my shoulder and whispered in my ear. "Siamang," she said. At that moment the leaves parted beside us: a rubbery little fellow emerged and motioned us to sit on a bench beneath a wicker birdcage. He was wearing a soiled loincloth and eight or ten necklaces of yellowed teeth. His hair flamed out like a brushfire. In the dim light from the braziers I noticed his nostrils—both shrunken and pinched, as if once pierced straight through. His face was of course inscrutable. As soon as we were seated he removed my socks and shoes, Jane's sneakers, and wrapped our feet in what I later learned were plantain leaves. I started to object—I bitterly resent anyone looking at my feet—but Jane shushed me. We had waited three months for reservations.

The maitre d' signed for us to follow, and led us through a dripping stone-walled tunnel to an outdoor garden where the flagstones gave way to dirt and we found ourselves on a narrow plant-choked path. He licked along like an iguana and we hurried to keep up. Wet fronds slapped back in my face, creepers snatched at my ankles, mud sucked at the plantain leaves on my feet. The scents of mold and damp and long-lying urine hung in the air, and I thought of the men's room at the subway station. It was dark as a womb. I offered Jane my hand, but she refused it. Her breathing was fast. The monkey chatter was loud as a zoo afire. "Far out," she said. I slapped a mosquito on my neck.

A moment later we found ourselves seated at a bamboo table overhung with branch and vine. Across from us sat Dr. and Mrs. U-Hwak-Lo, director of the Primate Center and wife. A candle guttered between them. I cleared my throat, and then began idly tracing my finger around the circular hole cut in the table's center. The Doctor's ears were the size of peanuts. "Glad you two could make it," he said. "I've long been urging Jane to sample some of our humble island fare." I smiled, crushed a spider against the back of my chair. The Doctor's English was perfect, pure Martha's Vineyard—he sounded like Ted Kennedy's insurance salesman. His wife's was weak: "Yes," she said, "nussing cook here, all roar." "How exciting!" said Jane. And then the conversation turned to primates, and the Center.

Mrs. U-Hwak-Lo and I smiled at one another. Jane and the Doctor were already deeply absorbed in a dialogue concerning the incidence of anal retention in chimps deprived of Frisbee coordination during the sensorimotor period. I gestured toward them with my head and arched my eyebrows wittily. Mrs. U-Hwak-Lo giggled. It was then that Jane's proximity began to affect me. The close wet air seemed to concentrate her essence, distill its potency. The U-Hwak-Los seemed unaffected. I began to feel queasy. I reached for the fingerbowl and drank down its contents. Mrs. U-Hwak-Lo smiled. It was coconut oil. Just then the waiter appeared carrying a wooden bowl the size of a truck tire. A single string of teeth slapped against his breastbone as he set the bowl down and slipped off into the shadows. The Doctor and Jane were oblivious—they were talking excitedly, occasionally lapsing into what I took to be ASL, ear- and nose- and lip-picking like a manager and his third-base coach. I peered into the bowl: it was filled to the rim with clean-picked chicken bones. Mrs. U-Hwak-Lo nodded, grinning: "No on-tray," she said. "Appeticer." At that moment a simian screamed somewhere close, screamed like death itself. Jane looked up. "Rhesus," she said.

On my return from the men's room I had some difficulty locating the table in the dark. I had already waded through two murky fountains and was preparing to plunge through my third when I heard Mrs. U-Hwak-Lo's voice behind me. "Here," she said. "Make quick, repass now serve." She took my hand and led me back to the table. "Oh, they're enormously resourceful," the Doctor was saying as I stumbled into my chair, pants wet to the knees. "They first employ a general anesthetic—a distillation of the chu-bok root—and then the chef (who logically doubles as village surgeon) makes a circular incision about the macaque's cranium, carefully peeling back the already-shaven scalp, and staunching the blood flow quite effectively with maura-ro, a highly absorbent powder derived from the tamana leaf. He then removes both the frontal and parietal plates to expose the brain . . ." I looked at Jane: she was rapt. I wasn't really listening. My attention was directed toward what I took to be the main course, which had appeared in my absence. An unsteady pinkish mound now occupied the center of the table, completely obscuring the circular hole—it looked like cherry vanilla yogurt, a carton and a half, perhaps two. On closer inspection I noticed several black hairs peeping out from around its flaccid edges. And thought immediately of the bush-headed maitre d'. I pointed to one of the hairs, remarking to Mrs. U-Hwak-Lo that the rudiments of culinary hygiene could be a little more rigorously observed among the staff. She smiled. Encouraged, I asked her what exactly the dish was. "Much delicacy," she said. "Very rare find in land of Lincoln." At that moment the waiter appeared and handed each of us a bamboo stick beaten flat and sharpened at one end.

". . . then the tribal elders or visiting dignitaries are seated around the table," the Doctor was saying. "The chef has previously of course located the macaque beneath the table, the exposed part of the creature's brain protruding from the hole in its center. After the feast, the lower ranks of the village population divide up the remnants. It's really quiet efficient."

"How fascinating!" said Jane. "Shall we try some?"

"By all means . . . but tell me, how has Konrad been coming with that Yerkish epic he's been working up?"

Jane turned to answer, bamboo stick poised: "Oh I'm so glad you asked—I'd almost forgotten. He's finished his tenth book and tells me he'll be doing two more—out of deference to the Miltonic tradition. Isn't that a groove?"

"Yes," said the Doctor, gesturing toward the rosy lump in the center of the table. "Yes it is. He's certainly—and I hope you won't mind the pun—a brainy fellow. Ho-ho."

"Oh, Doctor," Jane laughed, and plunged her stick into the pink. Beneath the table, in the dark, a tiny fist clutched at my pantleg.

I missed work again the following day. This time it took five Doriden to put me under. I had lain in bed sweating and tossing, listening to Jane's quiet breathing, inhaling her fumes. At dawn I dozed off, dreamed briefly of elementary school cafeterias swarming with knickered chimps and weltered with trays of cherry vanilla yogurt, and woke stale-mouthed. Then I took the pills. It was three-thirty when I woke again. There was a note from Jane: Bringing Konrad home for dinner. Vacuum rug and clean toilet.

Konrad was impeccably dressed—long pants, platform wedgies, cufflinks. He smelled of eau de cologne, Jane of used litter. They arrived during the seven o'clock news. I opened the door for them.

"Hello Jane," I said. We stood at the door, awkward, silent. "Well?" she said. "Aren't you going to greet our guest?" "Hello, Konrad," I said. And then: "I believe we met in the boys' room at the Center the other day?" He bowed deeply, straight-faced, his upper lip like a halved cantaloupe. Then he broke into a snicker, turned to Jane and juggled out an impossible series of gestures. Jane laughed. Something caught in my throat. "Is he trying to say something?" I asked. "Oh potpie," she said, "it was nothing—just a little quote from Yeats."

"Yeats?"

"Yes, you know: 'An aged man is but a paltry thing.' "[3]

Jane served watercress sandwiches and animal crackers as hors d'oeuvres. She brought them into the living room on a cut-glass serving tray and set them down before Konrad and me, where we sat on the sofa, watching the news. Then she returned to the kitchen. Konrad plucked up a tiny sandwich and swallowed it like a communion wafer, sucking the tips of his fingers. Then he lifted the tray and offered it to me. I declined. "No, thank you," I said. Konrad shrugged, set the plate down in his lap, and carefully stacked all the sandwiches in its center. I pretended to be absorbed with the news: actually I studied him, half-face. He was filling the gaps in his sandwich-construction with animal crackers. His lower lip protruded, his ears were rubbery, he was balding. With both hands he crushed the heap of crackers and sandwiches together and began kneading it until it took on the consistency of raw dough. Then he lifted the whole thing to his mouth and swallowed it without chewing. There were no whites to his eyes.

Konrad's only reaction to the newscast was a burst of excitement over a war story—the reporter stood against the wasteland of treadless tanks and recoilless guns in Thailand or Syria or Chile; huts were burning, old women weeping. "Wow-wow! Eeeeeeee! Er-er-er-er," Konrad said. Jane appeared in the kitchen doorway, hands dripping. "What is it, Konrad?" she said. He made a series of violent gestures. "Well?" I asked. She translated: 'Konrad says that 'the pig oppressors' genocidal tactics will lead to their mutual extermination and usher in a new golden age . . .' "—here she hesitated, looked up at him to continue (he was springing up and down on the couch, flailing his fists as though they held whips and scourges)—" '. . . of freedom and equality for all, regardless of race, creed, color—or genus.' I wouldn't worry," she added, "it's just his daily slice of revolutionary rhetoric. He'll calm down in a minute—he likes to play Che,[4] but he's basically nonviolent."

Ten minutes later Jane served dinner. Konrad, with remarkable

3. From "Sailing to Byzantium" by William Butler Yeats (1856–1939), Irish poet.
4. Che Guevara (1928–1967), Cuban revolutionary killed in Bolivia.

speed and coordination, consumed four cans of fruit cocktail, thirty-two spareribs, half a dozen each of oranges, apples, and pomegranates, two cheeseburgers and three quarts of chocolate malted. In the kitchen, clearing up, I commented to Jane about our guest's prodigious appetite. He was sitting in the other room, listening to *Don Giovanni*,[5] sipping brandy. Jane said that he was a big, active male and that she could attest to his need for so many calories. "How much does he weigh?" I asked. "Stripped," she said, "one eighty-one. When he stands up straight he's four eight and three quarters." I mulled over this information while I scraped away at the dishes, filed them in the dishwasher, neat ranks of blue china. A few moments later I stepped into the living room to observe Jane stroking Konrad's ears, his head in her lap. I stand five seven, one forty-three.

When I returned from work the following day, Jane was gone. Her dresser drawers were bare, the closet empty. There were white rectangles on the wall where her Rousseau[6] reproductions had hung. The top plank of the bookcase was ribbed with the dust-prints of her Edgar Rice Burroughs[7] collection. Her girls' softball trophy, her natural foods cookbook, her oaken cudgel, her moog, her wok: all gone. There were no notes. A pain jabbed at my sternum, tears started in my eyes. I was alone, deserted, friendless. I began to long even for the stink of her. On the pillow in the bedroom I found a fermenting chunk of pineapple. And sobbed.

By the time I thought of the Primate Center the sun was already on the wane. It was dark when I got there. Loose gravel grated beneath my shoes in the parking lot; the flag snapped at the top of its pole; the lights grinned lickerishly from the Center's windows. Inside the lighting was subdued, the building hushed. I began searching through the rooms, opening and slamming doors. The linoleum glowed all the way up the long corridor. At the far end I heard someone whistling "My Old Kentucky Home." It was the janitor. "Howdedo," he said. "Wut kin ah do fo yo at such a inauspicious hour ob de night?"

I was candid with him. "I'm looking for Miss Good."

"Ohhh, she leave bout fo-turdy evy day—sartinly yo should be well apprised ob dat fack."

"I thought she might be working late tonight."

"Noooo, no chance ob dat." He was staring at the floor.

"Mind if I look for myself?"

"Mah good man, ah trusts yo is not intimatin dat ah would dis-

5. Opera (1787) by Mozart. 6. Henri Rousseau (1844–1910), French painter. 7. Popular American novelist (1875–1950), author of the Tarzan books.

kise de troof . . . far be it fum me to pre-varicate just to proteck a young lady wut run off fum a man dat doan unnerstan her needs nor 'low her to spress de natchrul inclination ob her soul."

At that moment a girlish giggle sounded from down the hall. Jane's girlish giggle. The janitor's right hand spread itself across my chest. 'Ah wooden insinooate mahself in de middle ob a highly sinificant speriment if ah was yo, Jackson," he said, hissing through the gap in his teeth. I pushed by him and started down the corridor. Jane's laugh leaped out again. From the last door on my left. I hurried. Suddenly the Doctor and his wife stepped from the shadows to block the doorway. "Mr. Horne," said the Doctor, arms folded against his chest, "take hold of yourself. We are conducting a series of experiments here that I simply cannot allow you to—"

"A fig for your experiments," I shouted. "I want to speak to my, my—roommate." I could hear the janitor's footsteps behind me. "Get out of my way, Doctor," I said. Mrs. U-Hwak-Lo smiled. I felt panicky. Thought of the Tong Wars. "Is dey a problem here, Doc?" the janitor said, his breath hot on the back of my neck. I broke. Grabbed the Doctor by his elbows, wheeled around and shoved him into the janitor. They went down on the linoleum like spastic skaters. I applied my shoulder to the door and battered my way in, Mrs. U-Hwak-Lo's shrill in my ear: "You make big missake, Misser!" Inside I found Jane, legs and arms bare, pinching a lab smock across her chest. She looked puzzled at first, then annoyed. She stepped up to me, made some rude gestures in my face. I could hear scrambling in the hallway behind me. Then I saw Konrad—in a pair of baggy BVDs. I grabbed Jane. But Konrad was there in an instant—he hit me like a grill of a Cadillac and I spun across the room, tumbling desks and chairs as I went. I slumped against the chalkboard. The door slammed: Jane was gone. Konrad swelled his chest, swayed toward me, the fluorescent lights hissing overhead, the chalkboard cold against the back of my neck. And I looked up into the black eyes, teeth, fur, rock-ribbed arms.

RAYMOND CARVER

Where I'm Calling From

WE are on the front porch at Frank Martin's drying-out facility. Like the rest of us at Frank Martin's, J.P. is first and foremost a drunk. But he's also a chimney sweep. It's his first time here, and he's scared. I've been here once before. What's to say? I'm back. J.P.'s real name is Joe Penny, but he says I should call him J.P. He's about thirty years old. Younger than I am. Not much younger, but a little. He's telling me how he decided to go into his line of work, and he wants to use his hands when he talks. But his hands tremble. I mean, they won't keep still. "This has never happened to me before," he says. He means the trembling. I tell him I sympathize. I tell him the shakes will idle down. And they will. But it takes time.

We've only been in here a couple of days. We're not out of the woods yet. J.P. has these shakes, and every so often a nerve —maybe it isn't a nerve, but it's something—begins to jerk in my shoulder. Sometimes it's at the side of my neck. When this happens my mouth dries up. It's an effort just to swallow then. I know something's about to happen and I want to head it off. I want to hide from it, that's what I want to do. Just close my eyes and let it pass by, let it take the next man. J.P. can wait a minute.

I saw a seizure yesterday morning. A guy they call Tiny. A big fat guy, an electrician from Santa Rosa. They said he'd been in here for nearly two weeks and that he was over the hump. He was going home in a day or two and would spend New Year's Eve with his wife in front of the TV. On New Year's Eve, Tiny planned to drink hot chocolate and eat cookies. Yesterday morning he seemed just fine when he came down for breakfast. He was letting out with quacking noises, showing some guy how he called ducks right down onto his head. "Blam. Blam," said Tiny, picking off a couple. Tiny's hair was damp and was slicked back along the sides of his head. He'd just come out of the shower. He'd also nicked himself on the chin with his razor. But so what? Just about everybody at Frank Martin's has nicks on his face. It's something that happens. Tiny edged in at the head of the table and began telling about something that had happened on one of his drinking bouts. People at the table laughed and shook their heads as they shovelled up their eggs. Tiny would say something, grin, then look around the table for a sign of recognition. We'd all done things just as bad and crazy, so, sure, that's why we laughed. Tiny had scrambled eggs on his plate, and some biscuits and honey. I was at the table but I wasn't hungry. I had some coffee in front of me. Suddenly Tiny wasn't there anymore. He'd gone over in his chair with a big clatter. He was on his back on the floor with his eyes closed, his heels drumming the linoleum. People hollered for Frank Martin. But he was right there. A couple of guys got down on the floor beside Tiny. One of the guys put his fingers inside Tiny's mouth and tried to hold his tongue. Frank Martin yelled, "Everybody stand back!" Then I noticed that the bunch of us were leaning over Tiny, just looking at him, not able to take our eyes off him. "Give him air!" Frank Martin said. Then he ran into the office and called the ambulance.

Tiny is on board again today. Talk about bouncing back. This morning Frank Martin drove the station wagon to the hospital to get him. Tiny got back too late for his eggs, but he took some coffee into the dining room and sat down at the table anyway. Somebody in the kitchen made toast for him, but Tiny didn't eat it. He just sat with his coffee and looked into his cup. Every now and then he moved his cup back and forth in front of him.

I'd like to ask him if he had any signal just before it happened. I'd like to know if he felt his ticker skip a beat, or else begin to race. Did his eyelid twitch? But I'm not about to say anything. He doesn't look like he's hot to talk about it anyway. But what happened to Tiny is something I won't ever forget. Old Tiny flat on the floor, kicking his heels. So every time this little flitter starts up anywhere, I draw some breath and wait to find myself on my back, looking up, somebody's fingers in my mouth.

In his chair on the front porch, J.P. keeps his hands in his lap. I smoke cigarettes and use an old coal bucket for an ashtray. I listen to J.P. ramble on. It's eleven o'clock in the morning—an hour and a half until lunch. Neither one of us is hungry. But just the same we look forward to going inside and sitting down at the table. Maybe we'll get hungry.

What's J.P. talking about, anyway? He's saying how when he was twelve years old he fell into a well in the vicinity of the farm he grew up on. It was a dry well, lucky for him. "Or unlucky," he says, looking around him and shaking his head. He says how late that afternoon, after he'd been located, his dad hauled him out with a rope. J.P. had wet his pants down there. He'd suffered all kinds of terror in that well, hollering for help, waiting, and then hollering some more. He hollered himself hoarse before it was over. But he told me that being at the bottom of that well had made a lasting impression. He'd sat there and looked up at the well mouth. Way up at the top he could see a circle of blue sky. Every once in a while a white cloud passed over. A flock of birds flew across, and it seemed to J.P. their wingbeats set up this odd commotion. He heard other things. He heard tiny rustlings above him in the well, which made him wonder if things might fall down into his hair. He was thinking of insects. He heard wind blow over the well mouth, and that sound made an impression on him, too. In short, everything about his life was different for him at the bottom of that well. But nothing fell on him and nothing closed off that little circle of blue. Then his dad came along with the rope, and it wasn't long before J.P. was back in the world he'd always lived in.

"Keep talking, J.P. Then what?" I say.

When he was eighteen or nineteen years old and out of high

school and had nothing whatsoever he wanted to do with his life, he went across town one afternoon to visit a friend. This friend lived in a house with a fireplace. J.P. and his friend sat around drinking beer and batting the breeze. They played some records. Then the doorbell rings. The friend goes to the door. This young woman chimney sweep is there with her cleaning things. She's wearing a top hat, the sight of which knocked J.P. for a loop. She tells J.P.'s friend that she has an appointment to clean the fireplace. The friend lets her in and bows. The young woman doesn't pay him any mind. She spreads a blanket on the hearth and lays out her gear. She's wearing these black pants, black shirt, black shoes and socks. Of course by now she's taken her hat off. J.P. says it nearly drove him nuts to look at her. She does the work, she cleans the chimney, while J.P. and his friend play records and drink beer. But they watch her and they watch what she does. Now and then J.P. and his friend look at each other and grin, or else they wink. They raise their eyebrows when the upper half of the young woman disappears into the chimney. She was all-right-looking, too, J.P. said. She was about his age.

When she'd finished her work, she rolled her things up in the blanket. From J.P.'s friend she took a check that had been made out to her by his parents. And then she asks the friend if he wants to kiss her. "It's supposed to bring good luck," she says. That does it for J.P. The friend rolls his eyes. He clowns some more. Then, probably blushing, he kisses her on the cheek. At this minute J.P. made his mind up about something. He put his beer down. He got up from the sofa. He went over to the young woman as she was starting to go out the door.

"Me, too?" J.P. said to her. She swept her eyes over him. J.P. says he could feel his heart knocking. The young woman's name, it turns out, was Roxy.

"Sure," Roxy says. "Why not? I've got some extra kisses." And she kisses him a good one right on the lips and then turned to go.

Like that, quick as a wink, J.P. followed her onto the porch. He held the porch screen door for her. He went down the steps with her and out to the drive, where she'd parked her panel truck. It was something that was out of his hands. Nothing else in the world counted for anything. He knew he'd met somebody who could set his legs atremble. He could feel her kiss still burning on his lips, etc. At that minute J.P. couldn't begin to sort anything out. He was filled with sensations that were carrying him every which way.

He opened the rear door of the panel truck for her. He helped her store her things inside. "Thanks," she told him. Then he blurted it out—that he'd like to see her again. Would she go to a movie with him sometime? He'd realized, too, what he wanted to do with his life. He wanted to do what she did. He wanted to be a chimney sweep. But he didn't tell her that then.

J.P. says she put her hands on her hips and looked him over. Then she found a business card in the front seat of her truck. She gave it to him. She said, "Call this number after ten o'clock tonight. The answering machine will be turned off then. We can talk. I have to go now." She put the top hat on and then took it off. She looked at J.P. once more. She must have liked what she saw, because this time she grinned. He told her there was a smudge near her mouth. Then she got into her truck, tooted the horn, and drove away.

"Then what?" I say. "Don't stop now, J.P." I was interested. But I would have listened if he'd been going on about how one day he'd decided to start pitching horseshoes.

It rained last night. The clouds are banked up against the hills across the valley. J.P. clears his throat and looks at the hills and the clouds. He pulls his chin. Then he goes on with what he was saying.

Roxy starts going out with him on dates. And little by little he talks her into letting him go along on jobs with her. But Roxy's in business with her father and brother and they've got just the right amount of work. They don't need anybody else. Besides, who was this guy J.P.? J.P. what? Watch out, they warned her.

So she and J.P. saw some movies together. They went to a few dances. But mainly the courtship revolved around their cleaning chimneys together. Before you know it, J.P. says, they're talking about tying the knot. And after a while they do it, they get married. J.P.'s new father-in-law takes him in as a full partner. In a year or so, Roxy has a kid. She's quit being a chimney sweep. At any rate, she's quit doing the work. Pretty soon she has another kid. J.P.'s in his mid-twenties by now. He's buying a house. He says he was happy with his life. "I was happy with the way things were going," he says. "I had everything I wanted. I had a wife and kids I loved, and I was doing what I wanted to do with my life." But for some reason—who knows why we do what we do?—his drinking picks up. For a long time he drinks beer and beer only. Any kind of beer—it didn't matter. He says he could drink beer twenty-four hours a day. He'd drink beer at night while he watched TV. Sure, once in a while he drank hard stuff. But that was only if they went out on the town, which was not often, or else when they had company over. Then a time comes, he doesn't know why, when he makes the switch from beer to gin and tonic. And he'd have more gin and tonic after dinner, sitting in front of the TV. There was always a glass of gin and tonic in his hand. He says he actually liked the taste of it. He began stopping off after work for drinks before he went home to have more drinks. Then he began missing some dinners. He just wouldn't show up. Or else he'd show up but he wouldn't want anything to eat. He'd filled up on snacks at the bar. Sometimes he'd walk in the door and for no good reason throw his lunch pail across the living room. When Roxy yelled at him, he'd turn around and go out again. He moved his drinking time up to early afternoon, while he was still supposed to be working. He tells me that he was starting off the morning with a couple of drinks. He'd have a belt of the stuff before he brushed his teeth. Then he'd have his coffee. He'd go to work with a thermos bottle of vodka in his lunch pail.

J.P. quits talking. He just clams up. What's going on? I'm listening. It's helping me relax, for one thing. It's taking me away from my own situation. After a minute, I say, "What the hell? Go on, J.P." He's pulling his chin. But pretty soon he starts talking again.

J.P. and Roxy are having some real fights now. I mean *fights*. J.P. says that one time she hit him in the face with her fist and broke his nose. "Look at this," he says. "Right here." He shows me a line across the bridge of his nose. "That's a broken nose." He returned the favor. He dislocated her shoulder for her on that occasion. Another time he split her lip. They beat on each other in front of the kids. Things got out of hand. But he kept on drinking. He couldn't stop. And nothing could make him stop. Not even with Roxy's dad and her brother threatening to beat hell out of him. They told Roxy she should take the kids and clear out. But Roxy said it was her problem. She got herself into it, and she'd solve it.

Now J.P. gets real quiet again. He hunches his shoulders and pulls down in his chair. He watches a car driving down the road between this place and the hills.

I say, "I want to hear the rest of this, J.P. You better keep talking."

"I just don't know," he says. He shrugs.

"It's all right," I say. And I mean it's O.K. for him to tell it. "Go on, J.P."

One way she tried to solve things, J.P. says, was by finding a boyfriend. J.P. would like to know how she found the time with the house and kids.

I looked at him and I'm surprised. He's a grown man. "If you want to do that," I say, "you find the time. You make the time."

J.P. shakes his head. "I guess so," he says.

Anyway, he found out about it—about Roxy's boyfriend—and he went wild. He manages to get Roxy's wedding ring off her finger. And when he does he cuts it into several pieces with a pair of wire cutters. Good solid fun. They'd already gone a couple of rounds on this occasion. On his way to work the next morning he gets arrested on a drunk-driving charge. He loses his driver's license. He can't drive the truck to work anymore. Just as well, he says. He'd already fallen off a roof the week before and broken his thumb. It was just a matter of time until he broke his God-damned neck, he says.

He was here at Frank Martin's to dry out and to figure how to get his life back on track. But he wasn't here against his will, any more than I was. We weren't locked up. We could leave anytime we wanted. But a minimum stay of a week was recommended, and two weeks or a month was, as they put it, "strongly advised."

As I said, this is my second time at Frank Martin's. When I was trying to sign a check to pay in advance for a week's stay, Frank Martin said, "The holidays are always a bad time. Maybe you should think of sticking around a little longer this time? Think in terms of a couple of weeks. Can you do a couple of weeks? Think about it, anyway. You don't have to decide anything right now," he said. He held his thumb on the check and I signed my name. Then I walked my girlfriend to the front door and said goodbye. "Goodbye," she said, and she lurched into the doorjamb and then onto the porch. It's late afternoon. It's raining. I go from the door to the window. I move the curtain and watch her drive away. She's in my car. She's drunk. But I'm drunk, too, and there's nothing I can do. I make it to a big old chair that's close to the radiator, and I sit down. Some guys look up from their TV. Then slowly they shift back to what they were watching. I just sit there. Now and then I look up at something that's happening on the screen.

Later that afternoon the front door banged open and J.P. was brought in between these two big guys—his father-in-law and brother-in-law, I find out afterward. They steered J.P. across the room. The old guy signed him in and gave Frank Martin a check. Then these two guys helped J.P. upstairs. I guess they put him to bed. Pretty soon the old guy and the other guy came downstairs and headed for the front door. They couldn't seem to get out of this place fast enough. It was as if they couldn't wait to wash their hands of all this. I didn't blame them. Hell, no. I don't know how I'd act if I was in their shoes.

A day and a half later J.P. and I meet up on the front porch. We shake hands and comment on the weather. J.P. has a case of the shakes. We sit down and prop our feet on the railing. We lean back in our chairs as if we're just out there taking our ease, as if we might be getting ready to talk about our bird dogs. That's when J.P. gets going with his story.

It's cold out, but not too cold. It's a little overcast. At one point Frank Martin comes outside to finish his cigar. He has on a sweater buttoned up to his Adam's apple. Frank Martin is short and heavyset. He has curly gray hair and a small head. His head is out of proportion with the rest of his body. Frank Martin puts the cigar in his mouth and stands with his arms crossed over his chest. He works that cigar in his mouth and looks across the valley. He stands there like a prizefighter, like somebody who knows the score.

J.P. gets real quiet again. I mean, he's hardly breathing. I toss my cigarette into the coal bucket and look hard at J.P., who scoots farther down in his chair. J.P. pulls up his collar. What the hell's going on, I wonder. Frank Martin uncrosses his arms and takes a puff on the cigar. He lets the smoke carry out of his mouth. Then he raises his chin toward the hills and says, "Jack London[1] used to have a big place on the other side of this valley. Right over there behind that green hill you're looking at. But alcohol killed him. Let that be a lesson. He was a better man than any of us. But he couldn't handle the stuff, either." He looks at what's left of his cigar. It's gone out. He tosses it into the bucket. "You guys want to read something while you're here, read that book of his *The Call of the Wild*. You know the one I'm talking about? We have it inside, if you want to read something. It's about this animal that's half dog and half wolf. They don't write books like that anymore. But we could have helped Jack London, if we'd been here in those days. And if he'd let us. If he'd asked for our help. Hear me? Like we can help you. *If*. *If* you ask for it and *if* you listen. End of sermon. But don't forget. If," he says again. Then he hitches his pants and tugs his sweater down. "I'm going inside," he says. "See you at lunch."

"I feel like a bug when he's around," J.P. says. "He makes me feel like a bug. Something you could step on." J.P. shakes his head. Then he says, "Jack London. What a name! I wish I had me a name like that. Instead of the name I got."

Frank Martin talked about that "if" the first time I was here. My wife brought me up here that time. That's when we were still living together, trying to make things work out. She brought me here and she stayed around for an hour or two, talking to Frank

1. U.S. novelist and short-story writer (1876–1916).

Martin in private. Then she left. The next morning Frank Martin got me aside and said, "We can help you. If you want help and want to listen to what we say." But I didn't know if they could help me or not. Part of me wanted help. But there was another part. All said, it was a very big if.

This time around, six months after my first stay, it was my girlfriend who drove me here. She was driving my car. She drove us through a rainstorm. We drank champagne all the way. We were both drunk when she pulled up in the drive. She intended to drop me off, turn around, and drive home again. She had things to do. One thing she had to do was to go to work the next day. She was a secretary. She had an O.K. job with this electronic-parts firm. She also had this mouthy teen-age son. I wanted her to get a motel room in town, spend the night, and then drive home. I don't know if she got the room or not. I haven't heard from her since she led me up the front steps the other day and walked me into Frank Martin's office and said, "Guess who's here."

But I wasn't mad at her. In the first place she didn't have any idea what she was letting herself in for when she said I could stay with her after my wife asked me to leave. I felt sorry for her. The reason I felt sorry for her was on the day before Christmas her Pap smear[2] came back from the lab, and the news was not cheery. She'd have to go back to the doctor, and real soon. That kind of news was reason enough for both of us to start drinking. So what we did was get ourselves good and drunk. And on Christmas Day we were still drunk. We had to go out to a restaurant to eat, because she didn't feel anything like cooking. The two of us and her mouthy teen-age son opened some presents, and then we went to this steak house near her apartment. I wasn't hungry. I had some soup and a hot roll. I drank a bottle of wine with the soup. She drank some wine, too. Then we started in on Bloody Marys. For the next couple of days I didn't eat anything except cashew nuts. But I drank a lot of bourbon. On the morning of the twenty-eighth I said to her, "Sugar, I think I'd better pack up. I better go back to Frank Martin's. I need to try that place on again. Hey, how about you driving me?"

She tried to explain to her son that she was going to be gone that afternoon and evening, and he'd have to get his own dinner. But right as we were going out the door this God-damned kid screamed at us. He screamed, "You call this love? The hell with you both! I hope you never come back. I hope you kill yourselves!" Imagine this kid!

2. A test for cancer of the uterus.

Before we left town I had her stop at the liquor store, where I bought us three bottles of champagne. Quality stuff—Piper. We stopped someplace else for plastic glasses. Then we picked up a bucket of fried chicken. We set out for Frank Martin's in this rainstorm, drinking champagne and listening to music on the radio. She drove. I looked after the radio and poured champagne. We tried to make a little party out of it. But we were sad, too. There was that fried chicken, but we didn't eat any of it.

I guess she got home O.K. I think I would have heard something if she hadn't made it back. But she hasn't called me, and I haven't called her. Maybe she's had some news about herself by now. Then again, maybe she hasn't heard anything. Maybe it was all a mistake. Maybe it was somebody else's test. But she has my car, and I have things at her house. I know we'll be seeing each other again.

They clang an old farm bell here to signal mealtime. J.P. and I get out of our chairs slowly, like old geezers, and we go inside. It's starting to get too cold on the porch anyway. We can see our breath drifting out from us as we talk.

New Year's Eve morning I try to call my wife. There's no answer. It's O.K. But even if it wasn't O.K., what am I supposed to do? The last time we talked on the phone, a couple of weeks ago, we screamed at each other. I hung a few names on her. "Wet brain!" she said, and put the phone back where it belonged.

But I wanted to talk to her now. Something had to be done about my stuff. I still had things at her house, too.

One of the guys here is a guy who travels. He goes to Europe and the Middle East. That's what he says, anyway. Business, he says. He also says he has his drinking under control and doesn't have any idea why he's here at Frank Martin's. But he doesn't remember getting here. He laughs about it, about his not remembering. "Anyone can have a blackout," he says. "That doesn't prove a thing." He's not a drunk—he tells us this and we listen. "That's a serious charge to make," he says. "That kind of talk can ruin a good man's prospects." He further says that if he'd only stick to whiskey and water, no ice, he'd never get "intoxicated"—his word—and have these blackouts. It's the ice they put into your drink that does it. "Who do you know in Egypt?" he asks me. "I can use a few names over there."

For New Year's Eve dinner Frank Martin serves steak and baked potato. A green salad. My appetite's coming back. I eat the salad. I clean up everything on my plate and I could eat more. I look over at Tiny's plate. Hell, he's hardly touched anything. His steak is just sitting there getting cold. Tiny is not the same old Tiny. The poor bastard had planned to be at home tonight. He'd planned to be in his robe and slippers in front of the TV, holding hands with his wife. Now he's afraid to leave. I can understand. One seizure means you're a candidate for another. Tiny hasn't told any more nutty stories on himself since it happened. He's stayed quiet and kept to himself. Pretty soon I ask him if I can have his steak, and he pushes his plate over to me.

They let us keep the TV on until the New Year has been rung in at Times Square. Some of us are still up, sitting around the TV, watching the crowds on the screen, when Frank Martin comes in to show us his cake. He brings it around and shows it to each of us. I know he didn't make it. It's a God-damned bakery cake. But still it's a cake. It's a big white cake. Across the top of the cake there's writing in pink letters. The writing says "Happy New Year—1 Day At A Time."

"I don't want any stupid cake," says the guy who goes to Europe and the Middle East. "Where's the champagne?" he says, and laughs.

We all go into the dining room. Frank Martin cuts the cake. I sit next to J.P. J.P. eats two pieces and drinks a Coke. I eat a piece and wrap another piece in a napkin, thinking of later.

J.P. lights a cigarette—his hands are steady now—and he tells me his wife is coming to visit him in the morning. The first day of the New Year.

"That's great," I say. I nod. I lick the frosting off my finger. "That's good news, J.P."

"I'll introduce you," he says.

"I look forward to it," I say.

We say good night. We say Happy New Year. Sleep well. I use a napkin on my fingers. We shake hands.

I go to the pay phone once more, put in a dime, and call my wife collect. But nobody answers this time, either. I think about calling my girlfriend, and I'm dialing her number when I realize I don't want to talk to her. She's probably at home watching the same thing on TV that I've been watching. But maybe she isn't. Maybe she's out. Why shouldn't she be? Anyway, I don't want to talk to her. I hope she's O.K. But if she has something wrong with her I don't want to know about it. Not now. In any case, I won't talk to her tonight.

After breakfast J.P. and I take coffee out to the porch, where we plan to wait for his wife. The sky is clear, but it's cold enough so we're wearing our sweaters and jackets.

"She asked me if she should bring the kids," J.P. says. "I told her she should keep the kids at home. Can you imagine? My God, I don't want my kids up here."

We use the coal bucket for an ashtray. We look across the valley where Jack London used to live. We're drinking more coffee, when this car turns off the road and comes down the drive.

"That's her!" J.P. says. He puts his cup next to his chair. He gets up and goes down the steps to the drive.

I see this woman stop the car and set the brake. I see J.P. open the car door. I watch her get out, and I see them embrace. They hug each other. I look away. Then I look back. J.P. takes the woman's arm and they come up the stairs. This woman has crawled into chimneys. This woman broke a man's nose once. She has had two kids, and much trouble, but she loves this man who has her by the arm. I get up from the chair.

"This is my friend," J.P. says to his wife. "Hey, this is Roxy."

Roxy takes my hand. She's a tall, good-looking woman in a blue knit cap. She has on a coat, a heavy white sweater, and dark slacks. I recall what J.P. told me about the boyfriend and the wire cutters—all that—and I glance at her hands. Right. I don't see any wedding ring. That's in pieces somewhere. Her hands are broad and the fingers have these big knuckles. This is a woman who can make fists if she has to.

"I've heard about you," I say. "J.P. told me how you got acquainted. Something about a chimney, J.P. said."

"Yes, a chimney," she says. Her eyes move away from my face, then return. She nods. She's anxious to be alone with J.P., which I can understand. "There's probably a lot else he didn't tell you," she says. "I bet he didn't tell you everything," she says, and laughs. Then—she can't wait any longer—she slips her arm around J.P.'s waist and kisses him on the cheek. They start to move toward the door. "Nice meeting you," she says over her shoulder. "Hey, did he tell you he's the best sweep in the business?" She lets her hand down from J.P.'s waist onto his hip.

"Come on now, Roxy," J.P. says. He has his hand on the doorknob.

"He told me he learned everything he knew from you," I say.

"Well, that much is sure true," she says. She laughs again. But it's as if she's thinking about something else. J.P. turns the doorknob. Roxy lays her hand over his hand. "Joe, can't we go into town for lunch? Can't I take you someplace for lunch?"

J.P. clears his throat. He says, "It hasn't been a week yet." He takes his hand off the doorknob and brings his fingers to his chin. "I think they'd like it, you know, if I didn't leave the place for a little while yet. We can have some coffee inside," he says.

"That's fine," she says. Her eyes light on me once more. "I'm glad Joe's made a friend here. Nice to meet you," she says again.

They start to go inside. I know it's a foolish thing to do, but I do it anyway. "Roxy," I say. And they stop in the doorway and look at me. "I need some luck," I say. "No kidding. I could do with a kiss myself."

J.P. looks down. He's still holding the doorknob, even though the door is open. He turns the doorknob back and forth. He's embarrassed. I'm embarrassed, too. But I keep looking at her. Roxy doesn't know what to make of it. She grins. "I'm not a sweep anymore," she says. "Not for years. Didn't Joe tell you? What the hell. Sure, I'll kiss you. Sure. For luck."

She moves over, she takes me by the shoulders—I'm a big man—and she plants this kiss on my lips. "How's that?" she says.

"That's fine," I say.

"Nothing to it," she says. She's still holding me by the shoulders. She's looking me right in the eyes. "Good luck," she say, and then she let go of me.

"See you later, pal," J.P. says. He opens the door all the way, and they go inside.

I sit down on the front steps and light a cigarette. I watch what my hand does, then I blow out the match. I've got a case of the shakes. I started out with them this morning. This morning I wanted something to drink. It's depressing, and I didn't say anything about it to J.P. I try to put my mind on something else and for once it works.

I'm thinking about chimney sweeps—all that stuff I heard from J.P.—when for some reason I start to think about the house my wife and I lived in just after we were married. That house didn't have a chimney—hell, no—so I don't know what makes me remember it now. But I remember the house and how we'd only been in there a few weeks when I heard a noise outside one morning and woke up. It was Sunday morning and so early it was still dark in the bedroom. But there was this pale light coming in from the bedroom windows. I listened. I could hear something scrape against the side of the house. I jumped out of bed and went to the window.

"My God!" my wife says, sitting up in bed and shaking the hair away from her face. Then she starts to laugh. "It's Mr. Venturini," she says. "The landlord. I forgot to tell you. He said he was coming to paint the house today. Early. Before it gets too hot. I forgot all about it," she says, and laughs some more. "Come on back to bed, honey. It's just the landlord."

"In a minute," I say.

I push the curtain away from the window. Outside, this old guy in white coveralls is standing next to his ladder. The sun is just starting to break above the mountains. The old guy and I look each other over. It's the landlord, all right—this old guy in coveralls. But his coveralls are too big for him. He needs a shave, too. And he's wearing this baseball cap to cover his bald head. God damn it, I think, if he isn't a weird old hombre, then I've never seen one. And at that minute a wave of happiness comes over me that I'm not him—that I'm me and that I'm inside this bedroom with my wife. He jerks his thumb toward the sun. He pretends to wipe his forehead. He's letting me know he doesn't have all that much time. The old duffer breaks into a grin. It's then I realize I'm naked. I look down at myself. I look at him again and shrug. I'm smiling. What'd he expect?

My wife laughs. "Come *on,*" she says. "Get back in this bed. Right now. This minute. Come on back to bed."

I let go of the curtain. But I keep standing there at the window. I can see the landlord nod to himself as if to say, "Go on, sonny, go back to bed. I understand," as if he'd heard my wife calling me. He tugs the bill of his cap. Then he sets about his business. He picks up his bucket. He starts climbing the ladder.

I lean back into the step behind me now and cross one leg over the other. Maybe later this afternoon I'll try calling my wife again. And then I'll call to see what's happening with my girlfriend. But I don't want to get her mouthy son on the line. If I do call, I hope he'll be out somewhere doing whatever he does when he's not hanging around the house. I try to remember if I ever read any Jack London books. I can't remember. But there was a story of his I read in high school. "To Build a Fire" it was called. This guy in the Yukon is freezing. Imagine it—he's actually going to freeze to death if he can't get a fire going. With a fire he can dry his socks and clothing and warm himself. He gets his fire going, but then something happens to it. A branchful of snow drop on it. It goes out. Meanwhile, the temperature is falling. Night is coming on.

I bring some change out of my pocket. I'll try my wife first. If she answers, I'll wish her a Happy New Year. But that's it. I won't bring up business. I won't raise my voice. Not even if she starts something. She'll ask me where I'm calling from, and I'll have to tell her. I won't say anything about New Year's resolutions. There's no way to make a joke out of this. After I talk to her, I'll call my girlfriend. Maybe I'll call her first. I'll just have to hope I don't get her son on the line. "Hello, sugar," I'll say when she answers. "It's me."

ROBERT COOVER

The Babysitter

SHE arrives at 7:40, ten minutes late, but the children, Jimmy and Bitsy, are still eating supper, and their parents are not ready to go yet. From other rooms come the sounds of a baby screaming, water running, a television musical (no words: probably a dance number—patterns of gliding figures come to mind). Mrs. Tucker sweeps into the kitchen, fussing with her hair, and snatches a baby bottle full of milk out of a pan of warm water, rushes out again. "Harry!" she calls. "The babysitter's here already!"

• • •

That's My Desire? I'll Be Around?[1] He smiles toothily, beckons faintly with his head, rubs his fast balding pate. Bewitched, maybe? Or, What's the Reason? He pulls on his shorts, gives his hips a slap. The baby goes silent in mid-scream. Isn't this the one who used their tub last time? Who's Sorry Now, that's it.

• • •

Jack is wandering around town, not knowing what to do. His girlfriend is babysitting at the Tuckers', and later, when she's got the kids in bed, maybe he'll drop over there. Sometimes he watches TV with her when she's babysitting, it's about the only chance he gets to make out a little since he doesn't own wheels, but they have to be careful because most people don't like their sitters to have boyfriends over. Just kissing her makes her nervous. She won't close her eyes because she has to be watching the door all the time. Married people really have it good, he thinks.

• • •

"Hi," the babysitter says to the children, and puts her books on top of the refrigerator. "What's for supper?" The little girl, Bitsy, only stares at her obliquely. She joins them at the end of the kitchen table. "I don't have to go to bed until nine," the boy announces flatly, and stuffs his mouth full of potato chips. The babysitter catches a glimpse of Mr. Tucker hurrying out of the bathroom in his underwear.

• • •

Her tummy. Under her arms. And her feet. Those are the best places. She'll spank him, she says sometimes. Let her.

• • •

That sweet odor that girls have. The softness of her blouse. He catches a glimpse of the gentle shadows amid her thighs, as she curls her legs up under her. He stares hard at her. He has a lot of

1. Titles of popular songs, as are *What's the Reason* and *Who's Sorry Now*, below.

meaning packed into that stare, but she's not even looking. She's popping her gum and watching television. She's sitting right there, inches away, soft, fragrant, and ready: but what's his next move? He notices his buddy Mark in the drugstore, playing the pinball machine, and joins him. "Hey, this mama's cold, Jack baby! She needs your touch!"

• • •

Mrs. Tucker appears at the kitchen doorway, holding a rolled-up diaper. "Now, don't just eat potato chips, Jimmy! See that he eats his hamburger, dear." She hurried away to the bathroom. The boy glares sullenly at the babysitter, silently daring her to carry out the order. "How about a little of that good hamburger now, Jimmy?" she says perfunctorily. He lets half of it drop to the floor. The baby is silent and a man is singing a love song on the TV. The children crunch chips.

• • •

He loves her. She loves him. They whirl airily, stirring a light breeze, through a magical landscape of rose and emerald and deep blue. Her light brown hair coils and wisps softly in the breeze, and the soft folds of her white gown tug at her body and then float away. He smiles in a pulsing crescendo of sincerity and song.

• • •

"You mean she's alone?" Mark asks. "Well, there's two or three kids," Jack says. He slides the coin in. There's a rumble of steel balls tumbling, lining up. He pushes a plunger with his thumb, and one ball pops up in place, hard and glittering with promise. His stare? to say he loves her. That he cares for her and would protect her, would shield her, if need be, with his own body. Grinning, he bends over the ball to take careful aim: he and Mark have studied this machine and have it figured out, but still it's not that easy to beat.

• • •

On the drive to the party, his mind is partly on the girl, partly on his own high-school days, long past. Sitting at the end of the kitchen table there with his children, she had seemed to be self-consciously arching her back, jutting her pert breasts, twitching her thighs: and for whom if not for him? So she'd seen him coming out of there, after all. He smiles. Yet what could he ever do about it? Those good times are gone, old man. He glances over at his wife, who, readjusting a garter, asks: "What do you think of our babysitter?"

• • •

He loves her. She loves him. And then the babies come. And dirty diapers and one goddamn meal after another. Dishes. Noise. Clutter. And fat. Not just tight, her girdle actually hurts. Somewhere recently she's read about women getting heart attacks or cancer or something from too-tight girdles. Dolly pulls the car door shut with a grunt, strangely irritated, not knowing why. Party mood. Why is her husband humming, "Who's Sorry Now?" Pulling out of the drive, she glances back at the lighted kitchen window. "What do you think of our babysitter?" she asks. While her husband stumbles all over himself trying to answer, she pulls a stocking tight, biting deeper with the garters.

• • •

"Stop it!" she laughs. Bitsy is pulling on her skirt and he is tickling her in the ribs. "Jimmy! Don't!" But she is laughing too much to stop him. He leaps on her, wrapping his legs around her waist, and they all fall to the carpet in front of the TV, where just now a man in a tuxedo and a little girl in a flouncy white dress are doing a tapdance together. The babysitter's blouse is pulling out of her skirt, showing a patch of bare tummy: the target. "I'll spank!"

• • •

Jack pushes the plunger, thrusting up a steel ball, and bends studiously over the machine. "You getting any off her?" Mark asks, and clears his throat, flicks ash from his cigarette. "Well, not exactly, not yet," Jack says, grinning awkwardly, but trying to suggest more than he admits to, and fires. He heaves his weight gently against the machine as the ball bounds off a rubber bumper. He can feel her warming up under his hands, the flippers suddenly coming alive, delicate rapid-fire patterns emerging in the flashing of the lights. 1000 WHEN LIT: *now!* "Got my hand on it, that's about all." Mark glances up from the machine, cigarette dangling from his lip. "Maybe you need some help," he suggests with a wry one-sided grin. "Like maybe together, man, we could do it."

• • •

She likes the big tub. She uses the Tuckers' bath salts, and loves to sink into the hot fragrant suds. She can stretch out, submerged, up to her chin. It gives her a good sleepy tingly feeling.

• • •

"What do you think of our babysitter?" Dolly asks, adjusting a garter. "Oh, I hardly noticed," he says "Cute girl. She seems to get along fine with the kids. Why?" "I don't know." His wife tugs her skirt down, glances at a lighted window they are passing, adding: "I'm not sure I trust her completely, that's all. With the baby, I mean. She seems a little careless. And the other time, I'm almost sure she had a boyfriend over." He grins, claps one hand on his wife's broad gartered thigh. "What's wrong with that?" he asks. Still in anklets, too. Bare thighs, no girdles, nothing up there but a flimsy pair of panties and soft adolescent flesh. He's flooded with vague remembrances of football rallies and movie balconies.

• • •

How tiny and rubbery it is! she thinks, soaping between the boy's legs, giving him his bath. Just a funny jiggly little thing that looks like it shouldn't even be there at all. Is that what all the songs are about?

• • •

Jack watches Mark lunge and twist against the machine. Got her running now, racked them up. He's not too excited about the idea of Mark fooling around with his girlfriend, but Mark's a cooler operator than he is, and maybe, doing it together this once, he'd get over his own timidity. And if she didn't like it, there were other girls around. If Mark went too far, he could cut him off too. He feels his shoulders tense: enough's enough, man . . . but sees the flesh, too. "Maybe I'll call her later," he says.

• • •

"Hey, Harry! Dolly! Glad you could make it!" "I hope we're not late." "No, no, you're one of the first, come on in! By golly, Dolly, you're looking younger every day! How do you do it? Give my wife your secret, will you?" He pats her on her girdled bottom behind Mr. Tucker's back, leads them in for drinks.

• • •

8:00. The babysitter runs water in the tub, combs her hair in front of the bathroom mirror. There's a western on television, so she lets Jimmy watch it while she gives Bitsy her bath. But Bitsy doesn't want a bath. She's angry and crying because she has to be first. The babysitter tells her if she'll take her bath quickly, she'll let her watch television while Jimmy takes his bath, but it does no good. The little girl fights to get out of the bathroom, and the babysitter has to squat with her back against the door and forcibly undress the child. There are better places to babysit. Both children mind badly, and then, sooner or later, the baby is sure to wake up for a diaper change and more bottle. The Tuckers do have a good color TV, though, and she hopes things will be settled down enough to catch the 8:30 program. She thrusts the child into the tub, but she's still screaming and thrashing around. "Stop it now, Bitsy, or you'll wake the baby!" "I have to go potty!" the child wails, switching tactics. The babysitter sighs, lifts the girl out of the tub and onto the toilet, getting her skirt and blouse all wet in the process. She glances at herself in the mirror. Before she knows it, the girl is off the seat and out of the bathroom. "Bitsy! Come back here!"

• • •

"Okay, that's enough!" Her skirt is ripped and she's flushed and crying. "Who says?" "I do, man!" The bastard goes for her, but she tackles him. They roll and tumble. Tables tip, lights topple, the TV crashes to the floor. He slams a hard right to the guy's gut, clips his chin with a rolling left.

• • •

"We hope it's a girl." That's hardly surprising, since they already have four boys. Dolly congratulates the woman like everybody else, but she doesn't envy her, not a bit. That's all she needs about now. She stares across the room at Harry, who is slapping backs and getting loud, as usual. He's spreading out through the middle, so why the hell does he have to complain about her all the time? "Dolly, you're looking younger every day!" was the nice greeting she got tonight. "What's your secret?" And Harry: "It's all those calories. She's getting back her baby fat." "Haw haw! Harry, have a heart!"

• • •

"Get her feet" he hollers at Bitsy, his fingers in her ribs, running over her naked tummy, tangling in the underbrush of straps and strange clothing. "Get her shoes off!" He holds her pinned by pressing his head against her soft chest. "No! No, Jimmy! Bitsy, stop!" But though she kicks and twists and rolls around, she doesn't get up, she can't get up, she's laughing too hard, and the shoes come off, and he grabs a stockinged foot and scratches the sole ruthlessly, and she raises up her legs, trying to pitch him off, she's wild, boy, but he hangs on, and she's laughing, and on the screen there's a rattle of hooves, and he and Bitsy are rolling around and around on the floor in a crazy rodeo of long bucking legs.

• • •

He slips the coin in. There's a metallic fall and a sharp click as the dial tone begins. "I hope the Tuckers have gone," he says. "Don't worry, they're at our place," Mark says. "They're always the first ones to come and the last ones to go home. My old man's always bitching about them." Jack laughs nervously and dials the number. "Tell her we're coming over to protect her from getting raped," Mark suggests, and lights a cigarette. Jack grins, leaning casually against the door jamb of the phonebooth, chewing gum, one hand in his pocket. He's really pretty uneasy, though. He has the feeling he's somehow messing up a good thing.

• • •

Bitsy runs naked into the livingroom, keeping a hassock between herself and the babysitter. "Bitsy . . . !" the babysitter threatens. Artificial reds and greens and purples flicker over the child's wet body, as hooves clatter, guns crackle, and stagecoach wheels thunder over rutted terrain. "Get outa the way, Bitsy!" the boy complains. "I can't see!" Bitsy streaks past and the babysitter chases, cornering the girl in the back bedroom. Bitsy throws something that hits her softly in the face: a pair of men's undershorts. She grabs the girl scampering by, carries her struggling to the bathroom, and with a smart crack on her glistening bottom, pops her back into the tub. In spite, Bitsy peepees in the bathwater.

• • •

Mr. Tucker stirs a little water into his bourbon and kids with his host and another man, just arrived, about their golf games. They set up a match for the weekend, a threesome looking for a fourth. Holding his drink in his right hand, Mr. Tucker swings his left through the motion of a tee-shot. "You'll have to give me a stroke a hole," he says. "I'll give you a stroke!" says his host: "Bend over!" Laughing, the other man asks: "Where's your boy Mark tonight?" "I don't know," replies the host, gathering up a trayful of drinks. Then he adds in a low growl: "Out chasing tail probably." They chuckle loosely at that, then shrug in commiseration and return to the livingroom to join their women.

• • •

Shades pulled. Door locked. Watching the TV. Under a blanket maybe. Yes, that's right, under a blanket. Her eyes close when he kisses her. Her breasts, under both their hands, are soft and yielding.

• • •

A hard blow to the belly. The face. The dark beardy one staggers, the lean-jawed sheriff moves in, but gets a spurred boot in his face. The dark one hurls himself forward, drives his shoulder into the sheriff's hard midriff, her own tummy tightens, withstands, as the sheriff smashes the dark man's nose, slams him up against a wall, slugs him again! and again! The dark man grunts rhythmically, backs off, then plunges suicidally forward—her own knees draw up protectively—the sheriff staggers! caught low! but instead of following through, the other man steps back—a pistol! the dark one has a pistol! the sheriff draws! shoots from the hip! explosions! she clutches her hands between her thighs—no! the sheriff spins! wounded! the dark man hesitates, aims, her legs stiffen toward the set, the sheriff rolls desperately in the straw, fires: dead! the dark man is dead! groans, crumples, his pistol drooping in his collapsing hand, dropping, he drops. The sheriff, spent, nicked, watches weakly from the floor where he lies. Oh, to be whole! to be good and strong and right! to embrace and be embraced by harmony and wholeness! The sheriff, drawing himself painfully up on one elbow, rubs his bruised mouth with the back of his other hand.

• • •

"Well, we just sorta thought we'd drop over," he says, and winks broadly at Mark. "Who's we?" "Oh, me and Mark here." "Tell her, good thing like her, gotta pass it around," whispers Mark, dragging on his smoke, then flicking the butt over under the pinball machine. "What's that?" she asks. "Oh, Mark and I were just saying, like two's company, three's an orgy," Jack says, and winks again. She giggles. "Oh Jack!" Behind her, he can hear shouts and gunfire. "Well, okay, for just a little while, if you'll both be good." Way to go, man.

• • •

Probably some damn kid over there right now. Wrestling around on the couch in front of his TV. Maybe he should drop back to the house. Just to check. None of that stuff, she was there to do a job! Park the car a couple doors down, slip in the front door before she knows it. He sees the disarray of clothing, the young thighs exposed to the flickering television light, hears his baby crying. "Hey, what's going on here! Get outa here, son, before I call the police!" Of course, they haven't really been doing anything. They probably don't even know how. He stares benignly down upon the girl, her skirt rumpled loosely around her thighs. Flushed, frightened, yet excited, she stares back at him. He smiles. His finger touches a knee, approaches the hem. Another couple arrives. Filling up here with people. He wouldn't be missed. Just slip out, stop back casually to pick up something or other he forgot, never mind what. He remembers that the other time they had this babysitter, she took a bath in their house. She had a date afterwards, and she'd come from cheerleading practice or something. Aspirin maybe. Just drop quietly and casually into the bathroom to pick up some aspirin. "Oh, excuse me, dear! I only . . . !" She gazes back at him, astonished, yet strangely moved. Her soft wet breasts rise and fall in the water, and her tummy looks pale and ripply. He recalls that her pubic hairs, left in the tub, were brown. Light brown.

• • •

She's no more than stepped into the tub for a quick bath, when Jimmy announces from outside the door that he has to go to the bathroom. She sighs: just an excuse, she knows. "You'll have to wait." The little nuisance. "I can't wait." "Okay, then come ahead, but I'm taking a bath." She supposes that will stop him, but it doesn't. In he comes. She slides down into the suds until she's eye-level with the edge of the tub. He hesitates. "Go ahead, if you have to," she says, a little awkwardly, "but I'm not getting out." "Don't look," he says. She: "I will if I want to."

• • •

She's crying. Mark is rubbing his jaw where he's just slugged him. A lamp lies shattered. "Enough's enough, Mark! Now get outa here!" Her skirt is ripped to the waist, her bare hip bruised. Her panties lie on the floor like a broken balloon. Later, he'll wash her wounds, help her dress, he'll take care of her. Pity washes through him, giving him a sudden hard-on. Mark laughs at it, pointing. Jack crouches, waiting, ready for anything.

• • •

Laughing, they roll and tumble. Their little hands are all over her, digging and pinching. She struggles to her hands and knees, but Bitsy leaps astride her neck, bowing her head to the carpet. "Spank her, Jimmy!" His swats sting: is her skirt up? The phone rings. "The cavalry to the rescue!" she laughs, and throws them off to go answer.

• • •

Kissing Mark, her eyes closed, her hips nudge toward Jack. He stares at the TV screen, unsure of himself, one hand slipping cautiously under her skirt. Her hand touches his arm as though to resist, then brushes on by to rub his leg. This blanket they're under was a good idea. "Hi! This is Jack!"

• • •

Bitsy's out and the water's running. "Come on, Jimmy, your turn!" Last time, he told her he took his own baths, but she came in anyway. "I'm not gonna take a bath," he announces, eyes glued on the set. He readies for the struggle. "But I've already run your water. Come on, Jimmy, please!" He shakes his head. She can't make him, he's sure he's as strong as she is. She sighs. "Well, it's up to you. I'll use the water myself then," she says. He waits until he's pretty sure she's not going to change her mind, then sneaks in and peeks through the keyhole in the bathroom door: just in time to see her big bottom as she bends over to stir in the bubblebath. Then she disappears. Trying to see as far down as the keyhole will allow, he bumps his head on the knob. "Jimmy, is that you?" "I—I have to go to the bathroom!" he stammers.

• • •

Not actually in the tub, just getting in. One foot on the mat, the other in the water. Bent over slightly, buttocks flexed, teats swaying, holding on to the edge of the tub. "Oh, excuse me! I only wanted . . . . !" He passes over her astonishment, the awkward excuses, moves quickly to the part where he reaches out to— "What on earth are you doing, Harry?" his wife asks, staring at his hand. His host, passing, laughs. "He's practicing his swing for Sunday, Dolly, but it's not going to do him a damn bit of good!" Mr. Tucker laughs, sweeps his right hand on through the air as though lifting a seven-iron shot onto the green. He makes a *dok!* sound with his tongue. "In there!"

• • •

"No, Jack, I don't think you'd better." "Well, we just called, we just, uh, thought we'd, you know, stop by for a minute, watch television for thirty minutes, or, or something." "Who's we?" "Well, Mark's here, I'm with him, and he said he'd like to, you know, like if it's all right, just—" "Well, it's *not* all right. The Tuckers said no." "Yeah, but if we only—" "And they seemed awfully suspicious about last time." "Why? We didn't—I mean, I just thought —" "No, Jack, and that's period." She hangs up. She returns to the TV, but the commercial is on. Anyway, she's missed most of the show. She decides maybe she'll take a quick bath. Jack might come by anyway, it'd make her mad, that'd be the end as far as he was concerned, but if he should, she doesn't want to be all sweaty. And besides, she likes the big tub the Tuckers have.

• • •

He is self-conscious and stands with his back to her, his little neck flushed. It takes him forever to get started, and when it finally does come, it's just a tiny trickle. "See, it was just an excuse," she scolds, but she's giggling inwardly at the boy's embarrassment. "You're just a nuisance, Jimmy." At the door, his hand on the knob, he hesitates, staring timidly down on his shoes. "Jimmy?" She peeks at him over the edge of the tub, trying to keep a straight face, as he sneaks a nervous glance back over his shoulder. "As long as you bothered me," she says, "you might as well soap my back."

• • •

"The aspirin . . ." They embrace. She huddles in his arms like a child. Lovingly, paternally, knowledgeably, he wraps her nakedness. How compact, how tight and small her body is! Kissing her ear, he stares down past her rump at the still clear water. "I'll join you," he whispers hoarsely.

• • •

She picks up the shorts Bitsy threw at her. Men's underwear. She holds them in front of her, looks at herself in the bedroom mirror. About twenty sizes too big for her, of course. She runs her hand inside the opening in front, pulls out her thumb. How funny it must feel!

• • •

"Well, man, I say we just go rape her," Mark says flatly, and swings his weight against the pinball machine. "Uff! Ahh! Get in there, you mother! Look at that! Hah! Man, I'm gonna turn this baby over!" Jack is embarrassed about the phone conversation. Mark just snorted in disgust when he hung up. He cracks down hard on his gum, angry that he's such a chicken. "Well, I'm game if you are," he says coldly.

• • •

8:30 "Okay, come on, Jimmy, it's time." He ignores her. The western gives way to a spy show. Bitsy, in pajamas, pads into the livingroom. "No, Bitsy, it's time to go to bed." "You said I could watch!" the girl whines, and starts to throw another tantrum. "But you were too slow and it's late. Jimmy, you get in that bathroom, and right now!" Jimmy stares sullenly at the set, unmoving. The babysitter tries to catch the opening scene of the television program so she can follow it later, since Jimmy gives himself his own baths. When the commercial interrupts, she turns off the sound, stands in front of the screen. "Okay, into the tub, Jimmy Tucker, or I'll take you in there and give you your bath myself!" "Just try it," he says, "and see what happens."

• • •

They stand outside, in the dark, crouched in the bushes, peeking in. She's on the floor, playing with the kids. Too early. They seem to be tickling her. She gets to her hands and knees, but the little girl leaps on her head, pressing her face to the floor. There's an obvious target, and the little boy proceeds to beat on it. "Hey, look at that kid go!" whispers Mark, laughing and snapping his fingers softly. Jack feels uneasy out here. Too many neighbors, too many cars going by, too many people in the world. That little boy in there is one up on him, though: he's never thought about tickling her as a starter.

• • •

His little hand, clutching the bar of soap, lathers shyly a narrow space between her shoulderblades. She is doubled forward against her knees, buried in rich suds, peeking at him over the edge of her shoulder. The soap slithers out of his grip and plunks into the water. "I . . . I dropped the soap," he whispers. She: "Find it."

• • •

"I dream of Jeannie with the light brown pubic hair!"[2] "Harry! Stop that! You're drunk!" But they're laughing, they're all laughing, damn! he's feeling pretty goddamn good at that, and now he just knows he needs that aspirin. Watching her there, her thighs spread for him, on the couch, in the tub, hell, on the kitchen table for that matter, he tees off on Number Nine, and—*whap!*—swats his host's wife on the bottom. "Hole in one!" he shouts. "Harry!" Why can't his goddamn wife Dolly ever get happy-drunk instead of sour-drunk all the time? "Gonna be tough Sunday, old buddy!" "You're pretty tough right now, Harry," says his host.

• • •

The babysitter lunges forward, grabs the boy by the arms and hauls him off the couch, pulling two cushions with him, and drags him toward the bathroom. He lashes out, knocking over an endtable full of magazines and ashtrays. "You leave my brother alone!" Bitsy cries and grabs the sitter around the waist. Jimmy jumps on her and down they all go. On the silent screen, there's a fade-in to a dark passageway in an old apartment building in some foreign country. She kicks out and somebody falls between her legs. Somebody else is sitting on her face. "Jimmy! Stop that!" the babysitter laughs, her voice muffled.

• • •

She's watching television. All alone. It seems like a good time to go in. Just remember: really, no matter what she says, she wants it. They're standing in the bushes, trying to get up the nerve. "We'll tell her to be good," Mark whispers, "and if she's not good, we'll spank her." Jack giggles softly, but his knees are weak. She stands. They freeze. She looks right at them. "She can't see us." Mark whispers tensely. "Is she coming out?" "No," says Mark, "She's going into—that must be the bathroom!" Jack takes a deep breath, his heart pounding. "Hey, is there a window back there?" Mark asks.

2. Parody of actual song title, *I Dream of Jeannie with the Light Brown Hair.*

• • •

The phone rings. She leaves the tub, wrapped in a towel. Bitsy gives a tug on the towel. "Hey, Jimmy, get the towel!" she squeals. "Now stop that, Bitsy!" the babysitter hisses, but too late: with one hand on the phone, the other isn't enough to hang on to the towel. Her sudden nakedness awes them and it takes them a moment to remember about tickling her. By then, she's in the towel again. "I hope you got a good look," she says angrily. She feels chilled and oddly a little frightened. "Hello?" No answer. She glances at the window—is somebody out there? Something, she saw something, and a rustling—footsteps?

• • •

"Okay, I don't care, Jimmy, don't take a bath," she says irritably. Her blouse is pulled out and wrinkled, her hair is all mussed, and she feels sweaty. There's about a million things she'd rather be doing than babysitting with these two. Three: at least the baby's sleeping. She knocks on the overturned endtable for luck, rights it, replaces the magazines and ashtrays. The one thing that really makes her sick is a dirty diaper. "Just go on to bed." "I don't have to go to bed until nine," he reminds her. Really, she couldn't care less. She turns up the volume on the TV, settles down on the couch, poking her blouse back into her skirt, pushing her hair out of her eyes. Jimmy and Bitsy watch from the floor. Maybe, once they're in bed, she'll take a quick bath. She wishes Jack would come by. The man, no doubt the spy, is following a woman, but she doesn't know why. The woman passes another man. Something seems to happen, but it's not clear what. She's probably already missed too much. The phone rings.

• • •

Mark is kissing her. Jack is under the blanket, easing her panties down over her squirming hips. Her hand is in his pants, pulling it out, pulling it toward her, pulling it hard. She knew just where it was! Mark is stripping, too. God, it's really happening! he thinks with a kind of pious joy, and notices the open door. "Hey!" What's going on here?"

• • •

He soaps her back, smooth and slippery under his hand. She is doubled over, against her knees, between his legs. Her light brown hair, reaching to her gleaming shoulders, is wet at the edges. The soap slips, falls between his legs. He fishes for it, finds it, slips it behind him. "Help me find it," he whispers in her ear. "Sure Harry," says his host, going around behind him. "What'd you lose?"

• • •

Soon be nine, time to pack the kids off to bed. She clears the table, dumps paper plates and leftover hamburgers into the garbage, puts glasses and silverware into the sink, and the mayonnaise, mustard, and ketchup in the refrigerator. Neither child has eaten much supper finally, mostly potato chips and ice cream, but it's really not her problem. She glances at the books on the refrigerator. Not much chance she'll get to them, she's already pretty worn out. Maybe she'd feel better if she had a quick bath. She runs water into the tub, tosses in bubblebath salts, undresses. Before pushing down her panties, she stares for a moment at the smooth silken panel across her tummy, fingers the place where the opening would be if there were one. Then she steps quickly out of them, feeling somehow ashamed, unhooks her brassiere. She weighs her breasts in the palms of her hands, watching herself in the bathroom mirror, where, in the open window behind her, she sees a face. She screams.

• • •

She screams: "Jimmy! Give me that!" "What's the matter?" asks Jack on the other end. "Jimmy! Give me my towel! Right now!" "Hello? Hey, are you still there?" "I'm sorry, Jack," she says, panting. "You caught me in the tub. I'm just wrapped in a towel and these silly kids grabbed it away!" "Gee, I wish I'd been there!" "Jack—!" "To protect you, I mean." "Oh, sure," she says, giggling. "Well, what do you think, can I come over and watch TV with you?" "Well, not right this minute," she says. He laughs lightly. He feels very cool. "Jack?" "Yeah?" "Jack, I . . . I think there's somebody outside the window!"

• • •

She carries him, fighting all the way, to the tub, Bitsy pummeling her in the back and kicking her ankles. She can't hang on to him and undress him at the same time. "I'll throw you in, clothes and all, Jimmy Tucker!" she gasps. "You better not!" he cries. She sits on the toilet seat, locks her legs around him, whips his shirt up over his head before he knows what's happening. The pants are easier. Like all little boys his age, he has almost no hips at all. He hangs on desperately to his underpants, but when she succeeds in snapping these down out of his grip, too, he gives up, starts to bawl, and beats her wildly in the face with his fists. She ducks her head, laughing hysterically, oddly entranced by the spectacle of that pale little thing down there, bobbing and bouncing rubberlike about the boy's helpless fury and anguish.

• • •

"Aspirin? Whaddaya want aspirin for, Harry? I'm sure they got aspirin here, if you—" "Did I say aspirin? I meant uh, my glasses. And, you know, I thought, well, I'd sorta check to see if everything was okay at home." Why the hell is it his mouth feels like it's got about six sets of teeth packed in there, and a tongue the size of that liverwurst his host's wife is passing around? "Whaddaya want your glasses for, Harry? I don't understand you at all!" "Aw, well, honey,

I was feeling kind of dizzy or something, and I thought—" "Dizzy is right. If you want to check on the kids, why don't you just call on the phone?"

• • •

They can tell she's naked and about to get into the tub, but the bathroom window is frosted glass, and they can't see anything clearly. "I got an idea," Mark whispers. "One of us goes and calls her on the phone, and the other watches when she comes out." "Okay, but who calls?" "Both of us, we'll do it twice. Or more."

• • •

Down forbidden alleys. Into secret passageways. Unlocking the world's terrible secrets. Sudden shocks: a trapdoor! a fall! or the stunning report of a rifle shot, the *whaaii-ii-ing!* of the bullet biting concrete by your ear! Careful! Then edge forward once more, avoiding the light, inch at a time, now a quick dash for an open doorway—*look out!* there's a knife! a struggle! no! the long blade glistens! jerks! thrusts! *stabbed!* No, no, it missed! The assailant's down, yes! the spy's on top, pinning him, a terrific thrashing about, the spy rips off the assailant's mask: *a woman!*

• • •

Fumbling behind her, she finds it, wraps her hand around it, tugs. "Oh!" she gasps, pulling her hand back quickly, her ears turning crimson. "I . . . I thought it was the soap!" He squeezes her close between his thighs, pulls her back toward him, one hand sliding down her tummy between her legs. I Dream of Jeannie— "I have to go to the bathroom!" says someone outside the door.

• • •

She's combing her hair in the bathroom when the phone rings. She hurries to answer it before it wakes the baby. "Hello, Tuckers." There's no answer. "Hello?" A soft click. Strange. She feels suddenly alone in the big house, and goes in to watch TV with the children.

• • •

"Stop it!" she screams, "Please stop!" She's on her hands and knees, trying to get up, but they're too strong for her. Mark holds her head down. "Now, baby, we're gonna teach you how to be a nice girl," he says coldly, and nods at Jack. When she's doubled over like that, her skirt rides up her thighs to the leg bands of her panties. "C'mon, man, go! This baby's cold! She needs your touch!"

• • •

Parks the car a couple blocks away. Slips up to the house, glances in his window. Just like he's expected. Her blouse is off and the kid's shirt is unbuttoned. He watches, while slowly, clumsily, childishly, they fumble with each other's clothes. My God, it takes them forever. "Some party!" "You said it!" When they're more or less naked, he walks in. "Hey! What's going on here?" They go white as bleu cheese. Haw haw! "What's the little thing you got sticking out there, boy?" "Harry, behave yourself!" No, he doesn't let the kid get dressed, he sends him home bareassed. "Bareassed!" He drinks to that. "Promises, promises," says his host's wife. "I'll mail you your clothes, son!" He gazes down on the naked little girl on his couch. "Looks like you and me, we got a little secret to keep, honey," he says coolly. "Less you wanna go home the same way your boyfriend did!" He chuckles at his easy wit, leans down over her, and unbuckles his belt. "Might as well make it two secrets, right?" "What in God's name are you talking about, Harry?" He staggers out of there, drink in hand, and goes to look for his car.

• • •

"Hey! What's going on here?" They huddle half-naked under the blanket, caught utterly unawares. On television: the clickety-click of frightened running feet on foreign pavements. Jack is fumbling for his shorts, tangled somehow around his ankles. The blanket is snatched away. "On your feet there!" Mr. Tucker, Mrs. Tucker, and Mark's mom and dad, the police, the neighbors, everybody comes crowding in. Hopelessly, he has a terrific erection. So hard it hurts. Everybody stares down at it.

• • •

Bitsy's sleeping on the floor. The babysitter is taking a bath. For more than an hour now, he'd had to use the bathroom. He doesn't know how much longer he can wait. Finally, he goes to knock on the bathroom door. "I have to use the bathroom." "Well, come ahead, if you have to." "Not while you're in there." She sighs loudly. "Okay, okay, just a minute," she says, "but you're a real nuisance, Jimmy!" He's holding on, pinching it as tight as he can. "*Hurry!*" He holds his breath, squeezing shut his eyes. No. Too late. At last, she opens the door. "Jimmy!" "I *told* you to hurry!" he sobs. She drags him into the bathroom and pulls his pants down.

• • •

He arrives just in time to see her emerge from the bathroom, wrapped in a towel, to answer the phone. His two kids sneak up behind her and pull the towel away. She's trying to hang onto the phone and get the towel back at the same time. It's quite a picture. She's got a sweet ass. Standing there in the bushes, pawing himself with one hand, he lifts his glass with the other and toasts her sweet ass, which his son now swats. Haw haw, maybe that boy's gonna shape up, after all.

• • •

They're in the bushes, arguing about their next move, when she comes out of the bathroom, wrapped in a towel. They can hear the baby crying. Then it stops. They see her running, naked, back to the bathroom like she's scared or something. "I'm going in after her, man, whether you're with me or not!" Mark whispers, and he starts out of the bushes. But just then, a light comes sweeping up through the yard, as a car swings in the drive. They hit the dirt, hearts pounding. "Is it the cops?" "I don't know!" "Do you think they saw us?" "Sshh!" A man comes staggering up the walk from the drive, a drink in his hand, stumbles on in the kitchen door and then straight into the bathroom. "It's Mr. Tucker!" Mark whispers. A scream. "Let's get outa here, man!"

• • •

9:00. Having missed most of the spy show anyway and having little else to do, the babysitter has washed the dishes and cleaned the kitchen up a little. The books on the refrigerator remind her of her better intentions, but she decides that first she'll see what's next on TV. In the livingroom, she finds little Bitsy sound asleep on the floor. She lifts her gently, carries her into her bed, and tucks her in. "Okay, Jimmy, it's nine o'clock, I've let you stay up, now be a good boy." Sullenly, his sleepy eyes glued still to the set, the boy backs out of the room toward his bedroom. A drama comes on. She switches channels. A ballgame and a murder mystery. She switches back to the drama. It's a love story of some kind. A man married to an aging invalid wife, but in love with a younger girl. "Use the bathroom and brush your teeth before going to bed, Jimmy!" she calls, but as quickly regrets it, for she hears the baby stir in its crib.

• • •

Two of them are talking about mothers they've salted away in rest homes. Oh boy, that's just wonderful, this is one helluva party. She leaves them to use the john, takes advantage of the retreat to ease her girdle down awhile, get a few good deep breaths. She has this picture of her three kids carting her off to a rest home. In a wheelbarrow. That sure is something to look forward to, all right. When she pulls her girdle back up, she can't seem to squeeze into it. The host looks in. "Hey, Dolly, are you all right?" "Yeah, I just can't get into my damn girdle, that's all." "Here, let me help."

• • •

She pulls them on, over her own, standing in front of the bedroom mirror, holding her skirt bundled up around the waist. About twenty sizes too big for her, of course. She pulls them tight from behind, runs her hand inside the opening in front, pulls out her thumb. "And what a good boy am I!" She giggles: how funny it must feel! Then, in the mirror, she sees him: in the doorway behind her, sullenly watching. "Jimmy! You're supposed to be in bed!" "Those are my daddy's!" the boy says. "I'm gonna tell!"

• • •

"Jimmy!" She drags him into the bathroom and pulls his pants down. "Even your shoes are wet! Get them off!" She soaps up a warm washcloth she's had with her in the bathtub, scrubs him from the waist down with it. Bitsy stands in the doorway, staring. "Get out! Get out!" the boy screams at his sister. "Go back to bed, Bitsy. It's just an accident." "Get out!" The baby wakes and starts to howl.

• • •

The young lover feels sorry for her rival, the invalid wife; she believes the man has a duty toward the poor woman and insists she is willing to wait. But the man argues that he also has a duty toward himself: his life, too, is short, and he could not love his wife now even were she well. He embraces the young girl feverishly; she twists away in anguish. The door opens. They stand there grinning, looking devilish, but pretty silly at the same time. "Jack! I thought I told you not to come!" She's angry, but she's also glad in a way: she was beginning to feel a little too alone in the big house, with the children all sleeping. She should have taken that bath, after all. "We just came by to see if you were being a good girl," Jack says and blushes. The boys glance at each other nervously.

• • •

She's just sunk down into the tubful of warm fragrant suds, ready for a nice long soaking, when the phone rings. Wrapping a towel around her, she goes to answer: no one there. But now the baby's awake and bawling. She wonders if that's Jack bothering her all the time. If it is, brother, that's the end. Maybe it's the end anyway. She tries to calm the baby with the half-empty bottle, not wanting to change it until she's finished her bath. The bathroom's where the diapers go dirty, and they make it stink to high heaven. "Shush, shush!" she whispers, rocking the crib. The towel slips away, leaving an airy empty tingle up and down her backside. Even before she stoops for the towel, even before she turns around, she knows there's somebody behind her.

• • •

"We just came by to see if you were being a good girl," Jack says, grinning down at her. She's flushed and silent, her mouth half open. "Lean over," says Mark amiably. "We'll soap your back, as long as we're here." But she just huddles there, down in the suds, staring up at them with big eyes.

• • •

"Hey! What's going on here?" It's Mr. Tucker, stumbling through the door with a drink in his hand. She looks up from the TV. "What's the matter, Mr. Tucker?" "Oh, uh, I'm sorry, I got lost—no, I mean, I had to get some aspirin. Excuse me!" And he rushes past her into the bathroom, caroming off the livingroom door jamb on the way. The baby awakes.

• • •

"Okay, get off her, Mr. Tucker!" "Jack!" she cries, "what are *you* doing here?" He stares hard at them a moment: so that's where it goes. Then, as Mr. Tucker swings heavily off, he leans into the bastard with a hard right to the belly. Next thing he knows, though, he's got a face full of an old man's fist. He's not sure, as the lights go out, if that's his girlfriend screaming or the baby . . .

• • •

Her host pushes down on her fat fanny and tugs with all his might on her girdle, while she bawls on his shoulder: "I don't *wanna* go to a rest home!" "Now, now, take it easy, Dolly, nobody's gonna make you—" "Ouch! Hey, you're hurting!" "You should buy a bigger girdle, Dolly." "You're telling me?" Some other guy pokes his head in. "Whatsa-matter? Dolly fall in?" "No, she fell out. Give me a hand."

• • •

By the time she's chased Jack and Mark out of there, she's lost track of the program she's been watching on television. There's another woman in the story now for some reason. That guy lives a very complicated life. Impatiently, she switches channels. She hates ballgames, so she settles for the murder mystery. She switches just in time, too: there's a dead man sprawled out on the floor of what looks like an office or a study or something. A heavyset detective gazes up from his crouch over the body: "He's been strangled." Maybe she'll take that bath, after all.

• • •

She drags him into the bathroom and pulls his pants down. She soaps up a warm washcloth she's had in the tub with her, but just as she reaches between his legs, it starts to spurt, spraying her arms and hands. "Oh, Jimmy! I thought you were done!" she cries, pulling him toward the toilet and aiming it into the bowl. How moist and rubbery it is! And you can turn it every which way. How funny it must feel!

• • •

"Stop it!" she screams. "Please stop!" She's on her hands and knees and Jack is holding her head down. "Now we're gonna teach you how to be a nice girl," Mark says and lifts her skirt. "Well, I'll be damned!" "What's the matter?" asks Jack, his heart pounding. "Look at this big pair of men's underpants she's got on!" "Those are my daddy's!" says Jimmy, watching them from the doorway. "I'm gonna tell!"

• • •

People are shooting at each other in the murder mystery, but she's so mixed up, she doesn't know which ones are the good guys. She switches back to the love story. Something seems to have happened, because now the man is kissing his invalid wife tenderly. Maybe she's finally dying. The baby wakes, begins to scream. Let it. She turns up the volume on the TV.

• • •

Leaning down over her, unbuckling his belt. It's all happening just like he's known it would. Beautiful! The kid is gone, though his pants, poor lad, remain. Looks like you and me, we got a secret to keep, child!" But he's cramped on the couch and everything is too slippery and small. "Lift your legs up, honey. Put them around my back." But instead, she screams. He rolls off, crashing to the floor. There they all come, through the front door. On television, somebody is saying: "Am I a burden to you, darling?" "Dolly! My God! Dolly, I can explain . . . !"

• • •

The game of the night is Get Dolly Tucker Back in Her Girdle Again. They've got her down on her belly in the livingroom and the whole damn crowd is working on her. Several of them are stretching the girdle, while others try to jam the fat inside. "I think we made a couple inches on this side! Roll her over!" Harry?

• • •

She's just stepped into the tub, when the phone rings, waking the baby. She sinks down in the suds, trying not to hear. But that baby doesn't cry, it screams. Angrily, she wraps a towel around herself, stamps peevishly into the baby's room, just letting the phone jangle. She tosses the baby down on its back, unpins it diapers hastily, and gets yellowish baby stool all over her hands. Her towel drops away. She turns to find Jimmy staring at her like a little idiot. She slaps him in the face with her dirty hand, while the baby screams, the phone rings, and nagging voices argue on the TV. There are better things she might be doing.

• • •

What's happening? Now there's a young guy in it. Is he after the young girl or the old invalid? To tell the truth, it looks like he's after the same man the women are. In disgust, she switches channels. "The strangler again," growls the fat detective, hands on hips, staring down at the body of a half-naked girl. She's considering either switching back to the love story or taking a quick bath, when a hand suddenly clutches her mouth.

• • •

"You're both chicken," she says, staring up at them. "But what if Mr. Tucker comes home?" Mark asks nervously.

• • •

How did he get here? He's standing pissing in his own goddamn bathroom, his wife is still back at the party, the three of them are, like good kids, sitting in there in the livingroom watching TV. One of them is his host's boy Mark. "It's a good murder mystery, Mr. Tucker," Mark said, when he came staggering in on them a minute ago. "Sit still!" he shouted, "I am just home for a moment!" Then whump thump on into the bathroom. Long hike for a wee-wee,

Mister. But something keeps bothering him. Then it hits him: the girl's panties hanging like a broken balloon from the rabbit-ear antennae on the TV! He barges back in there, giving his shoulder a helluva crack on the livingroom door jamb on the way—but they're not hanging there any more. Maybe he's only imagined it. "Hey, Mr. Tucker," Mark says flatly. "Your fly's open."

• • •

The baby's dirty. Stinks to high heaven. She hurries back to the livingroom, hearing sirens and gunshots. The detective is crouched outside a house, peering in. Already, she's completely lost. The baby screams at the top of its lungs. She turns up the volume. But it's all confused. She hurries back in there, claps an angry hand to the baby's mouth. "Shut up!" she cries. She throws the baby down on its back, starts to unpin the diaper, as the baby tunes up again. The phone rings. She answers it, one eye on the TV. "*What?*" The baby cries so hard it starts to choke. Let it. "I said, hi, this is Jack!" Then it hits her: oh no! the diaper pin!

• • •

"The aspirin . . ." But she's already in the tub. Way down in the tub. Staring at him through the water. Her tummy looks pale and ripply. He hears sirens, people on the porch.

• • •

Jimmy gets up to go to the bathroom and gets his face slapped and smeared with baby poop. Then she hauls him off to the bathroom, yanks off his pajamas, and throws him into the tub. That's okay, but next she gets naked and acts like she's gonna get in the tub, too. The baby's screaming and the phone's ringing like crazy and in walks his dad. Saved! he thinks, but, no, his dad grabs him right back out of the tub and whales the dickens out of him, no questions asked, while she watches, then sends him—*whack!*—back to bed. So he's lying there, wet and dirty and naked and sore, and he still has to go to the bathroom, and outside his window he hears two older guys talking. "Listen, you know where to do it if we get her pinned?" "No! Don't you?"

• • •

"Yo ho heave ho! *Ugh!*" Dolly's on her back and they're working on the belly side. Somebody got the great idea of buttering her down first. Not to lose the ground they've gained, they've shot it inside with a basting syringe. But now suddenly there's this big tug-of-war under way between those who want to stuff her in and those who want to let her out. Something rips, but she feels better. The odor of hot butter makes her think of movie theaters and popcorn. "Hey, has anybody seen Harry?" she asks. "Where's Harry?"

• • •

Somebody's getting chased. She switches back to the love story, and now the man's back kissing the young lover again. What's going on?

She gives it up, decides to take a quick bath. She's just stepping into the tub, one foot in, one foot out, when Mr. Tucker walks in. "Oh, excuse me! I only wanted some aspirin . . ." She grabs for a towel, but he yanks it away. "Now, that's not how it's supposed to happen, child," he scolds. "Please! Mr. Tucker . . . !" He embraces her savagely, his calloused old hands clutching roughly at her backside. "Mr. Tucker!" she cries, squirming. "Your wife called—!" He's pushing something between her legs, hurting her. She slips, they both slip—something cold and hard slams her in the back, cracks her skull, she seems to be sinking into a sea . . .

• • •

They've got her over the hassock, skirt up and pants down. "Give her a little lesson there, Jack baby!" The television lights flicker and flash over her glossy flesh, 1000 WHEN LIT. Whack! Slap! Bumper to bumper! He leans into her, feeling her come alive.

• • •

The phone rings, waking the baby. "Jack, is that you? Now, you listen to me—" "No, dear, this is Mrs. Tucker. Isn't the TV awfully loud?" "Oh, I'm sorry, Mrs. Tucker! I've been getting—" "I tried to call you before, but I couldn't hang on. To the phone, I mean. I'm sorry, dear." "Just a minute, Mrs. Tucker, the baby's—" "Honey, listen! Is Harry there? Is Mr. Tucker there, dear?"

• • •

"Stop it!" she screams and claps a hand over the baby's mouth. "Stop it! Stop it! *Stop it!*" Her other hand is full of baby stool and she's afraid she's going to be sick. The phone rings. "No!" she cries. She's hanging on to the baby, leaning woozily away, listening to the phone ring. "Okay, okay," she sighs, getting ahold of herself. But when she lets go of the baby, it isn't screaming any more. She shakes it. Oh no . . .

• • •

"Hello?" No answer. Strange. She hangs up and, wrapped only in a towel, stares out the window at the cold face staring in—she screams!

• • •

She screams, scaring the hell out of him. He leaps out of the tub, glances up at the window she's gaping at just in time to see two faces duck away, then slips on the bathroom tiles, and crashes to his ass, whacking his head on the sink on the way down. She stares down at him, trembling, a towel over her narrow shoulders. "Mr. Tucker! Mr. Tucker, are you all right . . . ?" Who's Sorry Now? Yessir, who's back is breaking with each . . . He stares up at the little tufted locus of all his woes, and passes out, dreaming of Jeannie . . .

• • •

The phone rings. "Dolly! It's for you!" "Hello?" "Hello, Mrs. Tucker?" "Yes, speaking." "Mrs. Tucker, this is the police calling . . ."

• • •

It's cramped and awkward and slippery, but he's pretty sure he got it in her, once anyway. When he gets the suds out of his eyes, he sees her staring up at them. Through the water. "Hey, Mark! Let her up!"

• • •

Down in the suds. Feeling sleepy. The phone rings, startling her. Wrapped in a towel, she goes to answer. "No, he's not here, Mrs. Tucker." Strange. Married people act pretty funny sometimes. The baby is awake and screaming. Dirty, a real mess. Oh boy, there 's a lot of things she'd rather be doing than babysitting in this madhouse. She decides to wash the baby off in her own bathwater. She removes her towel, unplugs the tub, lowers the water level so the baby can sit. Glancing back over her shoulder, she sees Jimmy staring at her. "Go back to bed, Jimmy." "I have to go to the bathroom." "Good grief, Jimmy! It looks like you already have!" The phone rings. She doesn't bother with the towel—what can Jimmy see he hasn't already seen?—and goes to answer. "No, Jack, and that's final." Sirens, on the TV, as the police move in. But wasn't that the channel with the love story? Ambulance maybe. Get this over with so she can at least catch the news. "Get those wet pajamas off, Jimmy, and I'll find clean ones. Maybe you better get in the tub, too." "I think something's wrong with the baby," he says. "It's down in the water and it's not swimming or anything."

• • •

She's staring up at them from the rug. They slap her. Nothing happens. "You just tilted her, man!" Mark says softly. "We gotta get outa here!" Two little kids are standing wideeyed in the doorway. Mark looks hard at Jack. "No, Mark, they're just little kids . . . !" "We gotta, man, or we're dead."

• • •

"Dolly! My God! Dolly, I can explain!" She glowers down at them, her ripped girdle around her ankles. "What the four of you are doing in the bathtub with *my* babysitter?" she says sourly. "I can hardly wait!"

• • •

Police sirens wail, lights flash. "I heard the scream!" somebody shouts. "There were two boys!" "I saw a man!" "She was running with the baby!" "My God!" somebody screams "they're *all* dead!" Crowds come running. Spotlights probe the bushes.

• • •

"Harry, where the hell you been?" his wife whines, glaring blearily up at him from the carpet. "I can explain," he says. "Hey, whatsamatter, Harry?" his host asks, smeared with butter for some goddamn reason. "You look like you just seen a ghost!" Where did he leave his drink? Everybody's laughing, everybody except Dolly, whose cheeks are streaked with tears. "Hey, Harry, you won't let them take me to a rest home, will you, Harry?"

• • •

10:00. The dishes done, children to bed, her books read, she watches the news on television. Sleepy. The man's voice is gentle, soothing. She dozes—awakes with a start: a babysitter? Did the announcer say something about a babysitter?

• • •

"Just want to catch the weather," the host says, switching on the TV. Most of the guests are leaving, but the Tuckers stay to watch the news. As it comes on, the announcer is saying something about a babysitter. The host switches channels. "They got a better weatherman on four," he explains. "Wait!" says Mrs. Tucker. "There was something about a babysitter . . . !" The host switches back. "Details have not yet been released by the police," the announcer says. "Harry, maybe we'd better go . . ."

• • •

They stroll casually out of the drugstore, run into a buddy of theirs. "Hey! Did you hear about the babysitter?" the guy asks. Mark grunts, glances at Jack. "Got a smoke?" he asks the guy.

• • •

"I think I hear the baby screaming!" Mrs. Tucker cries, running across the lawn from the drive.

• • •

She wakes, startled, to find Mr. Tucker hovering over her. "I must have dozed off!" she exclaims. "Did you hear the news about the babysitter?" Mr. Tucker asks. "Part of it," she says, rising. "Too bad, wasn't it?" Mr. Tucker is watching the report of the ball scores and golf tournaments. "I'll drive you home in just a minute, dear," he says. "Why, how nice!" Mrs. Tucker exclaims from the kitchen. "The dishes are all done!"

• • •

"What can I say, Dolly?" the host says with a sigh, twisting the buttered strands of her ripped girdle between his fingers. "Your children are murdered, your husband gone, a corpse in your bathtub, and your house is wrecked. I'm sorry. But what can I say?" On the TV, the news is over, and they're selling aspirin. "Hell, *I* don't know," she says. "Let's see what's on the late late movie."

MARK COSTELLO

Murphy's Xmas

I

MURPHY'S drunk on the bright verge of still another Christmas and a car door slams. Then he's out in the headlights and in bed waking up the next afternoon with Annie kissing his crucified right fist. It's blue and swollen, and when he tries to move it, it tingles, it chimes and Annie says, How did you hurt your hand? Did you hit somebody?

Murphy waits while that question fades on her mouth, then the room glitters and he sniffs the old fractured acid of remorse asking: Was I sick?

Yes.

Where?

On the floor. And you fell out of bed twice. It was so terrible I don't think I could stand it if it happened again promise me you won't get drunk anymore, Glover had to teach both of your classes this morning you frighten me when you're this way and you've lost so much weight you should have seen yourself last night lying naked on the floor like something from a concentration camp in your own vomit you were so white you were blue

is the color of Annie's eyes as Murphy sinks into the stars and splinters of the sheets with her, making love to her and begging her forgiveness which she gives and gives until Murphy can feel her shy skeleton waltzing away with his in a fit of ribbons, the bursting bouquets of a Christmas they are going to spend apart and

bright the next morning they rise in sweet sorrow to part for Christmas; she to her parents' home in Missouri, he to haunted Illinois.

Murphy holds her head in his hands and whispers: I can't leave you. I won't be able to sleep. I know I won't. I'll get sick. I need you Annie.

She squeezes his shoulders, kisses his cheeks and tells him he can do it. It's only for two weeks. Good-bye. And be careful. Driving.

The door slams, the windows rattle and Annie walking through the snow is no bigger than her cello which she holds to her shoulder, a suitcase bangs against her left knee and the door opens and there's Glover jangling the keys of his Volkswagen, offering again to drive Murphy's family into Illinois for him.

Stricken by swerving visions of his son strewn across the wet December roadside, his toys and intestines glistening under the wheels of semi trucks, Murphy says no, he will drive and as he takes the proffered keys, Glover says: Is Annie gone already? I was supposed to give her a cello lesson before she left then he leaves, the door slams and Murphy hates him, his Byronesque[1] limp through the snow, his cello and his Volkswagen and sobriety. Rubbing his right fist, Murphy goes to the kitchen and drains a can of beer. Then he packs his bag and lights out for his abandoned home.

II

Now the trunks are tied down and the Volkswagen is overladen and they roll out of Kansas into Missouri with the big wind knocking them all over the road while vigilant Murphy fights the wheel and grins at the feather touches of his 5-year-old son, who kisses his neck and romps in the back seat, ready for Christmas.

In Mexico, Missouri, his wife looks at his swollen right fist and says: Tsk-tsk. You haven't grown up yet have you. Who did you hit this time?

Into the face of her challenge, Murphy blows blue cigarette smoke.

When they cross the Mighty Mississippi at Hannibal, she looks up at the old, well-kept houses, pats her swollen stomach and says: Maybe I could come here to live, to have my baby.

Murphy's son rushes into the crack of her voice. And he doesn't stop asking him to come back and be his daddy again until Murphy takes Dexamyl to keep awake and it is dark and his son is asleep and the Volkswagen hops and shudders over the flat mauve stretches of Illinois.

At Springfield, where they stop to take on gas, the fluorescent light of the filling station is like the clap of a blue hand across the face. Murphy's son wakes and his wife says: This is where President Lincoln lived and is buried.

Where?

In a tomb. Out there.

She points a finger past his nose and Murphy makes a promise he knows he can't keep: I know what. Do you want to hear a poem, Michael?

With his son at the back of his neck all snug in a car that he should never have presumed to borrow, he drives through Springfield trying to remember "When Lilacs Last in the Dooryard Bloom'd."[2] But he can't get past the first stanza. Three times he repeats "O powerful western fallen star," and then goes on in prose about the coffin moving across the country with the pomp of the inloop'd flags, through cities draped in black until his son is asleep again and

that coffin becomes his wife's womb and from deep in its copious satin Murphy hears the shy warble of the fetus: *you are my father,*

1. In the melodramatic, picturesque manner of George Gordon, Lord Byron, English Romantic poet (1788–1824). 2. Poem by Walt Whitman commemorating the death of President Lincoln.

you are my father, the throat bleeds, the song bubbles. Murphy is afraid enough to fight. He looks at his wife and remembers the wily sunlight of conception, the last time he made love to her amid the lace iron and miniature American flags of the Veterans Cemetery (it's the quietest place I know to talk, she said) while the crows slipped across the sun like blue razor blades and the chatter of their divorce sprang up around them

stone and pine, lilac and star, the cedars dusk and dim: *well it's final then, we're definitely going to get a divorce?* Murphy said *yes,* for good? *yes* and his wife caught him by the hip as he turned away *well it's almost dark now so why don't we just lie down and fuck once more for old time's sake here on the grass come on there are pine needles and they're soft*

Did you take your pill?

Yes

Ok, but no strings attached and

3½ months later Murphy is informed that he is going to be a father again and again, hurray, whoopee now

Murphy drives across slippery Illinois hearing a carol of death until the singer so shy becomes a child he will never hold or know, and the sweet chant of its breath gets caught in the whine of the tires as he imagines holding the child and naming it and kissing it, until it falls asleep on his shoulder—*how could you have tricked me this way? how could you have done it?*

That question keeps exploding behind Murphy's eyes, and when they hit his wife's hometown, he stops the car in front of a tavern and says: I can't do it.

What?

Face your parents.

He gets out: I'll wait here. Come back when you're unloaded.

His wife says *wait a minute,* and Murphy slams the door. He walks under the glittering Budweiser sign and she screams: I can't drive. I don't even know how to get this thing in reverse . . .

Push down.

Child!

Murphy hovers over the car: *I'm not a child!* and the motor roars, and the gears grind, and the Volkswagen hops and is dead. A red light flashes on in the middle of the speedometer and Murphy turns to the wakening face of 5-year-old Michael: Are we at Grandma's yet Daddy?

He slams his swollen right fist into his left palm: Yes we are!

Then he gets in and takes the wheel. And he drives them all the way home.

But he doesn't stop there. Murphy roars northwest out of Illinois into Iowa in search of friends and gin he can't find. Then he bangs back across the Mississippi, cuts down the heart of Illinois, and holes up in the YMCA in his wife's hometown, within visiting distance of his son.

Whom he loves and doesn't see. He keeps telling himself: *I think I'll surprise Michael and take him to the park this afternoon,* then he races down to the gym to run in circles and spit against the walls. He sits in the steam room, watches the clock and slaps his stomach, which is flat, but on the blink. To ease his pain, he drinks milk and eats cottage cheese and yogurt and calls Annie long distance in Missouri: God I love you and miss your body Annie I haven't slept for two days

and she says: Guess what?

What?

Glover was through town and gave me a cello lesson, he's a great guy his

gifts are stunning and relentless, he limps off to take your classes when you're too drunk to stand up in the morning—his hair is scrubbed, his skin cherubic, his wrists are opal and delicate; right now Murphy would like to seize them and break them off. Instead he says: Is he still in town?

"Who?

Glover.

Heavens no, he just stopped through for about two hours are you all right?

Yes. Listen Annie I love you

Murphy slams the phone down and bounds back upstairs to his room in the YMCA to sit alone while his cottage cheese and yogurt cartons fill up with snow on the window ledge and he imagines Annie back in their rooms in Kansas. When she walks across the floor her heels ring against the walls and every morning Murphy hears her before he sees her standing at the stove, her hair dark, her earrings silver, her robe wine, her thighs so cool, and the pearl flick of her tongue is like a beak when she kisses him

Murphy tastes unbelievable mint and blood and

imagines Glover limping across the floor of the living room with two glasses of gin in his hands. The betrayal is dazzling and quick. Bending under Glover's tongue, Annie whispers *no, no,* and as she goes down in their bed, her fingers make star-shaped wrinkles in the sheets

Murphy slams his fist down on his YMCA windowsill. Then popping them like white bullwhips over his head, he stuffs his towels and clothes into his bag, and lights out of there on lustrous Highway 47. The night is prodigal, the inane angels of the radio squawk out their thousand songs of Christmas and return. Bearing down on the wheel, Murphy murders the memory of Annie and Glover with the memory of his father, whom he has betrayed to old age, the stars and stripes of the U.S. Mail.

Composing them on the back of his American Legion 40 *and* 8 stationery, Murphy's father sends quick notes By Air to his grandson saying: I was feeling pretty low x until I got the pictures you drew for me Michael boy x then I bucked up x God bless you x I miss you x give my love to your daddy x who

unblessed and rocking in the slick crescents of Dexamyl and fatigue, is on his way home for still another Christmas. Now as he drives, he notes the dim absence of birds on the telephone lines, and thinking of the happy crows that Michael draws with smiles in their beaks, Murphy sees his father stumbling under the sign of the cross, crossing himself again and again on the forehead and lips, crossing himself on his tie clasp, wandering in a listless daze across the front lawn with a rake in his hands, not knowing whether to clean the gutter along the street or pray for his own son, who has sunk so low out in Kansas.

It is just dawning when Murphy breaks into the mauve and white outskirts of his dear dirty Decatur where billboards and *Newport* girls[3] in turquoise are crowned by the bursting golden crosses of Murphy's high school then

he's home. Pulled up and stopped in his own driveway. And sitting there with his hands crossed in his lap he feels agog like a Buddhistic time bomb about to go off, about to splinter and explode inside the dry sleep of his parents, the tears will smoulder, the braying angels of insomnia will shatter around the childless Christmas tree, there will be a fire, it will sputter and run up the walls and be Murphy's fault. Sitting there he feels hearts beginning to pump in the palms of his hands and he doesn't want to let anybody die

as he knocks on the dry oaken door of his parents' home and is welcomed with open arms and the sun rising behind his back

Inside the sockets of his mother's eyes, there are mauve circles and they have had the living room walls painted turquoise. Murphy blinks, shakes his father's hands, and his mother leads him into the kitchen.

There he drinks milk, eats cottage cheese and kisses his mother's hands. She cries and wants him to eat a big breakfast. With tears in her eyes, she offers him bacon, eggs, cornbread, coffee, butterchunk sweet rolls and Brazil nuts. When Murphy shakes his head she says: I think you're making the biggest mistake of your life, I think you'll live to regret it. Patricia is a lovely girl, you have a wonderful son and another child on the way. Isn't there any hope of you getting back together? I pray night and day and can't get little Michael off my mind. What's ever going to happen to him and the new child? Oh I wish I were twenty years younger

3. Advertisements for Newport cigarettes.

After breakfast they go shopping, and for his Christmas present Murphy picks out three packs of stainless steel razor blades and a pair of black oxford basketball shoes. Then he slips off for a workout at his high school gym. The basketball team is practicing and Murphy runs in wide circles around them, not bothering a soul.

Left to himself that afternoon, he drinks rum and eggnog and plays with the remote controls of the color television set. Then he roams the house and neighborhood and everything has changed. The sheets of his bed are blue. On the walls, where once there were newspaper photographs of himself in high school basketball uniform, there are now purple paintings of Jesus Christ kneeling on rocks in the Garden of Gethsemane.[4] Every place he looks, in corniced frames of diminishing size, there are color photographs of Murphy in tight-collared military attire. As he looks, the photographs get smaller and smaller and there is always a snub-nosed statue of St. Francis of Assisi[5] standing there, to measure himself by.

Up and down the block, birds bang in and out of bird feeders. The withering neighbors have put up fences within fences within fences. Half-drunk, Murphy keeps hitting the wrong switches and floodlights glare from the roof of the garage and light up the whole backyard. All night long his father keeps paying the encroaching negro carolers not to sing. Finally Murphy gets up from the sofa, and smiling, announces that he's going out. Taking his rum and eggnog with him, he sits in the Volkswagen and drinks until 3 o'clock in the morning. Then he gets out, vomits on the curb and goes back inside

Where his mother is awake in a nightgown of shriveled violet, with yellow spears of wheat sewn into the shoulders like cross-staves of static lightning about to go off and how

will Murphy hold her when she stops him on the carpet outside his bedroom door to tell him that she loves him, that he will always be her son no matter what happens she is so sorry that he had to leave his wife and children for

a mere girl, it is unbelievable that

in his hands her small skull buzzes and even before she mentions the fact of Annie, Murphy is holding Annie's skull in his hands and the sinking wings of his mother's sweet shoulders are Annie's shoulders in his mother's nightgown sinking: What are you talking about?

That girl you're living with. She called tonight

on Christmas Eve

4. The garden where Christ prayed before the Crucifixion (Mark 14:32). 5. St. Francis (1182?–1226), founder of the Franciscan order, was known for his humility and love of all living creatures.

Murphy hears the old familiar bells of his father's fury gonging
Your father answered, he was furious
Mother I'm not living with anyone
Michael I know you are

then the small lightning of her nightgown begins to strike across her shoulders and she is sobbing against his throat and Murphy is in bed holding his lie like a sheet up to his chin: Mother I told you I'm not living with anyone

Stroking his leg through the blankets, she disregards the crocked insomnia of his eyes, and makes him promise to try to sleep: Do you promise now?

Yes, Mother, I promise

and she leaves him sleepless between the blue sheets with Christ kneeling on the wall, the scent of his mother's handcream on the back of his neck and he hears her alone in her room coughing like a wife he has lost at last and picking at her rosary beads all night long

There is no sleep

or peace on earth. But with the muzzy dawn Murphy rises and goes to church with his parents. In the choir loft, the organs shudder; in his pew Murphy shivers and sniffs the contrition of Christmastide. All around him the faithful kneel in candle smoke and pray; all day long Murphy kneels and shuffles around trying to get Annie *long distance*, trying to tell her *never to call him at home again*. Then at 7 P.M. the phone rings and Murphy's simmering 70-year-old father answers it hissing: Long distance, for you

By the time Murphy hangs up, his father is dizzy. He staggers through the rooms slamming doors while Murphy's mother follows him whispering: Mike your blood pressure, your blood pressure

Then in the living room they face each other: The bitch! Calling here on Christmas Day! The little bitch!

Murphy turns to his mother and says, *I'm leaving* and his father spins him by the shoulder: You're not leaving, *I* am!

They both leave. Murphy by the back, his father by the front. Storm doors slam, crucifixes rattle on the walls. Murphy's father rounds the corner and screams: Come back here!

His voice is higher than Murphy has ever heard it, and the wind pulls at their clothes while they walk toward each other, his father in a slanting stagger, his overcoat too big for him, his eyes filled with tears.

I'm an old man. I'm dying. You won't see me again. Go back to your family, don't abandon your son.

Murphy reaches for his shoulder and says *Dad I can't* and his father slaps his hand away

Michael Murphy. You have a son named *Michael Murphy* and you tell me you can't go back to him?

Murphy lifts his hand and starts to speak, but his father screams: *Phony!* You're a phon*eee*, do you hear me?

They are at the door and Murphy's mother, in grief and her nightgown, pulls them in. His father stumbles to the wall and hits it: You phony. You ought to be in Vietnam!

Murphy's laughter is curdled and relieved. He slaps his hands together and screams: That's it, that's it!

Then he spins and bolts toward the back door, with his mother screaming: Michael! Where are you going?

To Vietnam, god damn it! To Vietnam

Which isn't far. 150 miles north. From a motel room deep in her own hometown, Murphy calls his wife and when he asks her to come over she says: Why *should* I come over?

You know why. I'm going out of my mind.

Be my guest.

Click

She opens the door during half-time of a TV football game and neither of them says a word as their clothes fly in slurred arcs onto the bed. Then standing naked in front of her, Murphy hunches up with holy quietude and smiles and breathes as he holds a glass of gin and tonic to her lips and she drinks and smiles as the lime skin nudges her teeth and she nods when she's had enough. While her mouth is still cool, Murphy kisses her tongue and gums and wants to push the bed against the wall and then to drive all the other guests to insomniac rack and ruin by humping and banging the bed with wet good health against the wall all afternoon but

his wife is sunk in an older despair. She runs her fingers up the vapid stack of Murphy's spine and says: You *are* handsome. I love to touch you.

Bare-chested Murphy turns on it, and the quick trick of her flattery gets them into bed, where to the pelvic thud of the innerspring she sucks on the spare skin of his collarbone and says: Tell me that you love me. You don't have to mean it. Just say it . . .

Murphy would like to but he can't. Both memory and flesh legislate against him. He looks down, and like painted furniture his wife's ribs now seem chipped by a thousand kicks; when he takes them in his mouth, her nipples taste as tight and deprived as walnuts; within the pregnant strop of her stomach against his, Murphy can feel the delicate strophes of Annie's waist, and moving like a pale liar before his wife's bared teeth, he remembers the beginning of the end of their marriage; the masks, mirrors and carrots that began to sprout around their bed like a bitter, 2 A.M. Victory garden,[6] one that Murphy had planted all by himself and was going to pick and shake in his wife's face on the sparkling, sacrosanct morn-

6. Garden planted to supplement food supply in World War II.

ing that he left for good and ever. Caught in the dowdy mosaics of their bedroom mirror, they would get down on their hands and knees and as the orange joke of a carrot disappeared between her legs, his wife would turn and ask, *who are you?* and Murphy would smile down from behind his mask and say: *who are you?* Then his smile would rot in his opened mouth, and Murphy *became* his impersonations; he played and moaned within an adultery so hypothetical it stunk and smoked the bedroom ceiling up like the induced death of love between them *Harder, Oh Harder* now Murphy and his father are standing outside the motel room window looking in at Murphy's marriage like peeping toms and his father is ordering Murphy back into the bed but Murphy resists and all of his reasons are rosy and shrill like a schoolboy he screams: *I wouldn't swap Annie for anybody, do you hear me, not anybody* and his father, in tears and death, screams: *Not for your son? Not for Michael Murphy? I'm*

Coming

and Murphy opens his eyes to endure his wife's orgasm like a slap across the face *Oh Thank You God, Oh Thank You.*

Thanking her with whispers and pecks about the neck and ears, Murphy sweeps his wife out into the brittle December afternoon and bright the next morning he picks up his son to take him home, 150 miles south, to his grandmother. Michael's raucous teeth glitter in the rearview mirror of the VW, and as they rattle into Decatur, Murphy loves him so much, he can't stop or share him with anybody just yet: I know what Michael. Do you want to go to the zoo before we go to Grandma's? Yes

he does. Right now. And Murphy, full of grins and flapdoodle, takes him there. He buys Michael a bag of popcorn, and as he goes back to the car to flick off the headlights, he turns to see the popcorn falling in white, jerky sprays among the ducks and geese.

The whole pause at the zoo is that way: spendthrift, inaugural and loving. Murphy squats and shows Michael how to feed the steaming billy goat with his bare hands. He flinches and giggles at the pink pluck of his lips, then they race over to look through the windows at the pacing leopards. Bare-handed and standing there, Murphy wonders how he would defend his son against a leopard. He can feel his fists and forearms being ripped away, but also he can feel his son escaping into the dusk and dim of the elm trees that surround the zoo.

Then he gets zany and amid giggles and protests, Murphy drives the borrowed VW up over the curb and through the park to Grandmother's house they go with the radio blaring: help I need somebody's help then

suddenly it's darker and cooler and their smiles are whiter when the subject changes like a slap across the face to

Michael's dreams. Five years old in a fatherless house, he sleeps alone and dreams of

snow. Murphy pulls him into the front seat, sets him on his lap and turns off the radio. Holding him too tight, he says: what kind of snow Michael?

You know. The kind that falls.

What do you dream?

That it's covering me up.

Then Michael begins to cry and says: I want somebody to sleep with me tonight and tomorrow night. I want *you* to sleep with me Daddy.

Murphy does. Three nights they stay in his parents' house and Murphy sleeps between the blue sheets while Michael sucks his thumb and urinates the first night against Murphy's leg, giving him the chance to be patient father loving his son

he carries him to the bathroom with sure avowals and tender kisses: That's all right Michael boy, Dad will take care of you

Always?

Always

and Murphy's mother is there in her nightgown in the stark light of the bedroom changing the sheets, putting down towels, kissing her grandson, wishing she were twenty years younger

In the lilac morning, quick with clouds and sunlight, Murphy and his mother and son go uptown. Standing in front of laughing mirrors in the Buster Brown Shoe Store, Murphy and Michael grow fat and skinny and tall and short together, then go to see Pinnochio not in the belly of a whale

but in the outer space of sure death and forgiveness, they eat silver sno-cones and Murphy is finally able to eat steak while his father roams through the rooms presenting his grandson with a plastic pistol on the barrel of which an assassin's scope has been mounted.

Compounding that armament with love, he displays, on the last afternoon, Murphy's basketball clippings. Spreading them out for his grandson on the bed, he whispers, smiles and gloats until 5-year-old Michael can't help himself. He walks over to Murphy and says: Grandpa says you were a great basketball player and played on TV

is that right Daddy?

That's right Michael, then they

are leaving. Clasping his toys to him, Michael cries pained and formal tears. Murphy stands on the curb, the wind in his eyes, and the apologies are yet to be made. Overhead the streetlight clangs and they are standing on the same corner where Murphy used to sit under the streetlight at night on the orange fire hydrant twirling his rosary beads like a black propeller over his head waiting for his parents to come home and light up the dark rooms with their voices and cigarettes then

he would see their headlights coming up the street and he would rise and put away his rosary beads to greet them now

he takes off his gloves and puts out his right hand to his father and says: Dad, I'm sorry.

When his apology cracks the air, his mother begins to cry. Grateful for that cue, his father takes his hand and says Goodbye, good luck, God bless you

III

Out there in Kansas the next afternoon, under a sere and benedictory sun, Murphy's Christmas comes to an end. He tools west away from home and the holidays, southwest toward the snaggled conclusion of still another New Year. His family rides in a swarm of shredded Kleenex, Cracker Jack, and terror referred

is terror refined: like the crucial envoy of his grandfather, Michael, sweet assassin, holds his plastic pistol to the base of Murphy's skull and says: Daddy? Why don't you come back and be my daddy?

Terse and perspirate, Murphy's wife takes a swipe at the pistol, but Michael moves out of her reach, and keeping it trained on the back of his father's skull, he repeats his question: Why don't you come back Daddy?

Before he can think or excuse himself, Murphy says, *Because.*

Because why?

Because Mommy and I fight.

You're not fighting now.

In tears and on her knees, Murphy's wife lunges into the back seat and disarms her son. But he begins to cry and find his ultimatum: Daddy

I'm too shy to have a new daddy, I want you to be my daddy, and if you won't come back and be my daddy

I'm going to kill you.

The moment of his threat is considered. And then it is foregone. Out of his fist and index finger, Michael makes a pistol and a patricide: Bang, bang, bang

you're dead Daddy

you're dead

Coffin that passes through lanes and streets, Volkswagen that blows and rattles under the new snow's perpetual clang, here, Murphy hands over his sprig of lilac and return, his modicum of rage and disbelief.

Certain that his son's aim was shy and hypothetical, he stops the Volkswagen in front of his apartment, flicks off the headlights, slams the door and hears the

dual squawk of tuned and funereal cellos

their notes curdle the snow, splinter the windows with a welcome so baroque and sepulchral, Murphy can't stand it. Roaring toward the door, he imagines Annie and Glover sitting on stiff-backed chairs, their cellos between their legs, their innocence arranged by Bach, certified by

the diagonal churn of their bows on string, the spiny octagons of their music stands, the opal bone and nylon of Annie's knees. Murphy rattles the door with his fist, and for a moment their music needles his rage, then squeaks to a stop. In turquoise slacks and sweater, with a smile brimful of tears and teeth so bright, Annie throws open the door and how

will Murphy return her kiss, while blurred in the corner of his eye, Glover scurries, gathering up his cello and his music: *Happy New Year did the car run all right* he takes the proffered keys and

guilty of nothing but his embarrassment

he says *don't mention it* as he leaves, slams out the door, and

left in the rattled vacuum of that departure, Murphy has no one to beat up or murder, no one on whom to avenge his Christmas; he is left with only the echo of the music, a suspicion founded on nothing but a cherub's limp and hustle through the chiming snow.

In bed, Annie is a sweet new anatomy of hope and extinction. She kisses him, the *Newport* flood of her hair gets in his eyes and Murphy cracks an elegiac and necessary joke: *Annie you'll never leave me for Glover will you?* She tells him not to be silly then

Murphy kisses her, and in a rush of flesh and new avowals, he puts everything into his lovemaking but his

heart

which hangs unbelievable and dead in his ribs, all shot to smithereens by Michael.

Outside the new snow falls and inside it is over. Annie is asleep in his arms and Murphy lies sleepless on a numb and chiming cross of his own making. On the walls there are no praying Christs, the turquoise Gethsemanes of Decatur are gone forever. The clock drones, the womb whirs, the shy trill of his wife's gestation comes to Murphy through the pines like Michael calling to him: *Sleep with me tonight and tomorrow night Daddy* the cradle's eloquence depends on pain, it is sewn in lilacs and shocks of wheat. Shy charlatan, Murphy sneaks up to it and in a roomfull of white, white sunlight, he looks in at his newborn child, and cannot look away or kid himself, his fatherhood is the fatherhood

of cottage cheese, the retreating footprints of snow and yogurt up his father's spine, the borrowed Volkswagen that will never run out of gas or plastic pistols. Then the dry bells of the furnace begin to hiss against Murphy's ankles, and he hears the whistling pines, the clangorous tombstones of the Veterans Cemetery. Flapping their arms like downed angels in the middle of winter, Murphy and

Annie make love and forgive each other until their ears and eye-sockets fill up with snow

then Michael stands over them, takes aim at Murphy and
makes his final declaration: Bang
bang, bang
you're dead Daddy
you're dead

IV

And for the first time in his life, Murphy lies there and knows it.

ANDRE DUBUS

A Father's Story

MY name is Luke Ripley, and here is what I call my life: I own a stable of thirty horses, and I have young people who teach riding, and we board some horses too. This is in northeastern Massachusetts. I have a barn with an indoor ring, and outside I've got two fenced-in rings and a pasture that ends at a woods with trails. I call it my life because it looks like it is, and people I know call it that, but it's a life I can get away from when I hunt and fish, and some nights after dinner when I sit in the dark in the front room and listen to opera. The room faces the lawn and the road, a two-lane country road. When cars come around the curve northwest of the house, they light up the lawn for an instant, the leaves of the maple out by the road and the hemlock closer to the window. Then I'm alone again, or I'd appear to be if someone crept up to the house and looked through a window: a big-gutted grey-haired guy, drinking tea and smoking cigarettes, staring out at the dark woods across the road, listening to a grieving soprano.

My real life is the only one nobody talks about anymore, except Father Paul LeBoeuf, another old buck. He has a decade on me: he's sixty-four, a big man, bald on top with grey at the sides; when he had hair, it was black. His face is ruddy, and he jokes about being a whiskey priest,[1] though he's not. He gets outdoors as much as he can, goes for a long walk every morning, and hunts and fishes with me. But I can't get him on a horse anymore. Ten years ago I could badger him into a trail ride! I had to give him a western saddle, and he'd hold the pommel and bounce through the woods with me, and be sore for days. He's looking at seventy with eyes that are younger than many I've seen in people in their twenties. I do not remember ever feeling the way they seem to; but I was lucky, because even as a child I knew that life would try me, and I

1. Vernacular term for a priest addicted to alcohol.

must be strong to endure, though in those early days I expected to be tortured and killed for my faith, like the saints I learned about in school.

Father Paul's family came down from Canada, and he grew up speaking more French than English, so he is different from the Irish priests who abound up here. I do not like to make general statements, or even to hold general beliefs, about people's blood, but the Irish do seem happiest when they're dealing with misfortune or guilt, either their own or somebody's else's, and if you think you're not a victim of either one, you can count on certain Irish priests to try to change your mind. On Wednesday nights Father Paul comes to dinner. Often he comes on other nights too, and once, in the old days when we couldn't eat meat on Fridays, we bagged our first ducks of the season on a Friday, and as we drove home from the marsh, he said: For the purposes of Holy Mother Church, I believe a duck is more a creature of water than land, and is not rightly meat. Sometimes he teases me about never putting anything in his Sunday collection, which he would not know about if I hadn't told him years ago. I would like to believe I told him so we could have a philosophical talk at dinner, but probably the truth is I suspected he knew, and I did not want him to think I so loved money that I would not even give his church a coin on Sunday. Certainly the ushers who pass the baskets know me as a miser.

I don't feel right about giving money for buildings, places. This starts with the Pope, and I cannot respect one of them till he sells his house and everything in it, and that church too, and uses the money to feed the poor. I have rarely, and maybe never, come across saintliness, but I feel certain it cannot exist in such a place. But I admit, also, that I know very little, and maybe the popes live on a different plane and are tried in ways I don't know about. Father Paul says his own church, St. John's, is hardly the Vatican. I like his church: it is made of wood, and has a simple altar and crucifix, and no padding on the kneelers. He does not have to lock its doors at night. Still it is a place. He could say Mass in my barn. I know this is stubborn, but I can find no mention by Christ of maintaining buildings, much less erecting them of stone or brick, and decorating them with pieces of metal and mineral and elements that people still fight over like barbarians. We had a Maltese woman taking riding lessons, she came over on the boat when she was ten, and once she told me how the nuns in Malta used to tell the little girls that if they wore jewelry, rings and bracelets and necklaces, in purgatory snakes would coil around their fingers and wrists and throats. I do not believe in frightening children or telling them lies, but if those nuns saved a few girls from devotion to things, maybe they were right. That Maltese woman laughed about it, but I noticed she wore only a watch, and that with a leather strap.

The money I give to the church goes in people's stomachs, and on their backs, down in New York City. I have no delusions about the worth of what I do, but I feel it's better to feed somebody than not. There's a priest in Times Square giving shelter to runaway kids, and some Franciscans who run a bread line; actually it's a morning line for coffee and a roll, and Father Paul calls it the continental breakfast for winos and bag ladies. He is curious about how much I am sending, and I know why: he guesses I send a lot, he has said probably more than tithing, and he is right; he wants to know how much because he believes I'm generous and good, and he is wrong about that; he has never had much money and does not know how easy it is to write a check when you have everything you will ever need, and the figures are mere numbers, and represent no sacrifice at all. Being a real Catholic is too hard; if I were one, I would do with my house and barn what I want the Pope to do with his. So I do not want to impress Father Paul, and when he asks me how much, I say I can't let my left hand know what my right is doing.

He came on Wednesday nights when Gloria and I were married, and the kids were young; Gloria was a very good cook (I assume she still is, but it is difficult to think of her in the present), and I liked sitting at the table with a friend who was also a priest. I was proud of my handsome and healthy children. This was long ago, and they were all very young and cheerful and often funny, and the three boys took care of their baby sister, and did not bully or tease her. Of course they did sometimes, with that excited cruelty children are prone to, but not enough so that it was part of her days. On the Wednesday after Gloria left with the kids and a U-Haul trailer, I was sitting on the front steps, it was summer, and I was watching cars go by on the road, when Father Paul drove around the curve and into the driveway. I was ashamed to see him because he is a priest and my family was gone, but I was relieved too. I went to the car to greet him. He got out smiling, with a bottle of wine, and shook my hand, then pulled me to him, gave me a quick hug, and said: 'It's Wednesday, isn't it? Let's open some cans.'

With arms about each other we walked to the house, and it was good to know he was doing his work but coming as a friend too, and I thought what good work he had. I have no calling. It is for me to keep horses.

In that other life, anyway. In my real one I go to bed early and sleep well and wake at four forty-five, for an hour of silence. I never want to get out of bed then, and every morning I know I can sleep for another four hours, and still not fail at any of my duties. But I get up, so have come to believe my life can be seen in miniature in that struggle in the dark of morning. While making the bed and boiling water for coffee, I talk to God: I offer Him my day, every act of my body and spirit, my thoughts and moods, as a prayer of thanksgiving, and for Gloria and my children and my friends and two women I made love with after Gloria left. This morning offertory is a habit from my boyhood in a Catholic school; or then it was a habit, but as I kept it and grew older it became a ritual. Then I say the Lord's Prayer, trying not to recite it, and one morning it occurred to me that a prayer, whether recited or said with concentration, is always an act of faith.

I sit in the kitchen at the rear of the house and drink coffee and smoke and watch the sky growing light before sunrise, the trees of the woods near the barn taking shape, becoming single pines and elms and oaks and maples. Sometimes a rabbit comes out of the treeline, or is already sitting there, invisible till the light finds him. The birds are awake in the trees and feeding on the ground, and the little ones, the purple finches and titmice and chickadees, are at the feeder I rigged outside the kitchen window; it is too small for pigeons to get a purchase. I sit and give myself to coffee and tobacco that get me brisk again, and I watch and listen. In the first year or so after I lost my family, I played the radio in the mornings. But I overcame that, and now I rarely play it at all. Once in the mail I received a questionnaire asking me to write down everything I watched on television during the week they had chosen. At the end of those seven days I wrote in *The Wizard of Oz* and returned it. That was in winter and was actually a busy week for my television, which normally sits out the cold months without once warming up. Had they sent the questionnaire during baseball season, they would have found me at my set. People at the stables talk about shows and performers I have never heard of, but I cannot get interested; when I am in the mood to watch television, I go to a movie or read a detective novel. There are always good detective novels to be found, and I like remembering them next morning with my coffee.

I also think of baseball and hunting and fishing, and of my children. It is not painful to think about them anymore, because even if we had lived together, they would be gone now, grown into their own lives, except Jennifer. I think of death too, not sadly, or with fear, though something like excitement does run through me, something more quickening than the coffee and tobacco. I suppose it is an intense interest, and an outright distrust: I never feel certain that I'll be here watching birds eating at tomorrow's daylight. Sometimes I try to think of other things, like the rabbit that is warm and breathing but not there till twilight. I feel on the brink of something about the life of the senses, but either am not equipped to go further or am not interested enough to concentrate. I have called all of this thinking, but it is not, because it is unintentional; what I'm really doing is feeling the day, in silence, and that is what Father Paul is doing too on his five-to-ten-mile walks.

When the hour ends I take an apple or carrot and I go to the stable and tack up a horse. We take good care of these horses, and no one rides them but students, instructors, and me, and nobody rides the horses we board unless an owner asks me to. The barn is dark and I turn on lights and take some deep breaths, smelling the hay and horses and their manure, both fresh and dried, a combined odor that you either like or you don't. I walk down the wide space of dirt between stalls, greeting the horses, joking with them about their quirks, and choose one for no reason at all other than the way it looks at me that morning. I get my old English saddle that has smoothed and darkened through the years, and go into the stall, talking to this beautiful creature who'll swerve out of a canter if a piece of paper blows in front of him, and if the barn catches fire and you manage to get him out he will, if he can get away from you, run back into the fire, to his stall. Like the smells that surround them, you either like them or you don't. I love them, so am spared having to try to explain why. I feed one the carrot or apple and tack up and lead him outside, where I mount, and we go down the driveway to the road and cross it and turn northwest and walk, then trot then canter to St. John's.

A few cars are on the road, their drivers looking serious about going to work. It is always strange for me to see a woman dressed for work so early in the morning. You know how long it takes them, with the makeup and hair and clothes, and I think of them waking in the dark of winter or early light of other seasons, and dressing as they might for an evening's entertainment. Probably this strikes me because I grew up seeing my father put on those suits he never wore on weekends or his two weeks off, and so am accustomed to the men, but when I see these women I think something went wrong, to send all those dressed-up people out on the road when the dew hasn't dried yet. Maybe it's because I so dislike getting up early, but am also doing what I choose to do, while they have no choice. At heart I am lazy, yet I find such peace and delight in it that I believe it is a natural state, and in what looks like my laziest periods I am closest to my center. The ride to St. John's is fifteen minutes. The horses and I do it in all weather; the road is well plowed in winter, and there are only a few days a year when ice makes me drive the pickup. People always look at someone on horseback, and for a moment their faces change and many drivers and I wave to each other. Then at St. John's, Father Paul and five or six regulars and I celebrate the Mass.

Do not think of me as a spiritual man whose every thought during those twenty-five minutes is at one with the words of the Mass.

Each morning I try, each morning I fail, and know that always I will be a creature who, looking at Father Paul and the altar, and uttering prayers, will be distracted by scrambled eggs, horses, the weather, and memories and daydreams that have nothing to do with the sacrament I am about to receive. I can receive, though: the Eucharist, and also, at Mass and at other times, moments and even minutes of contemplation. But I cannot achieve contemplation, as some can; and so, having to face and forgive my own failures, I have learned from them both the necessity and wonder of ritual. For ritual allows those who cannot will themselves out of the secular to perform the spiritual, as dancing allows the tongue-tied man a ceremony of love. And, while my mind dwells on breakfast, or Major or Duchess tethered under the church eave, there is, as I take the Host from Father Paul and place it on my tongue and return to the pew, a feeling that I am thankful I have not lost in the forty-eight years since my first Communion. At its center is excitement; spreading out from it is the peace of certainty. Or the certainty of peace. One night Father Paul and I talked about faith. It was long ago, and all I remember is him saying: Belief is believing in God; faith is believing that God believes in you. That is the excitement, and the peace; then the Mass is over, and I go into the sacristy and we have a cigarette and chat, the mystery ends, we are two men talking like any two men on a morning in America, about baseball, plane crashes, presidents, governors, murders, the sun, the clouds. Then I go to the horse and ride back to the life people see, the one in which I move and talk, and most days I enjoy it.

It is late summer now, the time between fishing and hunting, but a good time for baseball. It has been two weeks since Jennifer left, to drive home to Gloria's after her summer visit. She is the only one who still visits; the boys are married and have children, and sometimes fly up for a holiday, or I fly down or west to visit one of them. Jennifer is twenty, and I worry about her the way fathers worry about daughters but not sons. I want to know what she's up to, and at the same time I don't. She looks athletic, and she is: she swims and runs and of course rides. All my children do. When she comes for six weeks in summer, the house is loud with girls, friends of hers since childhood, and new ones. I am glad she kept the girl friends. They have been young company for me and, being with them, I have been able to gauge her growth between summers. On their riding days, I'd take them back to the house when their lessons were over and they had walked the horses and put them back in the stalls, and we'd have lemonade or Coke, and cookies if I had some, and talk until their parents came to drive them home. One year their breasts grew, so I wasn't startled when I saw Jennifer in

July. Then they were driving cars to the stable, and beginning to look like young women, and I was passing out beer and ashtrays and they were talking about college.

When Jennifer was here in summer, they were at the house most days. I would say generally that as they got older they became quieter, and though I enjoyed both, I sometimes missed the giggles and shouts. The quiet voices, just low enough for me not to hear from wherever I was, rising and falling in proportion to my distance from them, frightened me. Not that I believed they were planning or recounting anything really wicked, but there was a female seriousness about them, and it was secretive, and of course I thought: love, sex. But it was more than that: it was womanhood they were entering, the deep forest of it, and no matter how many women and men too are saying these days that there is little difference between us, the truth is that men find their way into that forest only on clearly marked trails, while women move about in it like birds. So hearing Jennifer and her friends talking so quietly, yet intensely, I wanted very much to have a wife.

But not as much as in the old days, when Gloria had left but her presence was still in the house as strongly as if she had only gone to visit her folks for a week. There were no clothes or cosmetics, but potted plants endured my neglectful care as long as they could, and slowly died; I did not kill them on purpose, to exorcise the house of her, but I could not remember to water them. For weeks, because I did not use it much, the house was as neat as she had kept it, though dust layered the order she had made. The kitchen went first: I got the dishes in and out of the dishwasher and wiped the top of the stove, but did not return cooking spoons and pot holders to their hooks on the wall, and soon the burners and oven were caked with spillings, the refrigerator had more space and was spotted with juices. The living room and my bedroom went next; I did not go into the children's rooms except on bad nights when I went from room to room and looked and touched and smelled, so they did not lose their order until a year later when the kids came for six weeks. It was three months before I ate the last of the food Gloria had cooked and frozen: I remember it was a beef stew, and very good. By then I had four cookbooks, and was boasting a bit, and talking about recipes with the women at the stables, and looking forward to cooking for Father Paul. But I never looked forward to cooking at night only for myself, though I made myself do it; on some nights I gave in to my daily temptation, and took a newspaper or detective novel to a restaurant. By the end of the second year, though, I had stopped turning on the radio as soon as I woke in the morning, and was able to be silent and alone in the evening too, and then I enjoyed my dinners.

It is not hard to live through a day, if you can live through a moment. What creates despair is the imagination, which pretends there is a future, and insists on predicting millions of moments, thousands of days, and so drains you that you cannot live the moment at hand. That is what Father Paul told me in those first two years, on some of the bad nights when I believed I could not bear what I had to: the most painful loss was my children, then the loss of Gloria, whom I still loved despite or maybe because of our long periods of sadness that rendered us helpless, so neither of us could break out of it to give a hand to the other. Twelve years later I believe ritual would have healed us more quickly than the repetitious talks we had, perhaps even kept us healed. Marriages have lost that, and I wish I had known then what I know now, and we had performed certain acts together every day, no matter how we felt, and perhaps then we could have subordinated feeling to action, for surely that is the essence of love. I know this from my distractions during Mass, and during everything else I do, so that my actions and feelings are seldom one. It does happen every day, but in proportion to everything else in a day, it is rare, like joy. The third most painful loss, which became second and sometimes first as months passed, was the knowledge that I could never marry again, and so dared not even keep company with a woman.

On some of the bad nights I was bitter about this with Father Paul, and I so pitied myself that I cried, or nearly did, speaking with damp eyes and breaking voice. I believe that celibacy is for him the same trial it is for me, not of the flesh, but the spirit: the heart longing to love. But the difference is he chose it, and did not wake one day to a life with thirty horses. In my anger I said I had done my service to love and chastity, and I told him of the actual physical and spiritual pain of practicing rhythm: nights of striking the mattress with a fist, two young animals lying side by side in heat, leaving the bed to pace, to smoke, to curse, and too passionate to question, for we were so angered and oppressed by our passion that we could see no further than our loins. So now I understand how people can be enslaved for generations before they throw down their tools or use them as weapons, the form of their slavery —the cotton fields, the shacks and puny cupboards and untended illnesses—absorbing their emotions and thoughts until finally they have little or none at all to direct with clarity and energy at the owners and legislators. And I told him of the trick of passion and its slaking: how during what we had to believe were safe periods, though all four children were conceived at those times, we were able with some coherence to question the tradition and reason and justice of the law against birth control, but not with enough conviction to soberly act against it, as though regular satisfaction in bed tempered our revolutionary as well as our erotic desires. Only when abstinence drove us hotly away from each other did we receive an urge so strong it lasted all the way to the drugstore and back; but always, after release, we threw away the remaining condoms; and after going through this a few times, we knew what would happen, and from then on we submitted to the calendar she so precisely marked on the bedroom wall. I told him that living two lives each month, one as celibates, one as lovers, made us tense and short-tempered, so we snapped at each other like dogs.

To have endured that, to have reached a time when we burned slowly and could gain from bed the comfort of lying down at night with one who loves you and whom you love, could for weeks on end go to bed tired and peacefully sleep after a kiss, a touch of the hands, and then to be thrown out of the marriage like a bundle from a moving freight car, was unjust, was intolerable, and I could not or would not muster the strength to endure it. But I did, a moment at a time, a day, a night, except twice, each time with a different woman and more than a year apart, and this was so long ago that I clearly see their faces in my memory, can hear the pitch of their voices, and the way they pronounced words, one with a Massachusetts accent, one midwestern, but I feel as though I only heard about them from someone else. Each rode at the stables and was with me for part of an evening; one was badly married, one divorced, so none of us was free. They did not understand this Catholic view, but they were understanding about my having it, and I remained friends with both of them until the married one left her husband and went to Boston, and the divorced one moved to Maine. After both those evenings, those good women, I went to Mass early while Father Paul was still in the confessional, and received his absolution. I did not tell him who I was, but of course he knew, though I never saw it in his eyes. Now my longing for a wife comes only once in a while, like a cold: on some late afternoons when I am alone in the barn, then I lock up and walk to the house, daydreaming, then suddenly look at it and see it empty, as though for the first time, and all at once I'm weary and feel I do not have the energy to broil meat, and I think of driving to a restaurant, then shake my head and go on to the house, the refrigerator, the oven; and some mornings when I wake in the dark and listen to the silence and run my hand over the cold sheet beside me; and some days in summer when Jennifer is here.

Gloria left first me, then the Church, and that was the end of religion for the children, though on visits they went to Sunday Mass with me, and still do, out of a respect for my life that they manage to keep free of patronage. Jennifer is an agnostic, though I doubt she would call herself that, any more than she would call herself any other name that implied she had made a decision, a choice, about existence, death, and God. In truth she tends to pantheism, a good sign, I think; but not wanting to be a father who tells his children what they ought to believe, I do not say to her that Catholicism includes pantheism, like onions in a stew. Besides, I have no missionary instincts and do not believe everyone should or even could live with the Catholic faith. It is Jennifer's womanhood that renders me awkward. And womanhood now is frank, not like when Gloria was twenty and there were symbols: high heels and cosmetics and dresses, a cigarette, a cocktail. I am glad that women are free now of false modesty and all its attention paid the flesh; but, still, it is difficult to see so much of your daughter, to hear her talk as only men and bawdy women used to, and most of all to see in her face the deep and unabashed sensuality of women, with no tricks of the eyes and mouth to hide the pleasure she feels at having a strong young body. I am certain, with the way things are now, that she has very happily not been a virgin for years. That does not bother me. What bothers me is my certainty about it, just from watching her walk across a room or light a cigarette or pour milk on cereal.

She told me all of it, waking me that night when I had gone to sleep listening to the wind in the trees and against the house, a wind so strong that I had to shut all but the lee windows, and still the house cooled; told it to me in such detail and so clearly that now, when she has driven the car to Florida, I remember it all as though I had been a passenger in the front seat, or even at the wheel. It started with a movie, then beer and driving to the sea to look at the waves in the night and the wind, Jennifer and Betsy and Liz. They drank a beer on the beach and wanted to go in naked but were afraid they would drown in the high surf. They bought another six-pack at a grocery store in New Hampshire, and drove home. I can see it now, feel it: the three girls and the beer and the ride on country roads where pines curved in the wind and the big deciduous trees swayed and shook as if they might leap from the earth. They would have some windows partly open so they could feel the wind; Jennifer would be playing a cassette, the music stirring them, as it does the young, to memories of another time, other people and places in what is for them the past.

She took Betsy home, then Liz, and sang with her cassette as she left the town west of us and started home, a twenty-minute drive on the road that passes my house. They had each had four beers, but now there were twelve empty bottles in the bag on the floor at the passenger seat, and I kept focusing on their sound against each other when the car shifted speeds or changed directions. For I want to understand that one moment out of all her heart's time on earth, and whether her history had any bearing on it, or whether her heart was then isolated from all it had known, and the sound of those bottles urged it. She was just leaving the town, accelerating past a night club on the right, gaining speed to climb a long, gradual hill, then she went up it, singing, patting the beat on the steering wheel, the wind loud through her few inches of open window, blowing her hair as it did the high branches alongside the road, and she looked up at them and watched the top of the hill for someone drunk or heedless coming over it in part of her lane. She crested to an open black road, and there he was: a bulk, a blur, a thing running across her headlights, and she swerved left and her foot went for the brake and was stomping air above its pedal when she hit him, saw his legs and body in the air, flying out of her light, into the dark. Her brakes were screaming into the wind, bottles clinking in the fallen bag, and with the music and wind inside the car was his sound, already a memory but as real as an echo, that car-shuddering thump as though she had struck a tree. Her foot was back on the accelerator. Then she shifted gears and pushed it. She ejected the cassette and closed the window. She did not start to cry until she knocked on my bedroom door, then called: "Dad?"

Her voice, her tears, broke through my dream and the wind I heard in my sleep, and I stepped into jeans and hurried to the door, thinking harm, rape, death. All were in her face, and I hugged her and pressed her cheek to my chest and smoothed her blown hair, then led her, weeping, to the kitchen and sat her at the table where still she could not speak, nor look at me; when she raised her face it fell forward again, as of its own weight, into her palms. I offered tea and she shook her head, so I offered beer twice, then she shook her head, so I offered whiskey and she nodded. I had some rye that Father Paul and I had not finished last hunting season, and I poured some over ice and set it in front of her and was putting away the ice but stopped and got another glass and poured one for myself too, and brought the ice and bottle to the table where she was trying to get one of her long menthols out of the pack, but her fingers jerked like severed snakes, and I took the pack and lit one for her and took one for myself. I watched her shudder with her first swallow of rye, and push hair back from her face, it is auburn and gleamed in the overhead light, and I remember how beautiful she looked riding a sorrel; she was smoking fast, then the sobs in her throat stopped, and she looked at me and said it, the words coming out with smoke: 'I hit somebody. With the *car*.'

Then she was crying and I was on my feet, moving back and forth, looking down at her, asking *Who? Where? Where?* She was pointing at the wall over the stove, jabbing her fingers and cigarette at it, her other hand at her eyes, and twice in horror I actually looked at the wall. She finished the whiskey in a swallow and I stopped pacing and asking and poured another, and either the drink or the exhaustion of tears quieted her, even the dry sobs, and she told me; not as I tell it now, for that was later as again and again we relived it in the kitchen or living room, and, if in daylight, fled it on horseback out on the trails through the woods and, if at night, walked quietly around in the moonlit pasture, walked around and around it, sweating through our clothes. She told it in bursts, like she was a child again, running to me, injured from play. I put on boots and a shirt and left her with the bottle and her streaked face and a cigarette twitching between her fingers, pushed the door open against the wind, and eased it shut. The wind squinted and watered my eyes as I leaned into it and went to the pickup.

When I passed St. John's I looked at it, and Father Paul's little white rectory in the rear, and wanted to stop, wished I could as I could if he were simply a friend who sold hardware or something. I had forgotten my watch but I always know the time within minutes, even when a sound or dream or my bladder wakes me in the night. It was nearly two; we had been in the kitchen about twenty minutes; she had hit him around one-fifteen. Or her. The road was empty and I drove between blowing trees; caught for an instant in my lights, they seemed to be in panic. I smoked and let hope play its tricks on me: it was neither man nor woman but an animal, a goat or calf or deer on the road; it was a man who had jumped away in time, the collision of metal and body glancing not direct, and he had limped home to nurse bruises and cuts. Then I threw the cigarette and hope both out the window and prayed that he was alive, while beneath that prayer, a reserve deeper in my heart, another one stirred: that if he were dead, they would not get Jennifer.

From our direction, east and a bit south, the road to that hill and the night club beyond it and finally the town is, for its last four or five miles, straight through farming country. When I reached that stretch I slowed the truck and opened my window for the fierce air; on both sides were scattered farmhouses and barns and sometimes a silo, looking not like shelters but like unsheltered things the wind would flatten. Corn bent toward the road from a field on my right, and always something blew in front of me: paper, leaves, dried weeds, branches. I slowed approaching the hill, and went up it in second, staring through my open window at the ditch on the left side of the road, its weeds alive, whipping, a mad dance with the trees above them. I went over the hill and down and, opposite the club, turned right onto a side street of houses, and parked there, in the leaping shadows of trees. I walked back across the road to the club's parking lot, the wind behind me, lifting me as I strode, and I could not hear my boots on pavement. I walked up the hill, on the shoulder, watching the branches above me, hearing their leaves and the creaking trunks and the wind.

Then I was at the top, looking down the road and at the farms and fields; the night was clear, and I could see a long way; clouds scudded past the half-moon and stars, blown out to sea.

I started down, watching the tall grass under the trees to my right, glancing into the dark of the ditch, listening for cars behind me; but as soon as I cleared one tree, its sound was gone, its flapping leaves and rattling branches far behind me, as though the greatest distance I had at my back was a matter of feet, while ahead of me I could see a barn two miles off. Then I saw her skid marks: short, and going left and downhill, into the other lane. I stood at the ditch, its weeds blowing; across it were trees and their moving shadows, like the clouds. I stepped onto its slope, and it took me sliding on my feet, then rump, to the bottom, where I sat still, my body gathered to itself, lest a part of me should touch him. But there was only tall grass, and I stood, my shoulders reaching the sides of the ditch, and I walked uphill, wishing for the flashlight in the pickup, walking slowly, and down in the ditch I could hear my feet in the grass and on the earth, and kicking cans and bottles. At the top of the hill I turned and went down, watching the ground above the ditch on my right, praying my prayer from the truck again, the first one, the one I would admit, that he was not dead, was in fact home, and began to hope again, memory telling me of lost pheasants and grouse I had shot, but they were small and the colors of their home, while a man was either there or not; and from that memory I left where I was and while walking in the ditch under the wind was in the deceit of imagination with Jennifer in the kitchen, telling her she had hit no one, or at least had not badly hurt anyone, when I realized he could be in the hospital now and I would have to think of a way to check there, something to say on the phone. I see now that, once hope returned, I should have been certain what it prepared me for: ahead of me, in high grass and the shadows of trees, I saw his shirt. Or that is all my mind would allow itself: a shirt, and I stood looking at it for the moments it took my mind to admit the arm and head and the dark length covered by pants. He lay face down, the arm I could see near his side, his head turned from me, on its cheek.

"Fella?" I said. I had meant to call, but it came out quiet and high, lost inches from my face in the wind. Then I said, 'Oh God,' and felt Him in the wind and the sky moving past the stars and moon and the field around me, but only watching me as He might have watched Cain or Job, I did not know which, and I said it again, and wanted to sink to the earth and weep till I slept there in the weeds. I climbed, scrambling up the side of the ditch, pulling at clutched grass, gained the top on hands and knees, and went to him like that, panting, moving through the grass as high and higher than my face, crawling under that sky, making sounds too, like some animal, there being no words to let him know I was here with him now. He was long; that is the word that came to me, not tall. I kneeled beside him, my hands on my legs. His right arm was by his side, his left arm straight out from the shoulder, but turned, so his palm was open to the tree above us. His left cheek was cleanshaven, his eye closed, and there was no blood. I leaned forward to look at his open mouth and saw the blood on it, going down into the grass. I straightened and looked ahead at the wind blowing past me through grass and trees to a distant light, and I stared at the light, imagining someone awake out there, wanting someone to be, a gathering of old friends, or someone alone listening to music or painting a picture, then I figured it was a night light at a farmyard whose house I couldn't see. *Going,* I thought. *Still going.* I leaned over again and looked at dripping blood.

So I had to touch his wrist, a thick one with a watch and expansion band that I pushed up his arm, thinking *he's left-handed,* my three fingers pressing his wrist, and all I felt was my tough fingertips on that smooth underside flesh and small bones, then relief, then certainty. But against my will, or only because of it, I still don't know, I touched his neck, ran my fingers down it as if petting, then pressed, and my hand sprang back as from fire. I lowered it again, held it there until it felt that faint beating that I could not believe. There was too much wind. Nothing could make a sound in it. A pulse could not be felt in it, nor could mere fingers in that wind feel the absolute silence of a dead man's artery. I was making sounds again; I grabbed his left arm and his waist, and pulled him toward me, and that side of him rose, turned, and I lowered him to his back, his face tilted up toward the tree that was groaning, the tree and I the only sounds in the wind. Turning my face from his, looking down the length of him at his sneakers, I placed my ear on his heart, and heard not that but something else, and I clamped a hand over my exposed ear, heard something liquid and alive, like when you pump a well and after a few strokes you hear air and water moving in the pipe, and I knew I must raise his legs and cover him and run to a phone, while still I listened to his chest, thinking *raise with what? cover with what?* and amid the liquid sound I heard the heart, then lost it, and pressed my ear against bone, but his chest was quiet, and I did not know when the liquid had stopped, and do not know now when I heard air, a faint rush of it, and whether under my ear or at his mouth or whether I heard it at all. I straightened and looked at the light, dim and yellow. Then I touched his throat, looking him full in the face. He was blond and young. He could have been sleeping in the shade of a tree, but for the smear of blood from his mouth to his hair, and the night sky, and the weeds blowing against his head, and the leaves shaking in the dark above us.

I stood. Then I kneeled again and prayed for his soul to join in peace and joy all the dead and living; and, doing so, confronted my first sin against him, not stopping for Father Paul, who could have given him the last rites, and immediately then my second one, or, I saw then, my first, not calling an ambulance to meet me there, and I stood and turned into the wind, slid down the ditch and crawled out of it, and went up the hill and down it, across the road to the street of houses whose people I had left behind forever, so that I moved with stealth in the shadows to my truck.

When I came around the bend near my house, I saw the kitchen light at the rear. She sat as I had left her, the ashtray filled, and I looked at the bottle, felt her eyes on me, felt what she was seeing too: the dirt from my crawling. She had not drunk much of the rye. I poured some in my glass, with the water from melted ice, and sat down and swallowed some and looked at her and swallowed some more, and said: 'He's dead.'

She rubbed her eyes with the heels of her hands, rubbed the cheeks under them, but she was dry now.

'He was probably dead when he hit the ground. I mean, that's probably what killed—'

'Where was he?'

'Across the ditch, under a tree.'

'Was he—did you see his face?'

'No, Not really. I just felt. For life, pulse. I'm going out to the car.'

'What for? Oh.'

I finished the rye, and pushed back the chair, then she was standing too.

'I'll go with you.'

'There's no need.'

'I'll go.'

I took a flashlight from a drawer and pushed open the door and held it while she went out. We turned our faces from the wind. It was like on the hill, when I was walking, and the wind closed the distance behind me: after three or four steps I felt there was no house back there. She took my hand, as I was reaching for hers. In the garage we let go, and squeezed between the pickup and her little car, to the front of it, where we had more room, and we stepped back from the grill and I shone the light on the fender, the smashed headlight turned into it, the concave chrome staring to the right, at the garage wall.

'We ought to get the bottles,' I said.

She moved between the garage and the car, on the passenger side, and had room to open the door and lift the bag. I reached out, and she gave me the bag and backed up and shut the door and came around the car. We sidled to the doorway, and she put her arm around my waist and I hugged her shoulders.

'I thought you'd call the police,' she said.

We crossed the yard, faces bowed from the wind, her hair blowing away from her neck, and in the kitchen I put the bag of bottles in the garbage basket. She was working at the table: capping the rye and putting it away, filling the ice tray, washing the glasses, emptying the ashtray, sponging the table.

'Try to sleep now,' I said.

She nodded at the sponge circling under her hand, gathering ashes. Then she dropped it in the sink and, looking me full in the face, as I had never seen her look, as perhaps she never had, being for so long a daughter on visits (or so it seemed to me and still does: that until then our eyes had never seriously met), she crossed to me from the sink and kissed my lips, then held me so tightly I lost balance, and would have stumbled forward had she not held me so hard.

I sat in the living room, the house darkened, and watched the maple and the hemlock. When I believed she was asleep I put on *La Boheme*,[2] and kept it at the same volume as the wind so it would not wake her. Then I listened to *Madame Butterfly*, and in the third act had to rise quickly to lower the sound: the wind was gone. I looked at the still maple near the window, and thought of the wind leaving farms and towns and the coast, going out over the sea to die on the waves. I smoked and gazed out the window. The sky was darker, and at daybreak the rain came. I listened to *Tosca*, and at six-fifteen went to the kitchen where Jennifer's purse lay on the table, a leather shoulder-purse crammed with the things of an adult woman, things she had begun accumulating only a few years back, and I nearly wept, thinking of what sandy foundations they were: driver's license, credit card, disposable lighter, cigarettes, checkbook, ballpoint pen, cash, cosmetics, comb, brush, Kleenex, these the rite of passage from childhood, and I took one of them—her keys—and went out, remembering a jacket and hat when the rain struck me, but I kept going to the car, and squeezed and lowered myself into it, pulled the seat belt over my shoulder and fastened it and backed out, turning in the drive, going forward into the road, toward St. John's and Father Paul.

Cars were on the road, the workers, and I did not worry about any of them noticing the fender and light. Only a horse distracted them from what they drove to. In front of St. John's is a parking lot; at its far side, past the church and at the edge of the lawn, is an

2. This and the two titles just below are operas by Giacomo Puccini (1858–1924).

old pine, taller than the steeple now. I shifted to third, left the road, and, aiming the right headlight at the tree, accelerated past the white blur of church, into the black trunk growing bigger till it was all I could see, then I rocked in that resonant thump she had heard, had felt, and when I turned off the ignition it was still in my ears, my blood, and I saw the boy flying in the wind. I lowered my forehead to the wheel. Father Paul opened the door, his face white in the rain.

'I'm all right.'

'What happened?'

'I don't know. I fainted.'

I got out and went around to the front of the car, looked at the smashed light, the crumpled and torn fender.

'Come to the house and lie down.'

'I'm all right.'

'When was your last physical?'

'I'm due for one. Let's get out of this rain.'

'You'd better lie down.'

'No. I want to receive.'

That was the time to say I want to confess, but I have not and will not. Though I could now, for Jennifer is in Florida, and weeks have passed, and perhaps now Father Paul would not feel that he must tell me to go to the police. And, for that very reason, to confess now would be unfair. It is a world of secrets, and now I have one from my best, in truth my only, friend. I have one from Jennifer too, but that is the nature of fatherhood.

Most of that day it rained, so it was only in early evening, when the sky cleared, with a setting sun, that two little boys, leaving their confinement for some play before dinner, found him. Jennifer and I got that on the local news, which we listened to every hour, meeting at the radio, standing with cigarettes, until the one at eight o'clock; when she stopped crying, we went out and walked on the wet grass, around the pasture, the last of sunlight still in the air and trees. His name was Patrick Mitchell, he was nineteen years old, was employed by CETA,[3] lived at home with his parents and brother and sister. The paper next day said he had been at a friend's house and was walking home, and I thought of that light I had seen, then knew it was not for him; he lived on one of the streets behind the club. The paper did not say then, or in the next few days, anything to make Jennifer think he was alive while she was with me in the kitchen. Nor do I know if we—I—could have saved him.

In keeping her secret from her friends, Jennifer had to perform

3. Comprehensive Employment and Training Act—a government program to assist people into the job market.

so often, as I did with Father Paul and at the stables, that I believe the acting, which took more of her than our daylight trail rides and our night walks in the pasture, was her healing. Her friends teased me about wrecking her car. When I carried her luggage out to the car on that last morning, we spoke only of the weather for her trip —the day was clear, with a dry cool breeze—and hugged and kissed, and I stood watching as she started the car and turned it around. But then she shifted to neutral and put on the parking brake and unclasped the belt, looking at me all the while, then she was coming to me, as she had that night in the kitchen, and I opened my ams.

I have said I talk with God in the mornings, as I start my day, and sometimes I sit with coffee, looking at the birds, and the woods. Of course He has never spoken to me, but that is not something I require. Nor does He need to. I know Him, as I know the part of myself that knows Him, that felt Him watching from the wind and the night as I kneeled over the dying boy. Lately I have taken to arguing with Him, as I can't with Father Paul, who, when he hears my monthly confession, has not heard and will not hear anything of failure to do all that one can to save an anonymous life, of injustice to a family in their grief, of deepening their pain at the chance and mystery of death by giving them nothing—no one—to hate. With Father Paul I feel lonely about this, but not with God. When I received the Eucharist while Jennifer's car sat twice-damaged, so redeemed, in the rain, I felt neither loneliness nor shame, but as though He were watching me, even from my tongue, intestines, blood, as I have watched my sons at times in their young lives when I was able to judge but without anger, and so keep silent while they, in the agony of their youth, decided how they must act; or found reasons, after their actions, for what they had done. Their reasons were never as good or as bad as their actions, but they needed to find them, to believe they were living by them, instead of the awful solitude of the heart.

I do not feel the peace I once did: not with God, nor the earth, or anyone on it. I have begun to prefer this state, to remember with fondness the other one as a period of peace I neither earned nor deserved. Now in the mornings while I watch purple finches driving larger titmice from the feeder, I say to Him: I would do it again. For when she knocked on my door, then called me, she woke what had flowed dormant in my blood since her birth, so that what rose from the bed was not a stable owner or a Catholic or any other Luke Ripley I had lived with for a long time, but the father of a girl.

And He says: I am a Father too.

Yes, I say, as You are a Son Whom this morning I will receive;

unless You kill me on the way to church, then I trust You will receive me. And as a Son You made Your plea.

Yes, He says, but I would not lift the cup.

True, and I don't want You to lift it from me either. And if one of my sons had come to me that night, I would have phoned the police and told them to meet us with an ambulance at the top of the hill.

Why? Do you love them less?

I tell Him no, it is not that I love them less, but that I could bear the pain of watching and knowing my sons' pain, could bear it with pride as they took the whip and nails. But You never had a daughter and, if You had, You could not have borne her passion.

So, He says, you love her more than you love Me.

I love her more than I love truth.

Then you love in weakness, He says.

As You love me, I say, and I go with an apple or carrot out to the barn.

LOUISE ERDRICH

Saint Marie

SO when I went there, I knew the dark fish must rise. Plumes of radiance had been soldered on me. No reservation girl had ever prayed so hard. There was no use in trying to ignore me any longer. I was going up there on the hill with the black-robe women. None were any lighter than me. I was going up there to pray as good as they could, because I don't have that much Indian blood. And they never thought they'd have a girl from this reservation as a saint they'd have to kneel to. But they were going to have me. And I'd be carved in pure gold. With ruby lips. And my toenails would be little pink ocean shells, which they would have to stoop down off their high horse to kiss.

I was ignorant. I was near age fourteen. The sky is just about the size of my ignorance. And just as pure. And that—the pure wideness of my ignorance—is what got me up the hill to the Sacred Heart Convent and brought me back down alive. For maybe Jesus did not take my bait, but them Sisters tried to cram me right down whole.

You ever see a walleye strike so bad the lure is practically on its back end before you reel it in? That is what they done with me. I don't like to make that low comparison, but I have seen a walleye do that once. And it's the same attempt as Sister Leopolda made to get me in her clutch.

I had the mail-order Catholic soul you get in a girl raised out in the bush, whose only thought is getting into town. Sunday Mass is the only time my father brought his children in except for school, when we were harnessed. Our souls went cheap. We were so anxious to get there we would have walked in on our hands and knees. We just craved going to the store, slinging bottle caps in the dust, making fool eyes at each other. And of course we went to church.

Where they have the convent is on top of the highest hill, so that from its windows the Sisters can be looking into the marrow of the town. Recently a windbreak was planted before the bar "for the purposes of tornado insurance." Don't tell me that. That poplar stand was put up to hide the drinkers as they get the transformation. As they are served into the beast of their burden. While they're drinking, that body comes upon them, and then they stagger or crawl out the bar door, pulling a weight they can't move past the poplars. They don't want no holy witness to their fall.

Anyway, I climbed. That was a long-ago day. A road for wagons wound in ruts to the top of the hill where they had their buildings of brick painted gleaming white. So white the sun glanced off in dazzling display to set forms whirling behind your eyelids. The face of God you could hardly look at. But that day it drizzled, so I could look all I wanted. I saw the homelier side. The cracked whitewash, and swallows nesting in the busted ends of eaves. I saw the boards sawed the size of broken windowpanes and the fruit trees, stripped. Only the tough wild rhubarb flourished. Goldenrod rubbed up their walls. It was a poor convent. I know that now. Compared with others it was humble, ragtag, out in the middle of no place. It was the end of the world to some. Where the maps stopped. Where God had only half a hand in the Creation. Where the Dark One had put in thick bush, liquor, wild dogs, and Indians.

I heard later that the Sacred Heart Convent was a place for nuns that don't get along elsewhere. Nuns that complain too much or lose their mind. I'll always wonder now, after hearing that, where they picked up Sister Leopolda. Perhaps she had scarred someone else, the way she left a mark on me. Perhaps she was just sent around to test her sisters' faith, here and there, like the spot-checker in a factory. For she was a definite hard trial for anyone, even for those who started out with veils of wretched love upon their eyes.

I was that girl who thought the hem of her black garment would help me rise. Veils of love, which was only hate petrified by longing, that was me. I was like those bush Indians who stole the holy black hat of a Jesuit and swallowed little scraps of it to cure their fevers. But the hat itself carried smallpox, and it was killing them with belief. Veils of faith! I had this confidence in Leopolda. She was different. The other Sisters had long ago gone blank and given up on Satan. He slept for them. They never noticed his comings and goings. But Leopolda kept track of him and knew his habits, the minds he burrowed in, the deep spaces where he hid. She knew as much about him as my grandma, who called him by other names and was not afraid.

In her class, Sister Leopolda carried a long oak pole for opening high windows. On one end it had a hook made of iron that could jerk a patch of your hair out or throttle you by the collar—all from a distance. She used this deadly hook-pole for catching Satan by surprise. He could have entered without your knowing it—through your lips or your nose or any one of your seven openings—and gained your mind. But she would see him. That pole would brain you from behind. And he would gasp, dazzled, and take the first thing she offered, which was pain.

She had a string of children who could breathe only if she said the word. I was the worst of them. She always said the Dark One wanted me most of all, and I believed this. I stood out. Evil was a common thing I trusted. Before sleep sometimes he came and whispered conversation in the old language of the bush. I listened. He told me things he never told anyone but Indians. I was privy to both worlds of his knowledge. I listened to him but, I had confidence in Leopolda. For she was the only one of the bunch he even noticed.

There came a day, though, when Leopolda turned the tide with her hook-pole.

It was a quiet day, with all of us working at our desks, when I heard him. He had sneaked into the closets in the back of the room. He was scratching around, tasting crumbs in our pockets, stealing buttons, squirting his dark juice in the linings and the boots. I was the only one who heard him, and I got bold. I smiled. I glanced back and smiled, and looked up at her sly to see if she had noticed. My heart jumped. For she was looking straight at me. And she sniffed. She had a big, stark, bony nose stuck to the front of her face, for smelling out brimstone and evil thoughts. She had smelled him on me. She stood up. Tall, pale, a blackness leading into the deeper blackness of the slate wall behind her. Her oak pole had flown into her grip. She had seen me glance at the closet. Oh, she knew. She knew just where he was. I watched her watch him in her mind's eye. The whole class was watching now. She was staring, sizing, following his scuffle. And all of a sudden she tensed down, poised on her bent kneesprings, cocked her arm back. She threw the oak pole singing over my head. It cracked through the thin wood door of the back closet and the heavy pointed hook drove through his heart. I turned. She'd speared her own black rubber overboot where he'd taken refuge, in the tip of her darkest toe.

Something howled in my mind. Loss and darkness. I understood. I was to suffer for my smile.

He rose up hard in my heart. I didn't blink when the pole cracked. My skull was tough. I didn't flinch when she shrieked in my ear. I only shrugged at the flowers of hell. He wanted me. More than anything he craved me. But then she did the worst. She did what broke my mind to her. She grabbed me by the collar and dragged me, feet flying, through the room and threw me in the closet with her dead black overboot. And I was there. The only light was a crack beneath the door. I asked the Dark One to enter into me and alert my mind. I asked him to restrain my tears, for they were pushing behind my eyes. But he was afraid to come back there. He was afraid of her sharp pole. And I was afraid of Leopolda's pole, too, for the first time. I felt the cold hook in my heart. It could crack through the door at any minute and drag me out, like a dead fish on a gaff, drop me on the floor like a gutshot squirrel.

I was nothing. I edged back to the wall as far as I could. I breathed the chalk dust. The hem of her full black cloak cut against my cheek. He had left me. Her spear could find me any time. Her keen ears would aim the hook into the beat of my heart.

What was that sound?

It filled the closet, filled it up until it spilled over, but I did not recognize the crying wailing voice as mine until the door cracked open, I saw brightness, and she hoisted me to her camphor-smelling lips.

"He *wants* you," she said. "That's the difference. I give you love."

Love. The black hook. The spear singing through the mind. I saw that she had tracked the Dark One to my heart and flushed him out into the open. So now my heart was an empty nest where she could lurk.

Well, I was weak. I was weak when I let her in but she got a foothold there. Hard to dislodge as the months passed. Sometimes I felt him—the brush of dim wings—but only rarely did his voice compel. It was between Marie and Leopolda now, and the struggle changed. I began to realize I had been on the wrong track with the fruits of hell. The real way to overcome Leopolda was this: I'd get to heaven first. And then, when I saw her coming, I'd shut the gate. She'd be out! That is why, besides the bowing and the scraping I'd be dealt, I wanted to sit on the altar as a saint.

To this end, I went on up the hill. Sister Leopolda was the consecrated nun who had sponsored me to come there.

"You're not vain," she had said. "You're too honest, looking into the mirror, for that. You're not smart. You don't have the ambition to get clear. You have two choices. One, you can marry a no-good Indian, bear his brats, die like a dog. Or two, you can give yourself to God."

"I'll come up there," I said, "but not because of what you think."

I could have had any damn man on the reservation at the time. And I could have made him treat me like his own life. I looked good. And I looked white. But I wanted Sister Leopolda's heart. And here was the thing: Sometimes I wanted her heart in love and admiration. Sometimes. And sometimes I wanted her heart to roast on a black stick.

She answered the back door, where they had instructed me to call. I stood there with my bundle. She looked me up and down.

"All right," she said finally. "Come in."

She took my hand. Her fingers were like a bundle of broom straws, so thin and dry, but the strength of them was unnatural. I couldn't have tugged loose if she had been leading me into rooms of white-hot coal. Her strength was a kind of perverse miracle, for she got it from fasting herself thin. Because of this hunger practice her lips were a wounded brown and her skin was deadly pale. Her eye sockets were two deep, lashless hollows. I told you about the nose. It stuck out far and made the place her eyes moved even deeper, as if she stared out of a gun barrel. She took the bundle from my hands and threw it in the corner.

"You'll be sleeping behind the stove, child."

It was immense, like a great furnace. A small cot was close behind it.

"Looks like it could get warm there," I said.

"Hot. It does."

"Do I get a habit?"

I wanted something like the thing she wore. Flowing black cotton. Her face was strapped in white bandages and a sharp crest of starched cardboard hung over her forehead like a glaring beak. If possible, I wanted a bigger, longer, whiter beak than hers.

"No," she said, grinning her great skull grin. "You don't get one yet. Who knows, you might not like us. Or we might not like you."

But she had loved me, or offered me love. And she had tried to hunt the Dark One down. So I had this confidence.

"I'll inherit your keys from you," I said.

She looked at me sharply, and her grin turned strange. She hissed, taking in her breath. Then she turned to the door and took a key from her belt. It was a giant key, and it unlocked the larder, where the food was stored.

Inside were all kinds of good stuff. Things I'd tasted only once or twice in my life. I saw sticks of dried fruit, jars of orange peel, spices like cinnamon. I saw tins of crackers with ships painted on the side. I saw pickles. Jars of herring and the rind of pigs. Cheese, a big brown block of it from the thick milk of goats. And the everyday stuff, in great quantities, the flour and the coffee.

The cheese got to me. When I saw it my stomach hollowed. My tongue dripped. I loved that goat-milk cheese better than anything I'd ever eaten. I stared at it. The rich curve in the buttery cloth.

"When you inherit my keys," she said sourly, slamming the door in my face, "you can eat all you want of the priest's cheese."

Then she seemed to consider what she'd done. She looked at me. She took the key from her belt and went back, sliced a hunk off, and put it in my hand.

"If you're good you'll taste this cheese again. When I'm dead and gone," she said.

Then she dragged out the big sack of flour. When I finished that heavenly stuff she told me to roll my sleeves up and begin doing God's labor. For a while we worked in silence, mixing up dough and pounding it out on stone slabs.

"God's work," I said after a while. "If this is God's work, then I've done it all my life."

"Well, you've done it with the Devil in your heart, then," she said. "Not God."

"How do you know?" I asked. But I knew she did. And I wished I had not brought up the subject.

"I see right into you like a clear glass," she said. "I always did."

"You don't know it," she continued after a while, "but he's come around here sulking. He's come around here brooding. You brought him in. He knows the smell of me and he's going to make a last-ditch try to get you back. Don't let him." She glared over at me. Her eyes were cold and lighted. "Don't let him touch you. We'll be a long time getting rid of him."

So I was careful. I was careful not to give him an inch. I said a rosary, two rosaries, three, underneath my breath. I said the Creed. I said every scrap of Latin I knew while we punched the dough with our fists. And still, I dropped the cup. It rolled under that monstrous iron stove, which was getting fired up for baking.

And she was on me. She saw he'd entered my distraction.

"Our good cup," she said. "Get it out of there, Marie."

I reached for the poker to snag it out from beneath the stove. But I had a sinking feeling in my stomach as I did this. Sure enough, her long arm darted past me like a whip. The poker landed in her hand.

"Reach," she said. "Reach with your arm for that cup. And when your flesh is hot, remember that the flames you feel are only one fraction of the heat you will feel in his hellish embrace."

She always did things this way, to teach you lessons. So I wasn't surprised. It was playacting anyway, because a stove isn't very hot underneath, right along the floor. They aren't made that way.

Otherwise, a wood floor would burn. So I said yes and got down on my stomach and reached under. I meant to grab it quick and jump up again, before she could think up another lesson, but here it happened. Although I groped for the cup, my hand closed on nothing. That cup was nowhere to be found. I heard her step toward me, a slow step. I heard the creak of thick shoe leather, the little *plat* as the folds of her heavy skirts met, a trickle of fine sand sifting somewhere, perhaps in the bowels of her, and I was afraid. I tried to scramble up, but her foot came down lightly behind my ear, and I was lowered. The foot came down more firmly at the base of my neck, and I was held.

"You're like I was," she said. "He wants you very much."

"He doesn't want me no more," I said. "He had his fill. I got the cup!"

I heard the valve opening, the hissed intake of breath, and knew that I should not have spoken.

"You lie," she said. "You're cold. There is a wicked ice forming in your blood. You don't have a shred of devotion for God. Only wild, cold, dark lust. I know it. I know how you feel. I see the beast . . . the beast watches me out of your eyes sometimes. Cold."

The urgent scrape of metal. It took a moment to know from where. Top of the stove. Kettle. She was steadying herself with the iron poker. I could feel it like pure certainty, driving into the wood floor. I would not remind her of pokers. I heard the water as it came, tipped from the spout, cooling as it fell but still scalding as it struck. I must have twitched beneath her foot because she steadied me, and then the poker nudged up beside my arm as if to guide. "To warm your cold-ash heart," she said. I felt how patient she would be. The water came. My mind was dead blank. Again. I could only think the kettle would be cooling slowly in her hand. I could not stand it. I bit my lip so as not to satisfy her with a sound. She gave me more reason to keep still.

"I will boil him from your mind if you make a peep," she said, "by filling up your ear."

Any sensible fool would have run back down the hill the minute Leopolda let them up from under her heel. But I was snared in her black intelligence by then. I could not think straight. I had prayed so hard I think I broke a cog in my mind. I prayed while her foot squeezed my throat. While my skin burst. I prayed even when I heard the wind come through, shrieking in the busted bird nests. I didn't stop when pure light fell, turning slowly behind my eyelids. God's face. Even that did not disrupt my continued praise. Words came. Words came from nowhere and flooded my mind.

Now I could pray much better than any one of them. Than all of them full force. This was proved. I turned to her in a daze when she let me up. My thoughts were gone, and yet I remember how surprised I was. Tears glittered in her eyes, deep down, like the sinking reflection in a well.

"It was so hard, Marie," she gasped. Her hands were shaking. The kettle clattered against the stove. "But I have used all the water up now. I think he is gone."

"I prayed," I said foolishly. "I prayed very hard."

"Yes," she said. "My dear one, I know."

We sat together quietly because we had no more words. We let the dough rise and punched it down once. She gave me a bowl of mush, unlocked the sausage from a special cupboard, and took that in to the Sisters. They sat down the hall, chewing their sausage, and I could hear them. I could hear their teeth bite through their bread and meat. I couldn't move. My shirt was dry but the cloth stuck to my back and I couldn't think straight. I was losing the sense to understand how her mind worked. She'd gotten past me with her poker and I would never be a saint. I despaired. I felt I had no inside voice, nothing to direct me, no darkness, no Marie. I was about to throw that cornmeal mush out to the birds and make a run for it, when the vision rose up blazing in my mind.

I was rippling gold. My breasts were bare and my nipples flashed and winked. Diamonds tipped them. I could walk through panes of glass. I could walk through windows. She was at my feet, swallowing the glass after each step I took. I broke through another and another. The glass she swallowed ground and cut until her starved insides were only a subtle dust. She coughed. She coughed a cloud of dust. And then she was only a black rag that flapped off, snagged in barbed wire, hung there for an age, and finally rotted into the breeze.

I saw this, mouth hanging open, gazing off into the waving trees.

"Get up!" she cried. "Stop dreaming. It is time to bake."

Two other Sisters had come in with her, wide women with hands like paddles. They were smoothing and evening out the firebox beneath the great jaws of the oven.

"Who is this one?" they asked Leopolda. "Is she yours?"

"She is mine," said Leopolda. "A very good girl."

"What is your name?" one asked me.

"Marie."

"Marie, Star of the Sea."

"She will shine," said Leopolda, "when we have burned off the dark corrosion."

The others laughed, but uncertainly. They were slow, heavy French, who did not understand Leopolda's twisted jokes, although they muttered respectfully at things she said. I knew they wouldn't believe what she had done with the kettle. So I kept quiet.

"*Elle est docile,*" they said approvingly as they left to starch the linens.

"Does it pain?" Leopolda asked me as soon as they were out the door.

I did not answer. I felt sick with the hurt.

"Come along," she said.

The building was quiet now. I followed her up the narrow staircase into a hall of little rooms, many doors, like a hotel. Her cell was at the very end. Inside was a rough straw mattress, a tiny bookcase with a picture of Saint Francis hanging over it, a ragged palm, and a crucifix. She told me to remove my shirt and sit down on her mattress. I did so. She took a pot of salve from the bookcase and began to smooth it upon my burns. Her stern hand made slow, wide circles, stopping the pain. I closed my eyes. I expected to see the docile blackness. Peace. But instead the vision reared up again. My chest was still tipped with diamonds. I was walking through windows. She was chewing up the broken litter I left behind.

"I am going," I said. "Let me go."

But she held me down.

"Don't go," she said quickly. "Don't. We have just begun."

I was weakening. My thoughts were whirling pitifully. The pain had kept me strong, and as it left me I began to forget, I couldn't hold on. I began to wonder if she had really scalded me with the kettle. I could not remember. To remember this seemed the most important thing in the world. But I was losing the memory. The scalding. The pouring. It began to vanish. I felt that my mind was coming off its hinge, flapping in the breeze, hanging by the hair of my own pain. I wrenched out of her grip.

"He was always in you," I said. "Even more than in me. He wanted you even more. And now he's got you. Get thee behind me!"

I shouted that, grabbed my shirt, and ran through the door, throwing the shirt on my body. I got down the stairs and into the kitchen, but no matter what I told myself, I couldn't get out the door. It wasn't finished. And she knew I would not leave. Her quiet step was immediately behind me.

"We must take the bread from the oven now," she said.

She was pretending nothing had happened. But for the first time I had gotten through some chink she'd left in her darkness. Touched some doubt. Her voice was so low and brittle it cracked off at the end of her sentence.

"Help me, Marie," she said slowly.

But I was not going to help her even though she calmly buttoned my shirt up and put the big cloth mittens in my hands for taking out the loaves. I could have bolted then. But I didn't. I knew that something was nearing completion. Something was about to happen. My back was a wall of singing flame. I was turning. I watched her take the long fork in one hand, to tap the loaves. In the other hand she gripped the black poker to hook the pans.

"Help me," she said again, and I thought, "Yes, this is part of it." I put the mittens on my hands and swung the door open on its hinges. The oven gaped. She stood back a moment, letting the first blast of heat rush by. I moved behind her. I could feel the heat at my front and at my back. Before, behind. My skin was turning to beaten gold. It was coming quicker than I had thought. The oven was like the gate of a personal hell. Just big enough and hot enough for one person, and that was her. One kick and Leopolda would fly in headfirst. And that would be one millionth of the heat she would feel when she finally collapsed in his hellish embrace.

Saints know these numbers.

She bent forward with her fork held out. I kicked her with all my might. She flew in. But the outstretched poker hit the back wall first, so she rebounded. The oven was not as deep as I had thought.

There was a moment when I felt a sort of thin, hot disappointment, as when a fish slips off the line. Only I was the one going to be lost. She was fearfully silent. She whirled. Her veil had cutting edges. She had the poker in one hand. In the other she held that long sharp fork she used to tap the delicate crusts of loaves. Her face turned upside-down on her shoulders. Her face turned blue. But saints are used to miracles. I felt no trace of fear.

If I was going to be lost, let the diamonds cut! Let her eat ground glass!

"Old she-devil bitch!" I shouted. "Kneel and beg! Lick the floor!"

That was when she stabbed me through the hand with the fork, then took the poker up alongside my head and knocked me out.

I came around maybe half an hour later. Things were so strange. So strange I can hardly tell it for delight at the remembrance. For when I came around this was actually taking place. I was being worshiped. I had somehow gained the altar of a saint.

I was lying back on the stiff couch in the Mother Superior's Office. I looked around me. It was as though my deepest dream had come to life. The Sisters of the convent were kneeling to me. Sister Bonaventure. Sister Dympna. Sister Celia Saint-Claire. The two with hands like paddles. They were down on their knees. Black capes were slung over some of their heads. My name was buzzing up and down the room like a fat autumn fly, lighting on the tips of the tongues between Latin, humming up the heavy, blood-dark curtains, circling their swaddled heads. Marie! Marie! A girl thrown in a closet. Who was afraid of a rubber overboot. Who was half overcome. A girl who came in the back door where they threw their garbage. Marie! Who never found the cup. Who had to eat their cold mush. Marie! Leopolda had her face buried in her knuckles. Saint Marie of the Holy Slops! Saint Marie of the Bread Fork! Saint Marie of the Burnt Back and Scalded Butt!

I broke out and laughed.

They looked up. All holy hell burst loose when they saw I was awake. I still did not understand what was happening. They were watching, talking, but not to me.

"The marks . . ."

"She has her hand closed."

"*Je ne peux pas voir.*"[1]

I was not stupid enough to ask what they were talking about. I couldn't tell why I was lying in white sheets. I couldn't tell why they were praying to me. But I'll tell you this. It seemed entirely natural. It was me. I lifted up my hand as in my dream. It was completely limp with sacredness.

"Peace be with you."

My arm was dried blood from the wrist down to the elbow. And it hurt. Their faces turned like fat flowers of adoration to follow that hand's movements. I let it swing through the air, imparting a saint's blessing. I had practiced. I knew exactly how to act.

They murmured. I heaved a sigh and a golden beam of light suddenly broke through the clouded window and flooded down directly on my face. A stroke of perfect luck! They had to be convinced.

Leopolda still knelt in the back of the room. Her knuckles were crammed halfway down her throat. Let me tell you, a saint has senses honed keen as a wolf's. I knew that she was over my barrel now. How it had happened did not matter. The last thing I remembered was that she flew from the oven and stabbed me. That one thing was most certainly true.

"Come forward, Sister Leopolda." I gestured with my heavenly wound. Oh, it hurt. It bled when I reopened the place where it had begun to heal. "Kneel beside me," I said.

She kneeled, but her voice box evidently did not work, for her mouth opened, shut, opened, but no sound came out. My throat clenched in the noble delight I had read of as befitting a saint. She could not speak. But she was beaten. It was in her eyes. She stared at me now with all the deep hate of the wheel of devilish dust that rolled wild within her emptiness.

"What is it you want to tell me?" I asked. And at last she spoke.

"I have told my sisters of your passion," she managed to choke

1. "I cannot see."

out. "How the stigmata . . . the marks of the nails . . . appeared in your palm and you swooned at the holy vision . . ."

"Yes," I said, curious.

And then, after a moment, I understood.

Leopolda had saved herself with her quick brain. She had witnessed a miracle. She had hid the fork and told this to the others. And of course they believed her, because they never knew how Satan came and went or where he took refuge.

"I saw it from the first," said the large one who had put the bread in the oven. "Humility of the spirit. So rare in these girls."

"I saw it too," said the other one with great satisfaction. She sighed quietly. "If only it was me."

Leopolda was kneeling bolt upright, face blazing and twitching, a barely held fountain of blasting poison.

"Christ has marked me," I agreed. I smiled a saint's smirk in her face. And then I looked at her. That was my mistake.

For I saw her kneeling there. Leopolda with her soul like a rubber overboot. With her face of a starved rat. With her desperate eyes drowning in the deep wells of her wrongness. There would be no one else after me. And I would leave. I saw Leopolda kneeling within the shambles of her love.

My heart had been about to surge from my chest with the blackness of my joyous heat. Now it dropped. I pitied her. I pitied her. Pity twisted in my stomach as if that hook-pole were driven through me at last. I was caught. It was a feeling more terrible than any amount of boiling water and worse than being forked. Still, still, I couldn't help what I did. I had already smiled in a saint's mealy forgiveness. I heard myself speaking gently.

"Receive the dispensation of my sacred blood," I whispered.

But there was no heart in it. No joy when she bent to touch the floor. No dark leaping. I fell back onto the white pillows. Blank dust was whirling through the light shafts. My skin was dust. Dust my lips. Dust the dirty spoons on the ends of my feet.

Rise up! I thought. Rise up and walk! There is no limit to this dust!

IRVIN FAUST

Roar Lion Roar

THE most bad thing is he don't see his beautiful school no more. His school is hid away on the other side of the big buildings, way in the west. Alma mater on the *Hudson* shore man, not a skinny river like the one stinkin under his window. They got a real hospital up there, a place they fix a guy up, not like Welfare where they stash him in a ward with faggot doctors who don't even know who he is. *Them* doctors, man, some day they will come and fix him, for don't he do it all for the Lions?[1] Don't they go out the very next week and take the Big Red? . . .

Ishmael Ramos tries to wriggle his little finger with happiness, but damn it don't work. He don't feel nothing from the neck down; but it don't matter. The sky outside his stinkin window is blue and white. The lion on the table is blue and white and so is the jacket on the foot of his bed. He is contented under the plaster and the bandages. He smiles at the little lion who smiles back, sharing his cool. Man they came a damn long way together . . .

Jesus he was green the first year up from Ponce. So green he don't even know who is the *Big* Green.[2] How stupido you can be?

All that blue outside the window, that was the color he saw every place the first day. From 110th and Amsterdam to Broadway and his street, 114. *Calle ciento quatorce*, his dumb old man called it and still calls it. Blue flags, blue signs, he found out later was saying Beat the Tigers and he don't even know who is the Tigers! Dig man, he wants to shake his head with pity, if only it would shake . . . That day he walked along the streets after the dragon subway let him go and he don't know nothing. *Nada.* All over the place blue jackets and white shoes and cool buildings on the grass, with tennis courts and hundreds of steps, like the governor's house in San Juan, only here nobody says beat it man, and he don't even dig . . .

He tried their school for awhile, Riverside Junior High, a smelly little place ain't even got no campus or tennis courts, but he don't go for it no way, and when they called him Sambo and Rastus, which ain't even his name, he cut out. They kept buggin him and pulled him back into the opportunity class where at least he had the opportunity to learn American and how to play it cool, but when he was sixteen they called him in with the old man who was sleeping off some pot and said he was wasting their time and society's time and he can't come back and after that whenever he hung around the school the cops said beat it Jack and kicked him in the ass. And then one day Miss Lefferts, the relief chick who always came around, said Ishmael I have a job for you where you can gain a little self-respect, and he began to deliver orders for Grand Union, but it was stupid and a bigger waste of time than junior high, so he cut out and the old man beat him up some more and Miss Lefferts said of course Grand Union does not meet your needs and she got him a job at John's Bargain Store on 109th and he quit that too when the boss bugged him and also a job on 93rd Street pushing

1. Ishmael's adopted alma mater is Columbia University. The Lions are their football team. The Big Red is Cornell's team. **2.** The Dartmouth team.

ladies' underwear which was embarrassing. Each time he got belted by the old man. Each time he was happier sitting around on the cool stone benches or beside the fountains, smelling the air and watching the boys and girls (coeds they were called). Next door to the Cambria Residence Hotel, where he lived with his stupido father and worn down old lady and six brothers and sisters, was Alpha Beta Pi House—oh such a beautiful name—and all night till one o'clock he would sit on his stoop and watch the blue jackets and white shoes walking in, sometime with a coed chick, sometime with a piece, and later at the window when his dumb family was snoring he would listen to the clack of the pool balls and the chicks jivin and the beer cans bangin on the sidewalk. After six months in New York he got his hair cut very short.

"Work," said Miss Lefferts, "is important to your eggo strength."

"*Trabaja!*" said his old man. "You got lazy blood. *Sangre mala.*"[3]

"What kind of job would involve you?" said Miss Lefferts, hard and skinny, with no belly or chest. "You're a difficult case, you know."

"He's bad fruit," said his father.

"No, no, he miss Ponce,"[4] said his mother.

"I want to work in Columbia," he said.

"You in America and you stayin," his father hissed.

"Columbia University."

"Have respect," his father said, slapping him.

"Oh oh be a good boy," his mother cried. "He always a little funny, missus."

"Why that's perfectly all right, Mrs. Ramos," said Miss Lefferts with a big smile. "Maybe he could teach Spanish."

"He couldn't teach the fish to swim," said his father.

"I can't teach Spanish," he said, "but I want to work there."

"Why in the world do you want to do that?" said Miss Lefferts with a loss of the smile.

"I like it."

"*Dios,*"[5] his mother crossed herself.

"What do you mean by you like it?"

"I don't know. I like it."

His father belted him.

"You mean," said Miss Lefferts, stepping between them, "it would satisfy a felt *need*, give you a sense of involvement?"

"I don't know. I like it."

"Forgive him," pleaded his mother.

"Scramble eggs," said his father, spinning his finger in his ear.

"Well," said Miss Lefferts, chewing her lip, "you really must recognize and live with your limitation." She sighed deep in her

3. "Work!" "Bad blood." **4.** City in Puerto Rico. **5.** "God."

skinny chest. "But let me see what I can do. My, you people certainly are a trial."

Man, he prayed. With Lady of Fatima on 98th Street and St. Christopher on 123rd and the Protestant saints in St. John's and Moses and the other Jew cats in their church on 110th and even in the big house on the Drive, where he bugged old United States Grant.[6] But most of all he prayed to the big, handsome chick named Alma on the front steps of Low Library.[7] Then he walked in great circles from 120th to 114th, from Broadway to Amsterdam, to seal off the island. On one side of that line he don't feel nothing good, the other—the inside—he was cool and safe, like he was sailing up the river in a brand new Buick. You feel that baby, you *have* to make it.

And he made it. Miss Lefferts she got the message; not only did she come through, but for all his prayers she reached out and found the beating heart of the island. In two weeks only he was making it far down inside the guts of University Gym, beside the giant pulsing boilers and the buzzing generators that pumped life through the scene and across the street to the coeds in their floppy shorts. He got the ten to four night shift—sweep up, mop up, watch out for pimps, whores, robbers and murderers, keep that pumping heart alive!

Sound man, that was a responsibility. A job that changed things, like the boilers was juicing him; a green cat cutting out and a big safe one cutting in. As soon as big, black Morris Brown checked out and he was alone with his boiler, his mops and brooms, his valves, he felt the newness, each night all over again. And at four in the morning, when Lewis Steiger came on, he left the cosy place with a last, deep breath, a look around, and then walked up and out to the paths that laced up to College Walk, where he said hello baby, how you doin, to Lefty the outside man, the plant workin real good man, cocked his head for the steady throb he had passed on to Lewis like a torch in the Olympic Games, and then walked across the line to the west side of Broadway, carrying in him the pure, warm, light blue of the campus.

He feels something now, inside the bandages—big wheel, hot dog on that cool turf. That's a feeling worth all the old man's puke, the old lady's dirty underwear. Dig that jive, faggot doctor, just sitting there, copying everything he says?

So one day when I ready as Freddy an cool as a fool I walk up and down outside the bookstore till it open and when it open I walk down the stairs an go through all the counters to where it hangin up

6. Nickname for Ulysses S. Grant; the "big house" would be Grant's tomb on Riverside Drive, New York. **7.** The statue of Alma Mater on the steps of Low Library on the Columbia campus.

on the wall like the sign upstairs say and it's blue with C O L U M-B I A over the pocket and across the back and I say how much to the cat with glasses.

"Eight-fifty with your bursar receipt," he say.

"I leave it home," I say.

"OK, eight-fifty without," he say.

An I give him the loot and reach for it an he say don you want to try it on and sure I want to try it on (but not in there Jackson) and I say OK I try on and I get the sleeves an pull up the zipper an so now I got this jacket (an right away it warm an light as smoke, Faggot, an cover me all over, like Maria Cruz when I cop her cherry in the sugar field in Ponce an when I look in the mirror, Jesus a cool blue boy is looking back at me).

"Nice feet," I say.

"It suit you," he say.

That was just the beginning man, for then came real kicks. In one month only he bought at Kenny's Kampus Korner white shoes with lots of bounce to the ounce and pants without no pleats, so tight his crotch buzzed, and a button-down shirt that had another cool button on the back of the neck, and every night with his jack and pants and shirt without a tie he walked through Livingston or Furnald or John Jay on his way to work. These cats was real old and important, each one a top Yankee and he was part of that big *blue* army, like man a Union cat, not a stinkin red, and he began to check in for cokes and Drake's Cakes in the Lion's Den in Ferris Booth, sitting under the great bronze seal like United States Grant, and one night without even thinking about it he sat in a class and the *maestro* smiled at him and he smiled back. Then cut into a class in Business and one in Mines and finally one in Hamilton,[8] which was the top because Alec he always looked so cool and knocked it off so young when he don't make it no more.

And all of a sudden, like he was smoking pot, which he wasn't, New York it don't bug him no more. Or put him down no more; he could walk down any street with his uniform and shoes and book and he don't feel *frijoles*[9] inside. Columbus Avenue and Manhattan and the whole stupid west side with all the spiks was a drag, streets to be walked over, not *through*, without his heart splitting his chest. Subways, man, overnight they cut out being dragons that was busting his ears and about to stomp him. He was ready man, with all the new cool inside him, ready for the pressed down ball that was bobbing up into his neck now that it was safe.

He was ready for a chick, man.

And with no sweat he found one. In Riverside Park, where each

8. Hamilton Hall, where most of Columbia's undergraduate classes are held. 9. Beans. In the context this means he doesn't feel jumpy or nervous.

afternoon after his duty he checked out the action in his bouncing white shoes. She was sun bathing and she said would he care to rub some Coppertan on her back and he said sure man why not, and there he was feeling up on her before they even jived around. Sandy Kurlop she made the whole bit swing so easy. She wasn't much of a chick, she don't have thick hair or a big juicy mouth; she was skinny, with pimples, and worst of all got no tits. But she was from Hunter and that made her a coed and like nothing her pimples and paper-thin chest don't even bug him. Like they was even a little cool. And man she dug.

"No, not Princeton men. They're too self-important if you know what I mean, too tradition conscious. And Yale men are so frivolous. And Harvard men are fags. But the Columbia man has a quality, a certain cosmopolitan independence. You know what I mean?"

"*Si*."[1]

And a week later when he was feeling the little nipples on her titless chest and she panted how she dug *dark* Columbia men, he knew exactly what she mean.

Ishmael sees Sandy in a tight little box in his head. She has this white line around her face and around her skinny body and she don't move; she hangs there over his bed and he understands. She is one of his stepping stones, the story of his life. Inside his head, attached to the weightless body he is loaded with stepping stones. One scene after another, you dig and then cut out and step up. A job, a uniform, a chick, when you ready the whistle blow and everybody go.

And man that coed and him they go. All over town. On the east side where there ain't no spiks and downtown in the Village and even out in Saint George, Staten Island, in the middle of a baseball field, they go. New York was with him, like holding him in her hand, *simpatico*,[2] no longer threatening to fall over and crush him. For all the time in the back of his head he knows he got the blue handle to latch onto. So he was ready for more stepping stones. Big important steppers. Like on the three-hour lecture cruise they took around his town, his big island he could control just by circling it, just as he used to circle his small island. And that small island, that was the heart of the whole scene, for the further they sailed the more he found how he got it all knocked up.

"This is Trinity Church," the cat on the mike said, "where Columbia first stood. They *still* own the property."

"That island within an island is Rockefeller Center," he said, "which stands on property owned by Columbia and rented to Rockefeller."

1. "Yes." 2. Understanding, sympathetic.

Rented to Rockefeller man!

And then they sailed out of the faggot little East River, which was skinny as Sandy, and floated in a big, quiet sea, which opened up to the cool Hudson in the north.

"This," said the cat, "looks calm, but don't let it pull the wool over your eyes. Underneath it is a raging torrent." His voice grew quiet and everybody on the boat cooled it. "They say it is stirred by . . . the devil. That is why it's called Spytin Dyvil." His voice grew darker still and then he told of the crazy old Dutch cat who swam to the other side through the raging torrent and then climbed out and said, "You see man, I do it IN SPITE OF THE DEVIL" . . . And man this was a true thing. You could see it. The water was thick and greasy and evil. Down there, way down, Señor Diablo was waiting, ready to thrash that water into a pot of boiling foam, like the head of a beer, only you don't drink it. He felt like full speed ahead, but the cat was still jivin.

"And up there on the cliff behind Spytin Dyvil is Baker Field, where the Columbia Lions play football."

Screw the faggot devil! He ran to the rail and as they sailed between the cliffs he saw it, cool and proud, sitting high on top of the biggest rock. And there facing him on the opposite rock as they glided by, a hundred feet high, was a beautiful blue C.

"The Columbia boys painted that before the Princeton game many years ago. They hung far out over the water to paint it, the crazy kids."

Yeah crazy all right! That big C was gliding past, he could almost reach out and touch it, that C, keeping the devil in line, cooling him, while up above, topping New York and the Hudson and everything else, the place where the Lion roared. Real crazy!

He would like so much to nod his head and agree with himself if he could. He sets her up instead. Sandy in her little white box, stashed away now. Well she served her purpose. When Baker Field cut in she cut out, just like that. He don't feel sorry for her, or glad, or nothing. She was just a step up and she had it. He got nothing for her no more. That night when he took her to her house on 158th Street and even while her mother was cooking in the kitchen and he was laying her on the couch in the living room for the last time, in a quiet part of his head he was high over the water, on the big grey cliffs.

"Morris, how I get to Baker Field?"

"Whachou want with Baker Field man?"

"I want to see football game."

"It's too early man. They just come back from trainin camp. They still practicin."

"When they start?"

"Two weeks man. Listen Ish, you come aroun early tomorra night an I show you a skull session an a runthrough. You like that. Right upstairs in the gym. Buff nevrybody be there."

"*Si si,* I with you man."

He lay in the dark and stared down.

Mother of Mary they was so cool and beautiful. A team of blue ghosts attached to four blue drivers. When the head driver cracked out numbers, like in a dream the ghosts floated forward, pulling the drivers with them, their soft shoes spattering the gym floor like raindrops. They stopped and crouched and a whistle blew and grey-haired Buff called softly and they sprang forward again. It like a smooth, silent mambo or chachacha they was doing all together. And Ishmael just lay there, on the cork track overhanging the gym, next to Morris, while the needles shot through him.

"That cat Savini," chuckled Morris, "man he got hips like a hoola hoop."

"He some story, morning glory," Ishmael breathed, nodding his head.

Morris nudged him. "Dig the pass man."

The head driver danced backward on his tiptoes as if he was about to fall and at the last instant shot the ball across the gym, where a tall, thin ghost reached up and plucked it like picking an apple off a tree. Ishmael could feel the ball nestle in his arms and he trembled all over.

"Buttonhook buttonhook,"[3] Morris whispered. "Federspiel he never miss."

"Man Federspiel a real cool baby."

Again they kneeled like they was praying, the ball slipped back and flitted through hands and bellies and he watched a big thick driver plunge ahead and open his arms. No BALL.

"Dig dig," Morris gurgled, turning over and waving his legs like a bug that flipped, "man what fakin, you see that handoff man?"

"*Si si,*" he slapped Morris. "Crazy man crazy."

"Vasell fake the Bulldogs[4] out their jock strops."

"Oh *si si si.*"

He crossed himself in the dark and he asked Mary very rapidly to look down and make the Bulldogs lose their goddam jocks.

When Saturday finally came he went straight from the boilers to early mass and begged for an hour. Then he took the subway up to Baker Field. It was still closed so he walked up and down the hilly streets and out to the cliffs, looking over the water where Sandy and he had sailed a long time ago when he was still moving up. He

3. Football pass pattern in which the receiving end curves back into a buttonhook path.
4. The Yale team.

sighted down the drop along the big, blue C and kneeled down and whispered again.

At noon the gates opened and he bought a ticket behind a goal post. He bought a program and studied the familiar names and numbers:

Savini 35
Haggerty 21
Warren 44
Vasell 16
Federspiel 53

Over and over he said them to himself as a few people sat down beside him. Then there was a scattered roar and the Bulldogs ran out, dark blue—almost black—and clumsy and mean-looking. Then another roar and the light Blues streamed out and his heart flopped and he had to cough to push it ahead. He remembered the rules on the blackboard in the gym.

"Ok gong," he yelled, "Les achiv mental guts."

They got the message and snapped into the familiar formations. They was a cool combination, light blue against the green and white like part of the sky had pulled together and formed a Vasell or a Haggerty, stamping them into line.

"Don be satisfied with secon best, gong," he yelled.

And then the eleven sky guys were strung out and the ball was flopping through the air straight at 44, who crossed himself quickly and gathered it in and was immediately swamped by lousy dark blue sweaters. But sound man, somehow the ball was gone and number 21 had it and was skittering crazily up the sidelines, doing a private mambo, while one dark blue after another dived and fell on his face or his ass; the cat next to him was screaming go go and he was on his feet screaming too, weaving a spell around Haggerty, who ran past every white line, past the goalpost, looked straight at him and threw the ball in the air, while the other ten grabbed him and lifted him up and a cannon went off. The band began to blow and all around him he could hear, "Oh who owns New York, oh who owns New York, C-O-L-U-M-B-I-A!"

"They haven't done that in nine years," the cat next to him said, quiet now, cleaning his glasses.

"One of those things," said the faggot with the derby. "Won't happen for nine more."

Pato[5] with the Bulldog heart, he thought, keep your horns off the Lions . . . He turned to the field. "Eef you think you con you con," he whispered, pouring strength onto the grass. The ball flew off Savini's foot and over the crossbar. "Dig," he murmured contentedly as the cannon blasted again. Then he whammied the Bulldogs . . .

5. Spanish obscenity.

They held. For a period and into half of another. Pale, thin, noble, while the fat Bulldogs fell all over their lard-asses trying to dig their cool. He sat quiet, concentrating on printing them in his head—Savini, wriggling out of sweaty hands; Vasell, whirling and leaving jocks all over the field; Haggerty, fluttering away from the clutching bulls. He was exhausted, but he hung in to the last quarter while they belted him, harder even than the old man, and ganged up, more even than the Rajahs when they stomped him and called him *poco loco*.[6] Man it was rugged.

"Here it comes, the deluge," said the four-eyed cat, "they've just run out of gas."

"It figured," said derby faggot, "same old Lions."

Smart cat. Lousy German, fat Jap, stinkin Russian . . . He dug in and belted back harder. But still they bulled in, like man they was stupid and don't know nothing else. They drove him under the stands . . .

When the gun went off he was retching against a hot dog counter, in the dark, all alone, spilling tears and yellow spit on the grass. It was bitter man, like nothing he ever tasted in his life. But sweeter too, than anything he ever tasted.

"Who own New Jork, who own New Jork," he whispered into the strings of hot puke . . .

Sure nosy doctor, he talk and make you happy, why he shouldn't, he ain't got nothing to hide? . . .

Well man we cut out an we go over the frot house an me an the gong we figure we sound on a few dumb Bulldogs but we play a little pool instead and do a couple coed chicks an puke over the rail after we drink a little gin, for if your school they loose you don feel so good man, this the way if you an Ivory[7] team, an then we throw a couple beer bottles over the rail at a few spiks livin nex door jus for kicks man an then I go up Ferris Booth to see my ace Vasell an I say Tom don be discouraged man, is not the size of the man what count but the size of his heart and he say buddy thanks a lot I feel cool now an he give me this lion an when I go back over my room at the frot me an my roomie we have a jive session an pray to the lion and then we hit the sock because we got a big test tomorra, *comprende*[8] man?

(*Oye Pato* from CCNY,[9] how you ever gonna dig? I feel sorry for you man. Shoot when the Lions they jive around in your head you don't want to know nothing else, they fill you up because they history man, when you still sucking tit they got the Rose Bowl gang and Cliff Montgomery and El Sid and the Gold Dust Twins,[1] man

6. A little crazy. **7.** Ismael's way of referring to an Ivy League team. **8.** "Understand?" **9.** City College of New York. **1.** Gene Rossides and Lou Lusserow, celebrated quarterback and fullback combination in the 1940's; Montgomery was a great Columbia quarterback on the victorious Rose Bowl team of 1934; Sid Luckman, a quarterback 1937–39, called El Sid by sportswriters in a play on the name of El Cid, legendary Spanish hero.

they fill you up like pot and rice and beans and you don't need nothing, the old man he don't bug you and the old lady can keep on screwing for Pedro Fish the faggot janitor and it don't slip you no more, you don't even got hot pants for chicks no more, they could lay down and spread wide open on Broadway and they nothing, *nada* man, you can read it in the books and newspapers how Big Bill Swiacki and Co.[2] even beat the goddam ARMY, man we got a *tradition* here on the Morningside, that the side the sun come up Sambo, and the whole scene it so goddam easy, all you do is eat, sleep and think nothing else and everything swing man, like you smoking brown ones[3] when the scene bug you a million ways, only the Lions they better then *brown* ones even.)

Si, he remembers the scene. In the stinkin bed where he's attached he remembers how cool it was on the island the time he got it all knocked.

Right away on that Sunday night he started getting ready for the Johnny Harvards from stinkin Boston. He prepared by dreaming. All week he dreamed. Beautiful and ugly, tough and easy dreams. Sometime every play made it like the Lions was running all on ball bearings, sometime every play was a fumble because the ball was a flat *taco* with two iron bars sticking out and nobody got hands to latch onto the handles no matter how hard he sweated and yelled. But Friday was a real cool dream, the ball was a round, fat tit and a *pato* Cantab[4] was sucking it when Vasell jumped to the rescue and then the Cantab stomped innocent Vasell and choked him and it looked real bad, when he cut in, belted this cat high and knocked him over and stomped his face and broke his neck. Vasell shook his hand and rolled out easy for the t.d. And when he got up for the game he wasn't even sweating no more.

Only that afternoon it don't go nothing like the miracle dream said. Those blood red Cantabs was big and mean and they was dirty man, clipping when nobody looked and holding and kicking the Lions in the nuts. The referee was blind, he don't see nothing, nobody sees nothing, or digs nothing or cares nothing. Only him.

"Hot dog guys," he yelled, clapping his hands till they went limp, as the Lions slouched off the field after the game. "We keel em nex week."

And his duty done, only then did he puke . . .

He wanted to stay sick all week it felt so good; he wanted to keep on crying, but there wasn't time. There was a job to do and he was the only cat in New York—in *America*—who cared; he *had* to pick them up all over again or the Big Green from the north mountains would roll them flat. And that wasn't right man. Jesus and Mary

2. Outstanding end who played with Rossides and Lusserow. **3.** Marijuana cigarettes.
4. Nickname for Harvard team member.

that was the whole bit nobody could see, the Bulldogs, the Cantabs and now the dirty Green, that it ain't right to torture the Lions. The Lions was KINGS, man, not dogs or a lousy color. Can't *no*body dig!

Hot and cool he dreamed and the hope seeped back in. Maybe this Saturday, maybe maybe, the little cat in his head said. Yeah man I listening, this Saturday we make it big, Green is flat, Green is cardboard, Green ain't alive, ain't real, we got them figured. Every way we got Green bugged . . .

Oh but man they was so stinkin real. Green sweaters wasn't flat, Green faces wasn't sawdust. They was all great fat cows, with faces that was all the same, one lousy look all the time, no laugh like Warren or cool sneer like Savini, only thick ugliness. And they kept on coming, streaming out like a dam broke and dirty green water was pouring out and drowning the twisting, snarling Lions. Like they was drowning him . . .

"Ishmael," said Miss Lefferts, "you simply have to face your concept of reality."

"Miss Lefferts she talkin to you mister," said the old man.

"*Dios mio*,"[5] said the old lady.

"*Todamente loco*,"[6] said Zapata, his brother.

"We do not think in those terms any more," said Miss Lefferts calmly. "He has merely dislocated his reality principles. Much like a shoulder sprain. We must simply set the joint. Ishmael," she said with a smile, "you are feeling badly because of an identification you have made."

"I kick his ass in," said the old man, "better talk nice."

"You are hurt inside, aren't you," said Miss Lefferts.

"Big shit from college," said Zapata. "Excuse me missus."

"Putting it another way," said Miss Lefferts, "you have been let down."

"He hear you missus, he playin cool."

"You are assuming all the blame, aren't you?"

"*Loco* cocoa," said the old man.

"By not taking nourishment that is rightly yours you are striking back in your own way. It is your symbol. Don't you see that?"

"Talk talk," said the old lady, "*una palabra, por favor*."[7]

"By lying inanimate in your bed you are expressing yourself. What are you expressing, Ishmael?"

"*Madre mia*,"[8] said the old lady. "He lay like he dead."

"Please," said Miss Lefferts, with a frown, "I understand this. My training has given me insights into behavior of various types. Now Ishmael, your family and I are with you a hundred percent. We accept you for what you are, you see. We understand, we do not

5. "My God." **6.** "Completely crazy." **7.** "One word, please." **8.** "Mother Mary mine."

reject, nothing is your fault. You are innocent. *Innocente. Comprende usted?*[9] Now tell me in your own words whatever is on your mind."

He sat up and looked out the window. "*Miracolo*,"[1] whispered the old lady.

"We eat up the Tigers Saturday," he said.

Man his heart is shooting crazy and it is so hard to swallow, like the first time he saw New York. If only he could cut out of this lousy bed like he jumped out of bed that Saturday morning . . .

Mira,[2] they was bright and shining orange as the sun. And his prayer had been answered, for they wasn't big or meanlooking or nothing. They was little and thin, thinner even than the Lions. And right away they don't hit so hard that it hurt each time. He sees the first play in his head. They DROPPED the ball, just like the Lions always did. And man they kept on dropping it. And when they dropped it just before the t.d. he realized, man these cats was *possible*. What a beautiful realization; it floods through him now, that knowledge. That was *paradiso*,[3] that quarter. First Warren went over. Then Savini. He pounded his hands till they was raw meat and stomped the stands.

"LES GO LI-YONS," clap clap clapclapclap, "LES GO LI-YONS," stomp stomp stompompomp, "HEET EM AGAIN HEET EM AGAIN. HODDER. HODDER."

And like a dumb green spik he fell right into the jaws of the dirty trap. For those little cats, after their big come-on, suddenly rose up and kicked him in the nuts and he would feel them aching now if he could feel. Like his second day up from Ponce and Jerry O'Brien slashed and wupped him till the nuts swelled up to baseballs. A Tiger, skinny as Jerry, sneaked down the field like a crook and when nobody was looking caught a stinkin pass and ran all the way for the paydirt. He lost his breath like he's losing it now. And he reached way down and came up with the juice to turn on the evil eye, which worked and the Lions they held. Right into the last stanza, *Gracias Dios*,[4] when the dirty Tigers struck again, harder. He moans as he see the same crooked Tiger cat bust away again and run through everybody on the field like the *Lions* was whammied. Oh he remembers how hard he hailed Mary, faster and faster beautiful lady, just for the Blue boys who adore you. But she left him all alone; in a minute another sick-looking Tiger reached up and stole Vasell's pretty buttonhook and went across and into their guts and the gun went off and he knew that never in this world in his whole life could he ever bring back that last terrible quarter. Oh man that scene:

Savini was on one knee, all alone, crying.

9. "Do you understand?" 1. "Miracle." 2. "Look!" 3. "Paradise." 4. "Thanks to God."

"Stiffs," the Pepsi-Cola in front of him screamed.

Vasell sat on the bench with his head in his hands. Beside him, Buff, old and tired, had his arm around Tom's shoulder, talking softly. Buff, a *real* father.

"It's simply a complex," the Pepsi's chick said, putting on her lipstick. "They can't beat Princeton because they feel inferior. They know it. Poor old Lions." . . .

Ishmael moans for his breath. He is so tired, like he just played sixty minutes offense and defense. He is homesick man. He thinks of the gym and the Alpha boys and the ball they having tonight with their chicks after the win over the Big Red. Do they know? Do anybody? Whatsa stinkin difference. The Lions they know an that's what counts. Poor old Lions, si faggot lady, but they roaring now. . .

That time he don't puke, he was so dried up. He walked away before the Pepsi and his chick could hear his heart stompin like it's stompin now. He kept on walking, underneath the stands and out over the rocks to the big one, where across the gap the big blue C curved underneath him in the cold sun. All around stretched the cool Hudson and her Valley. And below, flowing through the gap was that greasy water, the spittin devil, just like the cat on the boat said. And he was laughing up at him, soundin on[5] him. Man the stompin missed and then started up double time. Yeah, the *devil is a Tiger. Es verdad.*[6] And he know nobody cares now. *Si, el Diablo sabe.*[7] There ain't nobody to cool him no more like Cliff Montgomery and the Rose Bowl gang and El Sid cooled him regular and spit in his eye!

Man he can taste that knowledge again. You just got to show him up, that's all. You got to show the whole *world* what a real Blue do for the Lions . . . He sees everything so clear, like the slow motion movies at the West End. He sees the light Blue zipping up his jacket and sees him looking around slow and steady, up the Hudson Valley, and down river to Alma Mater on the Hudson shore. Now man his heart is one big whomp and he's breathing so hard . . . He sees again the other light Blue and hears him yelling, "It's the spik. Hey get a cop!" He sees the strong calm Blue nod his head and calls back reassuring:

"Thees one for you Cleef baby."

"Hey get offa there!"

Sees that light Blue fading away, hears his voice cutting out far over his head, "Hey, the crazy spik jumped . . ." as the great blue space swallowed him, even as the blue space is swallowing him now, as he aimed right for the eye of the stinkin devil . . . Is OK man, all OK, relax baby, it have to be done and we do it. Now we cool and

5. Mocking him (street slang). 6. "That's true." 7. "Yes, the devil knows."

safe man. Ol Devil Tiger he never bug us in the subways no more or in the street, or suck on our guts; he never drag us back no more to the bad green days . . . So go home, faggot doctor, who need you anyhow?

He checks out all the good safety things: Little Leo, the blue jack, the white shoes. Roger Willco over an out[8] *man.*

"Les Go Li-yons, we number one in the Ivory Leak," he whispers in the last cool breath he ever has.

8. Air Force jargon, often used in the streets. Essentially it means: "Understood." The words "over and out" signify that the speaker (on a radio) is abandoning transmission and leaving the channel open.

ERNEST J. GAINES

Just Like a Tree

I shall not;
I shall not be moved.
I shall not;
I shall not be moved.
Just like a tree that's
planted 'side the water.
Oh, I shall not be moved.

I made my home in glory;
I shall not be moved.
Made my home in glory;
I shall not be moved.
Just like a tree that's
planted 'side the water.
Oh, I shall not be moved.
(from an old Negro spiritual)

Chuckkie

PA hit him on the back and he jeck in them chains like he pulling, but ever'body in the wagon know he ain't, and Pa hit him on the back again. He jeck again like he pulling, but even Big Red know he ain't doing a thing.

"That's why I'm go'n get a horse," Pa say. "He'll kill that other mule. Get up there, Mr. Bascom."

"Oh, let him alone," Gran'mon say. "How would you like it if you was pulling a wagon in all that mud?"

Pa don't answer Gran'mon; he just hit Mr. Bascom on the back again.

"That's right, kill him," Gran'mon say. "See where you get mo' money to buy another one."

"Get up there, Mr. Bascom," Pa say.

"You hear me talking to you, Emile?" Gran'mon say. "You want me hit you with something?"

"Ma, he ain't pulling," Pa say.

"Leave him alone," Gran'mon say.

Pa shake the lines little bit, but Mr. Bascom don't even feel it, and you can see he letting Big Red do all the pulling again. Pa say something kind o' low to hisself, and I can't make out what it is.

I low' my head little bit, 'cause that wind and fine rain was hitting me in the face, and I can feel Mama pressing close to me to keep me warm. She sitting on one side o' me and Pa sitting on the other side o' me, and Gran'mon in the back o' me in her setting chair. Pa didn't want bring the setting chair, telling Gran'mon there was two boards in that wagon already and she could sit on one of 'em all by herself if she wanted to, but Gran'mon say she was taking her setting chair with her if Pa liked it or not. She say she didn't ride in no wagon on nobody board, and if Pa liked it or not, that setting chair was going.

"Let her take her setting chair," Mama say. "What's wrong with taking her setting chair."

"Ehhh, Lord," Pa say, and picked up the setting chair and took it out to the wagon. "I guess I'll have to bring it back in the house, too, when we come back from there."

Gran'mon went and clambed in the wagon and moved her setting chair back little bit and sat down and folded her arms, waiting for us to get in, too. I got in and knelt down 'side her, but Mama told me to come up there and sit on the board 'side her and Pa so I could stay warm. Soon 's I sat down, Pa hit Mr. Bascom on the back, saying what a trifling thing Mr. Bascom was, and soon 's he got some mo' money he was getting rid o' Mr. Bascom and getting him a horse.

I raise my head to look see how far we is.

"That's it, yonder," I say.

"Stop pointing," Mama say, "and keep your hand in your pocket."

"Where?" Gran'mon say, back there in her setting chair.

" 'Cross the ditch, yonder," I say.

"Can't see a thing for this rain," Gran'mon say.

"Can't hardly see it," I say. "But you can see the light little bit. That chinaball tree standing in the way."

"Poor soul," Gran'mon say. "Poor soul."

I know Gran'mon was go'n say "poor soul, poor soul," 'cause she had been saying "poor soul, poor soul," ever since she heard Aunt Fe was go'n leave from back there.

Emile

Darn cane crop to finish getting in and only a mule and a half to do it. If I had my way I'd take that shotgun and a load o' buckshots and—but what.'s the use.

"Get up, Mr. Bascom—please," I say to that little dried-up, long-eared, tobacco-color thing. "Please, come up. Do your share for God sake—if you don't mind. I know it's hard pulling in all that mud, but if you don't do your share, then Big Red'll have to do his and yours, too. So, please, if it ain't asking you too much to—"

"Oh, Emile, shut up," Leola say.

"I can't hit him," I say, "or Mama back there'll hit me. So I have to talk to him. Please, Mr. Bascom, if you don't mind it. For my sake. No, not for mine; for God sake. No, not even for His'n; for Big Red sake. A fellow mule just like yourself is. Please, come up."

"Now, your hear that boy blaspheming God right in front o' me there," Mama say. "Ehhh, Lord—just keep it up. All this bad weather there like this whole world coming apart—a clap o' thunder come there and knock the fool out you. Just keep it up."

Maybe she right, and I stop. I look at Mr. Bascom there doing nothing, and I just give up. That mule know long 's Mama's alive he go'n do just just what he want to do. He know when Papa was dying he told Mama to look after him, and he know no matter what he do, no matter what he don't do, Mama ain't go'n never let me do him anything. Sometimes I even feel Mama care mo' for Mr. Bascom 'an she care for me her own son.

We come up to the gate and I pull back on the lines.

"Whoa up, Big Red," I say. "You don't have to stop, Mr. Bascom. You never started."

I can feel Mama looking at me back there in that setting chair, but she don't say nothing.

"Here," I say to Chuckkie.

He take the lines and I jump down on the ground to open the old beat-up gate. I see Etienne's horse in the yard, and I see Chris new red tractor 'side the house, shining in the rain. When Mama die, I say to myself, Mr. Bascom, you going. Ever'body getting tractors and horses and I'm still stuck with you. You going, brother.

"Can you make it through?" I ask Chuckkie. "That gate ain't too wide."

"I can do it," he say.

"Be sure to make Mr. Bascom pull," I say.

"Emile, you better get back up here and drive 'em through," Leola say. "Chuckkie might break up that wagon."

"No, let him stay down there and give orders," Mama say, back there in that setting chair.

"He can do it," I say. "Come on, Chuckkie boy."

"Come up, here, mule," Chuckkie say.

And soon 's he say that, Big Red make a lunge for the yard, and Mr. Bascom don't even move, and 'fore I can bat my eyes I hear *pow-wow; sagg-sagg; pow-wow*. But above all that noise, Leola up there screaming her head off. And Mama—not a word; just sitting in that chair, looking at me with her arms still folded.

"Pull Big Red," I say. "Pull Big Red, Chuckkie."

Poor little Chuckkie up there pulling so hard till one of his little arms straight out in back; and Big Red throwing his shoulders and ever'thing else in it, and Mr. Bascom just walking there just 's loose and free, like he's suppose to be there just for his good looks. I move out the way just in time to let the wagon go by me, pulling half o' the fence in the yard behind it. I glance up again, and there's Leola still hollering and trying to jump out, but Mama not saying a word—just sitting there in that setting chair with her arms folded.

"Whoa," I hear little Chuckkie saying. "Whoa up, now."

Somebody open the door and a bunch o' people come out on the gallery.

"What the world—?" Etienne say. "Thought the whole place was coming to pieces there."

"Chuckkie had a little trouble coming in the yard," I say.

"Goodness," Etienne say. "Anybody hurt?"

Mama just sit there about ten seconds, then she say something to herself and start clambing out the wagon.

"Let me help you there, Aunt Lou," Etienne say, coming down the steps."

"I can make it,' 'Mama say. When she get on the ground she look up at Chuckkie. "Hand me my chair there, boy."

Poor little Chuckkie, up there with the lines in one hand, get the chair and hold it to the side, and Etienne catch it just 'fore it hit the ground. Mama start looking at me again, and it look like for at least a' hour she stand there looking at nobody but me. Then she say, "Ehhh, Lord," like that again, and go inside with Leola and the rest o' the people.

I look back at half o' the fence laying there in the yard, and I jump back on the wagon and guide the mules to the side o' the house. After unhitching 'em and tying 'em to the wheels, I look at Chris pretty red tractor again, and me and Chuckkie go inside: I make sure he kick all that mud off his shoes 'fore he go in the house.

Leola

Sitting over there by that fireplace, trying to look joyful when ever'body there know she ain't. But she trying, you know; smiling and bowing when people say something to her. How can she be joyful, I ask you; how can she be? Poor thing, she been here all her life—or the most of it, let's say. 'Fore they moved in this house, they lived in one back in the woods 'bout a mile from here. But for the past twenty-five or thirty years, she been right in this one house. I know ever since I been big enough to know people I been seeing her right here.

Aunt Fe, Aunt Fe, Aunt Fe, Aunt Fe; the name's been 'mongst us just like us own family name. Just like the name o' God. Like the name of town—the city. Aunt Fe, Aunt Fe, Aunt Fe, Aunt Fe.

Poor old thing; how many times I done come here and washed clothes for her when she couldn't do it herself. How many times I done hoed in that garden, ironed her clothes, wrung a chicken neck for her. You count the days in the year and you'll be pretty close. And I didn't mind it a bit. No, I didn't mind it a bit She there trying to pay me. Proud—Lord, talking 'bout pride. "Here." "No, Aunt Fe; no." "Here, here; you got a child there, you can use it." "No, Aunt Fe. No. No. What would Mama think if she knowed I took money from you? Aunt Fe, Mama would never forgive me. No. I love doing these thing for you. I just wish I could do more."

And there, now, trying to make 'tend she don't mind leaving. Ehhh, Lord.

I hear a bunch o' rattling round in the kitchen and I go back there. I see Louise stirring this big pot o' eggnog.

"Louise," I say.

"Leola," she say.

We look at each other and she stir the eggnog again. She know what I'm go'n say next, and she can't even look in my face.

"Louise, I wish there was some other way."

"There's no other way," she say.

"Louise, moving her from here's like moving a tree you been used to in your front yard all your life."

"What else can I do?"

"Oh, Louise, Louise."

"Nothing else but that."

"Louise, what people go'n do without her here?"

She stir the eggnog and don't answer.

"Louise, us'll take her in with us."

"You all no kin to Auntie. She go with me."

"And us'll never see her again."

She stir the eggnog. Her husband come back in the kitchen and kiss her on the back o' the neck and then look at me and grin. Right from the start I can see I ain't go'n like that nigger.

"Almost ready, honey?" he say.

"Almost."

He go to the safe and get one o' them bottles of whiskey he got in there and come back to the stove.

"No," Louise say. "Everybody don't like whiskey in it. Add the whiskey after you've poured it up."

"Okay, hon."

He kiss her on the back o' the neck again. Still don't like that nigger. Something 'bout him ain't right.

"You one o' the family?" he say.

"Same as one," I say. "And you?"

He don't like the way I say it, and I don't care if he like it or not.

He look at me there a second, and then he kiss her on the ear.

"Un-unnn," she say, stirring the pot.

"I love your ear, baby," he say.

"Go in the front room and talk with the people," she say.

He kiss her on the other ear. A nigger do all that front o' public got something to hide. He leave the kitchen, I look at Louise.

"Ain't nothing else I can do," she say.

"You sure, Louise? You positive?"

"I'm positive," she say.

The front door open and Emile and Chuckkie come in. A minute later Washington and Adrieu come in, too. Adrieu come back in the kitchen, and I can see she been crying. Aunt Fe is her godmother, you know.

"How you feel, Adrieu?"

"That weather out there," she say.

"Y'all walked?"

"Yes."

"Us here in the wagon. Y'all can go back with us."

"Y'all the one tore the fence down?" she ask.

"Yes, I guess so. That brother-in-law o' yours in there letting Chuckkie drive that wagon."

"Well, I don't guess it'll matter too much. Nobody go'n be here, anyhow."

And she start crying again. I take her in my arms and pat her on the shoulder, and I look at Louise stirring the egg-nog.

"What I'm go'n do and my nan-nane gone? I love her so much."

"Ever'body love her."

"Since my mama died, she been like my mama."

"Shhh," I say. "Don't let her hear you. Make her grieve. You don't want her grieving, now do you?"

She sniffs there 'gainst my dress few times.

"Oh, Lord," she say. "Lord, have mercy."

"Shhh," I say. "Shhh. That's what life's 'bout."

"That ain't what life's 'bout," she say. "It ain't fair. This been her home all her life. These the people she know. She don't know them people she going to. It ain't fair."

"Shhh, Adrieu," I say. "Now, you saying things that ain't your business."

She cry there some mo'.

"Oh, Lord, Lord," she say.

Louise turn from the stove.

"About ready now," she say, going to the middle door. "James, tell everybody to come back and get some."

James

Let me go on back here and show these country niggers how to have a good time. All they know is talk, talk, talk. Talk so much they make me buggy round here. Damn this weather—wind, rain. Must be a million cracks in this old house.

I go to that old beat-up safe in that corner and get that fifth of Mr. Harper[1] (in the South now; got to say Mister), give the seal one swipe, the stopper one jerk, and head back to that old wood stove. (Man, like, these cats are primitive—goodness. You know what I mean? I mean like wood stoves. Don't mention TV, man, these cats here never heard of that.) I start to dump Mr. Harper in the pot and Baby catches my hand again and say not all of them like it. You ever heard of anything like that? I mean a stud's going to drink eggnog, and he's not going to put whiskey in it. I mean he's going to drink it straight. I mean, you ever heard anything like that? Well, I wasn't pressing none of them on Mr. Harper. I mean, me and Mr. Harper get along too well together for me to go around there pressing.

I hold my cup there and let Baby put a few drops of this egg stuff in it; then I jerk my cup back and let Mr. Harper run a while. Couple of these cats come over (some of them aren't so lame) and set their cups, and I let Mr. Harper run for them. Then this cat says he's got 'nough. I let Mr. Harper run for this other stud, and pretty soon he says, "Hold it. Good." Country cat, you know. "Hold it. Good." Real country cat. So I raise the cup to see what Mr. Harper's doing. He's just right. I raise the cup again. Just right, Mr. Harper; just right.

I go to the door with Mr. Harper under my arm and the cup in my hand and I look into the front room where they all are. I mean, there's about ninety-nine of them in there. Old ones, young ones, little ones, big ones, yellow ones, black ones, brown ones—you name them, brother, and they were there. And what for? Brother, I'll tell you what for. Just because me and Baby are taking this old chick out of these sticks. Well, I'll tell you where I'd be at this moment if I was one of them. With that weather out there like it is, I'd be under about five blankets with some little warm belly pressing against mine. Brother, you can bet your hat I wouldn't be here. Man, listen to that thing out there. You can hear that rain beating on that old house like grains of rice; and that wind coming through them cracks like it does in those old Charlie Chaplin movies. Man, like you know—like *whooo-ee; whooo-ee.* Man, you talking about some weird cats.

I can feel Mr. Harper starting to massage my wig and I bat my eyes twice and look at the old girl over there. She's still sitting in that funny-looking little old rocking chair, and not saying a word to anybody. Just sitting there looking into the fireplace at them two pieces of wood that aren't giving out enough heat to warm a baby, let alone ninety-nine grown people. I mean, you know, like

1. A brand of whiskey.

that sleet's falling out there like all get-up-and-go, and them two pieces of wood'are lying there just as dead as the rest of these way-out cats.

One of the old cats—I don't know which one he is—Mose, Sam, or something like that—leans over and pokes in the fire a minute; then a little blaze shoots up, and he raises up, too, looking as satisfied as if he'd just sent a rocket into orbit. I mean, these cats are like that. They do these little bitty things, and they feel like they've really done something Well, back in these sticks, I guess there just isn't nothing big to do.

I feel Mr. Harper touching my skull now—and I notice this little chick passing by me with these two cups of eggnog. She goes over to the fireplace and gives one to each of these old chicks. The one sitting in that setting chair she brought with her from God knows where, and the other cup to the old chick that Baby and I are going to haul from here sometime tomorrow morning. Wait, man, I mean like, you ever heard of anybody going to somebody else's house with a chair? I mean, wouldn't you call that an insult at the basest point? I mean, now, like tell me what you think of that? I mean—dig—here I am at my pad, and in you come with your own stool. I mean, now, like man, you know. I mean that's an insult at the basest point. I mean, you know . . . you know, like way out. . . .

Mr. Harper, what you trying to do, boy?—I mean, *sir*. (Got to watch myself, I'm in the South. Got to keep watching myself.)

This stud touches me on the shoulder and raise his cup and say, "How 'bout a taste?" I know what the stud's talking about, so I let Mr. Harper run for him. But soon 's I let a drop get in, the stud say, " 'Nough." I mean I let about two drops get in, and already the stud's got enough. Man, I mean, like you know. I mean these studs are 'way out. I mean like 'way back there.

This stud takes a swig of his eggnog and say, "Ahhh." I mean this real downhome way of saying "Ahhhh." I mean, man, like these studs—I notice this little chick passing by me again, and this time she's crying. I mean weeping, you know. And just because this old ninety-nine-year-old chick's packing up and leaving. I mean, you ever heard of anything like that? I mean, here she is pretty as the day is long and crying because Baby and I are hauling this old chick away. Well, I'd like to make her cry. And I can assure you, brother, it wouldn't be from leaving her.

I turn and look at Baby over there by the stove, pouring eggnog in all these cups. I mean, there's about twenty of these cats lined up there. And I bet you not half of them will take Mr. Harper along. Some way-out cats, man. Some way-out cats.

I go up to Baby and kiss her on the back of the neck and give her a little pat where she likes for me to pat her when we're in the bed. She say, "Uh-uh," but I know she likes it anyhow.

Ben O

I back under the bed and touch the slop jar, and I pull back my leg and back somewhere else, and then I get me a good sight on it. I spin my aggie couple times and sight again and then I shoot. I hit it right square in the middle and it go flying over the fireplace. I crawl over there to get it and I see 'em all over there drinking they eggnog and they didn't even offer me and Chuckkie none. I find my marble on the bricks, and I go back and tell Chuckkie they over there drinking eggnog.

"You want some?" I say.

"I want shoot marble," Chuckkie say. "Yo' shot. Shoot up."

"I want some eggnog," I say.

"Shoot up. Ben O," he say. "I'm getting cold staying in one place so long. You feel that draft?"

"Coming from that crack under that bed," I say.

"Where?" Chuckkie say, looking for the crack.

"Over by that bedpost over there," I say.

"This sure's a beat-up old house," Chuckkie say.

"I want me some eggnog," I say.

"Well, you ain't getting none," Gran'mon say, from the fireplace. "It ain't good for you."

"I can drink eggnog," I say. "How come it ain't good for me? It ain't nothing but eggs and milk. I eat chicken, don't I? I eat beef, don't I?"

Gran'mon don't say nothing.

"I want me some eggnog," I say.

Gran'mon still don't say no more. Nobody else don't say nothing, neither.

"I want me some eggnog," I say.

"You go'n get a eggnog," Gran'mon say. "Just keep that noise up."

"I want me some eggnog," I say; "and I 'tend to get me some eggnog tonight."

Next thing I know, Gran'mon done picked up a chip out o' that corner and done sailed it back there where me and Chuckkie is. I duck just in time, and the chip catch old Chuckkie side the head.

"Hey, who that hitting me?" Chuckkie say.

"Move, and you won't get hit," Gran'mon say.

I laugh at old Chuckkie over there holding his head, and next thing I know here's Chuckkie done haul back there and hit me in my side. I jump up from here and give him two just to show him how it feel, and he jump up and hit me again. Then we grab each other and start tussling on the floor.

"You, Ben O," I hear Gran'mon saying. "You, Ben O, cut that out. Y'all cut that out."

But we don't stop, 'cause neither one o' us want be first. Then

I feel somebody pulling us apart.

"What I ought to do is whip both o' you," Mrs. Leola say. "Is that what y'all want?"

"No'm," I say.

"Then shake hand."

Me and Chuckkie shake hand.

"Kiss," Mrs. Leola say.

"No, ma'am," I say. "I ain't kissing no boy. I ain't that crazy."

"Kiss him, Chuckkie," she say.

Old Chuckkie kiss me on the jaw.

"Now, kiss him, Ben O."

"I ain't kissing no Chuckkie," I say. "No'm. Uh-uh. You kiss girls."

And the next thing I know, Mama done tipped up back o' me and done whop me on the leg with Daddy belt.

"Kiss Chuckkie," she say.

Chuckkie turn his jaw to me and I kiss him. I almost wipe my mouth. I even feel like spitting.

"Now, come back here and get you some eggnog," Mama say.

"That's right, spoil 'em," Gran'mon say. "Next thing you know, they be drinking from bottles."

"Little eggnog won't hurt 'em, Mama," Mama say.

"That's right, never listen," Gran'mon say. "It's you go'n suffer for it. I be dead and gone, me."

Aunt Clo

Be just like wrapping a chain round a tree and jecking and jecking, and then shifting the chain little bit and jecking and jecking some in that direction, and then shifting it some mo' and jecking and jecking in that direction. Jecking and jecking till you get it loose, and then pulling with all your might. Still it might not be loose enough and you have to back the tractor up some and fix the chain round the tree again and start jecking all over. Jeck, jeck, jeck. Then you hear the roots crying, and then you keep on jecking, and then it give, and you jeck some mo', and then it falls. And not till then you see the big hole in the ground and piece of the taproot still way down in it—a piece you won't never get out no matter if you dig till doomsday. Yes, you got the tree—least got it down on the ground, but did you get the taproot? No, sir, you didn't get the taproot. You stand there and look down in this hole at it and you grab yo' axe and jump down in it, and start chopping at the taproot, but do you get the taproot? No. You didn't get the taproot, sir. You never get the taproot. But, sir, I tell you what you do get. You get a big hole in the ground, sir; and you get another big hole in the air where the lovely branches been all these years. Yes, sir, that's what you get. The holes, sir, the holes. Two holes, sir, you can't never fill no matter how hard you try.

So you wrap yo' chain round yo' tree again, sir, and you start dragging it. But the dragging ain't so easy, sir, 'cause she's a heavy old tree—been there a long time, you know—heavy. And you make yo' tractor strain, sir, and the elements work 'gainst you, too, sir, 'cause the elements, they on her side, too, 'cause she part o' the elements, and the elements, they part o' her. So the elements, they do they little share to discourage you—yes, sir, they does. But you will not let the elements stop you. No, sir, you show the elements that they just elements, and man is stronger than elements, and you jeck and jeck on the chain, and soon she start to moving with you, sir, but if you look over yo' shoulder one second you see her leaving a trail—a trail, sir, that can be seen from miles and miles away. You see her trying to hook her little fine branches in different little cracks, in between pickets, round hills o' grass, round anything they might brush 'gainst. But you is a determined man, sir, and you jeck and you jeck, and she keep on grabbing and trying to hold, but you stronger, sir—course you the strongest—and you finally get her out on the pave road. But what you don't notice, sir, is just 'fore she get on the pave road she leave couple her little branches to remind the people that it ain't her that want leave, but you, sir, that think she ought to. So you just drag her and drag her, sir, and the folks that live in the houses 'side the pave road, they come out on they gallery and look at her go by, and then they go back in they house and sit by the fire and forget her. So you just go on, sir, and you just go and you go—and for how many days? I don't know. I don't have the least idea. The North to me, sir, is like the elements. It mystify me. But never mind, you finally get there, and then you try to find a place to set her. You look in this corner and you look in that corner, but no corner is good. She kind o' stand in the way no matter where you set her. So finally, sir, you say, "I just stand her up here a little while and see, and if it don't work out, if she keep getting in the way, I guess we'll just have to take her to the dump."

Chris

Just like him, though, standing up there telling them lies when everybody else feeling sad. I don't know what you do without people like him. And, yet, you see him there, he sad just like the rest. But he just got to be funny. Crying on the inside, but still got to be funny.

He didn't steal it, though; didn't steal it a bit. His grandpa was just like him. Mat? Mat Jefferson? Just like that. Mat could make you die laughing. 'Member once at a wake. Who was dead? Yes—Robert Lewis. Robert Lewis laying up in his coffin dead as a door nail. Everybody sad and droopy. Mat look at that and start his lying. Soon, half o' the place laughing. Funniest wake I ever went to, and yet—

Just like now. Look at 'em. Look at 'em laughing. Ten minutes ago you would 'a' thought you was at a funeral. But look at 'em now. Look at her there in that little old chair. How long she had it? Fifty years—a hundred? It ain't a chair no mo', it's little bit o' her. Just like her arm, just like her leg.

You know, I couldn't believe it. I couldn't. Emile passed the house there the other day, right after the bombing, and I was in my yard digging a water drain to let the water run out in the ditch. Emile, he stopped the wagon there 'fore the door. Little Chuckkie, he in there with him with that little rain cap buckled up over his head. I go out to the gate and I say, "Emile, it's the truth?"

"The truth," he say. And just like that he say it. "The truth."

I look at him there, and he looking up the road to keep from looking back at me. You know, they been pretty close to Aunt Fe ever since they was children coming up. His own mon, Aunt Lou, and Aunt Fe, they been like sisters, there, together.

Me and him, we talk there little while 'bout the cane cutting, then say he got to get on to the back. He shake the lines and drive on.

Inside me, my heart feel like it done swole up ten times the size it ought to be. Water come in my eyes, and I got to 'mit I cried right there. Yes sir, I cried right there by that front gate.

Louise come in the room and whisper something to Leola, and they go back in the kitchen. I can hear 'em moving things round back there, still getting things together they go'n be taking along. If they offer me anything, I'd like that big iron pot out there in the back yard. Good for boiling water when you killing hog, you know.

You can feel the sadness in the room again. Louise brought it in when she come in and whispered to Leola. Only, she didn't take it out when her and Leola left. Every pan they move, every pot they unhook keep telling you she leaving, she leaving.

Etienne turn over one o' them logs to make the fire pick up some, and I see that boy, Lionel, spreading out his hands over the fire. Watch out, I think to myself, here come another lie. People, he just getting started.

Anne-Marie Duvall

"You're not going?"

"I'm not going," he says, turning over the log with the poker. "And if you were in your right mind, you wouldn't go, either."

"You just don't understand, do you?"

"Oh, I understand. She cooked for your daddy. She nursed you when your mama died."

"And I'm trying to pay her back with a seventy-nine-cents scarf. Is that too much?"

He is silent, leaning against the mantel, looking down at the fire.

The fire throws strange shadows across the big, old room. Father looks down at me from against the wall. His eyes do not say go nor stay. But I know what he would do.

"Please go with me, Edward."

"You're wasting your breath."

I look at him a long time, then I get the small package from the coffee table.

"You're still going?"

"I am going."

"Don't call for me if you get bogged down anywhere back there."

I look at him and go out to the garage. The sky is black. The clouds are moving fast and low. A fine drizzle is falling, and the wind coming from the swamps blows in my face. I cannot recall a worse night in all my life.

I hurry into the car and drive out of the yard. The house stands big and black in back of me. Am I angry with Edward? No, I'm not angry with Edward. He's right. I should not go out into this kind of weather. But what he does not understand is I must. Father definitely would have gone if he were alive. Grandfather definitely would have gone, also. And, therefore, I must. Why? I cannot answer why. Only, I must go.

As soon as I turn down that old muddy road, I begin to pray. Don't let me go into that ditch, I pray. Don't let me go into that ditch. Please, don't let me go into that ditch.

The lights play on the big old trees along the road. Here and there the lights hit a sagging picket fence. But I know I haven't even started yet. She lives far back into the fields. Why? God, why does she have to live so far back? Why couldn't she have lived closer to the front? But the answer to that is as hard for me as is the answer to everything else. It was ordained before I—before father—was born—that she should live back there. So why should I try to understand it now?

The car slides towards the ditch, and I stop it dead and turn the wheel, and then come back into the road again. Thanks, father. I know you're with me. Because it was you who said that I must look after her, didn't you? No, you did not say it directly, father. You said it only with a glance. As grandfather must have said it to you, and as his father must have said it to him.

But now that she's gone, father, now what? I know. I know. Aunt Lou, Aunt Clo, and the rest.

The lights shine on the dead, wet grass along the road. There's an old pecan tree, looking dead and all alone. I wish I was a little nigger gal so I could pick pecans and eat them under the big old dead tree.

The car hits a rut, but bounces right out of it. I am frightened for a moment, but then I feel better. The windshield wipers are working well, slapping the water away as fast as it hits the glass. If I make the next half mile all right, the rest of the way will be good. It's not much over a mile now.

That was too bad about that bombing—killing that woman and her two children. That poor woman; poor children. What is the answer? What will happen? What do they want? Do they know what they want? Do they really know what they want? Are they positively sure? Have they any idea? Money to buy a car, is that it? If that is all, I pity them. Oh, how I pity them.

Not much farther. Just around that bend and—there's a water hole. Now what?

I stop the car and just stare out at the water a minute; then I get out to see how deep it is. The cold wind shoots through my body like needles. Lightning come from towards the swamps and lights up the place. For a split second the night is as bright as day. The next second it is blacker than it has ever been.

I look at the water, and I can see that it's too deep for the car to pass through. I must turn back or I must walk the rest of the way. I stand there a while wondering what to do. Is it worth it all? Can't I simply send the gift by someone tomorrow morning? But will there be someone tomorrow morning? Suppose she leaves without getting it, then what? What then? Father would never forgive me. Neither would grandfather or great-grandfather, either. No, they wouldn't.

The lightning flashes again and I look across the field, and I can see the tree in the yard a quarter of a mile away. I have but one choice: I must walk. I get the package out of the car and stuff it in my coat and start out.

I don't make any progress at first, but then I become a little warmer and I find I like walking. The lightning flashes just in time to show up a puddle of water, and I go around it. But there's no light to show up the second puddle, and I fall flat on my face. For a moment I'm completely blind, then I get slowly to my feet and check the package. It's dry, not harmed. I wash the mud off my raincoat, wash my hands, and I start out again.

The house appears in front of me, and as I come into the yard, I can hear the people laughing and talking. Sometimes I think niggers can laugh and joke even if they see somebody beaten to death. I go up on the porch and knock and an old one opens the door for me. I swear, when he sees me he looks as if he's seen a ghost. His mouth drops open, his eyes bulge—I swear.

I go into the old crowded and smelly room, and everyone of them looks at me the same way the first one did. All the joking and laughing has ceased. You would think I was the devil in person.

"Done, Lord," I hear her saying over by the fireplace. They

move to the side and I can see her sitting in that little rocking chair I bet you she's had since the beginning of time. "Done, Master," she says. "Child, what you doing in weather like this? Y'all move; let her get to that fire. Y'all move. Move, now. Let her warm herself."

They start scattering everywhere.

"I'm not cold, Aunt Fe," I say. "I just brought you something—something small—because you're leaving us. I'm going right back.

"Done, Master," she says. Fussing over me just like she's done all her life. "Done, Master. Child, you ain't got no business in a place like this. Get close to this fire. Get here. Done, Master."

I move closer, and the fire does feel warm and good.

"Done, Lord," she says.

I take out the package and pass it to her. The other niggers gather around with all kinds of smiles on their faces. Just think of it—a white lady coming through all of this for one old darky. It is all right for them to come from all over the plantation, from all over the area, in all kinds of weather: this is to be expected of them. But a white lady, a white lady. They must think we white people don't have their kind of feelings.

She unwraps the package, her bony little fingers working slowly and deliberately. When she sees the scarf—the seventy-nine-cents scarf—she brings it to her mouth and kisses it.

"Y'all look," she says. "Y'all look. Ain't it the prettiest little scarf y'all ever did see? Y'all look."

They move around her and look at the scarf. Some of them touch it.

"I go'n put it on right now," she says. "I go'n put it on right now, my lady."

She unfolds it and ties it round her head and looks up at everybody and smiles.

"Thank you, my lady," she says. "Thank you, ma'am, from the bottom of my heart."

"Oh, Aunt Fe." I say, kneeling down beside her. "Oh, Aunt Fe."

But I think about the other niggers there looking down at me, and I get up. But I look into that wrinkled old face again, and I must go back down again. And I lay my head in that bony old lap, and I cry and I cry—I don't know how long. And I feel those old fingers, like death itself, passing over my hair and my neck. I don't know how long I kneel there crying, and when I stop, I get out of there as fast as I can.

Etienne

The boy come in, and soon, right off, they get quiet, blaming the boy. If people could look little farther than the tip of they nose—No, they blame the boy. Not that they ain't behind the boy, what he doing, but they blame him for what she must do. What they don't know is that the boy didn't start it, and the people that bombed the house didn't start it, neither. It started a million years ago. It started when one man envied another man for having a penny mo' 'an he had, and then the man married a woman to help him work the field so he could get much 's the other man, but when the other man saw the man had married a woman to get much 's him, he, himself, he married a woman, too, so he could still have mo'. Then they start having children—not from love; but so the children could help 'em work so they could have mo'. But even with the children one man still had a penny mo' 'an the other, so the other man went and bought him a ox, and the other man did the same—to keep ahead of the other man. And soon the other man had bought him a slave to work the ox so he could get ahead of the other man. But the other man went out and bought him two slaves so he could stay ahead of the other man, and the other man went out and bought him three slaves. And soon they had a thousand slaves apiece, but they still wasn't satisfied. And one day the slaves all rose and kill the masters, but the masters (knowing slaves was men just like they was, and kind o' expected they might do this) organized theyself a good police force, and the police force, they come out and killed the two thousand slaves.

So it's not this boy you see standing here 'fore you, 'cause it happened a million years ago. And this boy here's just doing something the slaves done a million years ago. Just that this boy here ain't doing it they way. 'Stead of raising arms 'gainst the masters, he bow his head.

No, I say; don't blame the boy 'cause she must go. 'Cause when she's dead, and that won't be long after they get her up there, this boy's work will still be going on. She's not the only one that's go'n die from this boy's work. Many mo' of 'em go'n die f'ore it's over with. The whole place—everything. A big wind is rising, and when a big wind rise, the sea stirs, and the drop o' water you see laying on top the sea this day won't be there tomorrow. 'Cause that's what wind do, and that's what life is. She ain't nothing but one little drop o' water laying on top the sea, and what this boy's doing is called the wind . . . and she must be moved. No, don't blame the boy. Go out and blame the wind. No, don't blame him, 'cause tomorrow, what he's doing today, somebody go'n say he ain't done a thing. 'Cause tomorrow will be his time to be turned over just like it's hers today. And after that, be somebody else time to turn over. And it keep going like that till it ain't nothing left to turn—and nobody left to turn it.

"Sure, they bombed the house," he say; "because they want us to stop. But if we stopped today, then what good would we have done? What good? Those who have already died for the cause would have just died in vain."

"Maybe if they had bombed your house you wouldn't be so set on keeping this up."

"If they had killed my mother and my brothers and sisters, I'd press just that much harder. I can see you all point. I can see it very well. But I can't agree with you. You blame me for their being bombed. You blame me for Aunt Fe's leaving. They died for you and for your children. And I love Aunt Fe as much as anybody in here does. Nobody in here loves her more than I do. Not one of you." He looks at her. "Don't you believe me, Aunt Fe?"

She nods—that little white scarf still tied round her head.

"How many times have I eaten in your kitchen, Aunt Fe? A thousand times? How many times have I eaten tea cakes and drank milk on the back steps, Aunt Fe? A thousand times? How many times have I sat at this same fireplace with you, just the two of us, Aunt Fe? Another thousand times—two thousand times? How many times have I chopped wood for you, chopped grass for you, ran to the store for you? Five thousand times? How many times have we walked to church together, Aunt Fe? Gone fishing at the river together—how many times? I've spent as much time in this house as I've spent in my own. I know every crack in the wall. I know every corner. With my eyes shut, I can go anywhere in here without bumping into anything. How many of you can do that? Not many of you." He looks at her. "Aunt Fe?"

She looks at him.

"Do you think I love you, Aunt Fe?"

She nods.

"I love you, Aunt Fe, much as I do my own parents. I'm going to miss you much as I'd miss my own mother if she were going to leave me now. I'm going to miss you, Aunt Fe, but I'm not going to stop what I've started. You told me a story once, Aunt Fe, about my great-grandpa. Remember? Remember how he died?"

She looks in the fire and nods.

"Remember how they lynched him—chopped him into pieces?"

She nods.

"Just the two of us were sitting here beside the fire when you told me that. I was so angry I felt like killing. But it was you who told me get killing out of my mind. It was you who told me I would only bring harm to myself and sadness to the others if I killed. Do you remember that, Aunt Fe?"

She nods, still looking in the fire.

"You were right. We cannot raise our arms. Because it would mean death for ourselves, as well as for the others. But we will do something else—and that's what we will do." He looks at the people standing round him. "And if they were to bomb my own mother's house tomorrow, I would still go on."

"I'm not saying for you not to go on," Louise says. "That's up to you. I'm just taking Auntie from here before hers is the next house they bomb."

The boy look at Louise, and then at Aunt Fe. He go up to the chair where she sitting.

"Good-bye, Aunt Fe," he say, picking up her hand. The hand done shriveled up to almost nothing. Look like nothing but loose skin's covering the bones. "I'll miss you," he say.

"Good-bye, Emmanuel," she say. She look at him a long time. "God be with you."

He stand there holding the hand a while longer, then he nods his head, and leaves the house. The people stir around little bit, but nobody say anything.

Aunt Lou

They tell her good-bye, and half of 'em leave the house crying, or want cry, but she just sit there 'side the fireplace like she don't mind going at all. When Leola ask me if I'm ready to go, I tell her I'm staying right there till Fe leave that house. I tell her I ain't moving one step till she go out that door. I been knowing her for the past fifty some years now, and I ain't 'bout to leave her on her last night here.

That boy, Chuckkie, want stay with me, but I make him go. He follow his mon and paw out the house and soon I hear that wagon turning round. I hear Emile saying something to Mr. Bascom even 'fore that wagon get out the yard. I tell myself, well, Mr. Bascom, you sure go'n catch it, and me not there to take up for you—and I get up from my chair and go to the door.

"Emile?" I call.

"Whoa," he say.

"You leave that mule 'lone, you hear me?"

"I ain't done Mr. Bascom a thing, Mama," he say.

"Well, you just mind you don't," I say. "I'll sure find out."

"Yes'm," he say. "Come up here, Mr. Bascom."

"Now, you hear that boy. Emile?" I say.

"I'm sorry, Mama," he say. "I didn't mean no harm."

They go out in the road, and I go back to the fireplace and sit down again. Louise stir round in the kitchen a few minutes, then she come in the front where we at. Everybody else gone. That husband o' hers, there, got drunk long 'fore midnight, and Emile and them had to put him to bed in the other room.

She come there and stand by the fire.

"I'm dead on my feet," she say.

"Why don't you go to bed," I say. "I'm go'n be here."

"You all won't need anything?"

"They got wood in that corner?"

"Plenty."

"Then we won't need a thing."

She stand there and warm, and then she say good night and go round the other side.

"Well, Fe?" I say.

"I ain't leaving here tomorrow, Lou," she say.

" 'Course you is," I say. "Up there ain't that bad."

She shake her head. "No, I ain't going nowhere."

I look at her over in her chair, but I don't say nothing. The fire pops in the fireplace, and I look at the fire again. It's a good little fire—not too big, not too little. Just 'nough there to keep the place warm.

"You want sing, Lou?" she say, after a while. "I feel like singing my 'termination song."

"Sure," I say.

She start singing in that little light voice she got there, and I join with her. We sing two choruses, and then she stop.

"My 'termination for Heaven," she say. "Now—now—"

"What's the matter, Fe?" I say.

"Nothing," she say. "I want get in my bed. My gown hanging over there."

I get the gown for her and bring it back to the firehalf. She get out of her dress slowly, like she don't even have 'nough strength to do it. I help her on with her gown, and she kneel down there 'side the bed and say her prayers. I sit in my chair and look at the fire again.

She pray there a long time—half out loud, half to herself. I look at her kneeling down there, little like a little old girl. I see her making some kind o' jecking motion there, but I feel she crying 'cause this her last night here, and 'cause she got to go and leave ever'thing behind. I look at the fire.

She pray there ever so long, and then she start to get up. But she can't make it by herself. I go to help her, and when I put my hand on her shoulder, she say, "Lou? Lou?"

I say, "What's the matter, Fe?"

"Lou?" she say. "Lou?"

I feel her shaking in my hand with all her might. Shaking, shaking, shaking—like a person with the chill. Then I hear her take a long breath, longest I ever heard anybody take before. Then she ease back on the bed—calm, calm, calm.

"Sleep on, Fe," I tell her. "When you get up there, tell 'em all I ain't far behind."

EUGENE GARBER

The Poets

HER name was Sarah and she had performed many girlhood feats—ridden her jumper Jack to victory at the Windome Stakes against a field of fine male riders, won the senior mixed doubles at Salt Springs with Albert Hough, swum the Black Warrior, written the prize-winning poem for the university literary annual, which even her Uncle Carlton had conceded showed promise. This was the final stanza:

> *Now among the porcelain cats,*
> *Purple hum of listless chatter.*
> *Bend I to your chatoyant eye*
> *And supplicate your charity.*

"Nice, Essie," he wrote, "even if decadent ennui is as far from your character as gnats are to eagles." But she sent him no more poems.

A week after she was graduated from the university, the hottest June on record, 1934, she wrote from her hometown of Tumwah.

My dear bachelor barrister uncle, how are you faring in these lean times in the big city? Here the weekly is down to two pages. Even the Episcopalians can't afford to have the Sunday Bulletin printed any more. Miss Kendall's recital will not have a program this year, and the grocery store handy-bill business is defunct. So Daddy sits around the shop nipping with Tom, whom he will not let go. The county contracts go to Coggins in Melba again because, of course, old man Pelly tipped him off and he underbid Daddy by a fraction. Mama is waiting for me to accept Albert and save the family with "the only bank stocks that held up this side of Montgomery, honey." Your older sister of high ideals. Hope, *my* sister, whom I dearly love (won't you believe that, uncle dear, despite our horrendous fights?), must go to Mount Morris College for Women in North Carolina next year. (Mama judges that, unlike me, Hope would not be able to protect herself from certain undesirable elements at the university.) And where is the money to come from? My tan and exquisitely trained body, uncle dear, to fill Hope's empty head? Better that I should come to New Orleans and dance in Curly's infamous speakeasy. Can you get me on? . . .

Uncle Carlton wrote back, "Do not marry against your feelings, Essie. No good can come of it." But Sarah did marry Albert. Then, in early 1937, she wrote:

Dear uncle, let me be the first to bring you the joyous news, Mama's injunction notwithstanding. (Is the phrase juridically correct?) Your niece Hope has dropped out of Mount Morris, pregnant, paternity as yet undeclared, and therefore the child may be divine. Contemporaneously, I have declared to Albert that I wish to be free of the fetters of the marriage bed, requiring no settlement. Thus ends, uncle dear, my penitential years with the heaviest hands east of the Mississippi. And now what about that job at Curly's—or has repeal killed the business?

At Carlton's invitation Sarah went to New Orleans, arriving in time for Mardi Gras. She remained two months and left abruptly. Back at Tumwah she stayed only long enough to pack. She went to Atlanta and got a job as a receptionist at the Coca-Cola Company, winning out over a score of other applicants.

So, uncle dear, I have a job despite your gloomy prognostications. Even so, I apologize for failing twice to accept your avuncular counsel vis-à-vis matters of the heart. I should not have married Albert. You were certainly right about that. But I should not have dropped Maurice, you say? Dear Maurice. He was as gallant and passionate as my most romantic notions of the French. And his coffee money was certainly more fragrant than Albert's farmer-fingered bank notes. And what idealism! But I venture that he will not really, now that I am gone, hie him to Spain to fight the Falangists.[1] No matter. The truth is I do not love him. By now you know my dark secret. I want a man like you, Carlton—strong, intelligent, and unfamilied. Probably I want you. And, alas, the shadow of that forbidden desire falls over all my suitors. Why else do the men here seem as insipid and caramel-sweet as our product?

You asked about the family. The father of Hope's firstborn (due in late July, a sweaty labor) has manfully stepped forward, Charles Moore, son of a Virginia tobacco-man. Do not consult your Dun & Bradstreet[2] or other directories. Charles and Daddy became quickly if wordlessly reconciled by sharing an all-night bourbonic stupor. Mother continues to say that Hope and I have good blood and will eventually find ourselves. Where, Mother? Amid the quaint transformations of these southern nights, when we apple-cheeked Alabama virgins become roiling ladies in our husbands' stews? Anyway Hope and Charles have been married in a quiet (not to say secretive) ceremony at home by old Judge Lyle, without benefit of clergy, who preferred to remain aloof from the stain of this premature conception.

Shall I explain to Hope and Charles, her mental equal, how nature arranges these things in the unlikely eventuality that they wish to exercise some control over future occurrences? No. Because in the arcane recesses of my thorny heart I envy her.

Jack, my only true love, is sold and the money has gone into our

1. Right wing political party. **2.** Directory of financial standing.

Hope chest along with my works of hands and nights as the recent Mrs. Albert Hough.

Dear Essie, felicitations on the occasion of your reaching the quarter-century mark. And still alive! By what miracle of inner strength? Neither thrown to your death by the fiery stallion, nor swept away by the raging Black Warrior, nor immolated by alien tribes beyond the pale, nor lost questing for love through our torrid regions. Indomitable Essie! You are my epic. But do not imagine (do you know that I am forty?) that you suffer a fatal incestuous passion. That kind of junk only happens in bad southern novels. E.g., distraught niece succumbs to passion beyond reach of volition, confronts uncle with her towering desire, uncle's desire does not tower reciprocally because he has, alas, been emasculated by an overbearing father; finale: hopeless embrace and tears. No parts for a noble pair like us in that tawdry drama!

I have written Hope and congratulated her on the birth of Joel. The wire came yesterday. I have also bidden Sister Martha to accept all. Even in the worst of depressions, especially in the worst of depressions, nobody is going to stop smoking.

II

In 1939, when the war came to Europe, Sarah joined the Red Cross and went to England. During the Battle of Britain in 1941, she wrote from London.

. . . I have seen a terrible image in the ruins of the cathedral at Coventry,[3] Carlton. It was my body. I was charred, laid out, crucified, ruined, not three feet of me still standing erect. All my precious chalices and flagons melted down for easy transport, thieves' goods. I tried to soothe myself, saying: "There will be a resurrection. It's only your own ravaged past you have lost in the ruins here, you shallow egocentric." But it was not so. I saw us all there, all of us in this war I mean. One body would fit that blackened bed as well as another. Because I have seen under my hands too many broken bodies, Carlton, and my body under too many hands. Write me, learned uncle, who must I read to plumb this dark relationship between sex and war? Schopenhauer? Freud?[4]

When the war comes to America, don't you dare volunteer for anything. If I do not have you to come back to, I will die.

In 1944 Carlton wrote to Sarah, who was still in London.

Martha and Hope asked me to write you and tell you that Charles was killed in Normandy last month, several days after the invasion. Poor Charles, I saw him only the once, shortly before he went overseas. I never saw a man more certain of his death. We think

3. One of the first English cities to be heavily bombed in World War II. **4.** Arthur Schopenhauer, German philosopher (1788–1860) and Sigmund Freud, psychoanalyst (1856–1939).

that only the brave go toward the night with clairvoyant eyes. Our poets are in error. Simple Charles wore his death almost nobly, like a rare black flower on his breast. Finis.

Hope is not shattered. Martha is delighted with her role as grief-stricken mother, grateful to Charles for having the decency to get himself killed. Now her great hopes for her two beautiful daughters rise again. Do rise, Essie, like a phoenix, out of your ashes of Coventry. Come home and tell me, you my Nestor[5] now, what the meaning was that you discovered deep down in the eyes of the suffering. Here significance is occluded by boom, profits, power, and the approaching hysteria of victory.

Your father is drinking much less and working much more. The shop has a small government contract.

In 1945 shortly after V-J Day Sarah came home, the daughter, sister, niece seven years absent. She stayed in Tumwah about a month and then visited Carlton in New Orleans for a month. But before Sarah left for New Orleans, Hope wrote Carlton.

Mama told me to write you and tell you that we are depending on you to help Sarah. None of us can because she is too smart. What it amounts to is that all the suffering she saw has unsettled her. Dr. Thomas says many have come back this way. She shouldn't have stayed so long. You must be careful that she doesn't put on a courageous act for you because we know here that she is barely holding together. She lies awake at night and smokes and does not eat. She is thin as a rail. She won't see any of her old friends and she won't tell us anything that happened. Little Joel, who is bright for nine, says she looks like somebody who has come back from the grave. Little Joel is getting smart-alecky and generally out of hand. He needs a father and I am going to give him one, John Mullens, who is in roofing here. You might remember his daddy who played on the same team with Bully Vaught. Sarah doesn't know this because she doesn't take any interest in anything. She doesn't even know about Daddy's cancer and whether it is cured or just has remission. It takes two more years to tell. That is all our news. Sarah should be there before long. You are her favorite. In fact you are the only one she ever loved, though I would not tell that to Mama or Daddy. I hope you can help her.

III

So Sarah went to New Orleans. She spent a month with Carlton and then she went to San Francisco. From there she finally wrote him in early 1946.

Dear Carlton, I am finally settled in a small apartment near a park by the beach. I can see the ocean from my kitchen window. But I'm not writing to tell you about my life here except to say that I am

5. Oldest and wisest Greek in the Trojan War.

eating and that many hours of my sleep are at last dark and dreamless. I have not written before his because it has taken me a great while to digest that long month of talk, which I know was hell for you. Thank you. Maybe I will be able to do something for you some day, but I hope I never find you in that kind of need. You surprised me utterly. How could I have guessed that in New Orleans you were wrestling with the same thoughts that were destroying my sleep in London? And I was furious that you hadn't written to tell me, but when I saw how many nights it would take to say it all, I wasn't furious any more. That last sentence isn't quite accurate, is it? It didn't take so long to say it. Rather, it took a great while to find it there in the middle of all those words and then it took another great while to celebrate it, to dance around it. And then it took another little while to know that the dance was ended and it was time to part. I didn't share, there at the end, your exquisite sense of timing, Carlton. So you must forgive me for staying—what?—two days too long. I won't excuse myself by referring to all the old saws that establish the woman's greater passion for afterplay. And I won't apologize either for referring to our month as a sort of honeymoon. Because you will admit, Carlton, that there in the chaste and severe leather of your study, and surrounded by those great tomes of learning, we were lovers. You will admit that. Despite the perfectly unincestuous distance through which our words passed, we were lovers because our deeper bodies leapt out from us and clasped invisibly.

This is how it was. I came to you with a body so broken and bruised that I wanted to give it up, was in the process of giving it up. My Coventry cathedral, my charred ruin. And you kept asking me what I had seen. And I kept telling you about bodies wasted to the bone and about bodies hidden all in white except where the red and yellow suppurations appeared like little mouths crying out for love and about bodies with eyes in which the light slowly receded as if in a long tunnel and about how I would run down those black tunnels with my little nurse's torch of charity, but the dying light went too far and I always had to turn back. And I wondered, why is Carlton making me remember all these things? So I can die quicker? But when all the bodies were laid out in my mind's eye, you told me there is only one body. And you showed me how to see all of us as one great mole erected against the sea of death. And in that mole the bones and flesh constantly die and are born. The rote of the sea seeks out the dead, but the living cast the sea back. But in war comes death disproportionate. The mole begins to crumble and the shock of death runs through the whole body. That was what I felt, you said. But the war was over, you said, and the world's body was building. You said the sea of death would be pushed back and continents would touch like lovers. You said that for a while you, too, had wanted to die, but now you wanted to live more than ever, and I must live. At first I thought you were only a shallow optimist, for the tide of death was running hard in me. And then your words one by one began to stand up in me and staunch the flow. I felt them root in my bones and flourish in my blood until I conceived a little delta, barely a fingerlet, but I was reaching with you for another continent.

And now I don't ask myself, how did Carlton know how to save me? Because I know in that great mole of bodies our two lie contiguously, sharing, just as the old poems say, one heart in its temporary cage of ribs. And now I know that my poor little poem was to you, Carlton, my wise old cat with the deep green eyes, where all the lights that had fled me came back and glowed like verdant fire.

You said that everything that is given is restored sevenfold. It is true. Let me tell you how I feel now walking in the park. I feel like a virgin and a mother at the same time. I don't have any trouble understanding that old story. Obscenity and cynicism can never touch it. Do you see what I mean? Paradoxically your words have made me conceive. And that conception has closed all the old wounds and breaches. So, as the spring grows here, Carlton, I reach a kind of fullness. But whose hands can I trust it to?

I've read your letter dozens of times, Essie, and it has, as old Cousin Nan would say, warmed the cockles of my heart. The heat has risen up through every vein until my scalp tingles, as though your fingers were nested in my hair. But I cannot answer you in kind. Instead can we pretend that we both wrote your letter to each other? That it passes now perpetually from heart to heart like a quick-flying messenger-bird?

In my sleep the other night I saw you riding Jack by the bank of the Black Warrior. And suddenly I understood the meaning of your girlhood feats perfectly. But how could I have guessed then (when you were sometimes a beautiful girl, sometimes a sweaty raucous tomboy) that you were testing your strength, training arms, legs, lungs, and heart for that deep dive into the black waters of war. You have gone and come back, Essie. And you have brought us, my questing heroine, the only boon to be snatched from that wretched war—knowledge of the indestructible life at the center of everything.

IV

The forties passed into the fifties without striking news from Sarah. She tried several jobs with agencies specializing in the care of the poor or the mentally or physically handicapped. In her letters to Carlton she seemed to smile at herself, at this perhaps incongruous resurrection of the youthful idealism that had carried her off to England a decade before. She ended up as the receptionist in the office of a psychiatric clinic. "Here I sometimes take the disturbed by the hand, Carlton. I do not try to embrace them. I have learned the limits of my strength." But then in 1952 came news.

Dearest Carlton, this is the most difficult letter of all, bearing news of what must seem at first a defection. I thought that our invisible embrace in the russet air of your old study would be the last embrace of my life. And in a way it was. But I have found that I need to corporealize it. You will grant, Carlton, that if this is a failing it is more human than personal. I know you have the strength to go on alone. You remind me of Father Simms, the chaplain of the psychiatric ward here. He is so hirsute that the black hairs climb up above his white collar and burst from the sleeves of his cassock. He actually breathes with a sort of animal stertor, and not the strongest lotions can bury the odor of his sweat. I have to imagine that he has simian appetites. Smile if you like, but it seems to me that you two share that mysteriously ferocious celibate love of God, or whatever it is that the word of God stands for.

All of that is a kind of nervous, though true, introduction to a difficult declaration. Imagine, if my forty years will allow it, that I am a girl again sitting in your study drinking bourbon with fidgety hands and plucking smoke inexpertly from the end of one of your Chesterfields. I am trying to prepare myself to tell you that I am in love though I am particularly anxious not to use that debauched phrase. Imagine yourself bending toward me and soothing me with the wise light of your green old cat's eyes so that at last I can put away drink and cigarette, still my hands, and tell my story.

She came to our office several months ago. And though her troubles were endlessly complex, her fundamental need was simply love. I frightened her at first. My love growing six years since that month in your study must have seemed to her like some enormous and obscene yeasting. Here is how it was. I didn't recognize her when she came in, although I had seen her face on the jacket of her book, because she has to wear thick owlish glasses that discolor the flesh around her eyes and diminish the brown and black cores to tiny hollows. And yet I was not repulsed. In fact I went out strongly to those eyes. I was determined that they would not outrun me, as so many had in the war, to a place too dark for my courage. Later, when I found out who she was, the poems confirmed my intuition. But it is important that you understand that I knew her *essentially* before I knew her name, before I reread the book. Because I am not in love with a book.

There is no need to recount the small revelations and discoveries, the accidental meetings, the abrupt and embarrassed little exchanges, and then the long talks in which the words were less words than frail bridges of feeling bearing the two of us over dark waters. No courtship was more ordinary. I was the gallant and she the coy mistress. But, Carlton, I cannot describe for you our embrace. Unless every word were perfectly precise, every phrase as supple and warm as twined lovers' limbs, it would be a kind of breach of faith. And I haven't that power with words. But I address a prayer to you, Carlton, or perhaps through you, as I did in my old poem and have many times since. It is this. Because you are bigger and wiser in love, hold the two of us in your hand. Breathe upon us. Keep us warm. Because if this embrace grows cold, as in my marriage, as in the many wayward bestowals of my war-torn body, I do not think even you could snatch me from the sea again.

It is good that I have found her, Carlton, or else the new war might have cast me down, but she reaffirms for me your great thoughts of six years ago. She is my continent, all I can grasp, while you reach across the seas and perhaps across the skies to new planets. You are our loving giant, Carlton.

It is good, too, that the news from home is so bright—Daddy's cancer gone, business booming, Mama a burgeoning grandmother and pillar of the community, Hope and John breeding like rabbits for a future that needs all the life it can get. You were right, Carlton. The war that killed so many only confirmed in this curious species of ours its furious will to live, and this new war will not hurt so deeply So you see, even a maimed war victim like me, thanks to you, can reach out for her tiny share of the new love. I send you my love's book. Write me, Carlton, reach to me across the continent, for my love is yet a little in suspense, waiting for your nod, the wise wink of your green eye.

Carlton read Sarah's lover's book of poems, which was entitled Amyster, *Amyster being an imaginary horselike animal, lover, and alter ego. He sat down immediately to write Sarah. But the letter which he began with passionate heat he did not finish. Instead he mailed another. These are the two.*

Dear Essie, your letter was never so difficult as mine, for I must tell you that I have read *Amyster* and I am in great fear. These things are not so much poems as they are plunges into chaos. And this animal of hers is not so much a Pegasus as it is a Minotaur. And so far as I can see she is lost in the labyrinth. No, my own metaphor (or is it hers?) fails me. Because sometimes it seems that she herself is the Minotaur—those passionate descriptions of smoking gobbets of human flesh. They are not the necessary purgative images of a war-torn world, they are the wild bacchantic paeans of anthropophagi. No, Essie, I do not think you can be Theseus, or Ariadne to her Theseus,[6] or whatever in God's name she is and needs. No metaphor can hold her. How can you? Her own poem cannot give shape to her mind. Once I helped you, held you, you said, when you had

6. Ariadne gave Theseus the thread by which he escaped the labyrinth. Later he deserted her.

fallen into the pit. But you cannot help her similarly. She *is* the pit. . . .

Dear Essie, before I express my great joy in your new love, I have to take a moment, in mid-embrace, to subject you to a most gentle avuncular chiding. Hold your love in suspense for me? You know that everything dear to you is dear to me. In fact your letter and *Amyster* shower me with such varied treasures that I cannot as yet sort them. Again, as in the war, you have run ahead of me to new vistas. Wait for me. Better yet, come back and give me your hand, by which I mean write often, keep the sky bright with our heart-to-heart messenger-birds.

But Carlton received after this only short notes which explained their brevity as a consequence of the demands of clinic and apartment. "You would laugh to see me, Carlton. I am a caricature of the mid-century husband dutifully dashing between home and work, too prosperous and optimistic to need goals, but I do need a kind word from my wise old green-eyed cat." The kind word, however, was not answered, nor a subsequent one. Instead a letter came from Hope.

Dear Carlton, I don't know how I got to be the family correspondent, but here I am again. First, we're all very proud of you. Senior Partner in the best law firm in New Orleans! And old man Carter down at the *Bugle* got us a copy of the *Times-Picayune* with the big marine-disaster case you won against Gulf, because he knew you wouldn't send it yourself. When are you going to come and see us? We want to see you and we love you, but I won't lie about it: we want to show you off, too. Daddy is retiring next fall and some are planning a little festivity to mark the occasion. You can't say no to that. Mama says I'm to be very firm. It will be in October when it cools off. It's already getting hot. It's hotter every summer if you ask me. John says it's an effect of the bomb. Anyway mark your calendar.

But the real reason I wrote, Carlton, is not the good news. We called Sarah last night to wish her happy birthday, and something is wrong. Some woman answered the phone and said that Sarah was sick and that she was taking care of her. Sarah couldn't come to the phone, she said, but she wouldn't say what was the matter with her. The woman sounded like Billy-Goat Gruff. I wouldn't want her near me if I was sick. So we're suspicious. It's not like Sarah to refuse to answer, and I know she was there because I heard her say something in the background. So she's not in the hospital. I have a nightmare of one of those crazy people she works with getting hold of her. Anyway, we think you ought to call her on the telephone. Incidentally, I tried to call you, but couldn't get through. That's why I'm sending this air-mail special-delivery. I didn't know you were that big of a shot, Carlton. Anyway, if Sarah is in trouble again, you're the only one that can help her, as always. And please let us hear right away what you find out. Mama and Daddy are worried sick, though Sarah doesn't ever seem to think about that.

John and all my boys are fine.

Carlton flew immediately to San Francisco. Two days later he reported to Hope by phone that he had Sarah in the hospital under the best care available, after a nervous breakdown. A few days later he wrote a letter.

Dear Martha, Hope, and Colin. Tomorrow I am flying back to New Orleans. Essie's recovery, though it will take time, is now assured. The doctor's judgment and mine concur in this. So we can all take a deep breath and relax. But I will confess to you that I was frightened, because she would not talk to me for several days and was in a state of extreme physical debilitation. The doctor, however, says that it was probably not as close as it seemed, because Essie has vast reserves of strength which are beginning to show themselves now in the form of a firm new grasp on life. So she is on the way back. Martha, you mentioned on the phone the possibility of flying out. The doctor forbids it. I know that's painful for a mother. Perhaps my groping explanations that follow will help.

Essie has been on a long quest for love. She did not find it with Albert, as you know, because Albert's boorishness alienated her. She could not find it with you at home because love of family is not enough. And I, though we have had a few fine long visits, did not do well by her either, busy as I have always been with my work. All of this does not mean that we should heap our heads with ashes. In fact at this point Essie needs our love and understanding, not our regrets. But to go on.

In London once again Essie did not find love. I am sure she did not expect to, there amid all the bombings, the rubble, and broken bodies. But nevertheless she came back broken herself, as you saw. Then in San Francisco she steadied herself and got the job at the clinic, where everybody loves her to the point of idolatry. But that kind of love is not enough either. So a while back she began to see a brilliant poet somewhat younger that she. It looked as though it was going to work out, but finally it did not. That is what cast her down—yet one more failure of love.

There is no doubt, as I said, that Essie will recover completely. But she will still have her old need for love. And what must we do? Here is my advice to all of us. (Pardon me for offering it unasked.) First, of course, not a word of reproach of any kind. Shower her with love and good wishes. Invite her home, but do not insist on it. And I would not put too much emphasis on Colin's retirement festivities lest she feel compelled to attend before she has her strength back.

But you can depend on my coming, Colin, shipwrecks be damned, to lay claim to my share of the bourbon and Brunswick stew and to celebrate your honorable career.

On the Fourth of July 1954 Carlton wrote the following letter to Sarah.

Dear Essie, I have here in my study your fine and lucid letter of the 25th of last month written in your own firm hand at the desk in your new apartment overlooking the bay. I have called Dr. Temple to ask her permission, as you suggested, to write you the full account, which you request, of my experiences with Amyster. I have permission and now I have a holiday. So I in my turn sit to paper here at my desk, make abeyance to Mnemosyne and Justitia,[7] and begin. Headnote: I call her Amyster whenever I have to name her as a way of reminding you that your old rationalist uncle had an encounter not with a young woman of ordinary appellations but with a mythical being, and as a way of paying tribute to the courage and strength you must have had to live with that extraordinary being for two long years.

You must begin by understanding, Essie, that I came to San Francisco with my mind absolutely closed and a plan already laid out. I had always kept from you my true feelings about Amyster's poetry. From the very first it seemed to me absolutely frenzied, and (I think I said in a letter never mailed) even cannibalistic. When the second volume, *Woeman*, appeared with its gashed pages of dismembered images, and when I could recognize your poor body strewn in that wreckage more chaotic than any war's, and when you did not send me a copy, my heart was divided between hope and terror. On the one hand I hoped that you had seen Amyster for what she was and had freed yourself. On the other I feared that she had eaten you up and was vomiting you piecemeal in her poems. Forgive the horrible pun, the horrible image, but they are necessary to convey the revulsion I felt.

So when, after your long silence, I got Hope's letter telling of your illness, I went into high gear as only a compulsive legalist can. I arrived at your apartment with writs, injunctions, law officers, and court medical observers enough to snatch you away from ten Amysters. Thus is law, in this world, superior to myth. And though I try to keep the tone light, Essie, I am serious when I say that we must thank the law, for if I had been forced to face her nakedly, divested of my legal powers, I might very well have failed you. For one thing the ambiguous look you gave me from your sick bed might have undermined my resolve. Your eyes from the deep well of your suffering welcomed me, but they also seemed to say that I had no right to intervene—moral right or psychological right—but I had

7. Goddesses of memory and of justice.

my legal rights and I stood on those. So my gentlemen in white jackets whisked you away in a stretcher—hardly the right image for the rescue of the towered beauty by her prince charming. And Amyster was wise enough to retreat to higher ground. In fact she had not quite known what to do herself, she said, and was, though a bit ashamedly, glad that someone else had made a decision. She found it less agreeable that she was simultaneously being evicted from the apartment, and less agreeable still that she could not have her possessions until you returned to make division in the presence of an officer of the court. The locks, I told her, would be changed. Thus, Essie, I made her drink to the dregs my bitter legal prescriptions. She left with great dignity, promising that we would reunite under better circumstances. I thought not, having instructed hotel and hospital to reveal my whereabouts to no one. But she found me, and when you were clearly out of danger, I consented at last to meet her, agreeing on a neutral time and place, my hotel lounge at two. Our colloquy, my trial by combat with the mythical monster for the bound maiden, took almost three hours, the three longest hours of my fifty-seven years. And so desperate was the struggle that it seems to me the issue is still in doubt. You must be the final judge of that. But I am getting ahead of myself.

She came off the street in a long green gown and a white silken blouse that turned opalescent in the curious lighting of the lounge. She had pearls in her ears. And when she sat down across from me and took off her glasses, she was so extraordinarily beautiful that it almost took my breath away. To protect myself, I said inwardly: "The beauty is all my Essie's, veritably leeched from her flesh by this monstrous succubus." But what had I done except to impale myself even deeper on the paradox that already was bleeding away my courage—I mean that my love for you and your love for her were horribly entwined in her seductive person.

She began speaking in that undulant voice you have known so well—Lotus-eater, Siren, Nixie.[8] And I thought: How utterly is this not Amyster, not Woeman. But I did not know whether it was a true alternate self or a purely theatrical concoction. I will tell you my judgment of that later. So I was desperately afraid of her, but I had wisely brought with me, as a talisman, a powerful belief. This is what it was: that whatever power of words, profession of love for you, sweet moisture of eye she might produce, her essence was the ravening void, and because of that void even I, weak and tremulous as I was without my legal armor, was ultimately stronger than she—a proposition sorely to be tested.

Essie, you know us legalists, how we mercilessly demand of our

8. In Homer's *Odyssey* those who ate lotus forgot home and duty. Sirens lured mariners to their destruction. Nixies are water spirits in German folklore.

witnesses microscopic accuracy of image, word-for-word rendering of all that was said, etc. But here am I, unable to record verbatim more than a small fraction of what she said to me, and mistrustful of my recollection of all I saw. Perhaps my victory over her still seems to me so narrow and uncertain that I cannot with equanimity push my memory back into the rhythms of that remarkable voice. But I will try, where I can.

She began by saying that you had let her be everything for you. She was the child you never had, "conceived by the Word." And because of this virgin birth she sang meticulously of things still hidden in the bowels of earth. "I am her inner eye, her secret spelunker. All the tunnels of the war-torn body which frightened Nurse Sarah I have explored with unflickering candle." And then she had risen up and was the light-handed husband you never had and the father, too, you never had and the mother. "In the absolute dark, of unindividuate being we lie twined indissolubly. In the morning we release a butterfly of self onto the streets of the city and call it back at night to the woven core of our love which our hearts never leave." And this was her profound pun, that the poetry which rose from your twined being made the universe. And she said a great deal more in this line. Does it sound chaotic and farfetched here on my paper? You will know how to recast it, recapture its marvelous melody. And you will understand that when at last she finished this long paean, it seemed to me that the words I had planned to speak would be nothing more than a kind of floating ash blown across her beauteous vision as from an alley fire. But speak I must. "Between the vision and its incarnation fell the shadow of death. How do you explain that?"

She lit a cigarette, the fire orange and the paper purplish in that silly light of the lounge. But such was the ambiance of her presence that even that frightened me, as though she had power to skew the spectrum. As it turned out, my single thrust had sunk deeper than I knew. But at the moment I feared I was lost. Remember, I had chosen the lounge as a rendezvous because it was a public place demanding certain proprieties. But her opening speech had altered everything. The bartender and the meager midafternoon clientele seemed to me as removed as if they were projections, on clever translucent screens, of personages who in reality were in other places, perhaps other times. Thus we were utterly alone, beyond call of ordinary mortals.

She wished to hurt no one, she said, in a vastly altered tone, much more ordinary, to my relief; but I would soon learn that she had only climbed down from one poetic pinnacle to ascend another even more dizzying and terrible. She wished to hurt no one, but it was necessary to characterize the counterforces that worked against your happiness. "What was it that drove the child, like a homuncular Lear, out into thunderstorms?" (I had forgotten that curiosity of your childhood, Essie, forgotten that old Bessie once told Colin you were a changeling, a witch's child.) "Why did she ride wild Jack, embrace the swollen river, enter into combat against men, lay herself down in a loathsome marriage bed, and finally plunge into the hellfire of war? Because an older generation of child-eaters sent her on impossible missions in the hope of destroying her. But the subtlest of these conspirators, breathing on her his poisonous breath summer after slow summer, old serpent of the Mississippi, was an incestuous lover. This one wooed her with his 'messenger-birds,' birds that dipped their beaks in her heart's blood so that she could not love another." (So you had shown her my letters, Essie, as was proper—lovers should share everything.) But even the subtly amorous letters, she said, were not as wicked as my cunning sallies against other lovers. "For one poor lover he created the image of the labyrinth and set her down in the middle snorting and horned. And who but the incestuous one could play the hero of that scene, could follow the thread spun of the spittle of his own constant palaver?" In short, against such a family of death-dealers, the last one in particular, your vigilance had momentarily lapsed, a poisonous barb had pricked your heart, and you had sickened. In the hospital you were reasonably safe, but when you came out you would be vulnerable again. You would need her. Essie, I was stricken speechless. That image of the Minotaur I had once written to you but never mailed, and yet she had ferreted it out. Telepathy, divination, what? But she had thrown over me a shadow even deeper than the possibility of extrasensory powers, a shadow that cast everything beyond the table into a ghoulish gloom. All I could see was her face and beneath it the opalescent blouse like an image of unearthly light on ruffled water. The dark lips were saying: "Beware the green-eyed monster." And in my heart I was crying out to you: Essie, tell me quickly, did I imprison you in my affections? Never so unwilling a jailor, never one so anxious to give up the key. But you were not there to answer, and the dark lips were saying: "You always kill the thing you love." In another moment she would have taken you from me. I do not know what she would have done, what words would have passed. I only know I could feel you almost physically passing from me to her waiting embrace. So I had to speak. I said, "Yours is the ultimate sterility. Sweaty straining without issue. Endless naming of nothing to name, the animals in flight and the flowers rank. Words, words, words."

No, I did not ignite the air, did not exorcise that beautiful pearly face. It still hung there before me like a lamp of the moon. But my speaking gave me a little hope. I shut my eyes. I saw your hand, warm and still there on the hospital sheet where the sunlight lay boldly in a wide swath. I reached out and touched you. Then Amyster began to speak again. I opened my eyes. Her dark lunar lips eclipsed my sun. My soul, hunkering there in the shadows like a fear-frozen hare, shuddered. I can never forget those words. "You are going to instruct me in the arts of creation? Do you know who I am?" God knows I did not, Essie. Do not now. If she had said I AM THAT I AM, I could not have contradicted her. "I will tell you. I was born of earth, became a creature of the middle air, and later plumbed the bowels of my mother. In a moment I will show you the future. But, first, the past. One time when I was flying over the deserts of my childhood, I saw a black river, and beside it a beautiful rider on a white horse. I knew that someday the two of us would sit that stallion together and ford that stream." She is mad, I said to myself. But the words scraped about in my head like November leaves. "So when the time came I did my mating dance by the side of the road down which our warriors returned, because my mother told me my lover would be among the wounded. I crowed and danced such a madcap coxcomb's song as only my blackwater whitehorse rider could love—not knowing then that her left ear was stoppered with your chastely incestuous spittle." I must have winced. She reached out and touched me. I feared that hand on mine, but it seemed, to my great surprise, as warm as the one I had imagined lying on the sunny hospital sheet, and human. "That was only an aside. So when my lover came to me naked upon a white horse, we rode together across the black river and made on the other side such singing and wild whooping that the shades rose up and praised us. And we have mounted together into the sky and sung such ecstasy that the moon blushed. But all of this has only been a prelude to the time we ride into a white fire and consume each other utterly. And even that is only a prelude. We will rise again, a phoenix, flame and feather indistinguishable. And what flight could we not make after that?"

I was lost, Essie, blown on the wind of her words like dry husk toward an autumn flame. The barkeep and his trade posed motionlessly in the purple light that shone from behind the velvet valance—Amyster's Wax Museum of time past, my time, I as motionless as they. Well, twice before I had managed to speak. But this time there was not the slightest hope. I was a null. If I had opened my mouth I could not even have made that mouselike chittering which they say the souls of the dead make as they are ferried across. So I was lost, you were lost. You were hers. And then, the treasure hers for the taking, she cracked.

Maybe, paradoxically, it was the very frozenness which her words had created in me that defeated her. Maybe she thought she saw in my atrophied face stony stoicism, immovable opposition. At any rate her lips began to quiver. Her chest heaved and she began to weep. My senses came back to me. I saw the figures at the bar move and heard them make a burred noise. I smelled tobacco smoke and tasted the flat scotch on my tongue. The rug thickened under my feet and the cold slickness of the tabletop pressed itself against my fingers. So I was saved, because I was merely a ludicrous fat old man, sitting uncomfortably in a cocktail lounge beside a weeping younger woman. What tawdry images must have been in those turned heads at the bar! But Amyster began to recover herself. Her eyes crisped. I do not know what further flight she was capable of. I shudder to think, because I could not have survived it. I seized her hand and spoke to her. I said that she was an absolutely remarkable person, not remotely like any other I had ever known. But in another way, I said, I knew her of old. She was the demon lover of the old stories. In that mythic world she had her way with me. I gave her the victory without quarrel. I was the pompous avuncular adviser, fat and ineffective. But in this world the victory was mine. To wit, I was a rich man, I said, with many resources, all of which I would willingly array for the winning of your life and health. Therefore I had set people to watch. If I should learn that hereafter she ever approached you, even fleshlessly by letter or phone, I would build up around her such a legal, and if necessary extralegal, maze that she would never find her way out. In short let her keep to her haunts of the other world, where she had sway, for in this my vigilance wreathed around you a loving cordon impenetrable. I would like to think, Essie, that at that moment my leaden eyes recovered something of that green flashing which you have sometimes, perhaps only flatteringly, attributed to me. This I do know. She withdrew her hand and shrank away from me, down into that lair of the other world, where I did not dare to follow. Perhaps I only imagined it, but it seemed that she actually bared bright teeth. Amyster, I called after her, it is enough that you have invaded our dreams and stolen away our nights. It is more than enough that some ultimate day we will turn a corner, enter a door, and find ourselves again in your den, and this time without escape. But in the meantime, for whatever little time, I will have my days and my Essie will have hers. That is what I said and struck the table with my fist. So I was the secular judge of that day, Essie. And I will not yield to the judges of the underworld until I am forced to.

You will want to know of course, Essie, the precise facts which lie behind the threats I cast in Amyster's teeth. All were true. Private detectives in my hire watch you and watch her. Lawyers retained by me stand ready at my signal to prepare charges against her. The only falsification in my threats was one of omission, as you will already have surmised. That is, I stand ready to disband all of these adjutants when you advise me, for I have great hope that with Dr. Temple's help you are building up strength and wisdom which will stand proof against any revisitation of Amyster, whatever form it might take.

Well, Essie, I have filled much paper. My hand is cramped. Take it in your warm grasp. All of its recent deeds, well or ill performed, were lovingly done, for our old love's sake.

Dearest Carlton, now I fear the scales never can be balanced. You were always kind enough to say that I rode out to war for you and that you would have to spend a lifetime repaying me. But in truth, as I suspect you have always known, I rode out for myself, selfishly, compelled to explore that horror. But you rode out against Amyster for me. Yes, for me. I say it humbly, knowing nevertheless that nothing else could have tempted a wise one like you to challenge that darkness. So I remain eternally in your debt. I do not hope to repay you, because to do so I would have to find you in desperate need. So all I can do is say thank you.

I have read and reread your letter. Dr. Temple and I have made it the subject of several sessions. We agree that it does not matter that the Amyster I knew and the one you confronted are not quite the same. How could they be? The fact is that you saw deeply and acted correctly. However, in the heat of writing that marvelous letter, you left two questions unanswered. (Or did you, my sly old cat, leave those two little barbs, little knaps[9] a-purpose? Dr. Temple thinks you may indeed have been so ingenious, for they are, from her point of view, *the* questions.) Was Amyster acting out real alternate selves or was she putting on pure theater? I think that I myself would have said the former. But Dr. Temple has pretty well convinced me (remember A. was once her patient too) that the truth lies somewhere in between. A. was essentially unformed. I tried to give her form, but I couldn't. So she was forever, in life and in poetry, trying new possibilities. Gide,[1] incidentally, was a great hero of hers. But I was too weak to sustain her multiplicity. I began to lose my grip and go under. Now, you will be happy to know, I am back at work, only with a difference. Dr. Temple says that my experiences and insights are too valuable for the front office. I have become a "case recorder." I actually observe sessions and discuss results with Dr. Temple.

The other question you left hanging you will already have guessed the answer to. Did you really win the battle with A.? Of course you did. I have never seen her or heard from her again. She has not even shown up to get her clothes. Dr. Temple's prediction is that one day

9. Raps given as reminders. **1.** André Gide (1869–1951), French writer.

I will receive a letter which will tell of a new lover and a new book. It will be full of soft spite. And then a few years later, says Dr. Temple, we will read of her suicide. No one can handle so much chaos for very long. But I join you, Carlton, in your tribute to her. In fact I extend it. Not only does she possess our nights and our dreams and await us in death, she is, more than I ever was riding to war or you ever were riding against her, the ultimate rider against the night, the ultimate deep-river diver. Carlton, you remember I once wrote that I could not survive a parting from her, that if it happened you would not be able to pull me back from the sea of death. Yet I do seem to have survived. Here is how—and Dr. Temple knows it. A part of me rides with her yet, down the dark tunnels behind the bruised eyes of those who come to us too broken and loveless to go on alone.

Dr. Temple is a kind and clever old witch. Of course you can go to Tumwah next month, she says. I can get along without you for a few days. As though my own health were not in question. And perhaps it's not. But Tumwah at the moment seems to me such an alien place that it frightens me. Can I breathe the air there? Will I remember the language of my childhood? But you will be there, Carlton, to lend me your strong arm.

So in October of 1954 Carlton and Sarah joined the family and many of the townspeople of Tumwah to celebrate Colin's retirement. At Christmastime Hope sent out cards with a photograph of her four boys. On the one to Carlton she wrote a note.

Dear Carlton, what wonder you have done for Sarah. She looked like a queen. You looked like a Supreme Court judge (but not one of these new liberals) and she looked like a queen. Everyone said so. We were all so proud. Mama loved taking credit for having such a daughter who, she says, is practically running the most famous clinic in the West. But Daddy got tight and said something that made us all laugh. He said that it was clear to him that old Bessie was right. Sarah was not his and Mama's child. She was a foundling that Bessie brought in from the woods, left there by the royal witches, whatever they are. He said he wished he had made her tell the truth about it before she died. So you can see what a big thing it was the two of you coming. Out of room. All love. Hope.

V

A number of uneventful years passed. Sarah went on with her work at the clinic. Carlton in 1958 gave up his partnership and took a considerable financial loss to accept a seat as a federal judge. In a letter to Sarah he declared that he would not forget that the letter killeth and the spirit giveth life and that in court he would keep one eye on the law and the other on the future. In 1959 Carlton and Sarah returned to Tumwah for Colin's funeral. Martha, as widow, found it profoundly significant that he had died precisely at the biblical age of three score and ten in spite of having courted ruin and death at earlier ages. She herself would normally have two more years to live, but God had afflicted woman with longer life to punish her antics in the garden. The letters that Carlton, Hope, and Sarah wrote to each other were short and of settled affection. Even when in 1963 news came of the suicide of Amyster, there passed between Carlton and Sarah only gentle nods, as it were, of recognition and sad fulfillment. Then in 1965 Sarah wrote the following letter.

Dear Carlton, I have had occasion to look back over some of your letters. I'll tell you why in a minute. But first I have to ask pardon, my gentle judge, for a sin of omission. Do you remember that when you talked with A. she accused you of binding my heart with an incestuous love? You wrote in your account of the meeting that the accusation hit you so hard that you could not speak out to defend yourself. And I, unless I misremember, have never spoken of that in any letter since. Why was that? Perhaps I never wanted to deny the strength of my love for you under any circumstances, Carlton, even to exonerate us from incest. Well, I am not sure of my motives, but I am sure that you are blameless and that I ought to have said so long ago. Forgive me that omission. Before long I think I will know my motives and can report them to you. That is what I am writing to tell you, that at the age of fifty-three I discover, miraculously, that there are still two great adventures left to me. You have corrupted me with your flattering epic metaphors, Carlton. Suppose I tell you that I feel like Lord Alfred's Ulysses.[2] No, I am serious. After my spotted childhood, after my morbid marriage, after war, and after A., still two great adventures. One, of course, is death. The other I will already have embarked on by the time you receive this.

Some of the following is Dr. Temple's, some mine. We have talked so much that I can no longer distinguish. The surprising thing to me is that any of it (I mean aside from personal facts) is mine, that I have, as Dr. Temple constantly assures me, advanced her understanding of certain things. And now I am to be an emissary, as you said I was in the war. And I am to bring back understanding, as you also said I did from the war. I am going into my mind. But it is not only *my* mind. To begin another way. I have been dreaming again of Jack and the Black Warrior. I have been riding in the direction of the voice of someone who has gone before. It could be Daddy, or A. It is too distant to identify. And I always turn back. I lose courage. But, as Dr. Temple says, it is not only my white horse, my river, or my deceased loved one. In some

2. Poem by Alfred Lord Tennyson, British poet (1809–1892).

peculiar way my childhood and my adventures in the war and with A. and, yes, my love of you, Carlton, have tended to sum up in my mind this whole generation of fear. Are you wondering what exactly I mean by "this whole generation of fear"? Our generation, of course. But is it possible that our generation has summed up the whole history of man as brute? In that case, maybe what Dr. Temple and I are trying to do is plunge down past this brutal history to the deep place of light which, you always said, is the center of life. So we have arrayed our unheroic powers: my dreams, my old white horse, some crude potions from the pharmacopoeia of our time, and our strongest staff, Dr. Temple's wisdom and courage. Two aging and childless women in quest of nothing short of the omphalos.[3] What could be quainter, Carlton? And I am afraid, of course. But we will attempt it. We will keep a record, we do not know in what form—something I will write or say or sketch, or some combination. And you will see it all. Dr. Temple agrees to that.

So this is why I have been rereading your old letters, Carlton, to shore up my courage with the beams of your optimism. You were too modest when you wrote that you vanquished A. only in this world, that in the other she was the victor. In fact you pursued her very deep. No doubt I will meet her again. And perhaps this time I can snatch her up onto Jack and ride her to where her snakes are beautiful hair again. It is clearer and clearer to me that every act of mine is an extension of my love for you, Carlton. And all of your avuncular advice, which you used modestly to offer and humorously lament my ignoring, I have in essence taken. I take it now, searching for light. I ride my poor old Jack, saddlebags stuffed with your letters and love.

Immediately upon receiving this letter, Carlton sent Sarah a telegram. "Good-bye and Godspeed, Essie my love, who never waits for my valediction." He also wrote a note to Hope telling her that Sarah had embarked on a difficult psychological experiment and that she and Martha should not expect to hear from her for some time. But he himself did not have to wait long for news of Sarah. She and Dr. Temple were good to their word. In less than a week he began to receive typed transcriptions, fragments chosen by Dr. Temple from the various stages of Sarah's journey.

. . . I am writing a poem again. It is a lament for the body of my mother Martha standing naked by the little gas heater, drying before dressing for my father's funeral. Stomach creased, marsupial. Drooping dugs, withered bush. Broken blue veins match the flame behind. This open gas fire, they say, maddens. . . .

3. Point of origin, or central point of the world.

Here is my sister Hope floating on her back like a big-bellied island of easy entry. And here is my Uncle Carlton asleep in his chair like a big tom. His glasses are pushed up on his forehead where there are no eyes. Only I, the mischievous niece, know that behind the pale and veined lids burns the green entry of an endless tunnel. But I am not going to let old Bessie spank me, because I did not laugh at my father's funeral and because she stinks worse than a corpse and told stories on me. I am going to get on Jack and ride away. . . . You can tell when a horse is afraid of another beast. The ears quiver and the whinny is high-pitched. But I would not let Jack shy off the day we found the bull in old man Chrissum's second pasture. I made him jump two stiles. And we ran that bull until he could only stand smoking in the winter field. And I said, "Bull, if this was a sword instead of a crop, I would get down and kill you as nice as Manolete."[4] And I wrote a poem, too, about the bull which called attention to what has always been known, that a bull steaming in a winter field looks exactly like a cloudy continent. I gave the poem to my Uncle Carlton and he dropped it into his deep green eye, where it lies yet. The only thing I have not spoken of is the bodies that lie under the ground pierced by bullets and the mad old man who drew pictures of apple trees rotting in their hearts. I do not wish to speak of that. Let the earth have some secrets.

. . . This is one of the honey dreams. I can step slowly one two three. I can row slowly with my arms—stroke stroke stroke. But I will never get there against this tide. Is it the honey you put in my arm, doctor? I make a black shadow on the bottom, which hides all the little things. This is not going to work. I will not have a message for you when I get back. Everything down here is closed up tighter than a skin. What are the little things? Let me try to see. A path of white bones, leading to a skull, my Daddy's. A crab peeks out of the mouth. I do not know why but I am sure it is his. If I were a blind girl like that famous one I would know a face dead as well as alive. The fingers do not even have to enter the mouth. The other little things are my Uncle Carlton's green eyes. The honey does not allow me to bend over and peer down into them, but I know that they are laughing over my last poem. It is a wicked satiric poem. I got it out of my anthropology class. It is about old BM, M, M in Melanesia. About the maidens by the sea, by the sea, by the spermious sea. Rare but not unique, especially in certain foamy seasons, seasons, seasons for virgins to conceive. Do not under any circumstances show this to mother or father, say laughing Carlton's green eyes. No. But why did I, when the water was all my love, let Albert lay his pissy hands upon me, fill the sea with organ sounds,

4. Spanish bullfighter (1917–1947).

break the coral chapels? That was a poem, too, that your naughty niece wrote about second skins, Carlton, and never showed to you. . . .

. . . Two are up here I never expected to meet. One is Hope's Charles hunkered on the precipice. Sometimes he shifts his weight nervously from foot to foot and rotates his shoulders, but not the roaringest Andean wind of all our lives, Carlton, will ever bear this creature aloft. You said he could see far. Perhaps he can between the times the membranes and the fluids soup over his eyes. But what good is it to see and not be able to fly? You remember how you would not let me admire *I have slipped the surly bounds of earth on laugher-skittered wings?* I admire it still. The other is old Bessie sewing in the sun. I dance around her and tease her. You can't sew, Bessie, because you can't see to do it. Go away, child. You can't sew, Bessie, I can see the threads going ever-whichway. Go away, before I lay my hand to your bottom. I don't need that old dress anyway, Bessie. I'm going to fly away. No, you ain't. Not even a witch's child like you can fly. But didn't I fly, Carlton, on my laughter-skittered wings out of Bessie's reach? And later on Jack? And later didn't at least one or two of my poems mount up into your eyes? And later, didn't my letters join continents? Tell me I flew, Carlton, in spite of that old black woman. . . . Once I flew on the back of another, our lovely A., the longest dreaming of my life. Dark things can be high too, Carlton, and I knew she would be here with her great wind of words. They cannot drive her down. From the longest falls her defiance mounts up again. I do not even ask that she recognize me, dazzled by so many assaults on the sun. Because she already told me once: when you were just a little flower stalk of a girl making your slow way on Jack the first time down the river bank, your knees quivering against his flank and your arms trembling against the pull of the reins, I was already in you. . . .

Be sure to tell Carlton that, as only once before, I did not tell him quite all of the truth, that I was dying of cancer before we began—the little sea-bottom creature that has shuttled back and forth between Daddy and me for many years. It is fitting. We share what we can. . . . Who could guess? Wait. Father Simms once told me of one who believed the continuity of the inanimate, vegetative, and animate worlds. So I ought not to be surprised that mute stones still hold the scream and thunder of bombs. Put your ear to a conch shell and hear the roar of ocean. Put your ear to a stone of Coventry and hear the clangor of war. And do not tell me, my green-eyed uncle, that the sound is really behind my capped ear, that the war trills in my blood and clamors in my heart. I will write you a posthumous poem that you must publish to all, that the stones of graves must be chosen with the greatest care, examined by poets and paleontologists or we know not to what hells of din, from trumpeting mammoths to keening shells, we damn the dead. But how will I explain, Carlton, why the touch of all my doomed soldier-lovers hissed with a fire so beyond passion, even beyond love? Because some did think they loved me. The war had ignited them. Some, even before they were dead, floated around London like fox fires sporting the green glow of their putrescence. . . . Some cities lean against the sea, last projection of westering or eastering. Others, like mine, hold it in a mild embrace, calm its clamor and nest with it. That is the beginning of another posthumous poem which tells how a girl was raped by wild horsemen and thus had preview of the making of flesh. I already told who my child was, doomed in her green years like my consumed soldiers. This is the hardest way to follow, doctor, down into the fire, where she waits for me. I do not think I can tell it. I can tell you that the comical islanders and my sister at bridge tell it true, that the first one is a searing fire and the rest come teeming easily from the broken horn. But I do not want to lie to you. At first I did not have even an intimation that my lover was my child. I only knew the ecstasy of body when she came over me like a fiery-feathered thing. Here is where we ought to have been practicing those tricks of free drawing. I would choose a stylus varying in width according to the pitch of the hand. I would dip it in red ink and make such beautiful calligraphy and flourish that it would be the red-letter poem of all poems of love. You could read in it curling ecstasy, laced limbs, lovers' sighs like woven fires, and all else pertaining thereunto. . . . I am near the end, doctor, most fortunate in my double death. Drowning, see all past pass before me in an instant. Consumed by fire, know that the stars curve inward to consummate a second gathering. Tell Carlton, my green fire, that in my embrace I reconcile him to my red fire, that we three make a blanched and beautiful noon.

Once more Carlton used his legal powers in Sarah's behalf. Cowing courthouse, morticians, and family with complex claims of executorship, he had Sarah buried in a plain pine box in a stoneless grave, unbled and unembalmed, by the bank of the Black Warrior. In deference to the memory of Colin and to the feelings of Martha and Hope, friends of the family, brooking Carlton's eccentricity, walked the overgrown path to the grave in the mounting June heat to watch the clergyless noon burial and to hear the last words, of Carlton's own composing. "Here lies the body of Sarah, whose love for us we still see but through a glass darkly."

GABRIEL GARCÍA MÁRQUEZ

The Handsomest Drowned Man in the World[1]

A Tale for Children

THE first children who saw the dark and slinky bulge approaching through the sea let themselves think it was an enemy ship. Then they saw it had no flags or masts and they thought it was a whale. But when it washed up on the beach, they removed the clumps of seaweed, the jellyfish tentacles, and the remains of fish and flotsam, and only then did they see that it was a drowned man.

They had been playing with him all afternoon, burying him in the sand and digging him up again, when someone chanced to see them and spread the alarm in the village. The men who carried him to the nearest house noticed that he weighed more than any dead man they had ever known, almost as much as a horse, and they said to each other that maybe he'd been floating too long and the water had got into his bones. When they laid him on the floor they said he'd been taller than all other men because there was barely enough room for him in the house, but they thought that maybe the ability to keep on growing after death was part of the nature of certain drowned men. He had the smell of the sea about him and only his shape gave one to suppose that it was the corpse of a human being, because the skin was covered with a crust of mud and scales.

They did not even have to clean off his face to know that the dead man was a stranger. The village was made up of only twenty-odd wooden houses that had stone courtyards with no flowers and which were spread about on the end of a desertlike cape. There was so little land that mothers always went about with the fear that the wind would carry off their children and the few dead that the years had caused among them had to be thrown off the cliffs. But the sea was calm and bountiful and all the men fit into seven boats. So when they found the drowned man they simply had to look at one another to see that they were all there. That night they did not go out to work at sea. While the men went to find out if anyone was missing in neighboring villages, the women stayed behind to care for the drowned man. They took the mud off with grass swabs, they removed the underwater stones entangled in his hair, and they scraped the crust off with tools used for scaling fish. As they were doing that they noticed that the vegetation on him came from faraway oceans and deep water and that his clothes were in tatters,

1. Translated by Gregory Rabassa.

as if he had sailed through labyrinths of coral. They noticed too that he bore his death with pride, for he did not have the lonely look of other drowned men who came out of the sea or that haggard, needy look of men who drowned in rivers. But only when they finished cleaning him off did they become aware of the kind of man he was and it left them breathless. Not only was he the tallest, strongest, most virile, and best built man they had ever seen, but even though they were looking at him there was no room for him in their imagination.

They could not find a bed in the village large enough to lay him on nor was there a table solid enough to use for his wake. The tallest men's holiday pants would not fit him, nor the fattest ones' Sunday shirts, nor the shoes of the one with the biggest feet. Fascinated by his huge size and his beauty, the women then decided to make him some pants from a large piece of sail and a shirt from some bridal brabant linen so that he could continue through his death with dignity. As they sewed, sitting in a circle and gazing at the corpse between stitches, it seemed to them that the wind had never been so steady nor the sea so restless as on that night and they supposed that the change had something to do with the dead man. They thought that if that magnificent man had lived in the village, his house would have had the widest doors, the highest ceiling, and the strongest floor, his bedstead would have been made from a midship frame held together by iron bolts, and his wife would have been the happiest woman. They thought that he would have had so much authority that he could have drawn fish out of the sea simply by calling their names and that he would have put so much work into his land that springs would have burst forth from among the rocks so that he would have been able to plant flowers on the cliffs. They secretly compared him to their own men, thinking that for all their lives theirs were incapable of doing what he could do in one night, and they ended up dismissing them deep in their hearts as the weakest, meanest, and most useless creatures on earth. They were wandering through that maze of fantasy when the oldest woman, who as the oldest had looked upon the drowned man with more compassion than passion, sighed:

"He has the face of someone called Esteban."

It was true. Most of them had only to take another look at him to see that he could not have any other name. The more stubborn among them, who were the youngest, still lived for a few hours with the illusion that when they put his clothes on and he lay among the flowers in patent leather shoes his name might be Lautaro. But it was a vain illusion. There had not been enough canvas, the poorly cut and worse sewn pants were too tight, and the hidden strength of his heart popped the buttons on his shirt. After midnight the whistling of the wind died down and the sea fell into its Wednesday drowsiness. The silence put an end to any last doubts: he was Esteban. The women who had dressed him, who had combed his hair, had cut his nails and shaved him were unable to hold back a shudder of pity when they had to resign themselves to his being dragged along the ground. It was then that they understood how unhappy he must have been with that huge body since it bothered him even after death. They could see him in life, condemned to going through doors sideways, cracking his head on crossbeams, remaining on his feet during visits, not knowing what to do with his soft, pink, sea lion hands while the lady of the house looked for her most resistant chair and begged him, frightened to death, sit here, Esteban, please, and he, leaning against the wall, smiling, don't bother, ma'am, I'm fine where I am, his heels raw and his back roasted from having done the same thing so many times whenever he paid a visit, don't bother, ma'am, I'm fine where I am, just to avoid the embarrassment of breaking up the chair, and never knowing perhaps that the ones who said don't go, Esteban, at least wait till the coffee's ready, were the ones who later on would whisper the big boob finally left, how nice, the handsome fool has gone. That was what the women were thinking beside the body a little before dawn. Later, when they covered his face with a handkerchief so that the light would not bother him, he looked so forever dead, so defenseless, so much like their men that the first furrows of tears opened in their hearts. It was one of the younger ones who began the weeping. The others, coming to, went from sighs to wails, and the more they sobbed the more they felt like weeping, because the drowned man was becoming all the more Esteban for them, and so they wept so much, for he was the most destitute, most peaceful, and most obliging man on earth, poor Esteban. So when the men returned with the news that the drowned man was not from the neighboring villages either, the women felt an opening of jubilation in the midst of their tears.

"Praise the Lord," they sighed, "he's ours!"

The men thought the fuss was only womanish frivolity. Fatigued because of the difficult nighttime inquiries, all they wanted was to get rid of the bother of the newcomer once and for all before the sun grew strong on that arid, windless day. They improvised a litter with the remains of foremasts and gaffs, tying it together with rigging so that it would bear the weight of the body until they reached the cliffs. They wanted to tie the anchor from a cargo ship to him so that he would sink easily into the deepest waves, where fish are blind and divers die of nostalgia, and bad currents would not bring him back to shore, as had happened with other bodies. But the more they hurried, the more the women thought of ways to waste time. They walked about like startled hens, pecking with the sea charms on their breasts, some interfering on one side to put a scapular of the good wind on the drowned man, some on the other side to put a wrist compass on him, and after a great deal of *get away from there, woman, stay out of the way, look, you almost made me fall on top of the dead man,* the men began to feel mistrust in their livers and started grumbling about why so many main-altar decorations for a stranger, because no matter how many nails and holy-water jars he had on him, the sharks would chew him all the same, but the women kept piling on their junk relics, running back and forth, stumbling, while they released in sighs what they did not in tears, so that the men finally exploded with *since when has there ever been such a fuss over a drifting corpse, a drowned nobody, a piece of cold Wednesday meat.* One of the women, mortified by so much lack of care, then removed the handkerchief from the dead man's face and the men were left breathless too.

He was Esteban. It was not necessary to repeat it for them to recognize him. If they had been told Sir Walter Raleigh,[2] even they might have been impressed with his gringo accent, the macaw on his shoulder, his cannibal-killing blunderbuss, but there could be only one Esteban in the world and there he was, stretched out like a sperm whale, shoeless, wearing the pants of an undersized child, and with those stony nails that had to be cut with a knife. They only had to take the handkerchief off his face to see that he was ashamed, that it was not his fault that he was so big or so heavy or so handsome, and if he had known that this was going to happen, he would have looked for a more discreet place to drown in, seriously, I even would have tied the anchor off a galleon around my neck and staggered off a cliff like someone who doesn't like things in order not to be upsetting people now with this Wednesday dead body, as you people say, in order not to be bothering anyone with this filthy piece of cold meat that doesn't have anything to do with me. There was so much truth in his manner that even the most mistrustful men, the ones who felt the bitterness of endless nights at sea fearing that their women would tire of dreaming about them and begin to dream of drowned men, even they and others who were harder still shuddered in the marrow of their bones at Esteban's sincerity.

That was how they came to hold the most splendid funeral they could conceive of for an abandoned drowned man. Some women who had gone to get flowers in the neighboring villages returned with other women who could not believe what they had been told, and those women went back for more flowers when they saw the dead man, and they brought more and more until there were so many flowers and so many people that it was hard to walk about. At the final moment it pained them to return him to the waters as an orphan and they chose a father and mother from among the best

2. English navigator, statesman, courtier, and author (1552–1618).

people, and aunts and uncles and cousins, so that through him all the inhabitants of the village became kinsmen. Some sailors who heard the weeping from a distance went off course and people heard of one who had himself tied to the mainmast, remembering ancient fables about sirens.[3] While they fought for the privilege of carrying him on their shoulders along the steep escarpment by the cliffs, men and women became aware for the first time of the desolation of their streets, the dryness of their courtyards, the narrowness of their dreams as they faced the splendor and beauty of their drowned man. They let him go without an anchor so that he could come back if he wished and whenever he wished, and they all held their breath for the fraction of centuries the body took to fall into the abyss. They did not need to look at one another to realize that they were no longer all present, that they would never be. But they also knew that everything would be different from then on, that their houses would have wider doors, higher ceilings, and stronger floors so that Esteban's memory could go everywhere without bumping into beams and so that no one in the future would dare whisper the big boob finally died, too bad, the handsome fool has finally died, because they were going to paint their house fronts gay colors to make Esteban's memory eternal and they were going to break their backs digging for springs among the stones and planting flowers on the cliffs so that in future years at dawn the passengers on great liners would awaken, suffocated by the smell of gardens on the high seas, and the captain would have to come down from the bridge in his dress uniform, with his astrolabe, his pole star, and his row of war medals and, pointing to the promontory of roses on the horizon, he would say in fourteen languages, look there, where the wind is so peaceful now that it's gone to sleep beneath the beds, over there, where the sun's so bright that the sunflowers don't know which way to turn, yes, over there, that's Esteban's village.

3. In Greek and Roman mythology sirens were sea nymphs who lured mariners to their destruction.

GEORGE GARRETT

An Evening Performance

FOR several weeks, maybe a month or so, there she stood, a plump woman in a sequined one-piece bathing suit, poised on a stylized tower which rose into the very clouds, like Jacob's dreamy ladder, with here and there around it a few birds in tense swift V's, and below, far, far below, there was a tub, flaming and terrible, into which she was surely going to plunge. Beneath in fiery letters was printed: ONE OF THE FABULOUS WONDERS OF MODERN TIMES/ STELLA THE HIGH DIVER/SHE DIVES ONE HUNDRED FEET/INTO A FLAMING CAULDRON.

These posters had appeared mysteriously one Monday morning, and they were everywhere, on store windows, on the sides of buildings, on telephone and light poles, tacked to green trees; and you can believe they caused a stir. The children on the way to school (for it was just the beginning of the school year) bunched around them in excited clusters—staring at her buxom magnificence, wondering at her daring—and buzzed about it all day long like a hive of disturbed bees. By midmorning grumbling adults were ripping the posters down from windows and buildings, and a couple of policemen went up and down the main street and some of the side streets, taking them off telephone and light poles. But there were so many! And it was such a mystery. Lurid and unsettling as a blast of trumpets, they had come nevertheless in the night as silently as snow.

It would be later, much later, that the night counterman at the Paradise Diner on the outskirts of town, beyond the last glare of filling stations and the winking motels and the brilliant inanity of used-car lots—where, no matter how carnival-colorful with flags and whirligigs, no matter how brightly lit, the rows of cars stood lonesome like sad wooden horses from some carousel set out to graze—it would be later when he would remember that the man, the angry little man with the limp, had stopped there for coffee that same night that the posters had appeared.

In spite of all effort, a few of the posters remained, tantalizing in their vague promise of a future marvel, teased by the wind and the weather, faded by the still summer-savage sun and the first needling rains of autumn, the red letters blurring and dribbling away, fuzzy now as if they had been written by a shaking finger in something perishable like blood. Talked about for a while—and there were those who swore they remembered seeing such a thing and certainly those who had heard of it, a subject of some debate and even a little sermonizing in certain of the more fundamentalist churches, where amusement is, by definition, nearly equivalent to vice—the promise faded with the posters. There were few who hoped that Stella would ever dive there, fewer still who believed in her coming. It seemed, after all, only another joke of some kind, pointless, mirthless, and in a strange way deeply distressing.

Then one evening in late October with the weather now as cool and gray as wash water the truck came and parked in the field by the old Fairgrounds. At first it was nothing to take much notice of, merely a big, battered truck and pretty soon an Army surplus squad tent, sprouting (sagging in a most unmilitary, careless way) like a khaki mushroom beside it.

And there were people.

There were three of them. There was the man, gimpy (his left leg might have been wooden), his face puckered and fierce and jowly and quizzical like a Boston bulldog, his eyes glazed and almost lightless like the little button eyes of a doll; fierce and tired he seemed, spoke in mutters, showing from time to time a ruined mouth with teeth all awry and at all angles like an old fence; and sometimes around the town, shopping for groceries at the Supermarket, once taking a load of dirty clothes to the Washeteria, buying cigarettes and aspirins and comic books at the drugstore, and busily sorting out bolts and nuts and screws and clamps and brackets at the hardware store (for what?), he talked to himself, a harsh, steady, and indecipherable monotone. There was the little girl, a frail thing made entirely of glazed china with altogether unlikely eyes and hair as bright as new pennies, like a shower of money, richly brushed and shining and worn long to her waist. She wore white always, starched and ironed and fabulously clean; and the women had to wonder how her mother (?)—the woman anyhow—living in a sagging tent and a worn-out truck managed that. The little girl was heard to answer to the name of Angel and did not play with the other children who sometimes, after school, gathered in shrill clots around the tent and the truck to stare until the terrible man came out, limping, waving a pick handle, and chased them away.

The woman was an equal curiosity. She was short, broad-shouldered, wide-hipped, huge-handed, sturdy as a man. Her hair, dyed redder than you'd care to believe, was cut in a short bowl. She appeared to be in early middle age, though she might easily have been old—she wore such savage makeup, wild, accented, slanted eyes, a mouth of flame, and always two perfectly round spots of red like dying roses on her high cheekbones. Still, she had a smile that was a glory and she smiled often. She was not heard to speak to anyone and when she was talked to she smiled and stared, uncomprehending. It was not long before everyone knew she was a mute; it was proved when she was seen to communicate with the man, her hands as swift as wings and not a word.

The truth came out like a jack-in-the-box in a week or so. One fine morning the man had unloaded an enormous pile of boards and pipes beside the truck, and by noon he had erected in the center of the field what seemed to be the beginning of a good-size drilling derrick.

"For oil?" That was the joke around town before a few prominent men and a policeman went out there in cars, parked at the edge of the field, and walked to where he was working. He paid them no mind at all as they straggled toward him, and, as they drew near, they could see that he was sweat-soaked and working at his task with an unbecoming fury, all in hasty, jerky gestures like a comedian in a silent movie. He did not stop his work until they spoke to him.

"What are you trying to do here?" the policeman said.

The man spat and put his heavy wrench on the ground.

"What the hell does it look like I'm doing?" he said and someone giggled. "I'm putting up the tower."

"What kind of a tower?"

"The tower for Stella," the man said, sighing between his teeth. "How can she dive without a tower? That's logic, ain't it?"

"Oh," the policeman said. "You got to have a license to put on any kind of a exhibition around here."

The lame man lowered his head, seemed to shrink and sag like a slowly deflating balloon, and muttered to himself. Finally he raised his head and looked at them, and they could see the tears glisten in his eyes.

"How much do the license cost?" he said.

"Twenty-five dollars."

"We don't have to do the dive," the man said. "We got a lots of tricks. I can put up just a little bit of a trapeze and Angel can do things that would make your eyes pop out of your head. If worse come to worst we don't have to build nothing at all. If I have to I can stand on the back end of the truck and swallow swords and fire and Angel and Stella can dance."

"Any kind of exhibition costs twenty-five dollars for the license."

The man shrugged and hung his head again.

"Don't you have the money?"

He shook his head, but still would not look at them.

"Well, what the hell?" the policeman said. "You better take that tower down and get on out of town. We got a law—"

"Wait a minute," a merchant said. "You aim to sell tickets, don't you?"

The man nodded.

"If you put on the high dive, I reckon you may get as many as a thousand to see it, counting kids and all. What kind of a price do you charge?"

When the man looked up again, he had his ruined smile for them all. "Two bits a head," he said. "We got a roll of tickets printed up and everything."

The merchant made a hasty calculation. "All right," he said. "I'll tell you what I'll do. I'll get your license for you and you cut me in for half of what you take."

"*Half?*" the man said. "Half is too much. That's a dirty shame. It ain't hardly worth it for half. Besides, the high dive is dangerous."

"Take it or leave it."

"All right," the man said. "I can't do nothing but take it."

"Tell you what else I'll do," the merchant said. "I got a nigger boy helps me down to the store. I'll send him to help you put that tower up. How soon can you put on the show?"

"Tomorrow evening if the weather's good."

While they were standing there talking the woman had come across the field from the tent and stood holding the hand of the little girl, smiling her wonderful smile. She seemed to have not the least notion of what was going on, but as they walked away they saw that she had turned on the man, unsmiling, and as he shook and shook his head, her hands flashed at him like the wings of a wild bird in a cage.

All that day the tower grew and by noon of the next day it was finished. It stood not nearly so tall as the cloud- and bird-troubled structure on the posters, but menacingly high, a rickety skeleton that swayed a little in the light breeze. All the way to the top there was a rope ladder and on the top a small platform with an extended plank for a diving board. At the foot of the tower the lame man had created a large wooden and canvas tank into which he and the woman and the Negro who worked for the merchant poured buckets of water, drawn from a public spigot, all afternoon, until it was filled about to the depth of a tall man. There was a large GI can of gasoline nearby. The lame man rigged up a string of colored lights and two large searchlights intended to focus on the diver at the top. He set up a card table at the corner where the main road turned into the Fairgrounds. He put up a few of the posters on the poles and the side of the truck, and by midafternoon everything was ready.

Then the weather turned. The wind came from the north, steady, and with a thin rain like cold needles. The tower moved with the wind and shone with wet. The woman and the little girl stayed in the tent. The lame man stood at the card table, with a newspaper on his head to keep off the rain, waiting for the first customers to arrive.

Just at dark the merchant arrived. There was a good crowd, equal at least to their expectation, gathered in a ring around the tower, standing in raincoats and underneath umbrellas, silently waiting.

"Well," the merchant said, "it looks like we did all right irregardless of the weather."

"Yeah," the man replied. "Except she don't want to do it."

"What's that?"

"I mean it's too risky at a time like this."

"You should have thought of that before," the merchant said. "If you don't go through with it now, no telling what might happen."

"Oh, we'll give them a show," the man said. "I'll swallow swords if I have to. We'll do something."

"She's got to dive," the merchant said. "Or else you got a case of fraud on your hands."

After that the two of them went into the tent. Inside the woman was sitting on an Army cot, wrapped up in a man's bathrobe, and the little girl was beside her. It was cold and damp and foul in the tent. The merchant winced at the smell of it.

"Tell her she's got to do it."

The lame man waved his hands in deft code to her. She moved her hands slowly in reply and, smiling, shook her head. Outside the people had started to clap their hands in unison.

"She says it's too dangerous. It's dangerous anyhow, but on a night like this—"

"Come on," the merchant said. "It can't be that bad. There must be a trick to it."

The lame man shook his head.

"No, sir," he said. "It ain't no trick to it. It's the most dangerous activity in the world. She don't like to do it one bit."

"That's a fine thing," the merchant said. "Just fine and dandy. If she don't like it, why the hell do you put up posters and build towers and sell tickets, that's what I'd like to know."

"Somebody's got to do it. If it wasn't us, it would just have to be somebody else."

"Oh my God!" the merchant said, throwing up his hands. "Now you listen here. If you don't get the show going in five minutes, I'll have you all slapped right in the jail. Five minutes."

He opened the flap of the tent and went out into the dark and the chill rain. He could hear the little girl crying and the lame man muttering to himself.

Almost at once the lame man followed him. He started up the truck and turned on all the lights. Then the woman appeared in her outsize bathrobe and wearing now a white bathing cap. She walked to the foot of the tower and leaned against it, one hand clutching a rung of the rope ladder, smiling.

"Ladies and gentlemen," the lame man said. "You are about to witness a performance that defies the laws of nature and science. This little lady you see before you is fixing to climb to the top of the tower. There, at that terrible altitude, she's going to stand and dive into a flaming tank of water that's barely six feet deep. You won't believe your eyes. It's a marvel of the modern world. 'How does she do it?' some of you will ask. Now some show people will give you all kinds of fancy reasons for how and why they do their work. They'll tell you they learned it from the wise men of the East. They'll tell you about magicians and dreams and the Secrets of the Ancient World. Not us. The way that Stella does this dive is skill, skill pure and simple. When Stella climbs that tower and dives into the flames she's doing something anyone could do who has the heart and the skill and the nerve for it. That's what's different and special about our show. When Stella sails through the air and falls in the fire and comes up safe and smiling, she is the living and breathing proof of the boundless possibility of all mankind. It should make you happy. It should make you glad to be alive."

"Let's get on with it," someone shouted, and the crowd hollered and whistled.

"All right, we won't give you no special buildup," the lame man continued in an even voice. "We just say, there it is. See for yourself. And without further ado I give you Stella, the high diver."

He touched her. She removed the bathrobe and, opening her arms wide, showed herself, pale and stocky in the tight bathing suit with the winking sequins. Then she turned and began to climb the rope ladder. It was a perilous ascent and the ladder swung with the weight of her. When she reached the top, she rested, kneeling on the platform; then she stood up and unhitched the rope ladder and it fell away in a limp curve like a dead snake.

The crowd gasped.

"Do you see?" the lame man shouted. "Now there's no other way to get down except by diving!"

He hobbled over to the tank and sloshed gasoline on top of the water. He stood back and looked up at her. She stood on the diving plank and looked down. The tower rattled and moved in the wind and she seemed very small and far away. She stood on the end of the plank looking down, then she signaled to the man. He lit the gasoline and jumped back awkwardly as the flames shot up. Just at that instant she dived. Soaring and graceful, her arms wide apart, she seemed for a breathless time to hang at that great height in the wind, caught in the brilliant snare of the searchlights. Then she seemed to fold into herself like a fan and straight and swift as a thrown spear she descended, plummeting into the tank with a great and sparkling flash of fire and water.

There was a hushed moment while the crowd waited to see if she was still alive, but then she emerged, climbed out of the tank smiling, and showed herself to them, damp and unscathed. She put on her bathrobe and hurried back to the tent. Some of the people began to leave, but many stood gazing at the tower and the vacant tank. The lame man switched off the lights and followed after her, disappearing into the tent.

The merchant entered the tent. The three of them, sitting in a row along the edge of the cot, were eating something out of a can. A red lantern glared at their feet.

"Is that all?" the merchant said. "I mean is that all there is to it?"

The man nodded.

"Kind of brief, don't you think, for two bits a head?"

"That's all there is to it," the man said. "She could have killed herself. Ain't that enough for one evening? They ought to be glad."

The merchant looked at her. She was eating from the can and seemed as happy as could be.

"Can't you swallow some swords or something? We want everybody to feel they got their money's worth."

"Goddamnit, they did!" the lame man said. "They got all they're going to."

The merchant tried to persuade him to do something more, but he continued to refuse. So the merchant took his share of the money and left them. Soon the rest of the people left too.

The next morning the three of them were gone. The tower was gone, the truck, the tent, and they might never have been there at all, for all the trace they left. Except for the dark spots on the grass where the flaming water had splashed, except for a few posters remaining (and they were not true to fact or life), there was no trace of them.

But if the evening performance had been brief, it remained with them, haunting, a long time afterwards. Some of the preachers continued to denounce it as the work of the devil himself. The drunkards and tellers of tall tales embroidered on it and exaggerated it and preserved it until the legend of that high dive was like a beautiful tapestry before which they might act out their lives, strangely dwarfed and shamed. The children pestered and fidgeted and wanted to know when the three would come again.

A wise man said it had been a terrible thing.

"It made us all sophisticated," he said. "We can't be pleased by any ordinary marvels anymore—tightrope walkers, fire-eaters, pretty girls being fired out of cannons. It's going to take a regular apocalypse to make us raise our eyebrows again."

He was almost right, as nearly correct as a man could hope to be. How could he even imagine that more than one aging, loveless woman slept better ever after, smiled as she dreamed herself gloriously descending for all the world to see from a topless tower into a lake of flame?

WILLIAM H. GASS

In the Heart of the Heart of the Country

A Place

SO I have sailed the seas and come . . .
to B . . .[1]

a small town fastened to a field in Indiana. Twice there have been twelve hundred people here to answer to the census. The town is outstandingly neat and shady, and always puts its best side to the

1. Allusion to "Sailing to Byzantium" by William Butler Yeats, Irish poet, 1856–1939.

highway. On one lawn there's even a wood or plastic iron deer.

You can reach us by crossing a creek. In the spring the lawns are green, the forsythia is singing, and even the railroad that guts the town has straight bright rails which hum when the train is coming, and the train itself has a welcome horning sound.

Down the back streets the asphalt crumbles into gravel. There's Westbrook's, with the geraniums, Horsefall's, Mott's. The sidewalk shatters. Gravel dust rises like breath behind the wagons. And I am in retirement from love.

Weather

In the Midwest, around the lower Lakes, the sky in the winter is heavy and close, and it is a rare day, a day to remark on, when the sky lifts and allows the heart up. I am keeping count, and as I write this page, it is eleven days since I have seen the sun.

My House

There's a row of headless maples behind my house, cut to free the passage of electric wires. High stumps, ten feet tall, remain, and I climb these like a boy to watch the country sail away from me. They are ordinary fields, a little more uneven than they should be, since in the spring they puddle. The topsoil's thin, but only moderately stony. Corn is grown one year, soybeans another. At dusk starlings darken the single tree—a larch—which stands in the middle. When the sky moves, fields move under it. I feel, on my perch, that I've lost my years. It's as though I were living at last in my eyes, as I have always dreamed of doing, and I think then I know why I've come here: to see, and so to go out against new things—oh god how easily—like air in a breeze. It's true there are moments—foolish moments, ecstasy on a tree stump—when I'm all but gone, scattered I like to think like seed, for I'm the sort now in the fool's position of having love left over which I'd like to lose; what good is it now to me, candy ungiven after Halloween?

A Person

There are vacant lots on either side of Billy Holsclaw's house. As the weather improves, they fill with hollyhocks. From spring through fall, Billy collects coal and wood and puts the lumps and pieces in piles near his door, for keeping warm is his one work. I see him most often on mild days sitting on his doorsill in the sun. I notice he's squinting a little, which is perhaps the reason he doesn't cackle as I pass. His house is the size of a single garage, and very old. It shed its paint with its youth, and its boards are a warped and weathered gray. So is Billy. He wears a short lumpy faded black coat when it's cold, otherwise he always goes about in the same loose, grease-spotted shirt and trousers. I suspect his galluses were yellow once, when they were new.

Wires

These wires offend me. Three trees were maimed on their account, and now these wires deface the sky. They cross like a fence in front of me, enclosing the crows with the clouds. I can't reach in, but like a stick, I throw my feelings over. What is it that offends me? I am on my stump, I've built a platform there and the wires prevent my going out. The cut trees, the black wires, all the beyond birds therefore anger me. When I've wormed through a fence to reach a meadow, do I ever feel the same about the field?

The Church

The church has a steeple like the hat of a witch, and five birds, all doves, perch in its gutters.

My House

Leaves move in the windows. I cannot tell you yet how beautiful it is, what it means. But they do move. They move in the glass.

Politics

. . . for all those not in love.

I've heard Batista described as a Mason. A farmer who'd seen him in Miami made this claim. He's as nice a fellow as you'd ever want to meet. Of Castro, of course, no one speaks.

For all those not in love there's law: to rule . . . to regulate . . . to rectify. I cannot write the poetry of such proposals, the poetry of politics, though sometimes—often—always now—I am in that uneasy peace of equal powers which makes a State; then I communicate by passing papers, proclamations, orders, through my bowels. Yet I was not a State with you, nor were we both together any Indiana. A squad of Pershing Rifles at the moment, I make myself Right Face! Legislation packs the screw of my intestines. Well, king of the classroom's king of the hill. You used to waddle when you walked because my sperm between your legs was draining to a towel. Teacher, poet, folded lover—like the politician, like those drunkards, ill, or those who faucet-off while pissing heartily to preach upon the force and fullness of that stream, or pause from vomiting to praise the purity and passion of their puke—I chant, I beg, I orate, I command, I sing—

Come back to Indiana—not too late!
  (Or will you be a ranger to the end?)
Good-bye . . . Good-bye . . . oh, I shall always wait
  You, Larry, traveler—
                stranger,
                        son,
                        —my friend— .[2]

my little girl, my poem by heart, my self, my childhood.

But I've heard Batista described as a Mason. That dries up my pity, melts my hate. Back from the garage where I have overheard it, I slap the mended fender of my car to laugh, and listen to the metal stinging tartly in my hand.

2. Quote from "Indiana" by Hart Crane, American poet (1899–1932).

People

Their hair in curlers and their heads wrapped in loud scarves, young mothers, fattish in trousers, lounge about in the speedwash, smoking cigarettes, eating candy, drinking pop, thumbing magazines, and screaming at their children above the whir and rumble of the machines.

At the bank a young man freshly pressed is letting himself in with a key. Along the street, delicately teetering, many grandfathers move in a dream. During the murderous heat of summer, they perch on window ledges, their feet dangling just inside the narrow shelf of shade the store has made, staring steadily into the street. Where their consciousness has gone I can't say. It's not in the eyes. Perhaps it's diffuse, all temperature and skin, like an infant's, though more mild. Near the corner there are several large overalled men employed in standing. A truck turns to be weighed on the scales at the Feed and Grain. Images drift on the drugstore window. The wind has blown the smell of cattle into town. Our eyes have been driven in like the eyes of the old men. And there's no one to have mercy on us.

Vital Data

There are two restaurants here and a tearoom, two bars, one bank, three barbers, one with a green shade with which he blinds his window. two groceries. a dealer in Fords. one drug, one hardware, and one appliance store. several that sell feed, grain, and farm equipment, an antique shop. a poolroom. a laundromat. three doctors. a dentist. a plumber. a vet. a funeral home in elegant repair the color of a buttercup. numerous beauty parlors which open and shut like night-blooming plants. a tiny dime and department store of no width but several floors. a hutch, home-made, where you can order, after lying down or squirming in, furniture that's been fashioned from bent lengths of stainless tubing, glowing plastic, metallic thread, and clear shellac. an American Legion Post and a root beer stand. little agencies for this and that: cosmetics, brushes, insurance, greeting cards and garden produce—anything—sample shoes—which do their business out of hats and satchels, over coffee cups and dissolving sugar. a factory for making paper sacks and pasteboard boxes that's lodged in an old brick building bearing the legend OPERA HOUSE, still faintly golden, on its roof. a library given by Carnegie. a post office. a school. a railroad station. fire station. lumberyard. telephone company. welding shop. garage . . . and spotted through the town from one end to the other in a line along the highway, gas stations to the number five.

Education

In 1833, Colin Goodykoontz, an itinerant preacher with a name from a fairytale, summed up the situation in one Indiana town this way:

Ignorance and her squalid brood. A universal dearth of intellect. Total abstinence from literature is very generally practiced. . . . There is not a scholar in grammar or geography, or a *teacher capable* of *instructing* in them, to my knowledge. . . . Others are supplied a few months of the year with the most antiquated & unreasonable forms of teaching reading, writing & cyphering. . . . Need I stop to remind you of the host of loathsome reptiles such a stagnant pool is fitted to breed! Croaking jealousy; bloated bigotry; coiling suspicion; wormish blindness; crocodile malice!

Things have changed since then, but in none of the respects mentioned.

Business

One side section of street is blocked off with sawhorses. Hard, thin, bitter men in blue jeans, cowboy boots and hats, untruck a dinky carnival. The merchants are promoting themselves. There will be free rides, raucous music, parades and coneys, pop, popcorn, candy, cones, awards and drawings, with all you can endure of pinch, push, bawl, shove, shout, scream, shriek, and bellow. Children pedal past on decorated bicycles, their wheels a blur of color, streaming crinkled paper and excited dogs. A little later, there's a pet show for a prize—dogs, cats, birds, sheep, ponies, goats—none of which wins. The whirlabouts whirl about. The Ferris wheel climbs dizzily into the sky as far as a tall man on tiptoe might be persuaded to reach, and the irritated operators measure the height and weight of every child with sour eyes to see if they are safe for the machines. An electrical megaphone repeatedly trumpets the names of the generous sponsors. The following day they do not allow the refuse to remain long in the street.

My House, This Place and Body

I have met with some mischance, wings withering, as Plato says obscurely, and across the breadth of Ohio, like heaven on a table, I've fallen as far as the poet, to the sixth sort of body, this house in B, in Indiana, with its blue and gray bewitching windows, holy magical insides. Great thick evergreens protect its entry. And I live *in*.

Lost in the corn rows, I remember feeling just another stalk, and thus this country takes me over in the way I occupy myself when I am well . . . completely—to the edge of both my house and body. No one notices, when they walk by, that I am brimming in the doorways. My house, this place, and body, I've come in mourning to be born in. To anybody else it's pretty silly: love. Why should I feel a loss? How am I bereft? She was never mine; she was a fiction, always a golden tomgirl, barefoot, with an adolescent's slouch and a boy's taste for sports and fishing, a figure out of Twain, or worse, in Riley. Age cannot be kind.

There's little hand-in-hand here . . . not in B. No one touches except in rage. Occasionally girls will twine their arms about each other and lurch along, school out, toward home and play. I dreamed my lips would drift down your back like a skiff on a river. I'd follow a vein with the point of my finger, hold your bare feet in my naked hands.

The Same Person

Billy Holsclaw lives alone—how alone it is impossible to fathom. In the post office he talks greedily to me about the weather. His head bobs on a wild flood of words, and I take this violence to be a measure of his eagerness for speech. He badly needs a shave, coal dust has layered his face, he spits when he speaks, and his fingers pick at his tatters. He wobbles out in the wind when I leave him, a paper sack mashed in the fold of his arm, the leaves blowing past him, and our encounter drives me sadly home to poetry—where there's no answer. Billy closes his door and carries coal or wood to his fire and closes his eyes, and there's simply no way of knowing how lonely and empty he is or whether he's as vacant and barren and loveless as the rest of us are—here in the heart of the country.

Weather

For we're always out of luck here. That's just how it is—for instance in the winter. The sides of the buildings, the roofs, the limbs of the trees are gray. Streets, sidewalks, faces, feelings—they are gray. Speech is gray, and the grass where it shows. Every flank and front, each top is gray. Everything is gray: hair, eyes, window glass, the hawkers' bills and touters' posters, lips, teeth, poles and metal signs—they're gray, quite gray. Cars are gray. Boots, shoes, suits, hats, gloves are gray. Horses, sheep, and cows, cats killed in the road, squirrels in the same way, sparrows, doves, and pigeons, all are gray, everything is gray, and everyone is out of luck who lives here.

A similar haze turns the summer sky milky, and the air muffles your head and shoulders like a sweater you've got caught in. In the summer light, too, the sky darkens a moment when you open your eyes. The heat is pure distraction. Steeped in our fluids, miserable in the folds of our bodies, we can scarcely think of anything but our sticky parts. Hot cyclonic winds and storms of dust crisscross the country. In many places, given an indifferent push, the wind will still coast for miles, gathering resource and edge as it goes, cunning and force. According to the season, paper, leaves, field litter, seeds, snow, fill up the fences. Sometimes I think the land is flat because the winds have leveled it, they blow so constantly. In any case, a gale can grow in a field of corn that's as hot as a draft from hell, and to receive it is one of the most dismaying experiences of this life, though the smart of the same wind in winter is more humiliating, and in that sense even worse. But in the spring it rains as well, and the trees fill with ice.

Place

Many small Midwestern towns are nothing more than rural slums, and this community could easily become one. Principally, during the first decade of the century, though there were many earlier instances, well-to-do farmers moved to town and built fine homes to contain them in their retirement. Others desired a more social life, and so lived in, driving to their fields like storekeepers to their businesses. These houses are now dying like the bereaved who inhabit them; they are slowly losing their senses—deafness, blindness, forgetfulness, mumbling, an insecure gait, an uncontrollable trembling has overcome them. Some kind of Northern Snopes[3] will occupy them next: large-familied, Catholic, Democratic, scrambling, vigorous, poor; and since the parents will work in larger, nearby towns, the children will be loosed upon themselves and upon the hapless neighbors much as the fabulous Khan[4] loosed his legendary horde. These Snopes will undertake makeshift repairs with materials that other people have thrown away; paint halfway round their house, then quit; almost certainly maintain an ugly loud cantankerous dog and underfeed a pair of cats to keep the rodents down. They will collect piles of possibly useful junk in the back yard, park their cars in the front, live largely leaning over engines, give not a hoot for the land, the old community, the hallowed ways, the established clans. Weakening widow ladies have already begun to hire large rude youths from families such as these to rake and mow and tidy the grounds they will inherit.

People

In the cinders at the station, boys sit smoking steadily in darkened cars, their arms bent out the windows, white skirts glowing behind the glass. Nine o'clock is the best time. They sit in a line facing the highway—two or three or four of them—idling their engines. As you walk by a machine may growl at you or a pair of headlights flare up briefly. In a moment one will pull out, spinning cinders behind it, to stalk impatiently up and down the dark streets or roar half a mile into the country before returning to its place in line and pulling up.

My House, My Cat, My Company

I must organize myself. I must, as they say, pull myself together, dump this cat from my lap, stir—yes, resolve, move, do. But do what? My will is like the rosy dust-like light in this room: soft, diffuse, and gently comforting. It lets me do . . . anything . . . nothing. My ears hear what they happen to; I eat what's put before me; my eyes see what blunders into them; my thoughts are not thoughts, they are dreams. I'm empty or I'm full . . . depending; and I cannot choose. I sink my claws in Tick's fur and scratch the

3. The Snopes clan from William Faulkner's fiction have come to stand for trashy, no-good people of all regions. 4. Genghis Khan (1162–1227) was the Mongol conqueror of Asia and Eastern Europe.

bones of his back until his rear rises amorously. Mr. Tick, I murmur, I must organize myself. I must pull myself together. And Mr. Tick rolls over on his belly, all ooze.

I spill Mr. Tick when I've rubbed his stomach. Shoo. He steps away slowly, his long tail rhyming with his paws. How beautifully he moves, I think; how beautifully he accepts. So I rise and wander from room to room, up and down, gazing through most of my forty-one windows. How well this house receives its loving, too. Let out like Mr. Tick, my eyes sink in the shrubbery. I am not here; I've passed the glass, passed second-story spaces, flown by branches, brilliant berries, to the ground, grass high in seed and leafage every season; and it is the same as when I passed above you in my aged, ardent body; it's, in short, a kind of love; and I am learning to restore myself, my house, my body, by paying court to gardens, cats, and running water, and with neighbors keeping company.

Mrs. Desmond is my right-hand friend; she's eighty-five. A thin white mist of hair, fine and tangled, manifests the climate of her mind. She is habitually suspicious, fretful, nervous. Burglars break in at noon. Children trespass. Even now they are shaking the pear tree, stealing rhubarb, denting lawn. Flies caught in the screen and numbed by frost awake in the heat to buzz and scrape the metal cloth and frighten her, though she is deaf to me, and consequently cannot hear them. Boards creak, the wind whistles across the chimney mouth, drafts cruise like fish through the hollow rooms. It is herself she hears, her own flesh failing, for only death will preserve her from those daily chores she climbs like stairs, and all that anxious waiting. Is it now, she wonders. No? Then: is it now?

We do not converse. She visits me to talk. My task to murmur. She talks about her grandson, her daughter who lives in Delphi, her sister or her husband—both gone—obscure friends—dead—obscurer aunts and uncles—lost—ancient neighbors, members of her church or of her clubs—passed or passing on; and in this way she brings the ends of her life together with a terrifying rush: she is a girl, a wife, a mother, widow, all at once. All at once—appalling—but I believe it; I wince in expectation of the clap. Her talk's a fence—a shade drawn, window fastened, door that's locked—for no one dies taking tea in a kitchen; and as her years compress and begin to jumble, I really believe in the brevity of life; I sweat in my wonder; death is the dog down the street, the angry gander, bedroom spider, goblin who's come to get her; and it occurs to me that in my listening posture I'm the boy who suffered the winds of my grandfather with an exactly similar politeness, that I am, right now, all my ages, out in elbows, as angular as badly stacked cards. Thus was I, when I loved you, every man I could be, youth and child—far from enough—and you, so strangely ambiguous a being, met me, heart for spade, play after play, the whole run of our suits.

Mr. Tick, you do me honor. You not only lie in my lap, but you remain alive there, coiled like a fetus. Through your deep nap, I feel you hum. You are, and are not, a machine. You are alive, alive exactly, and it means nothing to you—much to me. You are a cat —you cannot understand—you are a cat so easily. Your nature is not something you must rise to. You, not I, live in: in house, in skin, in shrubbery. Yes. I think I shall hat my head with a steeple; turn church; devour people. Mr. Tick, though, has a tail he can twitch, he need not fly his Fancy. Claws, not metrical schema, poetry his paws; while smoothing . . . smoothing . . . smoothing roughly, his tongue laps its neatness. O Mr. Tick, I know you; you are an electrical penis. Go on now, shoo. Mrs. Desmond doesn't like you. She thinks you will tangle yourself in her legs and she will fall. You murder her birds, she knows, and walk upon her roof with death in your jaws. I must gather myself together for a bound. What age is it I'm at right now, I wonder. The heart, don't they always say, keeps the true time. Mrs. Desmond is knocking. Faintly, you'd think, but she pounds. She's brought me a cucumber. I believe she believes I'm a woman. Come in, Mrs. Desmond, thank you, be my company, it looks lovely, and have tea. I'll slice it, crisp, with cream, for luncheon, each slice as thin as me.

Politics

O all ye isolate and separate powers, Sing! Sing, and sing in such a way that from a distance it will seem a harmony, a Strindberg play, a friendship ring . . . so happy—happy, happy, happy—as here we go hand in handling, up and down. Our union was a singing, though we were silent in the songs we sang like single notes are silent in a symphony. In no sense sober, we barbershopped together and never heard the discords in our music or saw ourselves as dirty, cheap, or silly. Yet cats have worn out better shoes than those thrown through our love songs at us. Hush. Be patient—prudent—politic. Still, Cleveland killed you, Mr. Crane. Were you not politic enough and fond of being beaten? Like a piece of sewage, the city shat you from its stern three hundred miles from history—beyond the loving reach of sailors.[5] Well, I'm not a poet who puts Paris to his temple in his youth to blow himself from Idaho, or—fancy that—Missouri. My god, I said, this is my country, but must my country go so far as Terre Haute or Whiting, go so far as Gary?

When the Russians first announced the launching of their satellite, many people naturally refused to believe them. Later others were outraged that they had sent a dog around the earth. I wouldn't want to take that mutt from out that metal flying thing if he's still

5. Hart Crane committed suicide by jumping from a ship. A homosexual, he associated considerably with sailors.

living when he lands, our own dog catcher said; anybody knows you shut a dog up by himself to toss around the first thing he'll be setting on to do you let him out is bite somebody.

This Midwest. A dissonance of parts and people, we are a consonance of Towns. Like a man grown fat in everything but heart, we overlabor; our outlook never really urban, never rural either, we enlarge and linger at the same time. As Alice both changed and remained in her story. You are a blond. I put my hand upon your belly; feel it tremble from my trembling. We always drive large cars in my section of the country. How could you be a comfort to me now?

More Vital Data

The town is exactly fifty houses, trailers, stores, and miscellaneous buildings long, but in places no streets deep. It takes on width as you drive south, always adding to the east. Most of the dwellings are fairly spacious farm houses in the customary white, with wide wraparound porches and tall narrow windows, though there are many of the grander kind—fretted, scalloped, turreted, and decorated with clapboards set at angles or on end, with stained-glass windows at the stair landings and lots of wrought iron full of fancy curls—and a few of these look like castles in their rarer brick. Old stables serve as garages now, and the lots are large to contain them and the vegetable and flower gardens which, ultimately, widows plant and weed and then entirely disappear in. The shade is ample, the grass is good, the sky a glorious fall violet; the apple trees are heavy and red, the roads are calm and empty; corn has sifted from the chains of tractored wagons to speckle the streets with gold and with the russet fragments of the cob, and a man would be a fool who wanted, blessed with this, to live anywhere else in the world.

Education

Buses like great orange animals move through the early light to school. There the children will be taught to read and warned against Communism. By Miss Janet Jakes. That's not her name. Her name is Helen something—Scott or James. A teacher twenty years. She's now worn fine and smooth, and has a face, Wilfred says, like a mail-order ax. Her voice is hoarse, and she has a cough. For she screams abuse. The children stare, their faces blank. This is the thirteenth week. They are used to it. You will all, she shouts, you will all draw pictures of me. No. She is a Mrs.—someone's missus. And in silence they set to work while Miss Jakes jabs hairpins in her hair. Wilfred says an ax, but she has those rimless tinted glasses, graying hair, an almost dimpled chin. I must concentrate. I must stop making up things. I must give myself to life; let it mold me: that's what they say in *Wisdom's Monthly Digest* every day. Enough, enough—you've been at it long enough; and the children rise formally a row at a time to present their work to her desk. No, she wears rims; it's her chin that's dimpleless. Well, it will take more than a tablespoon of features to sweeten that face. So she grimly shuffles their sheets, examines her reflection crayoned on them. I would not dare . . . allow a child . . . to put a line around me. Though now and then she smiles like a nick in the blade, in the end these drawings depress her. I could not bear it—how can she ask?—that anyone . . . draw me. Her anger's lit. That's why she does it: flame. There go her eyes; the pink in her glasses brightens, dims. She is a pumpkin, and her rage is breathing like the candle in. No, she shouts, no—the cartoon trembling—no, John Mauck, John Stewart Mauck, this will not do. The picture flutters from her fingers. You've made me too muscular.

I work on my poetry. I remember my friends, associates, my students, by their names. Their names are Maypop, Dormouse, Upsydaisy. Their names are Gladiolus, Callow Bladder, Prince and Princess Oleo, Hieronymous, Cardinal Mummum, Mr. Fitchew, The Silken Howdah, Spot. Sometimes you're Tom Sawyer, Huckleberry Finn; it is perpetually summer; your buttocks are my pillow; we are adrift on a raft; your back is our river. Sometimes you are Major Barbara, sometimes a goddess who kills men in battle, sometimes you are soft like a shower of water; you are bread in my mouth.

I do not work on my poetry. I forget my friends, associates, my students, and their names: Gramophone, Blowgun, Pickle, Serenade . . . Marge the Barge, Arena, Uberhaupt . . . Doctor Dildoe, The Fog Machine. For I am now in B, in Indiana: out of job and out of patience, out of love and time and money, out of bread and out of body, in a temper, Mrs. Desmond, out of tea. So shut your fist up, bitch, you bag of death; go bang another door; go die, my dearie. Die, life-deaf old lady. Spill your breath. Fall over like a frozen board. Gray hair grows from the nose of your mind. You are a skull already—*memento mori*—the foreskin retracts from your teeth. Will your plastic gums last longer than your bones, and color their grinning? And is your twot still hazel-hairy, or are you bald as a ditch? . . . bitch . . . . . . bitch . . . . bitch. I wanted to be famous, but you bring me age—my emptiness. Was it *that* which I thought would balloon me above the rest? Love? where are you? . . . love me. I want to rise so high, I said, that when I shit I won't miss anybody.

Business

For most people, business is poor. Nearby cities have siphoned off all but a neighborhood trade. Except for feed and grain and farm supplies, you stand a chance to sell only what runs out to buy. Chevrolet has quit, and Frigidaire. A locker plant has left its afterimage. The lumberyard has been, so far, six months about its going. Gas stations change hands clumsily, a restaurant becomes available, a grocery closes. One day they came and knocked the cornices from the watch repair and pasted campaign posters on the windows. Torn across, by now, by boys, they urge you still to vote for half an orange beblazoned man who as a whole one failed two years ago to win at his election. Everywhere, in this manner, the past speaks, and it mostly speaks of failure. The empty stores, the old signs and dusty fixtures, the debris in alleys, the flaking paint and rusty gutters, the heavy locks and sagging boards: they say the same disagreeable things. What do the sightless windows see, I wonder, when the sun throws a passerby against them? Here a stair unfolds toward the street—dark, rickety, and treacherous—and I always feel, as I pass it, that if I just went carefully up and turned the corner at the landing, I would find myself out of the world. But I've never had the courage.

That Same Person

The weeds catch up with Billy. In pursuit of the hollyhocks, they rise in coarse clumps all around the front of his house. Billy has to stamp down a circle by his door like a dog or cat does turning round to nest up, they're so thick. What particularly troubles me is that winter will find the weeds still standing stiff and tindery to take the sparks which Billy's little mortarless chimney spouts. It's true that fires are fun here. The town whistle, which otherwise only blows for noon (and there's no noon on Sunday), signals the direction of the fire by the length and number of its blasts, the volunteer firemen rush past in their cars and trucks, houses empty their owners along the street every time like an illustration in a children's book. There are many bikes, too, and barking dogs, and sometimes —halleluiah—the fire's right here in town—a vacant lot of weeds and stubble flaming up. But I'd rather it weren't Billy or Billy's lot or house. Quite selfishly, I want him to remain the way he is—counting his sticks and logs, sitting on his sill in the soft early sun —though I'm not sure what his presence means to me . . . or to anyone. Nevertheless, I keep wondering whether, given time, I might not someday find a figure in our language which would serve him faithfully, and furnish his poverty and loneliness richly out.

Wires

Where sparrows sit like fists. Doves fly the steeple. In mist the wires change perspective, rise and twist. If they led to you, I would know what they were. Thoughts passing often, like the starlings who flock these fields at evening to sleep in the trees beyond, would form a family of paths like this; they'd foot down the natural height of air to just about a bird's perch. But they do not lead to you.

> Of whose beauty it was sung
> She shall make the old man young.

They fasten me.

If I walked straight on, in my present mood, I would reach the

Wabash. It's not a mood in which I'd choose to conjure you. Similes dangle like baubles from me. This time of year the river is slow and shallow, the clay banks crack in the sun, weeds surprise the sandbars. The air is moist and I am sweating. It's impossible to rhyme in this dust. Everything—sky, the cornfield, stump, wild daisies, my old clothes and pressless feelings—seem fabricated for installment purchase. Yes. Christ. I am suffering a summer Christmas; and I cannot walk under the wires. The sparrows scatter like handfuls of gravel. Really, wires are voices in thin strips. They are words wound in cables. Bars of connection.

Weather

I would rather it were the weather that was to blame for what I am and what my friends and neighbors are—we who live here in the heart of the country. Better the weather, the wind, the pale dying snow . . . the snow—why not the snow? There's never much really, not around the lower Lakes anyway, not enough to boast about, not enough to be useful. My father tells how the snow in the Dakotas would sweep to the roofs of the barns in the old days, and he and his friends could sled on the crust that would form because the snow was so fiercely driven. In Bemidji trees have been known to explode. That would be something—if the trees in Davenport or Francisville or Cardondale or Niles were to go blam some winter—blam! blam! blam! all the way down the gray, cindery, snow-sick streets.

A cold fall rain is blackening the trees or the air is like lilac and full of parachuting seeds. Who cares to live in any season but his own? Still I suspect the secret's in this snow, the secret of our sickness, if we could only diagnose it, for we are all dying like the elms in Urbana. This snow—like our skin it covers the country. Later dust will do it. Right now—snow. Mud presently. But it is snow without any laughter in it, a pale gray pudding thinly spread on stiff toast, and if that seems a strange description, it's accurate all the same. Of course soot blackens everything, but apart from that, we are never sufficiently cold here. The flakes as they come, alive and burning, we cannot retain, for if our temperatures fall, they rise promptly again, just as, in the summer, they bob about in the same feckless way. Suppose though . . . suppose they were to rise some August, climb and rise, and then hang in the hundreds like a hawk through December, what a desert we could make of ourselves—from Chicago to Cairo, from Hammond to Columbus—what beautiful Death Valleys.

Place

I would rather it were the weather. It drives us in upon ourselves —an unlucky fate. Of course there is enough to stir our wonder anywhere: there's enough to love, anywhere, if one is strong enough, if one is diligent enough, if one is perceptive, patient, kind enough—whatever it takes; and surely it's better to live in the country, to live on a prairie by a drawing of rivers, in Iowa or Illinois or Indiana, say, than in any city, in any stinking fog of human beings, in any blooming orchard of machines. It ought to be. The cities are swollen and poisonous with people. It ought to be better. Man has never been a fit environment for man—for rats, maybe, rats do nicely, or for dogs or cats and the household beetle.

And how long the street is, nowadays. These endless walls are fallen to keep back the tides of earth. Brick could be beautiful but we have covered it gradually with gray industrial vomits. Age does not make concrete genial and asphalt is always—like America—twenty-one, until it breaks up in crumbs like stale cake. The brick, the asphalt, the concrete, the dancing signs and garish posters, the feed and excrement of the automobile, the litter of its inhabitants: they compose, they decorate, they line our streets, and there is nowhere, nowadays, our streets can't reach.

A man in the city has no natural thing by which to measure himself. His parks are potted plants. Nothing can live and remain free where he resides but the pigeon, starling, sparrow, spider, cockroach, mouse, moth, fly and weed, and he laments the existence of even these and makes his plans to poison them. The zoo? There *is* the zoo. Through its bars the city man stares at the great cats and dully sucks his ice. Living, alas, among men and their marvels, the city man supposes that his happiness depends on establishing, somehow, a special kind of harmonious accord with others. The novelists of the city, of slums and crowds, they call it love—and break their pens.

Wordsworth feared the accumulation of men in cities. He foresaw their "degrading thirst after outrageous stimulation," and some of their hunger for love. Living in a city, among so many, dwelling in the heat and tumult of incessant movement, a man's affairs are touch and go—that's all. It's not surprising that the novelists of the slums, the cities, and the crowds, should find that sex is but a scratch to ease a tickle, that we're most human when we're sitting on the john, and that the justest image of our life is in full passage through the plumbing.

> The man, immur'd in cities, still retains
> His inborn inextinguishable thirst
> Of rural scenes, compensating his loss
> By supplemental shifts, the best he may.

Come into the country, then. The air nimbly and sweetly recommends itself unto our gentle senses. Here, growling tractors tear the earth. Dust roils up behind them. Drivers sit jouncing under bright umbrellas. They wear refrigerated hats and steer by looking at the tracks they've cut behind them, their transistors blaring. Close to the land, are they? good companions to the soil? Tell me: do they live in harmony with the alternating seasons?

It's a lie of old poetry. The modern husbandman uses chemicals from cylinders and sacks, spike-ball-and-claw machines, metal sheds, and cost accounting. Nature in the old sense does not matter. It does not exist. Our farmer's only mystical attachment is to parity. And if he does not realize that cows and corn are simply different kinds of chemical engine, he cannot expect to make a go of it.

It isn't necessary to suppose our cows have feelings; our neighbor hasn't as many as he used to have either; but think of it this way a moment, you can correct for the human imputations later: how would it feel to nurse those strange tentacled calves with their rubber, glass, and metal lips, their stainless eyes?

People

Aunt Pet's still able to drive her car—a high square Ford—even though she walks with difficulty and a stout stick. She has a watery gaze, a smooth plump face despite her age, and jet black hair in a bun. She has the slowest smile of anyone I ever saw, but she hates dogs, and not very long ago cracked the back of one she cornered in her garden. To prove her vigor she will tell you this, her smile breaking gently while she raises the knob of her stick to the level of your eyes.

House, My Breath and Window

My window is a grave, and all that lies within it's dead. No snow is falling. There's no haze. It is not still, not silent. Its images are not an animal that waits, for movement is no demonstration. I have seen the sea slack, life bubble through a body without a trace, its spheres impervious as soda's. Downwound, the whore at wagtag clicks and clicks. Leaves wiggle. Grass sways. A bird chirps, pecks the ground. An auto wheel in penning circles keeps its rigid spokes. These images are stones; they are memorials. Beneath this sea lies sea: god rest it . . . rest the world beyond my window, me in front of my reflection, above this page, my shade. Death is not so still, so silent, since silence implies a falling quiet, stillness a stopping, containing, holding in; for death is time in a clock, like Mr. Tick, electric . . . like wind through a windup poet. And my blear floats out to visible against the, glass, befog its country and bespill myself. The mist lifts slowly from the fields in the morning. No one now would say: the Earth throws back its covers; it is rising from sleep. Why is the feeling foolish? The image is too Greek. I used to gaze at you so wantonly your body blushed. Imagine: wonder: that my eyes could cause such flowering. Ah, my friend, your face is pale, the weather cloudy; a street has been felled through your chin, bare trees do nothing, houses take root in their rectangles, a steeple stands up in your head. You speak of loving; then give me a kiss. The pane is cold. On icy mornings the fog rises to greet me (as you always did); the barns and other buildings, rather than ghostly, seem all the more substantial for looming, as if they grew in themselves while I watched (as you always did). Oh, my approach, I suppose, was like breath in a rubber monkey. Nevertheless, on the road along the Wabash in the morning, though the trees are sometimes obscured by fog, their reflection floats serenely on the river, reasoning the banks, the sycamores in French rows. Magically, the world tips. I'm led to think that only those who grow down live (which will scarcely win me twenty-five from *Wisdom's Monthy Digest*), but I find I write that only those who live down grow; and what I write, I hold, whatever I really know. My every world's inverted, or reversed—or I am. I held you, too, that way. You were so utterly provisional, subject to my change. I could inflate your bosom with a kiss, disperse your skin with gentleness, enter your vagina from within, and make my love emerge like a fresh sex. The pane is cold. Honesty is cold, my inside lover. The sun looks, through the mist, like a plum on the tree of heaven, or a bruise on the slope of your belly. Which? The grass crawls with frost. We meet on this window, the world and I, inelegantly, swimmers of the glass; and swung wrong way round to one another, the world seems in. The world—how grand, how monumental, grave and deadly, that word is: the world, my house and poetry. All poets have their inside lovers. Wee penis does not belong to me, or any of this foggery. It is *his* property which he's thrust through what's womanly of me to set down this. These wooden houses in their squares, gray streets and fallen sidewalks, standing trees, your name I've written sentimentally across my breath into the whitening air, pale birds: they exist in me now because of him. I gazed with what intensity . . . A bush in the excitement of its roses could not have bloomed so beautifully as you did then. It was a look I'd like to give this page. For that is poetry: to bring within about, to change.

Politics

Sports, politics, and religion are the three passions of the badly educated. They are the Midwest's open sores. Ugly to see, a source of constant discontent, they sap the body's strength. Appalling quantities of money, time, and energy are wasted on them. The rural mind is narrow, passionate, and reckless on these matters. Greed, however shortsighted and direct, will not alone account for it. I have known men, for instance, who for years have voted squarely against their interests. Nor have I ever noticed that their surly Christian views prevented them from urging forward the smithereening, say, of Russia, China, Cuba, or Korea. And they tend to back their country like they back their local team: they have a fanatical desire to win; yelling is their forte; and if things go badly, they are inclined to sack the coach. All in all, then, Birch[6] is a good name. It stands for the bigot's stick, the wild-child-tamer's cane.

Forgetfulness—is that their object?

Oh, I was new, I thought. A fresh start; new cunt, new climate, and new country—there you were, and I was pioneer, and had no history. That language hurts me, too, my dear. You'll never hear it.

Final Vital Data

The Modern Homemakers' Demonstration Club. The Prairie Home Demonstration Club. The Night-outer's Home Demonstration Club. The IOOF, FFF, VFW, WCTU, WSCS, 4-H, 40 and 8, Psi Iota Chi, and PTA. The Boy and Girl Scouts, Rainbows, Masons, Indians and Rebekah Lodge. Also the Past Noble Grand Club of the Rebekah Lodge. As well as the Moose and the Ladies of the Moose. The Elks, the Eagles, the Jaynettes and the Eastern Star. The Women's Literary Club, the Hobby Club, the Art Club, the Sunshine Society, the Dorcas Society, the Pythian Sisters, the Pilgrim Youth Fellowship, the American Legion, the American Legion Auxiliary, the American Legion Junior Auxiliary, the Garden Club, the Bridge for Fun Club, the What-can-you-do? Club, the Get Together Club, the Coterie Club, the Worthwhile Club, the Let's Help Our Town Club, the No Name Club, the Forget-me-not Club, the Merry-go-round Club . . .

Education

Has a quarter disappeared from Paula Frosty's pocket book? Imagine the landscape of that face: no crayon could engender it; soft wax is wrong; thin wire in trifling snips might do the trick. Paula Frosty and Christopher Roger accuse the pale and splotchy Cheryl Pipes. But Miss Jakes, I *saw* her. Miss Jakes is so extremely vexed she snaps her pencil. What else is missing? I appoint you a detective, John: search her desk. Gum, candy, paper, pencils, marble, round eraser—whose? A thief. I can't watch her all the time, I'm here to teach. Poor pale fossetted Cheryl, it's determined, can't return the money because she took it home and spent it. Cindy, Janice, John, and Pete—you four who sit around her—you will be detectives this whole term to watch her. A thief. In all my time. Miss Jakes turns, unfists, and turns again. I'll handle you, she cries. To think. A thief. In all my years. Then she writes on the blackboard the name of Cheryl Pipes and beneath that the figure twenty-five with a large sign for cents. Now Cheryl, she says, this won't be taken off until you bring that money out of home, out of home straight up to here, Miss Jakes says, tapping her desk.

Which is three days.

6. Allusion to the John Birch Society, a right wing political group.

Another Person

I was raking leaves when Uncle Halley introduced himself to me. He said his name came from the comet, and that his mother had borne him prematurely in her fright of it. I thought of Hobbes,[7] whom fear of the Spanish Armada had hurried into birth, and so I believed Uncle Halley to honor the philosopher, though Uncle Halley is a liar, and neither the one hundred twenty-nine nor the fifty-three he ought to be. That fall the leaves had burned themselves out on the trees, the leaf lobes had curled, and now they flocked noisily down the street and were broken in the wires of my rake. Uncle Halley was himself (like Mrs. Desmond and history generally) both deaf and implacable, and he shooed me down his basement stairs to a room set aside there for stacks of newspapers reaching to the ceiling, boxes of leaflets and letters and programs, racks of photo albums, scrapbooks, bundles of rolled-up posters and maps, flags and pennants and slanting piles of dusty magazines devoted mostly to motoring and the Christian ethic. I saw a bird cage, a tray of butterflies, a bugle, a stiff straw boater and all kinds of tassels tied to a coat tree. He still possessed and had on display the steering lever from his first car, a linen duster, driving gloves and goggles, photographs along the wall of himself, his friends, and his various machines, a shell from the first war, a record of "Ramona" nailed through its hole to a post, walking sticks and fanciful umbrellas, shoes of all sorts (his baby shoes, their counters broken, were held in sorrow beneath my nose—they had not been bronzed, but he might have them done someday before he died, he said), countless boxes of medals, pins, beads, trinkets, toys, and keys (I scarcely saw—they flowed like jewels from his palms), pictures of downtown when it was only a path by the railroad station, a brightly colored globe of the world with a dent in Poland, antique guns, belt buckles, buttons, souvenir plates and cups and saucers (I can't remember all of it—I won't), but I recall how shamefully, how rudely, how abruptly, I fled, a good story in my mouth but death in my nostrils; and how afterward I busily, righteously, burned my leaves as if I were purging the world of its years. I still wonder if this town—its life, and mine now—isn't really a record like the one of "Ramona" that I used to crank around on my grandmother's mahogany Victrola through lonely rainy days as a kid.

The First Person

Billy's like the coal he's found: spilled, mislaid, discarded. The sky's no comfort. His house and his body are dying together. His windows are boarded. And now he's reduced to his hands. I suspect he has glaucoma. At any rate he can scarcely see, and weeds his

7. Thomas Hobbes (1588–1679), English philosopher.

yard of rubble on his hands and knees. Perhaps he's a surgeon cleansing a wound or an ardent and tactile lover. I watch, I must say, apprehensively. Like mine-war detectors, his hands graze in circles ahead of him. Your nipples were the color of your eyes. Pebble. Snarl of paper. Length of twine. He leans down closely, picks up something silvery, holds it near his nose. Foil? cap? coin? He has within him—what, I wonder? Does he know more now because he fingers everything and has to sniff to see? It would be romantic cruelty to think so. He bends the down on your arms like a breeze. You wrote me: something is strange when we don't understand. I write in return: I think when I loved you I fell to my death.

Billy, I could read to you from Beddoes,[8] he's your man perhaps; he held with dying, freed his blood of its arteries; and he said that there were many wretched love-ill fools like me lying alongside the last bone of their former selves, as full of spirit and speech, nonetheless, as Mrs. Desmond, Uncle Halley and the Ferris wheel, Aunt Pet, Miss Jakes, Ramona or the megaphone; yet I reverse him finally, Billy, on no evidence but braggadocio, and I declare that though my inner organs were devoured long ago, the worm which swallowed down my parts still throbs and glows like a crystal palace.

Yes, you were younger. I was Uncle Halley, the museum man and infrequent meteor. Here is my first piece of ass. They weren't so flat in those days, had more round, more juice. And over here's the sperm I've spilled, nicely jarred and clearly labeled. Look at this tape like lengths of intestine where I've stored my spew, the endless worm of words I've written, a hundred million emissions or more: oh I was quite a man right from the start; even when unconscious in my cradle, from crotch to cranium, I was erectile tissue; tough mostly, after the manner approved by Plato, I had intercourse by eye. Never mind, old Holsclaw, you are blind. We pull down darkness when we go to bed; put out like Oedipus the actually offending organ, and train our touch to lies. All cats are gray, says Mr. Tick; so under cover of glaucoma you are sack gray too, and cannot be distinguished from a stallion.

I must pull myself together, get a grip, just as they say, but I feel spilled, bewildered, quite mislaid. I did not restore my house to its youth, but to its age. Hunting, you hitch through the hollyhocks. I'm inclined to say you aren't half the cripple I am, for there is nothing left of me but mouth. However, I resist the impulse. It is another lie of poetry. My organs are all there, though it's there where I fail—at the roots of my experience. Poet of the spiritual, Rilke,[9] weren't you? yet that's what you said. Poetry, like love, is—in and out—a physical caress. I can't tolerate any more

8. Thomas Beddoes (1803–1849), English dramatist. **9.** Rainer Maria Rilke (1875–1926), Austrian poet.

of my sophistries about spirit, mind, and breath. Body equals being, and if your weight goes down, you are the less.

Household Apples

I knew nothing about apples. Why should I? My country came in my childhood, and I dreamed of sitting among the blooms like the bees. I failed to spray the pear tree too. I doubled up under them at first, admiring the sturdy low branches I should have pruned, and later I acclaimed the blossoms. Shortly after the fruit formed there were falls—not many—apples the size of goodish stones which made me wobble on my ankles when I walked about the yard. Sometimes a piece crushed by a heel would cling on the shoe to track the house. I gathered a few and heaved them over the wires. A slingshot would have been splendid. Hard, an unattractive green, the worms had them. Before long I realized the worms had them all. Even as the apples reddened, lit their tree, they were being swallowed. The birds preferred the pears, which were small —sugar pears I think they're called—with thick skins of graying green that ripen on toward violet. So the fruit fell, and once I made some applesauce by quartering and paring hundreds; but mostly I did nothing, left them, until suddenly, overnight it seemed, in that ugly late September heat we often have in Indiana, my problem was upon me.

My childhood came in the country. I remember, now, the flies on our snowy luncheon table. As we cleared away they would settle, fastidiously scrub themselves and stroll to the crumbs to feed where I would kill them in crowds with a swatter. It was quite a game to catch them taking off. I struck heavily since I didn't mind a few stains; they'd wash. The swatter was a square of screen bound down in red cloth. It drove no air ahead of it to give them warning. They might have thought they'd flown headlong into a summered window. The faint pink dot where they had died did not rub out as I'd supposed, and after years of use our luncheon linen would faintly, pinkly, speckle.

The country became my childhood. Flies braided themselves on the flypaper in my grandmother's house. I can smell the bakery and the grocery and the stables and the dairy in that small Dakota town I knew as a kid; knew as I dreamed I'd know your body, as I've known nothing, before or since; knew as the flies knew, in the honest, unchaste sense: the burned house, hose-wet, which drew a mist of insects like the blue smoke of its smolder, and gangs of boys, moist-lipped, destructive as its burning. Flies have always impressed me; they are so persistently alive. Now they were coating the ground beneath my trees. Some were ordinary flies; there were the large blue-green ones; there were swarms of fruit flies too, and the red-spotted scavenger beetle; there were a few wasps, several sorts of bees and butterflies—checkers, sulphurs, monarchs, commas, question marks—and delicate dragonflies . . . but principally houseflies and horseflies and bottleflies, flies and more flies in clusters around the rotting fruit. They loved the pears. Inside, they fed. If you picked up a pear, they flew, and the pear became skin and stem. They were everywhere the fruit was: in the tree still—apples like a hive for them—or where the fruit littered the ground, squashing itself as you stepped . . . there was no help for it. The flies droned, feasting on the sweet juice. No one could go near the trees; I could not climb; so I determined at last to labor like Hercules. There were fruit baskets in the barn. Collecting them and kneeling under the branches, I began to gather remains. Deep in the strong rich smell of the fruit, I began to hum myself. The fruit caved in at the touch. Glistening red apples, my lifting disclosed, had families of beetles, flies, and bugs, devouring their rotten undersides. There were streams of flies; there were lakes and cataracts and rivers of flies, seas, and oceans. The hum was heavier, higher, than the hum of the bees when they came to the blooms in the spring, though the bees were there, among the flies, ignoring me—ignoring everyone. As my work went on and juice covered my hands and arms, they would form a sleeve, black and moving, like knotty wool. No caress could have been more indifferently complete. Still I rose fearfully, ramming my head in the branches, apples bumping against me before falling, bursting with bugs. I'd snap my hand sharply but the flies would cling to the sweet. I could toss a whole cluster into a basket from several feet. As the pear or apple lit, they would explosively rise, like monads[1] for a moment, windowless, certainly, with respect to one another, sugar their harmony. I had to admit, though, despite my distaste, that my arm had never been more alive, oftener or more gently kissed. Those hundreds of feet were light. In washing them off, I pretended the hose was a pump. What have I missed? Childhood is a lie of poetry.

The Church

Friday night. Girls in dark skirts and white blouses sit in ranks and scream in concert. They carry funnels loosely stuffed with orange and black paper which they shake wildly, and small megaphones through which, as drilled, they direct and magnify their shouting. Their leaders, barely pubescent girls, prance and shake and whirl thei rskirts above their bloomers. The young men, leaping, extend their arms and race through puddles of amber light, their bodies glistening. In a lull, though it rarely occurs, you can hear the squeak of tennis shoes against the floor. Then the yelling begins again, and then continues; fathers, mothers, neighbors joining in to form a single pulsing ululation—a cry of the whole community—for in this gymnasium each body becomes the bodies

1. Simple, single-celled organism.

beside it, pressed as they are together, thigh to thigh, and the same shudder runs through all of them, and runs toward the same release. Only the ball moves serenely through this dazzling din. Obedient to law, it scarcely speaks but caroms quietly and lives at peace.

Business

It is the week of Christmas and the stores, to accommodate the rush they hope for, are remaining open in the evening. You can see snow falling in the cones of the street lamps. The roads are filling—undisturbed. Strings of red and green lights droop over the principal highway, and the water tower wears a star. The windows of the stores have been bedizened. Shamelessly they beckon. But I am alone, leaning against a pole—no . . . there is no one in sight. They're all at home, perhaps by their instruments, tuning in on their evenings, and like Ramona, tirelessly playing and replaying themselves. There's a speaker perched in the tower, and through the boughs of falling snow and over the vacant streets, it drapes the twisted and metallic strains of a tune that can barely be distinguished—yes, I believe it's one of the jolly ones, it's "Joy to the World." There's no one to hear the music but myself, and though I'm listening, I'm no longer certain. Perhaps the record's playing something else.

OAKLEY HALL

Horseman

IN my life I have been a fool with liquor and a wise man with horses. I was born on a horse, or just off one anyway, for my mother died in a fall a month before she was due to be light of me, and they cut me from her there. Which was the last time I was throwed, except by whiskey.

In those days before the Big Dry-up, I rode for the Castle Hundred and proud of it. That was when the squire's lands comprised a third of the Territory, who went to smash with the rest of the foreign owners when the country turned to desert.

I know that a man's memory will confuse him, and there is a true saying that the past has a rosier bottom than the present, but I can remember well the assemblies at the Castle, and the beautiful women, so fair-fleshed, with hair piled up to gleam like gem stones in the light of a thousand candles. You will ask if I remember the general at those affairs, and I will answer that he was only another youngster of an officer, though he had a powerful carriage even then. He was a hot-headed young fellow, and I am sure no better at fighting temptation than I have been in my life, and there was temptation and plenty amongst those ladies at the Castle.

The Hundred was green then, trees everywhere, and grassy meadows that would be a blanket of flowers in the spring. I remember the Squire and his guests hunting through the woods and meadows with that pack of white-and-liver-spotty hounds, the fox flying hell-for-leather with the dogs bellowing, and after them the riders coming. I was chief horsebreaker, and came to be trusted with more than mustangs, as I will relate. And did betray my trust which I would never have done if the liquor hadn't turned me into nothing more than a beast, as I will relate as well.

In those old times I remember the fat cattle, belly-down in grass like they were afloat in it. Cattle trailed down to the bottoms to drink at creeks that ran clear and fast and two yards wide. Those were prime days for man and beast, then.

The Dry-up came like a curse. The creeks dried up, and the Sweet-water turned to dry sand. Then you would see cattle baked into lumps of hide and horn in the dry bottoms, and all the fine foreign land-owners, the Squire among them, went back to where they had come from, and their foremen and cowboys turned into rustlers and desperados, and I will not deny I was among them.

Those were terrible times, with all men at their worst. Water was brought in in tank cars on the railroad until the railroad stopped running. Prospectors searching for the Lost Dutchman Mine died of thirst and you would find dried lumps of hide and hair in the bottoms that was man and donkey. But others died beside prospectors, and of lead, and scalping knives. For it seemed all men were turned into outlaws preying on each other, with Kimanches raiding out of the mountains to pick off stragglers, and not just stragglers. Many times the cavalry was too few to drive them off.

But little by little the general began beating them back. There would be a truce, then the hatchet dug up and more fighting, and another truce. In the main the general won the scraps, and that was a time when he was acquiring the little spreads that the Hundred had been cut up into. Putting it back together by hook and crook; for there were some to say that if a man didn't sell out cheap, that would be the next place Kimanche would come down on, and the cavalry slow to show.

I was riding with a bunch of turned-bad hands then, no better than the fellows next to me. But I saw that what the general was doing was right, putting things back together the way it used to be, and so I went to him and threw in with him.

So I became his horsebreaker, and trusted man besides. He confided in me secrets that will never pass my lips, and I was a help to him in many ways putting the Castle back in trim. Besides the Kimanche beat to where they scarcely troubled any more, it even rained a time or two, as it had not done in a coon's age. The grass came back a little, and Putaw Creek even ran a trickle, though the Sweetwater never did, and Bright City, where the fort was, became a considerable town.

And then the general asked me to undertake a task for him. I was to go east for a lady, and I knew that lady from the old days. I promised I would bring her safely back to him.

For I thought I saw that it was all coming around again, the great days returning. First the Kimanche beat back, then the rains coming, and the fine ladies and gentlemen returning to the Castle. For I know it can come round again if the right man shows up with his good sense, courage, and strength.

When I came to the place where the general had sent me, it was as though I had walked up to a mirror, spit and image of the Castle in the old days. There was green river bottom, and forests sweeping down from the hills, so that it seemed any minute there would be a horn call, and a fox streaking out with the hounds and riders after it. A great stone mansion lay on the far side of a creek with a covered bridge over it, and a road spiraling tan against the green hillside.

A plump fellow in a uniform of red trousers and stripe vest showed me up some stairs to where she was standing in a slant of sun from a window behind her, in a velvet gown with crisp ruching down the bosom and white lace at the sleeves. I thought she didn't remember me at first, but then she did, her rosebud mouth puckering once as though to blow a feather, and then softening into the winningest of smiles. All around her head was black hair in long sweet waves.

I told her what I had come for, and she nodded as though she knew it already. She said that we must hurry.

She went out of the room and came back with a carpet bag which she tossed some clothing into. She put on a hat that had a feather on it, and swung a cape over her shoulders.

I followed her carrying the carpet bag, which was heavy to pull my arm from its socket. Outside I swung the team around with the tassels on their harness nodding, while she whispered, "Hurry! Please hurry!" Then we were flying down the winding road. She never looked back one time.

She couldn't have said a dozen words to me on the long way to Cenotaph, where we booked seats on the train to San Hedrin and the Territory.

Jolting along the river and then through plains country in that coach, she watched out the window with her little chin braced on her hand like if she took her eyes off those mountains they would disappear.

For company we had a fat man and his fat wife in a poke bonnet, and a tall old drummer with hair like he'd been lightning-struck, and with him a pretty young woman with black hair, very demure most of the time looking down at her hands in black net gloves, though once in awhile her eye would catch mine sideways and smoulder like a hot coal. The other men would snicker and nudge each other whenever the drummer called her "daughter."

There were two prospectors with skin like bootleather, and those far-off looking chips of eyes; a half-grown boy playing cards with his old lady aunt; and a blind man with black-lensed spectacles and a terrible scar twisted across his forehead at the hairline like a pink centipede. He sat his seat with a very military bearing, both hands clasped on his long stick.

Once my lady took a sewing kit from her reticule to fasten a button back to her sleeve. When it was done she cut the thread with a tiny curved blade she sprung from her finger ring, like a cat's claw coming out. She showed it to me, a ring with a pale face in cameo on it. I couldn't make out where the shiny little blade had come from, which pleased her.

When a new conductor came on my heart sank, for it was Dan Slagle from the Castle Hundred crew that I knew well, stepping along the aisle with his eyes slitted at the fat couple, the drummer and his daughter, and me and my lady, like tallying stock. He gave me a nod.

"Well, hello, Dan," I said, and he said, "Well, hello, J.D."

When he'd gone on I eased my piece in its leather and never rested easy for a moment, for if it was Dan Slagle, King Mac was probably nearby.

And all of a sudden there was a jolt that flung everybody out of his seat. Another jolt tipped the coach up. It went over on its side with screeching metal, women squalling, and men shouting. My lady and I were tangled together from the wreck, and we extricated each other, moving a limb here and another there. The screaming had stopped and all through the car people were sorting themselves out. No one seemed much hurt. The coach being on its side, fellows climbed on the seats to try to open the windows. Just then glass was smashed with a boot kicking it in, and a man dropped through. It was Red Hoskins I had known all my life. As I reached for my revolver Jack Carew ducked in from the forward passage with a gun in either hand. My lady stood holding onto my arm as we faced these two fellows, and I was in a cold sweat over my task of bringing her safe back to the general.

We made our way outside with the rest, Jack relieving me of my revolver as I went by him, saying, "There's a good fellow, J.D." Outside, and right side up again, I saw they had broken the two coaches and the caboose off from the locomotive like wolves cutting a calf out of a herd.

King Mac was sitting on a big black looking over the scene, with a dozen riders in a half-circle with him. The coaches had been laid on their side by a log stabbed across the rails as I have seen done more times than I care to remember. All this while my lady kept her hand on my arm, not tight but reminding me I was responsible for her safety.

King Mac slumped on that seventeen-hands black, the corners of his mouth turned down steep and his eyes sleepy like he had seen everything there was to see and it bored him to extinction, but here it all came past again. His chins ran down to his neck, his belly hung out before him, and his black hat was turned down all around to keep the sun off his face, that was scabby with sun sores, and bristled with beard.

He didn't seem to take any notice of anything in particular, though some of his riders nudged each other to see me and my lady, and one or two nodded to me not unfriendly.

My lady leaned against me like she was taken faint, and whispered, "Who is that man?"

And I told her he was King Mac.

Just then she cried out in a muffled way when Jack Carew came up behind her to stick his ugly face against her neck.

"Oh, this one do smell so *good*, J.D.!"

I hit him, but he bounced back with his revolver out and slashed me across the face so I thought I was blinded and sank to my knees. My lady helped me up and daubed at my bloody face with a handkerchief. King Mac must have signaled Jack off, for he did no more.

They tied my hands behind my back then, with a chunk of sapling through the elbows, and tied hers too, though I noticed they were gentler with her than with the other women. Very nasty they were with the drummer's daughter, sticking dirty hands down the neck of her dress until she flinched back, then Red coming up behind to make her scream and jump forward. They were vile men that rode for King Mac out of Putaw Crossing.

They said he himself was not interested in women in a natural way but could only watch others in the exercise of their lusts, though I have also heard he could take his revolver barrel so cunning and skillful to those Putaw women they would beg him never to stop.

We set out with some of his riders alongside, up a stretch of dry creek, and then turned north through winding washes and big boulders. My lady looked elegant even with her hat gone and her hair loose and her cheeks streaked with sweat. Her bosom stuck out proud from the way her hands were tied behind.

King Mac rode drag, hulking along with the motion of his gelding. Once my lady whispered to ask where they were taking us, but

I shook my head I didn't know. I thought she and the other women were headed for Putaw Crossing, with some stops along the way. The men would be lucky to get much further at all. Though I noticed they had left the blind man his stick.

My lady spoke up to ask Jack Carew where we were going, and with a wink at me he said, "Oh, you'll find out soon enough, ma'am."

And she asked him who they were.

"Oh, just some fellows out rounding up the estrayed mares," he said, and grinned like he was the cleverest fellow alive.

The blind man had listened to this, and after it attached himself alongside us. I was able to help him step out faster by warning him what to watch out for in the path.

But the old woman, aunt to the boy, plumped herself down on a little pile of rocks with the boy crying and trying to tug her to her feet. She announced that she would just as soon die here as further along. Red Hoskins drew his rifle from its boot and laid it across the saddlehorn aimed at her. She folded her arms and gazed back at him, while the boy ran a few steps away, and then ran back. I saw nothing pass between Red and King Mac except that Red shrugged and put his piece away. We all marched on past where she sat straight-backed, with her arms folded. The boy kept sobbing and looking back until Red told him to shut up, which he did.

At sundown we came to sheds and a big corral, with a low adobe wall on two sides, and, rising from that, posts with barb wire strung between, and branches woven through the wire. In the corral we all sat on bales and gunnybags that were scattered around, and waited for what was to happen next. And I waited with my heart in my boots.

King Mac strolled by us, rolled by, I guess I should say, in his bulk. He wore a greasy cowhide jacket with fringes on it everywhere. Whenever he moved there was a haze of motion, so it seemed he moved swifter than another. He stood bellied out in front of us, scratching inside two buttons of his shirt and chewing on something like a cud, while he looked my lady over with his black-glass chips of eyes in his scabby, bristly face.

"You have brought us a rare one, fellow," he said, in his high voice.

I said I was bringing her to the general, whose guest she was to be, and who would not take it lightly that we had been interfered with.

"What'll he do about it, do you suppose?" King Mac said, taking a gold toothpick from his pocket and jabbing between his jagged, stumpy teeth with it. He scratched a thumbnail through the scabs of his chin, and asked if my lady had been educated.

She said she had.

"You know men's preferences, then, ma'am?"

She blushed very hot and did not answer him.

"Sometimes we must send the ladies to school for their lessons," King Mac said. "Other times it is unnecessary." There was a round of loutish laughter, to which he closed his eyes as though offended. When it was quiet he said to my lady, very low, "I will give you your freedom if you can discover mine. And much besides."

"Your what?" she said.

"My preferences." He swung away with his fringes all in a blurry motion, and minced over to where the drummer's daughter was sitting, with men crowding around him as men will around a bully. My lady was looking at me with her hot black eyes.

"You will tell me who he is," she said.

She pried at me until I told her he was in the business of seizing women and selling them into a certain slavery, but I did not tell her that Putaw Crossing was the call station for every kind of rustler, deserter, miner, trapper, and every other hard, lonely, and desperate man, and every color of nigger, breed, greaser, and Chinaman too. Nor that it was said King Mac sold women to the Kimanches, who paid well for white women.

All she said was, "I see."

The blind fellow, who was seated nearby, said, "He is not an entirely heartless man. Do not despair."

"Thank you," my lady said, as though she had taken comfort from that.

Dark came like a certain let down. King Mac's people had made a bonfire in the center of the corral, dragging in branches and pine knots, and my lady and I sat together on a pile of sacking as close to the abode wall and fence as we could get, with the blind man next to us. On a post nearby, but high up, I could see the rusty handles of a pair of wirecutters, though there was no way I could have reached them anyway, with my arms tied back aching as they were.

My lady moved closer so she was doing something behind me. She had the knifeblade out of her ring and was sawing rope, stopping once to catch her breath from exertion. Below us King Mac had climbed into a big highchair affair, like a judge's stand at a rodeo, made of saplings rawhided together. He had a jug which he lifted to his shoulder to suckle from, and, in the flickering of the bonfire, he cast a shadow over all that was a fearsome brooding thing.

When my lady sawed I could feel the heat of her breath on my ear. Then my hands were loosed, and in an instant I had the rope off, and her hands untied as well. Still I could not reach the wirecutters until my lady whispered to the blind man and borrowed his stick, and carefully I pried the cutters loose from their nail with the tip, flipped them toward me, and caught them as they fell. Squeezed up close to my lady and the blind man on the pile of sacking, I managed to clip one of the wires behind me with what seemed the loudest snap in the world. I clipped another, and another, finally turning to push a hole in the brush and loose wire. I helped my lady crawl through, and she dropped to the ground outside. Then I whispered to the blind fellow that it was his turn.

His fingers touched my face, quick and soft as the ghosts of fingers, exploring my features. "Do not worry about me," he whispered, "for men like these take me for good luck and will not molest me."

I swung through the wire after my lady, and we waited there, hardly breathing, but it didn't seem we had been missed.

There was a whicker, a horse tied to a post nearby. I helped my lady up behind the saddle, and swung up myself. I reined the animal away, whispering to him how I was counting on him, for likely he was one I had broke and trained myself like most in the Territory. He jerked his head like he understood, and we moved away from the big corral with my lady's arms locked around my waist. Then I touched my bootheel in and whispered again, and we made tracks away.

But as though King Mac, in his cunning, had laid a trap for my downfall, looped on the saddlehorn by its thong, was a leather-covered flask. And of course I must sample what was in it, and go on sampling. With whiskey-heat in my belly, and my lady pressed up against me, before much of that night of riding was gone we had tumbled off the horse to rut like beasts on the bare ground.

In full light she cried out my name. I came to my feet still drunken. There were two of them not fifty yards away, Jack Carew and another, with his rifle slanted at us, a rat-jawed dirty face showing under his hat brim.

Jack said, "Well, J.D., I allus said you was one selfish son-a-bitch. Now!"

There wasn't a thing in the world I could do while my lady scrambled to cover her limbs, except to back on over to the paint horse that had carried us here, with my hands raised to satisfy rat-jaw, who kept his rifle trained on me. Just then Jack Carew started to swing out of his saddle.

Well, there are those who say I can talk to a horse and know what the horse replies. I have had a hand in the gentling of most all the riding stock in the Territory, if I don't know each one by name, I know most, and Jack Carew's mare was called Magpie for her thieving habits. A horse will remember me because I chose to train him with words and whistles instead of hitting him over the face with a rope end like some ham-handed busters will do. Once I could whistle to bring in a horse at a gallop from a mile off.

So I called "Magpie'" just as Jack started to swing down. She jerked toward me, and Jack yelped as he started to fall. I whistled, not loud, and Magpie began trotting in a big arc, Jack with his boot caught in the stirrup bumping on the ground and squalling. The other fellow took up the chase, yelling to Jack to hold on and let go all at the same time. I had the lariat off the saddlehorn in a second, swinging a loop while rat-jaw raced up beside Magpie, grabbing for her bridle. I settled a loop over him and with a yelp he came out of the saddle and hung in the air about a minute before he came down with a jar to shake his grandmother. I sprinted barefoot through thorns and sharp pebbles for the rifle he had dropped, and laid it on him, his neck was broke where he sprawled here. His horse was high-tailing away, and Magpie had stopped to graze the dry grass. Jack Carew had managed to break his boot out of the stirrup. I took his revolver away from him while he sat there groaning. His face was scraped to raw bacon. "Jayd — Jayd — Jayd — ."

I grabbed his hair and shook him hard, calling him an evil toad who had once been a decent man. "Jayd — " he kept saying, "Jayd — " until I blew his brains out.

I took Magpie's reins and, with the revolver and rifle, tender-footed back to where my lady, with her clothing all together, stood watching me with those great dark eyes I would drown in every time I looked into them.

I got my clothes on to cover my nakedness, with Magpie pulled between us like a curtain. She mounted the other pony while I tended to the horses, feeling their legs and lifting each foot to look at shoe and hoof, talking to them both the while so they would know how we were depending on them. Then I swung up on Magpie and we made ourselves scarce from there.

My lady and I never spoke a word of what had happened that night I got into the whiskey. We never spoke of that or much else either in those days of riding and nights with a little cookfire, she sleeping on one side of it, and I pretending to on the other, staring at a red coal gleaming in the ashes and listening to the small sound of her breath. It was in small roundabout ways that we came to know each other, both of us, it seemed like, afraid of speaking more than good mornings and good nights, or how many days now? and maybe a word or two when I had shot a little game for supper and we sat braising bits of meat over the fire.

So I brought her safe to the Castle, which had been my charge. I had done the best I could, but failed in what the general might never come to know of, and I'll never know myself whether he did or didn't. He could see, on the outside of it anyway, that she was worn to a frazzle. He greeted her and me from the veranda of the Castle, very grateful to me, shaking my hand, and courtly with her, putting an arm around her and pecking at her cheek. And at that moment she looked past him at me, opening her eyes wide so I fell into them drowning, and smiled at me once and forever.

I had sworn off strong spirits and stuck with it for a long time after the flask was left on that pony's saddlehorn. I lived in the foreman's quarters just back of the Castle, and often, despite myself, dreamed of those nights with my lady across the cookfire, a little red coal winking a warning.

And one night when I was half-asleep, half-dreaming, I knew there was someone in the room with me. I jerked a hand for my revolver in its holster hanging from the bedpost, but did not touch it. There was a sniff of flowergarden in the room.

In the morning it seemed to me it must have been one of those dreams a man will have when he has been long without a woman and cannot control himself, until I got up from my bed with the covers thrown back, and there was a white flower with its petals mashed brown, one of the kind that grew in pots in the solarium of the Castle and that I had seen my lady wear in her hair.

After that once, though I would lie awake at night shivering to jar to pieces, it never happened again. Sometimes I would almost weep in my disappointment, and in the end I all but forgot it, as though it had been the dream I had first thought it was.

Meanwhile my lady became plumper and plumper until it was certain she was carrying child, and very near her term. And one day riding in from the corral I saw clouds rolling up black this side of the feathery clouds that hung over the Bucksaws. These had flashes of lightning streaking through them and were blackbelly rainclouds building up, so high all at once their shadow came sweeping over everything. And in the first real rainstorm for as long as anybody could remember, my lady was delivered of the most beautiful girl child as this world has ever seen. They called her Flora.

Before she was three she was sitting a mare fine as you please, a good seat on her, straight little back, and a commanding way she had of looking at you with her chin set and those eyes that seemed to gather in right away just what you were or weren't, but pink lips smiling as though to show she understood and forgave. She was her mother's very light and life when in her pinafore and a pink ribbon in her golden hair she ran to my lady, who would snatch her up to cover her with kisses. And the general's also, who often sat in the solarium when he was at the Castle, with his book, and a blanket over his knees, and Flora standing beside his chair touching his medals and asking about each one.

When it came time for the child to learn the ways of horses, it was me that was turned to. First, in the little ring I had had built, I would let her turn and turn at the end of a rope on the gentle mare Jessie, sidesaddle in her velvet riding habit like her mother's riding dress, and her black velvet cap with a feather in it. Then, with me beside her we rode close around the Castle, and later down the hill and splashing through Putaw Creek where water ran now.

I would only have to tell her once to hold the reins higher or tip her quirt a hair straighter, and she had done it and kept it that way, her mouth tight with her concentration. Now there was peace in the Territory, when we passed a band of Kimanche she would raise her quirt just so, while the young chief returned her greeting just the same, raising his rifle or spear as she had raised her quirt. The same with a squadron of cavalry, who would salute her very formal and as though she had been the general himself. Once we saw a pack of black riders off to the north that must be King Mac's, a great rush of hooves and dust and jammed-together men, too far off to make much out of, although I felt my blood turn to whey at the sight of them. But they showed no interest in us, and came no closer so that I thought we were safe from them here because of the general and cavalry at the fort.

But another time when we were out together we saw four riders trotting along a ridge line. At the distance we could make out that one of them was so small it might've been a monkey sitting his pinto horse, and another much bigger than the other two. Closer, they reined up to look us over, and I spurred Billy-bub so as to get between them and Flora. For the big one was King Mac, in a black slouch hat and about an acre of fringed white buckskin; with him one of the black riders, a boy that looked no older than Flora, with a mean, squinched face glowering down at us, and a woman seated sidesaddle, all in black velvet, with a cap of black feathers over a white face. It was the Drummer's daughter from the train. I didn't get my breath right until the four of them had swung away to disappear over the ridge, and we had got distance between us in the opposite direction.

Flora asked who they were, and I replied that they were from Putaw Crossing, which was on the other side of Helix Hill from the Castle, and was a place I hoped she would never see, for it was a filthy place.

"Are those bad people, J.D.?" she asked me.

"Yes. Bad."

"How can you tell?"

"For one, they have got different ways of looking at you, kind of sideways instead of straight on."

"But could you tell that from here?"
"So could you, which is why you asked about them."

The whiskey was after me again. It would gripe my insides like a half-hitch on the strain for one swallow of the stuff. I had sworn I would not drink in my room, and I did not, but I began to stash bottles here and there, one in a cairn of stones in a place Flora and I would pass when we rode out. I made sure we rode close by there, and with the excuse that I must relieve myself, which was true enough, walk down into the bottom and around a crag of rock, where I would take out my bottle and have a swig or two of whiskey.

And so I did this one day, taking the bottle from its hidey-hole with the glass blister hot where the sun had got to it, and uncorked it, and knocked back a long pull, standing there panting and hating myself and everything else. I tipped the bottle up for another dose to wash out the fire, and a third to drown the ashes, when there was a heavy drumming I could feel through my boot soles, like a flash flood bearing down from a cloudburst in the mountains. Then it was hooves, a herd of buffalo it seemed, so many, building and building but whatever it was invisible except for a rise of dust coming on. I began to run back to where I had left Flora, so slowfooted it was like running in quicksand, and my shouting drowned out by those beating hooves. Then they passed and went on, and the dust cloud passed along. I ran on panting and knowing I was too late. She was gone, with only the tracks of a great bunch of horses heading off to the north where the dust was still moving.

I set off riding hard following those tracks. The dust faded away before me. There was stony ground, and then a place where some tracks swung off to the left while the others ran straight ahead, and further along another party veering to the right. I didn't know what to do but keep spurring after the main body, though what I would do if I caught up I didn't know. Then there was hard ground for a spell, and a tangle of rocky draws, and night coming, and that was the end of it.

I rode back to the Castle with a half-moon sailing in scud cloud above me, slow and slower up the winding road toward the lights of the Castle windows. I dismounted there and climbed the steps with my hat in my hand.

Inside my lady came running toward me, with the general behind her, and two officers from the fort with him. "*Where is my child?*"

When I told her what had happened she didn't speak a word, and the officers made a great hub-bub that they would ride out, they would find her and bring her back, though I saw the general only crossed his arms on his chest in that way they lay dead men out sometimes. My lady crouched back against the marble fireplace there. She said, "*It is a judgment on me!*"

The two officers stopped their foolish talk and turned to try to comfort her. But she burst past them with the poker raised high to brain me, her face as fierce as a tigress. I did not even put up my hands to protect myself.

But she did not bring that poker down to kill me for my sins, for just then the general fell. He fell like a tree falling, not even trying to ease it, just toppling straight over with a crash on the parquet, like a dead man.

In the months of my wandering I took the pledge and failed, and pledged again and failed again in drunken shame, and misused myself in many ways. And one day, through an old acquaintance met by chance in a saloon in some trailhead town, I learned that my lady had never got over her grieving, that the Castle had been abandoned and was run down to ruin, and she and the general were moved into Bright City, where he never rested sending out cavalry troops to search for the band of renegade Kimanche that had stolen his daughter. But I knew it was not Kimanche that had taken Flora.

And so it was I returned to Bright City, coming in past the adobe fort, where a trooper with a rifle paced before the open gate and a bit of striped color hung from the flagpole as limp as I felt; and on along past the dump and Boot Hill, and into the town square with the dust from Blackie's hooves itching on my face. A carriage drawn by a fine team of grays came at me swaying on its thoroughbraces, a big sergeant with yellow chevrons on his sleeve up on the box. Seeing the two gold stars on the door I brought a hand up to jerk down on my hat brim, for I knew the general was inside that carriage, though I could not see him through the window.

I sat Blackie with my hand still pulling on my hat brim as though saluting, dust setting over me as the carriage jounced on by—heading for the fort where my lady was.

I gave Blackie a low whistle to start him along. For I knew I had not come back to Bright City, nor the fort either, but to Putaw Crossing where I must find Flora, and if King Mac decided to put me under for shooting Jack Carew and rat-jaw that time when I snatched my lady free of him, why that was all right; and if I had to go into harness like those other fellows I had known in the old days, in order to snatch Flora free, then that was as it must be too.

It was sunset, with the sun sinking blood-red into the western clouds when I rode out along the railroad tracks, the rails with rusty flashes of light along them. Coming into Putaw Crossing, the air was filled with dust mingled with smoke and the open-sewer stench that seemed to get caught in my clothes so that I could smell it on myself even when the breeze veered around.

At the crossroads I turned Blackie uphill, a bridge sounding hollow as a coffin beneath his hooves. In black night we mounted a pot-holed road past a solid front of storefronts under a wooden awning. There was a creak of a shutter in a wind I couldn't feel, and once a caterwauling and two cats tearing across the way in front of us. Blackie jumped pole-legged and then stood steady, shivering, while I patted and whispered to him.

There were sounds in the silence now, a voice raised somewhere, and laughter and a spate of tinny music shut off like a door had closed. I could remember when there'd been no more than a dozen adobe and tin shacks at the Crossing, and now the hill was thick with them.

Pretty soon I could make out dark forms of men, and lights showed where the road narrowed between two squatty 'dobes, with candles or lanterns inside. Women leaned out of windows, many of them in their bare flesh, calling out to the men passing, me among them, sometimes sweetly but more often coarse to chill your belly.

There was a big horse-barn at one of the turnings, there must have been a hundred horses stalled inside, and I left Blackie with the one-armed hostler there. King Mac's "palace" was on up the narrow, curving way another half a mile, he told me.

More men crowded the way, some few in town clothing, most in rough dress and many in leather jackets aping King Mac's buckskin fringes. There were hardrock miners in their sashes, workingmen in heavy boots, skinners, drifters, ruffians, and hardcases of every shade of color. From a window above me a redheaded woman opened the blouse of her dress to scoop her breasts at me. " 'Ey, 'andsome, you come see me, eh? Further up they's all clappy." When I went on past she spat down at me.

I could not even look down the side streets of cribs, though I might have to before I was through here.

The cobbled street led along a ridge where there was a breeze with the sewer stink blown away for a spell. Above the slot of a canyon a black peak towered, which, as I came up further, I saw was not part of the hill but a tented, sprawling structure with lights piercing its sides. Just here three of the black riders leaned together like blackbirds watching me come past them. One of them was Jim Eggers, who chose not to recognize me, nor I him.

There was another cross-street of cribs, with the whores hanging out the tops of the dutch-doors, and as I hurried on past I wondered if each one of the black riders had come here in this same way, with a blight on his conscience and no decency left him, or on some hunt that put a good face on his coming to Putaw Crossing and King Mac's service.

So at last I reached the top with the "palace" piled up before me in a confusion of lights and shadows. Nearer was a long building that had burned, with the roof timbers fallen in; all at once, like a kick in the belly. I understood the "palace" was no less than the Castle, for Putaw Crossing had grown up and over Helix Hill. Coming up the back way I had not realized that until now.

I stood there trying to catch my breath, staring at the Castle which was so changed, with the outbuildings burned. On a broad veranda I could make out the pale glow of cheroots where men lounged on benches. Someone sent a butt spinning sparks out into the dark. Each of the steps up to the veranda seemed three feet high as I climbed them.

The first person I saw, sitting above the pack of people inside, was a big, wall-eyed shotgun, slumped on his lookout stand between the faro layouts. He nodded to me just as though he had been certain I would come in the door at that very moment. Beyond him stairs curved to a landing. Walls had been knocked out to make the ballroom bigger, while the height seemed lower, as though the Castle had slumped down somehow.

I was nervy as a spooked horse as I made my way through bunches of men who paid me no attention, and whores with their bogus smiles and winks, until I came to the bar, where first I ordered a whiskey, then changed my mind. I jumped half out of my skin when there was a slap on my back.

"Well, hello, J.D.!"

It was Bobby Kettle from the old Hundred, in the rusty black the hands all seemed to wear here, scratchy little beard with a thin dark mouth grinning out of it.

"Well, hello, Kett," I said.

"Whiskey with an old pard, J.D.?"

I said I had taken the pledge, and he shrugged and set about swinging his elbows to clear a space for us among the men ganged around the bar. Those who weren't black-dressed were quick to make way for one who was, and the barkeep hurried to bring whiskey and a glass.

"Come out to join the boys, have you?" Bobby Kettle said.

"Just thought I'd look in, Kett. How is everybody?"

"Oh, everybody is healthy and prosperous," he said with a wink.

All at once there was shouting that shrilled to a screech, mixed with a snarling rousting. I switched around to see a man hurl himself out the door with a great black hound on his heels. There was laughter like the toadying laughter for a bully at another's expense. King Mac stood spread-legged on the landing, big as a grizzly in his pale buckskins, hat brim pulled down and a cigar stuck in his jaw. Beside him was a redheaded boy in a kind of dickey-shirt, with a nasty, freckled, squinched-up face. I had seen him with King Mac once before, and I looked for the drummer's daughter in the half-open door behind them, but didn't see her.

With a stirring and pushing this way and that, the black hound trotted back inside, nails clattering on the floor. He raced up the steps and haunched down beside the boy, who patted him and in the silence, in a shrill, mean voice, said, "Good dog, sir!"

"That's a big dog," I said to Kett.

"He will just take out after a man for no reason sometimes," he said, and giggled.

The boy took something from his pocket and dropped it bouncing down the stairs—a red ball. The hound lit out after it, down and across the room with people piling out of the way, some of them falling, and women squealing, until, with a scraping clatter, the dog caught the ball and trotted back up the stairs to return it to the boy, who patted him some more. All the while King Mac stood there sucking on his cigar and glancing around, so that I found myself sidling to get behind Kett.

Another rusty-black fellow clapped me on the shoulder and called me by name, though I couldn't recall his. Others came up to shake hands, and more whiskey was poured with me still managing to refuse a glass. And when I glanced back toward the landing, King Mac, the boy, and the hound were gone.

One of the fellows asked if I wasn't the one that was supposed to be able to talk to horses. "How about mules?" another wanted to know.

They were a hard-eyed, sharp-jawed bunch, dirty-faced like they hadn't washed this month. They were quick to nudge one another and have the laugh on someone else. Now they kept after me very scornful, who was the one supposed to be able to talk to horses, and I pretended to think it as funny as they did, though finally I said there might come a day and a reason for me to call in all the riding stock in the Territory, and then we'd see who was on foot.

This gave them a great laugh. They quieted down when a tall, bare-headed fellow came toward us. He had black spectacles on and swung a stick out before him, saying "Pardon. Pardon, gentlemen." He was greeted very polite by those around me, and called Lute. He was the blind man from the train, with that twisted scar on his forehead.

He came close to me and asked me my name, and, when I told him, if I would mind his touching my face: "For I must have other means of seeing than the sight of my eyes."

His fingers, that I remembered, chased over my features, light and quick, and like he was remembering me, too.

"Think you'll know him next time you see him, Lute?" Kett said, to snickers. And I heard another fellow whisper, "Damn-all how he knows when there's a stranger showed up."

"J.D. used to ride with the old Hundred bunch one time, Lute. Come back to join up again."

The blind man looked like a young fellow who had been struck old in an instant, his face young and old at the same time. A pulse ticked in the scar.

He said, "If you gentlemen would pardon us, I'd like to have a word with your friend. What I have felt in his features may be of value for him to know."

Kett said, "Lute can tell a man's fortune fine as any gypsy woman!"

"Do you see a table where we can have privacy?" the blind man said in a low voice. He took my arm, and I led him to a table in the corner. When we had seated ourselves he commanded me to put out my hand.

Leaning forward he made to be tracing lines in my palm, whispering, "You must tell me why you are here!"

I told him that I had come to find a child who had been stolen, a girl I thought must be in this place; and that her mother, who was out of her senses with grief, was the woman who had been with me when King Mac had derailed the train.

"And you are the father?"

I said that the general was the father.

He folded my fingers into my palm as though finished reading what was there, and leaned back with the round black lenses of his spectacles fixed on me. He said, "The child is here. She is an influence for the good."

My heart began to bang on my ribs. "It was my fault she was taken, you see," I said. He was silent, considering, his mouth a flat line. "The mother—" I started, but did not go on, for he had nodded in decision.

"Very well," he said. "I can help you take her from here. But how will you escape from the Crossing? There would be two hundred riders after you."

"You can leave that to me," I said.

"Very well. Listen to me: in five minutes' time you will leave this room. There is a door at the end of the veranda that will be unlocked. I will meet you inside." His chair jarred back as he rose. Without another word he headed across the room, stick flicking ahead of him, a head taller than anyone else there: "Pardon, please, gentlemen; ladies!"

I wandered among the gambling layouts, watching a play then moving along. One of the fancy-dressed women attached herself to my arm, but I shook her off, saying, "Later." When I judged five minutes had passed I strolled on outside, as though I was just stepping out for a breath of fresh air.

I opened the door at the end of the veranda on pitchy blackness. My arm was caught and I was pulled inside, the door closing behind me, a bolt rattling home. Lute thrust a bit of leather into my hand, the end of his belt.

"Hold to that. I know these passages well."

He set off at a good clip, pulling me behind him. I brushed a wall of splintery wood, then one of dressed stone. We were in a long passageway, very narrow. I remembered in the old days hearing of secret ways about the Castle.

"Steps," Lute said. It was a long flight up, making a right turn and then another. Once there were glimmers of dusty light from cracks in the wall, so that I had a glimpse of him climbing before me, holding the other end of the belt. Then there was another long passageway, and more stairs, until I had lost all sense of direction. At last he halted, so abruptly I banged into him from behind. He worked at something in the wall and became visible again in a dim square of light. It was a judas window. He pulled me into it.

In the exact center of the room Flora sat on the floor with her back to me. She was wearing a pinafore, and her long blonde hair, caught up in a blue bow, hung down her back. Squatting facing her was the redheaded boy. The big dog sat, tongue lolling, beside an open door in which the drummer's daughter stood, sumptuously dressed in black velvet with white lace, bare shoulders gleaming. Her lips were moving; she and Flora seemed to be conversing past the boy and the dog. I could make out voices, but not the words.

"Tell me what you see!" the blind man whispered in my ear.

I described the room and the people in it. Meanwhile the woman disappeared with a flick of her black skirt.

Flora gestured with her hand and the boy rose and retreated across the room. A shelf there held dolls seated against the wall. He brought one of these back to Flora, who incorporated it in some game she was playing, whch was invisible to me. He squatted before her again.

Tapping my arm, Lute demonstrated that the square of smoked glass could be slid to one side, and that we stood behind a secret door into the room, which was secured by bolts at the top and bottom.

Flora gestured again, I heard the distant voices again, there was considerable more back and forth talk, and the boy, hands in his pockets, stalked out of the room.

"The boy's gone," I whispered to Lute. "Now there is only the hound."

He nodded as though that was to be expected, and pressed something round into my hand. It was a red ball like the one the boy had tossed down the stairs. "You must be certain it goes out the far door," he whispered, and slid the glass aside.

I aimed the ball, flipped my wrist several times to limber it, and tossed the ball through the judas window. It flew over Flora's blonde head, bounced past the hound and out the door. The dog leaped after it, skidding around the corner and out of sight. Lute had slid the bolts and I pushed the door open. Flora's astonished face swung toward me.

"J.D.!" She scrambled to her feet and ran to me. I caught her in my arms, pulled her back through the door while Lute swung it closed behind us and threw the bolts just as the hound slammed into the door. I pressed my finger to Flora's lips in the dust-smelling dark.

Now the boy's voice was audible; "*Florrie.* You come out from where you're hiding, you hear—" Then Lute slid the judas window closed.

We hurried blind along the dark passageway, me holding to Lute's belt end with one hand and pulling Flora along with the other. "Step!" Lute whispered to me, and I whispered "Step down!" to Flora. We shuffled down the first stairs.

"Are you taking me to my mother and the general, J.D.?" Flora asked, and I said I was.

I touched dressed stone again, but Lute continued to descend, a ramp now instead of stairs, raw rock walls, mossy and damp. Further along I heard water trickling, and there was a feel of other passages drifted off this one, with puffs of cooler air sometimes and once a swatch of starry sky giving light enough for me to see the blind man hurrying along in the lead, and Flora's pale face behind, her tight hand gripping mine. We had to halt to pick our way over a rock fall.

"I knew you'd come, J.D.," Flora panted. "I'll be so happy to see my mother and the general again! Have they been very worried?"

"Very worried," I said, and asked if those people had been bad to her.

"They were as nice as they knew how to be. But they are a different kind of people, you see. They look at you out of the corners of their eyes the way you said, but then if you are straight with them they stop doing it."

"We must move swiftly," Lute said, and we hastened on. All at once we were under the stars again, with all around us the feverish clamor of Putaw Crossing. I saw we were not a hundred steps from the big stable where I had left Blackie. The blind man remained behind the pile of rubble, where the tunnel had come out. When I said he must come with us, he only shook his head.

"Others may need me here. But you must hurry. There will be many men in pursuit."

"You can trust *me* now," I said, clasped his hand once, and hurried Flora down to the corral. There was no light, but I found Blackie quickly and boosted Flora up behind the saddle. I gave a low whistle, and heard the answering stirring and whickering of the other animals in that place.

I sung up and cautioned Flora to hold on tight. Her arms came around me, and I could feel her warm face pressed to my back. I jammed my knuckles to my lips and blew such a blast as I had never blown before.

Behind us in the corral a terrific racket began, and the one-armed hostler, hurrying up with a lantern, gawked open-mouthed at Flora and me and the open doors of the horsebarn behind us. He backed away, swinging the lantern like a railroad switchman.

I pushed Blackie into a hard trot down the cobbled street, men jumping aside with yells and curses. I blew another whistle to rattle the windows. Just then one of the rusty-black riders leaped out to try to catch Blackie's reins, and I jerked out my piece and cold-cocked him with the barrel. We rode rattling on downhill.

The whole stampede of us, Blackie in the lead, and all the horseflesh of Putaw Crossing swarming after, surged on down the street between the dark shacks and storefronts, thundered across the bridge, and swung north on the road for Bright City. When I looked back over my shoulder it seemed that all the horses in the world were galloping after us in the starlight. Far back I saw a rider, but he had disappeared before I could unship my revolver. Her arms clasped around my waist, Flora spoke to me sometimes, but I couldn't make out what she said for the pounding of the hooves. Horses had caught up on either side of us, a big bay named Lopey on the right, and on the left a black and white pinto I couldn't recall the name of. Others were saddled, and many trailed ropes. I gave a whistle from time to time to keep them coming.

When we reached the fort, a white quarter-moon hung over the Bucksaws and the sky was paling for dawn. The trooper at the gate stood with his carbine at a half-ready, gaping out at Blackie and me with Flora pillion, and most of an acre of horses crowding around us. I swung out of the saddle to lift Flora down, so tired she could hardly stand.

"Take Miss Flora to the general, pronto!" I said, and the guard gasped. He clutched for her arm.

Flora said, "J.D., you just wait right there till my mother comes!"

"No," I said. No; I just wanted to secure these animals inside, for I'd bet the cavalry could use some remount. Then I'd be on my way.

The trooper rushed her inside the gate, with her little face turned back toward me and a hand raised up and waving to me to wait.

It took me some time to chouse those Putaws horses inside the fort, and swing the gate to, and mount up on Blackie again. My lady came running outside in her long wrapper, with her hair up in a cloth, to stop by me with her breast heaving and a hand held there, and those black discs of her eyes fixed on my face. The white knot of her hand sought mine where I held the reins. And she said, "You have brought me back my child!"

I said I had brought her back, who had lost her in the first place.

I drowned again in those black eyes, and she whispered the name of a place in Bright City. Just then the general trotted outside holding Flora by the hand. I raised up an arm in greeting to him, pulled Blackie to his haunches, whistled to make him jump, and lit out of there.

I found the place in town she had whispered to me, which was a hotel, and I lay there on the bed with my hands locked beneath my head staring up at the waterstains on the ceiling. Then I went down the street to buy a glass of whiskey for my dry throat, and ended up bringing the bottle back to my room.

The next morning I woke up not even sober yet, to smell on the pillow beside my face the scent of a white blossom laid there by someone who had come, and gone.

AMY HEMPEL

In the Cemetery Where Al Jolson Is Buried

for Jessica

TELL me things I won't mind forgetting," she said. "Make it useless stuff or skip it."

I began. I told her insects fly through rain, missing every drop, never getting wet. I told her no one in America owned a tape recorder before Bing Crosby did. I told her the shape of the moon is like a banana—you see it looking full, you're seeing it end-on.

The camera made me self-conscious and I stopped. It was trained on us from a ceiling mount—the kind of camera banks use to photograph robbers. It played our image to the nurses down the hall in Intensive Care.

"Go on, girl," she said, "you get used to it."

I had my audience. I went on. Did she know that Tammy Wynette had changed her tune? Really. That now she sings "Stand By Your *Friends*"? Paul Anka did it too, I said. Does "You're Having *Our* Baby." He got sick of all that feminist bitching.

"What else?" she said. "Have you got something else?"

Oh yes. For her I would always have something else.

"Did you know when they taught the first chimp to talk, it lied?

When they asked her who did it on the desk, she signed back Max, the janitor. And when they pressed her, she said she was sorry, that it was really the project director. But she was a mother, so I guess she had her reasons."

"Oh, that's good," she said. "A parable."

"There's more about the chimp," I said. "But it will break your heart."

"No thanks," she says, and scratches at her mask.

We look like good-guy outlaws. Good or bad, I am not used to the mask yet. I keep touching the warm spot where my breath, thank God, comes out. She is used to hers. She only ties the strings on top. The other ones—a pro by now—she lets hang loose.

We call this place the Marcus Welby Hospital. It's the white one with the palm trees under the opening credits of all those shows. A Hollywood hospital, though in fact it is several miles west. Off camera, there is a beach across the street.

She introduces me to a nurse as "the Best Friend." The impersonal article is more intimate. It tells me that *they* are intimate, my friend and her nurse.

"I was telling her we used to drink Canada Dry Ginger Ale and pretend we were in Canada."

"That's how dumb *we* were," I say.

"You could be sisters," the nurse says.

So how come, I'll bet they are wondering, it took me so long to get to such a glamorous place? But do they ask?

They do not ask.

Two months, and how long is the drive?

The best I can explain it is this—I have a friend who worked one summer in a mortuary. He used to tell me stories. The one that really got to me was not the grisliest, but it's the one that did. A man wrecked his car on 101 going south. He did not lose consciousness. But his arm was taken down to the wet bone—and when he looked at it—it scared him to death. I mean, he died.

So I didn't dare look any closer. But now I'm doing it—and hoping I won't be scared to death.

She shakes out a summer-weight blanket, showing a leg you did not want to see. Except for that, you look at her and understand the law that requires *two* people to be with the body at all times.

"I thought of something," she says. "I thought of it last night. I think there is a real and present need here. You know," she says, "like for someone to do it for you when you can't do it yourself. You call them up whenever you want—like when push comes to shove."

She grabs the bedside phone and loops the cord around her neck.

"Hey," she says, "the End o' the Line."

She keeps on, giddy with something. But I don't know with what.

"The giveaway was the solarium," she says. "That's where Marcus Welby broke the news to his patients. Then here's the real doctor suggesting we talk in the solarium. So I knew I was going to die.

"I can't remember," she says, "what does Kübler-Ross[1] say comes after Denial?"

It seems to me Anger must be next. Then Bargaining, Depression, and so on and so forth. But I keep my guesses to myself.

"The only thing is," she says, "is where's Resurrection? God knows I want to do it by the book. But she left out Resurrection."

She laughs, and I cling to the sound the way someone dangling above a ravine holds fast to the thrown rope.

We could have cried then, but when we didn't, we couldn't.

"Tell me," she says, "about that chimp with the talking hands. What do they do when the thing ends and the chimp says, 'I don't want to go back to the zoo'?"

When I don't say anything, she says, "O.K.—then tell me another animal story. I like animal stories. But not a sick one—I don't want to know about all the Seeing Eye dogs going blind."

No, I would not tell her a sick one.

"How about the hearing-ear dogs?" I say. "They're not going deaf, but they are getting very judgmental. For instance, there's this golden retriever in Jersey, he wakes up the deaf mother and drags her into the daughter's room because the kid has got a flashlight and is reading under the covers."

"Oh, you're killing me," she says. "Yes, you're definitely killing me."

"They say the smart dog obeys, but the smarter dog knows when to *dis*obey."

"Yes," she says, "the smarter *anything* knows when to disobey. Now, for example."

She is flirting with the Good Doctor, who has just appeared. Unlike the Bad Doctor, who checks the I.V. drip before saying good morning, the Good Doctor says things like "God didn't give epileptics a fair shake." He awards himself points for the cripples he could have hit in the parking lot. Because the Good Doctor is a little in love with her he says maybe a year. He pulls a chair up to her bed and suggests I might like to spend an hour on the beach.

"Bring me something back," she says. "Anything from the beach. Or the gift shop. Taste is no object."

The doctor slowly draws the curtain around her bed.

1. Elisabeth Kübler-Ross (1926–   ), author of popular books on death and dying.

"Wait!" she cries.

I look in at her.

"Anything," she says, "except a magazine subscription."

The doctor turns away.

I watch her mouth laugh.

What seems dangerous often is not—black snakes, for example, or clear-air turbulence. While things that just lie there, like this beach, are loaded with jeopardy. A yellow dust rising from the ground, the heat that ripens melons overnight—this is earthquake weather. You can sit here braiding the fringe on your towel and the sand will all of a sudden suck down like an hourglass. The air roars. In the cheap apartments onshore, bathtubs fill themselves and gardens roll up and over like green waves. If nothing happens, the dust will drift and the heat deepen till fear turns to desire. Nerves like that are only bought off by catastrophe.

"It never happens when you're thinking about it," she observed once.

"Earthquake, earthquake, earthquake," she said.

"Earthquake, earthquake, earthquake," I said.

Like the aviaphobe who keeps the plane aloft with prayer, we kept it up till an aftershock cracked the ceiling.

That was after the big one in '72. We were in college; our dormitory was five miles from the epicenter. When the ride was over and my jabbering pulse began to slow, she served five parts champagne to one part orange juice and joked about living in Ocean View, Kansas. I offered to drive her to Hawaii on the new world psychics predicted would surface the next time, or the next.

I could not say that now—next. *Whose* next? she could ask.

Was I the only one who noticed that the experts had stopped saying *if* and now spoke of *when*? Of course not; the fearful ran to thousands. We watched the traffic of Japanese beetles for deviation. Deviation might mean more natural violence.

I wanted her to be afraid with me, but she said, "I don't know. I'm just not."

She was afraid of nothing, not even of flying.

I have this dream before a flight where we buckle in and the plane moves down the runway. It takes off at thirty-five miles an hour, and then we're airborne, skimming the tree tops. Still, we arrive in New York on time. It is so pleasant. One night I flew to Moscow this way.

She flew with me once. That time she flew with me she ate macadamia nuts while the wings bounced. She knows the wing tips can bend thirty feet up and thirty feet down without coming off. She believes it. She trusts the laws of aerodynamics. My mind stampedes. I can almost accept that a battleship floats, and everybody knows steel sinks.

I see fear in her now and am not going to try to talk her out of it. She is right to be afraid.

After a quake, the six o'clock news airs a film clip of first-graders yelling at the broken playground per their teacher's instructions. "*Bad* earth!" they shout, because anger is stronger than fear.

But the beach is standing still today. Everyone on it is tranquilized, numb or asleep. Teenaged girls rub coconut oil on each other's hard-to-reach places. They smell like macaroons. They pry open compacts like clamshells; mirrors catch the sun and throw a spray of white rays across glazed shoulders. The girls arrange their wet hair with silk flowers the way they learned in *Seventeen*. They pose.

A formation of low-riders[2] pulls over to watch with a six-pack. They get vocal when the girls check their tan lines. When the beer is gone, so are they—flexing their cars on up the boulevard.

Above this aggressive health are the twin wrought-iron terraces, painted flamingo pink, of the Palm Royale. Someone dies there every time the sheets are changed. There's an ambulance in the driveway, so the remaining residents line the balconies, rocking and not talking, one-upped.

The ocean they stare at is dangerous, and not just the undertow. You can almost see the slapping tails of sand sharks keeping cruising bodies alive.

If she looked, she could see this, some of it, from her window. She would be the first to say how little it takes to make a thing all wrong.

There was a second bed in the room when I returned. For two beats I didn't get it. Then it hit me like an open coffin.

She wants every minute, I thought. She wants my life.

"You missed Gussie," she said.

Gussie is her parents' 300-pound narcoleptic maid. Her attacks often come at the ironing board. The pillowcases in that family are all bordered with scorch.

"It's a hard trip for her," I said. "How is she?"

"Well, she didn't fall asleep, if that's what you mean. Gussie's great—you know what she said? She said, 'Darlin' just keep prayin', down on your knees.' "

She shrugged. "See anybody good?"

"No," I said, "just the new Charlie's Angel. And I saw Cher's car down near the Arcade."

2. Drivers of rebuilt, underslung cars.

"Cher's car is worth *three* Charlie's Angels," she said, "What else am I missing?"

"It's earthquake weather," I told her.

"The best thing to do about earthquakes," she said, "is not to live in California."

"That's useful," I said. "You sound like Reverend Ike: 'The best thing to do for the poor is not be one of them.' "

We're crazy about Reverend Ike.

I noticed her face was bloated.

"You know," she said, "I feel like hell. I'm about to stop having fun."

"The ancients have a saying," I said. " 'There are times when the wolves are silent; there are times when the moon howls.' "

"What's that, Navajo?"

"Palm Royale lobby graffiti," I said. "I bought a paper there. I'll read to you."

"Even though I care about nothing?" she said.

I turned to page three, to a UPI filler datelined Mexico City. I read her "Man Robs Bank with Chicken," about a man who bought a barbecued chicken at a stand down the block from a bank. Passing the bank, he got the idea. He walked in and approached a teller. He pointed the brown paper bag at her and she handed over the day's receipts. It was the smell of barbecue sauce that eventually led to his capture.

The story made her hungry, she said, so I took the elevator down six floors to the cafeteria and brought back all the ice cream she wanted. We lay side by side, adjustable beds cranked up for optimal TV viewing, littering the sheets with Good Humor wrappers, picking toasted almonds out of the gauze. We were Lucy and Ethel, Mary and Rhoda in extremis. The blinds were closed to keep light off the screen.

We watched a movie starring men we used to think we wanted to sleep with. Hers was a tough cop out to stop mine, a vicious rapist who went after cocktail waitresses.

"This is a good movie," she said, when snipers felled them both.

I missed her already; my straight man, my diary.

A Filipino nurse tiptoed in and gave her an injection. She removed the pile of Popsicle sticks from the nightstand—enough to splint a small animal.

The injection made us sleepy—me in the way I picked up her inflection till her mother couldn't tell us apart on the phone. We slept.

I dreamed she was a decorator, come to furnish my house. She worked in secret, singing to herself. When she finished, she guided me proudly to the door. "How do you like it?" she asked, easing me inside.

Every beam and sill and shelf and knob was draped in black bunting, with streamers of black crepe looped around darkened mirrors.

"I have to go home," I said when she woke up.

She thought I meant home to her house in the Canyon, and I had to say No, *home* home. I twisted my hands in the hackneyed fashion of people in pain. I was supposed to offer something. The Best Friend. I could not even offer to come back.

I felt weak and small and failed. Also exhilarated. I had a convertible in the parking lot. Once out of that room, I would drive it too fast down the coast highway through the crab-smelling air. A stop in Malibu for sangria. The music in the place would be sexy and loud. They would serve papaya and shrimp and watermelon ice. After dinner I would pick up beach boys. I would shimmer with life, buzz with heat, vibrate with health, stay up all night with one and then the other.

Without a word, she yanked off her mask and threw it on the floor. She kicked at the blankets and moved to the door. She must have hated having to pause for breath and balance before slamming out of Isolation, and out of the second room, the one where you scrub and tie on the white masks.

A voice shouted her name in alarm, and people ran down the corridor. The Good Doctor was paged over the intercom. I opened the door and the nurses at the station stared hard, as if this flight had been my idea.

"Where is she?" I asked, and they nodded to the supply closet.

I looked in. Two nurses were kneeling beside her on the floor, talking to her in low voices. One held a mask over her nose and mouth, the other rubbed her back in slow circles. The nurses glanced up to see if I was the doctor, and when they saw I wasn't, they went back to what they were doing.

"There, there, honey," they cooed.

On the morning she was moved to the cemetery, the one where Al Jolson is buried, I enrolled in a Fear of Flying class. "What is your worst fear?" the instructor asked, and I answered, "That I will finish this course and still be afraid."

I sleep with a glass of water on the nightstand so I can see by its level if the coastal earth is trembling or if the shaking is still me.

What do I remember? I remember only the useless things I hear —that Bob Dylan's mother invented Wite-out, that twenty-three people must be in a room before there is a fifty-fifty chance two will have the same birthdate. Who cares whether or not it's true? In my head there are bath towels swaddling this stuff. Nothing else seeps through.

I review those things that will figure in the retelling: a kiss through surgical gauze, the pale hand correcting the position of the wig. I noted these gestures as they happened, not in any retrospect. Though I don't know why looking *back* should show us more than looking *at*. It is just possible I will say I stayed the night. And who is there that can say I did not?

Nothing else gets through until I think of the chimp, the one with the talking hands.

In the course of the experiment, that chimp had a baby. Imagine how her trainers must have thrilled when the mother, without prompting, began to sign to the newborn. Baby, drink milk. Baby, play ball. And when the baby died, the mother stood over the body, her wrinkled hands moving with animal grace, forming again and again the words, Baby, come hug, Baby, come hug, fluent now in the language of grief.

JINCY KORNHAUSER

Melinda Falling

THE very first time I saw her, Melinda was in midair, just below the summit of a long, winding staircase, on her way down. There were three other women on the wide carpeted stairs; two were prettier than Melinda, and all more chicly dressed (cocktail party, Newport; lawyers-bankers-brokers), but Melinda eclipsed them all, descending, as she did, by somersault and cartwheel. She was upside-down when I first caught sight of her, left profile to me, splayed hands poised above the stair upon which the uppermost chic woman was standing; long black skirt accordioned around her hips, plump pink face partially obscured by a curtain of brown hair. I thought: Oh, my. Her right foot came down first, glancing off the edge of a step, snapping free the golden heel of her plastic shoe, and, momentarily upright, she pivoted and went down the rest of the way sideways, arms and legs extended like spokes. She wheeled, in stately fashion, between the other two women, who stood motionless like handmaidens in a frieze, watching her. All watched her, all held their breath: she whirled in dignified silence, broken only by the soft thuds of hand and foot on thick red carpeting. She did not exactly defy gravity, but mastered it by the perfect rate of descent, so that, for instance, the hem of her skirt ebbed and flowed with tantalizing discretion. So deliberate, solemn, and utterly magical was her progress that it promised to go on forever. When finally she touched down on the floor, upright, there was a little collective sigh of disappointment and then spontaneous applause led, I believe, by me. "Magnificent!" I said. "Bravo!" And

I took her arm and led her away from the crowd; I was half in love already and wanted her all to myself. "Get me out of here," she said—her first words to me—and the expression on her flushed, round face was regal, impenetrable.

Stepping out of her ruined shoes she walked beside me like a queen, head high (though she was actually quite short), and we were out the door and halfway to my car before I realized she was trudging, uncomplaining, through ankle-deep snow in stockinged feet. "Allow me," I said, circling her midriff with one arm and stooping to cradle the backs of her knees; but she pretended not to understand and speeded up, high-stepping through the snow just ahead of me. Cursing my awkwardness I followed her, semi-attached in this absurd posture, and cursed myself again when, ushering her into my Mercedes, I heard the dull crack of her head colliding, *en passant*, against the doorframe.

"My name," I began, deferentially addressing not the shadowy form beside me but the red glow of the radio, "is Edwin Crapeau Foote. I am not a Newport Foote, but a Mattapoisett Foote. There is no ancestral excuse for my middle name; my mother just thought it sounded classy. I am a wildly successful investment lawyer, having in fifteen years made myself richer than half my clients and the social equal of the rest. I owe my present success to youthful ambition, and that ambition to precocious childhood revulsion toward the dullness and mediocrity of the smack dab middle of the middle class. I sought, you see, to move always among talented, challenging, unusual people: the witty, the sparkling, the unpredictable. Heady conversation, candlelit surprise. I thought, you see, that there must be some connection between money and memorable experience; between rare wine and rare intelligence. In short, I was a romantic idiot. Dear Lady, you have just provided me with the only moment in my entire life when I was not bored almost to the point of lunacy. With a single wordless act you have shown more daring, more devastating social awareness, more sheer imagination—"

"I tripped," she said.

I was silent for a long digestive moment. "That's impossible. Nobody could do that by accident."

"I do everything by accident," she said. "That's all you have to know about me. I'm a stupid secretary, that's all, and my stupid boss brought me to this stupid party because his wife is even homelier than me. And I would just like," she said, her voice rising in pitch and thinning out into a child's cry, "to do one goddamn simple thing in my life, like walk across a room or down the stupid stairs, without goddamn making a fool of myself." At the end of this remarkable speech (which, unlike my own, I am able to render verbatim) she fell silent, or almost silent: after awhile I became aware of soft gasps, breathy shudders, regularly spaced, almost imperceptible, and realized she was sobbing. (Melinda's sobs and Melinda's laughter were quiet affairs, practically indistinguishable.) And with a soothing cry I embraced the huddled bundle of her, and kissed her plump damp cheeks, and I was lost. She had astonished me twice in fifteen minutes. Are there really any better reasons for making a lifetime commitment?

"God, yes," said John Rittenhouse, my partner, with uncharacteristic animation. "Jesus, Ed, she's a typist over at Flink, Spitalny and Whatsit. She's a chubby little oaf. Young, okay, cute, possibly, but marriage—Good-Lord-have-you-lost-your-mind?" Rittenhouse and I have been friends since Chicago, so I let him get it off his chest and didn't take offense. "The trouble with you, Rittenhouse," I said, chuckling, "is you have no sense of vision. See you in church."

"Oh, of course, the Acrobat," said Kimberley Swanson, with her perfected silvery laugh. She was my current mistress and had, in fact, been one of the ladies on the stairs. "The Bouncing Ball. Dumpling Descending a Staircase." She stopped laughing when I asked her to clear her little toilet articles out of my bedroom, and my last glimpse of Kimberley, as she slammed out of the house, was a flash of long legs and elegant hips, swaying gracefully even in fury—a lovely woman, splendidly fashionable, utterly boring.

My mother, still alive at that time, was "tickled to death." I brought Melinda up to Mattapoisett one evening, and Mother celebrated us with pink champagne and great gobbets of her Famous Lasagna, the recipe for which she carefully copied out for my future bride on a "From the Kitchen of Mona Foote" index card, which I later incinerated. Mother was a good woman with execrable taste.

Melinda herself was more incredulous by far at my intentions than Rittenhouse or Kimberley. "All right, a joke's a joke," she said, after I arranged for our blood tests. This was at the end of a week-long courtship, during which she had received, with some apparent pleasure—Melinda was an eloquent blusher—my innumerable avowals of love. "But darling, you accepted my proposal just the other night. We're all set. You said, 'Sure thing, Mr. Foote.'" "I thought you were kidding," she said. Delightful Melinda! What I had taken for unbecoming flippancy (I *had* been rather hurt) was really her lovable attempt to humor a crazy man. It took me some time to convince her of the sincerity of my desire, but in the end she agreed, this time in earnest. "What the hell," said Melinda.

Under her own power Melinda was, in word and deed, as deliberate, stolid and utterly graceless as a basset hound. When she walked, she plodded; when she sat, she sank; she ran as though underwater and swam as if uphill, noisily, without propulsion, like a huge waterlogged bumblebee. Her expression was typically grave, ruminant; her voice was pleasantly low but often so vigilantly modulated as to be almost toneless; and except for the occasional blurt her speech had a regular stately rhythm—like a Sarabande—which imparted to her most casual remark the faintly ominous quality of pronouncement. She never gestured when talking, carefully trapping her hands, or busying them. Her smile was shy and pretty, transforming, but so long in coming that you could not watch its progress without conscious suspense.

Her enthusiasms were rare, bizarre, and zealously guarded. She loved two paintings, the only two with which, as far as I know, she was familiar: Hopper's "Sun in an Empty Room" and Edvard Munch's "The Shriek." Two old issues of Time magazine containing photographs of these were among the few personal effects she brought into our marriage; after much cajoling, she explained why she kept them, and when I presented her with decent prints, handsomely framed, she was startled into a wildfire smile; her hands rose up and opened out like flowers. She hung them, sun and shriek, in our bedroom, side by side.

Her literary appetites were limited to doctor-nurse romances and non-fiction accounts, with photographs, of natural and man-made disasters. Fearful, wholly without cause, of my contempt she cached her paperbacks around the house in the most unlikely places. Enchanted by my accidental discovery, in the clothes hamper, of *Clinical Passions* and *Nine Horrible Fires*, I searched out the rest, like a child on an Easter egg hunt, carefully replacing them in their niches. So secretive, so unfathomable was my Melinda that I half expected also to find collections of like-colored objects, ribbons and string and pieces of glass, nestled in the chandeliers; odd cufflinks and earrings under carpet corners.

She liked these few things—the paintings, the books—and sex, which I will get to in a moment; and not much else, really. She hated only her body. "It's out," she once confided, "to get me." Because of what she misconstrued as innate clumsiness (she was spectacularly wrong), she waged constant battle against spontaneity and impulse: what appeared to the untutored eye to be lumpishness of manner was really extreme caution. She was methodical about everything she did in the vain hope of avoiding accident. Of course, this had the same effect upon her body as the command "Don't think about green elephants" has upon the mind. I could have told her this, but never did.

For Melinda out of control, obedient to only the natural laws, was incomparably graceful. She fell the way we do in dreams, lazily and in profound silence. She never degraded her falls with unseemly attempts to save herself; she did not flail, or thrash, or clutch at things and knock them over; she did not shout or make funny noises; she never wore the lonely, humiliated expression of the commonplace stumblebum. She fell *glissando,* down every set of stairs in our three-story house, on the sidewalk, in the tub (backwards into bubbles, sending up aqueous sheets, puffs of foam), down a gentle grassy hill in Nova Scotia, off a stone wall in Salem, over the lap of a grateful old gentleman on the Super Chief. Every slip, tumble and langorous, effortless roll was as neatly executed as a movement in classical ballet.

Just how graceful, you may wonder, can a careening fat girl be? You fail to consider, for such is the tyranny of fashion, that the swan is not a slim animal; that the sea lion has no waist; you forget the patient, timeless arch of the surfacing whale.

Early on I learned to trust in the ingenuity and competence of her brilliant body—something she was never inclined to do—and I could watch her lose her balance, or rather gain imbalance, without my heart leaping to my throat; for I never knew her to acquire so much as the palest blue bruise, let alone do herself any serious damage. This is not to say that I stood idly by, a heartless voyeur, and offered her no protection from the anarchic forces which so distressed her. On the contrary, I installed extra handrails throughout the house, lowered the kitchen and pantry cabinets, laid down on tubs and tile those foot-shaped pads of ribbed rubber (so that our bathrooms looked like tiny dance studios), marred every extensive glass surface with gaily-colored safety decals (this following a sunny August morning when she joined me on the back patio without sliding open the glass door, exploding through it with casual magnificence, looking for all the world, I hardly need to say, like Danae at the visitation of Zeus);[1] and in general, as the sly Rittenhouse often observed, turned the house into a "paradise for shut-ins." I wanted her to be happy. After all, had I been the selfish decadent my old crowd thought me to be (for they eventually hit upon the consensus that I was keeping Melinda as some outlandish sort of pet, like a capybara or potto) I would, rather than trying to help her, have gone out of my way to precipitate her lovely disasters, bumping her as though by accident at the top of the stairs, absently stretching my legs out in front of her as she passed by. I would, for example, have bought her ice skates.

Her body was sleek, compact and rounded everywhere, each section as soft and solid as a peach. On our wedding night she came to bed in an outsized red flannel nightshirt, her brooding chubby face scrubbed and gleaming. She said, "I'll do whatever you want

1. Zeus transformed himself into a shower of gold to make sexual advances on Danae.

if you'll turn off the light." "And I'll do whatever you want," I replied, "with it on." We compromised, throughout our marriage, with indirect lighting from the hallway (and similar arrangements when we spent our nights away from home), and her skin curved in and out of shadow like dunes on a moonlit beach. "If it's all right with you, let's not do anything athletic," she said. She began, the first time and always, with terrible awkwardness, bucking, grasping, panting, without sincerity or sense; a savage if unconscious parody of the sexual technician. But in time she gave it up, and her breathing became slow and deep, and her arms circled my back, steadying me, and she took us out to sea: a night sea, some time after the passing of a storm. She moved with great power, beyond petty violence, beyond wildness, with the awesome elemental rhythm of nature in order. And though her cadence never varied, and the force of her surges never increased, at last she fell, and at the perfect moment, as if from a wonderful height. There was nothing of the flopping and hooting of her slender, acrobatic sisters. She fell with a low drawn-out sigh, smiling, her eyes wide and unseeing; her flesh and muscle rippled beneath me, and her hands fluttered against me, like wings. It was always this way. "I like that," she would say, almost as if she were realizing it for the first time; and I often wondered if she did forget, from one occasion to the next—if, in all her falls, she was in some kind of trance, or lapse.

Or perhaps, as Rittenhouse tactlessly suggested on the eve of our wedding, she was merely stupid. This is quite possible, and quite irrevelant. Melinda was the only woman I ever loved. I loved her dumpy and earthbound; I loved her floating free. It had often struck me that while we view the pairing of lovers with benign speculation, even envy, there is nothing so baffling, so grotesque, as another man's choice of wife, or a woman's of a husband. It occurs to me now that no explanation is possible.

During the first year I let my half of the practice go to hell and took an extended honeymoon. We spent the last six months touring Europe at a luxurious pace. My intent was not to "widen her horizons," for I was no Pygmalion, but to give her pleasure. On balance, then, the trip was not a great success, for only occasionally did her good-natured stoicism give way to genuine interest. At first I sought out, on the basis of the paltry clues she had provided, likely objects of delight: surprising her, for instance, with a detour to the Munch-Museum in Oslo. She trudged through the place without complaint, but it soon became apparent that the awful, hagridden lithographs and woodcuts did not move her; for all I could see they did not even ring a bell. I had better luck leaving our itinerary more or less to chance. She liked provincial French cuisine, so much that, with the aid of explicit instructions, she learned to duplicate it quite well when we got home. She liked the way the sheep clogged the cobblestone streets of Skye. In Paris, she coveted the voluminous dark robes and yashmaks of the Algerian women. I bought her a half dozen of the hideous things. (She never wore them in front of me, and I was startled to find, some months after our return, that she habitually wore them when she shopped for groceries. Whether she was enacting a fantasy or simply hiding out, I cannot say.)

Things ground to a halt in Salisbury, where, upon entering the nave of the great cathedral, she looked up at the immense vaulted expanse and, without even swaying, crashed heavily to her hands and knees. It was the only ugly fall she ever took; it was not her body's doing. "Makes me dizzy," she said, in a cranky mumble, and when I got her outside, "Can we go home now?" Overcome with remorse I begged pardon for my insensitivity, promising we would leave on the next available plane. And in bed that night she patted my shoulder in one of those rare bursts of offhand affection for which I was so grateful and said, "This isn't Europe. This is me in Europe."

I still have a photograph, taken earlier that day by a cooperative stranger, of the two of us framed between Stonehenge monoliths: a distinguished man of forty or so, an incongruous yet convincingly hearty smile on his urbane face; and beside him, crushed against him by his circling arm, a small, stout, frumpy young woman confronts the photographer with the wistful expression of a child mauled by a distant relative.

We were married for five years; during the first four I was deliriously happy and Melinda—well, Melinda rolled through them, like the great globe itself, in her own inscrutable way. The trouble started one evening early in the Fall, when we hosted a dinner party for the firm and a few important clients. It was partly Rittenhouse's fault, and partly mine.

Melinda had arranged a creditable feast—standing roast, mushrooms *à la Grecque*, braised endives and a risotto; she had also readied the fixings for crepes suzette, with the express condition that I would take care of the final preparations. She sat with the rest of us in the living room during cocktails, though she did not drink herself. In the interest of self-control she never drank. Banal chitchat filled the air and she listened intently, or did not hear at all, and fended off the occasional polite question with monosyllables, and regarded everyone, or no one, with an unblinking stare at once vacant and portentous, like a shell-shocked sphinx. All was as usual. And Rittenhouse, as usual, regarded her with bemused fascination, for the passing of years and my continued happiness had only worsened his obsessive incredulity. I was enmired in zinc futures with old man Winthrop and so did not notice exactly when and how Rittenhouse insinuated himself next to Melinda, and when I did see them he had what appeared to be her full attention and was obviously pouring on the not inconsiderable Rittenhouse charm. When I looked again they were gone—to the kitchen, as it turned out, where Rittenhouse, under the pretext of mixing himself a special drink, got her to try it. "I just wanted to see what she'd do," he told me the next morning, in a tone of mingled apology and awe. "Goddamn it," I said, too late, "she's not a toy."

They were gone a long time, and when they returned her face was flushed and happy, her brown eyes sparkled, and she carried in front of her, with monumental self-assurance, a tray holding two dozen frosted old fashioned glasses filled to the brim with a deep amber liquid; draped across each brim was an odorous gardenia, evidently culled from the back garden, withering visibly in its alcoholic bath. "Everybody try one," she commanded, graciously passing among us, and we all took at least one sip of her concoction, which was vile in a truly surprising way. "What is it?" I choked, not so much alarmed as amazed at the totality of her transformation. "A 'gin rummy,'" she said. "Jack says they make wonderful ones down at the HoHo Luau Pit." She frowned prettily. "They really should be drunk out of coconut shells." I shot Rittenhouse a look which collapsed his sheepish grin.

All hell broke loose that night, though if it had not been for the denouement I, at least, would have judged the party a success, for Melinda, who got steadily drunker throughout dinner, was a cynosure of all eyes, her body reveling wickedly in its unwonted release. There were no accidents, except for the finale: rather, she became more and more adroit as the evening progressed. Yet her unearthly competence contributed to a generally shared premonition of disaster. Conversation died as, long knife flashing in the candlelight, she carved and portioned out the huge roast with the blinding skill of a Japanese steakhouse chef; but she made up for it with a running patter of her own, commenting at length and very entertainingly upon our trip to Europe, which I had not until then realized had even registered with her; interlarding her account with aphorisms and opinions which I was startled to recognize as my own: "Neapolitans are the idiot-savants of life"; "When one meets the English, one understands the French." As she glided around the table replenishing wine glasses, Winthrop leaned over and punched my shoulder with a horny forefinger. "Remarkable woman," he said. At one point she excused herself, drove to the grocery store (she had no license) and returned in a twinkling with half a coconut, which she gutted and filled with yet another "gin rummy," which proved to be a mistake. For in the attempt simultaneously to propose an elaborate toast, something about "citizens of the world," and to dish out the crepes suzette she set the monstrous drink ablaze and bowled it over, sending a river of flame the length of the table. The immediate effect was magical: we rose to our feet as one with the hushed, appreciative cry of witnesses to a pyrotechnics display, but eventually the fire department had to be called, and though the damage was not extensive, the party broke up soon afterward.

She was disconsolate. For hours she lay face-down on the living room couch, sobbing wildly, angrily brushing off my comforting hand. When she became coherent she called herself "a freak, a freak, a freak," and threatened to run away to a side show. I told her that indeed, she was a freak, in a positive and glorious sense; that she was unique; that she was different, not in degree but in kind, from any woman I had ever known; and that therefore she was infinitely precious to me. She said I was crazy. How can it be crazy, I asked her, to love someone without reservation, just as she is, and to wish for nothing more. "I don't know," she said, "but it is."

I had known all along that she was indifferent to my love; that she had married me by accident, and stayed with me through inertia, in keeping with the overall random patterning of her life. Seeing that she was now actively wretched I determined to discover what I could offer her to make her happy. Your freedom, I said, if that's what you want. She appeared to think it over, and reject it as not worth the bother. "Melinda, we have a great deal of money. Just tell me what you want. Education? A summer house? A horse?" At first I could get nothing out of her but the general wish not to have been born, but finally she entered into the spirit of the thing. "Yes, there must be something I want," she said, for I had convinced her. And for long minutes she stared into space, her brow furrowed in mighty concentration. "Anything at all," I prompted from time to time. "Animal, vegetable or mineral." At last her face relaxed and she gave me a triumphant little smile. "What is it, Darling" "I want a baby," she said.

As a matter of fact, across the room from where she sat was a brass newspaper rack, and on that particular night the foremost newspaper bore the prominent headline, "Baby Survives Sub-Zero Ordeal." But her desire to get pregnant, from the moment she expressed it, was, whatever the nature of its origin, fierce and all-consuming. It consumed, first of all, the great pleasure she had always taken in lovemaking, for determined as she was to conceive she did not, in bed, allow her body a moment's peace, maintaining a deadly vigilance over its every motion. There were no more sea cruises for us, ever again. For six months she could talk of nothing but temperature charts and favorable positions, and with every failure she grew more single-minded. I tried to explain to her that she was going at it all wrong, that she should relax and think about other things. But she would not, or could not believe me, and so in the end her will consumed itself, and I found her one morning, shortly after her discovery of her sixth and final failure—for I could never persuade her to try again—sitting naked, cross-legged on the bed in a square of sunlight, her face unrecognizable in fury, pounding her poor innocent stomach with knotted fists. "Stupid bastard," she called it. "Stupid idiot sonofabitch." "We can adopt," I said. "That has nothing to do with it," she said, with a venomous look. "This is the last straw."

She proceeded, in spite of all I could do, to punish her body with starvation and grinding, relentless exercise. It was an all-out war, having nothing to do with self-improvement, but in the process, and of course by accident, she became a conventionally pretty woman, beautiful in fact, spare of hip, bony of ankle. She achieved in time the stick-like upper arm of the fashion model; high cheekbones, knifeblade collarbones and knobby spine emerged as her flesh dwindled and her skin tightened.

She was adopted by the Rittenhouse gang—my old crowd—and learned, through the meddling of the chic ladies, how to dress, how to shop, how to be like everybody else. So dispirited was her pummeled, malnourished body that it could not muster so much as a single misstep, and without the blurring effect of her envelope of flesh she seemed more ungainly than ever. Though she was a mere wisp, hers were still the leaden footfalls of a giantess, hers the ponderous gestures of the ungifted auditioner. But in the eyes of her new admirers there was something terribly piquant in the physical contradictions she posed, something almost *outré* in the spectacle of a slender, petite woman with an elephantine carriage; in fact, the more fashion-obsessed ladies in the circle began, unconsciously I suppose, to imitate her peculiar style, much as idiot women everywhere once affected the *Vogue* slouch, and after a time only the hopelessly gauche were light on their feet.

And though she was as close-mouthed as before, there was now a faint overlay of bitterness, of world-weariness, upon her speech and manner which intrigued the men, especially Rittenhouse, my partner, my old friend, my betrayer: Rittenhouse of the impish grin and silver tongue, the most eligible of society bachelors; who had, like me, refused to settle for anything less than the perfect woman.

I knew I would lose her. After all, I had won her by working her inertia to my own advantage, through the force of my desire; it was inevitable that the combined influence of so many would pull her away from me. What I could not have foreseen was the active nature of her defection. I never imagined she would fall in love.

What could he have told her that I had not, a thousand thousand times? What more can a woman wish to hear than that she is singular, peerless and rare; that you must have her, or die? In my blackest moods I see him snaking his arm around her pitiful waist, preening her with his hooded gaze, whispering, you are so beautifully right for this time, this place; you exemplify, typify and crystallize; you have that certain something; you look just like that television actress, you know, the one with the hyphenated name.

She did not have to tell me. I was there when it happened. I was witness; which is only fitting, since from the start I had been no less than her devout, adoring witness, and no more. I forget the place, the date, the occasion: some awful party, a humid night, tired laughter and tireless conversation, innocent of thought. My wife stood in a clearing at the other end of the room, leaning against a pillar of pink marble. She wore a sheath of olive brown chiffon, cut in the current severe style, and her hair was skinned back into an elaborate, gold-braised knot, and the corner of one ravaged hip pointed accusingly at me; and her eyes were clear and fathomless and gave away nothing, not a trace of desire or disappointment, or memory, or wonder. She was terrible, maddening; an impossible object; my only love. I thought: Oh, my. Then she swiveled her head to face, almost, in my direction, and her mouth widened slowly into a dazzling smile, and into her eyes dawned a light of intelligence and purpose; and she stirred and hurried forward, not to me but to another. The hem of her filmy skirt lapped gently at her ankles as she rushed, with step delicate and sure; she was suddenly, irrevocably, all elegance and heartbreaking grace. And I closed my eyes and turned away; for just this once I could not bear the sight of Melinda falling.

WILLIAM KOTZWINKLE

Follow the Eagle

Johnny Eagle climbed onto his 750-cubic-centimeter Arupa motorcycle and roared out of the Navaho Indian Reservation, followed by the Mexican, Domingo, on a rattling Japanese cycle stolen from a Colorado U law student.

Up the morning highway they rode toward the Colorado River, half-drunk and full-crazy in the sunlight, Eagle's slouch hat brim bent in the wind, Domingo's long black moustaches trailing in the air.

Yes, thought Eagle, wheeling easy over the flat land, yes indeed. And they came to Navaho Canyon where they shut down their bikes. Mist from the winding river far below rose up through the scarred plateau and the air was still.

Eagle and Domingo wheeled their bikes slowly to the edge of the Canyon. Domingo got off and threw a stone across the gorge. It struck the far wall, bounced, echoed, fell away in silence.

"Long way to the other side, man," he said, looking at Eagle.

Eagle said nothing, sat on his bike, staring across the gaping crack in the earth.

Domingo threw another stone, which cleared the gap, kicking up a little cloud of dust on top of the other cliff. "How fast you got to go—hunnert, hunnert twenty-five?"

Eagle spit into the canyon and tromped the starter of his bike.

"When you goin', man?" shouted Domingo over the roar.

"Tomorrow!"

That night was a party for Johnny Eagle on the Reservation. He danced with Red Wing in the long house, pressed her up against a corner. Medicine Man came by, gave Eagle a cougar tooth. "I been talkin' to it, Eagle," he said.

"Thanks, man," said Eagle and he put it around his neck and took Red Wing back to his shack, held her on the falling porch in the moonlight, looked at the moon over her shoulder.

She lay on his broken bed, hair undone on his ragged pillow, her buckskin jacket on the floor. Through the open window came music from the party, guitar strings and a drum head and Domingo singing

Uncle John have everything he need

"Don't go tomorrow," said Red Wing, unbuttoning Eagle's cowboy shirt.

"Gitchimanito[1] is watchin' out for me, baby," said Eagle, and he mounted her, riding bareback, up the draw, slow, to the drumbeat. His eyes were closed but he saw her tears, like silver beads, and he rode faster and shot his arrow through the moon.

"Oh, Johnny," she moaned, quivering beneath him, "don't go," and he felt her falling away, down the waving darkness.

They lay, looking out through the window. He hung the cat's tooth around her neck. "Stay with me," she said, holding him till dawn, and he rose up while she was sleeping. The Reservation was grey, the shacks crouching in the dawn light.

Eagle shook Domingo out of his filthy bed. The Mexican crawled

1. The Great Spirit.

across the floor, looking for his sombrero, and they walked across the camp to the garage where the pickup truck was stowed with Eagle's bike.

Eagle pulled the cycle off the kickstand and they rolled it up a wooden ramp into the back of the truck, then slid the ramp in the truck, roped it down, and drove quietly off the Reservation.

They went down the empty highway, Domingo at the wheel, Eagle slouched in the corner by the door. "Why you doin' this, man?" asked the Mexican, not looking at Eagle.

Eagle's hat was over his eyes. He slept a little, nodding with the bounces in and out of a dream. His head dropped against the cold window. The truck was stopped.

Eagle stepped down onto the silent mesa. My legs shakin, he thought and went round to the back of the truck, where Domingo was letting down the ramp. Eagle touched the cold handlebars of the bike and stopped shaking. They wheeled the cycle to the ground.

"I know a chick," said Domingo. They pushed the ramp to the edge of the canyon. "—with a fanstastic ass—" They faced the ramp to the misty hole, bracing it with cinder blocks. "She lives down in Ensenada, man, whattya say we go down there?"

Eagle climbed onto the bike, turned over the motor, breaking the morning stillness. He circled slowly, making bigger circles until the motor was running strong, then drove over to Domingo at the edge of the ramp.

"*Buena suerte, amigo!*"[2] shouted the Mexican over the roaring engine.

"On the other side!" called Eagle, and drove away from the ramp, fifty, a hundred, two, three, four hundred yards. He turned, lined the bike up with the ramp. A white chicken fluttered in his stomach. Domingo waved his black hat.

In neutral, Eagle gunned the big Arupa engine, once, twice, and engaging first gear spun out toward the ramp.

The sun was rising, the speedometer climbing as he shifted into second gear, fifty, sixty, seventy, eighty miles an hour. Eagle burned across the table land toward Navaho Canyon, into third gear, ninety, a hundred, had jumped twelve cars on this bike, had no job, saw Domingo from the corner of his eye, was going one twenty-five and that was it as he hit the ramp and sailed his ass off into space.

The cycle whined above the mist, floating like a thunder clap, and Johnny Eagle in his slouch hat rode lightly as an arrow, airborne in the glory of the moment as a sunbeam struck him in his arc of triumph, then his sunset came upon him and he saw the flaw in his life story, *one fifty, man, not one twenty-five,* as the far cliff for

2. "Good luck, friend!"

which he hungered came no closer, seemed to mock him through the mist, was impossible, always had been, and his slouch hat blew away.

Don't go, Johnny.

He strained to lift his falling horse, to carry her above the morning, to fly with her between his legs, rupturing several muscles in his passion and then as he fell for certain just clung sadly with the morning rising up his asshole, poor balls groaning Johnny Eagle, falling down Navaho Canyon, the geological formations quite apparent as the mist was clearing from the rock.

"SO LONG, MAN!" he shouted, with quite a way to go, falling like a regular comet, smoke and fire out the tailpipe as the bike turned slowly over, plunging through the hollow entry. Jesus Christ my blood is boiling there goes the engine.

He fell quietly, hissing through the mist, dreaming it was still dawn on Red Wing's red-brown thighs.

Johnny, don't go. O.K. babe I'll stay here.

But he saw the real rocks rushing past him.

I uster dance. Neck down in the fender. She held me in my screwloose, Johnny Eagle, be my old man, babe I'm crazy and mus' go to Gitchegumee.[3]

Down in Ensenada man

Domingo falling to the barroom laughing with his knife blade bloody, my look at that terra cotter there like faces in the Canyon, Sheriff you kin let us out now, won't do no harm. There goes my shoes man where am I.

A fantastic

Water lick rock. Thousand fist pound my brain out. Crack me, shell me, awful snot death crap death hunnert bucks that bike death cost me black death o no Colorado do not take me.

Yes I took you Johnny Eagle

Wham the arrow crossed the morning. I am shot from out my body whoooooooooooooo the endless sunrise.

Some time later a fledgling eagle was hatched by an old white-headed fierce-beaked queen of the Canyon. She pushed the little eagle into space where he learned to soar, crying *kyreeeee*, high above the morning, turning in the mist upon the wind.

And Domingo, riding down to Ensenada, to see the girl in Ensenada, crossed the border singing

He saw Aunt Mary comin' an'
He duck back in the alley

3. Place of the spirits.

URSULA K. LE GUIN

The New Atlantis

COMING back from my Wilderness Week I sat by an odd sort of man in the bus. For a long time we didn't talk; I was mending stockings and he was reading. Then the bus broke down a few miles outside Gresham. Boiler trouble, the way it generally is when the driver insists on trying to go over thirty. It was a Supersonic Superscenic Deluxe Longdistance coal-burner, with Home Comfort, that means a toilet, and the seats were pretty comfortable, at least those that hadn't yet worked loose from their bolts, so everybody waited inside the bus; besides, it was raining. We began talking, the way people do when there's a breakdown and a wait. He held up his pamphlet and tapped it—he was a dry-looking man with a schoolteacherish way of using his hands—and said, "This is interesting. I've been reading that a new continent is rising from the depths of the sea."

The blue stockings were hopeless. You have to have something besides holes to darn onto. "Which sea?"

"They're not sure yet. Most specialists think the Atlantic. But there's evidence it may be happening in the Pacific, too."

"Won't the oceans get a little crowded?" I said, not taking it seriously. I was a bit snappish, because of the breakdown and because those blue stockings had been good warm ones.

He tapped the pamphlet again and shook his head, quite serious. "No," he said. "The old continents are sinking, to make room for the new. You can see that that is happening."

You certainly can. Manhattan Island is now under eleven feet of water at low tide, and there are oyster beds in Ghirardelli Square.[1]

"I thought that was because the oceans are rising from polar melt."

He shook his head again. "That is a factor. Due to the greenhouse effect of pollution, indeed Antarctica may become inhabitable. But climatic factors will not explain the emergence of the new—or, possibly, very old—continents in the Atlantic and Pacific." He went on explaining about continental drift, but I liked the idea of inhabiting Antarctica and daydreamed about it for a while. I thought of it as very empty, very quiet, all white and blue, with a faint golden glow northward from the unrising sun behind the long peak of Mount Erebus.[2] There were a few people there; they were very quiet, too, and wore white tie and tails. Some of them carried oboes and violas. Southward the white land went up in a long silence toward the Pole.

1. A fancy shopping area in San Francisco. 2. Peak on west coast of Antarctica.

Just the opposite, in fact, of the Mount Hood Wilderness Area.[3] It had been a tiresome vacation. The other women in the dormitory were all right, but it was macaroni for breakfast, and there were so many organized sports. I had looked forward to the hike up to the National Forest Preserve, the largest forest left in the United States, but the trees didn't look at all the way they do in the postcards and brochures and Federal Beautification Bureau advertisements. They were spindly, and they all had little signs on saying which union they had been planted by. There were actually a lot more green picnic tables and cement Men's and Women's than there were trees. There was an electrified fence all around the forest to keep out unauthorized persons. The forest ranger talked about mountain jays, "bold little robbers," he said, "who will come and snatch the sandwich from your very hand," but I didn't see any. Perhaps because that was the weekly Watch Those Surplus Calories! Day for all the women, and so we didn't have any sandwiches. If I'd seen a mountain jay I might have snatched the sandwich from his very hand, who knows. Anyhow it was an exhausting week, and I wished I'd stayed home and practiced, even though I'd have lost a week's pay because staying home and practicing the viola doesn't count as planned implementation of recreational leisure as defined by the Federal Union of Unions.

When I came back from my Antarctican expedition, the man was reading again, and I got a look at his pamphlet; and that was the odd part of it. The pamphlet was called "Increasing Efficiency in Public Accountant Training Schools," and I could see from the one paragraph I got a glance at that there was nothing about new continents emerging from the ocean depths in it—nothing at all.

Then we had to get out and walk on into Gresham, because they had decided that the best thing for us all to do was get onto the Greater Portland Area Rapid Public Transit Lines, since there had been so many breakdowns that the charter bus company didn't have any more buses to send out to pick us up. The walk was wet, and rather dull, except when we passed the Cold Mountain Commune. They have a wall around it to keep out unauthorized persons, and a big neon sign out front saying COLD MOUNTAIN COMMUNE and there were some people in authentic jeans and ponchos by the highway selling macramé belts and sandcast candles and soybean bread to the tourists. In Gresham, I took the 4:40 GPARPTL Superjet Flyer train to Burnside and East 230th, and then walked to 217th and got the bus to the Goldschmidt Overpass, and transferred to the shuttlebus, but it had boiler trouble, so I didn't reach the downtown transfer point until ten after eight, and the buses go on a once-an-hour schedule at eight o'clock, so I got a meatless hamburger at the Longhorn Inch-Thick Steak House Dinerette and caught the nine

3. Mt. Hood is the highest point in Oregon.

o'clock bus and got home about ten. When I let myself into the apartment I flipped the switch to turn on the lights, but there still weren't any. There had been a power outage in West Portland for three weeks. So I went feeling about for the candles in the dark, and it was a minute or so before I noticed that somebody was lying on my bed.

I panicked, and tried again to turn the lights on.

It was a man, lying there in a long thin heap. I thought a burglar had got in somehow while I was away and died. I opened the door so I could get out quick or at least my yells could be heard, and then I managed not to shake long enough to strike a match, and lighted the candle, and came a little closer to the bed.

The light disturbed him. He made a sort of snorting in his throat and turned his head. I saw it was a stranger, but I knew his eyebrows, then the breadth of his closed eyelids, then I saw my husband.

He woke up while I was standing there over him with the candle in my hand. He laughed and said still half-asleep, "Ah, Psyche! From the regions which are holy land."[4]

Neither of us made much fuss. It was unexpected, but it did seem so natural for him to be there, after all, much more natural than for him not to be there, and he was too tired to be very emotional. We lay there together in the dark, and he explained that they had released him from the Rehabilitation Camp early because he had injured his back in an accident in the gravel quarry, and they were afraid it might get worse. If he died there it wouldn't be good publicity abroad, since there have been some nasty rumors about deaths from illness in the Rehabilitation Camps and the Federal Medical Association Hospitals; and there are scientists abroad who have heard of Simon, since somebody published his proof of Goldbach's Hypothesis in Peking. So they let him out early, with eight dollars in his pocket, which is what he had in his pocket when they arrested him, which made it, of course, fair. He had walked and hitched home from Coeur D'Alene, Idaho, with a couple of days in jail in Walla Walla[5] for being caught hitch-hiking. He almost fell asleep telling me this, and when he had told me, he did fall asleep. He needed a change of clothes and a bath but I didn't want to wake him. Besides, I was tired, too. We lay side by side and his head was on my arm. I don't suppose that I have ever been so happy. No; was it happiness? Something wider and darker, more like knowledge, more like the night: joy.

It was dark for so long, so very long. We were all blind. And there was the cold, a vast, unmoving, heavy cold. We could not move at

4. From the better known of two poems called *To Helen* by Edgar Allan Poe. Psyche, in classical mythology, was a princess of remarkable beauty, beloved by Cupid.
5. City in Washington.

all. We did not move. We did not speak. Our mouths were closed, pressed shut by the cold and by the weight. Our eyes were pressed shut. Our limbs were held still. Our minds were held still. For how long? There was no length of time; how long is death? And is one dead only after living, or before life as well? Certainly we thought, if we thought anything, that we were dead; but if we had ever been alive, we had forgotten it.

There was a change. It must have been the pressure that changed first, although we did not know it. The eyelids are sensitive to touch. They must have been weary of being shut. When the pressure upon them weakened a little, they opened. But there was no way for us to know that. It was too cold for us to feel anything. There was nothing to be seen. There was black.

But then—"then," for the event created time, created before and after, near and far, now and then—"then" there was the light. One light. One small, strange light that passed slowly, at what distance we could not tell. A small, greenish white, slightly blurred point of radiance, passing.

Our eyes were certainly open, "then," for we saw it. We saw the moment. The moment is a point of light. Whether in darkness or in the field of all light, the moment is small, and moves, but not quickly. And "then" it is gone.

It did not occur to us that there might be another moment. There was no reason to assume that there might be more than one. One was marvel enough: that in all the field of the dark, in the cold, heavy, dense, moveless, timeless, placeless, boundless black, there should have occurred, once, a small slightly blurred, moving light! Time need be created only once, we thought.

But we were mistaken. The difference between one and more than one is all the difference in the world. Indeed, that difference is the world.

The light returned.

The same light, or another one? There was no telling.

But, "this time," we wondered about the light: Was it small and near to us, or large and far away? Again there was no telling; but there was something about the way it moved, a trace of hesitation, a tentative quality, that did not seem proper to anything large and remote. The stars, for instance. We began to remember the stars.

The stars had never hesitated.

Perhaps the noble certainty of their gait had been a mere effect of distance. Perhaps in fact they had hurtled wildly, enormous furnace-fragments of a primal bomb thrown through the cosmic dark; but time and distance soften all agony. If the universe, as seems likely, began with an act of destruction, the stars we had used to see told no tales of it. They had been implacably serene.

The planets, however . . . We began to remember the planets. They had suffered certain changes both of appearance and of course.

At certain times of the year Mars would reverse its direction and go backward through the stars. Venus had been brighter and less bright as she went through her phases of crescent, full, and wane. Mercury had shuddered like a skidding drop of rain on the sky flushed with daybreak. The light we now watched had that erratic, trembling quality. We saw it, unmistakably, change direction and go backward. It then grew smaller and fainter; blinked—an eclipse?—and slowly disappeared.

Slowly, but not slowly enough for a planet.

Then—the third "then"!—arrived the indubitable and positive Wonder of the World, the Magic Trick, watch now, watch, you will not believe your eyes, mama, mama, look what I can do—

Seven lights in a row, proceeding fairly rapidly, with a darting movement, from left to right. Proceeding less rapidly from right to left, two dimmer, greenish lights. Two-lights halt, blink, reverse course, proceed hastily and in a wavering manner from left to right. Seven-lights increase speed, and catch up. Two-lights flash desperately, flicker, and are gone.

Seven-lights hang still for some while, then merge gradually into one streak, veering away, and little by little vanish into the immensity of the dark.

But in the dark now are growing other lights, many of them: lamps, dots, rows, scintillations—some near at hand, some far. Like the stars, yes, but not stars. It is not the great Existences we are seeing, but only the little lives.

In the morning Simon told me something about the Camp, but not until after he had had me check the apartment for bugs. I thought at first he had been given behavior mod and gone paranoid. We never had been infested. And I'd been living alone for a year and a half; surely they didn't want to hear me talking to myself? But he said, "They may have been expecting me to come here."

"But they let you go free!"

He just lay there and laughed at me. So I checked everywhere we could think of. I didn't find any bugs, but it did look as if somebody had gone through the bureau drawers while I was away in the Wilderness. Simon's papers were all at Max's so that didn't matter. I made tea on the Primus,[6] and washed and shaved Simon with the extra hot water in the kettle—he had a thick beard and wanted to get rid of it because of the lice he had brought from Camp—and while we were doing that he told me about the Camp. In fact he told me very little, but not much was necessary.

He had lost about twenty pounds. As he only weighed 140 to start with, this left little to go on with. His knees and wrist bones stuck out like rocks under the skin. His feet were all swollen and

6. Simple camp stove.

chewed-looking from the Camp boots; he hadn't dared take the boots off, the last three days of walking, because he was afraid he wouldn't be able to get them back on. When he had to move or sit up so I could wash him, he shut his eyes.

"Am I really here?" he asked. "Am I here?"

"Yes," I said. "You are here. What I don't understand is how you got here."

"Oh, it wasn't bad so long as I kept moving. All you need is to know where you're going—to have someplace to go. You know, some of the people in Camp, if they'd let them go, they wouldn't have had that. They couldn't have gone anywhere. Keeping moving was the main thing. See, my back's all seized up, now."

When he had to get up to go to the bathroom he moved like a ninety-year-old. He couldn't stand straight, but was all bent out of shape, and shuffled. I helped him put on clean clothes. When he lay down on the bed again, a sound of pain came out of him, like tearing thick paper. I went around the room putting things away. He asked me to come sit by him and said I was going to drown him if I went on crying. "You'll submerge the entire North American continent," he said. I can't remember what he said, but he made me laugh finally. It is hard to remember things Simon says, and hard not to laugh when he says them. This is not merely the partiality of affection: He makes everybody laugh. I doubt that he intends to. It is just that a mathematician's mind works differently from other people's. Then when they laugh, that pleases him.

It was strange, and it is strange, to be thinking about "him," the man I have known for ten years, the same man, while "he" lay there changed out of recognition, a different man. It is enough to make you understand why most languages have a word like "soul." There are various degrees of death, and time spares us none of them. Yet something endures, for which a word is needed.

I said what I had not been able to say for a year and a half: "I was afraid they'd brainwash you." He said, "Behavior mod is expensive. Even just the drugs. They save it mostly for the VIPs. But I'm afraid they got a notion I might be important after all. I got questioned a lot the last couple of months. About my 'foreign contacts.' " He snorted. "The stuff that got published abroad, I suppose. So I want to be careful and make sure it's just a Camp again next time, and not a Federal Hospital."

"Simon, were they . . . are they cruel, or just righteous?"

He did not answer for a while. He did not want to answer. He knew what I was asking. He knew by what thread hangs hope, the sword, above our heads.

"Some of them . . ." he said at last, mumbling.

Some of them had been cruel. Some of them had enjoyed their work. You cannot blame everything on society.

"Prisoners, as well as guards," he said.

You cannot blame everything on the enemy.

"Some of them, Belle," he said with energy, touching my hand, "some of them, there were men like gold there—"

The thread is tough; you cannot cut it with one stroke.

"What have you been playing?" he asked.

"Forrest, Schubert."

"With the quartet?"

"Trio, now. Janet went to Oakland with a new lover."

"Ah, poor Max."

"It's just as well, really. She isn't a good pianist."

I make Simon laugh, too, though I don't intend to. We talked until it was past time for me to go to work. My shift since the Full Employment Act last year is ten to two. I am an inspector in a recycled paper bag factory. I have never rejected a bag yet; the electronic inspector catches all the defective ones first. It is a rather depressing job. But it's only four hours a day, and it takes more time than that to go through all the lines and physical and mental examinations, and fill out all the forms, and talk to all the welfare counselors and inspectors every week in order to qualify as Unemployed, and then line up every day for the ration stamps and the dole. Simon thought I ought to go to work as usual. I tried to, but I couldn't. He had felt very hot to the touch when I kissed him goodbye. I went instead and got a black-market doctor. A girl at the factory had recommended her, for an abortion, if I ever wanted one without going through the regulation two years of sex-depressant drugs the fed-meds make you take when they give you an abortion. She was a jeweler's assistant in a shop on Alder Street, and the girl said she was convenient because if you didn't have enough cash you could leave something in pawn at the jeweler's as payment. Nobody ever does have enough cash, and of course credit cards aren't worth much on the black market.

The doctor was willing to come at once, so we rode home on the bus together. She gathered very soon that Simon and I were married, and it was funny to see her look at us and smile like a cat. Some people love illegality for its own sake. Men, more often than women. It's men who make laws, and enforce them, and break them, and think the whole performance is wonderful. Most women would rather just ignore them. You could see that this woman, like a man, actually enjoyed breaking them. That may have been what put her into an illegal business in the first place, a preference for the shady side. But there was more to it than that. No doubt she'd wanted to be a doctor, too; and the Federal Medical Association doesn't admit women into the medical schools. She probably got her training as some other doctor's private pupil, under the counter. Very much as Simon learned mathematics, since the universities don't teach much but Business Administration and Advertising and Media Skills anymore. However she learned it, she seemed to know her stuff. She fixed up a kind of homemade traction device for Simon very handily and informed him that if he did much more walking for two months he'd be crippled the rest of his life, but if he behaved himself he'd just be more or less lame. It isn't the kind of thing you'd expect to be grateful for being told, but we both were. Leaving, she gave me a bottle of about two hundred plain white pills, unlabeled. "Aspirin," she said. "He'll be in a good deal of pain off and on for weeks."

I looked at the bottle. I had never seen aspirin before, only the Super-Buffered Pane-Gon and the Triple-Power N-L-G-Zic and the Extra-Strength Apansprin with the miracle ingredient more doctors recommend, which the fed-meds always give you prescriptions for, to be filled at your FMA-approved private enterprise friendly drugstore at the low, low prices established by the Pure Food and Drug Administration in order to inspire competitive research.

"Aspirin," the doctor repeated. "The miracle ingredient more doctors recommend." She cat-grinned again. I think she liked us because we were living in sin. That bottle of black-market aspirin was probably worth more than the old Navajo bracelet I pawned for her fee.

I went out again to register Simon as temporarily domiciled at my address and to apply for Temporary Unemployment Compensation ration stamps for him. They only give them to you for two weeks and you have to come every day; but to register him as Temporarily Disabled meant getting the signatures of two fed-meds, and I thought I'd rather put that off for a while. It took three hours to go through the lines and get the forms he would have to fill out, and to answer the 'crats' questions about why he wasn't there in person. They smelled something fishy. Of course it's hard for them to prove that two people are married and aren't just adultering if you move now and then and your friends help out by sometimes registering one of you as living at their address; but they had all the back files on both of us and it was obvious that we had been around each other for a suspiciously long time. The State really does make things awfully hard for itself. It must have been simpler to enforce the laws back when marriage was legal and adultery was what got you into trouble. They only had to catch you once. But I'll bet people broke the law just as often then as they do now.

The lantern-creatures came close enough at last that we could see not only their light, but their bodies in the illumination of their light. They were not pretty. They were dark colored, most often a dark red, and they were all mouth. They ate one another whole. Light swallowed light, all swallowed together in the vaster mouth of the darkness. They moved slowly, for nothing, however small and hungry, could move fast under that weight, in that cold. Their eyes, round with fear, were never closed. Their bodies were tiny and bony behind the gaping jaws. They wore queer, ugly decorations on their lips and skulls: fringes, serrated wattles, featherlike fronds, gauds, bangles, lures. Poor little sheep of the deep pastures! Poor ragged, hunchjawed dwarfs squeezed to the bone by the weight of the darkness, chilled to the bone by the cold of the darkness, tiny monsters burning with bright hunger, who brought us back to life!

Occasionally, in the wan, sparse illumination of one of the lantern-creatures, we caught a momentary glimpse of other, large, unmoving shapes: the barest suggestion, off in the distance, not of a wall, nothing so solid and certain as a wall, but of a surface, an angle . . . Was it there?

Or something would glitter, faint, far off, far down. There was no use trying to make out what it might be. Probably it was only a fleck of sediment, mud or mica, disturbed by a struggle between the lantern-creatures, flickering like a bit of diamond dust as it rose and settled slowly. In any case, we could not move to go see what it was. We had not even the cold, narrow freedom of the lantern-creatures. We were immobilized, borne down, still shadows among the half-guessed shadow walls. Were we there?

The lantern-creatures showed no awareness of us. They passed before us, among us, perhaps even through us—it was impossible to be sure. They were not afraid, or curious.

Once something a little larger than a hand came crawling near, and for a moment we saw quite distinctly the clean angle where the foot of a wall rose from the pavement, in the glow cast by the crawling creature, which was covered with a foliage of plumes, each plume dotted with many tiny, bluish points of light. We saw the pavement beneath the creature and the wall beside it, heartbreaking in its exact, clear linearity, its opposition to all that was fluid, random, vast, and void. We saw the creature's claws, slowly reaching out and retracting like small stiff fingers, touch the wall. Its plumage of light quivering, it dragged itself along and vanished behind the corner of the wall.

So we knew that the wall was there; and that it was an outer wall, a housefront, perhaps, or the side of one of the towers of the city.

We remembered the towers. We remembered the city. We had forgotten it. We had forgotten who we were; but we remembered the city, now.

When I got home, the FBI had already been there. The computer at the police precinct where I registered Simon's address must have flashed it right over to the computer at the FBI building. They had questioned Simon for about an hour, mostly about what he had been doing during the twelve days it took him to get from the Camp to Portland. I suppose they thought he had flown to Peking or something. Having a police record in Walla Walla for hitchhiking helped him establish his story. He told me that one of them had gone to the bathroom. Sure enough I found a bug stuck on the top of the bathroom doorframe. I left it, as we figured it's really better to leave it when you know you have one, than to take it off and then never be sure they haven't planted another one you don't know about. As Simon said, if we felt we had to say something unpatriotic we could always flush the toilet at the same time.

I have a battery radio—there are so many work stoppages because of power failures, and days the water has to be boiled, and so on, that you really have to have a radio to save wasting time and dying of typhoid—and he turned it on while I was making supper on the Primus. The six o'clock All-American Broadcasting Company news announcer announced that peace was at hand in Uruguay, the president's confidential aide having been seen to smile at a passing blonde as he left the 613th day of the secret negotiations in a villa outside Katmandu. The war in Liberia[7] was going well; the enemy said they had shot down seventeen American planes but the Pentagon said we had shot down twenty-two enemy planes, and the capital city—I forget its name, but it hasn't been inhabitable for seven years anyway—was on the verge of being recaptured by the forces of freedom. The police action in Arizona was also successful. The Neo-Birch insurgents in Phoenix could not hold out much longer against the massed might of the American army and air force, since their underground supply of small tactical nukes from the Weathermen[8] in Los Angeles had been cut off. Then there was an advertisement for Fed-Cred cards, and a commercial for the Supreme Court: "Take your legal troubles to the Nine Wise Men!" Then there was something about why tariffs had gone up, and a report from the stock market, which had just closed at over two thousand, and a commercial for U.S. Government canned water, with a catchy little tune: "Don't be sorry when you drink/It's not as healthy as you think/Don't you think you really ought to/Drink coo-ool, puu-uure U.S.G. water?"—with three sopranos in close harmony on the last line. Then, just as the battery began to give out and his voice was dying away into a faraway tiny whisper, the announcer seemed to be saying something about a new continent emerging.

"What was that?"

"I didn't hear," Simon said, lying with his eyes shut and his face pale and sweaty. I gave him two aspirins before we ate. He ate little, and fell asleep while I was washing the dishes in the bathroom. I had been going to practice, but a viola is fairly wakeful in a one-room apartment. I read for a while instead. It was a best-seller Janet had given me when she left. She thought it was very good, but then

7. Liberia is a West African country; Katmandu is the capital of Nepal, at the foot of the Himalayas. **8.** Polar opposites on the political spectrum of the 1960's. The Weathermen was an extreme left-wing youth organization, while the John Birch Society (apparent forerunner of the "Neo-Birch insurgents") was very conservative.

she likes Franz Liszt too. I don't read much since the libraries were closed down, it's too hard to get books; all you can buy is best-sellers. I don't remember the title of this one, the cover just said "Ninety Million Copies in Print!!!" It was about small-town sex life in the last century, the dear old 1970s when there weren't any problems and life was so simple and nostalgic. The author squeezed all the naughty thrills he could out of the fact that all the main characters were married. I looked at the end and saw that all the married couples shot each other after all their children became schizophrenic hookers, except for one brave pair that divorced and then leapt into bed together with a clear-eyed pair of government-employed lovers for eight pages of healthy group sex as a brighter future dawned. I went to bed then, too. Simon was hot, but sleeping quietly. His breathing was like the sound of soft waves far away, and I went out to the dark sea on the sound of them.

I used to go out to the dark sea, often, as a child, falling asleep. I had almost forgotten it with my waking mind. As a child all I had to do was stretch out and think, "the dark sea . . . the dark sea . . ." and soon enough I'd be there, in the great depths, rocking. But after I grew up it only happened rarely, as a great gift. To know the abyss of the darkness and not to fear it, to entrust oneself to it and whatever may arise from it—what greater gift?

We watched the tiny lights come and go around us, and doing so, we gained a sense of space and of direction—near and far, at least, and higher and lower. It was that sense of space that allowed us to become aware of the currents. Space was no longer entirely still around us, suppressed by the enormous pressure of its own weight. Very dimly we were aware that the cold darkness moved, slowly, softly, pressing against us a little for a long time, then ceasing, in a vast oscillation. The empty darkness flowed slowly along our unmoving unseen bodies; along them, past them; perhaps through them; we could not tell.

Where did they come from, those dim, slow, vast tides? What pressure or attraction stirred the deeps to these slow drifting movements? We could not understand that; we could only feel their touch against us, but in straining our sense to guess their origin or end, we became aware of something else: something out there in the darkness of the great currents: sounds. We listened. We heard.

So our sense of space sharpened and localized to a sense of place. For sound is local, as sight is not. Sound is delimited by silence; and it does not rise out of the silence unless it is fairly close, both in space and in time. Though we stand where once the singer stood we cannot hear the voice singing; the years have carried it off on their tides, submerged it. Sound is a fragile thing, a tremor, as delicate as life itself. We may see the stars, but we cannot hear them. Even were the hollowness of outer space an atmosphere, an ether that transmitted the waves of sound, we could not hear the stars; they are too far away. At most if we listened we might hear our own sun, all the mighty, roiling, exploding storm of its burning, as a whisper at the edge of hearing.

A sea wave laps one's feet: It is the shock wave of a volcanic eruption on the far side of the world. But one hears nothing.

A red light flickers on the horizon: It is the reflection in smoke of a city on the distant mainland, burning. But one hears nothing.

Only on the slopes of the volcano, in the suburbs of the city, does one begin to hear the deep thunder, and the high voices crying.

Thus, when we became aware that we were hearing, we were sure that the sounds we heard were fairly close to us. And yet we may have been quite wrong. For we were in a strange place, a deep place. Sound travels fast and far in the deep places, and the silence there is perfect, letting the least noise be heard for hundreds of miles.

And these were not small noises. The lights were tiny, but the sounds were vast: not loud, but very large. Often they were below the range of hearing, long slow vibrations rather than sounds. The first we heard seemed to us to rise up through the currents from beneath us: immense groans, sighs felt along the bone, a rumbling, a deep uneasy whispering.

Later, certain sounds came down to us from above, or borne along the endless levels of the darkness, and these were stranger yet, for they were music. A huge calling, yearning music from far away in the darkness, calling not to us. Where are you? I am here.

Not to us.

They were the voices of the great souls, the great lives, the lonely ones, the voyagers. Calling. Not often answered. Where are you? Where have you gone?

But the bones, the keels and girders of white bones on icy isles of the South, the shores of bones did not reply.

Nor could we reply. But we listened, and the tears rose in our eyes, salt, not so salt as the oceans, the world-girdling deep bereaved currents, the abandoned roadways of the great lives; not so salt, but warmer.

I am here. Where have you gone?

No answer.

Only the whispering thunder from below.

But we knew now, though we could not answer, we knew because we heard, because we felt, because we wept, we knew that we were; and we remembered other voices.

Max came the next night. I sat on the toilet lid to practice, with the bathroom door shut. The FBI men on the other end of the bug got a solid half hour of scales and doublestops, and then a quite good performance of the Hindemith[9] unaccompanied viola sonata. The bathroom being very small and all hard surfaces, the noise I made was really tremendous. Not a good sound, far too much echo, but the sheer volume was contagious, and I played louder as I went on. The man up above knocked on his floor once; but if I have to listen to the weekly All-American Olympic Games at full blast every Sunday morning from his TV set, then he has to accept Paul Hindemith coming up out of his toilet now and then.

When I got tired I put a wad of cotton over the bug, and came out of the bathroom half-deaf. Simon and Max were on fire. Burning, unconsumed. Simon was scribbling formulae in traction, and Max was pumping his elbows up and down the way he does, like a boxer, and saying "The e-lec-tron emis-sion . . ." through his nose, with his eyes narrowed, and his mind evidently going light-years per second faster than his tongue, because he kept beginning over and saying "The e-lec-tron emis-sion . . ." and pumping his elbows.

Intellectuals at work are very strange to look at. As strange as artists. I never could understand how an audience can sit there and look at a fiddler rolling his eyes and biting his tongue, or a horn player collecting spit, or a pianist like a black cat strapped to an electrified bench, as if what they *saw* had anything to do with the music.

I damped the fires with a quart of black-market beer--the legal kind is better, but I never have enough ration stamps for beer; I'm not thirsty enough to go without eating—and gradually Max and Simon cooled down. Max would have stayed talking all night, but I drove him out because Simon was looking tired.

I put a new battery in the radio and left it playing in the bathroom, and blew out the candle and lay and talked with Simon; he was too excited to sleep. He said that Max had solved the problems that were bothering them before Simon was sent to Camp, and had fitted Simon's equations to (as Simon put it) the bare facts, which means they have achieved "direct energy conversion." Ten or twelve people have worked on it at different times since Simon published the theoretical part of it when he was twenty-two. The physicist Ann Jones had pointed out right away that the simplest practical application of the theory would be to build a "sun tap," a device for collecting and storing solar energy, only much cheaper and better than the U.S.G. Sola-Heetas that some rich people have on their houses. And it would have been simple only they kept hitting the same snag. Now Max has got around the snag.

I said that Simon published the theory, but that is inaccurate. Of course he's never been able to publish any of his papers, in print; he's not a federal employee and doesn't have a government clearance. But it did get circulated in what the scientists and poets call

9. Paul Hindemith, German composer and violinist (1895–1963).

Sammy's-dot,[1] that is, just handwritten or hectographed. It's an old joke that the FBI arrests everybody with purple fingers, because they have either been hectographing Sammy's-dots, or they have impetigo.

Anyhow, Simon was on top of the mountain that night. His true joy is in the pure math; but he had been working with Clara and Mac and the others in this effort to materialize the theory for ten years, and a taste of material victory is a good thing, once in a lifetime.

I asked him to explain what the sun tap would mean to the masses, with me as a representative mass. He explained that it means we can tap solar energy for power, using a device that's easier to build than a jar battery. The efficiency and storage capacity are such that about ten minutes of sunlight will power an apartment complex like ours, heat and lights and elevators and all, for twenty-four hours; and no pollution, particulate, thermal, or radioactive. "There isn't any danger of using up the sun?" I asked. He took it soberly—it was a stupid question, but after all not so long ago people thought there wasn't any danger of using up the earth—and said no, because we wouldn't be pulling out energy, as we did when we mined and lumbered and split atoms, but just using the energy that comes to us anyhow: as the plants, the trees and grass and rosebushes, always have done. "You could call it Flower Power,"[2] he said. He was high, high up on the mountain, ski-jumping in the sunlight.

"The State owns us," he said, "because the corporative State has a monopoly on power sources, and there's not enough power to go around. But now, anybody could build a generator on their roof that would furnish enough power to light a city."

I looked out the window at the dark city.

"We could completely decentralize industry and agriculture. Technology could serve life instead of serving capital. We could each run our own life. Power is power! . . . The State is a machine. We could unplug the machine, now. Power corrupts; absolute power corrupts absolutely.[3] But that's true only when there's a price on power. When groups can keep the power to themselves; when they can use physical power-to in order to exert spiritual power-over; when might makes right. But if power is free? If everybody is equally mighty? Then everybody's got to find a better way of showing that he's right. . . ."

"That's what Mr. Nobel[4] thought when he invented dynamite," I said. "Peace on earth."

He slid down the sunlit slope a couple of thousand feet and

1. Punning reference to *Samizdat*, a circuit of underground publications in the Soviet Union in the 1960's–70's. **2.** Youth slogan in the 1960's. **3.** Said by Lord Acton, English historian (1834–1902). **4.** Alfred Nobel (1833–1896), inventor of dynamite and donor of Nobel Prizes.

stopped beside me in a spray of snow, smiling. "Skull at the banquet," he said, "finger writing on the wall. Be still! Look, don't you see the sun shining on the Pentagon,[5] all the roofs are off, the sun shines at last into the corridors of power. . . . And they shrivel up, they wither away. The green grass grows through the carpets of the Oval Room, the Hot Line[6] is disconnected for nonpayment of the bill. The first thing we'll do is build an electrified fence outside the electrified fence around the White House. The inner one prevents unauthorized persons from getting in. The outer one will prevent authorized persons from getting out. . . ."

Of course he was bitter. Not many people come out of prison sweet.

But it was cruel, to be shown this great hope, and to know that there was no hope for it. He did know that. He knew it right along. He knew that there was no mountain, that he was skiing on the wind.

The tiny lights of the lantern-creatures died out one by one, sank away. The distant lonely voices were silent. The cold, slow currents flowed, vacant, only shaken from time to time by a shifting in the abyss.

It was dark again, and no voice spoke. All dark, dumb, cold.

Then the sun rose.

It was not like the dawns we had begun to remember: the change, manifold and subtle, in the smell and touch of the air; the hush that, instead of sleeping, wakes, holds still, and waits; the appearance of objects, looking gray, vague, and new, as if just created—distant mountains against the eastern sky, one's own hands, the hoary grass full of dew and shadow, the fold in the edge of a curtain hanging by the window—and then, before one is quite sure that one is indeed seeing again, that the light has returned, that day is breaking, the first, abrupt, sweet stammer of a waking bird. And after that the chorus, voice by voice: This is my nest, this is my tree, this is my egg, this is my day, this is my life, here I am, here I am, hurray for me! I'm here!—No, it wasn't like that at all, this dawn. It was completely silent, and it was blue.

In the dawns that we had begun to remember, one did not become aware of the light itself, but of the separate objects touched by the light, the things, the world. They were there, visible again, as if visibility were their own property, not a gift from the rising sun.

In this dawn, there was nothing but the light itself. Indeed there was not even light, we would have said, but only color: blue.

There was no compass bearing to it. It was not brighter in the east. There was no east or west. There was only up and down, below

5. Building in Arlington, Va., containing most of the United States Defense offices.
6. The Oval Room in the United States President's office; the Hot Line is a system for emergency communication between the American President and Soviet authorities.

and above. Below was dark. The blue light came from above. Brightness fell. Beneath, where the shaking thunder had stilled, the brightness died away through violet into blindness.

We, arising, watched light fall.

In a way it was more like an ethereal snowfall than like a sunrise. The light seemed to be in discrete particles, infinitesimal flecks, slowly descending, faint, fainter than flecks of fine snow on a dark night, and tinier; but blue. A soft, penetrating blue tending to the violet, the color of the shadows in an iceberg, the color of a streak of sky between gray clouds on a winter afternoon before snow: faint in intensity but vivid in hue: the color of the remote, the color of the cold, the color farthest from the sun.

On Saturday night they held a scientific congress in our room. Clara and Max came, of course, and the engineer Phil Drum and three others who had worked on the sun tap. Phil Drum was very pleased with himself because he had actually built one of the things, a solar cell, and brought it along. I don't think it had occurred to either Max or Simon to build one. Once they knew it could be done they were satisfied and wanted to get on with something else. But Phil unwrapped his baby with a lot of flourish, and people made remarks like, "Mr. Watson, will you come here a minute," and "Hey, Wilbur, you're off the ground!" and "I say, nasty mould you've got there, Alec, why don't you throw it out?" and "Ugh, ugh, burns, burns, wow, ow," the latter from Max, who does look a little pre-Mousterian.[7] Phil explained that he had exposed the cell for one minute at four in the afternoon up in Washington Park during a light rain. The lights were back on on the West Side since Thursday, so we could test it without being conspicious.

We turned off the lights, after Phil had wired the table-lamp cord to the cell. He turned on the lamp switch. The bulb came on, about twice as bright as before, at its full forty watts—city power of course was never full strength. We all looked at it. It was a dime-store table with a metallized gold base and a white plasticloth shade.

"Brighter than a thousand suns,"[8] Simon murmured from the bed.

"Could it be," said Clara Edmonds, "that we physicists have known sin[9]—and have come out the other side?"

"It really wouldn't be any good at all for making bombs with," Max said dreamily.

7. The remarks parody the first communication on a telephone by its inventor, Alexander Graham Bell (1847–1922); Wilbur Wright (1867–1912), who with his brother Orville (1871–1948), built the craft in which the first powered flight through air was made; Sir Alexander Fleming (1881–1955), discoverer of penicillin; and the first man to discover fire. Mousterians were Paleolithic cave dwellers in France. **8.** A reference to the first atomic explosion. **9.** Paraphrase of statement by J. Robert Oppenheimer, one of the scientists who perfected the atomic bomb.

"Bombs," Phil Drum said with scorn. "Bombs are obsolete. Don't you realize that we could move a mountain with this kind of power? I mean pick up Mount Hood, move it, and set it down. We could thaw Antarctica, we could freeze the Congo. We could sink a continent. Give me a fulcrum and I'll move the world.[1] Well, Archimedes, you've got your fulcrum. The sun."

"Christ," Simon said, "the radio, Belle!"

The bathroom door was shut and I had put cotton over the bug, but he was right; if they were going to go ahead at this rate there had better be some added static. And though I liked watching their faces in the clear light of the lamp—they all had good, interesting faces, well worn, like the handles of wooden tools or the rocks in a running stream—I did not much want to listen to them talk tonight. Not because I wasn't a scientist, that made no difference. And not because I disagreed or disapproved or disbelieved anything they said. Only because it grieved me terribly, their talking. Because they couldn't rejoice aloud over a job done and a discovery made, but had to hide there and whisper about it. Because they couldn't go out into the sun.

I went into the bathroom with my viola and sat on the toilet lid and did a long set of sautillé exercises. Then I tried to work at the Forrest trio, but it was too assertive. I played the solo part from *Harold in Italy*,[2] which is beautiful, but it wasn't quite the right mood either. They were still going strong in the other room. I began to improvise.

After a few minutes in E-minor the light over the shaving mirror began to flicker and dim; then it died. Another outage. The table lamp in the other room did not go out, being connected with the sun, not with the twenty-three atomic fission plants that power the Greater Portland Area. Within two seconds somebody had switched it off, too, so that we shouldn't be the only window in the West Hills left alight; and I could hear them rooting for candles and rattling matches. I went on improvising in the dark. Without light, when you couldn't see all the hard shiny surfaces of things, the sound seemed softer and less muddled. I went on, and it began to shape up. All the laws of harmonics sang together when the bow came down. The strings of the viola were the cords of my own voice, tightened by sorrow, tuned to the pitch of joy. The melody created itself out of air and energy, it raised up the valleys, and the mountains and hills were made low, and the crooked straight, and the rough places plain. And the music went out to the dark sea and sang in the darkness, over the abyss.

1. Said by Archimedes, Greek mathematician and inventor (287–212 B.C.). **2.** Symphony by Hector Berlioz (1803–1869).

When I came out they were all sitting there and none of them was talking. Max had been crying. I could see little candle flames in the tears around his eyes. Simon lay flat on the bed in the shadows, his eyes closed. Phil Drum sat hunched over, holding the solar cell in his hands.

I loosened the pegs, put the bow and the viola in the case, and cleared my throat. It was embarrassing. I finally said, "I'm sorry."

One of the women spoke: Rose Abramski, a private student of Simon's, a big shy woman who could hardly speak at all unless it was in mathematical symbols. "I saw it," she said. "I saw it. I saw the white towers, and the water streaming down their sides, and running back down to the sea. And the sunlight shining in the streets, after ten thousand years of darkness."

"I heard them," Simon said, very low, from the shadow. "I heard their voices."

"Oh, Christ! Stop it!" Max cried out, and got up and went blundering out into the unlit hall, without his coat. We heard him running down the stairs.

"Phil," said Simon, lying there, "could we raise up the white towers, with our lever and our fulcrum?"

After a long silence Phil Drum answered, "We have the power to do it."

"What else do we need?" Simon said. "What else do we need, besides power?"

Nobody answered him.

The blue changed. It became brighter, lighter, and at the same time thicker: impure. The ethereal luminosity of blue-violet turned to turquoise, intense and opaque. Still we could not have said that everything was now turquoise-colored, for there were still no things. There was nothing, except the color of turquoise.

The change continued. The opacity became veined and thinned. The dense, solid color began to appear translucent, transparent. Then it seemed as if we were in the heart of a sacred jade, or the brilliant crystal of a sapphire or an emerald.

As at the inner structure of a crystal, there was no motion. But there was something, now, to see. It was as if we saw the motionless, elegant inward structure of the molecules of a precious stone. Planes and angles appeared about us, shadowless and clear in that even, glowing, blue-green light.

These were the walls and towers of the city, the streets, the windows, the gates.

We knew them, but we did not recognize them. We did not dare to recognize them. It had been so long. And it was so strange. We had used to dream, when we lived in this city. We had lain down, nights, in the rooms behind the windows, and slept, and dreamed.

We had all dreamed of the ocean, of the deep sea. Were we not dreaming now?

Sometimes the thunder and tremor deep below us rolled again, but it was faint now, far away; as far away as our memory of the thunder and the tremor and the fire and the towers falling, long ago. Neither the sound nor the memory frightened us. We knew them.

The sapphire light brightened overhead to green, almost green-gold. We looked up. The tops of the highest towers were hard to see, glowing in the radiance of light. The streets and doorways were darker, more clearly defined.

In one of those long, jewel-dark streets something was moving—something not composed of planes and angles, but of curves and arcs. We all turned to look at it, slowly, wondering as we did so at the slow ease of our own motion, our freedom. Sinuous, with a beautiful flowing, gathering, rolling movement, now rapid and now tentative, the thing drifted across the street from a blank garden wall to the recess of a door. There, in the dark blue shadow, it was hard to see for a while. We watched. A pale blue curve appeared at the top of the doorway. A second followed, and a third. The moving thing clung or hovered there, above the door, like a swaying knot of silvery cords or a boneless hand, one arched finger pointing carelessly to something above the lintel of the door, something like itself, but motionless—a carving. A carving in jade light. A carving in stone.

Delicately and easily the long curving tentacle followed the curves of the carved figure, the eight petal-limbs, the round eyes. Did it recognize its image?

The living one swung suddenly, gathered its curves in a loose knot, and darted away down the street, swift and sinuous. Behind it a faint cloud of darker blue hung for a minute and dispersed, revealing again the carved figure above the door: the sea-flower, the cuttlefish, quick, great-eyed, graceful, evasive, the cherished sign, carved on a thousand walls, worked into the design of cornices, pavements, handles, lids of jewel boxes, canopies, tapestries, tabletops, gateways.

Down another street, about the level of the first-floor windows, came a flickering drift of hundreds of motes of silver. With a single motion all turned toward the cross street, and glittered off into the dark blue shadows.

There were shadows, now.

We looked up, up from the flight of silverfish, up from the streets where the jade-green currents flowed and the blue shadows fell. We moved and looked up, yearning, to the high towers of our city. They stood, the fallen towers. They glowed in the ever-brightening radiance, not blue or blue-green, up there, but gold. Far above them lay a vast, circular, trembling brightness: the sun's light on the surface of the sea.

We are here. When we break through the bright circle into life, *the water will break and stream white down the white sides of the towers, and run down the steep streets back into the sea. The water will glitter in dark hair, on the eyelids of dark eyes, and dry to a thin white film of salt.*

We are here.

Whose voice? Who called to us?

He was with me for twelve days. On January 28 the 'crats came from the Bureau of Health, Education and Welfare and said that since he was receiving Unemployment Compensation while suffering from an untreated illness, the government must look after him and restore him to health, because health is the inalienable right of the citizens of a democracy. He refused to sign the consent forms, so the chief health officer signed them. He refused to get up, so two of the policemen pulled him up off the bed. He started to try to fight them. The chief health officer pulled his gun and said that if he continued to struggle he would shoot him for resisting welfare, and arrest me for conspiracy to defraud the government. The man who was holding my arms behind my back said they could always arrest me for unreported pregnancy with intent to form a nuclear family.[3] At that Simon stopped trying to get free. It was really all he was trying to do, not to fight them, just to get his arms free. He looked at me, and they took him out.

He is in the federal hospital in Salem. I have not been able to find out whether he is in the regular hospital or the mental wards.

It was on the radio again yesterday, about the rising land masses in the South Atlantic and the Western Pacific. At Max's the other night I saw a TV special explaining about geophysical stresses and subsidence and faults. The U.S. Geodetic Service is doing a lot of advertising around town, the most common one is a big billboard that says IT'S NOT OUR FAULT! with a picture of a beaver pointing to a schematic map that shows how even if Oregon has a major earthquake and subsidence as California did last month, it will not affect Portland, or only the western suburbs perhaps. The news also said that they plan to halt the tidal waves in Florida by dropping nuclear bombs where Miami was. Then they will reattach Florida to the mainland with landfill. They are already advertising real estate for housing developments on the landfill. The president is staying at the Mile High White House in Aspen, Colorado. I don't think it will do him much good. Houseboats down on the Willamette are selling for $500,000. There are no trains or buses running south from Portland, because all the highways were badly damaged by the tremors and landslides last week, so I will have to see if I can get to Salem on foot. I still have the rucksack I bought for the Mount Hood

3. Parents and children regarded as a unit.

Wilderness Week. I got some dry lima beans and raisins with my Federal Fair Share Super Value Green Stamp minimal ration book for February—it took the whole book—and Phil Drum made me a tiny camp stove powered with the solar cell. I didn't want to take the Primus, it's too bulky, and I did want to be able to carry the viola. Max gave me a half pint of brandy. When the brandy is gone I expect I will stuff this notebook into the bottle and put the cap on tight and leave it on a hillside somewhere between here and Salem. I like to think of it being lifted up little by little by the water, and rocking, and going out to the dark sea.

Where are you?
We are here. Where have you gone?

DAVID MADDEN

No Trace

GASPING for air, his legs weak from the climb up the stairs, Ernest stopped outside the room, surprised to find the door wide open, almost sorry he had made it before the police. An upsurge of nausea, a wave of suffocation forced him to suck violently for breath as he stepped into Gordon's room—his *own* two decades before.

Tinted psychedelic emerald, the room looked like a hippie pad posing for a photograph in *Life*, but the monotonous electronic frenzy he heard was the seventeen-year locusts, chewing spring leaves outside. He wondered whether the sedative had so dazed him that he had stumbled into the wrong room. No, now, as every time in his own college years when he had entered this room, what struck him first was the light falling through the leaded, green-stained windowglass. As the light steeped him in the ambience of the early forties, it simultaneously illuminated the artifacts of the present. Though groggy from the sedative, he experienced, intermittently, moments of startling clarity when he saw each object separately.

Empty beer can pyramids.

James Dean, stark poster photograph.

Records leaning on orange crate.

Life-sized redheaded girl, banjo blocking her vagina, lurid color.

Rolltop desk, swivel chair, typewriter.

Poster photograph of a teen-age hero he didn't recognize.

Large *CORN FLAKES* carton.

Ernest recognized nothing, except the encyclopedias, as Gordon's. Debris left behind when Gordon's roommate ran away. Even so, knowing Gordon, Ernest had expected the cleanest room in De-

Lozier Hall, vacant except for suitcases sitting in a neat row, awaiting the end-of-ceremonies dash to the car. He shut the door quietly, listening to an automatic lock catch, as if concealing not just the few possible incriminating objects he had come to discover but the entire spectacle of a room startlingly overpopulated with objects, exhibits, that might bear witness, like archeological unearthings, to the life lived there.

He glanced into the closet. Gordon's suitcases did not have the look of imminent departure. Clothes hung, hangers crammed tightly together, on the rack above. The odor emanating from the closet convulsed him slightly, making him shut his eyes, see Gordon raise his arm, the sleeve of his gown slip down. revealing his white arm, the grenade in his hand. Shaking his head to shatter the image, Ernest opened his eyes.

Turning abruptly from the closet, he moved aimlessly about the room, distracted by objects that moved toward him. He had to hurry before someone discovered the cot downstairs empty, before police came to lock up Gordon's room. The green light drew him to the window where the babel of locusts was louder. Through the antique glass, he saw, as if under water, the broken folding chairs below, parodying postures into which the explosion had thrown the audience. The last of the curiosity seekers, turning away, trampling locusts, left three policemen alone among knocked over chairs.

I AM ANONYMOUS/ HELP ME. Nailed, buttons encrusted the windowframe. SUPPORT MENTAL HEALTH OR I'LL KILL YOU. SNOOPY FOR PRESIDENT. As he turned away, chalked, smudged lettering among the buttons drew him back: DOCTOR SPOCK IS AN ABORTIONIST. After his roommate ran away, why hadn't Gordon erased that? Jerking his head away from the buttons again, Ernest saw a ball-point pen sticking up in the desk top. On a piece of paper, the title "The Theme of Self-hatred in the Works of—", the rest obscured by a blue circular, a message scrawled in lipstick across it: GORDY BABY, LET ME HOLD SOME BREAD FOR THIS CAUSE. MY OLD LADY IS SENDING ME A CHECK NEXT WEEK. *The* CARTER. The circular pleaded for money for the Civil Liberties Union. Ernest shoved it aside, but "The Theme of Self-hatred in the Works of—" broke off anyway. Gordon's blue scrapbook, green in the light, startled him. Turning away, Ernest noticed *Revolution in a Revolution? A Tolkien Reader, Boy Scout Handbook* in a bookcase.

As he stepped toward the closet, something crunching harshly underfoot made him jump back. Among peanut shells, brown streaks in the green light. Gordon tracking smashed guts of locusts. Fresh streaks, green juices of leaves acid-turned to slime. He lifted one foot, trying to look at the sole of his shoe, lost balance, staggered backward, let himself drop on the edge of a cot. If investigators compared the stains—. Using his handkerchief, he wiped the soles.

Dying and dead locusts, *The Alumni Bulletin* had reported, had littered the campus paths for weeks. Everywhere, the racket of their devouring machinery, the reek of their putrefaction when they fell, gorged. Sniffing his lapels, he inhaled the stench of locusts and sweat, saw flecks of—. He shut his eyes, raked breath into his lungs, lay back on the cot.

Even as he tried to resist the resurgent power of the sedative, Ernest felt his exhausted mind and body sink into sleep. When sirens woke him, he thought for a moment he still lay on the bare mattress in the room downstairs, listening to the siren of that last ambulance. The injured, being carried away on stretchers, passed by him again. The Dean of Men had hustled Ernest into a vacated room, and sent to his house nearby for a sedative. Sinking into sleep, seeing the grenade go off again and again until the explosions became tiny, receding, mute puffs of smoke, Ernest had suddenly imagined Lydia's face when he would have to telephone her about Gordon, and the urgency of being prepared for the police had made him sit up in the bed. The hall was empty, everyone seemed to be outside, and he had sneaked up the narrow back stairway to Gordon's room.

Wondering which cot was Gordon's, which his roommate's, and why *both* had recently been slept in, Ernest sat up and looked along the wooden frame for the cigarette burn he had deliberately made the day before his own commencement when he and his roommate were packing for home. As he leaned across the cot, looking for the burn, his hand grazed a stiff yellow spot on the sheet. The top sheet stuck to the bottom sheet. An intuition of his son's climactic moment in an erotic dream the night before—the effort to keep from crying choked him. "I advocate—." Leaping away from the cot, he stopped, reeling, looked up at a road sign that hung over the door: DRIVE SLOWLY, WE LOVE OUR KIDS. Somewhere an unprotected street. What's-his-name's fault. *His* junk cluttered the room.

Wondering what the suitcases would reveal, Ernest stepped into the closet. Expecting them to be packed, he jerked up on them and jolted himself, they were so light. He opened them anyway. Crumbs of dirt, curls of lint. Gordon's clothes, that Lydia had helped him select, or sent him as birthday or Easter presents, hung in the closet, pressed. Fetid clothes Gordon's roommate—Carter, yes, Carter—had left behind dangled from hooks, looking more like costumes. A theatrical black leather jacket, faded denim pants, a wide black belt, ruby studs, a jade velvet cape, and, on the floor, boots and sandals. In a dark corner leaned the hooded golf clubs Ernest had handed down to Gordon, suspecting he would never lift them from the bag. "You don't like to hunt," he had blurted out one evening. "You don't like to fish. You don't get excited about football. Isn't there *some*thing we could do together?" "We could just sit and talk." They had ended up watching the Ed Sullivan Show.

Ernest's hand, paddling fish-like among the clothes in the dim closet, snagged on a pin that fastened a price tag to one of the suits he had bought Gordon for Christmas. Though he knew from Lydia that no girl came regularly on weekends from Melbourne's sister college to visit Gordon, surely he had had some occasion to wear the suit. Stacked on the shelf above: shirts, the cellophane packaging unbroken. His fingers inside one of the cowboy boots, Ernest stroked leather that was still flesh soft. Imagining Lydia's hysteria at the sight of Gordon, he saw a mortician handling Gordon's body, sorting, arranging pieces, saw not Gordon's, but the body of one of his clients on view, remembering how awed he had been by the miracle of skill that had put the man back together only three days after the factory explosion. Ernest stroked a damp polo shirt, unevenly stained pale green in the wash, sniffed it, realizing that Carter's body could not have left an odor that lasting. Now he understood what had disturbed him about Gordon's clothes, showing, informal and ragged, under the skirt of the black gown, at the sleeves, at the neck, as he sat on the platform, waiting to deliver the valedictory address.

Gripping the iron pipe that held hangers shoved tightly together, his body swinging forward as his knees sagged, Ernest let the grenade explode again. Gentle, almost delicate, Gordon suddenly raises his voice above the nerve-wearying shrill of the seventeen-year locusts that encrust the barks of the trees, a voice that had been too soft to be heard except by the men on the platform whose faces expressed shock—at *what* Ernest still did not know—and as that voice screams, a high-pitched nasal screech like brass, "I advocate a total revolution!" Gordon's left arm raises a grenade, holds it out before him, eclipsing his still-open mouth, and in his right hand, held down stiff at his side, the pin glitters on his finger. Frightened, raring back, as Ernest himself does, in their seats, many people try to laugh the grenade off as a bold but imprudent rhetorical gesture.

Tasting again Gordon's blood on his mouth, Ernest thrust his face between smothering wool coats, retched again, vomited at last.

As he tried to suck air into his lungs, gluey bands of vomit strangled him, lack of oxygen smothered him. Staggering backward out of the closet, he stood in the middle of the room, swaying. Avoiding Gordon's, he lowered himself carefully onto the edge of Carter's cot by the closet. He craved air but the stained-glass window, the only window in this corner room, wouldn't open, a disadvantage that came with the privilege of having the room with the magnificent light. The first time he had seen the room since his own graduation—he and Lydia had brought Gordon down to begin his freshman year—he had had to heave breath up from dry lungs to tell Gordon about the window. Early in the nineteenth century when DeLozier Hall was the entire school—and already one of the finest boys' colleges in the midwest—this corner room and the two adjacent comprised the chapel. From the fire that destroyed DeLozier Hall in 1938, three years before Ernest himself arrived as a freshman, only this window was saved. Except for the other chapel windows, DeLozier had been restored, brick by brick, exactly as it was originally. "First chance you get, go look in the cemetery at the grave of the only victim of the fire—nobody knows who it was, so the remains were never claimed. Probably somebody just passing through." He had deliberately saved that to leave Gordon with something interesting to think about. From the edge of the cot, he saw the bright eruption of vomit on Gordon's clothes.

The chapel steeple chimed four o'clock. The racket of the locusts' mandibles penetrated the room as if carried in through the green light. Photosynthesis. Chlorophyll. The D+ in biology that wrecked his average.

Rising, he took out his handkerchief and went into the closet. When the handkerchief was sopping wet, he dropped it into a large beer carton, tasting again the foaming beer at his lips, tingling beads on his tongue in the hot tent on the lawn as the ceremonies were beginning. He had reached the green just as the procession was forming: "You've been accepted by Harvard Grad School." Gordon had looked at him without a glimmer of recognition—Ernest had assumed that the shrilling of the locusts had drowned out his voice —then led his classmates toward the platfom.

Ernest was standing on a dirty tee shirt. He finished the job with that, leaving a corner to wipe his hands on, then he dropped it, also, into the carton.

He sat on the edge of the cot again, afraid to lie back on the mattress, sink into the gulley Carter had made over the four years and fall asleep. He only leaned back, propped on one arm. Having collected himself, he would make a thorough search, to prepare himself for whatever the police would find, tag, then show him for final identification. An exhibit of shocks. The police might even hold him responsible somehow—delinquently ignorant of his son's habits, associates. They might even find something that would bring in the F.B.I.—membership in some radical organization. What was *not* possible in a year like this? He had to arm himself against interrogation. "What sort of boy was your son?" "Typical, average, normal boy in every way. Ask my wife." But how many times had he read that in newspaper accounts of monstrous crimes? What did it mean anymore to be normal?

Glancing around the room, on the verge of an unsettling realization, Ernest saw a picture of Lydia leaning on Carter's rolltop desk.

Even in shadow, the enlarged snapshot he had taken himself was radiant. A lucid April sunburst in the budding trees behind her, bleached her green dress white, made her blond hair look almost platinum. Clowning, she had kicked out one foot, upraising and spreading her arms, and when her mouth finished yelling "Spring!" he had snapped her dimpled smile. On the campus of Melbourne's sister college Briarheath, locusts riddled those same trees, twenty years taller, forty miles from where he sat, while Lydia languished in bed alone—a mysterious disease, a lingering illness. Then the shunned realization came, made him stand up as though he were an intruder. On this cot, or perhaps the one across the room, he had made love to Lydia—that spring, the first and only time before their marriage. In August, she had discovered that she was pregnant. Gordon had never for a moment given them cause to regret that inducement to marriage. But Lydia's cautionary approach to sexual relations had made Gordon an only child.

Glancing around the room he hoped to discover a picture of himself. Seeing none, he sat down again. Under his thumb, he felt a rough texture on the wooden frame of the cot. The cigarette burn he had made himself in 1945. Then *this* had been Gordon's cot. Of course. By his desk. Flinging back the sheets, Ernest found nothing.

He crossed the room to Carter's cot where a dimestore reproduction of a famous painting of Jesus hung on the wall. Jerking hard to unstick the sheets, he lay bare Carter's bed. Twisted white sweat socks at the bottom. He shook them out. Much too large for Gordon. But Carter, then Gordon, had worn them with Carter's cowboy boots. Gordon had been sleeping in Carter's bed. Pressing one knee against the edge of the cot, Ernest leaned over and pushed his palms against the wall to examine closely what it was that had disturbed him about the painting. Tiny holes like acne scars in Jesus' upturned face. Ernest looked up. Ragged, feathered darts hung like bats from the ceiling. Someone had printed in Gothic script on the bottom white border: J. C. BLOWS. Using his fingernails, Ernest scraped at the edge of the tape, pulled carefully, but white wall paint chipped off, exposing the wallpaper design that dated back to his own life in the room. He stopped, aware that he had only started his search, that if he took this painting, he might be inclined to take other things. His intention, he stressed again to himself, was only to investigate, to be forewarned, not to search and destroy. But already he had the beer carton containing Carter's, or Gordon's, tee shirt and his own handkerchief to dispose of. He let the picture hang, one edge curling over, obscuring the lettering.

Backing into the center of the room, one leg painfully asleep, Ernest looked at the life-sized girl stuck to the wall with masking tape, holding a banjo over her vagina, the neck of it between her breasts, tip of her tongue touching one of the tuning knobs. His eye on a sticker stuck to the pane, he went to the window again: FRUIT OF THE LOOM 100% VIRGIN COTTON. More buttons forced him to read: WAR IS GOOD BUSINESS, INVEST YOUR SON. How would the police separate Carter's from Gordon's things? FLOWER POWER. He would simply tell them that Carter had left his junk behind when he bolted. But Gordon's failure to discard some of it, at least the most offensive items, bewildered Ernest. One thing appeared clear: living daily since January among Carter's possessions, Gordon had worn Carter's clothes, slept in Carter's bed.

From the ceiling above the four corners of the room hung the blank faces of four amplifiers, dark mouths gaping. Big Brother is listening. 1984. Late Show. Science fiction bored Ernest. Squatting, he flipped through records leaning in a Sunkist orange crate. MILES DAVIS/ THE GRATEFUL DEAD/ LEADBELLY/ THE BEATLES, their picture x-ed out/ MANTOVANI/ THE MAMAS AND THE PAPAS/ THE LOVING SPOONFUL. He was wasting time—Carter's records couldn't be used against Gordon. But then he found Glenn Miller's "In the Mood" and "Moonlight Serenade," a 78-rpm collector's item he had given Gordon. "Soothing background music for test-cramming time." TOM PAXTON/ THE MOTHERS OF INVENTION/ 1812 OVERTURE (Gordon's?)/ THE ELECTRONIC ERA/ JOAN BAEZ/ CHARLIE PARKER/ BARTOK.

Rising, he saw a poster he had not glimpsed before, stuck to the wall with a bowie knife, curled inward at its four corners: a color photograph of a real banana rising like a finger out of the middle of a cartoon fist.

Over the rolltop desk hung a guitar, its mouth crammed full of wilted roses. The vomit taste in his own mouth made Ernest retch. Hoping Carter had left some whiskey behind, he quickly searched the rolltop desk, and found a Jack Daniel's bottle in one of the cubbyholes. Had Gordon taken the last swallow himself this morning just before stepping out of this room?

Finding a single cigarette in a twisted package, Ernest lit it, quickly snuffed it in a hubcap used as an ashtray. The smell of fresh smoke would make the police suspicious. Recent daily activity had left Carter's desk a shambles. Across the room, Gordon's desk was merely a surface, strewn with junk. The Royal portable typewriter he had given Gordon for Christmas his freshman year sat on Carter's desk, the capital lock key set.

Among the papers on Carter's desk, Ernest searched for Gordon's notes for his speech. Ernest had been awed by the way Gordon prepared his senior project in high school—very carefully, starting with an outline, going through three versions, using cards, dividers, producing a forty-page research paper on Wordsworth. Lydia had said, "Why Ernest, he's been that way since junior high, worrying about college." On Carter's desk, Ernest found the beginnings of papers on Dryden, *The Iliad, Huckleberry Finn.* While he had always felt contentment in Gordon's perfect social behavior and exemplary academic conduct and achievements, sustained from grammar school right on through college, Ernest had sometimes felt, but quickly dismissed, a certain dismay. In her presence, Ernest agreed with Lydia's objections to Gordon's desire to major in English, but alone with him, he had told Gordon, "Satisfy yourself first of all." But he couldn't tell Gordon that he had pretended to agree with his mother to prevent her from exaggerating her suspicion that their marriage had kept him from switching to English himself after he got his B.S. in Business Administration. Each time she brought up the subject, Ernest wondered for weeks what his life would have been like had he become an English professor. As he hastily surveyed the contents of the desk, he felt the absence of the papers Gordon had written that had earned A's, helping to qualify him, as the student with the highest honors, to give the valedictory address.

Handling chewed pencils made Ernest sense the taste of lead and wood on his own tongue. He noticed a CORN FLAKES box but was distracted by a ball-point pen that only great force could have thrust so firmly into the oak desk. The buffalo side of a worn nickel leaned against a bright Kennedy half-dollar. Somewhere under this floor lay a buffalo nickel he had lost himself through a crack. Perhaps Gordon or Carter had found it. He unfolded a letter. It thanked Carter for his two-hundred-dollar contribution to a legal defense fund for students who had gone, without permission, to Cuba. Pulling another letter out of a pigeonhole, he discovered a bright gold piece resembling a medal. Trojan contraceptive. His own brand before Lydia became bedridden. Impression of it still on his wallet—no, that was the *old* wallet he carried as a senior. The letter thanked Carter for his inquiry about summer work with an organization sponsored by SNCC.[1] In another pigeonhole, he found a letter outlining Carter's duties during a summer voter campaign in Mississippi. "As for the friend you mention, we don't believe it would be in our best interests to attempt to persuade him to join in our work. If persuasion is desirable, who is more strategically situated than you, his own roommate?" Marginal scrawl in pencil: "This is the *man* talking, Baby!"

As he rifled through the numerous letters, folded hastily and slipped or stuffed into pigeonholes, Ernest felt he was getting an overview of liberal and left-wing activities, mostly student-oriented, over the past five years, for Carter's associations began in high school. He lifted his elbow off Gordon's scrapbook—birthday

1. Student National Coordinating Committee, a national radical student group.

present from Lydia—and flipped through it. Newspaper photo of students at a rally, red ink enringing a blurred head, a raised fist. Half full: clippings of Carter's activities. AP photo: Carter, bearded, burning his draft card. But no creep—handsome, hair and smile like Errol Flynn in "The Sea Hawk." Looking around at the poster photograph he hadn't recognized when he came in, Ernest saw Carter, wearing a Gestapo billcap, a monocle, an opera cape, black tights, Zorro boots, carrying a riding crop. When Ernest first noticed the ads—"Blow Yourself Up"—he had thought it a good deal at $2.99. Had Gordon given the scrapbook to Carter, or had he cut and pasted the items himself?

Ernest shoved the scrapbook aside and reached for a letter. "Gordy, This is just to tell you to save your tears over King.[2] We all wept over JFK our senior year in high school, and we haven't seen straight since. King just wasn't where the action's at. Okay, so I told you different a few months ago! How come you're always light years behind *me*? Catch up! Make the leap! I'm dumping all these creeps that try to play a rigged game. Look at Robert! I think I'm beginning to understand Oswald and Speck and Whitman.[3] They're the *real* individuals! They work alone while we run together like zebras. But, on the other hand, maybe the same cat did *all* those jobs. And maybe Carter knows who. Sleep on *that* one, Gordy, Baby." Boot camp. April 5. Suddenly, the first day back from Christmas vacation, Carter had impulsively walked out of this room. "See America first! Then the world!" That much Gordon had told them when Ernest and Lydia telephoned at Easter, made uneasy by his terse letter informing them that he was remaining on campus to "watch the locusts emerge from their seventeen-year buried infancy into appalling one-week adulthood," adding, parenthetically, that he had to finish his honors project. Marriage to Lydia had prevented Ernest's desire, like Carter's, to see the world. Not "prevented." Postponed perhaps. A vice-president of a large insurance company might hope to make such a dream come true—if only after he retired. Deep in a pigeonhole, Ernest found a snapshot of Gordon, costumed for a part in *Tom Sawyer*—one of the kids who saunter by in the whitewashing scene. False freckles. He had forgotten. On the back, tabs of fuzzy black paper—ripped out of the scrapbook.

Mixed in with Carter's were Lydia's letters. "Gordon Precious, You Promised—" Feverish eyes. Bed rashes. Blue Cross. Solitude. Solitaire. "Sleep, Lydia." Finding none of his own letters, Ernest remembered writing last week from his office, and the sense of solitude on the fifteenth floor, where he had seemed the only person

2. Martin Luther King Jr. (1929–1968). 3. Lee Harvey Oswald assassinated President Kennedy. Richard Speck and Charlie Whitman were notorious mass murderers.

stirring, came back momentarily. Perhaps in some drawer or secret compartment all his letters to Gordon (few though they had been) and perhaps other little mementos—his sharp-shooter's medal and the Korean coin that he had given Gordon, relics of his three years in the service, and matchbooks from the motels where he and Gordon had stayed on occasional weekend trips—were stored. Surely, somewhere in the room, he would turn up a picture of himself. He had always known that Gordon preferred his mother, but had he conscientiously excluded his father from his life, eliminating all trace? No, he shouldn't jump to conclusions. He had yet to gather and analyze all the evidence. Thinking in those terms about what he was doing, Ernest realized that not only was he going to destroy evidence to protect Gordon's memory as much as possible and shield Lydia, he was now deliberately searching for fragments of a new Gordon, hoping to know and understand him, each discovery destroying the old Gordon who would now always remain a stranger.

But he didn't have time to move so slowly, like a slow-motion movie. Turning quickly in Carter's swivel chair, Ernest bent over the large CORN FLAKES box, brimful of papers that had been dropped, perhaps tossed into it. Gordon's themes, including his honors thesis in a stiff black binder: "ANGUISH, SPIRITUAL AND PHYSICAL IN GERARD MANLEY HOPKINS' POETRY. Approved by: Alfred Hansen, Thorne Halpert (who had come to Melbourne in Ernest's own freshman year), Richard Kelp, John Morton." In red pencil at the bottom, haphazard scrawls, as if they were four different afterthoughts: "*Dis*approved by: Jason Carter, Gordon Foster, Lydia Foster, Gerard Manley Hopkins." Up the left margin, in lead pencil: "PISS ON ALL OF YOU!" Ernest saw Gordon burning the box in the community dump on the edge of the village.

Ernest stepped over to Gordon's desk, seeking some sort of perspective, some evidence of Gordon's life before he moved over to the rolltop desk and mingled his own things with Carter's. The gray steel drawers were empty. Not just empty. Clean. Wiped clean with a rag—a swipe in the middle drawer had dried in a soapy pattern of broken beads of moisture. Ernest saw there an image: a clean table that made him feel the presence behind him of another table where Gordon now, in pieces, lay. Under dirty clothes slung aside lay stacks of books and old newspapers, whose headlines of war, riot, murder, assassinations, negotiations seemed oddly remote in this room. The portable tape recorder Ernest had given Gordon last fall to help him through his senior year. He pressed the LISTEN button. Nothing. He pressed the REWIND. LISTEN. ". . . defy analysis. But let's examine this passage from Aristotle's 'De Interpretatione': 'In the case of that which is or which has taken place, propositions, whether positive or negative, must be true or false.' " "What did he say?" Someone whispering. "I didn't catch it." (Gordon's voice?) "Again, in the case of a pair of contraries—contradictories, that is. . . ." The professor's voice slipped into a fizzing silence. "I'm recording your speech, son," he had written to Gordon last week, "so your mother can hear it." But Ernest had forgotten his tape recorder.

The headline of a newspaper announced Charlie Whitman's sniper slaying of twelve people from the observation tower of the University administration building in Austin, Texas. But that was two summers past. Melbourne had no summer school. Folded, as though mailed. Had Carter sent it to Gordon from—Where *was* Carter from? Had Gordon received it at home?

A front page news photo showed a Buddhist monk burning on a Saigon street corner. Ernest's sneer faded in bewilderment as he saw that the caption identified an American woman burning on the steps of the Pentagon. Smudged pencil across the flames: THE MOTHER OF US ALL. Children bereft, left to a father, perhaps no father even. Ernest tried to remember the name of one of his clients, an English professor, who shot himself a week after the assassination of Martin Luther King. No note. Any connection? His wife showed Ernest the Student Guide to Courses—one anonymous, thus sexless, student's evaluation might have been a contributing factor: "This has got to be the most boring human being on the face of the earth." Since then, Ernest had tried to make his own presentations at company meetings more entertaining. Lately, many cases of middle-aged men who had mysteriously committed suicide hovered on the periphery of Ernest's consciousness. It struck him now that in every case, he had forgotten most of the "sensible" explanations, leaving nothing but mystery. Wondering whether those men had seen something in the eyes of their children, even their wives, that Ernest himself had been blind to, he shuddered but did not shake off a sudden clenching of muscles in his shoulders. "When the cause of death is legally ruled as suicide," he had often written, "the company is relieved of its obligations to—" Did Gordon *know* the grenade would explode? Or did he borrow it, perhaps steal it from a museum, and then did it, like the locusts, seventeen years dormant, suddenly come alive? Ernest had always been lukewarm about gun controls, but now he would insist on a thorough investigation to determine where Gordon purchased the grenade. Dealer in war surplus? Could they *prove* he meant it to go off? "When the cause of death is legally ruled—" Horrified that he was thinking so reflexively like an insurance executive, Ernest slammed his fist into his groin, and staggered back into the bed Gordon had abandoned.

His eyes half-opened, he saw his cigarette burn again on the wooden frame beside his hand. He recalled Gordon's vivid letter home the first week of his freshman year: "My roommate turns my stomach by the way he dresses, talks, acts, eats, sleeps." Ernest had thought that a boy so different from Gordon would be good for him, so his efforts, made at Lydia's fretful urgings, to have Carter replaced, or to have Gordon moved, were slapdash. He very much wanted his son to go through Melbourne in his old room. Books on Gordon's desk at the foot of the cot caught his attention. Some dating from junior high, these were all Gordon's, including the Great Books, with their marvelous Syntopicon. As the swelling pain in his groin subsided, Ernest stood up, hovering over the books.

A frayed copy of *Winnie the Pooh* startled him. "To Ernest, Christmas, 1928. All my love, Grandmother." The year he learned to write, Gordon had printed his own name in green crayon across the top of the next page. As Ernest leafed through the book, nostalgia eased his nerves. Penciled onto Winnie the Pooh was a gigantic penis extending across the page to Christopher Robin, who was bending over a daisy. "Damn you, Carter!" Ernest slammed it down—a pillar of books slurred, tumbled onto the floor. He stood still, staring into the green light, trying to detect the voices of people who might have heard in the rooms below. Ernest heard only the locusts in the light. A newspaper that had fallen leaned and sagged like a tent: Whitman's face looked up from the floor, two teeth in his high school graduation smile blacked out, a pencil-drawn tongue flopping out of his mouth. His name was scratched out and YOU AND ME, BABY was lettered in. Ernest kicked at the newspaper, twisted his heel into Whitman's face, and the paper rose up around his ankles like a yellowed flower, soot-dappled.

Ernest backed into the swivel chair, turned, rested his head in his hands on the rolltop desk, and breathed in fits and starts. He wanted to throw the hubcap ashtray through the stained-glass window and feel the spring air rush in upon his face and fill and stretch his lungs. Cigarillo butts, scorched Robert Burns bands, cigarette butts. Marijuana? He sniffed, but realized he couldn't recognize it if it *were*.

Was there nothing in the room but pale emanations of Carter's gradual transformation of Gordon? Closing his eyes, trying to conjure up Gordon's face, he saw, clearly, only Carter's smile, like a weapon, in the draft-card-burning photograph. *Wanting* to understood Gordon, he had only a shrill scream of defiance, an explosion, and this littered room with which to begin. He imagined the mortician, fitting pieces together, an arm on a drain board behind him. And when he was finished, what would he have accomplished? In the explosion, Gordon had vacated his body, and now the pieces had stopped moving, but the objects in his room twitched when Ernest touched them. Taking a deep breath, he inhaled the stench of spit and tobacco. He shoved the hubcap aside, and stood up.

Bending his head sideways, mashing his ear against his shoulder, Ernest read the titles of books crammed into cinderblock and pine-board shelves between Carter's cot and the window: *120 Days of Sodom,* the Marquis de Sade/ *Autobiography of Malcolm X/ The Postman Always Rings Twice,* James M. Cain/ *Mein Kampf*—. He caught himself reading title and authors aloud in a stupor. Silently, his lips still moving, he read: *Boy Scout Handbook.* Though he had never been a scout, Ernest had agreed with Lydia that, like a fraternity, it would be good for Gordon in future life. *Freedom Now,* Max Reiner/ *Nausea,* Jean-Paul Sartre/ *Atlas Shrugged,* Ayn Rand/ *The Scarlet Letter.* Heritage, leather-bound edition he had given Gordon for his sixteenth birthday. He had broken in the new Volkswagen, a surprise graduation present, driving it down. Late for the ceremonies, he had parked it, illegally, behind DeLozier Hall so it would be there when he and Gordon brought the suitcases and his other belongings down. *Castro's Cause,* Harvey Kreyborg/ *Notes from Underground,* Dostoyevski / *Lady Chatterley's Lover,* Ernest's own copy. Had Gordon sneaked it out of the house? Slumping to his knees, he squinted at titles he had been unable to make out: Carter had cynically shelved Ernest's own copy of *Profiles in Courage,* passed on to Gordon, next to *Oswald Resurrected* by Eugene Federogh.

There was a book with a library number on its spine. He would have to return that. The Gordon he had known would have done so before commencement. Afraid the police might come in suddenly and catch him there, Ernest rose to his feet. Glancing through several passages, highlighted with a yellow magic-marker, he realized that he was reading about "anguish, spiritual and physical, in Gerard Manley Hopkins' poetry." He rooted through the CORN FLAKES box again, took out Gordon's honors thesis. Flipping through the pages, he discovered a passage that duplicated, verbatim, a marked passage in the book. No footnote reference. The bibliography failed to cite the book that he held in his hand and now let drop, along with the honors thesis, into the beer carton onto Carter's fouled tee shirt and Ernest's handkerchief.

Why had he cheated? He never had before. Or had he plagiarized *all* those papers, from junior high on up to this one? No, surely, this time only. Ernest himself had felt the pressure in his senior year, and most of the boys in his fraternity had cheated when they really *had* to. Now he felt compelled to search thoroughly, examine everything carefully. The police had no right to invade a dead boy's privacy and plunge his invalid mother into grief.

In Carter's desk drawers, Ernest searched more systematically among letters and notes, still expecting to discover an early draft of Gordon's unfinished speech; perhaps it would be full of clues. He might even find the bill of sale for the grenade. Across the naked belly of a girl ripped from a magazine was written: "Gordy—" Carter had even renamed, rechristened Gordon. "Jeff and Conley and I are holding a peace vigil in the cold rain tonight, all night. Bring us a fresh jar of water at midnight. And leave your goddamn middle-class mottos in the room. Love, Carter."

A letter from Fort Jackson, South Carolina, April 20, 1968. "Dear Gordon, I am being shipped to Vietnam. I will never see you again. I have not forgotten what you said to me that night in our room across the Dark Gulf between our cots. As always, Carter." Without knowing what Carter meant, Ernest knew that gulf himself. He had tried to bridge it, touch Scott, his own roommate, whose lassitude about life's possibilities often provoked Ernest to wall-pounding rage. He had finally persuaded Scott to take a trip West with him right after graduation. Scott's nonchalant withdrawal at the last minute was so dispiriting that Earnest had accepted his father's offer of a summer internship with the insurance company as a claim adjustor.

A 1967 letter described in detail the march on the Pentagon. "What are you doing down there, you little fink? You should be up here with the rest of us. My brothers have been beaten by the cops. I'm not against the use of napalm in *some* instances. Just don't let me get my hands on any of it when those pig sonofabitches come swinging their sticks at us. We're rising up all over the world, Baby—or didn't you know it, with your nose in Chaucer's tales. Melbourne is about due to be hit so you'd better decide who's side you're on. I heard about this one campus demonstration where somebody set fire to this old fogey's life-long research on some obscure hang-up of his. I can think of a few at Melbourne that need shaking up." Ernest was shocked, then surprised at himself for being shocked. He wondered how Gordon had felt.

As Ernest pulled a postcard out of a pigeonhole, a white capsule rolled out into his hand. For a common cold, or LSD? He stifled an impulse to swallow it. By chance escape what chance might reveal. He flipped the capsule against the inside of the CORN FLAKES box and it popped like a cap pistol. Comic postcard—outhouse, hillbillies—mailed from Alabama, December 12, 1966. "Gordy, Baby, Wish you were here. You sure as hell ain't all *there*! Love, till death do us part, Carter." In several letters, Carter fervently attempted to persuade Gordon to abandon his "middle-class Puritan Upforcing" and embrace the cause of world brotherhood, which itself embraced all other great causes of "our time." But even through the serious ones ran a trace of self-mockery. He found Carter's draft notice, his *own* name crossed out, Gordon's typed in. Across the body of the form letter, dated February 1, 1968, was printed in Gothic script: NON SERVIUM.[4]

As Ernest reached for a bunch of postcards, he realized that he was eager not only to discover more about Gordon, but to assemble into some shape the fragments of Carter's life. A series of postcards with cryptic, taunting messages traced Carter's trail over the landscape of America, from early January to the middle of March, 1968. From Carmel, California, a view of a tower and cypress trees: "Violence is the sire of all the world's values."[5] Ernest remembered the card Gordon sent him from Washington, D.C., when he was in junior high: "Dear Dad, Our class went to see Congress but they were closed. Our teacher got mad. She dragged us all to the Smithsonian and showed us Lindbergh's airplane. It was called THE SPIRIT OF ST. LOUIS. I didn't think it looked so hot. Mrs. Landis said she saved the headlines when she was in high school. Did you? Your son, Gordon."

Ernest found a night letter from Lynn, Massachusetts. "Dear Gordon, Remembering that Jason spoke of you so often and so fondly, his father and I felt certain that you would not want to learn through the newspapers that our dear son has been reported missing in action. While no one can really approve in his heart of this war, Jason has always been the sort of boy who believed in dying for his convictions. We know that you will miss him. He loved you as though you were his own brother. Affectionate regards, Grace and Harold Carter." June 1, 1968, three days ago.

Trembling, Ernest sought more letters from Carter. One from boot camp summed up, in wild, impassioned prose, Carter's opinions on civil rights, the war, and "the American Dream that's turned into a nightmare." In another, "God is dead and buried on LBJ's ranch" dispensed with religion and politics, "inseparable." May 4, 1968: "Dear Gordy, We are in the jungle now, on a search and destroy mission. You have to admire some of these platoon leaders. I must admit I enjoy watching them act out their roles as all-American tough guys. They have a kind of style, anyway. In here you don't have time to analyze your thoughts. But I just thought a word or two written at the scene of battle might bring you the smell of smoke." Ernest sniffed the letter, uncertain whether the faint smell came from the paper.

He pulled a wadded letter out of a pigeonhole where someone had stuffed it. As he unwadded the note, vicious ballpoint pen markings wove a mesh over the words: "Gordon, I'm moving in with Conley. Pack my things and set them in the hall. I don't even want

4. "I will not serve." 5. From the poem "The Bloody Sire" by Robinson Jeffers (1887–1962).

to *enter* that room again. What you said last night made me sick. I've lived with you for three and a half years because I was always convinced that I could save your soul. But after last night, I know it's hopeless. Carter." Across the "Dark Gulf" between their beds, what could *Gordon* have said to shock Carter? Had Gordon persuaded him to stay after all? Or was it the next day that Carter had "impulsively" run away? Ernest searched quickly through the rest of the papers, hoping no answer existed, but knowing that if one did and he failed to find it, the police wouldn't fail.

"Gordy, Baby, Everything you read is lies! I've been in the field three weeks now. My whole life's search ends here, in this burning village, where I'm taking time to write to you. Listen, Baby, this is life! This is what it's all about. In the past weeks I've personally set fire to thirty-seven huts belonging to Viet Cong sympathizers. Don't listen to those sons-of-bitches who whine and gripe and piss and moan about the war. This is a *just* war. We're on the *right* side. This place has opened my eyes and heart, baby. With the bullets and the blood all around, you see things clearer. Words! To hell with words! All these beady-eyed little bastards understand is *bullets*, and a knife now and then. These bastards killed my buddy, a Black boy by the name of Bird. The greatest guy that ever lived. Well, there's ten Viet Cong that ain't alive today because of what they did to my buddy, and there'll be another hundred less Viet Cong if I can persuade them to send me out after I'm due to be pulled back. Yesterday, I found a Viet Cong in a hut with his goddamn wife and kids. I turned the flame thrower on the sons-of-bitches and when the hut burned down, I pissed on the hot ashes. I'm telling you all this to open your eyes, mister. This is the way it really is. Join your ass up, get over here where you belong. Forget everything I ever said to you or wrote to you before. I have seen the light. The future of the world will be decided right here. And I will fight until the last Viet Cong is dead. Always, your friend, Carter." May 21, 1968, two weeks ago.

Trying to feel as Gordon had felt reading this letter, feeling nothing, Ernest remembered Gordon's response to a different piece of information some kid in grammar school dealt him when he was eleven. Having informed Gordon that Santa Claus was a lie, he added the observation that nobody ever knows who his real father and mother are. Just as Ernest stepped into the house from the office, Gordon had asked: "Are you my real father?" In the living room where colored lights blazed on the tree, Lydia was weeping. It took two months to rid Gordon of the fantasy that he had been adopted. Or had he simply stopped interrogating them? But how did a man know *any*thing? Did that professor ever suspect that one day in print he would be labeled "the most boring man on the face of the earth?" Did Carter ever sense he would end up killing men in Vietnam? Did Gordon ever suspect that on his graduation day . . . ?

Now the day began to make sense. After Carter's letter from Vietnam, reversing everything he had preached to Gordon, Gordon had let his studies slide, and then the plagiarism had just happened, the way things will, because how could he really care anymore? Then did the night letter from Carter's mother shock him into pulling the grenade pin? Was "I advocate a total revolution!" Gordon's *own* climax to the attitude expressed in Carter's Vietnam letter? Or did the *old* Carter finally speak through Gordon's mouth? These possibilities made sense, but Ernest felt nothing.

His foot kicked a metal wastebasket under Carter's desk. Squatting, he pulled it out, and sitting again in the swivel chair, began to unwad several letters. "Dear Dad—" The rest blank. "Dear Dad—" Blank. "Dear Dad—" Blank. "Dear Father—" Blank. "Dear Dad—" Blank.

Ernest swung around in Carter's chair, rocked once, got to his feet, stood in the middle of the room, his hands dangling in front of him, the leaded moldings of the window cast black wavy lines over his suit, the green light stained his hands, his heart beat so fast he became aware that he was panting. Like a dog. His throat felt dry, his tongue swollen, eyes burning from reading in the oblique light. Dark spots of sweat on the floor. "Gordon. Gordon. Gordon."

Whatever Gordon had said in his valedictory address, Ernest knew that certain things in this room would give the public the wrong image of his son. Or perhaps—he faced it—the right image. Wrong or right, it would incite the disease in Lydia's body to riot and she would burn. He rolled the desk top down and began stuffing things into the beer carton. When it was full, he emptied the contents of the CORN FLAKES box onto the desk, throwing only the honors thesis back into it. When he jerked the bowie knife out of the wall, the banana poster fell. He scraped at the clotting vomit on the clothes hanging in the closet, and wiped the blade on the sole of his shoe. Then he filled the CORN FLAKES box with letters and other incriminating objects.

He opened the door and looked out. The hall was dim and deserted. The surviving seniors had gone home, though some must have lingered behind with wounded classmates, teachers, parents. The police would still be occupied with traffic. The back staircase was dark. He stacked the beer carton on top of the CORN FLAKES box, lifted both in his arms, and started to back out the door. But under the rolltop desk in a bed of lint lay a piece of paper that, even wadded up, resembled a telegram. Setting the boxes down, the cardboard already dark brown where he had pressed his forehead,

Ernest got on his knees and reached under the desk. Without rising, he unwadded the paper. URGENT YOU RENEW SUBSCRIPTION TO TIME AT STUDENT RATE. STOP. WORLD NEWS AT YOUR FINGERTIPS. STOP. Mock telegram technique, special reply pencil enclosed.

The boxes were heavier as Ernest lifted them again and backed out the door, almost certain that the grenade had not been a rhetorical flourish. Bracing the boxes against the wall, lifting his knee under them, Ernest quickly reached out, pulled at the door knob. When the door slammed, locked, startling him, he grabbed the boxes as they almost tipped over into the stairwell.

He had to descend very slowly. The narrow staircase curved twice before it reached the basement. His shoulder slid along the wall as he went down, carefully, step by step. The bottom of the box cut into his palms, sweat tickled his spine, and his thighs chafed each other as sweat dried on his flesh. He saw nothing until he reached the basement where twilight coming through the window of the door revealed the furnace. As he fumbled for the doorknob, already the devouring locusts jangled in his ears like a single note quivering relentlessly on a violin.

Locusts had dropped from the ivy onto the black hood of the Volkswagen, parked up tight against the building. He opened the trunk, set the boxes inside, closed the lid, locked it.

As he got in behind the wheel, a glimpse of the cemetery behind the dormitory made him recall the grave that had so awed him during his freshman year. From where he sat, turning the ignition key, the larger tombs of the historic dead obscured the small white stone, but he had not forgotten the epitaph: HERE LIES AN UNIDENTIFIED VICTIM OF THE FIRE THAT RAZED DELOZIER HALL, May 16, 1938. Since all the Melbourne students had been accounted for, he (or perhaps she) must have been a visitor.

Pulling off the highway, he drove along a dirt trail, new grass sprouting between the wheel ruts. Here, as visible evidence testified, Melbourne students brought the girls who came down from Briarheath. Parked, he let dusk turn to dark.

Then he left the woods, lights dimmed until he got onto the highway. On the outskirts of the town, looking at this distance like a village erected in one of those elaborate electric train sets, he turned onto a cinder road and stopped at a gate, got out, lifted the latch, drove through, then went back and closed the gate.

Headlights off, he eased over the soft, sooty dirt road, the rough bushes on each side a soft gray blur, into the main lot, where the faculty and other townspeople dumped junk and garbage.

The smell made him aware of the taste at the back of his mouth, the stench of burning rubber and plastic and dead animals made his headache pound more fiercely, his left eyelid beat like a pulse.

He unlocked the trunk, lifted out the CORN FLAKES box, and stumbled in the dark over tin cans and broken tools and springs and tires, set the box down, then went back and got the other box.

The boxes weren't far enough into the dump. He dragged them, one with each hand, backwards, up and over the rough terrain, stumbling, cutting his hands on rusty cans and nails in charred wood, thinking of tetanus, of Lydia without him.

Standing up, he sucked in the night air, feeling a dewy freshness mingled with the acrid smoke and fumes. He reached into his pocket for his lighter. His thumb began to hurt as he failed repeatedly to make the flint catch.

A bright beam shot out over the dump, another several yards beside it, then another—powerful flashlights—and as he crouched to avoid the lights, rifle fire shattered the silence over the dump. Reaching out, grabbing the cardboard flaps to keep his balance, Ernest squatted beside his boxes.

"Get that son-of-a-bitch, Doc!"

Twisting his neck around, Ernest saw the beam swing and dip through oily smoke coiling out of the debris and stop on a rat, crouched on a fire-blackened ice-box door. It started to run. But the slick porcelain allowed its feet no traction.

SUSAN MINOT

Lust

LEO was from a long time ago, the first one I ever saw nude. In the spring before the Hellmans filled their pool, we'd go down there in the deep end, with baby oil, and like that. I met him the first month away at boarding school. He had a halo from the campus light behind him. I flipped.

Roger was fast. In his illegal car, we drove to the reservoir, the radio blaring, talking fast, fast, fast. He was always going for my zipper. He got kicked out sophomore year.

By the time the band got around to playing "Wild Horses," I had tasted Bruce's tongue. We were clicking in the shadows on the other side of the amplifier, out of Mrs. Donovan's line of vision. It tasted like salt, with my neck bent back, because we had been dancing so hard before.

Tim's line: "I'd like to see you in a bathing suit." I knew it was his line when he said the exact same thing to Annie Hines.

You'd go on walks to get off campus. It was raining like hell, my sweater as sopped as a wet sheep. Tim pinned me to a tree, the woods light brown and dark brown, a white house half-hidden with the lights already on. The water was as loud as a crowd hissing. He made certain comments about my forehead, about my cheeks.

We started off sitting at one end of the couch and then our feet were squished against the armrest and then he went over to turn off the TV and came back after he had taken off his shirt and then we slid onto the floor and he got up again to close the door, then came back to me, a body waiting on the rug.

You'd try to wipe off the table or to do the dishes and Willie would untuck your shirt and get his hands up under in front, standing behind you, making puffy noises in your ear.

He likes it when I wash my hair. He covers his face with it and if I start to say something, he goes, "Shush."

For a long time, I had Philip on the brain. The less they noticed you, the more you got them on the brain.

My parents had no idea. Parents never really know what's going on, especially when you're away at school most of the time. If she met them, my mother might say, "Oliver seems nice" or "I like that one" without much of an opinion. If she didn't like them, "He's a funny fellow, isn't he?" or "Johnny's perfectly nice but a drink of water." My father was too shy to talk to them at all, unless they played sports and he'd ask them about that.

The sand was almost cold underneath because the sun was long gone. Eben piled a mound over my feet, patting around my ankles, the ghostly surf rumbling behind him in the dark. He was the first person I ever knew who died, later that summer, in a car crash. I thought about it for a long time.

"Come here," he says on the porch.

I go over to the hammock and he takes my wrist with two fingers.

"What?"

He kisses my palm then directs my hand to his fly.

Songs went with whichever boy it was. "Sugar Magnolia" was Tim, with the line "Rolling in the rushes/down by the riverside." With "Darkness Darkness," I'd picture Philip with his long hair. Hearing "Under my Thumb" there'd be the smell of Jamie's suede jacket.

We hid in the listening rooms during study hall. With a record cover over the door's window, the teacher on duty couldn't look in. I came out flushed and heady and back at the dorm was surprised how red my lips were in the mirror.

One weekend at Simon's brother's, we stayed inside all day with the shades down, in bed, then went out to Store 24 to get some ice cream. He stood at the magazine rack and read through *MAD* while I got butterscotch sauce, craving something sweet.

I could do some things well. Some things I was good at, like math or painting or even sports, but the second a boy put his arm around me, I forget about wanting to do anything else, which felt like a relief at first until it became like sinking into a muck.

It was different for a girl.

When we were little, the brothers next door tied up our ankles. They held the door of the goat house and wouldn't let us out till we showed them our underpants. Then they'd forget about being after us and when we played whiffle ball, I'd be just as good as them.

Then it got to be different. Just because you have on a short skirt, they yell from the cars, slowing down for a while and if you don't look, they screech off and call you a bitch.

"What's the matter with me?" they say, point-blank.

Or else, "Why won't you go out with me? I'm not asking you to get married," about to get mad.

Or it'd be, trying to be reasonable, in a regular voice, "Listen, I just want to have a good time."

So I'd go because I couldn't think of something to say back that wouldn't be obvious, and if you go out with them, you sort of have to do something.

I sat between Mack and Eddie in the front seat of the pickup. They were having a fight about something. I've a feeling about me.

Certain nights you'd feel a certain surrender, maybe if you'd had wine. The surrender would be forgetting yourself and you'd put your nose to his neck and feel like a squirrel, safe, at rest, in a restful dream. But then you'd start to slip from that and the dark would come in and there'd be a cave. You make out the dim shape of the windows and feel yourself become a cave, filled absolutely with air, or with a sadness that wouldn't stop.

Teenage years. You know just what you're doing and don't see the things that start to get in the way.

Lots of boys, but never two at the same time. One was plenty to keep you in a state. You'd start to see a boy and something would rush over you like a fast storm cloud and you couldn't possibly think of anyone else. Boys took it differently. Their eyes perked up at any little number that walked by. You'd act like you weren't noticing.

The joke was that the school doctor gave out the pill like aspirin. He didn't ask you anything. I was fifteen. We had a picture of him in assembly, holding up an IUD shaped like a T. Most girls were on the pill, if anything, because they couldn't handle a diaphragm. I kept the dial in my top drawer like my mother and thought of her each time I tipped out the yellow tablets in the morning before chapel.

If they were too shy, I'd be more so. Andrew was nervous. We stayed up with his family album, sharing a pack of Old Golds. Before it got light, we turned on the TV. A man was explaining how to plant seedlings. His mouth jerked to the side in a tic. Andrew thought it was a riot and kept imitating him. I laughed to be polite. When we finally dozed off, he dared to put his arm around me but that was it.

You wait till they come to you. With half fright, half swagger, they stand one step down. They dare to touch the button on your coat then lose their nerve and quickly drop their hand so you—you'd do anything for them. You touch their cheek.

The girls sit around in the common room and talk about boys, smoking their heads off.

"What are you complaining about?" says Jill to me when we talk about problems.

"Yeah," says Giddy. "You always have a boyfriend."

I look at them and think, As if.

I thought the worst thing anyone could call you was a cock-teaser. So, if you flirted, you had to be prepared to go through with it. Sleeping with someone was perfectly normal once you had done it. You didn't really worry about it. But there were other problems. The problems had to do with something else entirely.

Mack was during the hottest summer ever recorded. We were renting a house on an island with all sorts of other people. No one slept during the heat wave, walking around the house with nothing on which we were used to because of the nude beach. In the living room, Eddie lay on top of a coffee table to cool off. Mack and I, with the bedroom door open for air, sweated and sweated all night.

"I can't take this," he said at 3 A.M. "I'm going for a swim." He and some guys down the hall went to the beach. The heat put me on edge. I sat on a cracked chest by the open window and smoked and smoked till I felt even worse, waiting for something—I guess for him to get back.

One was on a camping trip in Colorado. We zipped our sleeping bags together, the coyotes' hysterical chatter far away. Other couples murmured in other tents. Paul was up before sunrise, starting a fire for breakfast. He wasn't much of a talker in the daytime. At night, his hand leafed about in the hair at my neck.

There'd be times when you overdid it. You'd get carried away. All the next day, you'd be in a total fog, delirious, absent-minded, crossing the street and nearly getting run over.

The more girls a boy has, the better. He has a bright look, having reaped fruits, blooming. He stalks around, sure-shouldered, and you have the feeling he's got more in him, a fatter heart, more stories to tell. For a girl, with each boy it's like a petal gets plucked each time.

Then you start to get tired. You begin to feel diluted, like watered-down stew.

Oliver came skiing with us. We lolled by the fire after everyone had gone to bed. Each creak you'd think was someone coming downstairs. The silver-loop bracelet he gave me had been a present from his girlfriend before.

On vacations, we went skiing, or you'd go south if someone invited you. Some people had apartments in New York that their families hardly ever used. Or summer houses, or older sisters. We always managed to find some place to go.

We made the plan at coffee hour. Simon snuck out and met me at Main Gate after lights-out. We crept to the chapel and spent the night in the balcony. He tasted like onions from a submarine sandwich.

The boys are one of two ways: either they can't sit still or they don't move. In front of the TV, they won't budge. On weekends they play touch football while we sit on the sidelines, picking blades of grass to chew on, and watch. We're always watching them run around. We shiver in the stands, knocking our boots together to keep our toes warm and they whizz across the ice, chopping their sticks around the puck. When they're in the rink, they refuse to look at you, only eyeing each other beneath low helmets. You cheer for them but they don't look up, even if it's a face-off when nothing's happening, even if they're doing drills before any game has started at all.

Dancing under the pink tent, he bent down and whispered in my ear. We slipped away to the lawn on the other side of the hedge. Much later, as he was leaving the buffet with two plates of eggs and sausage, I saw the grass stains on the knees of his white pants.

Tim's was shaped like a banana, with a graceful curve to it. They're all different. Willie's like a bunch of walnuts when nothing was happening, another's as thin as a thin hot dog. But it's like faces; you're never really surprised.

Still, you're not sure what to expect.

I look into his face and he looks back. I look into his eyes and they look back at mine. Then they look down at my mouth so I look at his mouth, then back to his eyes then, backing up, at his whole face. I think, Who? Who are you? His head tilts to one side.

I say, "Who are you?"

"What do you mean?"

"Nothing."

I look at his eyes again, deeper. Can't tell who he is, what he thinks.

"What?" he says. I look at his mouth.

"I'm just wondering," I say and go wandering across his face. Study the chin line. It's shaped like a persimmon.

"Who are you? What are you thinking?"

He says, "What the hell are you talking about?"

Then they get mad after when you say enough is enough. After, when it's easier to explain that you don't want to. You wouldn't dream of saying that maybe you weren't really ready to in the first place.

Gentle Eddie. We waded into the sea, the waves round and plowing in, buffalo-headed, slapping our thighs. I put my arms around his freckled shoulders and he held me up, buoyed by the water, and rocked me like a sea shell.

I had no idea whose party it was, the apartment jam-packed, stepping over people in the hallway. The room with the music was practically empty, the bare floor, me in red shoes. This fellow slides onto one knee and takes me around the waist and we rock to jazzy tunes, with my toes pointing heavenward, and waltz and spin and dip to "Smoke Gets in Your Eyes" or "I'll Love You Just for Now." He puts his head to my chest, runs a sweeping hand down my inside thigh and we go loose-limbed and sultry and as smooth as silk and I stamp my red heels and he takes me into a swoon. I never saw him again after that but I thought, I could have loved that one.

You wonder how long you can keep it up. You begin to feel like you're showing through, like a bathroom window that only lets in grey light, the kind you can't see out of.

They keep coming around. Johnny drives up at Easter vacation from Baltimore and I let him in the kitchen with everyone sound asleep. He has friends waiting in the car.

"What are you crazy? It's pouring out there," I say.

"It's okay," he says. "They understand."

So he gets some long kisses from me, against the refrigerator, before he goes because I hate those girls who push away a boy's face as if she were made out of Ivory soap, as if she's that much greater than he is.

The note on my cubby told me to see the headmaster. I had no idea for what. He had received complaints about my amorous displays on the town green. It was Willie that spring. The headmaster told me he didn't care what I did but that Casey Academy had a reputation to uphold in the town. He lowered his glasses on his nose. "We've got twenty acres of woods on this campus," he said. "Smooch with your boyfriend there."

Everybody'd get weekend permissions for different places then we'd all go to someone's house whose parents were away. Usually there'd be more boys than girls. We raided the liquor closet and smoked pot at the kitchen table and you'd never know who would end up where, or with whom. There were always disasters. Ceci got bombed and cracked her head open on the bannister and needed stitches. Then there was the time Wendel Blair walked through the picture window at the Lowe's and got slashed to ribbons.

He scared me. In bed, I didn't dare look at him. I lay back with my eyes closed, luxuriating because he knew all sorts of expert angles, his hands never fumbling, going over my whole body, pressing the hair up and off the back of my head, giving an extra hip shove, as if to say *There.* I parted my eyes slightly, keeping the screen of my lashes low because it was too much to look at him, his mouth loose and pink and parted, his eyes looking through my forehead, or kneeling up, looking through my throat. I was ashamed but couldn't look him in the eye.

You wonder about things feeling a little off-kilter. You begin to feel like a piece of pounded veal.

At boarding school, everyone gets depressed. We go in and see the housemother, Mrs. Gunther. She got married when she was eighteen. Mr. Gunther was her high-school sweetheart, the only boyfriend she ever had.

"And you knew you wanted to marry him right off?" we ask her.

She smiles and says, "Yes."

"They always want something from you," says Jill, complaining about her boyfriend.

"Yeah," says Giddy. "You always feel like you have to deliver something."

"You do," say Mrs. Gunther. "Babies."

After sex, you curl up like a shrimp, something deep inside you ruined, slammed in a place that sickens at slamming, and slowly you fill up with an overwhelming sadness, an elusive gaping worry. You don't try to explain it, filled with the knowledge that it's nothing after all, everything filling up finally and absolutely with death. After the briskness of loving, loving stops. And you roll over with death stretched out alongside you like a feather boa, or a snake, light as air, and you . . . you don't even ask for anything or try to say something to him because it's obviously your own damn fault. You haven't been able to—to what? To open your heart. You open your legs but can't, or don't dare anymore, to open your heart.

It starts this way:

You stare into their eyes. They flash like all the stars are out. They look at you seriously, their eyes at a low burn and their hands no matter what starting off shy and with such a gentle touch that the only thing you can do is take that tenderness and let yourself be swept away. When, with one attentive finger they tuck the hair behind your ear, you—

You do everything they want.

Then comes after. After when they don't look at you. They scratch their balls, stare at the ceiling. Or if they do turn, their gaze is altogether changed. They are surprised. They turn casually to look at you, distracted, and get a mild distracted surprise. You're gone. Their black look tells you that the girl they were fucking is not there anymore. You seem to have disappeared.

ALICE MUNRO

The Beggar Maid

PATRICK Blatchford was in love with Rose. This had become a fixed, even furious, idea with him. For her, a continual surprise. He wanted to marry her. He waited for her after classes, moved in and walked beside her, so that anybody she was talking to would have to reckon with his presence. He would not talk, when these friends or classmates of hers were around, but he would try to catch her eye, so that he could indicate by a cold incredulous look what he thought of their conversation. Rose was flattered, but nervous. A girl named Nancy Falls, a friend of hers, mispronounced Metternich[1] in front of him. He said to her later, "How can you be friends with people like that?"

Nancy and Rose had gone and sold their blood together, at Victoria Hospital. They each got fifteen dollars. They spent most of the money on evening shoes, tarty silver sandals. Then because they were sure the bloodletting had caused them to lose weight they had hot fudge sundaes at Boomers. Why was Rose unable to defend Nancy to Patrick?

Patrick was twenty-four years old, a graduate student, planning to be a history professor. He was tall, thin, fair, and good-looking, though he had a long pale-red birthmark, dribbling like a tear down his temple and his cheek. He apologized for it, but said it was fading, as he got older. When he was forty, it would have faded away. It was not the birthmark that canceled out his good looks, Rose thought. (Something did cancel them out, or at least diminish them, for her; she had to keep reminding herself they were there.) There was something edgy, jumpy, disconcerting, about him. His voice would break under stress—with her, it seemed he was always under stress—he knocked dishes and cups off tables, spilled drinks and bowls of peanuts, like a comedian. He was not a comedian; nothing could be further from his intentions. He came from British Columbia. His family was rich.

1. Austrian statesman (1773–1859).

He arrived early to pick Rose up, when they were going to the movies. He wouldn't knock, he knew he was early. He sat on the step outside Dr. Henshawe's door. This was in the winter, it was dark out, but there was a little coach lamp beside the door.

"Oh, Rose! Come and look!" called Dr. Henshawe, in her soft, amused voice, and they looked down together from the dark window of the study. "The poor young man," said Dr. Henshawe tenderly. Dr. Henshawe was in her seventies. She was a former English professor, fastidious and lively. She had a lame leg, but a still youthfully, charmingly tilted head, with white braids wound around it.

She called Patrick poor because he was in love, and perhaps also because he was a male, doomed to push and blunder. Even from up here he looked stubborn and pitiable, determined and dependent, sitting out there in the cold.

"Guarding the door," Dr. Henshawe said. "Oh, Rose!"

Another time she said disturbingly, "Oh, dear, I'm afraid he is after the wrong girl."

Rose didn't like her saying that. She didn't like her laughing at Patrick. She didn't like Patrick sitting out on the steps that way, either. He was asking to be laughed at. He was the most vulnerable person Rose had ever known, he made himself so, didn't know anything about protecting himself. But he was also full of cruel judgments, he was full of conceit.

"You are a scholar, Rose," Dr. Henshawe would say. "This will interest you." Then she would read aloud something from the paper, or, more likely, something from *Canadian Forum* or the *Atlantic Monthly*. Dr. Henshawe had at one time headed the city's school board; she was a founding member of Canada's socialist party. She still sat on committees, wrote letters to the paper, reviewed books. Her father and mother had been medical missionaries; she had been born in China. Her house was small and perfect. Polished floors, glowing rugs, Chinese vases, bowls and landscapes, black carved screens. Much that Rose could not appreciate, at the time. She could not really distinguish between the little jade animals on Dr. Henshawe's mantelpiece and the ornaments displayed in the jewelry store window, in Hanratty, though she could now distinguish between either of these and the things Flo bought from the five-and-ten.

She could not really decide how much she liked being at Dr. Henshawe's. At times she felt discouraged, sitting in the dining room with a linen napkin on her knee, eating from fine white plates on blue placemats. For one thing, there was never enough to eat, and she had taken to buying doughnuts and chocolate bars and hiding them in her room. The canary swung on its perch in the dining room window and Dr. Henshawe directed conversation. She talked about politics, about writers. She mentioned Frank Scott and Dorothy Livesay.[2] She said Rose must read them. Rose must read this, she must read that. Rose became sullenly determined not to. She was reading Thomas Mann. She was reading Tolstoy.

Before she came to Dr. Henshawe's, Rose had never heard of the working class. She took the designation home.

"This would have to be the last part of town where they put the sewers," Flo said.

"Of course," Rose said coolly. "This is the working-class part of town."

"*Working* class?" said Flo. "Not if the ones around here can help it."

Dr. Henshawe's house had done one thing. It had destroyed the naturalness, the taken-for-granted background, of home. To go back there was to go quite literally into a crude light. Flo had put fluorescent lights in the store and the kitchen. There was also, in a corner of the kitchen, a floor lamp Flo had won at Bingo; its shade was permanently wrapped in wide strips of cellophane. What Dr. Henshawe's house and Flo's house did best, in Rose's opinion, was discredit each other. In Dr. Henshawe's charming rooms there was always for Rose the raw knowledge of home, an indigestible lump, and at home, now, her sense of order and modulation elsewhere exposed such embarrassing sad poverty, in people who never thought themselves poor. Poverty was not just wretchedness, as Dr. Henshawe seemed to think, it was not just deprivation. It meant having those ugly tube lights and being proud of them. It meant continual talk of money and malicious talk about new things people had bought and whether they were paid for. It meant pride and jealousy flaring over something like the new pair of plastic curtains, imitating lace, that Flo had bought for the front window. That as well as hanging your clothes on nails behind the door and being able to hear every sound from the bathroom. It meant decorating your walls with a number of admonitions, pious and cheerful and mildly bawdy.

THE LORD IS MY SHEPHERD

BELIEVE IN THE LORD JESUS CHRIST AND THOU SHALL BE SAVED

Why did Flo have those, when she wasn't even religious? They were what people had, common as calendars.

THIS IS MY KITCHEN AND I WILL DO AS I DARNED PLEASE

MORE THAN TWO PERSONS TO A BED IS DANGEROUS AND UNLAWFUL

Billy Pope had brought that one. What would Patrick have to say about them? What would someone who was offended by a mispronunciation of Metternich think of Billy Pope's stories?

2. Canadian writers.

Billy Pope worked in Tyde's Butcher Shop. What he talked about most frequently now was the D.P.,[3] the Belgian, who had come to work there, and got on Billy Pope's nerves with his impudent singing of French songs and his naive notions of getting on in this country, buying a butcher shop of his own.

"Don't you think you can come over here and get yourself ideas," Billy Pope said to the D.P. "It's *youse* workin for *us*, and don't think that'll change into *us* workin for *youse*." That shut him up, Billy Pope said.

Patrick would say from time to time that since her home was only fifty miles away he ought to come up and meet Rose's family.

"There's only my stepmother."

"It's too bad I couldn't have met your father."

Rashly, she had presented her father to Patrick as a reader of history, an amateur scholar. That was not exactly a lie, but it did not give a truthful picture of the circumstances.

"Is your stepmother your guardian?"

Rose had to say she did not know.

"Well, your father must have appointed a guardian for you in his will. Who administers his estate?"

His *estate*. Rose thought an estate was land, such as people owned in England.

Patrick thought it was rather charming of her to think that.

"No, his money and stocks and so on. What he left."

"I don't think he left any."

"Don't be silly," Patrick said.

And sometimes Dr. Henshawe would say, "Well, you are a scholar, you are not interested in that." Usually she was speaking of some event at the college; a pep rally, a football game, a dance. And usually she was right; Rose was not interested. But she was not eager to admit it. She did not seek or relish that definition of herself.

On the stairway wall hung graduation photographs of all the other girls, scholarship girls, who had lived with Dr. Henshawe. Most of them had got to be teachers, then mothers. One was a dietician, two were librarians, one was a professor of English, like Dr. Henshawe herself. Rose did not care for the look of them, for their soft-focused meekly smiling gratitude, their large teeth and maidenly rolls of hair. They seemed to be urging on her some deadly secular piety. There were no actresses among them, no brassy magazine journalists; none of them had latched on to the sort of life Rose wanted for herself. She wanted to perform in public. She thought she wanted to be an actress but she never tried to act, was afraid to go near the college drama productions. She knew she

3. Displaced person, refugee from the Nazis.

couldn't sing or dance. She would really have liked to play the harp, but she had no ear for music. She wanted to be known and envied, slim and clever. She told Dr. Henshawe that if she had been a man she would have wanted to be a foreign correspondent.

"Then you must be one," cried Dr. Henshawe alarmingly. "The future will be wide open, for women. You must concentrate on languages. You must take courses in political science. And economics. Perhaps you could get a job on the paper for the summer. I have friends there."

Rose was frightened at the idea of working on a paper, and she hated the introductory economics course; she was looking for a way of dropping it. It was dangerous to mention things to Dr. Henshawe.

She had got to live with Dr. Henshawe by accident. Another girl had been picked to move in but she got sick; she had T.B., and went instead to a sanitarium. Dr. Henshawe came up to the college office on the second day of registration to get the names of some other scholarship freshmen.

Rose had been in the office just a little while before, asking where the meeting of the scholarship students was to be held. She had lost her notice. The Bursar was giving a talk to the new scholarship students, telling them of ways to earn money and live cheaply and explaining the high standards of performance to be expected of them here, if they wanted their payments to keep coming.

Rose found out the number of the room, and started up the stairs to the first floor. A girl came up beside her and said, "Are you on your way to three-oh-twelve, too?"

They walked together, telling each other the details of their scholarships. Rose did not yet have a place to live, she was staying at the Y. She did not really have enough money to be here at all. She had a scholarship for her tuition and the country prize to buy her books and a bursary of three hundred dollars to live on; that was all.

"You'll have to get a job," the other girl said. She had a larger bursary, because she was in Science (that's where the money is, the money's all in Science, she said seriously), but she was hoping to get a job in the cafeteria. She had a room in somebody's basement. How much does your room cost? How much does a hot plate cost? Rose asked her, her head swimming with anxious calculations.

This girl wore her hair in a roll. She wore a crepe blouse, yellowed and shining from washing and ironing. Her breasts were large and sagging. She probably wore a dirty-pink hooked-up-the-side brassiere. She had a scaly patch on one cheek.

"This must be it," she said.

There was a little window in the door. They could look through at the other scholarship winners already assembled and waiting. It seemed to Rose that she saw four or five girls of the same stooped and matronly type as the girl who was beside her, and several bright-eyed, self-satisfied babyish-looking boys. It seemed to be the rule that girl scholarship winners looked about forty and boys about twelve. It was not possible, of course, that they all looked like this. It was not possible that in one glance through the windows of the door Rose could detect traces of eczema, stained underarms, dandruff, moldy deposits on the teeth and crusty flakes in the corners of the eyes. That was only what she thought. But there was a pall over them, she was not mistaken, there was a true terrible pall of eagerness and docility. How else could they have supplied so many right answers, so many pleasing answers, how else distinguished themselves and got themselves here? And Rose had done the same.

"I have to go to the john," she said.

She could see herself, working in the cafeteria. Her figure, broad enough already, broadened out still more by the green cotton uniform, her face red and her hair stringy from the heat. Dishing up stew and fried chicken for those of inferior intelligence and handsomer means. Blocked off by the steam tables, the uniform, by decent hard work that nobody need be ashamed of, by publicly proclaimed braininess and poverty. Boys could get away with that, barely. For girls it was fatal. Poverty in girls is not attractive unless combined with sweet sluttishness, stupidity. Braininess is not attractive unless combined with some signs of elegance; *class*. Was this true, and was she foolish enough to care? It was; she was.

She went back to the first floor where the halls were crowded with ordinary students who were not on scholarship, who would not be expected to get A's and be grateful and live cheap. Enviable and innocent, they milled around the registration tables in their new purple and white blazers, their purple Frosh beanies, yelling reminders to each other, confused information, nonsensical insults. She walked among them feeling bitterly superior and despondent. The skirt of her green corduroy suit kept falling back between her legs as she walked. The material was limp; she should have spent more and bought the heavier weight. She thought now that the jacket was not properly cut either, though it had looked all right at home. The whole outfit had been made by a dressmaker in Hanratty, a friend of Flo's, whose main concern had been that there should be no revelation of the figure. When Rose asked if the skirt couldn't be made tighter this woman had said, "You wouldn't want your b.t.m. to show, now would you?" and Rose hadn't wanted to say she didn't care.

Another thing the dressmaker said was, "I thought now you was through school you'd be getting a job and help out at home."

A woman walking down the hall stopped Rose.

"Aren't you one of the scholarship girls?"

It was the Registrar's secretary. Rose thought she was going to be reprimanded, for not being at the meeting, and she was going to say she felt sick. She prepared her face for this lie. But the secretary said, "Come with me, now, I've got somebody I want you to meet."

Dr. Henshawe was making a charming nuisance of herself in the office. She liked poor girls, bright girls, but they had to be fairly good-looking girls.

"I think this could be your lucky day," the secretary said, leading Rose. "If you could put a pleasanter expression on your face."

Rose hated being told that, but she smiled obediently.

Within the hour she was taken home with Dr. Henshawe, installed in the house with the Chinese screens and vases, and told she was a scholar.

She got a job working in the Library of the college, instead of in the cafeteria. Dr. Henshawe was a friend of the Head Librarian. She worked on Saturday afternoons. She worked in the stacks, putting books away. On Saturday afternoons in the fall the Library was nearly empty, because of the football games. The narrow windows were open to the leafy campus, the football field, the dry fall country. The distant songs and shouts came drifting in.

The college buildings were not old at all, but they were built to look old. They were built of stone. The Arts building had a tower, and the Library had casement windows, which might have been designed for shooting arrows through. The buildings and the books in the Library were what pleased Rose most about the place. The life that usually filled it, and that was now drained away, concentrated around the football field, letting loose those noises, seemed to her inappropriate and distracting. The cheers and songs were idiotic, if you listened to the words. What did they want to build such dignified buildings for, if they were going to sing songs like that?

She knew enough not to reveal these opinions. If anybody said to her, "It's awful you have to work Saturdays and can't get to any of the games," she would fervently agree.

Once a man grabbed her bare leg, between her sock and her skirt. It happened in the Agriculture section, down at the bottom of the stacks. Only the faculty, graduate students, and employees had access to the stacks, though someone could have hoisted himself through a ground-floor window, if he was skinny. She had seen a man crouched down looking at the books on a low shelf, further along. As she reached up to push a book into place he passed behind her. He bent and grabbed her leg, all in one smooth startling motion, and then was gone. She could feel for quite a while where his fingers had dug in. It didn't seem to her a sexual touch, it was more like a joke, though not at all a friendly one. She heard him run away, or felt him running; the metal shelves were vibrating. Then they stopped. There was no sound of him. She walked around looking between the stacks, looking into the carrels. Suppose she did see him, or bumped into him around a corner, what did she intend to do? She did not know. It was simply necessary to look for him, as in some tense childish game. She looked down at the sturdy pinkish calf of her leg. Amazing, that out of the blue somebody had wanted to blotch and punish it.

There were usually a few graduate students working in the carrels, even on Saturday afternoons. More rarely, a professor. Every carrel she looked into was empty, until she came to one in the corner. She poked her head in freely, by this time not expecting anybody. Then she had to say she was sorry.

There was a young man with a book on his lap, books on the floor, papers all around him. Rose asked him if he had seen anybody run past. He said no.

She told him what had happened. She didn't tell him because she was frightened or disgusted, as he seemed afterward to think, but just because she had to tell somebody; it was so odd. She was not prepared at all for his response. His long neck and face turned red, the flush entirely absorbing a birthmark down the side of his cheek. He was thin and fair. He stood up without any thought for the book in his lap or the papers in front of him. The book thumped on the floor. A great sheaf of papers, pushed across the desk, upset his ink bottle.

"How vile," he said.

"Grab the ink," Rose said. He leaned to catch the bottle and knocked it on to the floor. Fortunately the top was on, and it did not break.

"Did he hurt you?"

"No, not really."

"Come on upstairs. We'll report it."

"Oh, no."

"He can't get away with that. It shouldn't be allowed."

"There isn't anybody to report to," Rose said with relief. "The Librarian goes off at noon on Saturdays."

"It's disgusting," he said in a high-pitched, excitable voice. Rose was sorry now that she had told him anything, and said she had to get back to work.

"Are you really all right?"

"Oh yes."

"I'll be right here. Just call me if he comes back."

That was Patrick. If she had been trying to make him fall in love with her, there was no better way she could have chosen. He had many chivalric notions, which he pretended to mock, by saying certain words and phrases as if in quotation marks. *The fair sex,* he would say, and *damsel in distress*. Coming to his carrel with that story, Rose had turned herself into a damsel in distress. The pretended irony would not fool anybody; it was clear that he did wish to operate in a world of knights and ladies; outrages; devotions.

She continued to see him in the Library, every Saturday, and often she met him walking across the campus or in the cafeteria. He made a point of greeting her with courtesy and concern, saying, "How are you," in a way that suggested she might have suffered a further attack, or might still be recovering from the first one. He always flushed deeply when he saw her, and she thought that this was because the memory of what she had told him so embarrassed him. Later she found out it was because he was in love.

He discovered her name, and where she lived. He phoned her at Dr. Henshawe's house and asked her to go to the movies. At first when he said, "This is Patrick Blatchford speaking," Rose could not think who it was, but after a moment she recognized the high, rather aggrieved and tremulous voice. She said she would go. This was partly because Dr. Henshawe was always saying she was glad Rose did not waste her time running with boys.

Rather soon after she started to go out with him, she said to Patrick, "Wouldn't it be funny if it was you grabbed my leg that day in the Library?"

He did not think it would be funny. He was horrified that she would think such a thing.

She said she was only joking. She said she meant that it would be a good twist in a story, maybe a Maugham story, or a Hitchcock movie. They had just been to see a Hitchcock movie.

"You know, if Hitchcock made a movie out of something like that, you could be a wild insatiable leg-grabber with one half of your personality, and the other half could be a timid scholar."

He didn't like that either.

"Is that how I seem to you, a timid scholar?" It seemed to her he deepened his voice, introduced a few growling notes, drew in his chin, as if for a joke. But he seldom joked with her; he didn't think joking was suitable when you were in love.

"I didn't say you were a timid scholar or a leg-grabber. It was just an idea."

After a while he said, "I suppose I don't seem very manly."

She was startled and irritated by such an exposure. He took such chances; had nothing ever taught him not to take such chances? But maybe he didn't, after all. He knew she would have to say something reassuring. Though she was longing not to, she longed to say judiciously, "Well, no. You don't."

But that would not actually be true. He did seem masculine to her. Because he took those chances. Only a man could be so careless and demanding.

"We come from two different worlds," she said to him, on another occasion. She felt like a character in a play, saying that. "My people are poor people. You would think the place I lived in was a dump."

Now she was the one who was being dishonest, pretending to throw herself on his mercy, for of course she did not expect him to say, oh, well, if you come from poor people and live in a dump, then I will have to withdraw my offer.

"But I'm glad," said Patrick. "I'm glad you're poor. You're so lovely. You're like the Beggar Maid."

"Who?"

"King Cophetua[4] and the Beggar Maid. You know. The painting. Don't you know that painting?"

Patrick had a trick—no, it was not a trick, Patrick had no tricks —Patrick had a way of expressing surprise, fairly scornful surprise, when people did not know something he knew, and similar scorn, similar surprise, whenever they had bothered to know something he did not. His arrogance and humility were both oddly exaggerated. The arrogance, Rose decided in time, must come from being rich, though Patrick was never arrogant about that in itself. His sisters, when she met them, turned out to be the same way, disgusted with anybody who did not know about horses or sailing, and just as disgusted by anybody knowing about music, say, or politics. Patrick and they could do little together but radiate disgust. But wasn't Billy Pope as bad, wasn't Flo as bad, when it came to arrogance? Maybe. There was a difference, though, and the difference was that Billy Pope and Flo were not protected. Things could get at them: D.P.'s; people speaking French on the radio; changes. Patrick and his sisters behaved as if things could never get at them. Their voices, when they quarreled at the table, were astonishingly childish; their demands for food they liked, their petulance at seeing anything on the table they didn't like, were those of children. They had never had to defer and polish themselves and win favor in the world, they never would have to, and that was because they were rich.

Rose had no idea at the beginning, how rich Patrick was. Nobody believed that. Everybody believed she had been calculating and clever, and she was so far from clever, in that way, that she really did not mind if they believed it. It turned out that other girls had been trying, and had not struck, as she had, the necessary note. Older girls, sorority girls, who had never noticed her before, began to look at her with puzzlement and respect. Even Dr. Henshawe, when she saw that things were more serious than she had supposed, and settled Rose down to have a talk about it, assumed that she would have an eye on the money.

4. This African king, the misogynist hero of a ballad, fell in love with a beggar maid he happened to see.

"It is no small triumph to attract the attentions of the heir to a mercantile empire," said Dr. Henshawe, being ironic and serious at the same time. "I don't despise wealth," she said. "Sometimes I wish I had some of it." (Did she really suppose she had not?) "I am sure you will learn how to put it to good uses. But what about your ambitions, Rose? What about your studies and your degree? Are you going to forget all that so soon?"

Mercantile Empire was a rather grand way of putting it. Patrick's family owned a chain of department stores in British Columbia. All Patrick had said to Rose was that his father owned some stores. When she said *two different worlds* to him she was thinking that he probably lived in some substantial house like the houses in Dr. Henshawe's neighborhood. She was thinking of the most prosperous merchants in Hanratty. She could not realize what a coup she had made because it would have been a coup for her if the butcher's son had fallen for her, or the jeweler's; people would say she had done well.

She had a look at that painting. She looked it up in an art book in the Library. She studied the Beggar Maid, meek and voluptuous, with her shy white feet. The milky surrender of her, the helplessness and gratitude. Was that how Patrick saw Rose? Was that how she could be? She would need that king, sharp and swarthy as he looked, even in his trance of passion, clever and barbaric. He could make a puddle of her, with his fierce desire. There would be no apologizing with him, none of that flinching, that lack of faith, that seemed to be revealed in all transactions with Patrick.

She could not turn Patrick down. She could not do it. It was not the amount of money but the amount of love he offered that she could not ignore; she believed that she felt sorry for him, that she had to help him out. It was as if he had come up to her in a crowd carrying a large, simple, dazzling object—a huge egg, maybe, of solid silver, something of doubtful use and punishing weight—and was offering it to her, in fact thrusting it at her, begging her to take some of the weight of it off him. If she thrust it back, how could he bear it? But that explanation left something out. It left out her own appetite, which was not for wealth but for worship. The size, the weight, the shine, of what he said was love (and she did not doubt him) had to impress her, even though she had never asked for it. It did not seem likely such an offering would come her way again. Patrick himself, though worshipful, did in some oblique way acknowledge her luck.

She had always thought this would happen, that somebody would look at her and love her totally and helplessly. At the same time she had thought that nobody would, nobody would want her at all, and up until now, nobody had. What made you wanted was nothing you did, it was something you had, and how could you ever tell whether you had it? She would look at herself in the glass and think: *wife, sweetheart*. Those mild lovely words. How could they apply to her? It was a miracle; it was a mistake. It was what she had dreamed of; it was not what she wanted.

She grew very tired, irritable, sleepless. She tried to think admiringly of Patrick. His lean, fair-skinned face was really very handsome. He must know a number of things. He graded papers, presided at examinations, he was finishing his thesis. There was a smell of pipe tobacco and rough wool about him, that she liked. He was twenty-four. No other girl she knew, who had a boyfriend, had one as old as that.

Then without warning she thought of him saying, "I suppose I don't seem very manly." She thought of him saying, "Do you love me? Do you really love me?" He would look at her in a scared and threatening way. Then when she said yes he said how lucky he was, how lucky they were, he mentioned friends of his and their girls, comparing their love affairs unfavorably to his and Rose's. Rose would shiver with irritation and misery. She was sick of herself as much as him, she was sick of the picture they made at this moment, walking across a snowy downtown park, her bare hand snuggled in Patrick's, in his pocket. Some outrageous and cruel things were being shouted, inside her. She had to do something, to keep them from getting out. She started tickling and teasing him.

Outside Dr. Henshawe's back door, in the snow, she kissed him, tried to make him open his mouth, she did scandalous things to him. When he kissed her his lips were soft; his tongue was shy; he collapsed over rather than held her, she could not find any force in him.

"You're lovely. You have lovely skin. Such fair eyebrows. You're so delicate."

She was pleased to hear that, anybody would be. But she said warningly, "I'm not so delicate, really. I'm quite large."

"You don't know how I love you. There's a book I have called *The White Goddess*.[5] Every time I look at the title it reminds me of *you*."

She wriggled away from him. She bent down and got a handful of snow from the drift by the steps and clapped it on his head.

"My White God."

He shook the snow out. She scooped up some more and threw it at him. He didn't laugh, he was surprised and alarmed. She brushed the snow off his eyebrows and licked it off his ears. She was laughing, though she felt desperate rather than merry. She didn't know what made her do this.

"Dr. *Hen*-shawe," Patrick hissed at her. The tender poetic voice

5. Collection of myths by English poet Robert Graves (1895–1985).

he used for rhapsodizing about her could entirely disappear, could change to remonstrance, exasperation, with no steps at all between.

"Dr. Henshawe will hear you!"

"Dr. Henshawe says you are an honorable young man," Rose said dreamily. "I think she's in love with you." It was true; Dr. Henshawe had said that. And it was true that he was. He couldn't bear the way Rose was talking. She blew at the snow in his hair. "Why don't you go in and deflower her? I'm sure she's a virgin. That's her window. Why don't you?" She rubbed his hair, then slipped her hand inside his overcoat and rubbed the front of his pants. "You're hard!" she said triumphantly. "Oh, Patrick! You've got a hard-on for Dr. Henshawe!" She had never said anything like this before, never come near behaving like this.

"Shut up!" said Patrick, tormented. But she couldn't. She raised her head and in a loud whisper pretended to call toward an upstairs window, "Dr. Henshawe! Come and see what Patrick's got for you!" Her bullying hand went for his fly.

To stop her, to keep her quiet, Patrick had to struggle with her. He got a hand over her mouth, with the other hand beat her away from his zipper. The big loose sleeves of his overcoat beat at her like floppy wings. As soon as he started to fight she was relieved—that was what she wanted from him, some sort of action. But she had to keep resisting, until he really proved himself stronger. She was afraid he might not be able to.

But he was. He forced her down, down, to her knees, face down in the snow. He pulled her arms back and rubbed her face in the snow. Then he let her go, and almost spoiled it.

"Are you all right? Are you? I'm sorry. Rose?"

She staggered up and shoved her snowy face into his. He backed off.

"Kiss me! Kiss the snow! I love you!"

"Do you?" he said plaintively, and brushed the snow from a corner of her mouth and kissed her, with understandable bewilderment. "Do you?"

Then the light came on, flooding them and the trampled snow, and Dr. Henshawe was calling over their heads.

"Rose! Rose!"

She called in a patient, encouraging voice, as if Rose was lost in a fog nearby, and needed directing home.

"Do you love him, Rose?" said Dr. Henshawe. "No, think about it. Do you?" Her voice was full of doubt and seriousness. Rose took a deep breath and answered as if filled with calm emotion, "Yes, I do."

"Well, then."

In the middle of the night Rose woke up and ate chocolate bars.

She craved sweets. Often in class or in the middle of a movie she started thinking about fudge cupcakes, brownies, some kind of cake Dr. Henshawe bought at the European Bakery; it was filled with dollops of rich bitter chocolate, that ran out on the plate. Whenever she tried to think about herself and Patrick, whenever she made up her mind to decide what she really felt, these cravings intervened.

She was putting on weight, and had developed a nest of pimples between her eyebrows.

Her bedroom was cold, being over the garage, with windows on three sides. Otherwise it was pleasant. Over by the bed hung framed photographs of Greek skies and ruins, taken by Dr. Henshawe herself on her Mediterranean trip.

She was writing an essay on Yeats's plays. In one of the plays a young bride is lured away by the fairies from her sensible unbearable marriage.

"Come away, O human child . . ." Rose read, and her eyes filled up with tears for herself, as if she was that shy elusive virgin, too fine for the bewildered peasants who have entrapped her. In actual fact she was the peasant, shocking high-minded Patrick, but he did not look for escape.

She took down one of those Greek photographs and defaced the wallpaper, writing the start of a poem which had come to her while she ate chocolate bars in bed and the wind from Gibbons Park banged at the garage walls.

> Heedless in my dark womb
> I bear a madman's child . . .

She never wrote any more of it, and wondered sometimes if she had meant headless. She never tried to rub it out, either.

Patrick shared an apartment with two other graduate students. He lived plainly, did not own a car or belong to a fraternity. His clothes had an ordinary academic shabbiness. His friends were the sons of teachers and ministers. He said his father had all but disowned him, for becoming an intellectual. He said he would never go into business.

They came back to the apartment in the early afternoon when they knew both the other students would be out. The apartment was the time. They clung together, shivering and giggling. Rose was doing the giggling. She felt a need to be continually playful. She was terrified that they could not manage it, that there was a great humiliation in store, a great exposure of their poor deceits and stratagems. But the deceits and stratagems were only hers. Patrick was never a fraud; he managed, in spite of gigantic embarrassment, apologies; he passed through some amazed pantings and flounderings, to peace. Rose was no help, presenting instead of an honest passivity much twisting and fluttering eagerness, unpracticed counterfeit of passion. She was pleased when it was accomplished; she did not have to counterfeit that. They had done what others did, they had done what lovers did. She thought of celebration. What occurred to her was something delicious to eat, a sundae at Boomers, apple pie with hot cinnamon sauce. She was not at all prepared for Patrick's idea, which was to stay where they were and try again.

When pleasure presented itself, the fifth or sixth time they were together, she was thrown out of gear entirely, her passionate carrying-on was silenced.

Patrick said, "What's the matter?"

"Nothing!" Rose said, turning herself radiant and attentive once more. But she kept forgetting, the new developments interfered, and she had finally to give in to that struggle, more or less ignoring Patrick. When she could take note of him again she overwhelmed him with gratitude; she was really grateful now, and she wanted to be forgiven, though she could not say so, for all her pretended gratitude, her patronizing, her doubts.

Why should she doubt so much, she thought, lying comfortably in the bed while Patrick went to make some instant coffee. Might it not be possible, to feel as she pretended? If this sexual surprise was possible, wasn't anything? Patrick was not much help; his chivalry and self-abasement, next door to his scoldings, did discourage her. But wasn't the real fault hers? Her conviction that anyone who could fall in love with her must be hopelessly lacking, must finally be revealed as a fool? So she took note of anything that was foolish about Patrick, even though she thought she was looking for things that were masterful, admirable. At this moment, in his bed, in his room, surrounded by his books and clothes, his shoe brushes and typewriter, some tacked-up cartoons—she sat up in bed to look at them, and they really were quite funny, he must allow things to be funny when she was not here—she could see him as a likable, intelligent, even humorous person; no hero; no fool. Perhaps they could be ordinary. If only, when he came back in, he would not start thanking and fondling and worshiping her. She didn't like worship, really; it was only the idea of it she liked. On the other hand, she didn't like it when he started to correct and criticize her. There was much he planned to change.

Patrick loved her. What did he love? Not her accent, which he was trying hard to alter, though she was often mutinous and unreasonable, declaring in the face of all evidence that she did not have a country accent, everybody talked the way she did. Not her jittery sexual boldness (his relief at her virginity matched hers at his competence). She could make him flinch at a vulgar word, a drawling tone. All the time, moving and speaking, she was destroying herself for him, yet he looked right through her, through all the distractions she was creating, and loved some obedient image that she herself could not see. And his hopes were high. Her accent could be eliminated, her friends could be discredited and removed, her vulgarity could be discouraged.

What about all the rest of her? Energy, laziness, vanity, discontent, ambition? She concealed all that. He had no idea. For all her doubts about him, she never wanted him to fall out of love with her.

They made two trips.

They went to British Columbia, on the train, during the Easter holidays. His parents sent Patrick money for his ticket. He paid for Rose, using up what he had in the bank and borrowing from one of his roommates. He told her not to reveal to his parents that she had not paid for her own ticket. She saw that he meant to conceal that she was poor. He knew nothing about women's clothes, or he would not have thought that possible. Though she had done the best she could. She had borrowed Dr. Henshawe's raincoat for the coastal weather. It was a bit long, but otherwise all right, due to Dr. Henshawe's classically youthful tastes. She had sold more blood and bought a fuzzy angora sweater, peach-colored, which was extremely messy and looked like a small-town girl's idea of dressing up. She always realized things like that as soon as a purchase was made, not before.

Patrick's parents lived on Vancouver Island, near Sidney. About half an acre of clipped green lawn—green in the middle of winter; March seemed like the middle of winter to Rose—sloped down to a stone wall and a narrow pebbly beach and salt water. The house was half stone, half stucco-and-timber. It was built in the Tudor style, and others. The windows of the living room, the dining room, the den, all faced the sea, and because of the strong winds that sometimes blew onshore, they were made of thick glass, plate glass Rose supposed, like the windows of the automobile showroom in Hanratty. The seaward wall of the dining room was all windows, curving out in a gentle bay; you looked through the thick curved glass as through the bottom of a bottle. The sideboard too had a curving, gleaming belly, and seemed as big as a boat. Size was noticeable everywhere and particularly thickness. Thickness of towels and rugs and handles of knives and forks, and silences. There was a terrible amount of luxury and unease. After a day or so there, Rose became so discouraged that her wrists and ankles felt weak. Picking up her knife and fork was a chore; cutting and chewing the perfect roast beef was almost beyond her; she got short of breath climbing the stairs. She had never known before how some places could choke you off, choke off your very life. She had not known this in spite of a number of very unfriendly places she had been in.

The first morning, Patrick's mother took her for a walk on the grounds, pointing out the greenhouse, the cottage where "the couple" lived: a charming, ivied, shuttered cottage, bigger than Dr. Henshawe's house. The couple, the servants, were more gentle-spoken, more discreet and dignified, than anyone Rose could think of in Hanratty, and indeed they were superior in these ways to Patrick's family.

Patrick's mother showed her the rose garden, the kitchen garden. There were many low stone walls.

"Patrick built them," said his mother. She explained anything with an indifference that bordered on distaste. "He built all these walls."

Rose's voice came out full of false assurance, eager and inappropriately enthusiastic.

"He must be a true Scot," she said. Patrick was a Scot, in spite of his name. The Blatchfords had come from Glasgow. "Weren't the best stonemasons always Scotsmen?" (She had learned quite recently not to say "Scotch.") "Maybe he had stonemason ancestors."

She cringed afterward, thinking of these efforts, the pretense of ease and gaiety, as cheap and imitative as her clothes.

"No," said Patrick's mother. "No. I don't think they were stonemasons." Something like fog went out from her: affront, disapproval, dismay. Rose thought that perhaps she had been offended by the suggestion that her husband's family might have worked with their hands. When she got to know her better—or had observed her longer; it was impossible to get to know her—she understood that Patrick's mother disliked anything fanciful, speculative, abstract, in conversation. She would also, of course, dislike Rose's chatty tone. Any interest beyond the factual consideration of the matter at hand—food, weather, invitations, furniture, servants—seemed to her sloppy, ill-bred, and dangerous. It was all right to say, "This is a warm day," but not, "This day reminds me of when we used to—" She hated people being *reminded*.

She was the only child of one of the early lumber barons of Vancouver Island. She had been born in a vanished northern settlement. But whenever Patrick tried to get her to talk about the past, whenever he asked her for the simplest sort of information—what steamers went up the coast, what year was the settlement abandoned, what was the route of the first logging railway—she would say irritably, "I don't know. How would I know about that?" This irritation was the strongest note that ever got into her words.

Neither did Patrick's father care for this concern about the past. Many things, most things, about Patrick, seemed to strike him as bad signs.

"What do you want to know all that for?" he shouted down the table. He was a short square-shouldered man, red-faced, astonishingly belligerent. Patrick looked like his mother, who was tall, fair, and elegant in the most muted way possible, as if her clothes, her make-up, her style, were chosen with an ideal neutrality in mind.

"Because I am interested in history," said Patrick in an angry, pompous, but nervously breaking voice.

"Because-I-am-interested-in-history," said his sister Marion in an immediate parody, break and all. "History!"

The sisters Joan and Marion were younger than Patrick, older than Rose. Unlike Patrick they showed no nervousness, no cracks in self-satisfaction. At an earlier meal they had questioned Rose.

"Do you ride?"

"No."

"Do you sail?"

"No."

"Play tennis? Play golf? Play badminton?"

No. No. No.

"Perhaps she is an intellectual genius, like Patrick," the father said. And Patrick, to Rose's horror and embarrassment, began to shout at the table in general an account of her scholarships and prizes. What did he hope for? Was he so witless as to think such bragging would subdue them, would bring out anything but further scorn? Against Patrick, against his shouting boasts, his contempt for sports and television, his so-called intellectual interests, the family seemed united. But this alliance was only temporary. The father's dislike of his daughters was minor only in comparison with his dislike of Patrick. He railed at them too, when he could spare a moment; he jeered at the amount of time they spent at their games, complained about the cost of their equipment, their boats, their horses. And they wrangled with each other, on obscure questions of scores and borrowings and damages. All complained to the mother about the food, which was plentiful and delicious. The mother spoke as little as possible to anyone and to tell the truth Rose did not blame her. She had never imagined so much true malevolence collected in one place. Billy Pope was a bigot and a grumbler, Flo was capricious, unjust, and gossipy, her father, when he was alive, had been capable of cold judgments and unremitting disapproval; but compared to Patrick's family, all Rose's own people seemed jovial and content.

"Are they always like this?" she said to Patrick. "Is it me? They don't like me."

"They don't like you because I chose you," said Patrick with some satisfaction.

They lay on the stony beach after dark, in their raincoats, hugged and kissed and uncomfortably, unsuccessfully, attempted more.

Rose got seaweed stains on Dr. Henshawe's coat. Patrick said, "You see why I need you? I need you so much!"

She took him to Hanratty. It was just as bad as she had thought it would be. Flo had gone to great trouble, and cooked a meal of scalloped potatoes, turnips, big country sausages which were a special present from Billy Pope, from the butcher shop. Patrick detested coarse-textured food, and made no pretense of eating it. The table was spread with a plastic cloth, they ate under the tube of fluorescent light. The centerpiece was new and especially for the occasion. A plastic swan, lime green in color, with slits in the wings, in which were stuck folded, colored paper napkins. Billy Pope, reminded to take one, grunted, refused. Otherwise he was on dismally good behavior. Word had reached him, word had reached both of them, of Rose's triumph. It had come from their superiors in Hanratty; otherwise they could not have believed it. Customers in the butcher shop—formidable ladies, the dentist's wife, the veterinarian's wife—had said to Billy Pope that they heard Rose had picked herself up a millionaire. Rose knew Billy Pope would go back to work tomorrow with stories of the millionaire, or millionaire's son, and that all these stories would focus on his—Billy Pope's—forthright and unintimidated behavior in the situation.

"We just set him down and give him some sausages, don't make no difference to us what he comes from!"

She knew Flo would have her comments too, that Patrick's nervousness would not escape her, that she would be able to mimic his voice and his flapping hands that had knocked over the ketchup bottle. But at present they both sat hunched over the table in miserable eclipse. Rose tried to start some conversation, talking brightly, unnaturally, rather as if she was an interviewer trying to draw out a couple of simple local people. She felt ashamed on more levels than she could count. She was ashamed of the food and the swan and the plastic tablecloth; ashamed for Patrick, the gloomy snob, who made a startled grimace when Flo passed him the toothpick-holder; ashamed for Flo with her timidity and hypocrisy and pretensions; most of all ashamed for herself. She didn't even have any way that she could talk, and sound natural. With Patrick there, she couldn't slip back into an accent closer to Flo's, Billy Pope's and Hanratty's. That accent jarred on her ears now, anyway. It seemed to involve not just a different pronunciation but a whole different approach to talking. Talking was shouting; the words were separated and emphasized so that people could bombard each other with them. And the things people said were like lines from the most hackneyed rural comedy. *Wal if a feller took a notion to,* they said. They really said that. Seeing them through Patrick's eyes, hearing them through his ears, Rose too had to be amazed.

She was trying to get them to talk about local history, some things she thought Patrick might be interested in. Presently Flo did begin to talk, she could only be held in so long, whatever her misgivings. The conversation took another line from anything Rose had intended.

"The line I lived on when I was just young," Flo said, "it was the worst place ever created for suiciding."

"A line is a concession road. In the township," Rose said to Patrick. She had doubts about what was coming, and rightly so, for then Patrick got to hear about a man who cut his own throat, *his own throat*, from ear to ear, a man who shot himself the first time and didn't do enough damage, so he loaded up and fired again and managed it, another man who hanged himself using a chain, the kind of chain you hook on a tractor with, so it was a wonder his head was not torn off.

Tore off, Flo said.

She went on to a woman who, though not a suicide, had been dead in her house a week before she was found, and that was in the summer. She asked Patrick to imagine it. All this happened, said Flo, within five miles of where she herself was born. She was presenting credentials, not trying to horrify Patrick, at least not more than was acceptable, in a social way; she did not mean to disconcert him. How could he understand that?

"You were right," said Patrick, as they left Hanratty on the bus. "It is a dump. You must be glad to get away."

Rose felt immediately that he should not have said that.

"Of course that's not your real mother," Patrick said. "Your real parents can't have been like that." Rose did not like his saying that either, though it was what she believed, herself. She saw that he was trying to provide for her a more genteel background, perhaps something like the homes of his poor friends: a few books about, a tea tray, and mended linen, worn good taste; proud, tired, educated people. What a coward he was, she thought angrily, but she knew that she herself was a coward, not knowing any way to be comfortable with her own people or the kitchen or any of it. Years later she would learn how to use it, she would be able to amuse or intimidate right-thinking people at dinner parties with glimpses of her early home. At the moment she felt confusion, misery.

Nevertheless her loyalty was starting. Now that she was sure of getting away, a layer of loyalty and protectiveness was hardening around every memory she had, around the store and the town, the flat, somewhat scrubby, unremarkable countryside. She would oppose this secretly to Patrick's views of mountains and ocean, his stone and timbered mansion. Her allegiances were far more proud and stubborn than his.

But it turned out he was not leaving anything behind.

Patrick gave her a diamond ring and announced that he was giving up being a historian for her sake. He was going into his father's business.

She said she thought he hated his father's business. He said that he could not afford to take such an attitude now that he would have a wife to support.

It seemed that Patrick's desire to marry, even to marry Rose, had been taken by his father as a sign of sanity. Great streaks of bounty were mixed in with all the ill will in that family. His father at once offered a job in one of the stores, offered to buy them a house. Patrick was as incapable of turning down this offer as Rose was of turning down Patrick's, and his reasons were as little mercenary as hers.

"Will we have a house like your parents?" Rose said. She really thought it might be necessary to start off in that style.

"Well, maybe not at first. Not quite so—"

"I don't want a house like that! I don't want to live like that!"

"We'll live however you like. We'll have whatever kind of house you like."

Provided it's not a dump, she thought nastily.

Girls she hardly knew stopped and asked to see her ring, admired it, wished her happiness. When she went back to Hanratty for a weekend, alone this time, thank God, she met the dentist's wife on the main street.

"Oh, Rose, isn't it wonderful! When are you coming back again? We're going to give a tea for you, the ladies in town all want to give a tea for you!"

This woman had never spoken to Rose, never given any sign before of knowing who she was. Paths were opening now, barriers were softening. And Rose—oh, this was the worst, this was the shame of it—Rose, instead of cutting the dentist's wife, was blushing and skittishly flashing her diamond and saying yes, that would be a lovely idea. When people said how happy she must be she did think herself happy. It was as simple as that. She dimpled and sparkled and turned herself into a fiancée with no trouble at all. Where will you live, people said and she said, Oh, in British Columbia! That added more magic to the tale. Is it really beautiful there, they said, is it never winter?

"Oh, yes!" cried Rose. "Oh, no!"

She woke up early, got up and dressed and let herself out of the side door of Dr. Henshawe's garage. It was too early for the buses to be running. She walked through the city to Patrick's apartment. She walked across the park. Around the South African War Memorial a pair of greyhounds were leaping and playing, an old woman standing by, holding their leashes. The sun was just up, shining on their pale hides. The grass was wet. Daffodils and narcissus in bloom.

Patrick came to the door, tousled, frowning sleepily, in his gray and maroon striped pajamas.

"Rose! What's the matter?"

She couldn't say anything. He pulled her into the apartment. She put her arms around him and hid her face against his chest and in a stagey voice said, "Please Patrick. Please let me not marry you."

"Are you sick? What's the matter?"

"Please let me not marry you," she said again, with even less conviction.

"You're crazy."

She didn't blame him for thinking so. Her voice sounded so unnatural, wheedling, silly. As soon as he opened the door and she faced the fact of him, his sleepy eyes, his pajamas, she saw that what she had come to do was enormous, impossible. She would have to explain everything to him, and of course she could not do it. She could not make him see her necessity. She could not find any tone of voice, any expression of the face, that would serve her.

"Are you upset?" said Patrick. "What's happened?"

"Nothing."

"How did you get here anyway?"

"Walked."

She had been fighting back a need to go to the bathroom. It seemed that if she went to the bathroom she would destroy some of the strength of her case. But she had to. She freed herself. She said, "Wait a minute, I'm going to the john."

When she came out Patrick had the electric kettle going, was measuring out instant coffee. He looked decent and bewildered.

"I'm not really awake," he said. "Now. Sit down. First of all, are you premenstrual?"

"No." But she realized with dismay that she was, and that he might be able to figure it out, because they had been worried last month.

"Well, if you're not premenstrual, and nothing's happened to upset you, then what is all this about?"

"I don't want to get married," she said, backing away from the cruelty of *I don't want to marry you.*

"When did you come to this decision?"

"Long ago. This morning."

They were talking in whispers. Rose looked at the clock. It was a little after seven.

"When do the others get up?"

"About eight."

"Is there milk for the coffee?" She went to the refrigerator.

"Quiet with the door," said Patrick, too late.

"I'm sorry," she said, in her strange silly voice.

"We went for a walk last night and everything was fine. You come this morning and tell me you don't want to get married. *Why* don't you want to get married?"

"I just don't. I don't want to be married."

"What else do you want to do?"

"I don't know."

Patrick kept staring at her sternly, drinking his coffee. He who used to plead with her *do you love me, do you really*, did not bring the subject up now.

"Well I know."

"What?"

"I know who's been talking to you."

"Nobody has been talking to me."

"Oh, no. Well, I bet Dr. Henshawe has."

"No."

"Some people don't have a very high opinion of her. They think she has an influence on girls. She doesn't like the girls who live with her to have boyfriends. Does she? You even told me that. She doesn't like them to be normal."

"That's not it."

"What did she say to you, Rose?"

"She didn't say anything." Rose began to cry.

"Are you sure?"

"Oh, Patrick, listen, please, I can't marry you, please, I don't know why, I can't, please, I'm sorry, believe me, I can't," Rose babbled at him, weeping, and Patrick saying, "Ssh! You'll wake them up!" lifted or dragged her out of the kitchen chair and took her to his room, where she sat on the bed. He shut the door. She held her arms across her stomach, and rocked back and forth.

"What is it, Rose? What's the matter? Are you sick!"

"It's just so hard to tell you!"

"Tell me what?"

"What I just did tell you!"

"I mean have you found out you have T.B. or something?"

"No!"

"Is there something in your family you haven't told me about? Insanity?" said Patrick encouragingly.

"No!" Rose rocked and wept.

"So what is it?"

"I don't love you!" she said. "I don't love you. I don't love you." She fell on the bed and put her head in the pillow. "I'm so sorry. I'm so sorry. I can't help it."

After a moment or two Patrick said, "Well. If you don't love me, you don't love me. I'm not forcing you to." His voice sounded strained and spiteful, against the reasonableness of what he was saying. "I just wonder," he said, "if you know what you do want. I don't think you do. I don't think you have any idea what you want. You're just in a state."

"I don't have to know what I want to know what I don't want!" Rose said, turning over. This released her. "I never loved you."

"Ssh. You'll wake them. We have to stop."

"I never loved you. I never wanted to. It was a mistake."

"All right. All right. You made your point."

"Why am I supposed to love you? Why do you act as if there was something wrong with me if I didn't? You despise me. You despise my family and my background and you think you are doing me a *great favor*—"

"I fell in love with you," Patrick said. "I don't despise you. Oh, Rose, I worship you."

"You're a sissy," Rose said. "You're a prude." She jumped off the bed with great pleasure as she said this. She felt full of energy. More was coming. Terrible things were coming.

"You don't even know how to make love right. I always wanted to get out of this from the very first. I felt sorry for you. You won't look where you're going, you're always knocking things over, just because you can't be bothered, you can't be bothered noticing anything, you're wrapped up in yourself, and you're always bragging, it's so stupid, you don't even know how to brag right, if you really want to impress people you'll never do it, the way you do it all they do is laugh at you!"

Patrick sat on the bed and looked up at her, his face open to whatever she would say. She wanted to beat him and beat him, to say worse and worse, uglier and crueller, things. She took a breath drew in air, to stop the things she felt rising in her from getting out.

"I don't want to see you, ever!" she said viciously. But at the door she turned and said in a normal and regretful voice, "Good-bye."

Patrick wrote her a note: "I don't understand what happened the other day and I want to talk to you about it. But I think we should wait for two weeks and not see or talk to each other and find out how we feel at the end of that time."

Rose had forgotten all about giving him back his ring. When she came out of his apartment building that morning she was still wearing it. She couldn't go back, and it seemed too valuable to send through the mail. She continued to wear it, mostly because she did not want to have to tell Dr. Henshawe what had happened. She was relieved to get Patrick's note. She thought that she could give him back the ring then.

She thought about what Patrick had said about Dr. Henshawe. No doubt there was some truth in that, else why should she be so reluctant to tell Dr. Henshawe she had broken her engagement, so unwilling to face her sensible approval, her restrained, relieved congratulations?

She told Dr. Henshawe that she was not seeing Patrick while she studied for her exams. Rose could see that even that pleased her.

She told no one that her situation had changed. It was not just Dr. Henshawe she didn't want knowing. She didn't like giving up being envied; the experience was so new to her.

She tried to think what to do next. She could not stay on at Dr. Henshawe's. It seemed clear that if she escaped from Patrick, she must escape from Dr. Henshawe too. And she did not want to stay on at the college, with people knowing about her broken engagement, with the girls who now congratulated her saying they had known all along it was a fluke, her getting Patrick. She would have to get a job.

The Head Librarian had offered her a job for the summer but that was perhaps at Dr. Henshawe's suggestion. Once she moved out, the offer might not hold. She knew that instead of studying for her exams she ought to be downtown, applying for work as a filing clerk at the insurance offices, applying at Bell Telephone, at the department stores. The idea frightened her. She kept on studying. That was the one thing she really knew how to do. She was a scholarship student after all.

On Saturday afternoon, when she was working at the Library, she saw Patrick. She did not see him by accident. She went down to the bottom floor, trying not to make a noise on the spiraling metal staircase. There was a place in the stacks where she could stand, almost in darkness, and see into his carrel. She did that. She couldn't see his face. She saw his long pink neck and the old plaid shirt he wore on Saturdays. His long neck. His bony shoulders. She was no longer irritated by him, no longer frightened by him; she was free. She could look at him as she would look at anybody. She could appreciate him. He had behaved well. He had not tried to rouse her pity, he had not bullied her, he had not molested her with pitiful telephone calls and letters. He had not come and sat on Dr. Henshawe's doorstep. He was an honorable person, and he would never know how she acknowledged that, how she was grateful for it. The things she had said to him made her ashamed now. And they were not even true. Not all of them. He did know how to make love. She was so moved, made so gentle and wistful, by the sight of him, that she wanted to give him something, some surprising bounty, she wished to undo his unhappiness.

Then she had a compelling picture of herself. She was running softly into Patrick's carrel, she was throwing her arms around him from behind, she was giving everything back to him. Would he take it from her, would he still want it? She saw them laughing and crying, explaining, forgiving. *I love you. I do love you, it's all right, I was terrible, I didn't mean it, I was just crazy, I love you, it's all right.* This was a violent temptation for her; it was barely resistable. She had an impulse to hurl herself. Whether it was off a cliff or into a warm bed of welcoming grass and flowers, she really could not tell.

It was not resistable, after all. She did it.

When Rose afterward reviewed and talked about this moment in her life—for she went through a period, like most people nowadays, of talking freely about her most private decisions, to friends and lovers and party acquaintances whom she might never see again, while they did the same—she said that comradely compassion had overcome her, she was not proof against the sight of a bare bent neck. Then she went further into it, and said greed, greed. She said she had run to him and clung to him and overcome his suspicions and kissed and cried and reinstated herself simply because she did not know how to do without his love and his promise to look after her; she was frightened of the world and she had not been able to think up any other plan for herself. When she was seeing life in economic terms, or was with people who did, she said that only middle-class people had choices anyway, that if she had had the price of a train ticket to Toronto her life would have been different.

Nonsense, she might say later, never mind that, it was really vanity, it was vanity pure and simple, to resurrect him, to bring him back his happiness. To see if she could do that. She could not resist such a test of power. She explained then that she had paid for it. She said that she and Patrick had been married ten years, and that during that time the scenes of the first breakup and reconciliation had been periodically repeated; with her saying again all the things she had said the first time, and the things she had held back, and many other things which occurred to her. She hopes she did not tell people (but thinks she did) that she used to beat her head against the bedpost, that she smashed a gravy boat through a dining-room window; that she was so frightened, so sickened by what she had done that she lay in bed, shivering, and begged and begged for his forgiveness. Which he granted. Sometimes she flew at him; sometimes he beat her. The next morning they would get up early and make a special breakfast, they would sit eating bacon and eggs and drinking filtered coffee, worn out, bewildered, treating each other with shamefaced kindness.

What do you think triggers the reaction? they would say.

Do you think we ought to take a holiday? A holiday together? Holidays alone?

A waste, a sham, those efforts, as it turned out. But they worked for the moment. Calmed down, they would say that most people probably went through the same things like this, in a marriage, and indeed they seemed to know mostly people who did. They could not separate until enough damage had been done, until nearly mortal damage had been done, to keep them apart. And until Rose could get a job and make her own money, so perhaps there was a very ordinary reason after all.

What she never said to anybody, never confided, was that she sometimes thought it had not been pity or greed or cowardice or vanity but something quite different, like a vision of happiness. In view of everything else she had told she could hardly tell that. It seems very odd; she can't justify it. She doesn't mean that they had perfectly ordinary, bearable times in their marriage, long busy stretches of wallpapering and vacationing and meals and shopping and worrying about a child's illness, but that sometimes, without reason or warning, happiness, the possibility of happiness, would surprise them. Then it was as if they were in different though identical-seeming skins, as if there existed a radiantly kind and innocent Rose and Patrick, hardly ever visible, in the shadow of their usual selves. Perhaps it was that Patrick she saw when she was free of him, invisible to him, looking into his carrel. Perhaps it was. She should have left him there.

She knew that was how she had seen him; she knows it, because it happened again. She was in Toronto Airport, in the middle of the night. This was about nine years after she and Patrick were divorced. She had become fairly well-known by this time, her face was familiar to many people in this country. She did a television program on which she interviewed politicians, actors, writers, *personalities,* and many ordinary people who were angry about something the government or the police or a union had done to them. Sometimes she talked to people who had seen strange sights. UFO's, or sea monsters, or who had unusual accomplishments or collections, or kept up some obsolete custom.

She was alone. No one was meeting her. She had just come in on a delayed flight from Yellowknife. She was tired and bedraggled. She saw Patrick standing with his back to her, at a coffee bar. He wore a raincoat. He was heavier than he had been, but she knew him at once. And she had the same feeling that this was a person she was bound to, that by a certain magical, yet possible trick, they could find and trust each other, and that to begin this all that she had to do was go up and touch him on the shoulder, surprise him with his happiness.

She did not do this, of course, but she did stop. She was standing still when he turned around, heading for one of the little plastic tables and curved seats grouped in front of the coffee bar. All his skinniness and academic shabbiness, his look of prim authoritarianism, was gone. He had smoothed out, filled out, into such a modish and agreeable, responsible, slightly complacent-looking man. His birthmark had faded. She thought how haggard and dreary she must look, in her rumpled trenchcoat, her long, graying hair fallen forward around her face, old mascara smudged under her eyes.

He made a face at her. It was a truly hateful, savagely warning, face; infantile, self-indulgent, yet calculated; it was a timed explosion of disgust and loathing. It was hard to believe. But she saw it.

Sometimes when Rose was talking to someone in front of the television cameras she would sense the desire in them to make a face. She would sense it in all sorts of people, in skillful politicians and witty liberal bishops and honored humanitarians, in housewives who had witnessed natural disasters and in workmen who had performed heroic rescues or been cheated out of disability pensions. They were longing to sabotage themselves, to make a face or say a dirty word. Was this the face they all wanted to make? To show somebody, to show everybody? They wouldn't do it, though; they wouldn't get the chance. Special circumstances were required. A lurid unreal place, the middle of the night, a staggering unhinging weariness, the sudden, hallucinatory appearance of your true enemy.

She hurried away then, down the long varicolored corridor, shaking. She had seen Patrick; Patrick had seen her; he had made that face. But she was not really able to understand how she could be an enemy. How could anybody hate Rose so much, at the very moment when she was ready to come forward with her good will, her smiling confession of exhaustion, her air of diffident faith in civilized overtures?

Oh, Patrick could. Patrick could.

BETH NUGENT

City of Boys

MY little sweetheart, she says, bringing her face close enough for me to see the fine net of lines that carves her skin into a weathered stone, you love me, don't you, little sweetheart, little lamb?

Whether or not she listens any more, I am not sure, but I always answer yes, yes, I always say, yes, I love you.

She is my mother, my father, my sister, brother, cousin, lover; she is everything I ever thought any one person needed in the world. She is everything but a boy.

—Boys, she tells me. Boys will only break you.

I know this. I watch them on the street corners, huddled under their puddles of blue smoke. They are as nervous as insects, always some part of their bodies in useless agitated motion, a foot tapping, a jaw clenching, a finger drawing circles against a thigh, eyes in restless, programmed movement, from breasts to face to legs to breasts. They are never still, and they twitch and jump when I walk by, but still I want them. I want them in the back seats of their cars, I want them under the bridge where the river meets the rocks in a slick slide of stone, I want them in the back rows of theaters and under the bushes and benches in the park.

—Boys, she says, don't think about boys. Boys would only make you do things you don't know how to do and things you'd never want to do if you knew what they were. I know, she says, I know plenty about boys.

She is everything to me. She is not my mother, although I have allowed myself the luxury of sometimes believing myself her child. My mother is in Fairborn, Ohio, where she waits with my father for me to come home and marry a boy and become the woman into whom she still believes it is not too late for me to grow. Fairborn is a city full of boys and parking meters and the Air Force, but most of all it is a city full of my mother and in my mind she looms over it like a cloud of radioactive dust. If I return it will be to her. She is not why I left, she is not why I am here; she is just one thing I left, like all the things that trail behind us when we go from place to place, from birth to birth and from becoming to becoming. She is just another breadcrumb, just another mother in the long series of mothers that let you go to become the women you have to become. But you are always coming back to them.

Where I live now is also a city full of boys, and coming here I passed through hundreds of cities and they were all full of boys.

—Boys, she tells me, are uninteresting, and when they grow up, they become men and become even more uninteresting.

I know this too. I see how boys spend their days, either standing around or playing basketball or engaged in irritating persistent harangue, and I can draw my own conclusions as to what they talk about and as to the heights of which they are capable and I see what they do all day, but still I want them.

The one time I pretended she was a boy, she knew it because I closed my eyes and I never close my eyes, and I imagined it was a boy there doing that, soft tongue between my thighs, and when I came she slapped me hard.

—I'm not a boy, she said, just you remember that. You know who I am and just remember that I love you and no boy could ever love you like I do.

Probably she is right. What boy could love with her slipping concentration; probably no boy could ever achieve what she lets go with every day that comes between us, what she has lost in her long history of love.

What I do sometimes is slip out under her absent gaze.—Where are you going, what are you going to do, she says, and wallowing in the luxury of thinking myself a child, I answer Nowhere, nothing. In their pure undirected intoxicating meaninglessness, our conversations carry more significance than either of us is strong enough to bear, together or alone, and I drag it out into the streets today, a long weight trailing behind me, as I look for boys.

Today, I tell myself, is a perfect day for losing things, love and innocence, illusions and expectations; it is a day through which I will walk and walk until I find the perfect boy.

Where we live, on the upper west side, the streets are full of Puerto Rican men watching women. Carefully they examine each woman that walks by, carefully they hold her with their eyes, as if they are somehow responsible for her continued existence on the street. Not a woman goes by untouched by the long leash of their looks.

Oh, they say, Mira Mira[1] ssssssssssss. In their eyes are all the women they have watched walk by and cook and comb their black hair; all the women they have touched with their hands, and all the women they have known live in their eyes and gleam out from within the dark. Their eyes are made only to see women on the streets.

Where we live, on West 83rd and Amsterdam, there are roaches and rats, but nothing matters as long as we're together, we say valiantly, longing. Nothing matters, I say, stomping a roach and nothing matters, she agrees, her eyes on a low-slung rat sidling by in the long hallway toward the little garbage room across from the door to our apartment. I told the super once that if he kept the garbage out on the street, perhaps the building would be less a home for vermin.—What's vermin, he wanted to know.—Vermin, I told him, is rats and roaches and huge black beetles scrabbling at the base of the toilet when you turn on the light at night. Vermin is all the noises at night, all the clicking and scratching and scurrying through the darkness.—No rats, he said, maybe a mouse or two, and maybe every now and then you'll see your roach eggs, but I keep this place clean. Together we watched as a big brown-shelled roach tried to creep past us on the wall. Neither of us moved to kill it, but when it stopped and waved its antennae, he brought his big fist down in a hard slam against the wall. He didn't look at the dead roach, but I could hardly take my eyes off it, perfectly flattened as though it had been steamrolled against the side of his palm.—

1. "Look, look."

Maybe a roach here and there, he said, flicking the roach onto the floor without looking at it, but I keep this place clean. Maybe if you had a man around the house, he said, trying to look past me into the apartment, you wouldn't have so much trouble with vermins.

I pretended not to understand what he meant and backed into the room. Rent control is not going to last forever in New York, and when it goes and all the Puerto Ricans have had to move to the Bronx, we will have to find jobs or hit the streets, but as long as we're together, as long as we have each other.—We'll always have each other, won't we, she says, lighting a cigarette and checking to see how many are left in her pack.

—Yes, I always say, wondering if she's listening or just lost in a cigarette count. You'll always have me, I say. Unless, I think, unless you leave me, or unless I grow up to become the woman my mother still thinks is possible.

Today is a day full of boys. They are everywhere, and I watch each of them, boys on motorcycles, in cars, on bicycles, leaning against walls, walking, to see which of them in this city of boys is mine.

I am not so young and she is not so old, but rent control is not going to last forever, and someday I will be a woman. She wants, I tell myself, nothing more than me. Sometimes I think she must have been my mother, the way she loves me, but when I asked her if she was ever my mother, she touched my narrow breasts and said, Would your mother do that, and ran her tongue over my nipple and said, Or that. Would your mother know what you want, Sweetheart? I'm not your mother, she said, I stole you from a mattress downtown, just around the corner where all the winos lie around in piss and wine and call for help and nobody listens. I saved you from that, she says, but I remember too clearly the trip out here, in the middle of a car full of people full of drugs, most of them, and I remember how she found me standing just outside the porn theater on 98th and Broadway and she slipped me right from under the gaze of about four hundred curious Puerto Ricans.—Does your mother know where you are? she said. I laughed and said, My mother knows all she needs to know, and she said, Come home with me, I have somebody I want you to meet. When she brought me home, she said to a big man who lay on the couch watching television, Tito, this is Princess Grace, and Tito raised his heavy head from the end of the couch and said, She don't look like no princess to me.

I never thought much of Tito, and she never let him touch me, even though our apartment is only one room, and he was sick with wanting it from me. At night after they'd done it just about as many times as anyone could, she crept over to me on little cat feet and whispered into my ear, Sweetheart you are my only one. As Tito slugged and snored his way through the nights, we'd do it at least one more time than they had, and she would sigh and say, Little sweetheart, you're the one I wanted all the time, even through all those boys and girls that loved me it was always you that I was looking for, you that I always wanted.

This is the kind of talk that kills me, this is the kind of talk that won me, in addition to the fact that she took me in from the hard streets full of boys and taxicabs and cops and everywhere I looked the hard eyes of innocence turned.

What it felt like with her that first time was my mother come back and curled up inside me, giving birth, so that I came out of her at the exact same second that I moved closest into her center.

The long car pulls up to the sidewalk and I bend to see if it has boys in it. It is full of them, so I say,

—Hey, can I have a ride.

—Hey, they say, Hey, the lady wants a ride. Where to, they ask.

—Oh, I say, wherever.

I look to see where they are heading;—Uptown, I say and the door swings open and I slide in. The oldest boy is probably sixteen and just got his driver's license and is driving his mother's car, a big Buick, or Chevrolet, or Monte Carlo, a mother's car. Each of the boys is different, but they are all exactly alike in the way that boys are, and right away I find the one I want. He's the one who does not look at me, and he's the oldest, only a couple of years younger than me, and it is his mother's car we are in.

—How about a party, they say, we know a good party uptown.

—Let's just see, I say, let's just ride uptown and see.

Sometimes I wake up to see her leaning on her thin knees against the wall that is stripped down to expose the rough brick beneath the plaster. I dream that she prays to keep me, but I am afraid that she prays for something else, a beginning or an end, or something I don't know about. She came to bed once and laid her face against my breast and I felt the imprint of the brick on the tender skin of her forehead.

She herself is not particularly religious, although the apartment is littered with the scraps of saints—holy relics of one sort or another; a strand of hair from the Christ child, a bit of fingernail from Paul, a shred of the Virgin's robe. They are left over from Tito, who collected holy relics the way some people collect lucky pennies or matchbooks, as some kind of hedge against some inarticulated sense of disaster. They are just clutter here, though, in this small apartment where we live and I suggested to her once that we throw them out. She picked up a piece of dried weed from Gethsemane and said, I don't think they're ours to throw out. Tito found them and if we got rid of them, who knows what might happen to Tito. Maybe they work is what I mean, she said; I don't think it's spiritually economic to be a skeptic about absolutely everything.

When Tito left, his relics abandoned for some new hope, she was depressed for a day or two, but said that it was really the best for everyone, especially for the two of us, the single reality to which our lives have been refined. Tito said he was getting sick of watching two dykes moon over each other all the time, though I think he was just angry because she wouldn't let him touch me. I was all for it, I wanted him to touch me. That's what I came to this city for, to have someone like Tito touch me, someone to whom touching is all the reality of being, someone who doesn't do it in basements and think he has to marry you, someone who does it and doesn't think about the glory of love. But she wouldn't have it; she said if he ever touched me, she would send me back to the 98th Street porn theater and let the Puerto Ricans make refried beans out of me, and as for Tito, he could go back to Rosa, his wife in Queens, and go back to work lugging papers for the *Daily News* and ride the subway every day and go home and listen to Rosa talk on the telephone all night, instead of hanging out on street corners and playing cards with the men outside the schoolyard. Because, she said, because she was paying the rent, and as long as rent control lasted in New York she would continue to pay the rent and she could live quite happily and satisfactorily by herself until she found the right sort of roommate; one, she said, fingering the shiny satin of Tito's shirt, who paid the rent.

So Tito kept his distance and kept us both sick with his desire and when she finally stopped sleeping with him on the bed and joined me on the mattress on the floor, even Tito could see that it wasn't going to be long before he would have to shift himself to the floor. To save himself from that he said one day that he guessed he was something of a fifth wheel around the joint, huh, and he'd found a nice Puerto Rican family that needed a man around the house and he guessed he'd move in with them. I think he was just covering for himself, though, because one day when she was out buying cigarettes, he roused himself from the couch and away from the television and said to me, You know, she was married before, you know.

—I know that, I said, I know all about that. How she pays the rent is with alimony money that still comes in from her marriage, and I know all about that and Tito wasn't telling me anything that I didn't know, so I looked back at the magazine I was reading and waited for him to go back to the television.

He kept looking at me, so I got up to look out the window to see if I could see her coming back and if she had anything for me.

—What I'm trying to say, he said, What I'm trying to tell you, is that you're not the only one, not you. I was the only one once too, the one she wanted all those years; I was the one before you and you're just the one before someone else.

I could see her rounding the corner from 83rd and Broadway and could see that she had something in a bag, doughnuts or something, for me. I said nothing but looked out the window and counted her steps toward our building. She was reeling slightly, and leaning toward the wall, so I guessed that she must have had a few drinks in the bar where she always buys her cigarettes. When I could hear her key turning in the lock to the street door, I went to open our door for her and Tito grabbed me by the arm and said, Listen, you just listen. Nobody is ever the only one for nobody, don't kid yourself. I pulled away and opened the door for her and she came in, cold skin and wet, and I put my face in her hair and breathed in the smell of gin and cigarettes and all the meaning of my life.

The next day Tito left, but he didn't go far, because I still see him hanging out on street corners. Now all the women he has known are in his eyes, but mostly there is her, and when he looks at me, I cannot bear to see her, lost in the dark there. Whenever I pass him, I always say

—Hey, Tiiiiiiito, Mira Mira, huh? and all his friends laugh, while Tito tries to look as though this is something he's planned himself, as though he has somehow elicited this remark from me.

One day I suppose Tito will use the key he forgot to leave behind to sneak in and cover me with his flagging desire, his fading regrets, and his disappointments, and she will move on, away from me; but rent control will not last forever in New York, and I cannot think ahead to the beginnings and the ends for which she prays.

The boys in the car lean against one another and leer and twitch like tortured insects and exchange glances that they think are far too subtle for me to understand, but I've come too far looking for too much to miss any of it. We drive too fast up Riverside, so that it's no time before the nice neighborhoods become slums full of women in windows and bright clothing slung over fire escapes, and salsa music laid over the thick city air like a layer of air all itself. Like the sound of crickets threading through Ohio summer nights, it sets the terms for everything.

—So, one of them says to me, so where are you going, anyways.

—Well, I say, Well. I was thinking about going to the Bronx Botanical Gardens. The Bronx Botanical Gardens is no place I'd ever really want to go, but I feel that it's important to maintain, at least in their eyes, some illusion of destination. If I were a bit more sure of myself, I'd suggest that we take the ferry over to Staten

Island and do it in the park there. Then I could think of her. When we went to Staten Island, it was cold and gray and windy; we got there and realized that there was nothing we wanted to see, that being in Staten Island was really not all that different from being in New York.—Or anywhere, she said, looking down a street into a corridor of rundown clothing stores and insurance offices. It was Sunday, so everything was closed up tight and no one was on the streets. Finally we found a coffee shop near the station, where we drank cokes and coffee and she smoked cigarettes while we waited for the boat to come in.

Lezzes, the counter man said to another man sitting at the counter eating a doughnut. What do you want to bet they're lezzes?

The man eating the doughnut turned and looked us over and said

—They're not so hot anyways, no big waste.

She smiled and held her hand to my face for a second; the smoke from the cigarette she held drifted past my eyes into my hair.

—What a moment, she said, to remember.

On the way back I watched the wind whip her face all out of any shape I knew, and when I caught the eyes of some boys on the ferry, she said, not looking at me, not taking her eyes off the concrete ripples of the robe at the foot of the Statue of Liberty just on our left, What you do is your own business, but don't expect me to love you forever if you do things like this. I'm not, she said, turning to look me full in the face, your mother, you know. All I am is your lover and nothing lasts forever.

When we got off the ferry, I said, I don't expect you to love me forever, and she said I was being promiscuous and quarrelsome, and she lit a cigarette as she walked down into the subway station. I watched her as she walked and it seemed to me to be the first time I had ever seen her back walking away from me, trailing a long blue string of smoke.

Something is going on with the boys, something has changed in the set of their faces, the way they hold their cigarettes, the way they nudge each other. Something changes when the light begins to fade and one of them says to me

—We have a clubhouse uptown, want to come there with us?

—What kind of club, I ask, what do you do there?

—We drink whiskey, they say, and take drugs and watch television.

My boy, the one I have picked out of this whole city of boys stares out the window, chewing at a toothpick he's got wedged somewhere in the depths of his jaw, and runs his finger over the slick plastic of the steering wheel. I can tell by his refusal to ask that he wants me to come.

This, I suppose, is how to get to the center of boys, to go to their club. Boys are like pack creatures, and they always form clubs; it's as though they cannot help themselves. It's the single law of human nature that I have observed, in my limited exposure to the world, that plays and plays and replays itself out with simple mindless consistency: where there are boys there are clubs, and anywhere there is a club it is bound to be full of boys, looking for the good times to be had just by being boys.

—Can I join? I ask. This is what I can take back to her, cigarettes and a boy's club; this will keep her for me forever, that I have gone to the center of boys and have come back a woman and I have come back to her.

—Well, they say and smirk and grin and itch at themselves, Well, there's an initiation.

The oldest of the boys is younger than me, and yet like boys everywhere, they think that I don't know nearly so much as they do, as if being a woman somehow short-circuits my capacity for input. They think they have a language that only boys can understand, but understanding their language is the key to my success, so I say, I will not fuck you all, separately or together.

My boy looks over at me and permits himself a cool half smile and I am irritated that he now holds me in higher regard because I can speak a language that any idiot could learn.

Between us there are no small moments; we do not speak at all or we speak everything. Heat bills and toothpaste and dinner and all the dailiness of living are given no language in our time together.

I realize that this kind of intensity cannot be sustained over a long period of time and that every small absence in our days signals an end between us. She tells me that I must never leave her, but what I know is that some day she will leave me with a fistfull of marriage money to pay the rent as long as rent control lasts in New York, and I will see her wandering down the streets, see her in the arms of another, and I say to her sometimes late at night when she blows smoke rings at my breasts, Don't leave me, don't ever ever ever leave me.

—Life, she always says to me, is one long leavetaking. Don't kid yourself, she says, Kid, and laughs.—Anyways, you are my little sweetheart, and how could I ever leave you and how could I leave this—soft touch of my skin—and this, and this.

She knows this kills me every time.

Their clubhouse is dirty and disorganized and everywhere there are mattresses and empty bottles and bags from McDonald's, and skittering through this mess are more roaches than I thought could exist in a single place, more roaches than there are boys in this city, more roaches than there are moments of love in this world.

The boys walk importantly in: This is their club, they are New York City boys and they take drugs and they have a club and I watch as they scatter around and sit in chairs and on mattresses and flip on the television. I hang back in the doorway and I reach out to snag the corner of the jacket my boy is wearing. He turns and I say

—How about some air.

—Let me just get high first, he says, and he walks over to a chair and sits down and pulls out his works and cooks up his dope and ties up his arm and spends a good two minutes searching for a vein to pop.

All over his hands and arms and probably his legs and feet and stomach are signs of collapse and ruin, as if his body had been created for a single purpose and he has spent a busy and productive life systematically mining it for good places to fix.

I watch him do this while the other boys do their dope or roll their joints or pop their pills and he offers me some; I say no, I'd rather keep a clear head and how about some air.

I don't want him to hit a nod before any of it's even happened, but this is my experience with junkies, that they exit right out of every situation before it's even become a situation.

—Let's take the car, he says.

You are my sweetheart, she says, and if you leave me, you will spend all your life coming back to me. With her tongue and her words and the quiet movements of her hand over my skin, she has drawn for me all the limits of my life and of my love. It is the one love that has created me and will contain me and if I left her I'd be lonely, and I'd rather sleep in the streets with her hand between my legs forever than be lonely.

In the car, the boy slides his hand between my legs and then puts it on the steering wheel. A chill in the air, empty streets, and it's late. Every second takes me further into the night away from her; every second brings me home. We drive to Inwood Park and climb the fence, so that we are only a few feet away from the Hudson.

—This is nothing like Ohio, I say to him, and he lights a cigarette and says

—Where's Ohio?

—Don't you go to school? I ask him; Don't you have to take geography?

—I know what I need to know, he says, and reaches over to unbutton my blouse. The thing about junkies is that they know they don't have much time, and the thing about boys is that they know how not to waste it.

—This is very romantic, I say, as his fingers hit my nipples like a piece of ice; Do you come here often?

What I like about this boy is that he just puts it right in. He just puts it in as though he does this all the time, as though he doesn't usually have to slide it through his fingers or in between his friends' rough lips; he just puts it in and comes like wet soap shooting out of a fist and this is what I wanted. This is what I wanted and I look at the Hudson rolling by over his shoulder; this is what I wanted but all I think about is the way it is with us; this is what I wanted but all I see is her face floating down the river, her eyes like pieces of moonlight caught in the water.

What I think is true doesn't matter any more; what I think is false doesn't matter any more. What I think at all doesn't matter any more because there is only her; like an image laid over my mind, she is superimposed on every thought I have. She sits by the window and looks out onto West 83rd Street as if she is waiting for something, waiting for rent control to end, or waiting for something else to begin. She sits by the window waiting for something and pulls a long string through her fingers. In the light from the window, I can see each of the bones in her hand; white and exposed, they make a delicate pattern that fades into the flesh and bone of her wrist.

—Don't ever change, I say to her. Don't ever ever change.

She smiles and lets the thin string dangle from her hand.

—Nothing ever stays the same, she says. You're old enough to know that, aren't you, little sweetheart? Permanence, she says, is nothing more than a desire for things to stay the same.

I know this.

—Life is hard for me, the boy says. What am I going to do with my life? I just hang around all day or drive my mother's car. Life is so hard. Everything will always be the same for me here in this city; it's going to eat me up and spit me out and I might as well have never been. He looks poetically out over the river.

—I wanted a boy, I say, not a poet.

—I'm not a poet, he says, I'm just a junkie, and you're nothing but a slut. You can get yourself home tonight.

I say nothing and watch the Hudson roll by.

—I'm sorry, he says. So what. So I'm a junkie and you're a slut, so what. Nothing ever changes. Besides, he says, my teacher wants me to be a track star because I can run faster than anyone else in gym class. That's what he says.

—Well, that sounds like a promising career, I say, although I can imagine the gym teacher's cock pressing against his baggy sweats as he stares at my boy and suggests afterschool workouts. Why don't you do that?

—I'd have to give up smoking, he says, and dope.

Together we watch the Hudson roll by and finally he says

—Well, it's about time I was getting my mother's car home.

—This is it? I ask him.

—What were you expecting? he says, I'm only a junkie. In two years I probably won't even be able to get it up any more.

—Look, I say, coming in and walking over to where she sits by the window. Look, I am a marked woman. There is blood between my legs and it isn't yours.

She looks at me, then looks back at what she was doing before I came in, blowing smoke rings that flatten against the dirty window.

—Did you bring me some cigarettes, she says, putting hers out in the ashtray that rests on the windowsill.

—A marked woman, I say. Can't you see the blood?

—I can't see anything, she says, and I won't look until I have a cigarette. I give her the cigarettes I bought earlier. Even in the midst of becoming a woman, I have remembered the small things that please her. She lights one and inhales the smoke, then lets it slowly out through her nose and her mouth at the same time. She knows this kills me.

—Don't you see it? I ask.

—I don't see anything, she says, I don't see why you had to do this.

She gets up and says, I'm going to bed now. I've been up all day and all night and I'm tired and I want to go to sleep before the sun comes up.

—I am a marked woman, I say, lying beside her, Don't you feel it?

—I don't feel anything, she says, but she holds me, and together we wait patiently for the light. She is everything to me. In the stiff morning before the full gloom of city light falls on us, I turn to her face full of shadows.

—I am a marked woman, I say, I am.

—Quiet, she says, and puts her dark hand gently over my mouth then moves it over my throat onto the rise of my chest. Across town, no one notices this, nothing is changed anywhere when she does this.

—Quiet, she says. She presses her hand against my heart and touches her face to mine and takes me with her into the motherless turning night. All moments stop here, this is the first and the last, and the only flesh is hers, the only touch her hand. Nothing else is, and together we turn under the stroke of the moon and the hiss of the stars and she is everything I will become and together we become every memory that has ever been known.

JOYCE CAROL OATES

How I Contemplated the World from the Detroit House of Correction and Began My Life Over Again

Notes for an Essay for an English Class at Baldwin Country Day School; Poking Around in Debris; Disgust and Curiosity; A Revelation of the Meaning of Life; A Happy Ending . . .

I. Events

THE girl (myself) is walking through Branden's, that excellent store. Suburb of a large famous city that is a symbol for large famous American cities. The event sneaks up on the girl, who believes she is herding it along with a small fixed smile, a girl of fifteen, innocently experienced. She dawdles in a certain style by a counter of costume jewelry. Rings, earrings, necklaces. Prices from $5 to $50, all within reach. All ugly. She eases over to the glove counter, where everything is ugly too. In her close-fitted coat with its black fur collar she contemplates the luxury of Branden's, which she has known for many years: its many mild pale lights, easy on the eye and the soul, its elaborate tinkly decorations, its women shoppers with their excellent shoes and coats and hairdos, all dawdling gracefully, in no hurry.

Who was ever in a hurry here?

2. The girl seated at home. A small library, paneled walls of oak. Some one is talking to me. An earnest, husky, female voice drives itself against my ears, nervous, frightened, groping around my heart, saying, "If you wanted gloves, why didn't you say so? Why didn't you ask for them?" That store, Branden's, is owned by Raymond Forrest who lives on Du Maurier Drive. We live on Sioux Drive. Raymond Forrest. A handsome man? An ugly man? A man of fifty or sixty, with gray hair, or a man of forty with earnest, courteous eyes, a good golf game; who is Raymond Forrest, this man who is my salvation? Father has been talking to him. Father is not his physician; Dr. Berg is his physician. Father and Dr. Berg refer patients to each other. There is a connection. Mother plays bridge with . . . On Mondays and Wednesdays our maid Billie works at . . . The strings draw together in a cat's cradle, making a net to save you when you fall. . . .

3. *Harriet Arnold's*. A small shop, better than Branden's. Mother in her black coat, I in my close-fitted blue coat. Shopping. Now look at this, isn't this cute, do you want this, why don't you want this, try this on, take this with you to the fitting room, take this

also, what's wrong with you, what can I do for you, why are you so strange . . . ? "I wanted to steal but not to buy," I don't tell her. The girl droops along in her coat and gloves and leather boots, her eyes scan the horizon, which is pastel pink and decorated like Branden's, tasteful walls and modern ceilings with graceful glimmering lights.

4. Weeks later, the girl at a bus stop. Two o'clock in the afternoon, a Tuesday; obviously she has walked out of school.

5. The girl stepping down from a bus. Afternoon, weather changing to colder. Detroit. Pavement and closed-up stores; grillwork over the windows of a pawnshop. What is a pawnshop, exactly?

II. Characters

1. The girl stands five feet five inches tall. An ordinary height. Baldwin Country Day School draws them up to that height. She dreams along the corridors and presses her face against the Thermoplex glass. No frost or steam can ever form on that glass. A smudge of grease from her forehead . . . could she be boiled down to grease? She wears her hair loose and long and straight in suburban teen-age style, 1968. Eyes smudged with pencil, dark brown. Brown hair. Vague green eyes. A pretty girl? An ugly girl? She sings to herself under her breath, idling in the corridor, thinking of her many secrets (the thirty dollars she once took from the purse of a friend's mother, just for fun, the basement window she smashed in her own house just for fun) and thinking of her brother who is at Susquehanna Boys' Academy, an excellent preparatory school in Maine, remembering him unclearly . . . he has long manic hair and a squeaking voice and he looks like one of the popular teen-age singers of 1968, one of those in a group, *The Certain Forces, The Way Out, The Maniacs Responsible.* The girl in her turn looks like one of those fieldsful of girls who listen to the boys' singing, dreaming and mooning restlessly, breaking into high sullen laughter, innocently experienced.

2. The mother. A Midwestern woman of Detroit and suburbs. Belongs to the Detroit Athletic Club. Also the Detroit Golf Club. Also the Bloomfield Hills Country Club. The Village Women's Club at which lectures are given each winter on Genet and Sartre and James Baldwin,[1] by the Director of the Adult Education Program at Wayne State University. . . . The Bloomfield Art Association. Also the Founders Society of the Detroit Institute of Arts. Also . . . Oh, she is in perpetual motion, this lady, hair like blown-up gold and finer than gold, hair and fingers and body of inestimable grace. Heavy weighs the gold on the back of her hairbrush and hand

1. Jean Genet (1910–), French novelist and playwright; Jean Paul Sartre (1905–1980), French novelist, dramatist, and philosopher; James Baldwin (1924–), American novelist and essayist.

mirror. Heavy heavy the candlesticks in the dining room. Very heavy is the big car, a Lincoln, long and black, that on one cool autumn day split a squirrel's body in two unequal parts.

3. The father. Dr. ______. He belongs to the same clubs as #2. A player of squash and golf; he has a golfer's umbrella of stripes. Candy stripes. In his mouth nothing turns to sugar, however; saliva works no miracles here. His doctoring is of the slightly sick. The sick are sent elsewhere (to Dr. Berg?), the deathly sick are sent back for more tests and their bills are sent to their homes, the unsick are sent to Dr. Coronet (Isabel, a lady), an excellent psychiatrist for unsick people who angrily believe they are sick and want to do something about it. If they demand a male psychiatrist, the unsick are sent by Dr. ______ (my father) to Dr. Lowenstein, a male psychiatrist, excellent and expensive, with a limited practice.

4. Clarita. She is twenty, twenty-five, she is thirty or more? Pretty, ugly, what? She is a woman lounging by the side of a road, in jeans and a sweater, hitchhiking, or she is slouched on a stool at a counter in some roadside diner. A hard line of jaw. Curious eyes. Amused eyes. Behind her eyes processions move, funeral pageants, cartoons. She says, "I never can figure out why girls like you bum around down here. What are you looking for anyway?" An odor of tobacco about her. Unwashed underclothes, or no underclothes, unwashed skin, gritty toes, hair long and falling into strands, not recently washed.

5. Simon. In this city the weather changes abruptly, so Simon's weather changes abruptly. He sleeps through the afternoon. He sleeps through the morning. Rising, he gropes around for something to get him going, for a cigarette or a pill to drive him out to the street, where the temperature is hovering around 35°. Why doesn't it drop? Why, why doesn't the cold clean air come down from Canada; will he have to go up into Canada to get it? will he have to leave the Country of his Birth and sink into Canada's frosty fields . . . ? Will the F.B.I. (which he dreams about constantly) chase him over the Canadian border on foot, hounded out in a blizzard of broken glass and horns . . . ?

"Once I was Huckleberry Finn," Simon says, "but now I am Roderick Usher."[2] Beset by frenzies and fears, this man who makes my spine go cold, he takes green pills, yellow pills, pills of white and capsules of dark blue and green . . . he takes other things I may not mention, for what if Simon seeks me out and climbs into my girl's bedroom here in Bloomfield Hills and strangles me, what then . . . ?

2. I.e., he has changed from a wholesome American boy into a morbid neurotic. Usher is the chief character in Edgar Alan Poe's *Fall of the House of Usher.* Huck Finn is the young hero of Mark Twain's novel *The Adventures of Huckleberry Finn.*

(As I write this I begin to shiver. Why do I shiver? I am now sixteen and sixteen is not an age for shivering.) It comes from Simon, who is always cold.

III. World Events

Nothing.

IV. People and Circumstances Contributing to This Delinquency

Nothing.

V. Sioux Drive

George, Clyde G. 240 Sioux. A manufacturer's representative; children, a dog, a wife. Georgian with the usual columns. You think of the White House, then of Thomas Jefferson, then your mind goes blank on the white pillars and you think of nothing. Norris, Ralph W. 246 Sioux. Public relations. Colonial. Bay window, brick, stone, concrete, wood, green shutters, sidewalk, lantern, grass, trees, blacktop drive, two children, one of them my classmate Esther (Esther Norris) at Baldwin. Wife, cars. Ramsey, Michael D. 250 Sioux. Colonial. Big living room, thirty by twenty-five, fireplaces in living room, library, recreation room, paneled walls wet bar five bathrooms five bedrooms two lavatories central air conditioning automatic sprinkler automatic garage door three children one wife two cars a breakfast room a patio a large fenced lot fourteen trees a front door with a brass knocker never knocked. Next is our house. Classic contemporary. Traditional modern. Attached garage, attached Florida room, attached patio, attached pool and cabana, attached roof. A front door mail slot through which pour *Time Magazine, Fortune, Life, Business Week,* the *Wall Street Journal,* the *New York Times,* the *New Yorker,* the *Saturday Review, M.D., Modern Medicine, Disease of the Month* . . . and also. . . . And in addition to all this, a quiet sealed letter from Baldwin saying: *Your daughter is not doing work compatible with her performance on the Stanford-Binet.*[3] . . . And your son is not doing well, not well at all, very sad. Where is your son anyway? Once he stole trick-and-treat candy from some six-year-old kids, he himself being a robust ten. The beginning. Now your daughter steals. In the Village Pharmacy she made off with, yes she did, don't deny it, she made off with a copy of *Pageant Magazine* for no reason, she swiped a roll of Life Savers in a green wrapper and was in no need of saving her life or even in need of sucking candy; when she was no more than eight years old she stole, don't blush, she stole a package of Tums only because it was out on the counter and available, and the nice lady behind the counter (now dead) said nothing. . . . Sioux Drive. Maples, oaks, elms. Diseased elms cut down. Sioux Drive runs into Roosevelt Drive. Slow, turning lanes, not streets, all drives and lanes and ways and passes. A private police force. Quiet private police, in

3. An intelligence test.

unmarked cars. Cruising on Saturday evenings with paternal smiles for the residents who are streaming in and out of houses, going to and from parties, a thousand parties, slightly staggering, the women in their furs alighting from automobiles bought of Ford and General Motors and Chrysler, very heavy automobiles. No foreign cars. Detroit. In 275 Sioux, down the block in that magnificent French-Normandy mansion, lives ______ himself, who has the C______ account itself, imagine that! Look at where he lives and look at the enormous trees and chimneys, imagine his many fireplaces, imagine his wife and children, imagine his wife's hair, imagine her fingernails, imagine her bathtub of smooth clean glowing pink, imagine their embraces, his trouser pockets filled with odd coins and keys and dust and peanuts, imagine their ecstasy on Sioux Drive, imagine their income tax returns, imagine their little boy's pride in his experimental car, a scaled down C______, as he roars round the neighborhood on the sidewalks frightening dogs and Negro maids, oh imagine all these things, imagine everything, let your mind roar out all over Sioux Drive and Du Maurier Drive and Roosevelt Drive and Ticonderoga Pass and Burning Bush Way and Lincolnshire Pass and Lois Lane.

When spring comes, its winds blow nothing to Sioux Drive, no odors of hollyhocks or forsythia, nothing Sioux Drive doesn't already possess, everything is planted and performing. The weather vanes, had they weather vanes, don't have to turn with the wind, don't have to contend with the weather. There is no weather.

VI. Detroit

There is always weather in Detroit. Detroit's temperature is always 32°. Fast-falling temperatures. Slow-rising temperatures. Wind from the north-northeast four to forty miles an hour, small-craft warnings, partly cloudy today and Wednesday changing to partly sunny through Thursday . . . small warnings of frost, soot warnings, traffic warnings, hazardous lake conditions for small craft and swimmers, restless Negro gangs, restless cloud formations, restless temperatures aching to fall out the very bottom of the thermometer or shoot up over the top and boil everything over in red mercury.

Detroit's temperature is 32°. Fast-falling temperatures. Slow-rising temperatures. Wind from the north-northeast four to forty miles an hour. . . .

VII. Events

1. The girl's heart is pounding. In her pocket is a pair of gloves! In a plastic bag! Airproof breathproof plastic bag, gloves selling for twenty-five dollars on Branden's counter! In her pocket! Shoplifted! . . . In her purse is a blue comb, not very clean. In her purse is a leather billfold (a birthday present from her grandmother in Philadelphia) with snapshots of the family in clean plastic windows, in the billfold are bills, she doesn't know how many bills. . . . In her

purse is an ominous note from her friend Tykie *What's this about Joe H. and the kids hanging around at Louise's Sat. night? You heard anything?* . . . passed in French class. In her purse is a lot of dirty yellow Kleenex, her mother's heart would break to see such very dirty Kleenex, and at the bottom of her purse are brown hairpins and safety pins and a broken pencil and a ballpoint pen (blue) stolen from somewhere forgotten and a purse-size compact of Cover Girl Make-Up, Ivory Rose. . . . Her lipstick is Broken Heart, a corrupt pink; her fingers are trembling like crazy; her teeth are beginning to chatter; her insides are alive; her eyes glow in her head; she is saying to her mother's astonished face *I want to steal but not to buy.*

2. At Clarita's. Day or night? What room is this? A bed, a regular bed, and a mattress on the floor nearby. Wallpaper hanging in strips. Clarita says she tore it like that with her teeth. She was fighting a barbaric tribe that night, high from some pills; she was battling for her life with men wearing helmets of heavy iron and their faces no more than Christian crosses to breathe through, every one of those bastards looking like her lover Simon, who seems to breathe with great difficulty through the slits of mouth and nostrils in his face. Clarita has never heard of Sioux Drive. Raymond Forrest cuts no ice with her, nor does the C______ account and its millions; Harvard Business School could be at the corner of Vernor and 12th Street for all she cares, and Vietnam might have sunk by now into the Dead Sea under its tons of debris, for all the amazement she could show . . . her face is overworked, overwrought, at the age of twenty (thirty?) it is already exhausted but fanciful and ready for a laugh. Clarita says mournfully to me *Honey somebody is going to turn you out let me give you warning.* In a movie shown on late television Clarita is not a mess like this but a nurse, with short neat hair and a dedicated look, in love with her doctor and her doctor's patients and their diseases, enamored of needles and sponges and rubbing alcohol. . . . Or no: she is a private secretary. Robert Cummings is her boss. She helps him with fantastic plots, the canned audience laughs, no, the audience doesn't laugh because nothing is funny, instead her boss is Robert Taylor and they are not boss and secretary but husband and wife, she is threatened by a young starlet, she is grim, handsome, wifely, a good companion for a good man. . . . She is Claudette Colbert. Her sister too is Claudette Colbert. They are twins, identical. Her husband Charles Boyer[4] is a very rich handsome man and her sister, Claudette Colbert, is plotting her death in order to take her place as the rich man's wife, no one will know because they are *twins*. . . . All these marvelous lives Clarita might have lived, but she fell out the bottom

4. Boyer, Colbert, Taylor, and Cummings are romantic film stars of the 1940's and '50's.

at the age of thirteen. At the age when I was packing my overnight case for a slumber party at Toni Deshield's she was tearing filthy sheets off a bed and scratching up a rash on her arms. . . . Thirteen is uncommonly young for a white girl in Detroit, Miss Brock of the Detroit House of Correction said in a sad newspaper interview for the *Detroit News*; fifteen and sixteen are more likely. Eleven, twelve, thirteen are not surprising in colored . . . they are more precocious. What can we do? Taxes are rising and the tax base is falling. The temperature rises slowly but falls rapidly. Everything is falling out the bottom, Woodward Avenue is filthy, Livernois Avenue is filthy! Scraps of paper flutter in the air like pigeons, dirt flies up and hits you right in the eye, oh Detroit is breaking up into dangerous bits of newspaper and dirt, watch out. . . .

Clarita's apartment is over a restaurant. Simon her lover emerges from the cracks at dark. Mrs. Olesko, a neighbor of Clarita's, an aged white wisp of a woman, doesn't complain but sniffs with contentment at Clarita's noisy life and doesn't tell the cops, hating cops, when the cops arrive. I should give more fake names, more blanks, instead of telling all these secrets. I myself am a secret; I am a minor.

3. My father reads a paper at a medical convention in Los Angeles. There he is, on the edge of the North American continent, when the unmarked detective put his hand so gently on my arm in the aisle of Branden's and said, "Miss, would you like to step over here for a minute?"

And where was he when Clarita put her hand on my arm, that wintry dark sulphurous aching day in Detroit, in the company of closed-down barber shops, closed-down diners, closed-down movie houses, homes, windows, basements, faces . . . she put her hand on my arm and said, "Honey, are you looking for somebody down here?"

And was he home worrying about me, gone for two weeks solid, when they carried me off . . . ? It took three of them to get me in the police cruiser, so they said, and they put more than their hands on my arm.

4. I work on this lesson. My English teacher is Mr. Forest, who is from Michigan State. Not handsome, Mr. Forest, and his name is plain, unlike Raymond Forrest's, but he is sweet and rodentlike, he has conferred with the principal and my parents, and everything is fixed . . . treat her as if nothing has happened, a new start, begin again, only sixteen years old, what a shame, how did it happen?—nothing happened, nothing could have happened, a slight physiological modification known only to a gynecologist or to Dr. Coronet. I work on my lesson. I sit in my pink room. I look around the room with my sad pink eyes. I sigh, I dawdle, I pause. I eat up time. I am

limp and happy to be home, I am sixteen years old suddenly, my head hangs heavy as a pumpkin on my shoulders, and my hair has just been cut by Mr. Faye at the Crystal Salon and is said to be very becoming.

(Simon too put his hand on my arm and said, "Honey, you have got to come with me," and in his six-by-six room we got to know each other. Would I go back to Simon again? Would I lie down with him in all that filth and craziness? Over and over again.

a Clarita is being betrayed as in front of a Cunningham Drug Store she is nervously eying a colored man who may or may not have money, or a nervous white boy of twenty with sideburns and an Appalachian look, who may or may not have a knife hidden in his jacket pocket, or a husky red-faced man of friendly countenance who may or may not be a member of the Vice Squad out for an early twilight walk.)

I work on my lesson for Mr. Forest. I have filled up eleven pages. Words pour out of me and won't stop. I want to tell everything . . . what was the song Simon was always humming, and who was Simon's friend in a very new trench coat with an old high school graduation ring on his finger . . . ? Simon's bearded friend? When I was down too low for him, Simon kicked me out and gave me to him for three days, I think, on Fourteenth Street in Detroit, an airy room of cold cruel drafts with newspapers on the floor. . . . Do I really remember that or am I piercing it together from what they told me? Did they tell the truth? Did they know much of the truth?

VIII. Characters

1. Wednesdays after school, at four; Saturday mornings at ten. Mother drives me to Dr. Coronet. Ferns in the office, plastic or real, they look the same. Dr. Coronet is queenly, an elegant nicotine-stained lady who would have studied with Freud had circumstances not prevented it, a bit of a Catholic, ready to offer you some mystery if your teeth will ache too much without it. Highly recommended by Father! Forty dollars an hour, Father's forty dollars! Progress! Looking up! Looking better! That new haircut is so becoming, says Dr. Coronet herself, showing how normal she is for a woman with an I.Q. of 180 and many advanced degrees.

2. Mother. A lady in a brown suede coat. Boots of shiny black material, black gloves, a black fur hat. She would be humiliated could she know that of all the people in the world it is my ex-lover Simon who walks most like her . . . self-conscious and unreal, listening to distant music, a little bowlegged with craftiness. . . .

3. Father. Tying a necktie. In a hurry. On my first evening home he put his hand on my arm and said, "Honey, we're going to forget all about this."

4. Simon. Outside, a plane is crossing the sky, in here we're in a hurry. Morning. It must be morning. The girl is half out of her mind, whimpering and vague; Simon her dear friend is wretched this morning . . . he is wretched with morning itself . . . he forces her to give him an injection with that needle she knows is filthy, she had a dread of needles and surgical instruments and the odor of things that are to be sent into the blood, thinking somehow of her father. . . . This is a bad morning, Simon says that his mind is being twisted out of shape, and so he submits to the needle that he usually scorns and bites his lip with his yellowish teeth, his face going very pale. *Ah baby!* he says in his soft mocking voice, which with all women is a mockery of love, *do it like this—Slowly*—And the girl, terrified, almost drops the precious needle but manages to turn it up to the light from the window . . . is it an extension of herself then? She can give him this gift then? I *wish you wouldn't do this to me,* she says, wise in her terror, because it seems to her that Simon's danger—in a few minutes he may be dead—is a way of pressing her against him that is more powerful than any other embrace. She has to work over his arm, the knotted corded veins of his arm, her forehead wet with perspiration as she pushes and releases the needle, staring at that mixture of liquid now stained with Simon's bright blood. . . . When the drug hits him she can feel it herself, she feels that magic that is more than any woman can give him, striking the back of his head and making his face stretch as if with the impact of a terrible sun. . . . She tries to embrace him but he pushes her aside and stumbles to his feet. *Jesus Christ,* he says. . . .

5. Princess, a Negro girl of eighteen. What is her charge? She is closed-mouthed about it, shrewd and silent, you know that no one had to wrestle her to the sidewalk to get her in here; she came with dignity. In the recreation room she sits reading *Nancy Drew and the Jewel Box Mystery,*[5] which inspires in her face tiny wrinkles of alarm and interest: what a face! Light brown skin, heavy shaded eyes, heavy eyelashes, a serious sinister dark brow, graceful fingers, graceful wristbones, graceful legs, lips, tongue, a sugar-sweet voice, a leggy stride more masculine than Simon's and my mother's, decked out in a dirty white blouse and dirty white slacks; vaguely nautical is Princess' style. . . . At breakfast she is in charge of clearing the table and leans over me, saying, *Honey you sure you ate enough?*

6. The girl lies sleepless, wondering. Why here, why not there? Why Bloomfield Hills and not jail? Why jail and not her pink room? Why downtown Detroit and not Sioux Drive? What is the difference? Is Simon all the difference? The girl's head is a parade of wonders. She is nearly sixteen, her breath is marvelous with won-

5. Mystery story for juveniles.

ders, not long ago she was coloring with crayons and now she is smearing the landscape with paints that won't come off and won't come off her fingers either. She says to the matron *I am not talking about anything,* not because everyone has warned her not to talk but because, because she will not talk; because she won't say anything about Simon, who is her secret. And she says to the matron, *I won't go home,* up until that night in the lavatory when everything was changed. . . . "No, I won't go home I want to stay here," she says, listening to her own words with amazement, thinking that weeds might climb everywhere over that marvelous $180,000 house and dinosaurs might return to muddy the beige carpeting, but never never will she reconcile four o'clock in the morning in Detroit with eight o'clock breakfasts in Bloomfield Hills. . . . oh, she aches still for Simon's hands and his caressing breath, though he gave her little pleasure, he took everything from her (five-dollar bills, ten-dollar bills, passed into her numb hands by men and taken out of her hands by Simon) until she herself was passed into the hands of other men, police, when Simon evidently got tired of her and her hysteria. . . . *No, I won't go home, I don't want to be bailed out.* The girl thinks as a *Stubborn and Wayward Child* (one of several charges lodged against her), and the matron understands her crazy white-rimmed eyes that are seeking out some new violence that will keep her in jail, should someone threaten to let her out. Such children try to strangle the matrons, the attendants, or one another . . . they want the locks locked forever, the doors nailed shut . . . and this girl is no different up until that night her mind is changed for her. . . .

IX. That Night

Princess and Dolly, a little white girl of maybe fifteen, hardy however as a sergeant and in the House of Correction for armed robbery, corner her in the lavatory at the farthest sink and the other girls look away and file out to bed, leaving her. God, how she is beaten up! Why is she beaten up? Why do they pound her, why such hatred? Princess vents all the hatred of a thousand silent Detroit winters on her body, this girl whose body belongs to me, fiercely she rides across the Midwestern plains on this girl's tender bruised body . . . revenge on the oppressed minorities of America! revenge on the slaughtered Indians! revenge on the female sex, on the male sex, revenge on Bloomfield Hills, revenge revenge. . . .

X. Detroit

In Detroit, weather weighs heavily upon everyone. The sky looms large. The horizon shimmers in smoke. Downtown the buildings are imprecise in the haze. Perpetual haze. Perpetual motion inside the haze. Across the choppy river is the city of Windsor, in Canada. Part of the continent has bunched up here and is bulging outward, at the tip of Detroit; a cold hard rain is forever falling on the expressways. . . . Shoppers shop grimly, their cars are not parked in safe places, their windshields may be smashed and graceful ebony hands may drag them out through their shatterproof smashed windshields, crying, *Revenge for the Indians!* Ah, they all fear leaving Hudson's and being dragged to the very tip of the city and thrown off the parking roof of Cobo Hall, that expensive tomb, into the river. . . .

XI. Characters We Are Forever Entwined With

1. Simon drew me into his tender rotting arms and breathed gravity into me. Then I came to earth, weighed down. He said, *You are such a little girl,* and he weighed me down with his delight. In the palms of his hands were teeth marks from his previous life experiences. He was thirty-five, they said. Imagine Simon in this room, in my pink room: he is about six feet tall and stoops slightly, in a feline cautious way, always thinking, always on guard, with his scuffed light suede shoes and his clothes that are anyone's clothes, slightly rumpled ordinary clothes that ordinary men might wear to not-bad jobs. Simon has fair long hair, curly hair, spent languid curls that are like . . . exactly like the curls of wood shavings to the touch, I am trying to be exact . . . and he smells of unheated mornings and coffee and too many pills coating his tongue with a faint green-white scum. . . . Dear Simon, who would be panicked in this room and in this house (right now Billie is vacuuming next door in my parents' room; a vacuum cleaner's roar is a sign of all good things), Simon who is said to have come from a home not much different from this, years ago, fleeing all the carpeting and the polished banisters . . . Simon has a deathly face, only desperate people fall in love with it. His face is bony and cautious, the bones of his cheeks prominent as if with the rigidity of his ceaseless thinking, plotting, for he has to make money out of girls to whom money means nothing, they're so far gone they can hardly count it, and in a sense money means nothing to him either except as a way of keeping on with his life. *Each Day's Proud Struggle,* the title of a novel we could read at jail. . . . Each day he needs a certain amount of money. He devours it. It wasn't love he uncoiled in me with his hollowed-out eyes and his courteous smile, that remnant of a prosperous past, but a dark terror that needed to press itself flat against him, or against another man . . . but he was the first, he came over to me and took my arm, a claim. We struggled on the stairs and I said, *Let me loose, you're hurting my neck, my face,* it was such a surprise that my skin hurt where he rubbed it, and afterward we lay face to face and he breathed everything into me. In the end I think he turned me in.

2. Raymond Forrest. I just read this morning that Raymond Forrest's father, the chairman of the board at ______, died of a heart attack on a plane bound for London. I would like to write

Raymond Forrest a note of sympathy. I would like to thank him for not pressing charges against me one hundred years ago, saving me, being so generous . . . well, men like Raymond Forrest are generous men, not like Simon. I would like to write him a letter telling of my love, or of some other emotion that is positive and healthy. Not like Simon and his poetry, which he scrawled down when he was high and never changed a word . . . but when I try to think of something to say, it is Simon's language that comes back to me, caught in my head like a bad song, it is always Simon's language:

There is no reality only dreams
Your neck may get snapped when you wake
My love is drawn to some violent end
She keeps wanting to get away
My love is heading downward
And I am heading upward
She is going to crash on the sidewalk
And I am going to dissolve into the clouds

XII. Events

1. Out of the hospital, bruised and saddened and converted, with Princess' grunts still tangled in my hair . . . and Father in his overcoat, looking like a prince himself, come to carry me off. Up the expressway and out north to home. Jesus Christ, but the air is thinner and cleaner here. Monumental houses. Heartbreaking sidewalks, so clean.

2. Weeping in the living room. The ceiling is two stories high and two chandeliers hang from it. Weeping, weeping, though Billie the maid is *probably listening*. I will never leave home again. Never. Never leave home. Never leave this home again, never.

3. Sugar doughnuts for breakfast. The toaster is very shiny and my face is distorted in it. Is that my face?

4. The car is turning in the driveway. Father brings me home. Mother embraces me. Sunlight breaks in movieland patches on the roof of our traditional-contemporary home, which was designed for the famous automotive stylist whose identity, if I told you the name of the famous car he designed, you would all know, so I can't tell you because my teeth chatter at the thought of being sued . . . or having someone climb into my bedroom window with a rope to strangle me. . . . The car turns up the blacktop drive. The house opens to me like a doll's house, so lovely in the sunlight, the big living room beckons to me with its walls falling away in a delirium of joy at my return, Billie the maid is *no doubt* listening from the kitchen as I burst into tears and the hysteria Simon got so sick of. Convulsed in Father's arms, I say I will never leave again, never,

why did I leave, where did I go, what happened, my mind is gone wrong, my body is one big bruise, my backbone was sucked dry, it wasn't the men who hurt me and Simon never hurt me but only those girls . . . my God, how they hurt me . . . I will never leave home again. . . . The car is perpetually turning up the drive and I am perpetually breaking down in the living room and we are perpetually taking the right exit from the expressway (Lahser Road) and the wall of the rest room is perpetually banging against my head and perpetually are Simon's hands moving across my body and adding everything up and so too are Father's hands on my shaking bruised back, far from the surface of my skin on the surface of my good blue cashmere coat (dry-cleaned for my release). . . . I weep for all the money here, for God in gold and beige carpeting, for the beauty of chandeliers and the miracle of a clean polished gleaming toaster and faucets that run both hot and cold water, and I tell them, *I will never leave home, this is my home, I love everything here, I am in love with everything here. . . .*

I am home.

TIM O'BRIEN

Going After Cacciato

IT was a bad time. Billy Boy Watkins was dead, and so was Frenchie Tucker. Billy Boy had died of fright, scared to death on the field of battle, and Frenchie Tucker had been shot through the neck. Lieutenants Sidney Martin and Walter Gleason had died in tunnels. Pederson was dead and Bernie Lynn was dead. Buff was dead. They were all among the dead. The war was always the same, and the rain was part of the war. The rain fed fungus that grew in the men's socks and boots, and their socks rotted, and their feet turned white and soft so that the skin could be scraped off with a fingernail, and Stink Harris woke up screaming one night with a leech on his tongue. When it was not raining, a low mist moved like sleep across the paddies, blending the elements into a single gray element, and the war was cold and pasty and rotten. Lieutenant Corson, who came to replace Lieutenant Martin, contracted the dysentery. The tripflares were useless. The ammunition corroded and the foxholes filled with mud and water during the nights and in the mornings there was always the next village and the war was always the same. In early September Vaught caught an infection. He'd been showing Oscar Johnson the sharp edge on his bayonet, drawing it swiftly along his forearm and peeling off a layer of mushy skin. "Like a Gillette Blueblade." Vaught had grinned. It did not bleed, but in a few days the bacteria soaked in and the arm turned yellow, and Vaught was carried aboard a Huey that dipped perpendicular, blades clutching at granite air, rising in its own wet wind and taking Vaught away. He never returned to the war. Later they had a letter from him that described Japan as smoky and full of bedbugs, but in the enclosed snapshot Vaught looked happy enough, posing with two sightly nurses, a long-stemmed bottle of wine rising from between his thighs. It was a shock to learn that he'd lost the arm. Soon afterward Ben Nystrom shot himself in the foot, but he did not die, and he wrote no letters. These were all things to talk about. The rain, too. Oscar said it made him think of Detroit in the month of May. "Not the rain," he liked to say. "Just the dark and gloom. It's Number One weather for rape and looting. The fact is, I do ninety-eight percent of my total rape and looting in weather just like this." Then somebody would say that Oscar had a pretty decent imagination for a nigger.

That was one of the jokes. There was a joke about Oscar. There were many jokes about Billy Boy Watkins, the way he'd collapsed in fright on the field of glorious battle. Another joke was about the lieutenant's dysentery, and another was about Paul Berlin's purple boils. Some of the jokes were about Cacciato, who was as dumb, Stink said, as a bullet, or, Harold Murphy said, as an oyster fart.

In October, at the end of the month, in the rain, Cacciato left the war.

"He's gone away," said Doc Peret. "Split for parts unknown."

The lieutenant didn't seem to hear. He was too old to be a lieutenant, anyway. The veins in his nose and cheeks were shattered by booze. Once he had been a captain on the way to being a major, but whiskey and the fourteen dull years between Korea and Vietnam had ended all that, and now he was just an old lieutenant with the dysentery. He lay on his back in the pagoda, naked except for green socks and green undershorts.

"Cacciato," Doc Peret repeated. "He's gone away. Split, departed."

The lieutenant did not sit up. He held his belly with both hands as if to contain the disease.

"He's gone to Paris," Doc said. "That's what he tells Paul Berlin, anyhow, and Paul Berlin tells me, so I'm telling you. He's gone, packed up and gone."

"Paree," the lieutenant said softly. "In France, Paree? *Gay* Paree?"

"Yes, sir. That's what he says. That's what he told Paul Berlin, and that's what I'm telling you. You ought to cover up, sir."

The lieutenant sighed. He pushed himself up, breathing loud, then sat stiffly before a can of Sterno. He lit the Sterno and cupped his hands around the flame and bent down, drawing in the heat.

Outside, the rain was steady. "Paree," he said wearily. "You're saying Cacciato's left for gay Paree, is that right?"

"That's what he said, sir. I'm just relaying what he told to Paul Berlin. Hey, really, you better cover yourself up."

"Who's Paul Berlin?"

"Right here, sir. This is Paul Berlin."

The lieutenant looked up. His eyes were bright blue, oddly out of place in the sallow face. "You Paul Berlin?"

"Yes, sir," said Paul Berlin. He pretended to smile.

"Geez, I thought you were Vaught."

"Vaught's the one who cut himself, sir."

"I thought that was you. How do you like that?"

"Fine, sir."

The lieutenant sighed and shook his head sadly. He held a boot to dry over the burning Sterno. Behind him in the shadows sat the crosslegged, roundfaced Buddha, smiling benignly from its elevated perch. The pagoda was cold. Dank and soggy from a month of rain, the place smelled of clays and silicates and old incense. It was a single square room, built like a pillbox, with a flat ceiling that forced the soldiers to stoop and kneel. Once it might have been an elegant house of worship, neatly tiled and painted and clean, candles burning in holders at the Buddha's feet, but now it was bombed-out junk. Sandbags blocked the windows. Bits of broken pottery lay under chipped pedestals. The Buddha's right arm was missing and his fat groin was gouged with shrapnel. Still, the smile was intact. Head cocked, he seemed interested in the lieutenant's long sigh. "So, Cacciato's gone away, is that it?"

"There it is," Doc Peret said. "You've got it now."

Paul Berlin smiled and nodded.

"To gay Paree," the lieutenant said. "Old Cacciato's going to Paree in France." He giggled, then shook his head gravely. "Still raining?"

"A bitch, sir."

"You ever seen rain like this? I mean, ever?"

"No, sir," Paul Berlin said.

"You Cacciato's buddy, I suppose?"

"No, sir," Paul Berlin said. "Sometimes he'd tag along, but not really."

"Who's his buddy?"

"Vaught, sir. I guess Vaught was, sometime."

"Well," the lieutenant said, dropping his nose inside the boot to smell the sweaty leather, "well, I guess we should just get Mister Vaught in here."

"Vaught's gone, sir. He's the one who cut himself—gangrene, remember?"

"Mother of Mercy."

Doc Peret draped a poncho over the lieutenant's shoulders. The rain was steady and thunderless and undramatic. Though it was mid-morning, the feeling was of endless dusk.

"Paree," the lieutenant murmured. "Cacciato's going to gay Paree —pretty girls and bare ass and Frogs everywhere. What's wrong with him?"

"Just dumb, sir. He's just awful dumb, that's all."

"And he's walking? He says he's walking to gay Paree?"

"That's what he says, sir, but you know how Cacciato can be."

"Does he know how far it is?"

"Six thousand eight hundred statute miles, sir. That's what he told me—six thousand eight hundred miles on the nose. He had it down pretty well. He had a compass and fresh water and maps and stuff."

"Maps," the lieutenant said. "Maps, flaps, schnaps. I guess those maps will help him cross the oceans, right? I guess he can just rig up a canoe out of those maps, no problem."

"Well, no," said Paul Berlin. He looked at Doc Peret, who shrugged. "No, sir. He showed me on the maps. See, he says he's going through Laos, then into Thailand and Burma, and then India, and then some other country, I forget, and then into Iran and Iraq, and then Turkey, and then Greece, and the rest is easy. That's exactly what he said. The rest is easy, he said. He had it all doped out."

"In other words," the lieutenant said, lying back, "in other words, fuckin AWOL."

"There it is," said Doc Peret. "There it is."

The lieutenant rubbed his eyes. His face was sallow and he needed a shave. For a time he lay very still, listening to the rain, hands on his belly, then he giggled and shook his head and laughed. "What for? Tell me—what the fuck for?"

"Easy," Doc said. "Really, you got to stay covered up, sir. I told you that."

"What for? I mean, what for?"

"Shhhhhhh, he's just dumb, that's all."

The lieutenant's face was yellow. He laughed, rolling onto his side and dropping the boot. "I mean, why? What sort of shit is this—walking to fucking gay Paree? What kind of bloody war is this, tell me, what's wrong with you people? Tell me—what's *wrong* with you?"

"Shhhhhh," Doc purred, covering him up and putting a hand on his forehead. "Easy does it."

"Angel of Mercy, Mother of Virgins, what's wrong with you guys? Walking to gay Paree, what's *wrong*?"

"Nothing, sir. It's just Cacciato. You know how Cacciato can be when he puts his head to it. Relax now and it'll be all fine. Fine. It's just that rockhead, Cacciato."

The lieutenant giggled. Without rising, he pulled on his pants and boots and a shirt, then rocked miserably before the blue Sterno flame. The pagoda smelled like the earth, and the rain was unending. "Shoot." The lieutenant sighed. He kept shaking his head, grinning, then looked at Paul Berlin. "What squad you in?"

"Third, sir."

"That's Cacciato's squad?"

"Yes, sir."

"Who else?"

"Me and Doc and Eddie Lazzutti and Stink and Oscar Johnson and Harold Murphy. That's all, except for Cacciato."

"What about Pederson and Buff?"

"They're the dead ones, sir."

"Shoot." The lieutenant rocked before the flame. He did not look well. "Okay." He sighed, getting up. "Third Squads goes after Cacciato."

Leading to the mountains were four clicks[1] of level paddy. The mountains jerked straight out of the rice, and beyond those mountains and other mountains was Paris.

The tops of the mountains coud not be seen for the mist and clouds. The rain was glue that stuck the sky to the land.

The squad spent the night camped at the base of the first mountain, then in the morning they began the ascent. At midday Paul Berlin spotted Cacciato. He was half a mile up, bent low and moving patiently, steadily. He was not wearing a helmet—surprising, because Cacciato always took great care to cover the pink bald spot at the crown of his skull. Paul Berlin spotted him, but it was Stink Harris who spoke up.

Lieutenant Corson took out the binoculars.

"Him, sir?"

The lieutenant watched while Cacciato climbed toward the clouds.

"That him?"

"It's him. Bald as an eagle's ass."

Stink giggled. "Bald as Friar Tuck—it's Cacciato, all right. Dumb as a dink."

They watched until Cacciato was swallowed in the rain and clouds.

"Dumb-dumb." Stink giggled.

They walked fast, staying in a loose column. First the lieutenant, then Oscar Johnson, then Stink, then Eddie Lazzutti, then Harold

1. Slang for measure of distance as indicated by the elevation of a gunsight.

Murphy, then Doc, then, at the rear, Paul Berlin. Who walked slowly, head down. He had nothing against Cacciato. The whole episode was silly, of course, a dumb and immature thing typical of Cacciato, but even so he had nothing special against him. It was just too bad. A waste of time in the midst of infinitely wider waste.

Climbing, he tried to picture Cacciato's face. The image came out fuzzed and amorphous and bland—entirely compatible with the boy's personality. Doc Peret, an acute observer of such things, hypothesized that Cacciato had missed Mongolian idiocy by the breadth of a single, wispy genetic hair. "Could have gone either way," Doc had said confidentially. "You see the slanting eyes? The pasty flesh, just like jelly, right? The odd-shaped head? I mean, hey, let's face it—the guy's fucking ugly. It's only a theory, mind you, but I'd wager big money that old Cacciato has more than a smidgen of the Mongol in him."

There may have been truth to it. Cacciato looked curiously unfinished, as though nature had struggled long and heroically but finally jettisoned him as a hopeless cause, not worth the diminishing returns. Open-faced, round, naive, plump, tender-complected, and boyish, Cacciato lacked the fine detail, the refinements and final touches that maturity ordinarily marks on a boy of seventeen years. All this, the men concluded, added up to a case of simple gross stupidity. He wasn't positively disliked—except perhaps by Stink Harris, who took instant displeasure with anything vaguely his inferior—but at the same time Cacciato was no one's friend. Vaught, maybe. But Vaught was dumb, too, and he was gone from the war. At best, Cacciato was tolerated. The way men will sometimes tolerate a pesky dog.

It was just too bad. Walking to Paris; it was one of those ridiculous things Cacciato would do. Like winning the Bronze Star for shooting a dink in the face. Dumb. The way he was forever whistling. Too blunt-headed to know better, blind to the bodily and spiritual dangers of human combat. In some ways this made him a good soldier. He walked point like a boy at his first county fair. He didn't mind the tunnel work. And his smile, more decoration than an expression of emotion, stayed with him in the most lethal of moments—when Billy Boy turned his last card, when Pederson floated face-up in a summer day's paddy, when Buff's helmet overflowed with an excess of red and gray fluids.

It was sad, a real pity.

Climbing the mountain, Paul Berlin felt an odd affection for the kid. Not friendship, exactly, but—real pity.

Not friendship. Not exactly. Pity, pity plus wonder. It was all silly, walking away in the rain, but it was something to think about.

They did not reach the summit of the mountain until midafternoon. The climb was hard, the rain sweeping down, the mountain oozing from beneath their feet. Below, the clouds were expansive, hiding the paddies and the war. Above, in more clouds, were more mountains.

Oscar Johnson found where Cacciato had spent the first night, a rock formation with an outcropping ledge as a roof, a can of burned-out Sterno, a chocolate wrapper, and a partly burned map. On the map, traced in red ink, was a dotted line that ran through the paddyland and up the first small mountain of the Annamese Cordillera. The dotted line ended there, apparently to be continued on another map.

"He's serious," the lieutenant said softly. "The blockhead's serious." He held the map as if it had a bad smell.

Stink and Oscar and Eddie Lazzutti nodded.

They rested in Cacciato's snug rock nest. Tucked away, looking out on the slate rain toward the next mountain, the men were quiet. Paul Berlin laid out a game of solitaire. Harold Murphy rolled a joint, inhaled, then passed it along, and they smoked and watched the rain and clouds and wilderness. It was peaceful. The rain was nice.

No one spoke until the ritual was complete.

Then, in a hush, all the lieutenant could say was, "Mercy."

"Shit" was what Stink Harris said.

The rain was unending.

"We could just go back," Doc Peret finally said. "You know, sir? Just head on back and forget him."

Stink Harris giggled.

"Seriously," Doc kept on, "we could just let the poor kid go. Make him M.I.A.,[2] strayed in battle, the lost lamb. Sooner or later he'll wake up, you know, and he'll see how insane it is and he'll come back."

The lieutenant stared into the rain. His face was yellow except for the network of broken veins.

"So what say you, sir? Let him go?"

"Dumber than a rock." Stink giggled.

"And smarter than Stink Harris."

"You know *what,* Doc."

"Pickle it."

"Who's saying to pickle it?"

"Just pickle it," said Doc Peret. "That's what."

Stink giggled but he shut up.

"What do you say, sir? Turn back?"

The lieutenant was quiet. At last he shivered and went into the rain with a wad of toilet paper. Paul Berlin sat alone, playing solitaire in the style of Las Vegas. Pretending, of course. Pretend-

2. Missing in action.

ing to pay thirty thousand dollars for the deck, pretending ways to spend his earnings.

When the lieutenant returned he told the men to saddle up.

"We turning back?" Doc asked.

The lieutenant shook his head. He looked sick.

"I knew it!" Stink crowed. "Damn straight, I knew it! Can't hump away from a war, isn't that right, sir? The dummy has got to learn you can't just hump your way out of a war." Stink grinned and flicked his eyebrows at Doc Peret. "I knew it. By golly, I knew it!"

Cacciato had reached the top of the second mountain. Standing bareheaded, hands loosely at his sides, he was looking down on them through a blur of rain. Lieutenant Corson had the binoculars on him.

"Maybe he don't see us," Oscar said. "Maybe he's lost."

"Oh, he sees us. He sees us fine. Sees us real fine. And he's not lost. Believe me, he's not."

"Throw out smoke, sir?"

"Why not? the lieutenant said. "Sure, why not throw out pretty smoke, why not?" He watched Cacciato through the glasses while Oscar threw out the smoke. It fizzled for a time and then puffed up in a heavy cloud of lavender. "Oh, he sees us," the lieutenant whispered. "He sees us fine."

"The bastard's *waving!*"

"I can see that, thank you. Mother of Saints."

As if stricken, the lieutenant suddenly sat down in a puddle, put his head in his hands and began to rock as the lavender smoke drifted up the face of the mountain. Cacciato was waving both arms. Not quite waving. The arms were flapping. Paul Berlin watched through the glasses. Cacciato's head was huge, floating like a balloon in the high fog, and he did not look at all frightened. He looked young and stupid. His face was shiny. He was smiling, and he looked happy.

"I'm sick," the lieutenant said. He kept rocking. "I tell you, I'm a sick, sick man."

"Should I shout up to him?"

"Sick." The lieutenant moaned. "Sick, sick. It wasn't this way on Pusan,[3] I'll tell you that. Sure, call up to him—I'm sick."

Oscar Johnson cupped his hands and hollered, and Paul Berlin watched through the glasses. For a moment Cacciato stopped waving. He spread his arms wide, as if to show them empty, slowly spreading them out like wings, palms up. Then his mouth opened wide, and in the mountains there was thunder.

3. In Korea, in another war.

"What'd he say?" The lieutenant rocked on his haunches. He was clutching himself and shivering. "Tell me what he said."

"Can't hear, sir. Oscar—?"

There was more thunder, long-lasting thunder that came in waves from deep in the mountains. It rolled down and moved the trees and grasses.

"Shut the shit up!" The lieutenant was rocking and shouting at the rain and wind and thunder. "What'd the dumb fucker say?"

Paul Berlin watched through the glasses, and Cacciato's mouth opened and closed and opened, but there was only more thunder. Then his arms began flapping again. Flying, Paul Berlin suddenly realized. The poor kid was perched up there, arms flapping, trying to fly. Fly! Incredibly, the flapping motion was smooth and practiced and graceful.

"A chicken!" Stink squealed. "Look it! A squawking chicken!"

"Mother of Children."

"Look it!"

"A miserable chicken, you see that? A chicken!"

The thunder came again, breaking like Elephant Feet across the mountains, and the lieutenant rocked and held himself.

"For Christ sake." He moaned. "What'd he say? Tell me."

Paul Berlin could not hear. But he saw Cacciato's lips move, and the happy smile.

"Tell me."

So Paul Berlin, watching Cacciato fly, repeated it. "He said goodbye."

In the night the rain hardened into fog, and the fog was cold. They camped in the fog, near the top of the mountains, and the thunder stayed through the night. The lieutenant vomited. Then he radioed that he was in pursuit of the enemy.

"Gunships, Papa Two-Niner?" came the answer from far away.

"Negative," said the old lieutenant.

"Arty?[4] Tell you what. You got a real sweet voice, Papa Two-Niner. No shit, a lovely voice." The radio voice paused. "So, here's what I'll do, I'll give you a bargain on the arty—two for the price of one, no strings and a warranty to boot. How's that? See, we got this terrific batch of new one–fifty-five in, first-class ordinance, I promise you, and what we do, what we do is this. What we do is we go heavy on volume here, you know? Keeps the prices low."

"Negative," the lieutenant said.

"Well, geez. Hard to please, right? Maybe some nice illum, then? Willie Peter,[5] real boomers with some genuine sparkles mixed in. We're having this close-out sale, one time only."

4. Artillery. **5.** White phosphorous; illum: illumination.

"Negative. Negative, negative, negative."

"You'll be missing out on some fine shit."

"Negative, you monster."

"Okay," the radio voice said, disappointed-sounding, "but you'll wish . . . No offense, Papa Two-Niner. Have some happy hunting."

"Mercy," said the lieutenant into a blaze of static.

The night fog was worse than the rain, colder and more saddening. They lay under a sagging lean-to that seemed to catch and hold the fog like a net. Oscar and Harold Murphy and Stink and Eddie Lazzutti slept anyway, curled around one another like lovers. They could sleep and sleep.

"I hope he's moving," Paul Berlin whispered to Doc Peret. "I just hope he keeps moving. He does that, we'll never get him."

"Then they'll chase him with choppers. Or planes or something."

"Not if he gets himself lost," Paul Berlin said. "Not if he hides."

"What time is it?"

"Don't know."

"What time you got, sir?"

"Very lousy late," said the lieutenant from the bushes.

"Come on."

"Four o'clock. O-four-hundred, which is to say A.M. Got it?"

"Thanks."

"Charmed." His ass, hanging six inches from the earth, made a soft warm glow in the dark.

"You okay, sir?"

"I'm wonderful. Can't you see how wonderful I am?"

"I just hope Cacciato keeps moving," Paul Berlin whispered. "That's all I hope—I hope he uses his head and keeps moving."

"It won't get him anywhere."

"Get him to Paris maybe."

"Maybe." Doc sighed, turning onto his side. "And where is he then?"

"In Paris."

"No way. I like adventure, too, but, see, you can't walk to Paris from here. You just can't."

"He's smarter than you think," Paul Berlin said, not quite believing it. "He's not all that dumb."

"I know," the lieutenant said. He came from the bushes. "I know all about that."

"Impossible. None of the roads go to Paris."

"Can we light a Sterno, sir?"

"No," the lieutenant said, crawling under the lean-to and lying flat on his back. His breath came hard. "No, you can't light a fucking Sterno, and no, you can't go out to play without your mufflers and galoshes, and no, kiddies and combatants, no, you can't have chocolate sauce on your broccoli. No."

"All right."

"No!"

"You saying no, sir?"

"No." The lieutenant sighed with doom. "It's still a war, isn't it?"

"I guess."

"There you have it. It's still a war."

The rain resumed. It started with thunder, then lightning lighted the valley deep below in green and mystery, then more thunder, then it was just the rain. They lay quietly and listened. Paul Berlin, who considered himself abnormally sane, uncluttered by high ideas or lofty ambitions or philosophy, was suddenly struck between the eyes by a vision of murder. Butchery, no less. Cacciato's right temple caving inward, a moment of black silence, then the enormous explosion of outward-going brains. It was no metaphor; he didn't think in metaphors. No, it was a simple scary vision. He tried to reconstruct the thoughts that had led to it, but there was nothing to be found—the rain, the discomfort of mushy flesh. Nothing to justify such a bloody image, no origins. Just Cacciato's round head suddenly exploding like a pricked bag of helium: boom.

Where, he thought, was all this taking him, and where would it end? Murder was the logical circuit-stopper, of course; it was Cacciato's rightful, maybe inevitable due. Nobody can get away with stupidity forever, and in war the final price for it is always paid in purely biological currency, hunks of toe or pieces of femur or bits of exploded brain. And it *was* still a war, wasn't it?

Pitying Cacciato with wee-hour tenderness, and pitying himself for the affliction that produced such visions, Paul Berlin hoped for a miracle. He was tired of murder. Not scared by it—not at that particular moment—and not awed by it, just fatigued.

"He did some awfully brave things," he whispered. Then realized that Doc was listening. "He did. The time he dragged that dink out of his bunker, remember that."

"Yeah."

"The time he shot the kid in the kisser."

"I remember."

"At least you can't call him a coward, can you? You can't say he ran away because he was scared."

"You can say a lot of other shit, though."

"True. But you can't say he wasn't brave. You can't say that."

"Fair enough," Doc said. He sounded sleepy.

"I wonder if he talks French."

"You kidding, partner?"

"Just wondering. You think it's hard to learn French, Doc?"

"Cacciato?"

"Yeah, I guess not. It's a neat thing to think about, though, old Cacciato walking to Paris."

"Go to sleep," Doc Peret advised. "Remember, pal, you got your own health to think of."

They were in the high country.

It was country far from the war, high and peaceful country with trees and thick grass, no people and no dogs and no lowland drudgery. Real wilderness, through which a single trail, liquid and shiny, kept taking them up.

The men walked with their heads down. Stink at point, then Eddie Lazzutti and Oscar, next Harold Murphy with the machine gun, then Doc, then the lieutenant, and last Paul Berlin.

They were tired and did not talk. Their thoughts were in their legs and feet, and their legs and feet were heavy with blood, for they'd been on the march many hours and the day was soggy with the endless rain. There was nothing symbolic, or melancholy, about the rain. It was simple rain, everywhere.

They camped that night beside the trail, then in the morning continued the climb. Though there were no signs of Cacciato, the mountain had only one trail and they were on it, the only way west.

Paul Berlin marched mechanically. At his sides, balancing him evenly and keeping him upright, two canteens of Kool-Aid lifted and fell with his hips, and the hips rolled in their ball-and-socket joints. He respired and sweated. His heart hard, his back strong, up the high country.

They did not see Cacciato, and for a time Paul Berlin thought they might have lost him forever. It made him feel better, and he climbed the trail and enjoyed the scenery and the sensations of being high and far from the real war, and then Oscar found the second map.

The red dotted line crossed the border into Laos.

Farther ahead they found Cacciato's helmet and armored vest, then his dogtags, then his entrenching tool and knife.

"Dummy just keeps to the trail." The lieutenant moaned. "Tell me why? Why doesn't he leave the trail?"

"It's the only way to Paris," Paul Berlin said.

"A rockhead," said Stink Harris. "That's why."

Liquid and shiny, a mix of rain and red clay, the trail took them higher.

Cacciato eluded them but he left behind the wastes of his march—empty tins, bits of bread, a belt of golden ammo dangling from a dwarf pine, a leaking canteen, candy wrappers, and worn rope.

Clues that kept them going. Tantalizing them on, one step then the next—a glimpse of his bald head, the hot ash of a breakfast fire, a handkerchief dropped coyly along the path.

So they kept after him, following the trails that linked one to the next westward in a simple linear direction without deception. It was deep, jagged, complex country, dark with the elements of the season, and ahead was the frontier.

"He makes it that far," Doc Peret said, pointing to the next line of mountains, "and we can't touch him."

"How now?"

"The border," Doc said. The trail had leveled out and the march was easier. "He makes it to the border and it's bye-bye Cacciato."

"How far?"

"Two clicks maybe. Not far."

"Then he's made it," whispered Paul Berlin.

"Maybe so."

"By God!"

"Maybe so," Doc said.

"Boy, lunch at Tour d'Argent![6] A night at the old opera!"

"Maybe so."

The trail narrowed, then climbed, and a half hour later they saw him.

He stood at the top of a small grassy hill, two hundred meters ahead. Loose and at ease, smiling, Cacciato already looked like a civilian. His hands were in his pockets and he was not trying to hide himself. He might have been waiting for a bus, patient and serene and not at all frightened.

"Got him!" Stink yelped. "I knew it! Now we got him!"

The lieutenant came forward with the glasses.

"I knew it," Stink crowed, pressed forward. "The blockhead's finally giving it up—giving up the old ghost, I knew it!"

"What do we do, sir?"

The lieutenant shrugged and stared through the glasses.

"Fire a shot?" Stink held his rifle up and before the lieutenant could speak he squeezed off two quick rounds, one a tracer that turned like a corkscrew through the mist. Cacciato smiled and waved.

"Look at him," Oscar Johnson said. "I do think we got ourselves a predicament. Truly a predicament."

"There it is," Eddie said, and they both laughed, and Cacciato kept smiling and waving.

"A true predicament."

Stink Harris took the point, walking fast and chattering, and Cacciato stopped waving and watched him come, arms folded and his big head cocked as if listening for something. He looked amused.

6. A famous and expensive restaurant in Paris.

There was no avoiding it.

Stink saw the wire as he tripped it, but there was no avoiding it.

The first sound was that of a zipper suddenly yanked up; next, a popping noise, the spoon releasing and primer detonating; then the sound of the grenade dropping; then the fizzling sound. The sounds came separately but quickly.

Stink knew it as it happened. With the next step, in one fuzzed motion, he flung himself down and away, rolling, covering his skull, mouth open, yelping a funny, trivial little yelp.

They all knew it.

Eddie and Oscar and Doc Peret dropped flat, and Harold Murphy bent double and did an oddly graceful jackknife for a man of his size, and the lieutenant coughed and collapsed, and Paul Berlin, seeing purple, closed his eyes and fists and mouth, brought his knees to his belly, coiling, and let himself fall.

Count, he thought, but the numbers came in a tangle without sequence.

His belly hurt. That was where it started. First the belly, a release of fluids in the bowels next, a shitting feeling, a draining of all the pretensions and silly hopes for himself, and he was back where he started, writhing. The lieutenant was beside him. The air was windless—just the misty rain. His teeth hurt. Count, he thought, but his teeth hurt and no numbers came. I don't want to die, he thought lucidly, with hurting teeth.

There was no explosion. His teeth kept hurting and his belly was floating in funny ways.

He was ready, steeled. His lungs hurt now. He was ready, but there was no explosion. Then came a fragile pop. Smoke, he thought without thinking, smoke.

"Smoke." The lieutenant moaned, then repeated it. "Fucking smoke."

Paul Berlin smelled it. He imagined its velvet color, purple, but he could not open his eyes. He tried, but he could not open his eyes or unclench his fists or uncoil his legs, and the heavy fluids in his stomach were holding him down, and he could not wiggle or run to escape. There was no explosion.

"Smoke," Doc said softly. "Just smoke."

It was red smoke, and the message seemed clear. It was all over them. Brilliant red, thick, acid-tasting. It spread out over the earth like paint, then began to climb against gravity in a lazy red spiral.

"Smoke," Doc said. "Smoke."

Stink Harris was crying. He was on his hands and knees, chin against his throat, bawling and bawling. Oscar and Eddie had not moved.

"He had us," the lieutenant whispered. His voice was hollowed out, senile-sounding, almost a reminiscence. "He could've had all of us."

"Just smoke," Doc said. "Lousy smoke is all."

"The dumb fucker could've had us."

Paul Berlin could not move. He felt entirely conscious, a little embarrassed but not yet humiliated, and he heard their voices, heard Stink weeping and saw him beside the trail on his hands and knees, and he saw the red smoke everywhere, but he could not move.

"He won't come," said Oscar Johnson, returning under a white flag. "Believe me, I tried, but the dude just won't play her cool."

It was dusk and the seven soldiers sat in pow-wow.

"I told him all the right stuff, but he won't give it up. Told him it was crazy as shit and he'd probably end up dead, and I told him how he'd end up court-martialed at the best, and I told him how his old man would shit when he heard about it. Told him maybe things wouldn't go so hard if he just gave up and came back right now. I went through the whole spiel, top to bottom. The dude just don't listen."

The lieutenant was lying prone, Doc's thermometer in his mouth, sick-looking. It wasn't his war. The skin on his arms and neck was loose around deteriorating muscle.

"I told him—I told him all that good shit. Told him it's ridiculous, dig? I told him it won't work, no matter what, and I told him we're fed up. Fed up."

"You tell him we're out of rations?"

"Shit, yes, I told him that. And I told him he's gonna starve his own ass if he keeps going, and I told him we'd have to call in gunships if it came to it."

"You tell him he can't walk to France?"

Oscar grinned. He was black enough to be indistinct in the dusk. "Maybe I forgot to tell him that."

"You should've told him."

The lieutenant slid a hand behind his neck and pushed against it as if to relieve some spinal pressure. "What else?" he asked. "What else did he say?"

"Nothing, sir. He said he's doing okay. Said he was sorry to scare us with the smoke."

"The bastard." Stink kept rubbing his hands against the black stock of his rifle.

"What else?"

"Nothing. You know how he is, sir. Just a lot of smiles and stupid stuff. He asked how everybody was, so I said we're fine, except for the scare with the smoke boobytrap, and then he said he was sorry about that, so I told him it was okay. What can you say to a dude like that?"

The lieutenant nodded, pushing against his neck. He was quiet a while. He seemed to be making up his mind. "All right." He finally sighed. "What'd he have with him?"

"Sir?"

"Musketry," the lieutenant said. "What kind of weapons?"

"His rifle. That's all, his rifle and some bullets. I didn't get much of a look.

"Claymores?"

Oscar shook his head. "I didn't see none. Maybe so."

"Grenades?"

"I don't know. Maybe a couple."

"Beautiful recon job, Oscar. Real pretty."

"Sorry, sir. He had his stuff tight, though."

"I'm sick."

"Yes, sir."

"Dysentery's going through me like coffee. What you got for me, Doc?"

Doc Peret shook his head. "Nothing, sir. Rest."

"That's it," the lieutenant said. "What I need is rest."

"Why not let him go, sir?"

"Rest," the lieutenant said, "is what I need."

Paul Berlin did not sleep. Instead he watched Cacciato's small hill and tried to imagine a proper ending.

There were only a few possibilities remaining, and after what had happened it was hard to see a happy end to it. Not impossible, of course. It could still be done. With skill and boldness, Cacciato might slip away and cross the frontier mountains and be gone. He tried to picture it. Many new places. Villages at night with barking dogs, people whose eyes and skins would change in slow evolution and counterevolution as Cacciato moved westward with whole continents before him and the war far behind him and all the trails connecting and leading toward Paris. It could be done. He imagined the many dangers of Cacciato's march, treachery and deceit at every turn, but he also imagined the many good times ahead, the stinging feel of aloneness, and new leanness and knowledge of strange places. The rains would end and the trails would go dry and be baked to dust, and there would be changing foliage and great expanses of silence and songs and pretty girls in straw huts and, finally, Paris.

It could be done. The odds were like poison, but it could be done.

Later, as if a mask had been peeled off, the rain ended and the sky cleared and Paul Berlin woke to see the stars.

They were in their familiar places. It wasn't so cold. He lay on his back and counted the stars and named those that he knew, named the constellations and the valleys of the moon. It was just too bad. Crazy, but still sad. He should've kept going—left the trails and waded through streams to rinse away the scent, buried his feces, swung from the trees branch to branch; he should've slept through the days and ran through the nights. It might have been done.

Toward dawn he saw Cacciato's breakfast fire. He heard Stink playing with the safety catch on his M-16, a clicking noise like a slow morning cricket. The sky lit itself in patches.

"Let's do it," the lieutenant whispered.

Eddie Lazzutti and Oscar and Harold Murphy crept away toward the south. Doc and the lieutenant waited a time then began to circle west to block a retreat. Stink Harris and Paul Berlin were to continue up the trail.

Waiting, trying to imagine a rightful and still happy ending, Paul Berlin found himself pretending, in a vague sort of way, that before long the war would reach a climax beyond which everything else would become completely commonplace. At that point he would stop being afraid. All the bad things, the painful and grotesque things, would be in the past, and the things ahead, if not lovely, would at least be tolerable. He pretended he had crossed that threshold.

When the sky was half-light, Doc and the lieutenant fired a red flare that streaked high over Cacciato's grassy hill, hung there, then exploded in a fanning starburst like the start of a celebration. Cacciato Day, it might have been called. October something, in the year 1968, the Year of the Pig.

In the trees at the southern slope of the hill Oscar and Eddie and Harold Murphy each fired red flares to signal their advance.

Stink went into the weeds and hurried back, zipping up his trousers. He was very excited and happy. Deftly, he released the bolt on his weapon and it slammed hard into place.

"Fire the flare," he said, "and let's go."

Paul Berlin took a long time opening his pack.

But he found the flare, unscrewed its lid, laid the firing pin against the primer, then jammed it in.

The flare jumped away from him. It went high and fast, rocketing upward and taking a smooth arc that followed the course of the trail, leaving behind a dirty wake of smoke.

At its apex, with barely a sound, the flare exploded in a green dazzle over Cacciato's hill. It was a fine, brilliant shade of green.

"Go," whispered Paul Berlin. It did not seem enough. "Go," he said, and then he shouted, "Go."

JONATHAN PENNER

Emotion Recollected in Tranquillity[1]

AFTER I got out of the service, I moved back in with my mother. Our temple was teaching contract bridge, and my mother drafted me as her partner, at least one generation younger than anybody else in the room. No matter which of us was declarer, my mother played the hand (her card sense was amazing, I give her that) while I sat behind the dummy.

Mrs. Leonard was another regular, a huge woman who always toadied up to my mother. I was the reason why. "Tell Philly," she'd beg my mother, as though we had food and she were starving, "to give Diane a little phone call." Then she'd squeeze my arm or sometimes, under the bridge table, always frightening me, my thigh. She was terrified her daughter would marry Richard Dean, a Gentile whose pharmacist uncle had been heard to pass anti-Semitic remarks.

"In addition to which," she would tell me sadly, taking me aside afterward during coffee and cake, "the boy is AC-DC."

Though this was close enough to the truth, I was silent out of loyalty. Mrs. Leonard thought I hadn't understood. She narrowed her eyes. "Do I need to spell it out?" She puffed at her cigarette in the way she used to signal sophistication. "A switch-hitter."

What Mrs. Leonard didn't know was that Diane had been on my mind as far back as my memory went. I had felt for her, starting in kindergarten, an unforgettable hatred. Even then she was considered pretty, which I especially hated, because it drew attention to her, therefore to me. Back then, and through the first six grades, she and I were the only Jews in our class.

Diane was incredibly stupid, incredibly something—nobody minding the store, was how my mother put it. In class, teachers had to yell at her to pay attention. It was always the same. Her vagueness, her dreamy sweetness, made me want to hit her, but I was afraid to. And year after year, fat Mrs. Leonard, whenever we met, would reach out a hand to stroke my head, which I didn't dare lean away more than slightly. The smell of her sweat and perfume intoxicated me, and I watched in fascination as the flesh hanging from her upper arm swung like a water-filled balloon.

"Philly, let me take you home," she'd say. "You'll write a little poem for me." Her voice was so melodious, humorous, and inviting that I would nervously feel myself falling under her spell.

"You and Diane are some pair. A little bride and groom."

1. Famous definition of poetry from the Preface to the *Lyrical Ballads,* by William Wordsworth (1770–1850), English poet.

The idea of my marrying anyone was humiliating. When her mother maneuvered us face to face at temple "events," I stared at Diane expressionlessly, while she wore a simple-minded smile and tried to back away. At last she would escape to the temple's front steps and sit reading a book, whose title she would hide when she saw me looking at it, and I would join my friends in back of the building, humming rocks at the garbage cans with as vicious a sidearm whip as possible.

In high school, to her mother's despair, she hung around with a brotherhood of tough guys we all called—I never knew why—the Baldies. Their leader, Rodney Cooper, would take her to movies, and then, late at night, to a deserted golf course. Big Ones, he always called her, Big Ones, and she'd only smile. Her mother was right to worry. Loathsome as Rodney was, he made himself the love of her life. Maybe it was just his being the first: Diane was soft, and would have retained anyone's impress.

"Sucks and fucks," he claimed, standing with his friends on the baseball field, all of them smoking and strewing the ground with butts. "Shakespeare!" Seeing me on the fringe of the group he drew me apart and put his arm over my shoulder. "Jew girls are the best," he told me, as a compliment. "Right, Shakespeare?" I imagined myself dividing his grinning face into diamonds by pushing it through the chain-link backstop, but in a fight he would have destroyed me.

Oh, she loved him. He didn't go to college, so she didn't—she enrolled in Hammersmith Secretarial School, whose billboard showed a giant hammer striking a door marked GOOD JOB, HI PAY. When Mrs. Leonard saw me at temple, escorting my mother to a bar mitzvah, she stared reproachfully. At the reception afterward she cornered us, holding out a paper napkin laden with rugaluch.[2] "And you, Philly," she said bitterly. "What are your plans? Yale? Harvard? Brandeis?"

"I may go into the Army," I said.

She looked at my mother, who flushed but shrugged. Mrs. Leonard brightened. "A young man has time," she said, folding her napkin around the rugaluch and stuffing it into her pocketbook. "Are you still writing your lovely poems?"

"It's harder now."

"Explain to Mrs. Leonard about the Army," said my mother cruelly.

So I must have been able to explain my reasoning, then—I had to repeatedly, until the very day I left. But now don't ask me. It turned out I never wrote a poem about the Army. You see novels about the Army, but did you ever see a poem? They sent me to

2. Pastry.

Germany—no poems about that, either. But once while I was there I got drunk and helped overturn some parked cars. And in jail I did write a poem, not about jail, but about Diane's face, which I remembered as too big, a pale floating target.

When I returned home she was working in a department store, going to the local college part-time. I enrolled there too. Rodney had gone to Texas to seek his fortune. Diane missed him badly, but was falling in love with someone new, the one her mother, squinting through cigarette smoke, called the switch-hitter, AC-DC.

This was unfair, but it was true that Richard Dean was (and God knows how Mrs. Leonard found out) a transvestite. Once a week or so he liked to go into the city dressed as a woman. Diane, who had taken to confiding in me (her oldest friend, she remarked sentimentally) about her love life, said it was the deception he liked. That and the whiff of danger.

"He knows he isn't a homo," she explained. Saying the word made her squirm. "He just likes to see if he can pass. Can you understand that a little?"

"Sure," I said, and I thought I could. "When I was small I liked to go around the house in my mother's heels."

Our temple had started a theater group, and my mother was there night after night for rehearsals. I usually stayed home alone. Though I met girls at college, they weren't right—that was all I would say whenever my mother raised the subject. To my surprise I'd turned out to be a serious, no, a gloomy person, and could hardly stand frivolity or even cheerfulness. Since getting out of the Army I'd had acceptances from a few literary magazines, and was starting to think about a book of poems. If I could accumulate forty I liked, I'd try for the Yale Younger Poets Award. That was enough to dream about.

But, as though I were forever back in jail in Germany, seeing her pale face float before me, I was disturbed to find myself—after all these years—contracting Diane like a kind of disease. I might have become infected in childhood. Like leprosy, its stain could have taken decades to surface. In any case, the way Richard Dean would slide his hand around under her armpit—as though he were sticking it between two cushions—made me furious.

It was Diane's cowlike submissiveness to him that bothered me most. She was pitifully afraid of his leaving her, already afraid—something I could hardly believe, in such a luscious girl—of being single all her life, and alone in her old age. "If I looked younger," she said (she wasn't yet twenty-five), cranning to peer in my car's rear-view mirror, stretching her face with her fingertips. Her sweater rode up, exposing an inch of white back.

Finally Richard told her she shouldn't talk to me so much. That amazed Diane.

"It's natural," I said, because I could understand his jealousy. Sometimes, after rehearsals, my mother was spending the night with her theater group's director, a retired actor. It wasn't the same, but upsetting enough. "I'd be nervous too," I said, "in Richard's position."

"You wouldn't if I were your girl," said Diane—protesting her loyalty to him, and not hinting at anything at all.

Her mindless subservience made me angry enough to think she was right, he was certain to leave her—who could be happy with her for long? But at night, waiting to fall asleep, I had visions of Richard Dean dying in a car accident—sometimes my mother was in the car too—visions so clear that I frightened myself, and beamed into my pillow the thought that I didn't mean it.

At other times I imagined myself catching him in a homosexual act, and beating him up in spite of his being dressed as a woman, and telling him never to see Diane again. But I knew I would never lift a finger to him. He said he was a karate expert, and once, in a sudden rage, had half-squatted into combat position, hands stiffened like hatchets. "I can break twelve of your bones in two seconds," he told me softly. I laughed and backed away. Though the Army had tried teaching me a little of that, I had failed to learn it. In a fight he would demolish me.

Ghazir—he was a Christian Lebanese, raised in France, but an Arab was all Mrs. Leonard ever saw—was twenty years older than we were, with enormous shoulders and a walrus mustache. Divorced, he lived in a cottage he had built out in the country. Less than a month after she met him, Diane was living with him.

What, she asked me with a hopeless little smile, could she tell her mother? I didn't know. When Mrs. Leonard saw me in the supermarket, she rose from the freezer bin, a quart of ice cream in each hand. "Philly," she said distractedly, pointing at me with one of the quarts, the pendulous flesh of her arm swaying, the look on her face telling the world—while I pretended not to see, hurrying to the checkout—that I, my stubbornness, disloyalty, unmanliness, was the cause of it all.

I guess there are periods in everyone's life, like childhood, that seem to last forever, but when you look back at them later they're collapsed as flat as packing cartons, and everything's squashed together. That's what it started to be like for me now. Diane lived with Ghazir and finally married him. I got a job distributing newspapers, and didn't win the Yale Younger Poets Award. I began to send my book of poems to little presses named after things like planets and trees. Diane and Ghazir fought, were divorced, but continued to live together—their trouble was her fault, she was too demanding, she told me. Mrs. Leonard died. I wept at her funeral, but when I saw Richard Dean there, crying too, a guy who knew she'd hated him, I dried right up. My mother, svelte leading lady, was there with her boy friend, the director of the Temple B'Nai Israel Players. "The weight this woman carried," said my mother, "she's got no kick coming."

Ghazir began to beat Diane. When I, drunk, tried to return the favor, he hugged me until one of my ribs cracked. I paid to have my book of poems published, and stacked the boxed copies in my bedroom. Ghazir was seeing other women, blaming Diane, who agreed that she was driving him crazy, she wanted so much to remarry him. My mother married her director, they bought a condo in Miami, and she gave me a hug and sold the house out from under me. "This is my chance for happiness," she explained. "Not so many years are left. What about you?" She made claws in the air. "When are you going to grab hold?"

I moved, then, to a furnished room nearer the university. My landlord was an old man who swept his sidewalk with painful care early each morning. He was completely deaf. I communicated with him in writing, but seldom, because my childish script irritated him. On a ledge in the dim downstairs hall, beside the disconnected telephone, lay a tract titled "What to Do in Time of Sorrow." It lay there, slowly growing a skin of dust, the three years I lived in that house.

Ghazir had been having an affair with a French girl who lived with a wealthy family as a baby-sitter. She met him at his cottage, often bringing the children, when Diane was at work. Diane knew about it. Ghazir vehemently denied that anything sexual was going on. But when the girl returned to France he was broken-hearted, and wept with his face pressed into Diane's lap, she told me. Then he said he was going to Europe.

His picture postcards arrived with decreasing frequency, with no return address and no mention of his coming back. Diane still lived at the cottage, where, every time I visited her, she would talk to me for hours about nothing but Ghazir. The surrounding vegetation grew wild. I attacked it with a sickle. Winter came, and Ghazir wrote that he was working in a bicycle shop, thinking of getting married. He had asked his cousin to look into selling the cottage.

And a sign, FOR SALE, did appear, hammered through the snow into the frozen ground. No buyers came. Ghazir stopped writing. The cold wind oozed in; each time I visited I tacked up more cardboard. I left my deaf old man and slept in Diane's front room. Evenings, we made a fire and talked about our childhood, which she, to my amazement, remembered as perfect. Spring came early. I pounded open the windows, bruising the heel of my palm, and patched the torn screens. On a night with a full moon and a scented breeze, Diane and I became lovers. As we lay together in the valley of Ghazir's mattress, as she slept in my arms, I beamed a promise into her damp forehead: to compensate her for every insult and betrayal.

We moved back to town, which had grown disturbingly since we were children, and rented a garden apartment in what I remembered as empty marshland. I got a job at an aerospace plant—it had to do with missile nosecones, they said, but I never learned how. I emptied boxes of head-sized plastic hunks into a hopper atop a machine. They came out at the bottom fist-sized, warm, and smelling like model airplane glue. Diane, who was working as a secretary at the telephone company, joined their Executive-in-Training Program. We bought chairs and a sofa, rough-hewn wood slung with leather, the style that year. New sets of everything that came in sets—linens, pots and pans, china, glasses, silverware. It was the nicest place I ever lived in.

Except when we were at our jobs, we were together, even if I was just taking a ten-minute trip to the drug store. "You don't think I'm too clingy?" she asked.

"I love it," I told her. "Don't use that word."

Diane knew from the start how badly I was going to fail her, and her difficult job was to teach me that. She started practically at once asking whether she disappointed me, whether I was upset with her, as though I were a doctor withholding news of fatal illness.

"You look nervous," she'd say, or "You look unhappy," when I wasn't aware of feeling those things. If I did tell her something was bothering me, a backache, or something from work, she was more upset than I was, as though the trouble were her fault. She saw things in my expression that I never meant to be there. She heard them in my voice. She heard them in my silence.

And at last it became maddening, when I had been thinking about something, to look up and see her little smile of guilty fear. "I wasn't being cold," I'd shout, before she had a chance to say it.

But now I began to criticize everything about her. I said she spent too much on clothes—her dresses filled her closet and half of mine, many more than my mother had owned.

"That's because she threw them out whenever the style changed," said Diane. And it was true, I had been unfair, most of Diane's clothes were old, I thought I could remember some from the days of Richard Dean—old and unflattering, tight around the stomach and rear. And how strangely somber. When I saw them by the dozen, packed together on hangers, I realized that she never wore anything vivid.

"You should try bright colors," I told her.

But she only looked worried and asked me, smiling a little, her voice as hopeless as though I'd suggested she leap the moon, "Do you think I should?"

Diane. I saw now that I was stuck with her, her with me, forever. We weren't unhappy. I shouted, but not often; she rarely cried. We bought a second car, used. She dyed her hair to conceal the white. I had an extra drink each evening. We bought a little outboard cruiser and moored it in the river. I hardly remembered, would barely have wanted, any other life.

And then one night—out for supper at Howard Johnson's—we saw someone who looked familiar. "It couldn't be," said Diane.

I doubted it too. But Rodney Cooper recognized us at once, grinned, waved, and came to join us in our booth. "Shakespeare," he laughed, squeezing my hand. His face was deeply tanned, his hair silver, his wrinkles full of sly good humor. He was just back for a visit, he said—he came every year to see his family. He'd done, oh, pretty well in Texas, had his own business, now. Contractor, laying pipe, starting to bid on some pretty big jobs. His lawyer and his accountant were both Jews, he told us, then grinned, showing us that he admired the sharpness and shadiness of our race. Diane, with an unconscious half-smile, was staring at him—trying to read his face, I knew, wondering what he was thinking of her. It was exactly the same as always. "Big Ones," said Rodney, as he reached for our checks, "I gotta ask. You two married, or what?" Diane and I shook our heads slowly, as though in time to the same music.

They live in Houston now—I know from the postmark on their Christmas card. It's the same card every year, the one his secretary must mail to his customers and suppliers. The signature, Rodney and Diane Cooper, is in red Old English type, within a wreath of green holly. I wonder how many others come to our town, whether he sends them to his grade school teachers in their retirement, or any of the old Baldies.

The missile nosecone business hasn't been good. But by the time the layoffs came, I had enough seniority to bump a younger man in what we call the Publications Division. Now I edit and mostly write *Inner Space*, a weekly that's distributed throughout the plant. News about the company, contracts we've been awarded, results from the bowling league, necrology—the Director of Publications lets me do whatever I want. Lately I've tried some light verse. I don't sign it, but the other publications people know who wrote it, and they say it's not bad. One of them is a woman, Lila. She hasn't been to where I live, but someday I think I'll open Diane's old closet and show her the boxes full of my book of poems.

Last week I saw Ghazir. He must be close to seventy, now. But he still has his swagger, and I stopped on the sidewalk to watch him. He emerged from a barbershop, thin hair and great mustache beautifully trimmed, and jaywalked across the street. I wanted to stop him there in the middle of traffic and ask when he'd gotten back from France. I'd have liked to know what he thought of his ex-wife's marriage, whether it would last or whether we'd see Diane back in town one of these years, alone in her old age as she'd always predicted. I wished we could go to a bar together, he and I, and have some drinks and talk about our lives. But Ghazir was across the street now. He hopped into an idling Thunderbird, where a young woman had just slid from the driver's seat to make room for him, and drove away with his arm around her.

And when I saw that, I knew it was good I hadn't spoken to him. I might have told him that he'd never loved Diane, none of them had, that they'd ruined her. If we'd gone to that bar and had those drinks I'd probably have cried and said that I was the only one in the world who had tried to save her. If even a shadow of mockery crossed his face I might have grabbed his thick neck and squeezed. And it would have been the same as always—no matter how I fought, old as he was, he would have crucified me.

JAYNE ANNE PHILLIPS

Souvenir

KATE always sent her mother a card on Valentine's Day. She timed the mails from wherever she was so that the cards arrived on February 14th. Her parents had celebrated the day in some small fashion, and since her father's death six years before, Kate made a gesture of compensatory remembrance. At first, she made the cards herself: collage and pressed grass on construction paper sewn in fabric. Now she settled for art reproductions, glossy cards with blank insides. Kate wrote in them with colored inks, "You have always been my Valentine," or simply "Hey, take care of yourself." She might enclose a present as well, something small enough to fit into an envelope; a sachet, a perfumed soap, a funny tintype of a prune-faced man in a bowler hat.

This time, she forgot. Despite the garish displays of paper cupids and heart-shaped boxes in drugstore windows, she let the day nearly approach before remembering. It was too late to send anything in the mail. She called her mother long-distance at night when the rates were low.

"Mom? How are you?"

"It's you! How are *you?*" Her mother's voice grew suddenly brighter; Kate recognized a tone reserved for welcome company.

Sometimes it took a while to warm up.

"I'm fine," answered Kate. "What have you been doing?"

"Well, actually I was trying to sleep."

"Sleep? You should be out setting the old hometown on fire."

"The old hometown can burn up without me tonight."

"Really? What's going on?"

"I'm running in-service training sessions for the primary teachers." Kate's mother was a school superintendent. "They're driving me batty. You'd think their brains were rubber."

"They are," Kate said. "Or you wouldn't have to train them. Think of them as a salvation, They create a need for your job."

"Some salvation. Besides, your logic is ridiculous. Just because someone needs training doesn't mean they're stupid."

"I'm just kidding. But *I'm* stupid. I forgot to send you a Valentine's card."

"You did? That's bad. I'm trained to receive one. They bring me luck."

"You're receiving a phone call instead," Kate said. "Won't that do?"

"Of course," said her mother, "but this is costing you money. Tell me quick, how are you?"

"Oh, you know. Doctoral pursuits. Doing my student trip, grooving with the professors."

"The professors? You'd better watch yourself."

"It's a joke, Mom, a joke. But what about you? Any men on the horizon?"

"No, not really. A married salesman or two asking me to dinner when they come through the office. Thank heavens I never let those things get started."

"You should do what you want to," Kate said.

"Sure," said her mother. "And where would I be then?"

"I don't know. Maybe Venezuela."

"They don't even have plumbing in Venezuela."

"Yes, but their sunsets are perfect, and the villages are full of dark passionate men in blousy shirts."

"That's your department, not mine."

"Ha," Kate said, "I wish it were my department. Sounds a lot more exciting than teaching undergraduates."

Her mother laughed. "Be careful," she said. "You'll get what you want. End up sweeping a dirt floor with a squawling baby around your neck."

"A dark baby," Kate said, "to stir up the family blood."

"Nothing would surprise me," her mother said as the line went fuzzy. Her voice was submerged in static, then surfaced. "Listen," she was saying. "Write to me. You seem so far away."

They hung up and Kate sat watching the windows of the neighboring house. The curtains were transparent and flowered and none of them matched. Silhouettes of the window frames spread across them like single dark bars. Her mother's curtains were all the same, white cotton hemmed with a ruffle, tiebacks blousing the cloth into identical shapes. From the street it looked as if the house was always in order.

Kate made a cup of strong Chinese tea, turned the lights off, and sat holding the warm cup in the dark. Her mother kept no real tea in the house, just packets of instant diabetic mixture which tasted of chemical sweetener and had a bitter aftertaste. The packets sat on the shelf next to her mother's miniature scales. The scales were white. Kate saw clearly the face of the metal dial on the front, its markings and trembling needle. Her mother weighed portions of food for meals: frozen broccoli, slices of plastic-wrapped Kraft cheese, careful chunks of roast beef. A dog-eared copy of *The Diabetic Diet* had remained propped against the salt shaker for the last two years.

Kate rubbed her forehead. Often at night she had headaches. Sometimes she wondered if there were an agent in her body, a secret in her blood making ready to work against her.

The phone blared repeatedly, careening into her sleep. Kate scrambled out of bed, naked and cold, stumbling, before she recognized the striped wallpaper of her bedroom and realized the phone was right there on the bedside table, as always. She picked up the receiver.

"Kate?" said her brother's voice. "It's Robert. Mom is in the hospital. They don't know what's wrong but she's in for tests."

"Tests? What's happened? I just talked to her last night."

"I'm not sure. She called the neighbors and they took her to the emergency room around dawn." Robert's voice still had that slight twang Kate knew was disappearing from her own. He would be calling from his insurance office, nine o'clock their time, in his thick glasses and wide, perfectly knotted tie. He was a member of the million-dollar club[1] and his picture, tiny, the size of a postage stamp, appeared in the Mutual of Omaha magazine. His voice seemed small too over the distance. Kate felt heavy and dull. She would never make much money, and recently she had begun wearing make-up again, waking in smeared mascara as she had in high school.

"Is Mom all right?" she managed now. "How serious is it?"

"They're not sure," Robert said. "Her doctor thinks it could have been any of several things, but they're doing X rays."

1. I.e., has been honored by his employees for selling more than a million dollars worth of insurance.

"Her doctor *thinks?* Doesn't he know? Get her to someone else. There aren't any doctors in that one-horse town."

"I don't know about that," Robert said defensively. "Anyway, I can't force her. You know how she is about money."

"Money? She could have a stroke and drop dead while her doctor wonders what's wrong."

"Doesn't matter. You know you can't tell her what to do."

"Could I call her somehow?"

"No, not yet. And don't get her all worried. She's been scared enough as it is. I'll tell her what you said about getting another opinion, and I'll call you back in a few hours when I have some news. Meanwhile, she's all right, do you hear?"

The line went dead with a click and Kate walked to the bathroom to wash her face. She splashed her eyes and felt guilty about the Valentine's card. Slogans danced in her head like reprimands. *For A Special One. Dearest Mother. My Best Friend.* Despite Robert, after breakfast she would call the hospital.

She sat a long time with her coffee, waiting for minutes to pass, considering how many meals she and her mother ate alone. Similar times of day, hundreds of miles apart. Women by themselves. The last person Kate had eaten breakfast with had been someone she'd met in a bar. He was passing through town. He liked his fried eggs gelatinized in the center, only slightly runny, and Kate had studiously looked away as he ate. The night before he'd looked down from above her as he finished and she still moved under him. "You're still wanting," he'd said. "That's nice." Mornings now, Kate saw her own face in the mirror and was glad she'd forgotten his name. When she looked at her reflection from the side, she saw a faint etching of lines beside her mouth. She hadn't slept with anyone for five weeks, and the skin beneath her eyes had taken on a creamy darkness.

She reached for the phone but drew back. It seemed bad luck to ask for news, to push toward whatever was coming as though she had no respect for it.

Standing in the kitchen last summer, her mother had stirred gravy and argued with her.

"I'm thinking of your own good, not mine," she'd said. "Thinking of what you put yourself through. And how can you feel right about it? You were born here, I don't care what you say." Her voice broke and she looked, perplexed, at the broth in the pan.

"But, hypothetically," Kate continued, her own voice unaccountably shaking, "if I'm willing to endure whatever I have to, do you have a right to object? You're my mother. You're supposed to defend my choices."

"You'll have enough trouble without choosing more for yourself.

Using birth control that'll ruin your insides, moving from one place to another. I can't defend your choices. I can't even defend myself against you." She wiped her eyes on a napkin.

"Why do you have to make me feel so guilty?" Kate said, fighting tears of frustration. "I'm not attacking you."

"You're not? Then who are you talking to?"

"Oh Mom, give me a break."

"I've tried to give you more than that," her mother said. "I know what your choices are saying to me." She set the steaming gravy off the stove. "You may feel very differently later on. It's just a shame I won't be around to see it."

"Oh? Where will you be?"

"Floating around on a fleecy cloud."

Kate got up to set the table before she realized her mother had already done it.

The days went by. They'd gone shopping before Kate left. Standing at the cash register in an antique shop on Main Street, they bought each other pewter candle holders. "A souvenir," her mother said. "A reminder to always be nice to yourself. If you live alone you should eat by candlelight."

"Listen," Kate said, "I eat in a heart-shaped tub with bubbles to my chin. I sleep on satin sheets and my mattress has a built-in massage engine. My overnight guests are impressed. You don't have to tell me about the solitary pleasures."

They laughed and touched hands.

"Well," her mother said. "If you like yourself, I must have done something right."

Robert didn't phone until evening. His voice was fatigued and thin. "I've moved her to the university hospital," he said. "They can't deal with it at home."

Kate waited, saying nothing. She concentrated on the toes of her shoes. They needed shining. *You never take care of anything,* her mother would say.

"She has a tumor in her head." He said it firmly, as though Kate might challenge him.

"I'll take a plane tomorrow morning," Kate answered, "I'll be there by noon."

Robert exhaled. "Look," he said, "don't even come back here unless you can keep your mouth shut and do it my way."

"Get to the point."

"The point is they believe she has a malignancy and we're not going to tell her. I almost didn't tell you." His voice faltered. "They're going to operate but if they find what they're expecting, they don't think they can stop it."

For a moment there was no sound except an oceanic vibration of distance on the wire. Even that sound grew still. Robert breathed. Kate could almost see him, in a booth at the hospital, staring straight ahead at the plastic instructions screwed to the narrow rectangular body of the telephone. It seemed to her that she was hurtling toward him.

"I'll do it your way," she said.

The hospital cafeteria was a large room full of orange Formica tables. Its southern wall was glass. Across the highway, Kate saw a small park modestly dotted with amusement rides and bordered by a narrow band of river. How odd, to build a children's park across from a medical center. The sight was pleasant in a cruel way. The rolling lawn of the little park was perfectly, relentlessly green.

Robert sat down. Their mother was to have surgery in two days.

"After it's over," he said, "they're not certain what will happen. The tumor is in a bad place. There may be some paralysis."

"What kind of paralysis?" Kate said. She watched him twist the green-edged coffee cup around and around on its saucer.

"Facial. And maybe worse."

"You've told her this?"

He didn't answer.

"Robert, what is she going to think if she wakes up and—"

He leaned forward, grasping the cup and speaking through clenched teeth. "Don't you think I thought of that?" He gripped the sides of the table and the cup rolled onto the carpeted floor with a dull thud. He seemed ready to throw the table after it, then grabbed Kate's wrists and squeezed them hard.

"You didn't drive her here," he said. "She was so scared she couldn't talk. How much do you want to hand her at once?"

Kate watched the cup sitting solidly on the nubby carpet.

"We've told her it's benign," Robert said, "that the surgery will cause complications, but she can learn back whatever is lost."

Kate looked at him. "Is that true?"

"They hope so."

"We're lying to her, all of us, more and more." Kate pulled her hands away and Robert touched her shoulder.

"What do *you* want to tell her, Kate? 'You're fifty-five and you're done for'?"

She stiffened. "Why put her through the operation at all?"

He sat back and dropped his arms, lowering his head. "Because without it she'd be in bad pain. Soon." They were silent, then he looked up. "And anyway," he said softly, "we don't *know*, do we? She may have a better chance than they think."

Kate put her hands on her face. Behind her closed eyes she saw a succession of blocks tumbling over.

They took the elevator up to the hospital room. They were alone and they stood close together. Above the door red numerals lit up, flashing. Behind the illuminated shapes droned an impersonal hum of machinery.

Then the doors opened with a sucking sound. Three nurses stood waiting with a lunch cart, identical covered trays stacked in tiers. There was a hot bland smell, like warm cardboard. One of the women caught the thick steel door with her arm and smiled. Kate looked quickly at their rubber-soled shoes. White polish, the kind that rubs off. And their legs seemed only white shapes, boneless and two-dimensional, stepping silently into the metal cage.

She looked smaller in the white bed. The chrome side rails were pulled up and she seemed powerless behind them, her dark hair pushed back from her face and her forearms delicate in the baggy hospital gown. Her eyes were different in some nearly imperceptible way; she held them wider, they were shiny with a veiled wetness. For a moment the room seemed empty of all else; there were only her eyes and the dark blossoms of the flowers on the table beside her. Red roses with pine. Everyone had sent the same thing.

Robert walked close to the bed with his hands clasped behind his back, as though afraid to touch. "Where did all the flowers come from?" he asked.

"From school, and the neighbors. And Katie." She smiled.

"FTD," Kate said. "Before I left home. I felt so bad for not being here all along."

"That's silly," said their mother. "You can hardly sit at home and wait for some problem to arise."

"Speaking of problems," Robert said, "the doctor tells me you're not eating. Do I have to urge you a little?" He sat down on the edge of the bed and shook the silverware from its paper sleeve.

Kate touched the plastic tray. "Jell-O and canned cream of chicken soup. Looks great. We should have brought you something."

"They don't *want* us to bring her anything," Robert said. "This is a hospital. And I'm sure your comments make her lunch seem even more appetizing."

"I'll eat it!" said their mother in mock dismay. "Admit they sent you in here to stage a battle until I gave in."

"I'm sorry," Kate said. "He's right."

Robert grinned. "Did you hear that? She says I'm right. I don't believe it." He pushed the tray closer to his mother's chest and made a show of tucking a napkin under her chin.

"Of course you're right, dear." She smiled and gave Kate an obvious wink.

"Yeah," Robert said, "I know you two. But seriously, you eat this. I have to go make some business calls from the motel room."

Their mother frowned. "That motel must be costing you a fortune."

"No, it's reasonable," he said. "Kate can stay for a week or two and I'll drive back and forth from home. If you think this food is bad, you should see the meals in that motel restaurant." He got up to go, flashing Kate a glance of collusion. "I'll be back after supper."

His footsteps echoed down the hallway. Kate and her mother looked wordlessly at each other, relieved. Kate looked away guiltily. Then her mother spoke, apologetic. "He's so tired," she said. "He's been with me since yesterday."

She looked at Kate, then into the air of the room. "I'm in a fix," she said. "Except for when the pain comes, it's all a show that goes on without me. I'm like an invalid, or a lunatic."

Kate moved close and touched her mother's arms. "That's all right, we're going to get you through it. Someone's covering for you at work?"

"I had to take a leave of absence. It's going to take a while afterward—"

"I know. But it's the last thing to worry about, it can't be helped."

"Like spilt milk. Isn't that what they say?"

"I don't know what they say. But why didn't you tell me? Didn't you know something was wrong?"

"Yes . . . bad headaches. Migraines, I thought, or the diabetes getting worse. I was afraid they'd start me on insulin." She tightened the corner of her mouth. "Little did I know . . ."

They heard the shuffle of slippers. An old woman stood at the open door of the room, looking in confusedly. She seemed about to speak, then moved on.

"Oh," said Kate's mother in exasperation, "shut that door, please? They let these old women wander around like refugees." She sat up, reaching for a robe. "And let's get me out of this bed."

They sat near the window while she finished eating. Bars of moted yellow banded the floor of the room. The light held a tinge of spring which seemed painful because it might vanish. They heard the rattle of the meal cart outside the closed door, and the clunk-slide of patients with aluminum walkers. Kate's mother sighed and pushed away the half-empty soup bowl.

"They'll be here after me any minute. More tests. I just want to stay with you." Her face was warm and smooth in the slanted light, lines in her skin delicate, unreal; as though a face behind her face was now apparent after many years. She sat looking at Kate and smiled.

"One day when you were about four you were dragging a broom around the kitchen. I asked what you were doing and you told me that when you got old you were going to be an angel and sweep the rotten rain off the clouds."

"What did you say to that?"

"I said that when you were old I was sure God would see to it," Her mother laughed. "I'm glad you weren't such a smart aleck then," she said. "You would have told me my view of God was paternalistic."

"Ah yes," sighed Kate. "God, that famous dude. Here I am, getting old, facing unemployment, alone, and where is He?"

"You're not alone," her mother said, "I'm right here."

Kate didn't answer. She sat motionless and felt her heart begin to open like a box with a hinged lid. The fullness had no edges.

Her mother stood. She rubbed her hands slowly, twisting her wedding rings. "My hands are so dry in the winter," she said softly, "I brought some hand cream with me but I can't find it anywhere, my suitcase is so jumbled. Thank heavens spring is early this year. . . . They told me that little park over there doesn't usually open till the end of March . . ."

She's helping me, thought Kate, I'm not supposed to let her down.

". . . but they're already running it on weekends. Even past dusk. We'll see the lights tonight. You can't see the shapes this far away, just the motion . . ."

A nurse came in with a wheelchair. Kate's mother pulled a wry face. "This wheelchair is a bit much," she said.

"We don't want to tire you out," said the nurse.

The chair took her weight quietly. At the door she put out her hand to stop, turned, and said anxiously, "Kate, see if you can find that hand cream?"

It was the blue suitcase from years ago, still almost new. She's brought things she never used for everyday; a cashmere sweater, lace slips, silk underpants wrapped in tissue. Folded beneath was a stack of postmarked envelopes, slightly ragged, tied with twine. Kate opened one and realized that all the cards were there, beginning with the first of the marriage. There were a few photographs of her and Robert, baby pitchers almost indistinguishable from each other, and then Kate's homemade Valentines, fastened together with rubber bands. Kate stared. *What will I do with these things?* She wanted air; she needed to breathe. She walked to the window and put the bundled papers on the sill. She'd raised the glass and pushed back the screen when suddenly, her mother's clock radio went off with a flat buzz. Kate moved to switch it off and brushed the cards with her arm. Envelopes shifted and slid, scattering on the floor of the room. A few snapshots wafted silently out the window. They dipped and turned, twirling. Kate didn't try to reach them. They seemed only scraps, buoyant and yellowed, blown away, the faces small as pennies. Somewhere far-off there were sirens, almost musical, drawn out and carefully approaching.

The nurse came in with evening medication. Kate's mother lay in bed. "I hope this is strong enough," she said. "Last night I couldn't sleep at all. So many sounds in a hospital . . ."

"You'll sleep tonight," the nurse assured her.

Kate winked at her mother. "That's right," she said, "I'll help you out if I have to."

They stayed up for an hour, watching the moving lights outside and the stationary glows of houses across the distant river. The halls grew darker, were lit with night lights, and the hospital dimmed. Kate waited. Her mother's eyes fluttered and finally she slept. Her breathing was low and regular.

Kate didn't move. Robert had said he'd be back; where was he? She felt a sunken anger and shook her head. She'd been on the point of telling her mother everything. The secrets were a travesty. What if there were things her mother wanted done, people she needed to see? Kate wanted to wake her before these hours passed in the dark and confess that she had lied. Between them, through the tension, there had always been a trusted clarity. Now it was twisted. Kate sat leaning forward, nearly touching the hospital bed.

Suddenly her mother sat bolt upright, her eyes open and her face transfixed. She looked blindly toward Kate but seemed to see nothing. "Who are you?" she whispered. Kate stood, at first unable to move. The woman in the bed opened and closed her mouth several times, as though she were gasping. Then she said loudly, "Stop moving the table. Stop it this instant!" Her eyes were wide with fright and her body was vibrating.

Kate reached her. "Mama, wake up, you're dreaming." Her mother jerked, flinging her arms out. Kate held her tightly.

"I can hear the wheels," she moaned.

"No, no," Kate said. "You're here with me."

"It's not so?"

"No," Kate said. "It's not so."

She went limp. Kate felt for her pulse and found it rapid, then regular. She sat rocking her mother. In a few minutes she lay her back on the pillows and smoothed the damp hair at her temples, smoothed the sheets of the bed. Later she slept fitfully in a chair, waking repeatedly to assure herself that her mother was breathing.

Near dawn she got up, exhausted, and left the room to walk in the corridor. In front of the window at the end of the hallway she saw a man slumped on a couch; the man slowly stood and wavered before her like a specter. It was Robert.

"Kate?" he said.

Years ago he had flunked out of a small junior college and their mother sat in her bedroom rocker, crying hard for over an hour while Kate tried in vain to comfort her. Kate went to the university the next fall, so anxious that she studied frantically, outlining whole textbooks in yellow ink. She sat in the front rows of large classrooms to take voluminous notes, writing quickly in her thick notebook. Robert had gone home, held a job in a plant that manufactured business forms and worked his way through the hometown college. By that time their father was dead, and Robert became, always and forever, the man of the house.

"Robert," Kate said, "I'll stay. Go home."

After breakfast they sat waiting for Robert, who had called and said he'd arrive soon. Kate's fatigue had given way to an intense awareness of every sound, every gesture. How would they get through the day? Her mother had awakened from the drugged sleep still groggy, unable to eat. The meal was sent away untouched and she watched the window as though she feared the walls of the room.

"I'm glad your father isn't here to see this," she said. There was a silence and Kate opened her mouth to speak. "I mean," said her mother quickly, "I'm going to look horrible for a few weeks, with my head all shaved." She pulled an afghan up around her lap and straightened the magazines on the table beside her chair.

"Mom," Kate said, "your hair will grow back."

Her mother pulled the afghan closer. "I've been thinking of your father," she said. "It's not that I'd have wanted him to suffer. But if he had to die, sometimes I wish he'd done it more gently. That heart attack, so finished; never a warning. I wish I'd had some time to nurse him. In a way, it's a chance to settle things."

"Did things need settling?"

"They always do, don't they?" She sat looking out the window, then said softly, "I wonder where I'm headed."

"You're not headed anywhere." Kate said. "I want you right here to see me settle down into normal American womanhood."

Her mother smiled reassuringly. "Where are my grandchildren?" she said. "That's what I'd like to know."

"You stick around," said Kate, "and I promise to start working on it." She moved her chair closer, so that their knees were touching and they could both see out the window. Below them cars moved on the highway and the Ferris wheel in the little park was turning.

"I remember when you were one of the little girls in the parade at the country fair. You weren't even in school yet; you were beautiful in that white organdy dress and pinafore. You wore those shiny black patent shoes and a crown of real apple blossoms. Do you remember?"

"Yes," Kate said. "That long parade. They told me not to move and I sat so still my legs went to sleep. When they lifted me off the float I couldn't stand up. They put me under a tree to wait for you, and you came, in a full white skirt and white sandals, your hair tied back in a red scarf. I can see you yet."

Her mother laughed. "Sounds like a pretty exaggerated picture."

Kate nodded. "I was little. You were big."

"You loved the county fair. You were wild about the carnivals." They looked down at the little park. "Magic, isn't it?" her mother said.

"Maybe we could go see it," said Kate. "I'll ask the doctor."

They walked across a pedestrian footbridge spanning the highway. Kate had bundled her mother into a winter coat and gloves despite the sunny weather. The day was sharp, nearly still, holding its bright air like illusion. Kate tasted the brittle water of her breath, felt for the cool handrail and thin steel of the webbed fencing. Cars moved steadily under the bridge. Beyond a muted roar of motors the park spread green and wooded, its limits clearly visible.

Kate's mother had combed her hair and put on lipstick. Her mouth was defined and brilliant; she linked arms with Kate like an escort. "I was afraid they'd tell us no," she said. "I was ready to run away!"

"I promised I wouldn't let you. And we only have ten minutes, long enough for the Ferris wheel." Kate grinned.

"I haven't ridden one in years. I wonder if I still know how."

"Of course you do. Ferris wheels are genetic knowledge."

"All right, whatever you say." She smiled. "We'll just hold on."

They drew closer and walked quickly through the sounds of the highway. When they reached the grass it was ankle-high and thick, longer and more ragged than it appeared from a distance. The Ferris wheel sat squarely near a grove of swaying elms, squat and laboring, taller than trees. Its neon lights still burned, pale in the sun, spiraling from inside like an imagined bloom. The naked elms surrounded it, their topmost branches tapping. Steel ribs of the machine were graceful and slightly rusted, squeaking faintly above a tinkling music. Only a few people were riding.

"Looks a little rickety," Kate said.

"Oh, don't worry," said her mother.

Kate tried to buy tickets but the ride was free. The old man running the motor wore an engineer's cap and patched overalls. He stopped the wheel and led them on a short ramp to an open car. It dipped gently, padded with black cushions. An orderly and his children rode in the car above. Kate saw their dangling feet, the girls' dusty sandals and gray socks beside their father's shoes and the hem of his white pants. The youngest one swung her feet absently, so it seemed the breeze blew her legs like fabric hung on a line.

Kate looked at her mother. "Are you ready for the big sky?" They laughed. Beyond them the river moved lazily. Houses on the opposite bank seemed empty, but a few rowboats bobbed at the docks. The surface of the water lapped and reflected clouds, and as Kate watched, searching for a definition of line, the Ferris wheel jerked into motion. The car rocked. They looked into the distance and Kate caught her mother's hand as they ascended.

Far away the hospital rose up white and glistening, its windows catching the glint of the sun. Directly below, the park was nearly deserted. There were a few cars in the parking lot and several dogs chasing each other across the grass. Two or three lone women held children on the teeter-totters and a wind was coming up. The forlorn swings moved on their chains. Kate had a vision of the park at night, totally empty, wind weaving heavily through the trees and children's playthings like a great black fish about to surface. She felt a chill on her arms. The light had gone darker, quietly, like a minor chord.

"Mom," Kate said, "it's going to storm." Her own voice seemed distant, the sound strained through layers of screen or gauze.

"No," said her mother, "it's going to pass over." She moved her hand to Kate's knee and touched the cloth of her daughter's skirt.

Kate gripped the metal bar at their waists and looked straight ahead. They were rising again and she felt she would scream. She tried to breathe rhythmically, steadily. She felt the immense weight of the air as they moved through it.

They came almost to the top and stopped. The little car swayed back and forth.

"You're sick, aren't you," her mother said.

Kate shook her head. Below them the grass seemed to glitter coldly, like a sea. Kate sat wordless, feeling the touch of her mother's hand. The hand moved away and Kate felt the absence of the warmth.

They looked at each other levelly.

"I know all about it," her mother said, "I know what you haven't told me."

The sky circled around them, a sure gray movement. Kate swallowed calmly and let their gaze grow endless. She saw herself in her mother's wide brown eyes and felt she was falling slowly into them.

KIT REED

Winter

IT was late fall when he come to us, there was a scum of ice on all the puddles and I could feel the winter cold and fearsome in my bones, the hunger inside me was already uncurling, it would pace through the first of the year but by spring it would be raging like a tiger, consuming me until the thaw when Maude could hunt again and we would get the truck down the road to town. I was done canning but I got the tomatoes we had hanging in the cellar and I canned some more; Maude went out and brought back every piece of meat she could shoot and all the grain and flour and powdered milk she could bring in one truckload, we had to lay in everything we could before the snow could come and seal us in. The week he come Maud found a jack-rabbit stone dead in the road, it was frozen with its feet sticking straight up, and all the meat hanging in the cold room had froze. Friday there was rime on the grass and when I looked out I seen footprints in the rime, I said Maude, someone is in the playhouse and we went out and there he was. He was asleep in the mess of clothes we always dressed up in, he had his head on the velvet gown my mother wore to the Exposition and his feet on the satin gown she married Father in, he had pulled her feather boa around his neck and her fox fur was wrapped around his loins.

Before he come, Maude and me would pass the winter talking about how it used to be, we would call up the past between us and look at it and Maude would end by blaming me. I could of married either Lister Hoffman or Harry Mead and left this place for good if it hadn't been for you, Lizzie. I'd tell her, Hell, I never needed you. You didn't marry them because you didn't marry them, you was scared of it and you would use me for an excuse. She would get mad then. It's a lie. Have it your way, I would tell her, just to keep the peace.

We both knew I would of married the first man that asked me, but nobody would, not even with all my money, nobody would ask me because of the taint. If nobody had of known then some man might of married me, but I went down to the field with Miles Harrison once while Father was still alive, and Miles and me, we almost, except that the blackness took me, right there in front of him, and so I never did. Nobody needed to know, but then Miles saw me fall down in the field. I guess it was him that put something between my teeth, but when I come to myself he was gone. Next time I went to town they all looked at me funny, some of them would try and face up to me and be polite but they was all jumpy, thinking would I do it right there in front of them, would I froth much, would they be hurt, as soon as was decent they would say Excuse me, I got to, anything to get out of there fast. When I run into Miles that day he wouldn't look at me and there hasn't been a man near me since then, not in more than fifty years, but Miles and me, we almost, and I have never stopped thinking about that.

Now Father is gone and my mother is gone and even Lister Hoffman and Miles Harrison and half the town kids that used to laugh at me, they are all gone, but Maude still reproaches me, we sit after supper and she says If it hadn't been for you I would have grandchildren now and I tell her I would have had them before she ever did because she never liked men, she would only suffer them to get children and that would be too much trouble, it would hurt. That's a lie, Lizzie, she would say, Harry and me used to . . . and I would tell her You never, but Miles and me . . . Then we would both think about being young and having people's hands on us but memory turns Maude bitter and she can never leave it at that, she says, It's all your fault, but I know in my heart that people make their lives what they want them, and all she ever wanted was to be locked in here with nobody to make demands on her, she wanted to stay in this house with me, her dried-up sister, cold and safe, and if the hunger is on her, it has come on her late.

After a while we would start to make up stuff: Once I went with a boy all the way to Portland . . . Once I danced all night and half the morning, he wanted to kiss me on the place where my elbow bends . . . We would try to spin out the winter but even that was not enough and so we would always be left with the hunger; no matter how much we laid in, the meat was always gone before the thaw and I suppose it was really our lives we was judging but we would decide nothing in the cans looked good to us and so we would sit and dream and hunger and wonder if we would die of it, but finally the thaw would come and Maude would look at me and sigh: If only we had another chance.

Well now perhaps we will.

We found him in the playhouse, maybe it was seeing him being in the playhouse, where we pretended so many times, asleep in the middle of my mother's clothes or maybe it was but there was this boy, or man, and something about him called up our best memories, there was promise wrote all over him. I am too old, I am all dried out, but I have never stopped thinking about that one time and seeing that boy there, I could pretend he was Miles and I was still young. I guess he sensed us, he woke up fast and went into a crouch, maybe he had a knife, and then I guess he saw it was just two big old ladies in Army boots, he said, I run away from the Marines, I needed a place to sleep.

Maude said, I don't care what you need, you got to get out of here, but when he stood up he wobbled. His hair fell across his head like the hair on a boy I used to know and I said, Maude, why don't you say yes to something just this once.

He had on this denim shirt and pants like no uniform I ever seen and he was saying, Two things happened, I found out I might have to shoot somebody in the war and then I made a mistake and they beat me so I cut out of there. He smiled and he looked open. I stared hard at Maude and Maude finally looked at me and said, All right, come up to the house and get something to eat.

He said his name was Arnold but when we asked him Arnold what, he said Never mind. He was in the kitchen by then, he had his head bent over a bowl of oatmeal and some biscuits I had made, and when I looked at Maude she was watching the way the light slid across his hair. When we told him our names he said, You are both beautiful ladies. I could see Maude's hands go up to her face and she went into her room and when she come back I saw she had put colour on her cheeks. While we was alone he said how good the biscuits was and wasn't that beautiful silver, did I keep it polished all myself and I said well yes, Maude brings in supplies but I am in charge of the house and making all the food. She come back then and saw us with our heads together and said to Arnold, I guess you'll be leaving soon.

I don't know, he said, they'll be out looking for me with guns and dogs.

That's no never mind of ours.

I never done nothing bad in the Marines, we just had different ideas. We both figured it was something worse but he looked so sad and tired and besides, it was nice to have him to talk to, he said, I just need a place to hole up for a while.

Maude said, You could always go back to your family.

He said, They never wanted me. They was always mean-hearted, not like you.

I took her side and said, It wouldn't kill you to let him stay on, Maude, it's time we had a little life around here.

There won't be enough food for three.

He won't stay long. Besides, he can help you with the chores.

She was looking at his bright hair again, she said, like it was all my doing, If you want to let him stay I guess we can let him stay.

He was saying, I could work for my keep.

All right, I said, you can stay on until you get your strength.

My heart jumped. A man, I thought. A man. How can I explain it? It was like being young, having him around. I looked at Maude and saw some of the same things in her eyes, hunger and hope, and I thought, You are ours now, Arnold, you are all ours. We will feed you and take care of you and when you want to wander we will let you wander, but we will never let you go.

Just until things die down a little, he was saying.

Maude had a funny grin. Just until things die down.

Well it must of started snowing right after dark that afternoon, because when we all waked up the house was surrounded. I said, Good thing you got the meat in, Maude, and she looked out, it was still blowing snow and it showed no signs of stopping, she looked out and said, I guess it is.

He was still asleep, he slept the day through except he stumbled down at dusk and dreamed over a bowl of my rabbit stew, I turned to the sink and when I looked back the stew was gone and the biscuits was gone and all the extra in the pot was gone, I had a little flash of fright, it was all disappearing too fast. Then Maude come over to me and hissed, The food, he's eating all the food and I looked at his brown hands and his tender neck and I said, It don't matter, Maude, he's young and strong and if we run short he can go out into the snow and hunt. When we looked around next time he was gone, he had dreamed his way through half a pie and gone right back to bed.

Next morning he was up before the light, we sat together around the kitchen table and I thought how nice it was to have a man in the house, I could look at him and imagine anything I wanted. Then he got up and said, Look, I want to thank you for everything, I got to get along now and I said, You can't, and he said, I got things to do, I been here long enough, but I told him You can't, and took him over to the window. The sun was up by then and there it was, snow almost to the window ledges, like we have every winter, and all the trees was shrouded, we could watch the sun take the snow and make it sparkle and I said, Beautiful snow, beautiful, and he only shrugged and said, I guess I'll have to wait till it clears off some. I touched his shoulder. I guess it will. I knew not to tell him it would never clear off, not until late spring; maybe he guessed, anyway he looked so sad I gave him Father's silver snuffbox to cheer him up.

He would divide his time between Maude and me, he played Rook with her and made her laugh so hard she gave him her pearl earrings and the brooch Father brought her back from Quebec. I gave him Grandfather's diamond stickpin because he admired it, and for Christmas we gave him the cameos and Father's gold-headed cane. Maude got the flu over New Year and Arnold and me spent New Year's Eve together, I mulled some wine and he hung up some of Mama's jewelry from the centre light, and touched it and made it twirl. We lit candles and played the radio, New Year's Eve in Times Square and somebody's Make-believe Ballroom, I went to pour another cup of wine and his hand was on mine on the bottle, I knew my lips was red for once and next day I gave him Papa's fur-lined coat.

I guess Maude suspected there was something between us, she looked pinched and mean when I went in with her broth at lunch, she said, Where were you at breakfast and I said, Maude, it's New Year's Day, I thought I would like to sleep in for once. She was quick and spiteful. You were with him. I thought, If she wants to think that about me, let her, and I let my eyes go sleepy and I said, We had to see the New Year in, didn't we? She was out of bed in two days, I have never seen anybody get up so fast after the flu. I think she couldn't stand us being where she couldn't see what we was up to every living minute. Then I got sick and I knew what torture it must have been for her, just laying there, I would call Maude and I would call her, and sometimes she would come and sometimes she wouldn't come and when she finally did look in on me I would say, Maude, where have you been and she would only giggle and not answer. There was meat cooking all the time, roasts and chops and chicken fricassee, when I said Maude, you're going to use it up, she would only smile and say, I just had to show him who's who in the kitchen, he tells me I'm a better cook than you ever was. After a while I got up, I had to even if I was dizzy and like to throw up, I had to get downstairs where I could keep an eye on them. As soon as I was up to it I made a roast of venison that would put hair on an egg and after that we would vie with each other in the kitchen, Maude and me. Once I had my hand on the skillet handle and she come over and tried to take it away, she was saying, Let me serve it up for him. I said, you're a fool, Maude, I cooked this and she hissed at me, through the steam, it won't do you no good, Lizzie, it's me he loves, and I just pushed her away and said, you goddam fool, he loves me, and I give him my amethysts just to prove it. A couple of days later I couldn't find neither of them nowhere, I thought I heard noises up in the back room and I went up there and if they was in there they wouldn't answer, the door was locked and they wouldn't say nothing, not even when I knocked and knocked and knocked. So the next day I took him up in my room and we locked the door and I told him a story about every piece in my jewel box, even the cheap ones, when Maude tapped and whined outside the door we would just shush, and when we did come out and she said, All right, Lizzie, what was you doing in there, I only giggled and wouldn't tell.

She shouldn't of done it, we was all sitting around the table after dinner and she looked at me hard and said, You know something, Arnold, I wouldn't get too close to Lizzie, she has fits. Arnold only tried to look like it didn't matter, but after Maude went to bed I went down to make sure it was all right. He was still in the kitchen, whittling, and when I tried to touch his hand he pulled away.

I said, Don't be scared, I only throw one in a blue moon.

He said, That don't matter.

Then what's the matter?

I don't know, Miss Lizzie, I just don't think you trust me.

Course I trust you, Arnold, don't I give you everything?

He just looked sad. Everything but trust.

I owe you so much, Arnold, you make me feel so young.

He just smiled for me then. You look younger, Miss Lizzie, you been getting younger every day I been here.

You did it.

If you let me, I could make you really young.

Yes, Arnold, yes.

But I have to know you trust me.

Yes, Arnold.

So I showed him where the money was. By then it was past midnight and we was both tired, he said, Tomorrow, and I let him go off to get his rest.

I don't know what roused us both and brought us out into the hall but I bumped into Maude at dawn, we was both standing in our nightgowns like two ghosts. We crept downstairs together and there was light in the kitchen, the place where we kept the money was open, empty, and there was a crack of light in the door to the coldroom. I remember looking through and thinking, The meat is almost gone. Then we opened the door a crack wider and there he was, he had made a sledge, he must of sneaked down there and worked on it every night. It was piled with stuff, our stuff, and now he had the door to the outside open, he had dug himself a ramp out of the snow and he was lashing some home-made snowshoes on his feet, in another minute he would cut out of there.

When he heard us he turned.

I had the shotgun and Maude had the axe.

He said, You can have all your stuff.

We said, We don't care about the stuff, Arnold, How could we tell him it was our youth he was taking away?

He looked at us, wall-eyed. You can have it all, just let me out.

You said you loved us, Arnold.

He was scrabbling up the snow ramp. Never mind what I told you, let me out of here.

He was going to get away in another minute, so Maude let him have it with the axe.

Afterward we closed the way to the outside and stood there and looked at each other, I couldn't say what was in my heart so I only looked at Maude, we was both sad, sad, I said. The food is almost gone.

Maude said, Everything is gone. We'll never make it to spring.

Maude looked at him laying there. You know what he told me? He said, I can make you young.

Me too, I said. There was something in his eyes that made me believe it.

Maude's eyes was aglitter, she said, The food is almost gone.

I knew what she meant, he was going to make us young. I don't know how it will work in us, but he is going to make us young, it will be as if the fits had never took me, never in all them years. Maude was looking at me, waiting, and after a minute I looked square at her and I said, I know.

So we et him.

TOM ROBBINS

The Chink and the Clock People

TO NEITHER the Siwash nor the Chinese does the Chink belong.

As are many of the best and worse contributions to the human race, the Chink is Japanese. With their flair for inventive imitation, the Japanese made the Chink.

He was born on an island in the Ryukyu chain. It was called an island, but in actuality it was a volcano, a half-submerged dunce cap that Nature had once placed on the noggin of the sea for forgetting which had come first, land or water. For centuries this volcano had sent shock after shock of purple smoke into the sky. It was a chain smoker. A Ryukyu chain smoker.

Upon the sides of this smoking volcanic cone the Chink's parents had raised yams, and the little Chink had played. Once when he was six, he climbed to the top of the volcano. His sister found him there, on the edge of the crater, unconscious from the fumes, his hair and eyebrows singed. He had been looking in.

When he was eight, he emigrated to the United States of America, where his uncle tended gardens in San Francisco. The Chink picked up English and other bad habits. He went to high school and other dangerous places. He earned American citizenship and other dubious distinctions.

When asked what he wished to do with his life, he answered (although he had learned to appreciate movies, jukebox music, and cheerleaders) that he wanted to grow yams on the side of a volcano—but as that was impractical in the city of San Francisco, he became, like Uncle, a gardener. For more than a dozen years he made the grass greener and the flowers flowerier on the campus of the University of California at Berkeley.

By special arrangement with his employers, the Chink attended one class a day at the university. Over a twelve-year span he completed a good many courses. He was never graduated, but it would be a mistake to assume he did not receive an education.

He was astute enough to warn his relatives, on December 8, 1941, the day after Pearl Harbor, "We'd better get our yellow asses back to some safe volcano and eat yams till this blows over." They didn't listen. After all, they were patriotic, property-owning, tax-paying American citizens.

The Chink wasn't anxious to flee, either. He was in love again. Camping on the rim of a different volcano.

On February 20, 1942, came the order. Two weeks later, the army took steps. In March, evacuation was in full swing. Some 110,000 people of Japanese ancestry were moved out of their homes in "strategic" areas of the West Coast and settled in ten "relocation" camps farther inland. They could bring to camp only what they could carry. Left behind were houses, businesses, farms, home furnishings, personal treasures, liberty. Americans of non-Nip ancestry bought up their farmland at ten cents on the dollar (the crops failed). Seventy percent of the relocated people had been born and reared in the U.S.

"Loyal" Japanese were separated from "disloyal." If one would swear allegiance to the American war effort—and could pass an FBI investigation—one had the choice of remaining in a relocation camp or finding employment in some nonstrategic area. The camps were militaristic formations of tarpaper barracks, supplied with canvas cots and pot-bellied stoves. Six to nine families lived in a barracks. Partitions between "apartments" were as thin as crackers and did not reach the ceiling (even so, there were an average of twenty-five births per month in most camps). There was no great rush to leave the camps: a loyal family that had been relocated on an Arkansas farm had been killed by an irate anti-Jap mob.

Disloyal Japanese-Americans—those who expressed excessive bitterness over the loss of their property and the disruption of their lives, or who for various other reasons were suspected of being dangeous to national security—were given the pleasure of one another's company at a special camp, the Tule Lake Segregation Center in Siskiyou County, California. The Chink had been asked if he supported the American war effort. "Hell, no!" he replied. "Ha ha ho ho and hee hee." He waited for the logical next question, did he support the Japanese war effort, to which he would have given the same negative response. He was still waiting when the military police shoved him on the train to Tule Lake.

Tule was even less of a lake than Siwash. It had been drained so that land could be "reclaimed" for farming.

The detention camp had been built on that part of the dry lake bottom that was unsuitable for cultivation. However, the inmates (or "segregees," as the War Relocation Authority preferred to label them) were put to work on surrounding farmland, building dikes, digging irrigation ditches, and producing crops that proved once again that the greenest thumbs are often yellow.

(Perhaps the author is telling you more about Tule Lake than you want to know. But the camp, in northern California near the Oregon border, still exists, and while time, that ultimate diet pill, has reduced its 1032 buildings to their concrete foundations, the government may have plans for them which may someday be your concern.)

Baked in summer, dust-blinded in fall, frozen in winter and mud-up-to-elbows in spring, the Tule Lake camp was surrounded by a high barbed fence. Soldiers in lookout towers kept constant watch on—kids swimming in ditches, adolescents hunting rattlesnakes, old men playing Go, and women shopping for notions in a commissary where the latest issues of *True Confessions* were always on the racks. It was reported that even if the guards were removed, the segregees would not try to escape. They were afraid of Tule Lake farmers.

The Chink petitioned to be allowed to join his family in a less restrictive camp. But his FBI check disclosed that he had, over a period of years, pursued such heathen practices as jujitsu, ikebana, Sanskrit, mushroom magic, and Zen archery; that at UC he had written academic papers which suggested anarchist leanings; and that he had had repeated intimate relations with Caucasian women, including the niece of an admiral in the U.S. Navy. Please to remain at Tule Lake.

In early November of 1943, there was trouble at Tule Lake. A careless GI truckdriver accidentally killed a Japanese farm worker. Angered, the segregees refused to complete the harvest. There followed a confrontation which army spokesmen identified as a "riot." Among the 155 ringleader troublemakers who were beaten and imprisoned in the stockade was the man we now call the Chink. The Chink had not participated in the "riot," had, in fact, been looking forward to the rhythm of harvest, but camp authorities claimed that his notorious insubordinate attitude (not to mention the crazed way he had of venerating plants, vegetables, and other men's wives) contributed to unrest at the camp.

If he liked the segregation center little, he liked the stockade less. For several days and nights he meditated upon the yam, that tuber that, while remaining sweet to the taste and soft to the touch, is so tough it will thrive on the sides of live volcanos. "Yam" became his mantra. *Om mani padme yam. Hare yam-a. Wham, bam, thank-*

you yam. Hellfire and yam nation. Then, like the yam, he went underground. He tunneled out of the stockade, out of the camp.

He headed for the proverbial hills. The Cascade Mountains lay to the west, across twenty or more miles of lava beds. The lava felt sharply familiar. Each rip in his shoes brought him closer to his childhood. All night, he jogged, walked, rested, jogged. At sunrise, Mt. Shasta, a cone of diamond ice cream, a volcano on a sabbatical, adorned (like the whooping cranes) with the power of white, was waiting. Encouraging him. An hour after dawn he was in tree-cover.

His plan was to follow the crest trail through the Cascades, down the full length of the Sierra Nevada, and into Mexico. In the spring, perhaps, he would wetback into the U.S. again and work the crops. There weren't many farmers who could distinguish a Nip from a Spick, not under a straw hat, not with spine bent to the rutabagas. Alas, Mexico was a thousand miles away, the month was November, there was already snow at the higher altitudes, flop flap was the song of his shoes.

Fortunately, the Chink knew which plants to chomp, which nuts and mushrooms to toast over tiny minimum-smoke fires. As best he could, he patched his shoes with bark. His journey went well for a week or more. Then, out of the mysterious dwelling place of weather, there rode an abrupt and burly storm. For a while it toyed with him, blowing in his ears, aging his normally black hair, hanging flakes artfully from the tip of his nose. But the storm was on serious business, and soon the Chink, crouched though he was in the lee of a cliff, realized that, by comparison, the passion of this storm to storm made puny his own desire to reach Mexico. Snow snow snow snow snow snow. The last thing a person sees before he dies he will be obliged to carry with him through all the baggage rooms of lasting death. The Chink strained to squint a sequoia or at least a huckleberry bush, but all his freezing eyes saw was snow. And the snow wanted to lie atop him as badly as any male ever wanted to lie on female.

The storm had its way with him. He lost consciousness trying to think of God, but thinking instead of a radiant woman cooking yams.

Of course, he was rescued. He was rescued by the only people who possibly could have rescued him. He was discovered, hauled in, bedded down, and thawed out by members of an American Indian culture that, for several reasons, cannot be identified beyond this fanciful description: the Clock People.

It is not easy, perhaps, to accept the fact of the Clock People's existence. You might read through every issue of the *National*

Geographic since the Year One and not find an exact parallel to the Clock People's particular distinctions. However, if you think about it for a while—the way the author has—it becomes obvious that the civilizing process has left pockets of vacuum which only Clock People could have filled.

The room in which the fugitive regained consciousness was large and well-heated, draped with crude blankets and the skins of animals. Whether it was a cave, a camouflaged cabin, or an elaborate tepee/hogan-type dwelling, the Chink would never say. He was careful not to disclose any details that might aid in pinpointing the location of his hosts.

As has been written, the Clock People are an American Indian culture. Ethnically speaking, however, they are not a tribe. Rather, they are a gathering of Indians from various tribes. They have lived together since 1906.

At the dawning of April 18, 1906, the city of San Francisco awakened to a terrible roar, mounting in intensity. For sixty-five seconds the city shook like a rubber meatball in the jaws of Teddy Roosevelt. There followed a silence almost as terrible as the roar. The heart of San Francisco lay in ruins. Buildings had tumbled into creviced streets, twisted bodies of humans and horses colored the rubble, gas hissed like the Snake of All Bad Dreams from dozens of broken mains. During the next three days, flames enveloped 490 blocks, unquenched by the teardrops of the homeless and lame.

History knows the catastrophe as the Great San Francisco Earthquake. That is not how the Clock People know it, but, then, the Clock People don't believe in earthquakes.

Among the crowds who watched the blazing devastation from surrounding hills was a scattering of American Indians. Largely from California tribes, though including folk from Nevada and Oregon, and in whose midst there moved representatives of the few but notorious Siwash, they were the first of the urbanized Indians. Poor, generally, they held jobs of menial and disreputable stature along the Barbary Coast (it should be emphasized, however, that they had been drawn into the city, each and every one of them, not by desire for money—they needed no money where they came from—but by *curiosity* alone). The white San Franciscans camping on the smoky hilltops surveyed the ruins in a state of shock. Perhaps the Indians, too, were overwhelmed by the spectacle, but they, as always, appeared as inscrutable as the other side of a nickel. Yet, the Indians were to display shock aplenty. It was when the fires were at last controlled and the citizens began to rush back into the still-warm ashes, singing, praising the Lord, and shouting to one another their plans for rebuilding their metropolis, that Indian eyes widened in disbelief. They simply could not comprehend what they were witnessing. They realized that the White Man lacked wisdom, but was he completely goofy? Couldn't he read the largest and most lurid of signs? Even those Indians who had grown to trust the White Man were grievously disappointed. Rebuild the city? They shook their heads and muttered.

For several weeks they remained on the hill, strangers united by shock and disappointment as well as by a common cultural comprehension of what had transpired below. Then, through communications the nature of which is known best to them, several of the Indians led a migration of a small band of souls into the Sierras, where, in a period of thirteen full moons, they generated the stalk of a new culture. (Or, should we say, under their impetus, the ancient stalk of Life Religion put forth unexpected and portentous shoots.)

On behalf of the Susquehanna, the Winnebago, the Kickapoo, the Chickasaw, the Kwakiutl, the Potawatomi, and all the other splendidly appellated aborigines who came to be labeled "Indians" through the ignorance of an Italian sailor with a taste for oranges, it is only fitting that "Indians" misnamed our Japanese-American hero "Chink."

There were very few Japanese in San Francisco in 1906, but Chinese were plentiful. Already there was a Chinatown, and its exotic trappings were a lure to tourists. Drugs, gambling, and prostitution abounded in the Chinese quarter, just as they did on the Barbary Coast, and the Indians often had overheard their employers speaking of the competition from the "Chinks."

In the years between 1906 and 1943, the Clock People had, naturally, discussed on many occasions the circumstances of their Sierra migration. More than once, they had wondered aloud why the yellow people had been so unenlightened as to join the whites in resurrecting San Francisco. It had been astonishing enough to watch the White Man set about to repeat his mistake, but to watch the Orientals follow him . . . !

Their curiosity about yellow men probably had influenced their decision to rescue this near-frozen outsider. During his days of recuperation, the storm victim had heard various of his hosts inquire about the condition of "the Chink." His sense of irony was not so frost-bitten that he could refrain from perpetuating, once he had recovered, the misnomer.

Eventually, perhaps, he confessed to his Japanese ancestry. Certainly and soon, he confessed to being a fugitive. The Clock People elected to harbor him, and were never to regret it. In the years that followed, the Chink performed them many services. In return, he was accepted as one of them, and gained privity to all of the secrets of the clockworks.

The pivotal function of the Clock People is the keeping and observing of the clockworks. The clockworks is a real thing. It is kept at the center, at the soul, of the Great Burrow.

The Great Burrow is a maze or labyrinthine sequence of tunnels, partly manmade, partly of geological origin. More specifically, a natural network of narrow caves, lying beneath a large knoll in the Sierra wilderness, was lengthened and elaborated upon by the Indians who exiled themselves from San Francisco in 1906. Many, if not most, of the tunnels are dead ends.

The Clock People, as we now know them, divided themselves into 13 families, not necessarily along tribal lines. (What is the numerical significance of the Clock People's taking 13 months to structure their ritual, then separating into 13 families? Well, briefly, they consider 13 a more natural number than 12. To the Babylonians, 13 was unlucky. That is why, when they invented astrology, they willfully overlooked a major constellation, erroneously assigning to the zodiac only 12 houses. The Clock People knew nothing of Babylonian superstition, but they knew the stars, and it was partly in an effort to override the unnatural 12-mindedness of Western culture that they chose to give 13 its due.) To each family was assigned the responsibility for one section of the Great Burrow. Each family knows one section inch by inch, but is completely ignorant of the other 12 sections. So, no family nor no individual knows the Way. The Way, of course, being the true path that takes one through the Great Burrow maze to the clockworks. Moreover, it is not possible for the families to compile a map of the Way, for each family holds as a sacred secret its knowledge of its burrow or section of the Way.

(In naming these tunnel sections "burrows," the Clock People were not particularly identifying with animals—no more so than were the Indians in whose culture totems played such a large and vivid role. Totemically-oriented Indians utilized the characteristics of certain animals *metaphorically*. It was simply a form of poetic symbolism. They used animals to think with.)

Okay. Who gets to the clockworks, how, and when? Each morning at sunrise, that day's designated guides—one from each of the 13 families—gather at the portal, or entrance, to the Great Burrow. Then, they are all blindfolded except for the guide representing the Family of the First Burrow. The blindfolded 12 link hands and are led by the first guide through any of several routes he or she may take to reach the beginning of the Second Burrow. A guide will purposefully attempt never to use the same route twice.

Often a guide will backtrack, and sometimes he or she will instruct the others in the party to let go of each other's hands and spin. Since, by this date, there are around 20 members in each family, an individual acts as guide only about 13 times a year.

Now, when the first guide reaches the terminus of his burrow and the beginning of the next, he instructs the guide for the Second Burrow to remove his blindfold, while binding his own eyes. And so it goes until the group is at the large central chamber, which contains the clockworks. There, they go about "keeping the time" until the hour for the return trip. Theoretically, the 13 daily guides emerge from the Great Burrow at sunset, although this occurs in actuality only upon those days when there are 13 hours of daylight.

Occasionally, other people accompany the guides on their mission. An aged or sickly person who is about to die or a pregnant woman commencing labor is led, blindfolded, to the central burrow, for insomuch as it is possible, all Clock People deaths and births occur in the presence of the clockworks. Aside from birthing or dying, the reason for the daily visit to the clockworks is to check the time.

Maybe we should say "check the *times*," for the clockworks is really two clocks and the sort of time each one measures is quite distinct.

First, there is a huge hourglass, at least 7 feet in diameter and 13 feet tall, made from the finely stitched and tightly stretched internal membranes of large beasts (elk, bears, mountain lions). The hourglass is filled with acorns, enough so that it takes them approximately 13 hours to pour, or funnel, one by one, through the slender passage in the waist of the transparent device. When the daily guides enter the soul burrow, the hourglass is turned upon its opposite end. When they depart—in approximately 13 hours—they flip it again. So, "checking the time," or "keeping the time" is, in the 26-hour day of the Clock People, the same as "making time," or, more generally, "making history." The Clock People believe that they are making history and that the end of history will come with the destruction of the clockworks.

Please do not construe the "end of history" or the "end of time" to mean "the end of life" or what is normally meant by the apocalyptically-minded when they speak (almost wishfully, it seems) of the "end of the world." That is paranoiac rubbish, and however one may finally evaluate the Clock People, their philosophy must be appreciated on a higher plane than doomsday drivel.

Well, then, what do the Clock People mean by the "end of history" and how will the clockworks be destroyed?

Zoom in on this: these people, these clandestinely exiled Indians, have no other ritual than this one: THE CHECKING OF THE

CLOCKWORKS—the keeping/making of history. Likewise, they have but one legend or cultural myth: that of a continuum they call the Eternity of Joy. It is the Eternity of Joy that they believe all men will pass into once the clockworks is destroyed. They look forward to a state of timelessness, when bored, frustrated, and unfulfilled people will no longer have to "kill time" for time will be finally dead.

They are preparing for timelessness by eliminating from their culture all rules, schedules, and moral standards other than those that are directly involved with the keeping of the clockworks. The Clock People may be the most completely anarchistic community that has ever existed. Rather, they may be the first community so far in which anarchy has come close to working. That is impressive in itself and should fan with peacock tails of optimism all those who dream of the ideal social condition.

The Clock People manage their anarchism (if that is not a contradiction) simply because they have channeled all of their authoritarian compulsions and control mania into a single ritual. It is clearly understood by all members of the community that there is no other ritual, no other required belief than this ONE—and, furthermore, that they themselves created the ritual: they have no silly superstitions about gods or ancestor spirits who hold this ritual over their heads in return for homage and/or "good" conduct.

Ritual, usually, is an action or ceremony employed to create a unity of mind among a congregation or community. The Clock People see the keeping of the clockworks as the *last* of the *communal* rituals. With the destruction of the clockworks, i.e., at the end of time, all rituals will be personal and idiosyncratic, serving not to unify a community/cult in a common cause but to link each single individual with the universe in whatever manner suits him or her best. Unity will give way to plurality in the Eternity of Joy, although, since the universe is simultaneously Many and One, whatever links the individual to the universe will automatically link him or her to all others, even while it enhances his or her completely separate identity in an eternal milkshake unclabbered by time. Thus, paradoxically, the replacement of societal with individual rituals will bring about an ultimate unity vastly more universal than the plexus of communal rites which presently divides peoples into unwieldy, agitating, and competing groups.

Now, the Clock People, being visionaries, are not content with their time-checking ritual. After all, it is the lone authoritarian, compulsive action which binds them. They chafe to dispense with it. If it could be eliminated, they could pass out of history and into the Eternity of Joy. Timeless, they could bear their children and bury their dead wherever they chose. However, they understand that at this evolutionary stage they still require the ritual even as they realize that destroying the clockworks is entirely within their power.

They will not destroy it. They have agreed—and this is central to their mythos—that the destruction must come from the outside, must come by natural means, must come at the will (whim is more like it) of that gesticulating planet whose more acute stirrings thoughtless people call "earthquakes."

Here, we can understand a bit more about the origins of their culture. The great rumble of 1906, which destroyed practically the whole of San Francisco, was taken by the Indians as a sign. They had left the land and gone to the city. That the city could be destroyed by the land in 65 seconds gave them a clue as to where the real power lay.

Within a natural context the phenomenon would never have appeared as a holocaust. Away from the herding centers we prize as cities, an "earthquake" would only manifest itself as a surface quickening of the globe's protoplastic movements, which, at various depths and various intensities, are occurring all of the time, and so not in time but all over time. Being "all over time" is the same as being out of time, because the notion of time is welded inseparably to the notion of progression, but what is already everywhere cannot possibly progress.

From there, it is a short leap to the ledge of the dream: the Eternity of Joy (a continuous present in which everything, including the dance of aging which we mistake as a chronological unfolding rather than a fixed posture of deepening cellular awareness, is taken together and always).

When the citizens of San Francisco began immediately to rebuild their city, the Indians were understandably very disappointed. The white (and yellow) San Franciscans hadn't learned a thing. They had been given a sign—a powerful, lucid sign—that urban herding and its concomitant technologies are not the proper way to partake of this planet's hospitality. Actually, there are countless ways to live upon this tremorous sphere in mirth and good health, and probably only one way—the industrialized, urbanized, herding way—to live here stupidly, and man has hit upon that one wrong way. The people of San Francisco failed to heed the sign. They capitulated, opting to stay in time and so out of eternity.

Readers may wonder why the Indians, who recognized the "earthquake" for what it really was, did not simply usher in the Eternity of Joy then and there. Well, they had both a realistic view and a sense of humor regarding their situation. They understood that it would take at least three or four generations to cleanse themselves of previous cultural deposits. The patriarchs—only two or three of whom are still alive—reasoned that if they could channel all of their fellows' frustrations and self-destructive compulsions into a single, simple ritual, then two things would follow. One, outside of that ritual, the community could experiment freely with styles of life instead of the attractions of death. Two, sooner or later, the Earth would issue another potent sign, one powerful enough to destroy their last icon of time-bound culture, the clockworks, ending the ritual even while it was reshaping much of American civilization.

Which brings us, ticking, to the matter of the second clock. The first clock in the original clockworks, the membrane hourglass, sits in a pool of water. The Great Burrow is situated upon a deep fracture, a major branch of the San Andreas Fault. The Sierra fault is clearly shown on geological maps of northern California (which does hint at the location of the original clockworks, doesn't it? even though the fracture is very long). In addition, the underground stream that feeds the Great Burrow pool flows directly into the San Andreas Fault. That pool of water is the second clock in the clockworks system. Consider its components.

Moments prior to an earthquake, certain sensitive persons experience nausea. Animals, such as cattle, are even more sensitive to prequake vibrations, feeling them earlier and more strongly. By far the most quake-sensitive creatures in existence are catfish. Readers, this is scientific fact; the dubious among you should not hesitate to check it out. Catfish.

Now, there is a species of catfish, hereditarily sightless, that dwells exclusively in subterranean streams. Its Latin name is *Satan eurystomus*, again for the skeptical, but spelunkers know the fish as blindcats. Relatively rare in California, blindcats are quite common in the caverns and caves of the Ozark states and Texas.

The clockworks pool is inhabited by such catfish. Their innate catfish earthquake sensitivity is compounded by the fact that they are tuned in, fin and whisker, to the vibrations of one of the globe's largest and most frenetic fault systems. When a tremor of any Ricterian passion is building, the catfish go into a state of shock. They cease feeding, and when they move at all, it is erratically. By constantly monitoring changes in the Earth's magnetic field or the tilt of the Earth's surface or the rate of movement and intensity of stress where faults are slowly creeping, seismologists have correctly predicted a handful of minor tremors, though with no great exactitude. The clockworks catfish, on the other hand, have registered upcoming quakes as far away as Los Angeles (in 1971) and as early as four weeks in advance.

On the earthen walls of the Central Burrow, the Clock People have marked in sequence the dates and intensities of all tremors, mad or mild, that have occurred along the 2000 miles of West

Coast faults since 1908. The whole pattern, transcribed from the catfish clock, reveals a rhythmic structure that indicates to the rhythmic minds of the Indians that something emphatic is going to be coming along any week now.

This peek on destruction is Pythagorean only in the sense that with the cataclysmic konking of the last vestige of cultural ritual will come the kind of complete social and psychic freedom that only natural, timeless anarchy can offer, the birth of a new people into the Eternity of Joy.

The Clock People regard civilization as an insanely complex set of symbols that obscure natural processes and encumber free movement. The Earth is alive. She burns inside with the heat of cosmic longing. She longs to be with her husband again. She moans. She turns softly in her sleep. When the symbologies of civilization are destroyed, there will be no more "earthquakes." Earthquakes are a manifestation of man's consciousness. Without manmade follies, there could not be earthquakes. In the Eternity of Joy, pluralized, deurbanized man, at ease with his gentle technologies, will smile and sigh when the Earth begins to shake. "She is restless tonight," they will say.

"She dreams of loving."

"She has the blues."

Among the Clock People, who never had tasted a yam, the Chink dwelt for 26 years.

For the first eight of those years, he lived virtually as a Clock Person himself, an honorary member of the Family of the Thirteenth Burrow, sharing their food, lodging, and women. (Being an anarchistic, or more precisely, a pluralistic society, some of the Clock People were monogamous, some, perhaps most, practitioners of free love. In a pluralistic society, love quickly shows all of its many smeared and smiling faces, and it should be noted that the term "family" was relevant only to the clockworks ritual, outside of which there was uninhibited intermingling. For example, a man from the Family of the Fifth Burrow might impregnate an Eleventh Burrow lady, and the resulting child, once of age, might be assigned to the Family of the Ninth Burrow.)

In 1951, the war now only a glint in the American Legion's shell-popped eye, the Chink moved into a shack that he built some nine or ten miles from the Great Burrow. The shack was strategically erected at the narrow entrance to the valley which, with a creek as its racing stripe, totaled out against the base of the tunnel-filled knoll. In the other direction, a couple of miles farther beyond the shack, was a trail that led to a dirt road that led to a paved highway that led past, eventually, a combination gas station, café, and general store. The Chink began to take fortnightly hikes to that store, where, among other supplies, he picked up newspapers and magazines. These he read to those Clock People (all spoke English but few could read it) who were interested, which was mainly the younger ones, the older Indians regarding that "news" that did not have to do with quakes, hurricanes, floods, and other geophysical shenanigans as trivia. The belch of civilization, they called it. Maybe the older Indians were right. It was the Eisenhower Years, remember, and the news read as if it had been washed out of a Pentagon desk commander's golf socks.

The Chink also linked the older Indians with the rest of the world, but in a different manner. Throughout the decades, the Clock People had mysteriously maintained periodic contact with certain Indians on the outside. These outside contacts were medicine men, or shamans, although exactly what was their relationship to the clockworks ritual and Eternity of Joy legend the Chink was never to ascertain. However, in the mid-50s, one or more of these outsiders took to showing up at the Sierra store at the precise hours of the Chink's unannounced visits. They'd drink a beer with him, and give him a piece or two of seemingly insignificant gossip which he would feel compelled to pass along once he was back at the Great Burrow. Thus, he functioned as a medium, like the air is the medium for drumbeats, connecting Clock People, young and old, with distant drummers.

He also functioned as an agent of diversion. When hunters, hikers, or prospectors entered the area, the Chink used his wiles to guide them away from the vicinity of the Great Burrow. Often, studding conversation with tips about game, scenic waterfalls, or ore deposits was enough to divert the intruders, but occasionally a small rockslide or other mishap would have to be arranged. Even so, a few interlopers, especially rangers of the U.S. Forest Service, slipped through the Chink's net. Those who got too close were slain by the Clock People. From 1965 to 1969, seven outsiders took arrows through their breasts and were buried inside the Great Burrow.

These slayings were a source of contention between the Chink and the Clock People, the latter regarding them as the regrettable but necessary price of protection, the former declaring: "There are many things worth living for, there are a few things worth dying for, but there is nothing worth killing for."

The Chink tried to impress upon the Clock People that, with the increase in air traffic over the mountains, as well as in the number of outdoorsmen whom civilization was driving into the wilderness, it was only a matter of "time" before their culture was exposed. What would they do then? Obviously, the System would not be gracious enough to leave them alone. "We will hide in the tunnels," answered some of the middle-aged. "We will defend ourselves to the death," answered some of the youth. "The movements of the Earth will take care of all that," answered the elders, smiling enigmatically.

If the killings upset him, the Chink accepted other contradictions in the Clock People's philosophy with ease. When faced with a contradiction, as he was—as we all are—daily if not hourly, it seemed only fair to him to take both sides.

Yet, he grew increasingly impatient with the Clock People's notions, and toward the end of his Sierra stay his hickory-dickory mouse of mockery ran frequently up their clock.

Now, a number of the young men of the Great Burrow had lost patience, too. Through the Chink's news broadcasts they had learned of mushrooming militancy among American Indians. They learned of "Red Power" and of proud reservations whose residents were freshly painted—and armed to the teeth. In early spring of 1969, a quartet of bucks slipped away from the Great Burrow, venturing into the strange world beyond the still snowy mountains to see for themselves. A couple of months later, they returned, excited, feathered, beaded, buzzing of revolution. Two comrades threw in with them, and they deserted the Clock People to go face the White Man on his own terms—and in his own time. The bucks called at the Chink's shack on their way down the mountains. "You're as tired as we are of sitting around waiting for a motherfucking earthquake," they said in the idiom they had recently adopted. "You're strong and smart and have taught us much. Come with us and join the movement."

"This movement of yours, does it have slogans?" inquired the Chink.

"Right on!" they cried, and they quoted him some.

"Your movement, does it have a flag?" asked the Chink.

"You bet," and they described their emblem.

"And does your movement have leaders?"

"Great leaders."

"Then shove it up your butts," said the Chink. "I have taught you nothing." He skipped down to the creek to gather watercress.

A few weeks later, he accepted the invitation of an aged Siwash chief, who was the principal outside confederate of the Clock People, a degenerated warlock who could turn urine into beer, to be initiated as a shaman, an honor which gave him right of occupancy in the sacred cave on faraway Siwash Ridge. At once he left for the Dakota hills to construct a clockworks whose ticks might more accurately echo the ticks of the universe, which, as he listened, sounded more and more like "ha ha ho ho and hee hee."

MARY ROBISON

Coach

THE August two-a-day practice sessions were sixty-seven days away, Coach calculated. He was drying breakfast dishes. He swabbed a coffee cup and made himself listen to his wife, who was across the kitchen, sponging the stove's burner coils.

"I know I'm no Rembrandt," Sherry said, "but I have so damn much fun trying, and this little studio—this room—we can afford. I could get out of your way by going there and get you and Daphne out of my way. No offense."

"I'm thinking," Coach said.

His wife coasted from appliance to appliance. She swiped the face of the oven clock with her sponge. "You're thinking too slow. Your reporter's coming at nine and it's way after eight now. Should I give them a deposit on the studio or not? Yes or no?"

Coach was staring at the sink, at a thread of water that came from one of the taps. He thought of the lake place where they used to go in North Carolina. He saw green water being thickly sliced by a power boat; the boat towing Sherry, who was blonde and laughing on her skis, her rounded back strong, her suit shining red.

"Of course, of course, give them the money," he said.

Their daughter, Daphne, wandered into the kitchen. She was dark-haired, lazy-looking, fifteen. Her eyes were lost behind bangs. She drew open the enormous door of the refrigerator.

"Don't hang, Daphne, you'll unhinge things," her mother said. "What are you after?"

"Food mainly," Daphne said.

Sherry went away, to the little sun patio off the kitchen. Coach pushed the glass door sideways after her and it smacked shut.

"Eat and run," he said to Daphne. "I've got a reporter coming in short order. Get dressed." He spoke firmly but in the smaller voice he always used for his child.

"Yes, sir," Daphne said. She broke into the freezer compartment and ducked to let its gate pass over head. "Looks bad. Nothing in here but Eggos."

"I ate Eggos. Just hustle up," Coach said.

"Can I be here for this guy?" Daphne asked.

"Who guy? The reporter? Nuh-uh. He's just from the college, Daph. Coming to see if the new freshman coach has three heads or just two."

Daphne was nodding at the food jars racked on the wide refrigerator door. "Hey, lookit," she said. She blew a breath in front of the freezer compartment and made a short jet of mist.

Coach remembered a fall night, a Friday-game night, long ago, when he had put Daphne on the playing field. It was during the ceremonies before his unbeaten squad had taken on Ignatius South High School. Parents' Night. He had laced shoulder pads on Daphne and draped the trainer's gag jersey—number 1/2—over her, and balanced Tim-somebody's helmet on her eight-year-old head. She was lost in the getup, a small pile of equipment out on the fifty-yard line. She had applauded when the loudspeaker announced her name, when the p.a. voice, garbled by amplification and echo, had rung out, "Daughter of our coach, Harry Noonan, and his wife—number one-half, Daphne Noonan!" She had stood in the bath of floodlights, shaking as the players and their folks strolled by—the players grim in their war gear, the parents tiny and apologetic-seeming in civilian clothes. The co-captain of the team, awesome in his pads and cleats and steaming from warm-up running, had palmed Daphne's big helmet and twisted it sideways. From behind, from the home stands, Coach had heard, "Haaa!" as Daphne turned circles of happy confusion, trying to right the helmet. Through the ear hole her left eye had twinkled, Coach remembered. He had heard, "God, that's funny," and "Coach's kid."

On the sun porch now, his wife was doing a set of tennis exercises. She was between Coach and the morning sun, framed by the glass doors. He could see through the careless weave of her caftan, enough to make out the white flesh left by her swimsuit.

"I knew you wouldn't let me," Daphne said. She had poured a glass of chocolate milk. She pulled open a chilled banana. "I bet Mom gets to be here."

"Daph, this isn't a big deal. We've been through it all before," Coach said.

"Not for a college paper," Daphne said. "Wait a minute, I'll be right back." She left the kitchen.

"I'll hold my breath and count the heartbeats," Coach said to the space she had left behind.

They were new to the little town, new to Pennsylvania. Coach was assuming charge of the freshman squad, in a league where freshmen weren't eligible for the varsity. He had taken the job, not sure if it was a step up for him or a serious misstep. The money was so-so. But he wanted the college setting for his family—especially for Daphne. She had been seeming to lose interest in the small celebrity they achieved in high-school towns. She had acted bored at the Noonans' Sunday spaghetti dinners for standout players. She had stopped fetching plates of food for the boys, who were too game-sore to get their own. She had even stopped wearing the charm bracelet her parents had put together for her—a silver bracelet with a tiny megaphone, the numerals 68—a league championship year—and, of course, a miniature football.

Coach took a seat at the kitchen table. He ate grapes from a bowl. He spilled bottled wheat germ into his palm. On the table were four chunky ring binders, their black leatherette covers printed with the college seal—which still looked strange to him. These were his playbooks, and he was having trouble getting the play tactics into his head.

"Will you turn off the radio?" he yelled.

The bleat from Daphne's upstairs bedroom ceased. A minute later she came down and into the kitchen. She had a cardboard folder and some textbooks with her. "Later on, would you look at this stuff and help me? Can you do these?" she asked Coach.

He glanced over one of her papers. It was penciled with algebra equations, smutty with erasures and scribbled-out parts. "I'd have to see the book, but no. Not now, not later. I don't want to and I don't have time."

"That's just great," Daphne said.

"Your mother and I got our Algebra homework done already, Daph. We turned ours in," Coach said. "This was in nineteen fifty-six."

"Mom!" Daphne said, pushing aside the glass door.

"Forget it," Sherry said.

2

Toby, the boy sent from *The Rooter* to interview Coach, was unshaven and bleary-eyed. He wore a rumpled cerise polo shirt and faded Levi's. He asked few questions, dragging his words. Now and then he grumbled of a hangover and no sleep. He yawned during Coach's answers. He took no notes.

"You're getting this now?" Coach said.

"Oh, yeah, it's writing itself, I'm such a pro," Toby said, and Coach wasn't certain if the boy was kidding.

"So, you've been here just a little while. Lucky you," Toby said. "Less than a month?"

"Is that like a question? It seems less than less than a month—less than a week—a day and a half," Coach said.

For the interview, he had put on white sports slacks and a maroon pullover with a gold collar—the college's colors. The pullover he had bought at Campus World. The clothes had a snug fit that flattered Coach and showed off his flat stomach and heavy biceps.

He and Toby were on either end of the sofa in the living room of the house, a wooden two-story Coach had found and would be paying off for decades, he was sure.

Toby said, "Well, believe it or not, I've got enough for a couple sticks, which is shoptalk among we press men for two columns. If you're going to be home tomorrow, there's a girl who'll come and take your picture—Marcia. She's a drag, I warn you."

"One thing about this town, there aren't any damn sidewalks, and the cars don't give you much room if you're jogging," Coach said, standing up.

"Hey, tell me about it. When I'm hitching, I wear an orange poncho and carry a red flag and paint a big X on my back. Of course, I'm probably just making a better target," the reporter said.

"I jog down at the track now. It's a great facility, comparable to a Big Ten's. I like the layout," Coach said.

"Okay, but the interview's over," Toby said.

"Well, I came from high schools, remember. In Indiana and Ohio—good schools with good budgets, mind you, but high schools, nonetheless."

"Yeah, I got where you're coming from," Toby said.

"Did you need to know what courses I'll be handling? Fall quarter, they've got me lined up for two things: The Atlantic World is the first one, and Colloquium on European Industrial Development, I think it is. Before, I always taught World History. P.O.D.,[1] once or twice."

"That three-eighty-one you're going to teach is a tit course, in case nobody's informed you. It's what we call lunch," Toby said.

"It's, in nature, a refresher class," Coach said.

"Yeah, or out of nature," Toby said.

Daphne came from the long hall steps into the living room. Her dark hair was brushed and lifting with static. Her eyes seemed to Coach larger than usual, and a little sooty around the lashes.

"You're just leaving, aren't you, buster?" Coach said to her.

"Retrieving a pencil," Daphne said.

"Is your name really Buster?" Toby asked.

"Get your pencil and scoot. This is Toby here. Toby, this is my daughter, Daphne," Coach said.

"Nice to meet you," Daphne said. She slipped into a deep chair at the far corner of the long living room.

"Can she hear us over in that country?" Toby said. "Do you read me?" he shouted.

Daphne smiled. Coach saw bangs and her very white teeth.

"Come on, Daph, hit the trail," he said.

"I've got a joke for her first," Toby said. "What's green and moves very fast?"

"Frog in a blender," Daphne said. "Dad? Some friends invited me to go swimming with them at the Natatorium. May I?"

1. Problems of Democracy.

"You've got to see the Nat. It's the best thing," Toby said.

"What about your class, though? She's in makeup school here, Toby, catching up on some algebra that didn't take the first time around."

Toby wrinkled his nose at Daphne. "At first, I thought you meant *makeup* school, like lipstick and rouge."

"I wish," Daphne said.

She slipped her left foot from her leather sandal and casually stroked the toes.

"She's a nut for swimming," Coach said.

"You'll be so bored here. Most nights, your options are either ordering a pizza or slashing your wrists," Toby told Daphne.

"Oh," she said, rolling her chin on her shoulder in a rather seductive way.

"Take it from Toby," he said.

Coach let Toby through the front door, and watched until he was down the street.

"He was nice," Daphne said.

"Aw, Daph. That's what you say about everybody. There's a lot better things you could say—more on-the-beam things."

"I guess you're mad," she said.

Coach went to the kitchen, to sit down with his playbooks again. Daphne came after him.

"Aren't you?" she said.

"I guess you thought he was cute," Coach said. He flapped through some mimeographed pages, turning them on the notebook's silver rings. "I don't mean to shock you about it, but you'd be wasting your time there, Daph. You'd be trying to start a fire with a wet match."

Daphne stared at her father. "That's sick!" she said.

"I'm not criticizing him for it. I'm just telling you," Coach said.

3

"This is completely wrong," Coach said sadly. He read further. "Oh, no," he said. He drowned the newspaper in his bath water and slogged the pages over into a corner by the commode.

His wife handed him a dry edition, one of the ten or twelve *Rooters* Daphne had brought home.

Sherry was parallel to Coach on the edge of the tub, sitting with her back braced against the wall. "Oh, cheer up," she said. "Nobody reads a free newspaper."

Coach quartered the dry *Rooter* into a package around Toby's article. "Well, I wasn't head coach at Elmgrove, and I sure wasn't Phi Beta Kappa. And look at this picture," Coach said.

"What's wrong with it?" Sherry said.

"Where did he get that you were at Mt. Holyoke? And I didn't bitch about the sidewalks this much."

"You didn't?" Sherry said. "That's almost too bad. I thought that was the best part of the article."

Coach slunk farther into the warm water until it crowded his chin. He kept the newspaper aloft. "Oh, come on, give me some credit here! Don't they have any supervision over in Journalism? I don't see how he could get away with this shit. It's an unbelievably sloppy job."

"It's just a dinky article in a handout paper, Coach. What do you care? It wouldn't matter if he said we were a bright-green family with scales," Sherry said.

"He didn't think of that or he would have. This breaks my heart," Coach said.

"Daph liked it," Sherry said.

Coach wearily chopped bath water with the side of his hand and threw a splash at the soap recess in the tiled wall. "I tell you, I'm going to be spending my whole first year here explaining how none of it's true."

"What difference does true make?" Sherry said.

4

Coach was seated awkwardly on an iron stool at a white table on the patio of the Dairy Frost. Daphne was across from him, fighting the early evening heat for her mocha-fudge cone. She tilted her head at the cone, lapping at it.

"You aren't saying anything," Coach said.

"Wait," Daphne said.

She worked on the cone.

"I've been waiting."

"If you two want to separate, it's none of my business," she said.

They were facing the busy parking lot when a new Pontiac turned in off the highway, glided easily onto the gravel, took a parking slot close by. In the driver's seat was a boy with built-up shoulders—a boy who looked very familiar to Coach. In back was a couple in their fifties—the boy's parents, Coach thought—both talking at once.

"Have I been spilling all this breath for nothing? *Not* a separation," Coach said. "Not anything like it."

"All right, not," Daphne said. She stopped in her attack on the cone long enough to watch the Pontiac boy step out. Dark brown ice cream streamed between her knuckles and down the inside of her wrist.

"You're losing it, honey," Coach said.

Daphne dabbed around the cone and her hand, making repairs.

"Hell, *real* trouble your father wouldn't tell you about at a *Dairy* Frost. This apartment your mom found is like an office or something. A studio for her to go to and get away every now and then. That kid's in my backfield. What the *hell's* his name?"

They watched as the young man took orders from his parents, then went inside the Dairy Frost. He looked both wider and taller than the other patrons, out of their scale. His rump and haunches were thick with muscle. His neck was fat but tight.

"Bobby Stark!" Coach said, and smiled very quickly at the parents in the Pontiac. He turned back to his daughter.

"She wants to get away from us," Daphne said.

"Definitely not. She gave me a list, is how this whole thing started. She's got stuff she wants to do, and you with your school problems and me with the team—we're too much for her, see? She could spend her entire day on us, if you think about it, and never have one second for herself. If you think about it fairly, Daphne, you'll agree."

Daphne seemed to consider. She was focused on the inside of the Dairy Frost building, and for a while she kept still.

"That guy looks dumb. One of the truly dumb," she said.

"My halfback? He's not. He was his class salutatorian," Coach said.

"He doesn't know *you*."

"Just embarrassed," Coach said. "Can we stick to the point, Daph? And quit rocking the boat. Look what you're doing." Daphne's arm was on the table and she was violently swinging her legs under her chair.

She made a sigh and marched over to a trash can to deposit her slumping cone. Then she washed up at the children's drinking fountain and rejoined Coach, who had finished his Brown Cow but had kept the plastic spoon in his mouth.

"What was on this list of Mom's?" Daphne asked.

"Adult stuff," Coach said.

"Just give me an example."

Coach removed the plastic spoon and cracked it in half.

"Your mother's list is for five years. In that time, she wants to be speaking French regularly. She wants to follow up on her printmaking."

"This is adult stuff?" Daphne said.

Coach raised a hand to Bobby Stark. Stark had three malt cups in a cardboard carrier and he was moving toward the parking lot.

"Hey, those all for you?" Coach called out.

"I got a month to get fat, Coach. You'll have five months to beat it off me," the boy called back.

The people at some of the tables around Coach's lit up with grins. Bobby Stark's parents were grinning.

"Every hit of that junk takes a second off your time in the forty—just remember that!" Coach shouted.

Stark wagged his head ruefully, his cheeks blushing. He pretended to hide the malts behind his arm.

"Duh," Daphne said in a hoarse voice. "Which way to the door, Coach?"

"He can hear you," Coach said.

"Duh, kin I have a candy bar, Coach?" she rasped.

They faced Stark, who smiled a little crookedly at Daphne, and threw her a wink so dazzling, she went silent.

5

Coach was in the basement laundry room, both arms busy hugging a bundle of jogging clothes. He was waiting on the washer, waiting for Sherry to unload her clothes.

"The Cowboys are soaking their players in a sense-deprivation tub of warm saltwater," she said.

"We know," Coach said.

"If Dallas is doing it, I just thought you might want to consider it."

"We have. Hustle up a little with your stuff, will you?" Coach said.

"It's like my apartment," Sherry said. "A place apart."

Coach cut her off. "Don't go on about how much you love your apartment."

"I wasn't going to," Sherry said. She slung her wet slacks and blouses into the dryer.

Coach had just two weeks before the start of the heavy practices. His team would have him then, he knew, almost straight through the Christmas holidays.

"I like that," Coach said. "A place apart."

A half hour later, Coach and his wife were on the side patio. They could hear the tick of the clothes dryer downstairs. Sherry had changed into a halter top. She was taking sun on her back, adding to her tan.

"You know what's odd?" she said. "Daphne's popularity here. I don't mean it's odd."

"She's always done terrific with people, always gone over well," Coach said.

"*Your* people, though. These are hers," Sherry said. "Like that reporter."

"Yeah, they're like sisters," Coach said.

6

It was a week before the two-a-day practice sessions would begin. The sky was colorless and glazed, like milk glass. When Coach looked at the sun, his eyes ached, his head screamed.

He had run some wind sprints on the stadium field, and now he was doing an easy lap. A stopwatch on a noose of ribbon swung against his chest. He cut through the goalposts and trotted for the sidelines, for the twenty, where he had dumped his clipboard and a towel.

Someone called to him.

Blond Bobby Stark came out from under the stands. His football shoes were laced together and draped around his neck. He wore a midriff-cut T-shirt and shorts. He walked gingerly in white wool socks.

"Did everybody go? Or am I the first one here?" he called to Coach.

" 'Bout a half hour," Coach said, heaving.

Stark sat down to untangle his shoes, and Coach, sweating, stood over him.

Coach spat. He folded his arms in a way that pushed out his muscles. He sniffed, twisting his whole nose and mouth to the left. He said, "You know Stark, you were salutatorian for your class."

"High school," the boy said. He grinned up at Coach, an eye pinched against the glare.

"That counts, believe me. Maybe we can use you to help some of our slower players along—some of the linemen, maybe I'm thinking."

"What do you mean—tutor?" Stark said.

"Naw. Teach them to eat without biting off their fingers. How to tie a necktie. Some of your style," Coach said, and Stark bobbed his head.

Stark settled the fit of his right shoe. He said, "But there aren't any really dumb ones on our squad, because they'd just get flunked out. Recruiters won't touch them in this league. There wouldn't be any percentage in it."

"Then I'm greatly relieved," Coach said.

He planted his feet along a furrow of lime-eaten grass. He faced the open end of the stadium, where the enormous library building stood shimmering and uncertain behind sheets of heat that rose from the parking area.

Stark stood up and studied his shoes as he began jogging in place. He danced twenty yards down the field; loped back.

Other players were arriving for the informal session. Coach meant to time them in the mile, and in some dashes.

Stark looked jittery. He walked in semicircles, crowding Coach.

"What're you worried about?" Coach asked him. "Girl problems you got? You pull a muscle already?"

Stark glanced quickly around them. He said, "I live all my life two doors down from Coach Burton's house. My mom and Burton's wife are best friends, so I always know what's going on."

Burton had been the head coach of the varsity team for over a decade.

"You probably know about it already, anyway," Stark said. "Do you?"

"What the hell are you talking about, Stark?"

"You don't know? Typical. Burton's leaving, see? Like at the end of this year. His wife wants him out real bad, and the alumni want him out because they're tired of losing seasons. So what I heard was you were brought in because of it. And if we do okay this season, like you'll be varsity coach next year."

"That's conjecture," Coach said. But he was excited.

It was three o'clock, still hot. Coach was moving along a sidewalk with Bobby Stark, who was balanced on a racing bicycle, moving just enough to keep the machine upright.

"Three things," Coach said. "I've seen all the game films from last year, and I came here personally and witnessed the Tech game. No one lost because of the coaching. A coach can work miracles with a good team, but he is *helpless* if his personnel don't want it bad enough. That's the worst part about running a team—you can't climb down into your people's hearts and change them."

Some college girls in a large expensive car went past. They shrieked and whistled at Bobby Stark.

"Lifeguards at the pool," he explained.

"I don't know if Burton's leaving or not," Coach continued. "But if his wife wants him to go, he probably will. If you're ever thinking about a career in coaching someday, Bob, think about that. Your family's either with you or you've had it. And remember, whether you stay someplace or not depends completely on a bunch of *kids*. I swear, I'd give up a leg for a chance to get in a game myself—just one play, with what I know now."

Stark nodded. They went on a block, and he said, "I turn off here. You going to tell your daughter about the job?"

"My daughter?" Coach said, and smiled.

7

No one was home. A magnet under a plastic ladybug held a note to the face of the refrigerator. The note read:

> *Harry, I'm at my place. Daph's with Toby K. somewhere, fooling around. Be good now, Sherry Baby.*

"Dope," Coach said.

He felt very good.

He took a beer upstairs and drank it while he showered. He cinched on a pair of sweat pants and, wearing only these, went back down and fetched another beer.

He watched some of a baseball game on cable. He thought over his conversation with Bobby Stark. "Boy, is that true!" Coach said, and then was not at all sure why he had said it.

He frowned, remembering that in his second year of college, the only year he had been on the varsity team, he had proved an indifferent player.

"Not now," he whispered. "Not anymore."

He squashed the shape out of his beer can and stood it on top of the television.

There was a thump over his head. The ceiling creaked.

"Someone came home while I was in the shower," he said to himself, and ran his hand over his belly, feeling for signs of bloat from the beer.

He took the stairs in three leaps, strode into the master bedroom, calling, "Sherry?"

The dark figure in the room surprised Coach.

He yelled, "Hey!"

Daphne was dancing in front of the full-length mirror. She had improvised a look—sweeping her hair over her right ear, and stretching the neck of her shirt until her right shoulder was bared. A thing by the Commodores shrieked from her transistor.

"Nothing," she said.

"You're not home. Aren't you with whoosis? You're supposed to be out. You are *beet* red," Coach said.

Daphne lowered her head and squared her shirt, which bagged around her small torso. "Okay, Dad," she said.

"No, but how did your audience like the show? I bet they loved it," Coach said. He smiled at himself in the mirror. "I'm just kidding you, Daph. You looked great."

"Come *on*, Dad," she said, and tried to pass.

Coach chimed in with the radio. He shuffled his feet. "Hey, Daph, you know what time it is?" he said.

"Let me out, please," Daphne said.

"It's monkey time'" Coach did a jerky turn, keeping in the way of the exit door. "Do the shing-a-ling. Do the Daphne." He rolled his shoulder vampishly. He kissed his own hand. He sang along.

"Thanks a lot," Daphne said. She gave up on trying to get around him. She leaned over and snapped off her radio. "You've got to use a mirror so you don't look stupid," she said. "Everybody does."

"I was only kidding. Seriously. I know dancing is important," Coach said.

"May I go now? I've got algebra." Daphne brought her hair from behind her ear.

"Before that, you have to hear the news. Here's a news bulletin, flash extra."

"You're drunk. You and Mom are going to live in different cities," Daphne said. "Somebody shot somebody."

"No, this is good news. I'm going to be coach here of the varsity. Me." Coach pointed to his chest.

"Now let me out, please," Daphne said.

Coach let her pass. He followed her down the narrow hallway to her bedroom.

"More money," he said. "I'll even be on TV. I'll have my own show on Sundays. And I'll get written up in the press all the time. By *real* reporters. Hey! Why am I yelling at wood, here?"

8

Coach was drunk at the kitchen table. He was enjoying the largeness of the room, and he was making out a roster for his dream team. He had put the best kids from his fifteen years of coaching in the positions they had played for him. He was puzzling over the tight-end spot. "Jim Wyckoff or Jerry Kinney?" he said aloud. He penciled "Kinney" into his diagram.

He heard Daphne on the stairs. It occurred to him to clear the beer cans from the table. Instead, he snapped open a fresh can. "Daphne?" he called.

"Wait a second. What?" she said from the living room.

"Just wondered who else was alive besides me," Coach said. "Your mom's still not home."

Daphne entered the kitchen.

"You're sorry you were rude before? That's perfectly okay, honey, just forget it. All right, Father, but I really am ashamed of myself anyway," Coach said.

"You guzzled all those?" Daphne said.

"Hold still. What've you got on?" Coach asked her. He hauled his chair around so that he could see his daughter.

"Two, four, five," Daphne said, counting the cans.

She was wearing one of the fan shirts that Coach had seen on a few summer coeds. On the front, against a maroon field, in gold, was GO. Across the back was GRIFFINS.

"Now you're talking," Coach said.

"It was free. This guy I met—well, these two guys, really—who work at Campus World, they gave it to me. It's dumb, but I want you to see I care. I do care. Not just for you, but because I want to stay here. Do you think we can maybe? Do your people look any good this year?"

"Winners," Coach said.

"Yeah," Daphne said.

Coach skidded his chair forward. "Have a beer," he said. "Sit down here and let me show you on paper the material they've given me to work with. Then maybe you'll be a believer. Now these guys are fast and big for once. I'm not overestimating them, either. I've seen what I've seen," Coach said.

A car crept into the drive, and then its engine noise filled the garage. Coach and Daphne were quiet until Sherry bustled down the short hall that connected the garage to the kitchen.

"Really late. Sorry, sorry," she said.

"It's a party in here, I warn you," Coach said.

"So I noticed." Sherry had a grocery sack, but it was almost empty. There were bright streaks of paint on her brown arms.

Daphne plucked a bag of Oreo cookies from the groceries.

"Shoot me one of those," Coach said.

"Is there any beer left for me?" Sherry said. "I want to drown my disappointment. I can't paint!"

"You *can* paint," Coach said.

"Let's face it," Sherry said. "An artist? The wife of a coach?"

JANET BEELER SHAW

No Place to Be on Christmas

ALTHOUGH the bus station was crammed, Gary noticed the woman the minute she came in the door. He thought she was in the wrong place, should be at the airport, maybe, in that blue coat shaped like a dress and those lizardy shoes that matched her purse. The crowd pressed around her, but she stood in the doorway—maybe she thought she'd made a mistake, too. Then she took off her leather gloves, passed her fingers through her dark hair, and, as if she'd made an appointment, walked right past the line to Gary's ticket window.

"Are those arrival times correct?" She pointed to the board above him. Giving her a dirty look, a soldier in a parka reached around her to slap down his bucks on the counter.

"You bet." Gary made change. Now that she was up close, he saw she was older than he'd thought from across the room, but prettier, too: a small chin, short nose, tilty eyes—a cat's face.

"You mean the bus from Minneapolis won't be in until *morning*?" She checked her jeweled watch against the wall clock: 12:15 A.M.

"Traffic's held up all over because of the storm." He peeled off a ticket to Chicago and handed it to the soldier.

"Are the passengers all right?"

"Cooling their heels in the Minneapolis bus station, just like these folks here. When the roads are plowed out they'll be on their way."

"But it's Christmas eve!"

"It sure is."

"Would you please phone the stationmaster in Minneapolis for me? I want to speak to Miss Jane Monroe."

The soldier winked at Gary.

"Public phones are against the far wall."

She put her elbow on the counter. "Why can't you call for me?"

So she was going to stay right there, blocking the line. He wrote down the number of the Minneapolis station and handed it to her. "Regulations."

"You know what you can do with your regulations!"

He had to smile—slim little broad. "Merry Christmas!" he called to her back.

While he sold tickets he watched her. When she finally got a phone she cupped her hands around the receiver as though she were telling a secret. Her straight-cut hair slipped forward on her cheeks like curtains. When she hung up she stepped away and just stood there. Even from that distance he saw she was crying.

She chose a seat between a girl who leaned on her duffle and a sleeping boy with a ponytail. She crossed her legs, took out a cigarette, and held it to her lips as though someone would come to light it for her. After a moment she put it away and folded her hands on her purse. She closed her eyes.

Pretending she's not here at all, he thought. Too good for this place. The edge of lace at her skirt hem made him angry. The chicks he knew wore mostly jeans. "Some folks have more than they purely *need*," he said to Fat Roy, who was setting his change tray into the next drawer.

"God gonna fix 'em, gonna make it even in the end." Fat Roy's palms were silvery-pink. Gary thought of the secret colors inside a dog's mouth.

"He's sure taking his own sweet time about it."

"Hush, you," said Fat Roy, counting bills.

By 6:00 A.M., when Gary got off, the roads were plowed, the waiting room almost empty. The woman in the blue coat slept bent over, her head on her folded arms, her purse under her cheek. Gary stepped outside for a breath.

The cold air tasted of rust, like well water. A fine-edged light, aluminum foil, tented the buildings and the power plant. He jammed his hands into his pockets. The whole world was like Grandpa's wall-eyed mare. For seven years Gary had ridden her every day, and yet every time he came near her she'd start and shy away like he was a stranger, or stare straight through him. No matter what, he couldn't bring her around, make her pay attention.

He caught sight of his reflection in the glass doors. He'd been told often enough that he was good-looking, but all he could see was an outline, no features at all. Just a twenty-seven year blank.

He bought a carton of milk and two cupcakes from the machine. He sat down by the woman. When she didn't wake, he jostled her foot. She jumped and rubbed her eyes.

"The bus that had you so worried is due in at eight-ten."

He could see she'd forgotten where she was. A crease from her purse scarred her cheek. Without paint on them, her lips looked fuller. "Who *are* you?"

"I sell tickets."

"I know that. What's your name?" A sleep-flush gathered on her throat above the neckline of the white blouse.

"Gary Kreuger."

"Gary, I'm going to have you fired."

He laughed—being rich didn't make you smart. "For telling you when to meet your bus? My boss'll give me a medal."

"For not giving me some decent help last night. I'm waiting for my daughter."

That surprised him. "A little kid?"

"Eighteen. But believe me, she needs help."

"If I'd have made a personal call for you, I'd have had to for everyone else here. You'll have her home with you soon enough, opening her Christmas stocking."

She snapped wide her purse, took out a cigarette again, put it back. "I'm just so tired."

"Trying to quit smoking?" He put his arm along the back of the seat and stretched his legs.

"I wish I could. But what can you do instead?" She combed at her hair with her fingers.

He offered her the second of his cupcakes. He thought she looked grateful.

"No, thanks," she said after a moment.

"Coffee, then? There's a machine."

She shook her head. Then she pulled a wallet out of her purse and peeled a single off the solidest stack of bills he'd seen in maybe years. She handed him the single. "Milk, please. Like yours."

He made change from Fat Roy's drawer, and brought her a carton of milk. She sipped from it. "Do you live here in town?" he asked.

"This isn't a talk show."

"I've been up all night, and it takes me a while to wind down."

She shrugged. "Milwaukee. I drove here so Jane wouldn't have to change buses."

"You're far from home."

"I should have gone to a motel. I didn't know I'd have to wait all night."

He smelled flowers, now that he was close to her. "I think you should know something."

She looked at him over the rim of the milk carton, her gray eyes wide. "Now what?"

"You had some pretty bad dreams last night. You moaned in your sleep."

"Do you get paid to watch people sleep?"

"Don't get mad. I couldn't help but notice. There's all kinds of sleepers, but I could see you were troubled." He gave her his best smile.

"Of course I'm troubled! My daughter's stranded, I had no place to sleep, and the ticket agent wouldn't help me."

"I'm not your enemy." Wondering if she was his.

She eyed him. He kept his smile pinned on. She took out her cigarettes, handed him one, took one for herself. He lit them. She inhaled like she was starving. "She's pregnant," she said, as though that was his fault, too.

He took a drag—what was there to say? "She's not married, she's pregnant, she's only eighteen. And she wants to have the baby." She watched him through the smoke.

He tried to think. "It's not herpes."

"For god's sake!" She leaned back to toss the carton into the trash container. Slam-dunk. "Men really *are* all alike. I've fought that idea but it's true." She touched his wrist, as if his attention might be wandering when she had such an important point to make. "Men are a different *breed*. If you think you've ever understood a woman, think again. You haven't."

"I've known a few." A lot, but bragging didn't pay.

"You may have thought you did, but no, you did not know them. I've just told you a young girl is going through the greatest crisis in her life and all you can say is that it's not herpes."

"I meant, you can't cure herpes."

"You think there's a cure for motherhood?" She was getting loud. Fat Roy looked up from where he snoozed at the counter. "You think that's something you can just quit, like smoking?"

"Listen, I—"

"You think you're a normal person, don't you, Gary? But you are probably crazy. Men *are*."

"Your husband will talk sense to your daughter—"

"Husband! He's in Bermuda with a radiologist, and by now she's probably pregnant, too. God." She started to cry.

It seemed a chance—for what, he wasn't sure. He heard himself saying, "Look, I should have helped you more last night. I'm real sorry. I live just a block from here on Jennifer Street, and that bus won't be in for a couple of hours yet. At my place you can wash up, have some breakfast, pull yourself together before your daughter gets here." The ease of his speech surprised him, as if he'd practiced it.

She rubbed her nose. The rash on her throat had spread over her cheeks like a mask. She peered around the waiting room, the cigarette smoke ribboned in the air, sniffed—maybe at the stink of exhaust fumes and the chemical they used on the floor. No one left but a few soldiers sleeping.

"This is no place to be on Christmas morning." He summed it up.

She took a look at Fat Roy staring at her, his pink birthmark a butterfly on his black cheek. She stood, buttoning her coat. He held the door for her.

"Men don't know what it's like to be a mother," she said.

"Mine drowned when my dad's boat overturned on the Wisconsin river. They were fishing. My grandfolks raised me."

She took his arm to step over the oil slick at the garage entrance. In the west a fingernail moon dangled like a fish lure on the horizon.

"It's not even morning." Her shoulders trembled and her breath blossomed white. She pulled her printed scarf up over her mouth, though it was too thin to do much good, he thought.

"We'll take my car." Before he could repeat that he only lived a block away, she'd turned into the parking lot behind the station and was fumbling in her purse for keys. She dropped them, pulled them out of the snow, brushed crystals from her ankles. Her blue Mercedes was the only car in the lot.

Like leaping off a bridge into a creek, he took a breath deep enough to make his lungs ache before he ducked in and closed the door on his side.

The engine groaned, then roared. "I must be out of my mind to be doing this," she said, as though taking her pulse.

He kept quiet. Let her argue with herself.

"I guess it doesn't matter."

He had her park behind his apartment building, but he walked her around to the front staircase. It was bad enough—the carpet smelling of dog pee and pot, bikes locked to the landing railings, bare, dirty windows. She didn't touch the railing.

When he unlocked his door and stood back for her to pass him, he saw how she looked at the walls, his three rooms; no posters, not even curtains. He pulled his bedroom door shut before she could see he didn't even have a bedstead for his mattress.

She put a finger on his grandmother's dowry chest by the kitchen door. "I like antiques." She took off her coat, folded it, laid it on the chest, then stepped out of her shoes and she went into his bathroom with her purse; she closed, then locked the door. He heard water running. So what happens now? he asked himself, feeling like he was speeding down a sledding-hill too fast, might hit the snow bank, crash into the barn.

In his bedroom he stripped off his uniform, skinnied quick into his jeans, sweatshirt and boots. He splashed tap water on his face at the kitchen sink, then got out pancake mix, eggs and bacon for breakfast.

His kitchen was all right—he'd hung some Christmas cards, tinsel, and colored glass ornaments on a string across the windows—next year he'd get a tree. He put candles on the formica table, laid out plastic mats and paper napkins. By the time she came out of the bathroom he'd started bacon frying and coffee heating. The radiators were knocking.

She'd brushed her hair and put on glasses, aviator-style, with no rims. Stocking-footed, she looked girlish. She was a cat stepping silently into a barn where there were mice to be caught. "What can I do?"

"Just relax." He reached down the griddle. She straightened her blouse collar and laid her purse down on her folded coat before she sat at his table.

The bacon was popping and he only half-listened while she talked about her daughter, her only child, Jane, always a problem—allergies, asthma, a time in her early teens when she couldn't be made to eat, a gymnast, played the piano, but never really stuck with anything. The business of the upcoming divorce really upset her. At her college up in St. Paul she'd started seeing a counselor who had written that she spoke of suicide.

She took a handkerchief from her skirt pocket to wipe her eyes with. "My name's Lee." As if he'd asked just then.

"Been tough on you, Lee."

"I guess it shows. I got this call from her a couple of days ago. She was at her roommate's house, but she decided she wanted to come home after all. She said she was pregnant. So right away I said, 'Come on home, baby. I'll take care of everything.' But no, she said she wants to have the baby. As though she was choosing a puppy to raise! She just doesn't know, and I don't know how to tell her. I made an appointment for her with my therapist."

He handed Lee a cup of coffee.

"Do you have anything to drink?"

He looked in the cupboard. "Peppermint Schnapps."

"Ugh." Then. "All right."

He poured a shot for each of them into plastic glasses.

"This tastes like candy."

The smell of it reminded him of Grandpa, thin and old in his big overalls and baseball cap. He'd worked hard all his life and had less than when he'd begun. The government, he said, but his land was poor. There'd been hardly enough money to bury him and Grandma.

She held out her glass for more; he poured and set the bottle by her on the table. He brushed oil on the griddle, spooned on batter.

"Actually, Jeff had been seeing this woman he works with for two years. Doctors are devious, let me tell you. Lots of reasons to be away from home at odd hours. I suppose it would have just gone on like that, but the woman decided she wanted to get married. Isn't that the most common story in the world? I don't miss him, if you're wondering. I'm through with men. I don't like the things you have to do to please them."

He checked the schnapps bottle, figured only a couple of shots left, and poured himself a glass of milk. Then he dished up the pancakes, started more cooking, and set the plate of bacon between them.

"I couldn't even eat supper last night. I was just so frantic, driving here through all that snow."

He watched her pour syrup, lick her fingers. "How is it?"

She looked up from her plate like she'd forgotten he was there. "Oh, lovely." Then she shut up while they ate.

When they'd finished the second stack of cakes and all the bacon, he poured them each a cup of coffee. She glanced at her purse, so he offered her one of his Luckies and she tipped her head back to exhale.

"You feel better, now, don't you." He wanted her to notice that.

"What's your last name again?"

"Kreuger. My folks were Swiss-German."

"Tell me about yourself, Gary."

There wasn't much to tell—that he wanted to tell her, anyway. His grandpa's farm, not saying how poor and small it had been. A couple years working in his uncle's grain store. "I gave college a try. At Whitewater. But I couldn't see much point to it. For good times I play the fiddle."

"A musician."

"A fiddler. Polkas, waltzes and such."

"I thought there was something unusual about you." The schnapps had brought up the color in her pale face as if she were flushed again. She looked rested. "Play some," she told him.

But another idea came to him real quick. He got out a tape of his group he played with—three fiddles and two accordions—and pushed back his grandma's little hooked rug. The rocker went into the hall. When the polka started up, he held out his hand.

Taking off her glasses, she stood up right away, like dancing had been her idea all along. "Do I need to see where I'm going? I could put my contacts back in."

He took her hand—small, warm, lightly sticky; he showed her how to hold him at his shoulder. "Just hang on."

Her back tensed and she stared up at him like she'd lose her balance if she looked away. Then she got into it—he gave the schnapps credit for that—and she was as good as most. After the polka, they waltzed.

Through the steamed-up windows he saw Christmas tree lights coming on in the houses down the street. The sun was a pink hedge-rose above the frozen lake. When he turned the tape, she said, "Can we waltz some more?"

"I'll twirl your head off."

It was a spinning waltz, and, instead of holding his shoulders, she hung on around his neck. On every turn the inside of her legs brushed his, her slip rustling. Silk. She was the kind to wear it. Her feet whispered across the floor. Her face was turned up, her eyes narrowed, sweat on her temples and upper lip. He thought of the wall-eyed mare running away with him, galloping flat out through the pine copse, scrub pine stinging his hands and face; she'd tried to scrape him off on the trees. Lee hung on tight.

Then she leaned against him, her silky leg still between his from the last turn. "I'm dizzy."

He couldn't help it; he clutched her to him. He wanted to pull her on top of him to feel her weight, her breasts pressed between them. He wanted silk in his hands, on his face. He pushed his face against her throat and damp hair.

She pushed out of his arms, looked at her watch. "What time's that bus?"

"What bus?"

"My daughter!"

"Oh, right. Eight-ten."

"I've got to get back!"

He steadied her, his hands on her waist. Steadied himself—because it all came together, as though he'd been swimming under dark water and burst into the flashing air before he'd expected to reach the surface. Cool, so cool. He turned his back. "I'll call the station, check on that bus, and you wash up. You're only three minutes away."

When she banged the bathroom door closed, he rattled the phone in its cradle. "Morning, Roy. How about the bus coming down from Minneapolis?" He slid his hand into Lee's purse, pulled the wallet out, opened it. "About eight-ten for sure?" Slipped his fingers between the folds of smooth leather. "Sounds good, Roy."

No bills! He caught his breath and tipped her purse to look inside. Car keys, an address book, handkerchief, comb, lipstick. That was all.

She unlocked the bathroom door; he closed the purse. "Thanks, Roy."

"I'm hurrying." She stepped into her high heels, grabbed her purse, and disappeared again into the bathroom. She didn't bother to close the door, so he watched her draw lipstick on, lean forward to whip her comb through her hair.

The vision came to him as clearly as though he'd seen it happen—she'd dropped that roll of money in the snow with her car keys. The bills lay waiting for him in the drift by her tire tracks.

She looped her scarf around her throat, buttoned her coat crooked. "You saved the day, Gary."

"Sure I did." Like a parent hurrying along a child when the school bus is coming, he turned up the collar of her coat, handed her her glasses. "Maybe your daughter will listen to reason."

"If there's a girl in the world who needs a mother, she's the one."

As she ran down the front stairs, her purse bumping the bannister, she called back, "Merry Christmas!"

He grabbed his parka. He took the back stairs two at a time down to the alley door; the alley ran behind the parking lot. He peered through the streaked window.

She still stood working the lock of her car. Her breath drifted up around her bent head. Then the key turned and she slid inside. Liquid jetted onto her windshield. While she waited for the wipers to clear it, she reached into the collar of her coat, into her blouse between her breasts, and came out with the roll of bills.

He let himself back into his apartment. When he hurled his parka across the kitchen, it knocked down the string of Christmas cards and colored ornaments before it fell against the radiator into the tinkling pieces of red and green glass. She'd known what he was going to do before he'd known—that was the worst part.

He groaned at the dirty dishes, the coffee grounds in the sink, the schnapps bottle overturned on the table. Then he leaned on the window sill to look down at the bus coming in at last from Milwaukee, bringing poor little Jane into the arms of her mother. "Relax, kid," he said out loud. "You got no problems. Your old lady will think of everything."

GRAHAM SWIFT

Learning to Swim

MRS. Singleton had three times thought of leaving her husband. The first time was before they were married, on a charter plane coming back from a holiday in Greece. They were students who had just graduated. They had rucksacks and faded jeans. In Greece they had stayed part of the time by a beach on an island. The island was dry and rocky with great grey and vermilion coloured rocks and when you lay on the beach it seemed that you too became a hot, basking rock. Behind the beach there were eucalyptus trees like dry, leafy bones, old men with mules and gold teeth, a fragrance of thyme, and a café with melon seeds on the floor and a jukebox which played bouzouki music and songs by Cliff Richard. All this Mr. Singleton failed to appreciate. He'd only liked the milk-warm, clear blue sea, in which he'd stayed most of the time as if afraid of foreign soil. On the plane she'd thought: He hadn't enjoyed the holiday, hadn't liked Greece at all. All that sunshine. Then she'd thought she ought not to marry him.

Though she had, a year later.

The second time was about a year after Mr. Singleton, who was a civil engineer, had begun his first big job. He became a junior partner in a firm with a growing reputation. She ought to have been pleased by this. It brought money and comfort; it enabled them to move to a house with a large garden, to live well, to think about raising a family. They spent weekends in country hotels. But Mr. Singleton seemed untouched by this. He became withdrawn and incommunicative. He went to his work austere-faced. She thought: He likes his bridges and tunnels better than me.

The third time, which was really a phase, not a single moment, was when she began to calculate how often Mr. Singleton made love to her. When she started this it was about once every fortnight on average. Then it became every three weeks. The interval had been widening for some time. This was not a predicament Mrs. Singleton viewed selfishly. Love-making had been a problem before, in their earliest days together, which, thanks to her patience and initiative, had been overcome. It was Mr. Singleton's unhappiness, not her own, that she saw in their present plight. He was distrustful of happiness as some people fear heights or open spaces. She would reassure him, encourage him again. But the averages seemed to defy her personal effort: once every three weeks, once every month . . . She thought: Things go back to as they were.

But then, by sheer chance, she became pregnant.

Now she lay on her back, eyes closed, on the coarse sand of the beach in Cornwall. It was hot and, if she opened her eyes, the sky was clear blue. This and the previous summer had been fine enough to make her husband's refusal to go abroad for holidays tolerable. If you kept your eyes closed it could be Greece or Italy or Ibiza. She wore a chocolate-brown bikini, sunglasses, and her skin, which seldom suffered from sunburn, was already beginning to tan. She let her arms trail idly by her side, scooping up little handfuls of sand. If she turned her head to the right and looked towards the sea she could see Mr. Singleton and their son Paul standing in the shallow water. Mr. Singleton was teaching Paul to swim. "Kick!" he was saying. From here, against the gentle waves, they looked like no more than two rippling silhouettes.

"Kick!" said Mr. Singleton, "Kick!" He was like a punisher administering lashes.

She turned her head away to face upwards. If you shut your eyes you could imagine you were the only one on the beach; if you held them shut you could be part of the beach. Mrs. Singleton imagined that in order to acquire a tan you had to let the sun make love to you.

She dug her heels in the sand and smiled involuntarily.

When she was a thin, flat-chested, studious girl in a grey school uniform, Mrs. Singleton had assuaged her fear and desperation about sex with fantasies which took away from men the brute physicality she expected of them. All her lovers would be artists. Poets would write poems to her, composers would dedicate their works to her. She would even pose, naked and immaculate, for painters, who having committed her true, her eternal form to canvas, would make love to her in an impalpable, ethereal way, under the power of which her bodily and temporal self would melt away, perhaps for ever. These fantasies (for she had never entirely renounced them) had crystallized for her in the image of a sculptor, who from a cold intractable piece of stone would fashion her very essence—which would be vibrant and full of sunlight, like the statues they had seen in Greece.

At university she had worked on the assumption that all men lusted uncontrollably and insatiably after women. She had not yet encountered a man who, whilst prone to the usual instincts, possessing moreover a magnificent body with which to fulfil them, yet had scruples about doing so, seemed ashamed of his own capacities. It did not matter that Mr. Singleton was reading engineering, was scarcely artistic at all, or that his powerful physique was unlike the nebulous creatures of her dreams. She found she loved this solid man-flesh. Mrs. Singleton had thought she was the shy, inexperienced, timid girl. Overnight she discovered that she wasn't this at all. He wore tough denim shirts, spoke and smiled very little and had a way of standing very straight and upright as if he didn't need any help from anyone. She had to educate him into moments of passion, of self-forgetfulness which made her glow with her own achievement. She was happy because she had not thought she was happy and she believed she could make someone else happy. At the university girls were starting to wear jeans, record-players played the Rolling Stones and in the hush of the Modern Languages Library she read Leopardi and Verlaine.[1] She seemed to float with confidence in a swirling, buoyant element she had never suspected would be her own.

"Kick!" she heard again from the water.

Mr. Singleton had twice thought of leaving his wife. Once was after a symphony concert they had gone to in London when they had not known each other very long and she still tried to get him to read books, to listen to music, to take an interest in art. She would buy concert or theatre tickets, and he had to seem pleased. At this concert a visiting orchestra was playing some titanic, large-scale work by a late nineteenth-century composer. A note in the programme said it represented the triumph of life over death. He had sat on his plush seat amidst the swirling barrage of sound. He had no idea what he had to do with it or the triumph of life over death. He had thought the same thought about the rapt girl on his left, the future Mrs. Singleton, who now and then bobbed, swayed or rose in her seat at if the music physically lifted her. There were at least seventy musicians on the platform. As the piece worked to its final crescendo the conductor, whose arms were flailing frantically so that his white shirt back appeared under his flying tails, looked so absurd Mr. Singleton thought he would laugh. When the music stopped and was immediately supplanted by wild cheering and clapping he thought the world had gone mad. He had struck his own hands together so as to appear to be sharing the ecstasy. Then, as they filed out, he had almost wept because he felt like an insect. He even thought she had arranged the whole business so as to humiliate him.

He thought he would not marry her.

The second time was after they had been married some years. He was one of a team of engineers working on a suspension bridge over an estuary in Ireland. They took it in turns to stay on the site and to inspect the construction work personally. Once he had to go to the very top of one of the two piers of the bridge to examine work on the bearings and housing for the main overhead cables. A lift ran up between the twin towers of the pier amidst a network of scaffolding and power cables to where a working platform was positioned. The engineer, with the supervisor and the foreman, had only

1. Giacomo Leopardi (1798–1837), Italian poet, and Paul Verlaine (1844–1896), French poet.

to stay on the platform from where all the main features of construction were visible. The men at work on the upper sections of the towers, specialists in their trade, earning up to two hundred pounds a week—who balanced on precarious cat-walks and walked along exposed reinforcing girders—often jibed at the engineers who never left the platform. He thought he would show them. He walked out on to one of the cat-walks on the outer face of the pier where they were fitting huge grip-bolts. This was quite safe if you held on to the rails but still took some nerve. He wore a check cheesecloth shirt and his white safety helmet. It was a grey, humid August day. The cat-walk hung over greyness. The water of the estuary was the colour of dead fish. A dredger was chugging near the base of the pier. He thought, I could swim the estuary; but there is a bridge. Below him the yellow helmets of workers moved over the girders for the roadway like beetles. He took his hands from the rail. He wasn't at all afraid. He had been away from his wife all week. He thought: She knows nothing of this. If he were to step out now into the grey air he would be quite by himself, no harm would come to him . . .

Now Mr. Singleton stood in the water, teaching his son to swim. They were doing the water-wings exercise. The boy wore a pair of water-wings, red underneath, yellow on top, which ballooned up under his arms and chin. With this to support him, he would splutter and splash towards his father who stood facing him some feet away. After a while at this they would try the same procedure, his father moving a little nearer, but without the water-wings, and this the boy dreaded. "Kick!" said Mr. Singleton. "Use your legs!" He watched his son draw painfully towards him. The boy had not yet grasped that the body naturally floated and that if you added to this certain mechanical effects, you swam. He thought that in order to swim you had to make as much frantic movement as possible. As he struggled towards Mr. Singleton his head, which was too high out of the water, jerked messily from side to side, and his eyes which were half closed swivelled in every direction but straight ahead. "Towards me!" shouted Mr. Singleton. He held out his arms in front of him for Paul to grasp. As his son was on the point of clutching them he would step back a little, pulling his hands away, in the hope that the last desperate lunge to reach his father might really teach the boy the art of propelling himself in water. But he sometimes wondered if this were his only motive.

"Good boy. Now again."

At school Mr. Singleton had been an excellent swimmer. He had won various school titles, broken numerous records and competed successfully in ASA championships. There was a period between the ages of about thirteen and seventeen which he remembered as the happiest in his life. It wasn't the medals and trophies that made him glad, but the knowledge that he didn't have to bother about anything else. Swimming vindicated him. He would get up every morning at six and train for two hours in the baths, and again before lunch; and when he fell asleep, exhausted, in French and English periods in the afternoon, he didn't have to bother about the indignation of the masters—lank, ill-conditioned creatures—for he had his excuse. He didn't have to bother about the physics teacher who complained to the headmaster that he would never get the exam results he needed if he didn't cut down his swimming, for the headmaster (who was an advocate of sport) came to his aid and told the physics teacher not to interfere with a boy who was a credit to the school. Nor did he have to bother about a host of other things which were supposed to be going on inside him, which made the question of what to do in the evening, at week-ends, fraught and tantalizing, which drove other boys to moodiness and recklessness. For once in the cool water of the baths, his arms reaching, his eyes fixed on the blue marker line on the bottom, his ears full so that he could hear nothing around him, he would feel quite by himself, quite sufficient. At the end of races, when for one brief instant he clung panting alone like a survivor to the finishing rail which his rivals had yet to touch, he felt an infinite peace. He went to bed early, slept soundly, kept to his training regimen; and he enjoyed this Spartan purity which disdained pleasure and dis-order. Some of his schoolmates mocked him—for not going to dances on Saturdays or to pubs, under age, or the Expresso after school. But he did not mind. He didn't need them. He knew they were weak. None of them could hold out, depend on themselves, spurn comfort if they had to. Some of them would go under in life. And none of them could cleave the water as he did or possessed a hard, stream-lined, perfectly tuned body as he did.

Then, when he was nearly seventeen all this changed. His father, who was an engineer, though proud of his son's trophies, suddenly pressed him to different forms of success. The headmaster no longer shielded him from the physics master. He said: "You can't swim into your future." Out of spite perhaps or an odd consistency of self-denial, he dropped swimming altogether rather than cut it down. For a year and a half he worked at his maths and physics with the same single-mindedness with which he had perfected his sport. He knew about mechanics and engineering because he knew how to make his body move through water. His work was not merely competent but good. He got to university where he might have had the leisure, if he wished, to resume his swimming. But he did not. Two years are a long gap in a swimmer's training; two years when you are near your peak can mean you will never get back to your true form. Sometimes he went for a dip in the university pool and swam slowly up and down amongst practising members of the university team, whom perhaps he could still have beaten, as a kind of relief.

Often, Mr. Singleton dreamt about swimming. He would be moving through vast expanses of water, an ocean. As he moved it did not require any effort at all. Sometimes he would go for long distances under water, but he did not have to bother about breathing. The water would be silvery-grey. And as always it seemed that as he swam he was really trying to get beyond the water, to put it behind him, as if it were a veil he were parting and he would emerge on the other side of it at last, on to some pristine shore, where he would step where no one else had stepped before.

When he made love to his wife her body got in the way; he wanted to swim through her.

Mrs. Singleton raised herself, pushed her sun-glasses up over her dark hair and sat with her arms stretched straight behind her back. A trickle of sweat ran between her breasts. They had developed to a good size since her schoolgirl days. Her skinniness in youth had stood her in good stead against the filling out of middle age, and her body was probably more mellow, more lithe and better proportioned now than it had ever been. She looked at Paul and Mr. Singleton half immersed in the shallows. It seemed to her that her husband was the real boy, standing stubbornly upright with his hands before him, and that Paul was some toy being pulled and swung relentlessly around him and towards him as though on some string. They had seen her sit up. Her husband waved, holding the boy's hand, as though for the two of them. Paul did not wave; he seemed more concerned with the water in his eyes. Mrs. Singleton did not wave back. She would have done if her son had waved. When they had left for their holiday Mr. Singleton had said to Paul, "You'll learn to swim this time. In salt water, you know, it's easier." Mrs. Singleton hoped her son wouldn't swim; so that she could wrap him, still, in the big yellow towel when he came out, rub him dry and warm, and watch her husband stand apart, his hands empty.

She watched Mr. Singleton drop his arm back to his side. "If you wouldn't splash it wouldn't go in your eyes," she just caught him say.

The night before, in their hotel room, they had argued. They always argued about half way through their holidays. It was symbolic, perhaps, of that first trip to Greece, when he had somehow refused to enjoy himself. They had to incur injuries so that they could then appreciate their leisure, like convalescents. For the first four days or so of their holiday Mr. Singleton would tend to be moody, on edge. He would excuse this as "winding down," the not-to-be-hurried process of dispelling the pressures of work. Mrs. Singleton would be patient. On about the fifth day Mrs. Singleton would begin to suspect that the winding down would never end and indeed (which she had known all along) that it was not winding down at all—he was clinging, as to a defence, to his bridges and tunnels; and she would show her resentment. At this point Mr. Singleton would retaliate by an attack upon her indolence.

Last night he had called her "flabby." He could not mean, of course, "flabby-bodied" (she could glance down, now, at her still flat belly), though such a sensual attack would have been simpler, almost heartening, from him. He meant "flabby of attitude." And what he meant by this, or what he wanted to mean, was that *he* was not flabby; that he worked, facing the real world, erecting great solid things on the face of the land, and that, whilst he worked, he disdained work's rewards—money, pleasure, rich food, holidays abroad—that he hadn't "gone soft," as she had done since they graduated eleven years ago, with their credentials for the future and their plane tickets to Greece. She knew this toughness of her husband was only a cover for his own failure to relax and his need to keep his distance. She knew that he found no particular virtue in his bridges and tunnels (it was the last thing he wanted to do really —build); it didn't matter if they were right or wrong, they were there, he could point to them as if it vindicated him—just as when he made his infrequent, if seismic, love to her it was not a case of enjoyment or satisfaction; he just did it.

It was hot in their hotel room. Mr. Singleton stood in his blue pyjama bottoms, feet apart, like a PT instructor.

"Flabby? What do you mean—'flabby'!?" she had said, looking daunted.

But Mrs. Singleton had the advantage whenever Mr. Singleton accused her in this way of complacency, of weakness. She knew he only did it to hurt her, and so to feel guilty, and so to feel the remorse which would release his own affection for her, his vulnerability, his own need to be loved. Mrs. Singleton was used to this process, to the tenderness that was the tenderness of successively opened and reopened wounds. And she was used to being the nurse who took care of the healing scars. For though Mr. Singleton inflicted the first blow he would always make himself more guilty than he made her suffer, and Mrs. Singleton, though in pain herself, could not resist wanting to clasp and cherish her husband, wanting to wrap him up safe when his own weakness and submissiveness showed and his body became liquid and soft against her; could not resist the old spur that her husband was unhappy and it was for her to make him happy. Mr. Singleton was extraordinarily lovable when he was guilty. She would even have yielded indefinitely, foregoing her own grievance, to this extreme of comforting him for the pain he caused her, had she not discovered, in time, that this only pushed the process a stage further. Her forgiveness of him became only another level of comfort, of softness he must reject. His flesh shrank from her restoring touch.

She thought: Men go round in circles, women don't move.

She kept to her side of the hotel bed, he, with his face turned, to his. He lay like a person washed up on a beach. She reached out her hand and stroked the nape of his neck. She felt him tense. All this was a pattern.

"I'm sorry," he said, "I didn't mean—"

"It's all right, it doesn't matter."

"Doesn't it matter?" he said.

When they reached this point they were like miners racing each other for deeper and deeper seams of guilt and recrimination.

But Mrs. Singleton had given up delving to rock bottom. Perhaps it was five years ago when she had thought for the third time of leaving her husband, perhaps long before that. When they were students she'd made allowances for his constraints, his reluctances. An unhappy childhood perhaps, a strict upbringing. She thought his inhibition might be lifted by the sanction of marriage. She'd thought, after all, it would be a good thing if he married her. She had not thought what would be good for her. They stood outside Gatwick Airport, back from Greece, in the grey, wet August light. Their tanned skin had seemed to glow. Yet she'd known this mood of promise would pass. She watched him kick against contentment, against ease, against the long, glittering life-line she threw at him; and, after a while, she ceased to try to haul him in. She began to imagine again her phantom artists. She thought: People slip off the shores of the real world, back into dreams. She hadn't "gone soft," only gone back to herself. Hidden inside her like treasure there were lines of Leopardi, of Verlaine her husband would never appreciate. She thought, he doesn't need me, things run off him, like water. She even thought that her husband's neglect in making love to her was not a problem he had but a deliberate scheme to deny her. When Mrs. Singleton desired her husband she could not help herself. She would stretch back on the bed with the sheets pulled off like a blissful nude in a Modigliani.[2] She thought this ought to gladden a man. Mr. Singleton would stand at the foot of the bed and gaze down at her. He looked like some strong, chaste knight in the legend of the Grail. He would respond to her invitation, but before he did so there would be this expression,

2. Amedeo Modigliani (1884–1920), Italian painter.

half stern, half innocent, in his eyes. It was the sort of expression that good men in books and films are supposed to make to prostitutes. It would ensure that their love-making was marred and that afterward it would seem as if he had performed something out of duty that only she wanted. Her body would feel like stone. It was at such times, when she felt the cold, dead-weight feel of abused happiness, that Mrs. Singleton most thought she was through with Mr. Singleton. She would watch his strong, compact torso already lifting itself off the bed. She would think: He thinks he is tough, contained in himself, but he won't see what I offer him, he doesn't see how it is I who can help him.

Mrs. Singleton lay back on her striped towel on the sand. Once again she became part of the beach. The careless sounds of the seaside, of excited children's voices, of languid grownups', of wooden bats on balls, fluttered over her as she shut her eyes. She thought: It is the sort of day on which someone suddenly shouts, "Someone is drowning."

When Mrs. Singleton became pregnant she felt she had outmanoeuvered her husband. He did not really want a child (it was the last thing he wanted, Mrs. Singleton thought, a child), but he was jealous of her condition, as of some achievement he himself could attain. He was excluded from the little circle of herself and her womb, and, as though to puncture it, he began for the first time to make love to her of a kind where he took the insistent initiative. Mrs. Singleton was not greatly pleased. She seemed buoyed up by her own bigness. She noticed that her husband began to do exercises in the morning, in his underpants, press-ups, squat-jumps, as if he were getting in training for something. He was like a boy. He even became, as the term of her pregnancy drew near its end, resilient and detached again, the virile father waiting to receive the son (Mr. Singleton knew it would be a son, so did Mrs. Singleton) that she, at the appointed time, would deliver him. When the moment arrived he insisted on being present so as to prove he wasn't squeamish and to make sure he wouldn't be tricked in the transaction. Mrs. Singleton was not daunted. When the pains became frequent she wasn't at all afraid. There were big, watery lights clawing down from the ceiling of the delivery room like the lights in dentists' surgeries. She could just see her husband looking down at her. His face was white and clammy. It was his fault for wanting to be there. She had to push, as though away from him. Then she knew it was happening. She stretched back. She was a great surface of warm, splitting rock and Paul was struggling bravely up into the sunlight. She had to coax him with her cries. She felt him emerge like a trapped survivor. The doctor groped with rubber gloves. "There we are," he said. She managed to look at Mr.

Singleton. She wanted suddenly to put him back inside for good where Paul had come from. With a fleeting pity she saw that this was what Mr. Singleton wanted too. His eyes were half closed. She kept hers on him. He seemed to wilt under her gaze. All his toughness and control were draining from him and she was glad. She lay back triumphant and glad. The doctor was holding Paul; but she looked, beyond, at Mr. Singleton. He was far away like an insect. She knew he couldn't hold out. He was going to faint. He was looking where her legs were spread. His eyes went out of focus. He was going to faint, keel over, right there on the spot.

Mrs. Singleton grew restless, though she lay unmoving on the beach. Wasps were buzzing close to her head, round their picnic bag. She thought that Mr. Singleton and Paul had been too long at their swimming lesson. They should come out. It never struck her, hot as she was, to get up and join her husband and son in the sea. Whenever Mrs. Singleton wanted a swim she would wait until there was an opportunity to go in by herself; then she would wade out, dip her shoulders under suddenly and paddle about contentedly, keeping her hair dry, as though she were soaking herself in a large bath. They did not bathe as a family; nor did Mrs. Singleton swim with Mr. Singleton—who now and then, too, would get up by himself and enter the sea, swim at once about fifty yards out, then cruise for long stretches, with a powerful crawl or butterfly, back and forth across the bay. When this happened Mrs. Singleton would engage her son in talk so he would not watch his father. Mrs. Singleton did not swim with Paul either. He was too old now to cradle between her knees in the very shallow water, and she was somehow afraid that while Paul splashed and kicked around her he would suddenly learn how to swim. She had this feeling that Paul would only swim while she was in the sea, too. She did not want this to happen, but it reassured her and gave her sufficient confidence to let Mr. Singleton continue his swimming lessons with Paul. These lessons were obsessive, indefatigable. Every Sunday morning at seven, when they were at home, Mr. Singleton would take Paul to the baths for yet another attempt. Part of this, of course, was that Mr. Singleton was determined that his son should swim; but it enabled him also to avoid the Sunday morning languor: extra hours in bed, leisurely love-making.

Once, in a room at college, Mr. Singleton had told Mrs. Singleton about his swimming, about his training sessions, races; about what it felt like when you could swim really well. She had run her fingers over his long, naked back.

Mrs. Singleton sat up and rubbed sun-tan lotion on to her thighs. Down near the water's edge, Mr. Singleton was standing about waist deep, supporting Paul who, gripped by his father's hands, water wings still on, was flailing, face down, at the surface. Mr. Singleton kept saying, "No, keep still." He was trying to get Paul to hold his body straight and relaxed so he would float. But each time as Paul nearly succeeded he would panic, fearing his father would let go, and thrash wildly. When he calmed down and Mr. Singleton held him, Mrs. Singleton could see the water running off his face like tears.

Mrs. Singleton did not alarm herself at this distress of her son. It was a guarantee against Mr. Singleton's influence, an assurance that Paul was not going to swim; nor was he to be imbued with any of his father's sullen hardiness. When Mrs. Singleton saw her son suffer, it pleased her and she felt loving toward him. She felt that an invisible thread ran between her and the boy which commanded him not to swim, and she felt that Mr. Singleton knew that it was because of her that his efforts with Paul were in vain. Even now, as Mr. Singleton prepared for another attempt, the boy was looking at her smoothing the sun-tan oil on to her legs.

"Come on, Paul," said Mr. Singleton. His wet shoulders shone like metal.

When Paul was born it seemed to Mrs. Singleton that her life with her husband was dissolved, as a mirage dissolves, and that she could return again to what she was before she knew him. She let her staved-off hunger for happiness and her old suppressed dreams revive. But then they were not dreams, because they had a physical object and she knew she needed them in order to live. She did not disguise from herself what she needed. She knew that she wanted the kind of close, even erotic relationship with her son that women who have rejected their husbands have been known to have. The kind of relationship in which the son must hurt the mother, the mother the son. But she willed it, as if there would be no pain. Mrs. Singleton waited for her son to grow. She trembled when she thought of him at eighteen or twenty. When he was grown he would be slim and light and slender, like a boy even though he was a man. He would not need a strong body because all his power would be inside. He would be all fire and life in essence. He would become an artist, a sculptor. She would pose for him naked (she would keep her body trim for this), and he would sculpt her. He would hold the chisel. His hands would guide the cold metal over the stone and its blows would strike sunlight.

Mrs. Singleton thought: All the best statues they had seen in Greece seemed to have been dredged up from the sea.

She finished rubbing the lotion on to her insteps and put the cap back on the tube. As she did so she heard something that made her truly alarmed. It was Mr. Singleton saying, "That's it, that's the way! At last! Now keep it going!" She looked up. Paul was in the same position as before but he had learnt to make slower, regular motions with his limbs and his body no longer sagged in the middle. Though he still wore the water-wings he was moving, somewhat laboriously, forwards so that Mr. Singleton had to walk along with him; and at one point Mr. Singleton removed one of his hands from under the boy's ribs and simultaneously looked at his wife and smiled. His shoulders flashed. It was not a smile meant for her. She could see that. And it was not one of her husband's usual, infrequent, rather mechanical smiles. It was the smile a person makes about some joy inside, hidden and incommunicable.

"That's enough," thought Mrs. Singleton, getting to her feet, pretending not to have noticed, behind her sun-glasses, what had happened in the water. It *was* enough: They had been in the water for what seemed like an hour. He was only doing it because of their row last night, to make her feel he was not outmatched by using the reserve weapon of Paul. And, she added with relief to herself, Paul still had the water-wings and one hand to support him.

"That's enough now!" she shouted aloud, as if she were slightly, but not ill-humouredly, peeved at being neglected. "Come on in now!" She had picked up her purse as a quickly conceived ruse as she got up, and as she walked towards the water's edge she waved it above her head. "Who wants an ice-cream?"

Mr. Singleton ignored his wife. "Well done, Paul," he said. "Let's try that again."

Mrs. Singleton knew he would do this. She stood on the little ridge of sand just above where the beach, becoming fine shingle, shelved into the sea. She replaced a loose strap of her bikini over her shoulder and with a finger of each hand pulled the bottom half down over her buttocks. She stood feet apart, slightly on her toes, like a gymnast. She knew other eyes on the beach would be on her. It flattered her that she—and her husband, too—received admiring glances from those around. She thought, with relish for the irony: Perhaps they think we are happy, beautiful people. For all her girlhood diffidence, Mrs. Singleton enjoyed displaying her attractions and she liked to see other people's pleasure. When she lay sunbathing she imagined making love to all the moody, pubescent boys on holiday with their parents, with their slim waists and their quick heels.

"See if you can do it without me holding you," said Mr. Singleton. "I'll help you at first." He stooped over Paul. He looked like a mechanic making final adjustments to some prototype machine.

"Don't you want an ice-cream then, Paul?" said Mrs. Singleton. "They've got those chocolate ones."

Paul looked up. His short wet hair stood up in spikes. He looked like a prisoner offered a chance of escape, but the plastic water-wings, like some absurd pillory, kept him fixed.

Mrs. Singleton thought: He crawled out of me; now I have to lure him back with ice-cream.

"Can't you see he was getting the hang of it?" Mr. Singleton said. "If he comes out now he'll—"

"Hang of it! It was you. You were holding him all the time."

She thought: Perhaps I am hurting my son.

Mr. Singleton glared at Mrs. Singleton. He gripped Paul's shoulders. "You don't want to get out now, do you Paul?" He looked suddenly as if he really might drown Paul rather than let him come out.

Mrs. Singleton's heart raced. She wasn't good at rescues, at resuscitations. She knew this because of her life with her husband.

"Come on, you can go back in later," she said.

Paul was a hostage. She was playing for time, not wanting to harm the innocent.

She stood on the sand like a marooned woman watching for ships. The sea, in the sheltered bay, was almost flat calm. A few, glassy waves idled in but were smoothed out before they could break. On the headlands there were outcrops of scaly rocks like basking lizards. The island in Greece had been where Theseus left Ariadne.[3] Out over the blue water, beyond the heads of bobbing swimmers, seagulls flapped like scraps of paper.

Mr. Singleton looked at Mrs. Singleton. She was a fussy mother daubed with Ambre Solaire, trying to bribe her son with silly ice-creams; though if you forgot this she was a beautiful, tanned girl, like the girls men imagine on desert islands. But then, in Mr. Singleton's dreams, there was no one else on the untouched shore he ceaselessly swam to.

He thought, If Paul could swim, then I could leave her.

Mrs. Singleton looked at her husband. She felt afraid. The water's edge was like a dividing line between them which marked off the territory in which each existed. Perhaps they could never cross over.

"Well, I'm getting the ice-creams: you'd better get out."

She turned and paced up the sand. Behind the beach was an ice-cream van painted like a fairground.

Paul Singleton looked at his mother. He thought: She is deserting me—or I am deserting her. He wanted to get out to follow her. Her feet made puffs of sand which stuck to her ankles, and you could see all her body as she strode up the beach. But he was afraid of his father and his gripping hands. And he was afraid of his mother, too. How she would wrap him, if he came out,

3. Theseus deserted his lover and benefactor after carrying her away.

in the big yellow towel like egg yolk, how she would want him to get close to her smooth, sticky body, like a mouth that would swallow him. He thought: The yellow towel humiliated him, his father's hands humiliated him. The water-wings humiliated him: You put them on and became a puppet. So much of life is humiliation. It was how you won love. His father was taking off the water-wings like a man unlocking a chastity belt. He said: "Now try the same, coming towards me." His father stood some feet away from him. He was a huge, straight man, like the pier of a bridge. "Try." Paul Singleton was six. He was terrified of water. Every time he entered it he had to fight down fear. His father never realized this. He thought it was simple; you said: "Only water, no need to be afraid." His father did not know what fear was; the same as he did not know what fun was. Paul Singleton hated water. He hated it in his mouth and in his eyes. He hated the chlorine smell of the swimming baths, the wet, slippery tiles, the echoing whoops and screams. He hated it when his father read to him from *The Water Babies*.[4] It was the only story his father read, because, since he didn't know fear or fun, he was really sentimental. His mother read lots of stories. "Come on then. I'll catch you." Paul Singleton held out his arms and raised one leg. This was the worst moment. Perhaps having no help was most humiliating. If you did not swim you sank like a statue. They would drag him out, his skin streaming. His father would say: "I didn't mean . . ." But if he swam his mother would be forsaken. She would stand on the beach with chocolate ice-cream running down her arm. There was no way out; there were all these things to be afraid of and no weapons. But then, perhaps he was not afraid of his mother nor his father, nor of water, but of something else. He had felt it just now—when he'd struck out with rhythmic, reaching strokes and his feet had come off the bottom and his father's hand had slipped from under his chest: as if he had mistaken what his fear was; as if he had been unconsciously pretending, even to himself, so as to execute some plan. He lowered his chin into the water. "Come on!" said Mr. Singleton. He launched himself forward and felt the sand leave his feet and his legs wriggle like cut ropes. "There," said his father as he realized. "There!" His father stood like a man waiting to clasp a lover; there was a gleam on his face. "Towards me! Towards me!" said his father suddenly. But he kicked and struck, half in panic, half in pride, away from his father, away from the shore, away, in this strange new element that seemed all his own.

4. A fairy tale by Charles Kingsley (1819–1875), English novelist.

WILLIAM TREVOR

Beyond the Pale

WE always went to Ireland in June.

Ever since the four of us began to go on holidays together, in 1965 it must have been, we had spent the first fortnight of the month at Glencorn Lodge in Co. Antrim. Perfection, as Dekko put it once, and none of us disagreed. It's a Georgian house by the sea, not far from the village of Ardbeag. It's quite majestic in its rather elegant way, a garden running to the very edge of a cliff, its long rhododendron drive—or avenue, as they say in Ireland. The English couple who bought the house in the early sixties, the Malseeds, have had to build on quite a bit but it's all been discreetly done, the Georgian style preserved throughout. Figs grow in the sheltered gardens, and apricots, and peaches in the greenhouses which old Mr Saxton presides over. He's Mrs Malseed's father actually. They brought him with them from Surrey, and their Dalmatians, Charger and Snooze.

It was Strafe who found Glencorn for us. He'd come across an advertisement in the *Lady* in the days when the Malseeds still felt the need to advertise. 'How about this?' he said one evening at the end of the second rubber, and then read out the details. We had gone away together the summer before, to a hotel that had been recommended on the Costa del Sol, but it hadn't been a success because the food was so appalling. 'We could try this Irish one,' Dekko suggested cautiously, which is what eventually we did.

The four of us have been playing bridge together for ages, Dekko, Strafe, Cynthia and myself. They call me Milly, though strictly speaking my name is Dorothy Milson. Dekko picked up his nickname at school, Dekko Deakin sounding rather good, I dare say. He and Strafe were in fact at school together, which must be why we all call Strafe by his surname: Major R. B. Strafe he is, the initials standing for Robert Buchanan. We're of an age, the four of us, all in the early fifties: the prime of life, so Dekko insists. We live quite close to Leatherhead, where the Malseeds were before they decided to make the change from Surrey to Co. Antrim. Quite a coincidence, we always think.

'How *very* nice,' Mrs Malseed said, smiling her welcome again this year. Some instinct seems to tell her when guests are about to arrive, for she's rarely not waiting in the large low-ceilinged hall that always smells of flowers. She dresses beautifully, differently every day, and changing of course in the evening. Her blouse on this occasion was scarlet and silver, in stripes, her skirt black. This choice gave her a brisk look, which was fitting because being so busy she often has to be a little on the brisk side. She has smooth grey hair which she once told me she entirely looks after herself, and she almost always wears a black velvet band in it. Her face is well made up, and for one who arranges so many vases of flowers and otherwise has to use her hands she manages to keep them marvellously in condition. Her fingernails are varnished a soft pink, and a small gold bangle always adorns her right wrist, a wedding present from her husband.

'Arthur, take the party's luggage,' she commanded the old porter, who doubles as odd-job man. 'Rose, Geranium, Hydrangea, Fuchsia.' She referred to the titles of the rooms reserved for us: in winter, when no one much comes to Glencorn Lodge, pleasant little details like that are seen to. Mrs Malseed herself painted the flower-plaques that are attached to the doors of the hotel instead of numbers; her husband sees to redecoration and repairs.

'Well, well, well,' Mr Malseed said now, entering the hall through the door that leads to the kitchen regions. 'A hundred thousand welcomes,' he greeted us in the Irish manner. He's rather shorter than Mrs Malseed, who's handsomely tall. He wears Donegal tweed suits and is brown as a berry, including his head, which is bald. His dark brown eyes twinkle at you, making you feel rather more than just another hotel guest. They run the place like a country house, really.

'Good trip?' Mr Malseed enquired.

'Super,' Dekko said. 'Not a worry all the way.'

'Splendid.'

'The wretched boat sailed an hour early one day last week,' Mrs Malseed said. 'Quite a little band were left stranded at Stranraer.'

Strafe laughed. 'Typical of that steamship company,' he said. 'Catching the tide, I dare say?'

'They caught a rocket from me,' Mrs Malseed replied good-humouredly. 'A couple of old dears were due with us on Tuesday and had to spend the night in some awful Scottish lodging-house. It nearly finished them.'

Everyone laughed, and I could feel the others thinking that our holiday had truly begun. Nothing had changed at Glencorn Lodge, all was well with its Irish world. Kitty from the dining-room came out to greet us, spotless in her uniform. 'Ach, you're looking younger,' she said, paying the compliment to all four of us, causing everyone in the hall to laugh again. Kitty's a bit of a card.

Arthur led the way to the rooms called Rose, Geranium, Hydrangea and Fuchsia, carrying as much of our luggage as he could manage and returning for the remainder. Arthur has a beaten, fisherman's face and short grey hair. He wears a green baize apron, and a white shirt with an imitation-silk scarf tucked into it at the neck. The scarf, in different swirling greens which blend nicely with the green of his apron, is an idea of Mrs Malseed's and one appreciates the effort, if not at a uniform, at least at tidiness.

'Thank you very much,' I said to Arthur in my room, smiling and finding him a coin.

We played a couple of rubbers after dinner as usual, but not of course going on for as long as we might have because we were still quite tired after the journey. In the lounge there was a French family, two girls and their parents, and a honeymoon couple—or so we had speculated during dinner—and a man on his own. There had been other people at dinner of course, because in June Glencorn Lodge is always full: from where we sat in the window we could see some of them strolling about the lawns, a few taking the cliff path down to the seashore. In the morning we'd do the same: we'd walk along the sands to Ardbeag and have coffee in the hotel there, back in time for lunch. In the afternoon we'd drive somewhere.

I knew all that because over the years this kind of pattern had developed. We had our walks and our drives, tweed to buy in Cushendall, Strafe's and Dekko's fishing day when Cynthia and I just sat on the beach, our visit to the Giant's Causeway and one to Donegal perhaps, though that meant an early start and taking potluck for dinner somewhere. We'd come to adore Co. Antrim, its glens and coastline, Rathlin Island and Tievebulliagh. Since first we got to know it, in 1965, we'd all four fallen hopelessly in love with every variation of this remarkable landscape. People in England thought us mad of course: they see so much of the troubles on television that it's naturally difficult for them to realize that most places are just as they've always been. Yet coming as we did, taking the road along the coast, dawdling through Ballygally, it was impossible to believe that somewhere else the unpleasantness was going on. We'd never seen a thing, nor even heard people talking about incidents that might have taken place. It's true that after a particularly nasty carry-on a few winters ago we did consider finding somewhere else, in Scotland perhaps, or Wales. But as Strafe put it at the time, we felt we owed a certain loyalty to the Malseeds and indeed to everyone we'd come to know round about, people who'd always been glad to welcome us back. It seemed silly to lose our heads, and when we returned the following summer we knew immediately we'd been right. Dekko said that nothing could be further away from all the violence than Glencorn Lodge, and though his remark could hardly be taken literally I think we all knew what he meant.

'Cynthia's tired,' I said because she'd been stifling yawns. 'I think we should call it a day.'

'Oh, not at all,' Cynthia protested. 'No, please.'

But Dekko agreed with me that she was tired, and Strafe said he didn't mind stopping now. He suggested a nightcap, as he always does, and as we always do also, Cynthia and I declined. Dekko said he'd like a Cointreau.

The conversation drifted about. Dekko told us an Irish joke about a drunk who couldn't find his way out of a telephone box, and then Strafe remembered an incident at school concerning his and Dekko's housemaster, A. D. Cowley-Stubbs, and the house wag, Thrive Major. A. D. Cowley-Stubbs had been known as Cows and often featured in our after-bridge reminiscing. So did Thrive Major.

'Perhaps I *am* sleepy,' Cynthia said. 'I don't think I closed my eyes once last night.'

She never does on a sea crossing. Personally I'm out like a light the moment my head touches the pillow; I often think it must be the salt in the air because normally I'm an uneasy sleeper at the best of times.

'You run along, old girl,' Strafe advised.

'Brekky at nine,' Dekko said.

Cynthia said good-night and went, and we didn't remark on her tiredness because as a kind of unwritten rule we never comment on one another. We're four people who play bridge. The companionship it offers, and the holidays we have together, are all part of that. We share everything: the cost of petrol, the cups of coffee or drinks we have; we even each make a contribution towards the use of Strafe's car because it's always his we go on holiday in, a Rover it was on this occasion.

'Funny, being here on your own,' Strafe said, glancing across what the Malseeds call the After-Dinner Lounge at the man who didn't have a companion. He was a red-haired man of about thirty, not wearing a tie, his collar open at the neck and folded back over the jacket of his blue serge suit. He was uncouth-looking, though it's a hard thing to say, not at all the kind of person one usually sees at Glencorn Lodge. He sat in the After-Dinner Lounge as he had in the dining-room, lost in some concentration of his own, as if calculating sums in his mind. There had been a folded newspaper on his table in the dining-room. It now reposed tidily on the arm of his chair, still unopened.

'Commercial gent,' Dekko said. 'Fertilizers.'

'Good heavens, never. You wouldn't get a rep in here.'

I took no part in the argument. The lone man didn't much interest me, but I felt that Strafe was probably right: if there was anything dubious about the man's credentials he might have found it difficult to secure a room. In the hall of Glencorn Lodge there's a notice which reads: *We prefer not to feature in hotel guides, and we would be grateful to our guests if they did not seek to include*

Glencorn Lodge in the Good Food Guide, the Good Hotel Guide, the Michelin, Egon Ronay or any others. We have not advertised Glencorn since our early days, and prefer our recommendations to be by word of mouth.

'Ah, thank you,' Strafe said when Kitty brought his whiskey and Dekko's Cointreau. 'Sure you won't have something?' he said to me, although he knew I never did.

Strafe is on the stout side, I suppose you could say, with a gingery moustache and gingery hair, hardly touched at all by grey. He left the Army years ago, I suppose because of me in a sense, because he didn't want to be posted abroad again. He's in the Ministry of Defence now.

I'm still quite pretty in my way, though nothing like as striking as Mrs Malseed, for I've never been that kind of woman. I've put on weight, and wouldn't have allowed myself to do so if Strafe hadn't kept saying he can't stand a bag of bones. I'm careful about my hair and, unlike Mrs Malseed, I have it very regularly seen to because if I don't it gets a salt and pepper look, which I hate. My husband, Ralph, who died of food-poisoning when we were still quite young, used to say I wouldn't lose a single look in middle age, and to some extent that's true. We were still putting off having children when he died, which is why I haven't any. Then I met Strafe, which meant I didn't marry again.

Strafe is married himself, to Cynthia. She's small and ineffectual, I suppose you'd say without being untruthful or unkind. Not that Cynthia and I don't get on or anything like that, in fact we get on extremely well. It's Strafe and Cynthia who don't seem quite to hit it off, and I often think how much happier all round it would have been if Cynthia had married someone completely different, someone like Dekko in a way, except that that mightn't quite have worked out either. The Strafes have two sons, both very like their father, both of them in the Army. And the very sad thing is they think nothing of poor Cynthia.

'Who's that chap?' Dekko asked Mr Malseed, who'd come over to wish us good-night.

'Awfully sorry about that, Mr Deakin. My fault entirely, a booking that came over the phone.'

'Good heavens, not at all,' Strafe protested, and Dekko looked horrified in case it should be thought he was objecting to the locals. 'Splendid-looking fellow,' he said, overdoing it.

Mr Malseed murmured that the man had only booked in for a single night, and I smiled the whole thing away, reassuring him with a nod. It's one of the pleasantest of the traditions at Glencorn Lodge that every evening Mr Malseed makes the rounds of his guests just to say good-night. It's because of little touches like that that I, too, wished Dekko hadn't questioned Mr Malseed about the man because it's the kind of thing one doesn't do at Glencorn Lodge. But Dekko is a law unto himself, very tall and gangling, always immaculately suited, a beaky face underneath mousy hair in which flecks of grey add a certain distinction. Dekko has money of his own and though he takes out girls who are half his age he has never managed to get around to marriage. The uncharitable might say he has a rather gormless laugh; certainly it's sometimes on the loud side.

We watched while Mr Malseed bade the lone man good-night. The man didn't respond, but just sat gazing. It was ill-mannered, but this lack of courtesy didn't appear to be intentional: the man was clearly in a mood of some kind, miles away.

'Well, I'll go up,' I said. 'Good-night, you two.'

'Cherry-bye, Milly,' Dekko said. 'Brekky at nine, remember.'

'Good-night, Milly,' Strafe said.

The Strafes always occupy different rooms on holidays, and at home also. This time he was in Geranium and she in Fuchsia. I was in Rose, and in a little while Strafe would come to see me. He stays with her out of kindness, because he fears for her on her own. He's a sentimental, good-hearted man, easily moved to tears: he simply cannot bear the thought of Cynthia with no one to talk to in the evenings, with no one to make her life around. 'And besides,' he often says when he's being jocular, 'it would break up our bridge four.' Naturally we never discuss her shortcomings or in any way analyse the marriage. The unwritten rule that exists among the four of us seems to extend as far as that.

He slipped into my room after he'd had another drink or two, and I was waiting for him as he likes me to wait, in bed but not quite undressed. He has never said so, but I know that that is something Cynthia would not understand in him, or ever attempt to comply with. Ralph, of course, would not have understood either; poor old Ralph would have been shocked. Actually it's all rather sweet, Strafe and his little ways.

'I love you, dear,' I whispered to him in the darkness, but just then he didn't wish to speak of love and referred instead to my body.

If Cynthia hadn't decided to remain in the hotel the next morning instead of accompanying us on our walk to Ardbeag everything might have been different. As it happened, when she said at breakfast she thought she'd just potter about the garden and sit with her book out of the wind somewhere, I can't say I was displeased. For a moment I hoped Dekko might say he'd stay with her, allowing Strafe and myself to go off on our own, but Dekko—who doesn't go in for saying what you want him to say—didn't. 'Poor old sausage,' he said instead, examining Cynthia with a solicitude that suggested she was close to the grave, rather than just a little lowered by the change of life or whatever it was.

'I'll be perfectly all right,' Cynthia assured him. 'Honestly.'

'Cynthia likes to mooch, you know,' Strafe pointed out, which of course is only the truth. She reads too much, I always think. You often see her putting down a book with the most melancholy look in her eyes, which can't be good for her. She's an imaginative woman, I suppose you would say, and of course her habit of reading so much is often useful on our holidays: over the years she has read her way through dozens of Irish guide-books. 'That's where the garrison pushed the natives over the cliffs,' she once remarked on a drive. 'Those rocks are known as the Maidens,' she remarked on another occasion. She has led us to places of interest which we had no idea existed: Garron Tower on Garron Point, the mausoleum at Bonamargy, the Devil's Backbone. As well as which, Cynthia is extremely knowledgeable about all matters relating to Irish history. Again she has read endlessly: biographies and autobiographies, long accounts of the centuries of battling and politics there've been. There's hardly a town or village we ever pass through that hasn't some significance for Cynthia, although I'm afraid her impressive fund of information doesn't always receive the attention it deserves. Not that Cynthia ever minds; it doesn't seem to worry her when no one listens. My own opinion is that she'd have made a much better job of her relationship with Strafe and her sons if she could have somehow developed a bit more character.

We left her in the garden and proceeded down the cliff path to the shingle beneath. I was wearing slacks and a blouse, with the arms of a cardigan looped round my neck in case it turned chilly: the outfit was new, specially bought for the holiday, in shades of tangerine. Strafe never cares how he dresses and of course she doesn't keep him up to the mark: that morning, as far as I remember, he wore rather shapeless corduroy trousers, the kind men sometimes garden in, and a navy-blue fisherman's jersey. Dekko as usual was a fashion plate: a pale green linen suit with pleated jacket pockets, a maroon shirt open at the neck, revealing a medallion on a fine gold chain. We didn't converse as we crossed the rather difficult shingle, but when we reached the sand Dekko began to talk about some girl or other, someone called Juliet who had apparently proposed marriage to him just before we'd left Surrey. He'd told her, so he said, that he'd think about it while on holiday and he wondered now about dispatching a telegram from Ardbeag saying, *Still thinking*. Strafe, who has a simple sense of humour, considered this hugely funny and spent most of the walk persuading Dekko that the telegram must certainly be sent, and other telegrams later on, all with the same message. Dekko kept laughing, throwing his head back in a way that always reminds me of an Australian bird I once saw in a nature film on television. I could see this was going to become one of those jokes that would accompany us all through the holiday, a man's thing really, but of course I didn't mind. The girl called Juliet was nearly thirty years younger than Dekko. I supposed she knew what she was doing.

Since the subject of telegrams had come up, Strafe recalled the occasion when Thrive Major had sent one to A. D. Cowley-Stubbs: *Darling regret three months gone love Rowena.* Carefully timed, it had arrived during one of Cows' Thursday evening coffee sessions. Rowena was a maid, known as the Bicycle, who had been sacked the previous term, and old Cows had something of a reputation as a misogynist. When he read the message he apparently went white and collapsed into an armchair. Warrington P. J. managed to read it too, and after that the fat was in the fire. The consequences went on rather, but I never minded listening when Strafe and Dekko drifted back to their schooldays. I just wish I'd known Strafe then, before either of us had gone and got married.

We had our coffee at Ardbeag, the telegram was sent off, and then Strafe and Dekko wanted to see a man called Henry O'Reilly whom we'd met on previous holidays, who organizes mackerel-fishing trips. I waited on my own, picking out postcards in the village shop that sells almost everything, and then I wandered down towards the shore. I knew that they would be having a drink with the boatman because a year had passed since they'd seen him last. They joined me after about twenty minutes, Dekko apologizing but Strafe not seeming to be aware that I'd had to wait because Strafe is not a man who notices little things. It was almost one o'clock when we reached Glencorn Lodge and were told by Mr Malseed that Cynthia needed looking after.

The hotel, in fact, was in a turmoil. I have never seen anyone as ashen-faced as Mr Malseed; his wife, in a forget-me-not dress, was limp. It wasn't explained to us immediately what had happened, because in the middle of telling us that Cynthia needed looking after Mr Malseed was summoned to the telephone. I could see through the half-open door of their little office a glass of whiskey or brandy on the desk and Mrs Malseed's bangled arm reaching out for it. Not for ages did we realize that it all had to do with the lone man whom we'd speculated about the night before.

'He just wanted to talk to me,' Cynthia kept repeating hysterically in the hall. 'He sat with me by the magnolias.'

I made her lie down. Strafe and I stood on either side of her bed as she lay there with her shoes off, her rather unattractively cut plain pink dress crumpled and actually damp from her tears. I wanted to make her take it off and to slip under the bed-clothes in her petticoat but somehow it seemed all wrong, in the circumstances, for Strafe's wife to do anything so intimate in my presence.

'I couldn't stop him,' Cynthia said, the rims of her eyes crimson by now, her nose beginning to run again. 'From half past ten till well after twelve. He had to talk to someone, he said.'

I could sense that Strafe was thinking precisely the same as I was: that the red-haired man had insinuated himself into Cynthia's company by talking about himself and had then put a hand on her knee. Instead of simply standing up and going away Cynthia would have stayed where she was, embarrassed or tongue-tied, at any rate unable to cope. And when the moment came she would have turned hysterical. I could picture her screaming in the garden, running across the lawn to the hotel, and then the pandemonium in the hall. I could sense Strafe picturing that also.

'My God, it's terrible,' Cynthia said.

'I think she should sleep,' I said quietly to Strafe. 'Try to sleep, dear,' I said to her, but she shook her head, tossing her jumble of hair about on the pillow.

'Milly's right,' Strafe urged. 'You'll feel much better after a little rest. We'll bring you a cup of tea later on."

'My God!' she cried again. 'My God, how could I sleep?'

I went away to borrow a couple of mild sleeping pills from Dekko, who is never without them, relying on the things too much in my opinion. He was tidying himself in his room, but found the pills immediately. Strangely enough, Dekko's always sound in a crisis.

I gave them to her with water and she took them without asking what they were. She was in a kind of daze, one moment making a fuss and weeping, the next just peering ahead of her, as if frightened. In a way she was like someone who'd just had a bad nightmare and hadn't yet completely returned to reality. I remarked as much to Strafe while we made our way down to lunch, and he said he quite agreed.

'Poor old Cynth!' Dekko said when we'd all ordered lobster bisque and entrecôte béarnaise. 'Poor old sausage.'

You could see that the little waitress, a new girl this year, was bubbling over with excitement; but Kitty, serving the other half of the dining-room, was grim, which was most unusual. Everyone was talking in hushed tones and when Dekko said, 'Poor old Cynth!' a couple of heads were turned in our direction because he can never keep his voice down. The little vases of roses with which Mrs Malseed must have decorated each table before the fracas had occurred seemed strangely out of place in the atmosphere which had developed.

The waitress had just taken away our soup-plates when Mr Malseed hurried into the dining-room and came straight to our table. The lobster bisque surprisingly hadn't been quite up to scratch, and in passing I couldn't help wondering if the fuss had caused the kitchen to go to pieces also.

'I wonder if I might have a word, Major Strafe,' Mr Malseed said, and Strafe rose at once and accompanied him from the dining-room. A total silence had fallen, everyone in the dining-room pretending to be intent on eating. I had an odd feeling that we had perhaps got it all wrong, that because we'd been out for our walk when it had happened all the other guests knew more of the details than Strafe and Dekko and I did. I began to wonder if poor Cynthia had been raped.

Afterward Strafe told us what occurred in the Malseeds' office, how Mrs Malseed had been sitting there, slumped, as he put it, and how two policemen had questioned him. 'Look, what on earth's all this about?' he had demanded rather sharply.

'It concerns this incident that's taken place, sir,' one of the policemen explained in an unhurried voice. 'On account of your wife—'

'My wife's lying down. She must not be questioned or in any way disturbed.'

'Ach, we'd never do that, sir.'

Strafe does a good Co. Antrim brogue and in relating all this to us he couldn't resist making full use of it. The two policemen were in uniform and their natural slowness of intellect was rendered more noticeable by the lugubrious air the tragedy had inspired in the hotel. For tragedy was what it was; after talking to Cynthia for nearly two hours the lone man had walked down to the rocks and been drowned.

When Strafe finished speaking I placed my knife and fork together on my plate, unable to eat another mouthful. The facts appeared to be that the man, having left Cynthia by the magnolias, had clambered down the cliff to a place no one ever went to, on the other side of the hotel from the sands we had walked along to Ardbeag. No one had seen him except Cynthia, who from the cliff-top had apparently witnessed his battering by the treacherous waves. The tide had been coming in, but by the time old Arthur and Mr Malseed reached the rocks it had begun to turn, leaving behind it the fully dressed corpse. Mr Malseed's impression was that the man had lost his footing on the seaweed and accidentally stumbled into the depths, for the rocks were so slippery it was difficult to carry the corpse more than a matter of yards. But at least it had been placed out of view, while Mr Malseed hurried back to the hotel to telephone for assistance. He told Strafe that Cynthia had been most confused, insisting that the man had walked out among the rocks and then into the sea, knowing what he was doing.

Listening to it all, I no longer felt sorry for Cynthia. It was typical of her that she should so sillily have involved us in all this. Why on earth had she sat in the garden with a man of that kind instead of standing up and making a fuss the moment he'd begun to paw her? If she'd acted intelligently the whole unfortunate episode could clearly have been avoided. Since it hadn't there was no point whatsoever in insisting that the man had committed suicide when at that distance no one could possibly be sure.

'It really does astonish me,' I said at the lunch table, unable to prevent myself from breaking our unwritten rule. 'Whatever came over her?'

'It can't be good for the hotel,' Dekko commented, and I was glad to see Strafe giving him a little glance of irritation.

'It's hardly the point,' I said coolly.

'What I meant was, hotels occasionally hush things like this up.'

'Well, they haven't this time.' It seemed an age since I had waited for them in Ardbeag, since we had been so happily laughing over the effect of Dekko's telegram. He'd included his address in it so that the girl could send a message back, and as we'd returned to the hotel along the seashore there'd been much speculation between the two men about the form this would take.

'I suppose what Cynthia's thinking,' Strafe said, 'is that after he'd tried something on with her he became depressed.'

'Oh, but he could just as easily have lost his footing. He'd have been on edge anyway, worried in case she reported him.'

'Dreadful kind of death,' Dekko said. His tone suggested that that was that, that the subject should now be closed, and so it was.

After lunch we went to our rooms, as we always do at Glencorn Lodge, to rest for an hour. I took my slacks and blouse off, hoping that Strafe would knock on my door, but he didn't and of course that was understandable. Oddly enough I found myself thinking of Dekko, picturing his long form stretched out in the room called Hydrangea, his beaky face in profile on his pillow. The precise nature of Dekko's relationship with these girls he picks up has always privately intrigued me: was it really possible that somewhere in London there was a girl called Juliet who was prepared to marry him for his not inconsiderate money?

I slept and briefly dreamed. Thrive Major and Warrington P. J. were running the post office in Ardbeag, sending telegrams to everyone they could think of, including Dekko's friend Juliet. Cynthia had been found dead beside the magnolias and people were waiting for Hercule Poirot[1] to arrive. 'Promise me you didn't do it,' I whis-

1. Fictional detective in many of the works of Agatha Christie.

pered to Strafe, but when Strafe replied it was to say that Cynthia's body reminded him of a bag of old chicken bones.

Strafe and Dekko and I met for tea in the tea-lounge. Strafe had looked in to see if Cynthia had woken, but apparently she hadn't. The police officers had left the hotel, Dekko said, because he'd noticed their car wasn't parked at the front any more. None of the three of us said, but I think we presumed, that the man's body had been removed from the rocks during the quietness of the afternoon. From where we sat I caught a glimpse of Mrs Malseed passing quite briskly through the hall, seeming almost herself again. Certainly our holiday would be affected, but it might not be totally ruined. All that remained to hope for was Cynthia's recovery, and then everyone could set about forgetting the unpleasantness. The nicest thing would be if a jolly young couple turned up and occupied the man's room, exorcising the incident, as newcomers would.

The family from France—the two little girls and their parents—were chattering away in the tea-lounge, and an elderly trio who'd arrived that morning were speaking in American accents. The honeymoon couple appeared, looking rather shy, and began to whisper and giggle in a corner. People who occupied the table next to ours in the dining-room, a Wing-Commander Orfell and his wife, from Guildford, nodded and smiled as they passed. Everyone was making an effort, and I knew it would help matters further if Cynthia felt up to a rubber or two before dinner. That life should continue as normally as possible was essential for Glencorn Lodge, the example already set by Mrs Malseed.

Because of our interrupted lunch I felt quite hungry, and the Malseeds pride themselves on their teas. The chef, Mr McBride, whom of course we've met, has the lightest touch I know with sponge cakes and little curranty scones. I was, in fact, buttering a scone when Strafe said:

'Here she is.'

And there indeed she was. By the look of her she had simply pushed herself off her bed and come straight down. Her pink dress was even more crumpled than it had been. She hadn't so much as run a comb through her hair, her face was puffy and unpowdered. For a moment I really thought she was walking in her sleep.

Strafe and Dekko stood up. 'Feeling better, dear?' Strafe said, but she didn't answer.

'Sit down, Cynth,' Dekko urged, pushing back a chair to make room for her.

'He told me a story I can never forget. I've dreamed about it all over again.' Cynthia swayed in front of us, not even attempting to sit down. To tell the truth, she sounded inane.

'Story, dear?' Strafe enquired, humouring her.

She said it was the story of two children who had apparently ridden bicycles through the streets of Belfast, out into Co. Antrim. The bicycles were dilapidated, she said; she didn't know if they were stolen or not. She didn't know about the children's homes because the man hadn't spoken of them, but she claimed to know instinctively that they had ridden away from poverty and unhappiness. 'From the clatter and the quarrelling,' Cynthia said. 'Two children who later fell in love.'

'Horrid old dream,' Strafe said. 'Horrid for you, dear.'

She shook her head, and then sat down. I poured another cup of tea. 'I had the oddest dream myself,' I said. 'Thrive Major was running the post office in Ardbeag.'

Strafe smiled and Dekko gave his laugh, but Cynthia didn't in any way acknowledge what I'd said.

'A fragile thing the girl was, with depths of mystery in her wide brown eyes. Red-haired of course he was himself, thin as a rake in those days. Glencorn Lodge was derelict then.'

'You've had a bit of a shock, old thing,' Dekko said.

Strafe agreed, kindly adding, 'Look, dear, if the chap actually interfered with you—'

'Why on earth should he do that?' Her voice was shrill in the tea-lounge, edged with a note of hysteria. I glanced at Strafe, who was frowning into his tea-cup. Dekko began to say something, but broke off before his meaning emerged. Rather more calmly Cynthia said:

'It was summer when they came here. Honeysuckle he described. And mother of thyme. He didn't know the name of either.'

No one attempted any kind of reply, not that it was necessary, for Cynthia just continued.

'At school there were the facts of geography and arithmetic. And the legends of scholars and of heroes, of Queen Maeve and Finn MacCool.[2] There was the coming of St. Patrick to a heathen people. History was full of kings and high-kings, and Silken Thomas and Wolfe Tone, the Flight of the Earls, the Siege of Limerick.'

When Cynthia said that, it was impossible not to believe that the unfortunate events of the morning had touched her with some kind of madness. It seemed astonishing that she had walked into the tea-lounge without having combed her hair, and that she'd stood there swaying before sitting down, that out of the blue she had started on about two children. None of it made an iota of sense, and surely she could see that the nasty experience she'd suffered should not be dwelt upon? I offered her the plate of scones, hoping

2. Legendary figures. Below: St. Patrick is credited with bringing Catholicism to Ireland. Silken Thomas was the 10th Earl of Kildare. Wolfe Tone was a patriot and nationalist who killed himself in prison in 1798. The Flight of the Earls involves the departure of 99 persons for France to escape religious persecution.

that if she began to eat she would stop talking, but she took no notice of my gesture.

'Look, dear,' Strafe said, 'there's not one of us who knows what you're talking about.'

'I'm talking about a children's story, I'm talking about a girl and a boy who visited this place we visit also. He hadn't been here for years, but he returned last night, making one final effort to understand. And then he walked out into the sea.'

She had taken a piece of her dress and was agitatedly crumpling it between the finger and thumb of her left hand. It was dreadful really, having her so grubby-looking. For some odd reason I suddenly thought of her cooking, how she wasn't in the least interested in it or in anything about the house. She certainly hadn't succeeded in making a home for Strafe.

'They rode those worn-out bicycles through a hot afternoon. Can you feel all that? A newly surfaced road, the snap of chippings beneath their tyres, the smell of tar? Dust from a passing car, the city they left behind?'

'Cynthia dear,' I said, 'drink your tea, and why not have a scone?'

'They swam and sunbathed on the beach you walked along today. They went to a spring for water. There were no magnolias then. There was no garden, no neat little cliff paths to the beach. Surely you can see it clearly?'

'No,' Strafe said. 'No, we really cannot, dear.'

'This place that is an idyll for us was an idyll for them too: the trees, the ferns, the wild roses near the water spring, the very sea and sun they shared. There was a cottage lost in the middle of the woods: they sometimes looked for that. They played a game, a kind of hide and seek. People in a white farmhouse gave them milk.'

For the second time I offered Cynthia the plate of scones and for the second time she pointedly ignored me. Her cup of tea hadn't been touched. Dekko took a scone and cheerfully said:

'All's well that's over.'

But Cynthia appeared to have drifted back into a daze, and I wondered again if it could really be possible that the experience had unhinged her. Unable to help myself, I saw her being led away from the hotel, helped into the back of a blue van, something like an ambulance. She was talking about the children again, how they had planned to marry and keep a sweetshop.

'Take it easy, dear,' Strafe said, which I followed up by suggesting for the second time that she should make an effort to drink her tea.

'Has it to do with the streets they came from? Or the history they learnt, he from his Christian Brothers, she from her nuns? History is unfinished in this island; long since it has come to a stop in Surrey.'

Dekko said, and I really had to hand it to him:

'Cynth, we have to put it behind us.'

It didn't do any good. Cynthia just went rambling on, speaking again of the girl being taught by nuns, and the boy by Christian Brothers. She began to recite the history they might have learnt, the way she sometimes did when we were driving through an area that had historical connections. "Can you imagine,' she embarrassingly asked, 'our very favourite places bitter with disaffection, with plotting and revenge? Can you imagine the treacherous murder of Shane O'Neill the Proud?'[3]

Dekko made a little sideways gesture of his head, politely marvelling. Strafe seemed about to say something, but changed his mind. Confusion ran through Irish history, Cynthia said, like convolvulus in a hedgerow. On May 24th, 1487, a boy of ten called Lambert Simnel, brought to Dublin by a priest from Oxford, was declared Edward VI of all England and Ireland, crowned with a golden circlet taken from a statue of the Virgin Mary. On May 24th, 1798, here in Antrim, Presbyterian farmers fought for a common cause with their Catholic labourers. She paused and looked at Strafe. Chaos and contradiction, she informed him, were hidden everywhere beneath nice-sounding names. 'The Battle of the Yellow Ford,' she suddenly chanted in a sing-song way that sounded thoroughly peculiar, the Statutes of Kilkenny. The Battle of Glenmama, the Convention of Drumceat. The Act of Settlement, the Renunciation Act. The Act of Union, the Toleration Act.[4] Just so much history it sounds like now, yet people starved or died while other people watched. A language was lost, a faith forbidden. Famine followed revolt, plantation followed that. But it was people who were struck into the soil of other people's land, not forests of new trees; and it was greed and treachery that spread as a disease among them all. No wonder unease clings to these shreds of history and shots ring out in answer to the mockery of drums. No wonder the air is nervy with suspicion.'

There was an extremely awkward silence when she ceased to speak. Dekko nodded, doing his best to be companionable. Strafe nodded also. I simply examined the pattern of roses on our tea-time china, not knowing what else to do. Eventually Dekko said:

'What an awful lot you know, Cynth!'

'Cynthia's always been interested,' Strafe said. 'Always had a first-rate memory.'

'Those children of the streets are part of the battles and the Acts,' she went on, seeming quite unaware that her talk was literally almost crazy. 'They're part of the blood that flowed around

3. Shane O'Neill fought against the English forces of Elizabeth I, but was killed by Irish foes. **4.** Milestones in the long history of Irish troubles.

those nice-sounding names.' She paused, and for a moment seemed disinclined to continue. Then she said:

'The second time they came here the house was being built. There were concrete-mixers, and lorries drawn up on the grass, noise and scaffolding everywhere. They watched all through another afternoon and then they went their different ways: their childhood was over, lost with their idyll. He became a dockyard clerk. She went to London, to work in a betting shop.'

'My dear,' Strafe said very gently, 'it's interesting, everything you say, but it really hardly concerns us.'

'No, of course not.' Quite emphatically Cynthia shook her head, appearing wholly to agree. 'They were degenerate, awful creatures They must have been.'

'No one's saying that, my dear.'

'Their story should have ended there, he in the docklands of Belfast, she recording bets. Their complicated childhood love should just have dissipated, as such love often does. But somehow nothing was as neat as that.'

Dekko, in an effort to lighten the conversation, mentioned a boy called Gollsol who'd been at school with Strafe and himself, who'd formed a romantic attachment for the daughter of one of the groundsmen and had later actually married her. There was a silence for a moment, then Cynthia, without emotion, said:

'You none of you care. You sit there not caring that two people are dead.'

'Two people, Cynthia?' I said.

'For God's sake, I'm telling you!' she cried. 'That girl was murdered in a room in Maida Vale.'[5]

Although there is something between Strafe and myself, I do try my best to be at peace about it. I go to church and take communion, and I know Strafe occasionally does too, though not as often as perhaps he might. Cynthia has no interest in that side of life, and it rankled with me now to hear her blaspheming so casually, and so casually speaking about death in Maida Vale on top of all this stuff about history and children. Strafe was shaking his head, clearly believing that Cynthia didn't know what she was talking about.

'Cynthia dear,' I began, 'are you sure you're not muddling something up here? You've been upset, you've had a nightmare: don't you think your imagination, or something you've been reading—'

'Bombs don't go off on their own. Death doesn't just happen to occur in Derry and Belfast, in London and Amsterdam and Dublin, in Berlin and Jerusalem. There are people who are murderers: that is what this children's story is about.'

5. A section of London.

A silence fell, no one knowing what to say. It didn't matter of course because without any prompting Cynthia continued.

'We drink our gin with Angostura bitters, there's lamb or chicken Kiev. Old Kitty's kind to us in the dining-room and old Arthur in the hall. Flowers are everywhere, we have our special table.'

'Please let us take you to your room now,' Strafe begged, and as he spoke I reached out a hand in friendship and placed it on her arm. 'Come on, old thing,' Dekko said.

'The limbless are left on the streets, blood spatters the car-parks. *Brits Out* it says on a rockface, but we know it doesn't mean us.'

I spoke quietly then, measuring my words, measuring the pause between each so that its effect might be registered. I felt the statement had to be made, whether it was my place to make it or not. I said:

'You are very confused, Cynthia.'

The French family left the tea-lounge. The two Dalmatians, Charger and Snooze, ambled in and sniffed and went away again. Kitty came to clear the French family's tea things. I could hear her speaking to the honeymoon couple, saying the weather forecast was good.

'Cynthia,' Strafe said, standing up, 'we've been very patient with you but this is now becoming silly.'

I nodded just a little. 'I really think,' I softly said, but Cynthia didn't permit me to go on.

'Someone told him about her. Someone mentioned her name, and he couldn't believe it. She sat alone in Maida Vale, putting together the mechanisms of her bombs: this girl who had laughed on the seashore, whom he had loved.'

'Cynthia,' Strafe began, but he wasn't permitted to continue either. Hopelessly, he just sat down again.

'Whenever he heard of bombs exploding he thought of her, and couldn't understand. He wept when he said that; her violence haunted him, he said. He couldn't work, he couldn't sleep at night. His mind filled up with images of her, their awkward childhood kisses, her fingers working neatly now. He saw her with a carrier-bag, hurrying it through a crowd, leaving it where it could cause most death. In front of the mouldering old house that had once been Glencorn Lodge they'd made a fire and cooked their food. They'd lain for ages on the grass. They'd cycled home to their city streets.'

It suddenly dawned on me that Cynthia was knitting this whole fantasy out of nothing. It all worked backwards from the moment when she'd had the misfortune to witness the man's death in the sea. A few minutes before he'd been chatting quite normally to her, he'd probably even mentioned a holiday in his childhood and some girl there'd been: all of it would have been natural in the circumstances, possibly even the holiday had taken place at Glencorn. He'd said good-bye and then unfortunately he'd had his accident. As she watched from the cliff edge, something had cracked in poor Cynthia's brain, she having always been a prey to melancholy. I suppose it must be hard having two sons who don't think much of you, and a marriage not offering you a great deal, bridge and holidays probably the best part of it. For some odd reason of her own she'd created her fantasy about a child turning into a terrorist. The violence of the man's death had clearly filled her imagination with Irish violence, so regularly seen on television. If we'd been on holiday in Suffolk I wondered how it would have seemed to the poor creature.

I could feel Strafe and Dekko beginning to put all that together also, beginning to realize that the whole story of the red-haired man and the girl was clearly Cynthia's invention. 'Poor creature,' I wanted to say, but did not do so.

'For months he searched for her, pushing his way among the people of London, the people who were her victims. When he found her she just looked at him, as if the past hadn't even existed. She didn't smile, as if incapable of smiling. He wanted to take her away, back to where they came from, but she didn't reply when he suggested that. Bitterness was like a disease in her, and when he left her he felt the bitterness in himself.'

Again Strafe and Dekko nodded, and I could feel Strafe thinking that there really was no point in protesting further. All we could hope for was that the end of the saga was in sight.

'He remained in London, working on the railways. But in the same way as before he was haunted by the person she'd become, and the haunting was more awful now. He bought a gun from a man he'd been told about and kept it hidden in a shoe-box in his rented room. Now and again he took it out and looked at it, then put it back. He hated the violence that possessed her, yet he was full of it himself: he knew he couldn't betray her with anything but death. Humanity had left both of them when he visited her again in Maida Vale.'

To my enormous relief and, I could feel, to Strafe's and Dekko's too, Mr and Mrs Malseed appeared beside us. Like his wife, Mr Malseed had considerably recovered. He spoke in an even voice, clearly wishing to dispose of the matter. It was just the diversion we needed.

'I must apologize, Mrs Strafe,' he said. 'I cannot say how sorry we are that you were bothered by that man.'

'My wife is still a little dicky,' Strafe explained, 'but after a decent night's rest I think we can say she'll be as right as rain again.'

'I only wish, Mrs Strafe, you had made contact with my wife or myself when he first approached you.' There was a spark of irritation in Mr Malseed's eyes, but his voice was still controlled. 'I mean, the unpleasantness you suffered might just have been averted.'

'Nothing would have been averted, Mr Malseed, and certainly not the horror we are left with. Can you see her as the girl she became, seated at a chipped white table, her wires and fuses spread around her? What were her thoughts in that room, Mr Malseed? What happens in the mind of anyone who wishes to destroy? In a back street he bought his gun for too much money. When did it first occur to him to kill her?'

'We really are a bit at sea,' Mr Malseed replied without the slightest hesitation. He humoured Cynthia by displaying no surprise, by speaking very quietly.

'All I am saying, Mr Malseed, is that we should root our heads out of the sand and wonder about two people who are beyond the pale.'

'My dear,' Strafe said, 'Mr Malseed is a busy man.'

Still quietly, still perfectly in control of every intonation, without a single glance around the tea-lounge to ascertain where his guests' attention was, Mr Malseed said:

'There is unrest here, Mrs Strafe, but we do our best to live with it.'

'All I am saying is that perhaps there can be regret when two children end like this.'

Mr Malseed did not reply. His wife did her best to smile away the awkwardness. Strafe murmured privately to Cynthia, no doubt beseeching her to come to her senses. Again I imagined a blue van drawn up in front of Glencorn Lodge, for it was quite understandable now that an imaginative woman should go mad, affected by the ugliness of death. The garbled speculation about the man and the girl, the jumble in the poor thing's mind—a children's story as she called it—all somehow hung together when you realized they didn't have to make any sense whatsoever.

'Murderers are beyond the pale, Mr Malseed, and England has always had its pales. The one in Ireland began in 1395.'

'Dear,' I said, 'what has happened has nothing whatsoever to do with calling people murderers and placing them beyond some pale or other. You witnessed a most unpleasant accident, dear, and it's only to be expected that you've become just a little lost. The man had a chat with you when you were sitting by the magnolias and then the shock of seeing him slip on the seaweed—'

'He didn't slip on the seaweed,' she suddenly screamed. 'My God, he didn't slip on the seaweed.'

Strafe closed his eyes. The other guests in the tea-lounge had fallen silent ages ago, openly listening. Arthur was standing near the door and was listening also. Kitty was waiting to clear away our tea things, but didn't like to because of what was happening.

'I must request you to take Mrs Strafe to her room, Major,' Mr Malseed said. 'And I must make it clear that we cannot tolerate further upset in Glencorn Lodge.'

Strafe reached for her arm, but Cynthia took no notice.

'An Irish joke,' she said, and then she stared at Mr and Mrs Malseed, her eyes passing over each feature of their faces. She stared at Dekko and Strafe, and last of all at me. She said eventually:

'An Irish joke, an unbecoming tale: of course it can't be true. Ridiculous, that a man returned here. Ridiculous, that he walked again by the seashore and through the woods, hoping to understand where a woman's cruelty had come from.'

'This talk is most offensive,' Mr Malseed protested, his calmness slipping just a little. The ashen look that had earlier been in his face returned. I could see he was beside himself with rage. 'You are trying to bring something to our doorstep which most certainly does not belong there.'

'On your doorstep they talked about a sweetshop: Cadbury's bars and different-flavoured creams, nut-milk toffee, Aero and Crunchie.'

'For God's sake pull yourself together,' I clearly heard Strafe whispering, and Mrs Malseed attempted to smile. 'Come along now, Mrs Strafe,' she said, making a gesture. 'Just to please us, dear. Kitty wants to clear away the dishes. Kitty!' she called out, endeavouring to bring matters down to earth.

Kitty crossed the lounge with her tray and gathered up the cups and saucers. The Malseeds, naturally still anxious, hovered. No one was surprised when Cynthia began all over again, by crazily asking Kitty what she thought of us.

'I think, dear,' Mrs Malseed began, 'Kitty's quite busy really.'

'Stop this at once,' Strafe quietly ordered.

'For fourteen years, Kitty, you've served us with food and cleared away the tea-cups we've drunk from. For fourteen years we've played our bridge and walked about the garden. We've gone for drives, we've bought our tweed, we've bathed as those children did.'

'Stop it,' Strafe said again, a little louder. Bewildered and getting red in the face, Kitty hastily bundled china on to her tray. I made a sign at Strafe because for some reason I felt that the end was really in sight. I wanted him to retain his patience, but what Cynthia said next was almost unbelievable.

'In Surrey we while away the time, we clip our hedges. On a bridge night there's coffee at nine o'clock, with macaroons or *petits fours*. Last thing of all we watch the late-night News, packing away our cards and scoring-pads, our sharpened pencils. There's been an incident in Armagh, one soldier's had his head shot off, another's run amok. Our lovely Glens of Antrim, we all four think, our coastal drives: we hope that nothing disturbs the peace. We think of Mr Malseed, still busy in Glencorn Lodge, and Mrs Malseed finishing her flower-plaques for the rooms of the completed annexe.'

'Will you for God's sake shut up?' Strafe suddenly shouted. I could see him struggling with himself, but it didn't do any good. He called Cynthia a bloody spectacle, sitting there talking rubbish. I don't believe she even heard him.

'Through honey-tinted glasses we love you and we love your island, Kitty. We love the lilt of your racy history, we love your earls and heroes. Yet we made a sensible pale here once, as civilized people create a garden, pretty as a picture.'

Strafe's outburst had been quite noisy and I could sense him being ashamed of it. He muttered that he was sorry, but Cynthia simply took advantage of his generosity, continuing about a pale.

'Beyond it lie the bleak untouchables, best kept as dots on the horizon, too terrible to contemplate. How can we be blamed if we make neither head nor tail of anything, Kitty, your past and your present, those battles and Acts of Parliament? We people of Surrey: how can we know? Yet I stupidly thought, you see, that the tragedy of two children could at least be understood. He didn't discover where her cruelty had come from because perhaps you never can: evil breeds in a mysterious way. That's the story the red-haired stranger passed on to me, the story you huddled away from.'

Poor Strafe was pulling at Cynthia, pleading with her, still saying he was sorry.

'Mrs Strafe,' Mr Malseed tried to say, but got no further. To my horror Cynthia abruptly pointed at me.

'That woman,' she said, 'is my husband's mistress, a fact I am supposed to be unaware of, Kitty.'

'My God!' Strafe said.

'My husband is perverted in his sexual desires. His friend, who shared his schooldays, has never quite recovered from that time. I myself am a pathetic creature who has closed her eyes to a husband's infidelity and his mistress's viciousness. I am dragged into the days of Thrive Major and A. D. Cowley-Stubbs: mechanically I smile. I hardly exist, Kitty.'

There was a most unpleasant silence, and then Strafe said:

'None of that's true. For God's sake, Cynthia,' he suddenly shouted, 'go and rest yourself.'

Cynthia shook her head and continued to address the waitress. She'd had a rest, she told her. 'But it didn't do any good, Kitty, because hell has invaded the paradise of Glencorn, as so often it has invaded your island. And we, who have so often brought it, pretend it isn't there. Who cares about children made into murderers?'

Strafe shouted again. 'You fleshless ugly bitch!' he cried. 'You bloody old fool!' He was on his feet, trying to get her to hers. The blood was thumping in his bronzed face, his eyes had a fury in them

I'd never seen before. 'Fleshless!' he shouted at her, not caring that so many people were listening. He closed his eyes in misery and in shame again, and I wanted to reach out and take his hand but of course I could not. You could see the Malseeds didn't blame him, you could see them thinking that everything was ruined for us. I wanted to shout at Cynthia too, to batter the silliness out of her, but of course I could not do that. I could feel the tears behind my eyes, and I couldn't help noticing that Dekko's hands were shaking. He's quite sensitive behind his joky manner, and had quite obviously taken to heart her statement that he had never recovered from his schooldays. Nor had it been pleasant, hearing myself described as vicious.

'No one cares,' Cynthia said in the same unbalanced way, as if she hadn't just been called ugly and a bitch. 'No one cares, and on our journey home we shall all four be silent. Yet is the truth about ourselves at least a beginning? Will we wonder in the end about the hell that frightens us?'

Strafe still looked wretched, his face deliberately turned away from us. Mrs Malseed gave a little sigh and raised the fingers of her left hand to her cheek, as if something tickled it. Her husband breathed heavily. Dekko seemed on the point of tears.

Cynthia stumbled off, leaving a silence behind her. Before it was broken I knew she was right when she said we would just go home, away from this country we had come to love. And I knew as well that neither here nor at home would she be led to a blue van that was not quite an ambulance. Strafe would stay with her because Strafe is made like that, honourable in his own particular way. I felt a pain where perhaps my heart is, and again I wanted to cry. Why couldn't it have been she who had gone down to the rocks and slipped on the seaweed or just walked into the sea, it didn't matter which? Her awful rigmarole hung about us as the last of the tea things were gathered up—the earls who'd fled, the famine and the people planted. The children were there too, grown up into murdering riff-raff.

JOHN UPDIKE

The Other

ROB Arnold met Priscilla Hunter at college in the fifties, and the fact that she was a twin seemed to matter as little as the fact she had been raised as an Episcopalian and he as a Baptist. How blissfully little did seem to matter in the fifties! Politics, religion, class—all beside the point. Young lives then, once Eisenhower had settled for a draw in Korea[1] and McCarthy had self-destructed like a fairy-tale goblin, seemed to be composed of timeless simplicities and old verities, of weather and works of art on opposite sides of a museum wall, of ancient professors, arrogant and scarcely audible from within the security of their tenure, lecturing from yellowing notes upon Dante and Kant while in the tall windows at their backs sunlight filtered through the feathery leaves of overarching elms. In those days Harvard Yard was innocent of Dutch-elm disease. And in those days a large and not laughable sexual territory existed within the borders of virginity, where physical parts were fed to the partner one at a time, beginning with the lips and hands. Strangely, Rob and Priscilla had been traversing this territory for several weeks before she confided to him that she was an identical twin. One of her breasts, clothed in an angora sweater and the underlying stiffness of a brassiere, was held in his hand at the time. Their faces were so close together that he could smell the mentholated tobacco in the breath of her confession. "Rob, I ought to tell you. I have a sister who looks just like me." Priscilla seemed to think it slightly shameful, and in fact it was exciting.

Her twin, the other, was named Susan, and attended the University of Chicago, though she, too, had been admitted to Radcliffe. Their parents—two Minneapolis lawyers, the father a specialist in corporation law and the mother in divorce and legal-aid work—had always encouraged the girls to be different; they had dressed them in different clothes from the start and had sent them to different private schools at an early age. A myth had been fostered in the family that Priscilla was the "artistic" one and Susan the more "practical" and "scientific," though to the twins themselves their interests and attitudes seemed close to identical. As children, they had succumbed simultaneously to the same diseases—chicken pox, mumps—and even when sent to different summer camps had a way, their conversations in September revealed, of undergoing the same trials and initiations. They learned to swim the same week, in widely separated lakes, and had let themselves be necked with in different forests. They fell in love with the same movie star (Montgomery Clift), had the same favorite song ("Two Loves Have I," as sung by Frankie Laine), and preferred the same Everly brother (Don, the darker and slicker-looking). Rob asked Priscilla if she missed her twin. She said, "No," but to have said otherwise might have been insulting, for she was lying entangled with him, mussed and overheated, in his fifth-floor room, with its single dormer window, in Winthrop House.

Rob was an only child, with a widowed mother, and asked, "What does it feel like, having a twin?"

1. President Eisenhower brought the Korean War to a conclusion with a compromise. Senator Joseph McCarthy was a notorious politician (1909–1957).

Priscilla made a thoughtful mouth; prim little creases appeared in her pursed upper lip. "Nice," she answered, after a long pause that had dried the amorous moisture from her eyes. They were brown eyes, a delicious candy color, darker than caramel but paler than Hershey's kisses. "You have a backup, seeing the same things you do. A kind of insurance policy, in a funny way."

"Even when you're sent to different schools and all that?"

"That doesn't matter so much, it turns out. Suzie and I always knew we weren't the other and were going to have to lead different lives. It's just that when I'm with her there's so much less explaining to do. Maybe that's why I'm not much good at explaining things. Sorry," Priscilla said. Her face was still pink from the soft struggle they had been having on his bed.

"You're good enough," Rob said, and dropped the subject, for it had interrupted this slow journey they were making, bit by bit, into one another. He considered himself lucky to have landed her. She had, Priscilla, a lovely athletic figure, long-muscled and hippy and with wide sloping shoulders, yet narrowed to a fine firmness at the ankles and wrists; his pleasure at seeing her undressed at first disconcerted her in its intensity, and time passed before she could accept it as her due and, still a virgin, coolly give him, in his room, in the narrow space between his iron frame bed and standard oak desk, little one-woman "parades." Though they could not, for all those good fifties reasons (pregnancy, the social worth of female chastity), make love, he had talked her into this piece of display. She held her chin up bravely and slowly turned in mock-model style, showing all sides of herself; the sight was so glorious Rob had to avert his eyes, and saw how her bare feet, fresh from chilly boots and rimmed in pink, slowly pivoted on the oval rug of braided rags his mother had given him to make his room more cozy. When his minute of drinking in Priscilla was up, she would scramble, suddenly blushing and laughing at herself, into bed beside him, under rough blue blankets that Harvard issued in those days as if to soldiers or monks. They would try to read from the same book; they were taking a course together—Philosophy 10, Idealism from Plato to Whitehead.[2]

Once she had told him that she was a twin, he could not forget it, or quite forgive her. The monstrous idea flirted at the back of his head that she was half a person; there was something withheld, something hollowbacked and tinny about the figure she cut in his mind even as their courtship proceeded smoothly toward marriage. He wanted to become a lawyer; she was doubly the daughter of lawyers and in all things ideal, given the inevitable small differences

2. Alfred North Whitehead, British philosopher (1861–1947).

between two individuals. She had been raised rather rich and he rather poor. His drab and pious upbringing embarrassed him. He had felt indignantly drowned on that absurd day when, dressed in a sleazy white gown, he had submitted to the shock of immersion, tipped backward and all the way under by the murderous hands of a minister wearing hip waders; whereas Priscilla kept in her room like a girlhood Teddy bear the embossed prayer book given her upon confirmation and sometimes carried it, in white-gloved hands, to services at the pretty little Church of New Jerusalem across from the Busch-Reisinger.[3] Both young people were for Stevenson in 1956, but she seemed secretly pleased when Eisenhower won again and Rob had wished Henry Wallace[4] were still running. He wanted to become a lawyer for a perverse reason: to avenge his father. His father, not yet fifty when he died of Hodgkin's disease, in the days before chemotherapy, had been an auto mechanic who had borrowed heavily to open a garage of his own, and it had been lawyers —lawyers for the bank and other creditors—who had briskly, with perfect legality, administered the financial ruin and thwarted the dying man's attempts to divert money to his survivors.

None of this at the time seemed to matter; what mattered was her beauty and his ardor and gratitude and her cool appraisal of the future value of his gratitude as she dazzlingly, with a silver poise faintly resembling cruelty, displayed herself to him. The fact of her being a twin put a halo around her form, a shimmer of duplication, a suggestion, curiously platonic, that there was, somewhere else, unseen, another version of this reality, this body.

Priscilla's parents lived in St. Paul, in a big, cream-colored, many-dormered house a few blocks from the gorge holding the Mississippi, which was not especially wide this far north. Though Rob several times travelled there to display himself, in his best clothes, to his prospective in-laws, he did not meet Susan until the wedding. She had always been away—on a package tour of Europe or waitressing in Southern California, a part of the world where she had been led by some of her racier U. of C. friends. When Rob met her at last, she had come from Santa Barbara to be Priscilla's maid of honor. Though it was early June and cool in Minnesota, she had a surfer's deep tan and a fluffy haircut short as a boy's. A stranger to the family might not have spotted her, amid the welter of siblings and cousins, as the bride's twin. But Rob had been long alerted, and as he clasped her warm hand the current of identity stunned him to wordlessness. Her face was Priscilla's down to the protruding, determined cut of her upper lip and the slightly sad droop of the lashes at the outside corners of her eyes. He reddened, and imagined that Susan did, though her manner with him was instantly ironical—

3. Museum on the Harvard campus. **4. American politician (1888–1965).**

bantering and languid in perhaps the West Coast manner. Enclosed within Priscilla's body, the coolness of a stranger seemed rude, even hostile. Rob noted what seemed to be a ray or two less of caramel in her irises, a smoother consistency of chocolate. These darker eyes made her seem more passionate, more impudent and flitting, as she moved through her old home with none of a bride's responsibilities. And Susan was, Rob thought, appraising her repeatedly through the social flurry, distinctly bigger, if only by a centimetre and an ounce.

His impressions, Priscilla told him when they were alone, were wrong: Susan had expected to like him and did, very much. And though she had been the firstborn, she had never been, as often happens, the stronger or heavier. Their heights and weights had always been precisely the same. Priscilla thought that, indeed, Suzie had lost some weight, chasing around with that creepy crowd of beach bums out there. Their parents were up in arms because she had announced her intention to do graduate work in art history at U.C.L.A., where there really wasn't any art, when there was that entire wonderful Chester Dale collection at the Art Institute, along with everything else in Chicago. Or why not go East, like Priscilla? Their parents had hoped Susan would become a physicist, or at least a psychologist. Rob liked hearing Priscilla, not normally much of an explainer, run on this way about her sister; being near her twin did seem to embolden her, to loosen her tongue. He enjoyed the tumble of an extensive, ambitious family, amid whose many branches his own mother, their guest for the weekend, seemed a wan, doomed graft. The big house was loaded with pale padded furniture and vacation souvenirs; his mother found a safe corner in a little-used library and worked at a needlepoint footstool cover she had brought from North Carolina.

In church, the twins, the one majestic in white tulle and the other rather mousy in mauve taffeta, were vividly distinguishable. Rob, however, standing at the altar in a daze of high Episcopalianism, the musk of incense in his nostrils and a gold-leafed panel of apostles flickering off to the side, had a disquieting thrill of confusion, as if the mocking-eyed maid of honor might be his intimate from Winthrop House days and the mysterious figure on their father's arm a woman virtually unknown to him, tanned and crop-haired beneath her veil and garland of florets. Susan's voice was just a grain or two the huskier, so he knew it was Priscilla who, in a shy, true voice, recited the archaic vows with him. At the reception, amid all the kissing, he kissed his sister-in-law and was startled at the awkwardly averted, rather stubbornly downcast cheek; Rob had reflexively expected Priscilla's habituated frontal ease. And when they danced, Susan was stiff in his arms. Yet none of this marred her fascination, the superior authenticity she enjoyed over the actual reality as the wedding night untidily proceeded through champagne and forced jollity to its trite, closeted climax. Susan was with them (her remembered stiffness, as if she and Rob had too much to say to dare a word, and her imagined slightly greater size and heft) during the botch of defloration, exciting him, urging him on through Priscilla's pain. Though he knew he had put an unfortunate crimp in this infant marriage, and had given his long-cherished ardor a bad name, he fell asleep with happy exhaustion, as if all his guilt were shifted onto the body of a twin of his own.

Rob was not accepted at Harvard Law School; but good-hearted Yale took him. It was all for the best, for if Cambridge in those years was the path to Washington, New Haven was closer to New York and Wall Street, where the real money was. After a few years in the city, the Arnolds settled in Greenwich and had children—a girl, a boy, and a girl. Having married a La Jolla builder of million-dollar homes. Susan kept pace with a girl, a boy, and then another boy. This break in symmetry led them both, it seemed, to stop bearing children. Also, the Pill had come along and made birth control irresistible. Kennedy had been shot, and something called rock blasted from the radio however you twisted the dial. The twins, though, had their nests safely made. Susan's husband was named Jeb Herrera; he claimed descent from one of the old Spanish ranching families of Alta California, but in joying moods asserted that his great-great-grandfather had been a missionary's illegitimate son. He was a curly-haired, heavy, gracious, enthusiastic man, a bit too proclaimedly, for Rob's taste, in love with life. His small, even teeth looked piratical, when he smiled through the black curls of his beard. He was one of the first men Rob knew to wear a full beard and to own a computer—a tan metal box taller than a man, a freestanding broom closet that spat paper. Jeb had programmed it to respond to the children's questions with jokes in printout. His office was a made-over wharf shed where dozens shuffled paper beside canted windows full of the Pacific. None of his employees wore neckties. Though the twins, as they eased into matronhood, might still be mistaken for one another, there was no mistaking the husbands. Susan, it would appear, had the artistic taste, and Priscilla had bet on practicality. Rob had become a specialist in tax law, saw his name enrolled in the list of junior partners on the engraved firm stationery, and forgot about avenging his father.

The growing families visited back and forth; there was something concordant about the homes, though one was white clapboard set primly on watered green lawn, and the other was redwood and stucco wedged into a hillside where fat little cactuses intricate as snowflakes flourished among expensively transplanted rocks. Both houses were cheerful for children, with back stairs and big windows and a certain sporty airiness. The Arnolds had a long sun room with a Ping-Pong table and, above it on the second floor, a sleeping porch with a hammock. As soon as they could afford it, they crowded a composition tennis court into the space between the garage and the line fence, where the lawn had always been scruffy anyway and the vegetable garden had gone to weeds every July. The La Jolla house, which overlooked the fifteenth fairway of a golf course, shuffled indoors and outdoors with its sliding glass doors and cantilevered deck and its family-sized hot tub out on the deck.

Rob first saw his wife's sister naked one warm evening in Christmas vacation when Susan let fall a large white towel behind her and slid her silent silhouette into this hot tub. Rob and his wife were already in, coping with the slithering, giggling bodies of their excited children; so the moment passed almost unnoticed amid the family tumble. Almost. Susan was distinctly not Priscilla; their skins had aged differently on the two different coasts. Priscilla's was dead pale this time of year, its summer tan long faded, whereas there was something thickened and delicately crinkled and permanently golden about Susan's. With an accustomed motion she had eased her weight from her buttocks into the steaming wide circle of water. Her expression looked solemn, dented by shadow. Rob remembered the same resolute, unfocussed expression on Priscilla's face in the days when she would grant him her little "parade" in the shadows of his narrow college room. Both sisters had brown eyes in deep sockets and noses that looked upturned, with long nostrils and sharp central dents in their upper lips. Both were wearing bangs that winter. Their heads and shoulders floated side by side; Susan's breasts seemed the whiter for the contrast with her year-round bathing-suit tan.

"How much do you do this sort of thing?" Priscilla asked her twin, a touch nervously, glancing toward Rob.

"Oh, now and then, with people you know, usually. You get used to it—it's a local custom. You sort of let yourself dissolve."

Yet she, too, gave Rob an alert glance. He had already passed into dissolution, his vapor of double love one with the heat, the steam, the abundant dinner wine, the scent of the eucalyptus trees brooding above the deck, the stars beyond them, the strangeness of this all being a few days before Christmas. Immersed, their bodies had become foreshortened stumps of flesh, comical blobs of mercury. Jeb appeared on the deck holding a naked baby—little Lucas—in one crooked arm and a fresh half gallon of Gallo Chablis in the other. Early in his thirties, Jeb had a pendulous belly. He descended to them like a hairy Nepture; the tub overflowed. When the water calmed, his penis drifted under Rob's eyes like a lead-colored fish swimming nowhere.

The families stopped travelling back and forth in complete units as the maturing children developed local attachments and summer jobs. The two oldest cousins, Karen and Rose, had been fast friends from the start, though there was no mistaking them for twins: Karen had become as washed-out and mild-faced a blonde as Rob's mother (now dead), and Rose was so dark that boys on the street catcalled to her in Spanish. The two older boys, Henry and Gabriel, made a more awkward matchup, the one burdened with all of Rob's allergies and a drowsy shyness all his own, and the other a macho little athlete with a wedge-shaped back and the unthinking cruelty of those whose bodies are perfectly connected to their wills. The girl and the boy that completed the sets, Jennifer and Lucas, claimed to detest each other, and, indeed, did squabble tediously, perhaps in defense against any notion that they would someday marry. The bigger the children became, the harder they pulled apart, and the more frayed the lines between their parents became. Once little Lucas became too big to hold in one arm and strike a pose with, Jeb's interest seemed to wander away from families and family get-togethers. There were late-night long-distance calls between the sisters, and secrets from the children.

Susan suddenly had more gray hair than Priscilla. Rob felt touched by her, and drawn in a new fashion, when she would visit them for a few weeks in the summer without Jeb, with perhaps an inscrutable Rose and a resentful Lucas in tow. More than once, Rob met the L.A. red-eye at LaGuardia and was kissed at the gate as if he were Susan's savior; there had been drunks on the plane, college kids, nobody could sleep, Lucas had insisted on watching a ghastly Jerry Lewis movie, Rose threw up over Nebraska somewhere, they had gone way north around some thunderheads, an old lech in an admiral's uniform kept trying to buy her drinks at three in the morning, my God, never again. As Rob gently swung the car up the summer-green curves of the Merritt Parkway, Susan nodded asleep, and seemed his wife. Priscilla's skin, too, now sagged in those defenseless puckers when she slept.

As a guest in their home, Susan slept on the upstairs porch. The swish of cars headed toward the railroad station, and the birds—so much more aggressive, she said, than those on the West Coast—awakened her too early; and then at night the Arnolds took her to too many parties. "How do you stand it?" she would ask her twin.

"Oh, it gets to be a habit. Try taking a nap in the afternoon. That's what I do."

"Jeb and I hardly go out at all anymore. We decided other people weren't helping our marriage." This was a clue, and far from the only one. There was a hungry boniness to her figure now. Like a sick person willing to try any cure, Susan drank only herbal tea—

no caffeine, no alcohol—and ate as little meat as she politely could. Whereas Priscilla, who had once appeared so distinctly a centimetre smaller, now was relatively hefty. Broad of shoulder and hip, she moved through parties with a certain roll, a practiced cruiser who knew where the ports were—the confiding women and the unhappy men and the bar table in the corner. Sometimes after midnight Rob watched her undress in their bedroom and thought of all the Martinis and Manhattans, the celery sticks and devilled eggs that had gone into those haunches and upper arms.

"Other people don't help *it*," was Priscilla's answer to Susan. "But they might do something for *you*. You, a woman. Aren't you a woman, or are you only a part of a marriage?" She had never forgiven him, Rob feared, for that unideal wedding night.

Poor Susan seemed a vision of chastity whom they would discover each morning at the breakfast table, frazzled after another night's poor sleep, her hair drooping onto the lapels of a borrowed bathrobe, her ascetic breakfast of grapefruit and granola long eaten, the *Times* scattered about her in pieces read with a desperate thoroughness. Rob wanted to urge bacon and waffles upon her, and to make up good news to counteract the bad news that had been turning her hair gray. Priscilla knew what it was, but was no good at explaining. "Jeb's a bastard," she would say simply in their bedroom. "He always was. My parents knew it, but what could they do? She had to get married, once I did. And all men are bastards, more or less."

"My, you've gotten tough. He was always very dear with the kids, I thought. At least when they were little. And he builds those million-dollar houses."

"Not so much anymore he doesn't," she said. As she pivoted on their plush carpet, yellow calluses showed at her heels.

"What do you mean?"

"Ask *her*, if you're so interested."

But he never could. He could no more have asked Susan to confide her private life than he could have tiptoed onto the sleeping porch and looked down at—what he held so clearly in his mind—his wife's very face, transposed into another, chastened existence, fragilely asleep in this alien house, this alien climate and time zone. So magical a stranger might awake under the pressure of his regard. He would have trespassed. He would have spoiled something he was saving.

The 1973–75 recession gave Jeb's tottering, overextended business the last push it needed; everything coming undone at once, the Herreras began to divorce amid the liquidation. When Susan visited them in the bicentennial year, it was as a single woman, her thinness now whittled to a certain point, a renewed availability. But not, of course, available to Rob; the collapse of one marriage made the other doubly precious.

As in other summers, Rob was touched by Susan's zeal with the children, ushering as many as could be captured onto the train and into the city for a visit to the Museum of Natural History or to see the tall ships that beautiful hazy July day. Rose was not with her; the girl had drawn closer to her father in his distress, and was waitressing in a taco joint in San Diego. And Karen, now stunning with her flaxen hair and pale moonface above a slender body, was above everything except boys and ballet. One Saturday while Priscilla stayed home, having contracted for a lunch at the club with one of those similarly boozy women she called "girlfriends," Rob accompanied Susan on an excursion she had cooked up for the just barely willing Jennifer and Lucas, all the way to New Haven to see the Beinecke Library, with its translucent marble and the three Noguchis[5] so marvelously toylike and monumental in their sunken well. Rob had not see these wonders himself; they had come to Yale after his time. And he rather enjoyed these excursions with his sister-in-law; all that old tumble of family life had fallen to them to perpetuate. He let her drive his Mercedes and sat beside her, taking secret inventory of all the minute ways in which she differed from Priscilla—the slight extra sharpness to the thrust of her upper lip, the sea scallop of shallow wrinkles the sun had engraved at the corner of her eye, the hair or two more of bulk or wildness to her eyebrow on its crest of bone. The hair of her head, once shorter, then grayer, was now dyed too even a dark brown, with unnatural reddish lights. She turned to him for a second on a long straight-away. "You've never asked about me and Jeb," she said.

"What was to ask? Things speak for themselves."

"I loved that about you," Susan pronounced. Her verb alarmed him; "love" was a word he associated with the tacky sermons of his youth. "It's been a nightmare for years," she went on, and he realized that she was offering to present herself in a new way to him, as more than a strange ghost behind a familiar mask. She was in a sense naked. But he, after nearly two decades of playing the good husband, had discovered affairs, and had fallen in love locally. The image of his mistress—she was one of Priscilla's "girlfriends"—rose up, her head tipped back, her lipstick smeared, and deafened him to the woman he was with; without hearing the words, he saw Susan's mouth, that distinctive complicated mouth the sisters shared, making a pursy, careful expression, like a schoolteacher emphasizing a crucial point.

Lucas, in the back seat, was listening and cried out, "Mom, stop bitching about Dad to Uncle Rob—you do it to *everybody!*"

Jennifer said, "Oh listen to big man here, protecting his awful

5. Isamu Noguchi (1904–   ), American sculptor.

daddy," and there was a thump, and the girl sobbed in spite of her scorn.

"You make me barf, you know that?" Lucas told her, his own voice shakily full of tears. "You've always been the most god-awful germ, no kidding."

"Daddy," Jennifer said, with something of womanly aloofness. "This little spic just broke my arm."

The adult conversation was not resumed. Priscilla a few days later drove her sister back to LaGuardia, to begin a new life. Susan was planning to take her half of what money was left when the La Jolla house was sold and move with the two younger children to the Bay area and study ceramics at Berkeley.

"I told her she's crazy," Priscilla said to him. "There's nothing but gays in San Francisco."

"Maybe she's not as needful of male consolation as some."

"What's that supposed to mean? You're not above a little consolation yourself, from what I've been hearing."

"Easy, easy. The kids are upstairs."

"Karen isn't upstairs; she's in New York, letting that cradle robber she met at the club take her to the Alvin Ailey.[6] Wake up. You know what your trouble has always been? You're an only child. You never loved me, you just loved the idea of sneaking into a family. You loved my family, the idea of there being so many of us, rich and Episcopalian and all that."

"I didn't need the Episcopalian so much. I thought I was going to sneeze all through the wedding. Incense, I couldn't believe it."

"You poor little Baptist boy. You know what my father said at the time? I've never told you this."

"Then don't."

"He said, 'He'll never fit in. He's a guttersnipe, Prissy.' "

"Wow. Did he really say 'guttersnipe'? And fit into what—the St. Paul Order of the Moose? Gee, I always rather liked him, too. Especially early in the mornings, when you could catch him sober."

"He *despised* you. But then Sue picked Jeb, and he was so much worse."

"That *was* lucky."

"He made you look good, it's a crazy fact."

"Yes, and you make Sue look good, so it evens out. Come on, let's save this for midnight. Here comes Henry."

But the boy, six feet tall suddenly, was wearing earphones plugged into a satchel-sized radio; on his way to the porch he gave his parents a glassy, oblivious smile.

Any smugness the Arnolds may have felt in relation to the Herreras' disasters lasted less than a year. An ingenious tax shelter Rob had directed a number of clients into was ruled invalid by the

6. A dance troupe.

I.R.S., and these clients suddenly owed the government hundreds of thousands of dollars, including tens of thousands in penalties. Though they had been duly cautioned and no criminal offense was charged, the firm could not keep him; his divorce soon followed. One of the men Priscilla had been seeing had freed himself from his own wife and was prepared to take her on; Rob wondered what Priscilla did now, all hundred and fifty pounds of her, that was so wonderful. To think that he had started it all off with those formalized, chaste "parades."

She resettled with the children in Cos Cob. Having fouled his professional nest in the East, Rob accepted with gratitude the offer of a former colleague to join a firm in Los Angeles, as less than a junior partner. He had always been happy on their visits to Southern California and, though a one-bedroom condo in Westwood wasn't a redwood house overlooking a fairway in La Jolla, Old Man Hunter had been right: he fitted in better here. Southern California had a Baptist flavor that helped him heal. The people mostly came from small Midwestern towns, and there was a naïveté in even the sin—the naked acts in the bars and the painted little-girl hookers in jogging shorts along Hollywood Boulevard. The great stucco movie theatres of the thirties had been given over to X-rated films; freckle-faced young couples watched them holding hands and eating popcorn. In this city where sex was a kind of official currency, Rob made up for the fun he had missed while catching the train and raising the children in Greenwich, and evened the score with his former wife. Los Angeles was like that earlier immersion, at the age of religious decision, which coincided with puberty; that bullying big hand had shoved him under and he had come up feeling, as well as indignant, cleansed and born again.

One day downtown on the escalator from Figueroa Street up to the Bonaventure,[7] he found himself riding behind a vivid black-haired girl whom he slowly recognized as his niece, Rose. He touched her naked shoulder and bought her a drink in the lobby lounge, amid all the noisy, curving pools. Rose was all of twenty-four now; he could hardly believe it. She told him her father had a job as foreman for another builder and had bought himself a stinkpot and kept taking weekend runs into Mexico; his dope-snorting friends that kept putting a move on her drove her crazy, so she had split. Now she worked as a salesgirl in a failing imported-leather-goods shop in the underground Arco Plaza while her chances of becoming an actress became geometrically smaller with each passing year. These days, she explained, if you haven't got your face somewhere by the time you're nineteen you're *finito*. And indeed, Rob thought, her face was unsubtle for a career of pretense; framed by a poodle cut of tight black curls, it had too much of Jeb's raw hopefulness,

7. A large hotel in downtown Los Angeles.

a shiny candor somehow coarse. Rob was excited by this disappointed young beauty, but women her age, with their round breasts and enormous pure eye whites, rather frightened him, like machines that are too new and expensive. He asked about her mother, and was given Susan's address. "She's doing real well," Rose warned him.

An exchange of letters followed; Susan's handwriting was a touch rounder than Priscilla's, but with the same "g"s that looked like "s"s and "t"s that had lost their crossings, like hats blown off by the wind. One autumn Saturday, he flew up to the Bay area. Three hundred miles of coast were cloudless and the hills had put on their inflammable tawny summer coats, that golden color the Californian loves as a New Englander loves the scarlet of turning maples. Berkeley looked surprisingly like Cambridge, once you ascended out of Oakland's slough: big homes built by a species of the middle class that had migrated elsewhere, and Xeroxed protest posters in many colors pasted to mailboxes and tacked to trees. Susan lived in the second-floor-back of a great yellow house that, but for its flaking paint and improvised outside stairways, reminded him of her ancestral home in St. Paul. She had been watching for him, and they kissed awkwardly halfway up her access stairs.

The apartment was dominated by old photos of her children and by examples of her own ceramics—crusty, oddly lovely things, with a preponderance of turquoise and muddy orange in the glazes. She was even selling a few, at a shop a friend of hers ran in Sausalito. A female friend. And she taught part time at a private elementary school. And still took classes—the other students called her Granny, but she loved them; their notions of what mattered were so utterly different from what ours were at that age. All this came out in a rapid voice, with a diffident stabbing of hands and a way of pushing her hair back from her ears as if to improve her hearing. Something in her manner implied that this was a slightly tiresome duty he had invented for them. He was an old relative, a page from the past. She was thinner than ever and had let her hair go back to gray, no longer just streaked but solidly gray, hanging down past the shoulders of a russet wool turtleneck sweater such as men wear in Scotch ads. He had never seen Priscilla look like this. In tight, spattered jeans and bare feet, Susan's skinniness was exciting; he wanted to seize her before she dwindled away entirely.

She took him for a drive, in her Mazda, just as if they still had children to entertain together. The golden slashed hills interwoven with ocean and lagoons, the curving paths full of cyclists and joggers and young parents with infants in backpacks looked idyllic, a vision of the future, an enchanted land not of perpetual summer, as where he lived, but of eternal spring. She had put on spike heels with her jeans and a vest of sheepskin patches over her sweater, and these additions made her startlingly stylish. They went out to eat at a local place where tabbouleh[8] followed artichoke soup. Unlike most couples on a first date, they had no lack of things to talk about. Reminiscence shied away from old grievances and turned to the six children, their varying and still uncertain fates; fates seemed so much slower to shape up than when they had been young. Priscilla was hardly mentioned. As the evening wore on, Priscilla became an immense hole in their talk, a kind of cave they were dwelling in, while their voices slurred and their table candle flickered. Was it that Susan was trying to spare him acknowledging what had been, after all, a great marital defeat; or was Rob trying not to cast upon her a shadow of comparison, an onus of being half a person? She took him back to her apartment; indeed, he had not arranged for anywhere else to go.

Suzie kicked off her shoes and turned on an electric heater and dragged a magnum of Gallo from the refrigerator. She was tired; he liked that, since he was, too, as though they had been pulling at the same load in tandem all these years. They sat on the floor, on opposite sides of a glass coffee table in whose surface her face was mirrored—the swinging witchy hair, the deep eye sockets and thoughtful upper lip. "You've come a long way," she announced, in that voice which had once struck him as huskier than another but that in this room felt as fragile as the pots blushing turquoise on the shelves.

"How do you mean?"

"To see me. *Do* you see me? *Me*, I mean."

"Who else? I've always liked you. Loved, should I say? Or would that be too much?"

"I think it would. Things between us have always been . . ."

"Complicated," Rob finished.

"Exactly. I don't want to be just a way of correcting a mistake."

He thought a long time, so long her face became anxious, before answering, "Why not?" He knew that most people, including Susan, had more options than he, but he had faith that in an affluent nation a need, honestly confessed, has a good chance of being met.

This being the eighties, she was nervous about herpes, and even after his reassurances was still nervous. She asked him to hold off for a while, until she really felt trust. Meanwhile, there were things they *could* do. Seeing her undress and move self-consciously, chin up, through a little parade in the room, he thought her majestic, for being nearly skeletal. Plato was wrong, what is is absolute.[9] The delay Susan imposed, the distances between them that could not be quickly changed, helped Rob grasp the blissful truth that she was only another woman.

8. A Middle Eastern salad made with bulgur wheat. 9. A somewhat garbled reference to Plato's doctrine that the apparent world is illusory while ideas are absolute.

GUY VANDERHAEGHE

Going to Russia

"ANOTHER of your letters arrived at my house yesterday," the doctor announces. "That makes four now." He says this in a colourless, insipid voice, in the way he says most things.

It is only the significant pause which follows that alerts me I am expected to respond, and distracts my attention from the scene outside his office window. For several minutes I have been watching two children as they tramp stiffly off into the distance. They lead me to think of my daughter, and to wonder if she misses my visits.

Here, we are on the outskirts of the city, where the new suburbs dwindle into prairie, and prairie into winter sky. The children, stuffed into bulky snowsuits, totter along, their arms stiffly extended like tiny astronauts foraging on the frozen cinder of a spent star.

Suburban tots often come to explore these splendid spaces. I have navigated them too, in my imagination, warm behind a double pane of glass. I find it strange that this blank sweep of land terrifies some of my fellow inmates and that they feel the need to keep their blinds down night and day. I like it. It makes me think of Russia.

"Yes?" I say finally, a little late, but nevertheless meaning to politely encourage him.

"Mr. Caragan, I thought when we met last Wednesday we agreed there would be no more letters."

The man has me there. But I am an impulsive fellow and that was Wednesday. By Thursday I felt I owed him some kind of explanation as to what had moved me to write the first three letters. "That's true," I admit, "that was the understanding."

"But?"

I shrug.

Dr. Herzl spreads a sheet of paper on his desk. His fingers rub diligently at the fold marks. When he is satisfied everything is shipshape, he begins to read to himself. I note a barely perceptible flicker in his upper lip. When he finishes, he looks up at me sharply. An old tactic that I recognize immediately. "This doesn't make much sense to me," he says.

"No?"

"Excuse me," he says, pausing. "I'm not a critic. . . . " The doctor smiles to signal me that this is an offering from his store of inexhaustible wit. "But I find your language rather . . . formal, stilted," he says at last, finding the words he wants. "As if you are under great strain, as if you are trying to keep a lid on your feelings when you write me these letters." He searches the page. "For instance, there's this: 'I answer in writing because my thought will thus be more fully expressed, and more distinctly perceived, like a sound amid silence.' Doesn't that sound a bit unusual to you?"

"There's quotation marks around that."

"Pardon?"

"I didn't write that. There's quotation marks around that."

"Oh." The doctor hesitates. "Who *did* write it then?"

"Mikhail Osipovich Gershenzon."[1]

A doubtful look passes over his face. He suspects me of pulling his leg. Dr. Herzl considers me a great joker, albeit an unbalanced, a lunatic one.

"It's true," I assure him.

"I am not familiar . . ."

"So who is? But then, you don't need to be," I say. "I explained it all in the letter. It's all in there. I used Gershenzon as an example. I was trying to help you see why I write—"

I am interrupted. "Yes, I'm sure. But you understand—fourteen pages in your tiny handwriting—I only skimmed it."

"Of course." I don't know whatever led me to believe he would profit from the story of the Corner-to-Corner Correspondence. Or that anyone else would, for that matter. When I told Janet, who is young, an artist, and believes herself to be in possession of a sensitive soul, about the series of letters exchanged between Gershenzon and Viacheslav Ivanovitch Ivanov[2] while they recuperated in a rest-home in Russia, she said: "I don't get it. What's a corner-to-corner correspondence?"

"It was called that because each of the correspondents was in opposite corners of the same room. That's why it was called the Corner-to-Corner Correspondence," I said, ending my obvious explanation lamely.

"They couldn't talk? What was it, throat cancer?"

"No, as I said before, these guys were poets, philosophers, men of letters. Remember?" I prodded. "It was just that they felt more comfortable, surer of themselves, when writing. They had time to reflect on what they wanted to say, to test their ideas. To compose."

"That's the weirdest thing I ever heard—writing to someone in the same room," she said. "That sort of thing just gets in the way of real feelings. It's a kind of mask to hide who you really are, and what you're all about."

That was her final judgment, and from Janet's considered decisions there is no appeal, as I have learned to my sorrow. Still, I was

1. (1869–1925), Russian writer. **2.** (1866–1949), Russian writer.

almost in love, and at that precarious point one imagines it is important to be understood. So at our next planned meeting, two days later, I took along with me a passage I had copied from one of Gershenzon's letters. It was to demonstrate to her the subtleties which are the province of the written word, and, more importantly, to signal her what was going on in my mind.

"You see, honey," I said, trying to explain what Gershenzon meant to me, "he felt out of step with things going on around him. He might have said to old Ivanov: 'Viacheslav, what's the matter with me? I don't feel I belong. I don't feel right. Why is it I don't think what other people think, or feel what other people say they feel?' He could have put it that way. He could have, but he didn't. What he did do was write:

> This is the life I lead by day. But on a deeper level of consciousness I lead a different life. There, an insistent, persistent, hidden voice has been saying for years: No, no, this is not it! Some other kind of will in me turns away in misery and distaste from all of culture, from all that is being said and done around me. It finds all this tedious and vain, like a struggle of phantoms flailing away in a void; it seems to know another world, to foresee a different life, not yet to be found on earth but which will come and cannot fail to come, for only then will true reality be achieved. To me this voice is the voice of my real self. I live like a foreigner acclimatized in an alien land; the natives like me and I like them, I diligently work for their good, share their sorrows and rejoice in their joys, but at the same time I know that I am a stranger. I secretly long for the fields of my homeland, for its different spring, the smell of its flowers, and the way its women speak. Where is my homeland? I shall never see it, I shall die in foreign parts."

Of course, when I looked up from the page, it was only to discover that Janet had gone to the bathroom to apply her contraceptive foam.

"I hear that you're still refusing to see your wife," says Dr. Herzl, introducing a new topic.

"That's not entirely true. I said I wouldn't see her alone. If she brings our daughter with her, well, that's a different story."

"Why won't you speak to your wife alone?"

"I explain that in my second letter—"

"Why don't you explain it to me now. Face to face, without the pretences of these letters." There is a measure of asperity in the good doctor's voice. From the very beginning I knew he didn't like me. I do not have a confessional nature and he holds that against me.

I stare back stolidly.

"Is it because you're ashamed? Is that why you won't allow your wife to visit?"

"Yes." There is little harm in agreeing with him. He has made up his mind on this point long ago.

"Ashamed of what? Your affair? Or what you did at the gallery?"

Why not? "Both," I affirm, blithely shouldering a double load, the tawdry fardels of sexual guilt.

"Speaking of the gallery," says Dr. Herzl, "your wife agrees with me. She believes that the depiction of the penis was what triggered the incident there."

"She does, does she?"

"She thinks you felt it was undersized. She says you're prone to read a disproportionate significance into that sort of thing."

This is so like Miriam that I offer no complaint against this preposterous interpretation of my actions. I had my reasons.

Dr. Herzl clears his throat. "How am I to understand your silence?"

"The suggestion is too silly to grace with a comment."

"How did you feel when you did it?"

"Cold."

"I see," says the doctor, letting his fingers wander through the paper on his desk. "Well, I believe we've made some progress. We've begun to talk to one another, at any rate. Now is as good a time to stop as any." He closes my file. Perhaps the fact that it bulges with my correspondence reminds him. "You do see that writing letters is a way of avoiding the problem?" he asks hopefully.

"I want to see my daughter. You tell Miriam to bring Cynthia here."

"I'm sorry," says Dr. Herzl. "Mrs. Caragan says that would be impossible."

In my room I lie down on my bed and speculate how Miriam is making out. I know she is not starving. I am on full salary while incapacitated. The teachers' federation knows how to negotiate a collective agreement, and insanity is paid its rich deserts.

As far as the other things go—the neighbours' whispers, the long, woeful faces of acquaintances—the proud prow of Miriam's clipper can cleave those mundane waters. And her real friends, the ones that never liked me, will be intent on keeping her busy, or, as they would prefer, "involved".

For a number of years, I was "involved" too. Miriam demanded it. She was terribly concerned that we didn't trade our ideals for a mortgage, that we didn't become ordinary people. The flight from ordinariness kept me on a pretty strenuous schedule. I'd get home from the high school where I teach something called social studies just in time to grab a cheese sandwich and receive a briefing while the paint dried on my placard. Then we'd all load into a Volkswagen van owned by a troll with a social conscience, a short, hairy guy who made pieces of knotty-pine furniture capacious and sturdy enough to stand up to hard use by the giants I assumed were his clients, and drive off to let our opinions be known.

But about four years ago, when Miriam and I were fighting about Cynthia, and I was drinking even more than I was just before I got tossed in here, I gave up being involved and began my own journey; and there is no way that I'm going to give Miriam the chance to coax me back to Canada, now that I'm safely here, on the borders of Russia.

There's an irony, too, in how my travels began. They commenced at one of Miriam's protest rallies. About a dozen lonely souls were picketing a Liberal Fund-Raising Dinner—the reason why I now fail to recollect. It was the usual dispirited occasion. I was a little drunk and bored. The cars kept pulling up to the front of the hotel and discharging Liberals who slunk tight-lipped through our righteous gauntlet. One particularly incensed woman of our number kept demanding to know whether the Liberals were dining on macaroni and cheese that night. "Are you?" she shrilled in their faces. "Are you eating macaroni and cheese tonight?" The implication being that her own feisty spirit was sustained solely on that starchy, plebeian fuel.

It was all going more or less our way until a large, ruddy, drunk, middle-aged Liberal turned a passionate eye on our assembly. He was very angry. He seemed to have missed the point about macaroni and cheese. He thought we were objecting to our country. "Hey, you bastards!" he bellowed, while his wife tried to drag him into the lobby, "I love my country! I love Canada!" he yelled, actually striking his chest with his fist. "And if you don't, why don't you get out! *Why don't you go to Russia if you don't like it here?*"

The poor man's obvious sincerity touched me as much as his logic bewildered me. Why did he presume those people had any interest in going to Russia? Didn't he know it was *Sweden* they wanted to get to? Volvos, guiltless sex, Bergman films, functional furniture. Hey, I wanted to shout back, these people would prefer Sweden! And realizing for the first time where my wife and her friends were bound, I admitted I didn't want to go along. I was the one the gentleman was addressing. Although at the time I didn't know my longing was for Russia.

Oh, not the Russia he meant. Not Soviet Russia. But nineteenth-century Russia, the Russia of Dostoevsky's saintly prostitutes and Alyosha; of Tolstoy's Pierre; and Aksionov, the sufferer in "God Sees The Truth But Waits".[3] A country where the characters in books were allowed to ask one another the questions: How must

3. A story by Tolstoy. Pierre appears in *War and Peace*; Alyosha, in *The Brothers Karamazov*.

I live to be happy? What is goodness? Why does man suffer? What is to be done?

I had set a timid foot on that Eurasian continent years ago when, as a student in a course on European literature in translation, I had read some of the Russian masters. I returned because I was unhappy and because I sensed that only in Russia does unhappiness find a meaning. Like Aksionov, who suffered in place of the real murderer and thief, I felt a hundred times worse, a hundred times more guilt. I don't suppose I let it show much. I punished Miriam by putting our daughter's framed photograph on the end table, by drinking too much, and by being rude to people she wished desperately to impress.

Still, I was faithful to her in a purely technical sense until I met Janet several months ago. Janet is a young artist who supports herself as a substitute teacher; we met in the staffroom of my high school. At the end of that particular day, a bitterly cold one late in November, I spotted her waiting at the bus stop, looking hypothermic in the kind of tatty old fur coat creative people buy at Salvation Army thrift stores. I offered her a ride. She, in turn, when I had driven her home, offered me coffee.

I think it was the splendour of the drawings and paintings lending life to her old, decaying, high-ceilinged apartment that attracted me to her. Perhaps I felt she could salvage any wreck and breathe life into it, as she had that apartment. *Here,* I thought, gazing at the fire on her walls, *is a Russian soul.*

I asked if I could come back another day to make a purchase. She assured me that I could, that she would be delighted. I returned, bought a drawing. Returned again and carried away a canvas. Simply put, one thing led to another. We became lovers. Regularly, on school-days between three-thirty and four-thirty, p.m., she screwed me with clinical detachment. If I close my eyes I can see her hard little jockey-body rocking above me, muscles strained and taut (I could pluck the cords on her neck) as she mutely galloped me hither and thither, while I snorted away under her like old Dobbin.

That it was nothing more than a little equestrian exercise I lacked the courage to see.

Dr. Herzl makes a point of telling me how pleased he is that there have been no more letters since last we met. He sits behind his desk, bathed in pale March sunshine and self-assurance. I am struck by his aseptic smile and unlined face, hardly the face of a man privy to so many sorrows. More than most men, certainly.

Out of the blue he asks: "I think we're ready to talk about the Opening. And Janet. Don't you?"

"We could." I clear my throat and look at my hands. They're

very soft. The therapists here have tried to encourage me to take up handicrafts. However, if I cannot make boots like Tolstoy I will do nothing in that line.

"I'm interested to know the reasons why you posed for her. Particularly in light of what subsequently happened, it seems an odd thing for you to do."

"I didn't want to."

"But you did nevertheless."

"Obviously."

"Why?"

"Because she said she needed to sketch from life, and now that she wasn't a student she didn't get the opportunity. She couldn't afford to pay a model."

"So you wanted to help her with her work?"

"Yes." I knew how much it meant to her. Even then I knew what she was: a gifted, intense, ambitious girl, who was also a little bit stupid about things that had nothing to do with her art, and therefore did not concern her.

I can see by the look in the doctor's eyes that he is about to chance something. "Could it have been that modelling was a way of exposing yourself? Exposing yourself without having to fear consequences?"

"No."

He presses his hands together. "Why did you take such violent exception when you learned that the sketches were to be shown?" he asks softly.

"You can't be serious."

"Perfectly. I am perfectly serious. Tell me why."

"Because she didn't tell me," I say. I am unable to keep the anger out of my voice. "I saw it on a poster. 'Janet Markowsky: Studies in the Male Nude'."

"Any other reason?"

"Sure. This is a small city. I'm a teacher. Somebody would recognize me. How the hell could I walk into a classroom after every kid in the school had gone down to take a gander at old Caragan's wazoo?"

"You're exaggerating."

"And you don't know kids. Anyway, it was the principle of the thing. Don't you see?" My hands have begun to tremble, I trap them between my knees.

"Were you disturbed that there were drawings of other men?"

"No."

"Are you sure?"

"I went to Janet and I said, 'For God's sake, what are you doing to me? I can't take this right now. Please, take the sketches out of the show.' " It *was* a bad time for me. Cynthia's birthday was coming up and every year she gets older, the more her face haunts me.

"And?"

"She said she was very sorry but this opportunity had suddenly presented itself. A small gallery had an immediate opening because the artist slotted had decided to show in Calgary. Janet said she hadn't time to produce new work. She had to go with the drawings. With what she had. 'Janet,' I said, 'I'm a teacher, put a mustache on me. Anything!'

" 'I can't touch them,' she said. 'I could screw them up really badly. You can never tell what you'll do when you start mucking around with things.' "

"I phoned Ms. Markowsky yesterday and I asked her a question," says Herzl severely.

"What question?"' I am surprised.

"I asked her if you wanted her to change the penises. It was just a hunch," he says, very much the clever, smug detective. "She said you did. She said you wanted them made bigger."

I put my head in my hands. I should have known it. The little bitch is the type to make sure she gets even. She won't forgive me for ruining her Opening. Herzl, the moron, gave her the clue she needed to do it. Not that I really mind. "I wanted a mustache," I say tiredly.

Herzl is really on a roll now. "Why did you take all your clothes off and walk through the gallery, Mr. Caragan? Did you think you would frighten people with your penis? Do you think it is menacing?"

"Because I'm crazy," I say. "Because I thought Life should imitate Art."

The hospital is silent at night. Nothing like I would have imagined—no dim cries, or the muffled sounds of sleepers dreaming bad dreams. Everyone has sunk into the opaque slumber of the correctly dosed and medicated. Except me. I hide my pills under my tongue and make a magnificent show of swallowing.

I hear the night-duty nurse go by. The moon is so bright tonight, so full and white and gleaming, that I can write my fifth letter to Dr. Herzl without showing a light under my door and risking detection at three o'clock in the morning.

On my shaky plastic desk my books are piled. I have Herzen, Dostoevsky, Gogol, Turgenev, Lermontov, Soloviev, Leontiev, Gorky, Chekhov, Pushkin, Tolstoy and Rozanov to keep me company in exile. Day by day I feel a little of my guilt subside as I share her sentence. Like her father, Cynthia sleeps in an institution.

The people who care for her tell me she doesn't remember me from visit to visit. That is why Miriam never goes to visit the child.

It is pointless, she says. *Cynthia is profoundly retarded, and nothing will ever change that. I refuse to feel guilt.*

But my daughter is four years old now. She is no longer a baby. She must remember me.

And whenever I look into her wise, calm eyes set like stones in their Asiatic folds, I sense the grandeur of Russia, the infinite, colossal steppes sleeping there.

ALICE WALKER

Everyday Use

for your grandmamma

I WILL wait for her in the yard that Maggie and I made so clean and wavy yesterday afternoon. A yard like this is more comfortable than most people know. It is not just a yard. It is like an extended living room. When the hard clay is swept clean as a floor and the fine sand around the edges lined with tiny, irregular grooves, anyone can come and sit and look up into the elm tree and wait for the breezes that never come inside the house.

Maggie will be nervous until after her sister goes: she will stand hopelessly in corners, homely and ashamed of the burn scars down her arms and legs, eying her sister with a mixture of envy and awe. She thinks her sister has held life always in the palm of one hand, that "no" is a word the world never learned to say to her.

You've no doubt seen those TV shows where the child who has "made it" is confronted, as a surprise, by her own mother and father, tottering in weakly from backstage. (A pleasant surprise, of course: What would they do if parent and child came on the show only to curse out and insult each other?) On TV mother and child embrace and smile into each other's faces. Sometimes the mother and father weep, the child wraps them in her arms and leans across the table to tell how she would not have made it without their help. I have seen these programs.

Sometimes I dream a dream in which Dee and I are suddenly brought together on a TV program of this sort. Out of a dark and soft-seated limousine I am ushered into a bright room filled with many people. There I meet a smiling, gray, sporty man like Johnny Carson who shakes my hand and tells me what a fine girl I have. Then we are on the stage and Dee is embracing me with tears in her eyes. She pins on my dress a large orchid, even though she has told me once that she thinks orchids are tacky flowers.

In real life I am a large, big-boned woman with rough, man-working hands. In the winter I wear flannel nightgowns to bed and overalls during the day. I can kill and clean a hog as mercilessly as a man. My fat keeps me hot in zero weather. I can work outside all day, breaking ice to get water for washing; I can eat pork liver cooked over the open fire minutes after it comes steaming from the hog. One winter I knocked a bull calf straight in the brain between the eyes with a sledge hammer and had the meat hung up to chill before nightfall. But of course all this does not show on television. I am the way my daughter would want me to be: a hundred pounds lighter, my skin like an uncooked barley pancake. My hair glistens in the hot bright lights. Johnny Carson has much to do to keep up with my quick and witty tongue.

But that is a mistake. I know even before I wake up. Who ever knew a Johnson with a quick tongue? Who can even imagine me looking a strange white man in the eye? It seems to me I have talked to them always with one foot raised in flight, with my head turned in whichever way is farthest from them. Dee, though. She would always look anyone in the eye. Hesitation was no part of her nature.

"How do I look, Mama?" Maggie says, showing just enough of her thin body enveloped in pink skirt and red blouse for me to know she's there, almost hidden by the door.

"Come out into the yard," I say.

Have you ever seen a lame animal, perhaps a dog run over by some careless person rich enough to own a car, sidle up to someone who is ignorant enough to be kind to him? That is the way my Maggie walks. She has been like this, chin on chest, eyes on ground, feet in shuffle, ever since the fire that burned the other house to the ground.

Dee is lighter than Maggie, with nicer hair and a fuller figure. She's a woman now, though sometimes I forget. How long ago was it that the other house burned? Ten, twelve years? Sometimes I can still hear the flames and feel Maggie's arms sticking to me, her hair smoking and her dress falling off her in little black papery flakes. Her eyes seemed stretched open, blazed open by the flames reflected in them. And Dee. I see her standing off under the sweet gum tree she used to dig gum out of; a look of concentration on her face as she watched the last dingy gray board of the house fall in toward the red-hot brick chimney. Why don't you do a dance around the ashes? I'd wanted to ask her. She had hated the house that much.

I used to think she hated Maggie, too. But that was before we raised the money, the church and me, to send her to Augusta to school. She used to read to us without pity; forcing words, lies, other folks' habits, whole lives upon us two, sitting trapped and ignorant underneath her voice. She washed us in a river of make-believe, burned us with a lot of knowledge we didn't necessarily need to know. Pressed us to her with the serious way she read, to shove us away at just the moment, like dimwits, we seemed about to understand.

Dee wanted nice things. A yellow organdy dress to wear to her graduation from high school; black pumps to match a green suit she'd made from an old suit somebody gave me. She was determined to stare down any disaster in her efforts. Her eyelids would not flicker for minutes at a time. Often I fought off the temptation to shake her. At sixteen she had a style of her own: and knew what style was.

I never had an education myself. After second grade the school was closed down. Don't ask me why: in 1927 colored asked fewer questions than they do now. Sometimes Maggie reads to me. She stumbles along good-naturedly but can't see well. She knows she is not bright. Like good looks and money, quickness passed her by. She will marry John Thomas (who has mossy teeth in an earnest face) and then I'll be free to sit here and I guess just sing church songs to myself. Although I never was a good singer. Never could carry a tune. I was always better at a man's job. I used to love to milk till I was hooked[1] in the side in '49. Cows are soothing and slow and don't bother you, unless you try to milk them the wrong way.

I have deliberately turned my back on the house. It is three rooms, just like the one that burned, except the roof is tin; they don't make shingle roofs any more. There are no real windows, just some holes cut in the sides, like the portholes in a ship, but not round and not square, with rawhide holding the shutters up on the outside. This house is in a pasture, too, like the other one. No doubt when Dee sees it she will want to tear it down. She wrote me once that no matter where we "choose" to live, she will manage to come see us. But she will never bring her friends. Maggie and I thought about this and Maggie asked me, "Mama, when did Dee ever *have* any friends?"

She had a few. Furtive boys in pink shirts hanging about on washday after school. Nervous girls who never laughed. Impressed with her they worshiped the well-turned phrase, the cute shape, the scalding humor that erupted like bubbles in lye. She read to them.

When she was courting Jimmy T she didn't have much time to pay to us, but turned all her faultfinding power on him. He *flew* to marry a cheap city girl from a family of ignorant flashy people. She hardly had time to recompose herself.

When she comes I will meet—but there they are!

Maggie attempts to make a dash for the house, in her shuffling

1. I.e., by the horn of the cow being milked.

way, but I stay her with my hand. "Come back here," I say. And she stops and tries to dig a well in the sand with her toe.

It is hard to see them clearly through the strong sun. But even the first glimpse of leg out of the car tells me it is Dee. Her feet were always neat-looking, as if God himself had shaped them with a certain style. From the other side of the car comes a short, stocky man. Hair is all over his head a foot long and hanging from his chin like a kinky mule tail. I hear Maggie suck in her breath. "Uhnnnh," is what it sounds like. Like when you see the wriggling end of a snake just in front of your foot on the road. "Uhnnnh."

Dee next. A dress down to the ground, in this hot weather. A dress so loud it hurts my eyes. There are yellows and oranges enough to throw back the light of the sun. I feel my whole face warming from the heat waves it throws out. Earrings gold, too, and hanging down to her shoulders. Bracelets dangling and making noises when she moves her arm up to shake the folds of the dress out of her armpits. The dress is loose and flows, and as she walks closer, I like it. I hear Maggie go "Uhnnnh" again. It is her sister's hair. It stands straight up like the wool on a sheep. It is black as night and around the edges are two long pigtails that rope about like small lizards disappearing behind her ears.

"Wa-su-zo-Tean-o!" she says, coming on in that gliding way the dress makes her move. The short stocky fellow with the hair to his navel is all grinning and he follows up with "Asalamalakim,[2] my mother and sister!" He moves to hug Maggie but she falls back, right up against the back of my chair. I feel her trembling there and when I look up I see the perspiration falling off her chin.

"Don't get up," says Dee. Since I am stout it takes something of a push. You can see me trying to move a second or two before I make it. She turns, showing white heels through her sandals, and goes back to the car. Out she peeks next with a Polaroid. She stoops down quickly and lines up picture after picture of me sitting there in front of the house with Maggie cowering behind me. She never takes a shot without making sure the house is included. When a cow comes nibbling around the edge of the yard she snaps it and me and Maggie *and* the house. Then she puts the Polaroid in the back seat of the car, and comes up and kisses me on the forehead.

Meanwhile Asalamalakim is going through motions with Maggie's hand. Maggie's hand is as limp as a fish, and probably as cold, despite the sweat, and she keeps trying to pull it back. It looks like Asalamalakim wants to shake hands but wants to do it fancy. Or maybe he don't know how people shake hands. Anyhow, he soon gives up on Maggie.

"Well," I say. "Dee."

2. Phonetic rendering of a Muslim greeting. "Wa-su-zo-Tean-o" is a similar rendering of an African dialect salutation.

"No, Mama," she says. "Not 'Dee,' Wangero Leewanika Kemanjo!"

"What happened to 'Dee'?" I wanted to know.

"She's dead," Wangero said. "I couldn't bear it any longer, being named after the people who oppress me."

"You know as well as me you was named after your aunt Dicie," I said. Dicie is my sister. She named Dee. We called her "Big Dee" after Dee was born.

"But who was *she* named after?" asked Wangero.

"I guess after Grandma Dee," I said.

"And who was she named after?" asked Wangero.

"Her mother," I said, and saw Wangero was getting tired. "That's about as far back as I can trace it," I said. Though, in fact, I probably could have carried it back beyond the Civil War through the branches.

"Well," said Asalamalakim, "there you are."

"Uhnnnh," I heard Maggie say.

"There I was not," I said, "before 'Dicie' cropped up in our family, so why should I try to trace it that far back?"

He just stood there grinning, looking down on me like somebody inspecting a Model A car. Every once in a while he and Wangero sent eye signals over my head.

"How do you pronounce this name?" I asked.

"You don't have to call me by it if you don't want to," said Wangero.

"Why shouldn't I?" I asked. "If that's what you want us to call you, we'll call you."

"I know it might sound awkward at first," said Wangero.

"I'll get used to it," I said. "Ream it out again."

Well, soon we got the name out of the way. Asalamalakim had a name twice as long and three times as hard. After I tripped over it two or three times he told me to just call him Hakim-a-barber. I wanted to ask him was he a barber, but I didn't really think he was, so I didn't ask.

"You must belong to those beef-cattle peoples down the road," I said. They said "Asalamalakim" when they met you, too, but they didn't shake hands. Always too busy: feeding the cattle, fixing the fences, putting up salt-lick shelters, throwing down hay. When the white folks poisoned some of the herd the men stayed up all night with rifles in their hands. I walked a mile and a half just to see the sight.

Hakim-a-barber said, "I accept some of their doctrines, but farming and raising cattle is not my style." (They didn't tell me, and I didn't ask, whether Wangero (Dee) had really gone and married him.)

We sat down to eat and right away he said he didn't eat collards and pork was unclean. Wangero, though, went on through the chitlins and corn bread, the greens and everything else. She talked a blue streak over the sweet potatoes. Everything delighted her. Even the fact that we still used the benches her daddy made for the table when we couldn't afford to buy chairs.

"Oh, Mama!" she cried. Then turned to Hakim-a-barber. "I never knew how lovely these benches are. You can feel the rump prints," she said, running her hands underneath her and along the bench. Then she gave a sigh and her hand closed over Grandma Dee's butter dish. "That's it!" she said. "I knew there was something I wanted to ask you if I could have." She jumped up from the table and went over in the corner where the churn stood, the milk in it clabber by now. She looked at the churn and looked at it.

"This churn top is what I need," she said. "Didn't Uncle Buddy whittle it out of a tree you all used to have?"

"Yes," I said.

"Uh huh," she said happily. "And I want the dasher, too."

"Uncle Buddy whittle that, too?" asked the barber.

Dee (Wangero) looked up at me.

"Aunt Dee's first husband whittled the dash," said Maggie so low you almost couldn't hear her. "His name was Henry, but they called him Stash."

"Maggie's brain is like an elephant's," Wangero said, laughing. "I can use the churn top as a centerpiece for the alcove table," she said, sliding a plate over the churn, "and I'll think of something artistic to do with the dasher."

When she finished wrapping the dasher the handle stuck out. I took it for a moment in my hands. You didn't even have to look close to see where hands pushing the dasher up and down to make butter had left a kind of sink in the wood. In fact, there were a lot of small sinks; you could see where thumbs and fingers had sunk into the wood. It was beautiful light yellow wood, from a tree that grew in the yard where Big Dee and Stash had lived.

After dinner Dee (Wangero) went to the trunk at the foot of my bed and started rifling through it. Maggie hung back in the kitchen over the dishpan. Out came Wangero with two quilts. They had been pieced by Grandma Dee and then Big Dee and me had hung them on the quilt frames on the front porch and quilted them. One was in the Lone Star pattern. The other was Walk Around the Mountain. In both of them were scraps of dresses Grandma Dee had worn fifty and more years ago. Bits and pieces of Grandpa Jarrell's Paisley shirts. And one teeny faded blue piece, about the size of a penny matchbox, that was from Great Grandpa Ezra's uniform that he wore in the Civil War.

"Mama," Wangero said sweet as a bird. "Can I have these old quilts?"

I heard something fall in the kitchen, and a minute later the kitchen door slammed.

"Why don't you take one or two of the others?" I asked. "These old things was just done by me and Big Dee from some tops your grandma pieced before she died."

"No," said Wangero. "I don't want those. They are stitched around the borders by machine."

"That'll make them last better," I said.

"That's not the point," said Wangero. "These are all pieces of dresses Grandma used to wear. She did all this stitching by hand. Imagine!" She held the quilts securely in her arms, stroking them.

"Some of the pieces, like those lavender ones, come from old clothes her mother handed down to her," I said, moving up to touch the quilts. Dee (Wangero) moved back just enough so that I couldn't reach the quilts. They already belonged to her.

"Imagine!" she breathed again, clutching them closely to her bosom.

"The truth is," I said, "I promised to give them quilts to Maggie, for when she marries John Thomas."

She gasped like a bee had stung her.

"Maggie can't appreciate these quilts!" she said. "She'd probably be backward enough to put them to everyday use."

"I reckon she would," I said. "God knows I been saving 'em for long enough with nobody using 'em. I hope she will!" I didn't want to bring up how I had offered Dee (Wangero) a quilt when she went away to college. Then she had told me they were old-fashioned, out of style.

"But they're *priceless!*" she was saying now, furiously; for she has a temper. "Maggie would put them on the bed and in five years they'd be in rags. Less than that!" "She can always make some more," I said. "Maggie knows how to quilt."

Dee (Wangero) looked at me with hatred. "You just will not understand. The point is these quilts, *these* quilts!"

"Well," I said, stumped. "What would *you* do with them?"

"Hang them," she said. As if that was the only thing you *could* do with quilts.

Maggie by now was standing in the door. I could almost hear the sound her feet made as they scraped over each other.

"She can have them, Mama," she said, like somebody used to never winning anything, or having anything reserved for her. "I can 'member Grandma Dee without the quilts."

I looked at her hard. She had filled her bottom lip with checkerberry snuff and it gave her face a kind of dopey, hangdog look. It was Grandma Dee and Big Dee who taught her how to quilt herself. She stood there with her scarred hands hidden in the folds of her skirt. She looked at her sister with something like fear but she wasn't mad at her. This was Maggie's portion. This was the way she knew God to work.

When I looked at her like that something hit me in the top of my head and ran down to the soles of my feet. Just like when I'm in church and the spirit of God touches me and I get happy and shout. I did something I never had done before: hugged Maggie to me, then dragged her on into the room, snatched the quilts out of Miss Wangero's hands and dumped them into Maggie's lap. Maggie just sat there on my bed with her mouth open.

"Take one or two of the others," I said to Dee.

But she turned without a word and went out to Hakim-a-barber.

"You just don't understand," she said, as Maggie and I came out to the car.

"What don't I understand?" I wanted to know.

"Your heritage," she said. And then she turned to Maggie, kissed her, and said, "You ought to try to make something of yourself, too, Maggie. It's really a new day for us. But from the way you and Mama still live you'd never know it."

She put on some sunglasses that hid everything above the tip of her nose and her chin.

Maggie smiled; maybe at the sunglasses. But a real smile, not scared. After we watched the car dust settle I asked Maggie to bring me a dip of snuff. And then the two of us sat there just enjoying, until it was time to go in the house and go to bed.

JOY WILLIAMS

Taking Care

I

JONES, the preacher, has been in love all his life. He is baffled by this because as far as he can see, it has never helped anyone, even when they have acknowledged it, which is not often. Jones' love is much too apparent and arouses neglect. He is like an animal in a traveling show who, through some aberration, wears a vital organ outside the skin, awkward and unfortunate, something that shouldn't be seen, certainly something that shouldn't be watched working. Now he sits on a bed beside his wife in the self-care unit of a hospital fifteen miles from their home. She has been committed here for tests. She is so weak, so tired. There is something wrong with her blood. Her arms are covered with bruises where they have gone into the veins. Her hip, too, is blue and swollen where they have drawn out samples of bone marrow. All of this is frightening. The doctors are severe and wise, answering Jones' questions in a way that makes him feel hopelessly deaf. They have told him that there really is no such thing as a disease of the blood, for the blood is not a living tissue but a passive vehicle for the transportation of food, oxygen and waste. They have told him that abnormalities in the blood corpucles, which his wife seems to have, must be regarded as symptoms of disease elsewhere in the body. They have shown him, upon request, slides and charts of normal and pathological blood cells which look to Jones like canapés. They speak (for he insists) of leukocytosis, myelocytes and megaloblasts. None of this takes into account the love he has for his wife! Jones sits beside her in this dim pleasant room, wearing a gray suit and his clerical collar, for when he leaves her he must visit other parishioners who are patients here. This part of the hospital is like a motel. One may wear one's regular clothes. The rooms have ice-buckets, rugs and colorful bedspreads. How he wishes that they were traveling and staying overnight, this night, in a motel. A nurse comes in with a tiny paper cup full of pills. There are three pills, or rather, capsules, and they are not for his wife but for her blood. The cup is the smallest of its type that Jones has ever seen. All perspective, all sense of time and scale seem abandoned in this hospital. For example, when Jones turns to kiss his wife's hair, he nicks the air instead.

II

Jones and his wife have one child, a daughter, who, in turn, has a single child, a girl, born one-half year ago. Jones' daughter has fallen in with the stars and is using the heavens, as Jones would be the first to admit, more than he ever has. It has, however, brought her only grief and confusion. She has left her husband and brought the baby to Jones. She has also given him her dog, a German shepherd. She is going to Mexico where soon, in the mountains, she will have a nervous breakdown. Jones does not know this, but his daughter has seen it in the stars and is going out to meet it. Jones quickly agrees to care for both the baby and the dog, as this seems to be the only thing his daughter needs from him. The day of the baby's birth is secondary to the position of the planets and the terms of houses, quadrants and gradients.[1] Her symbol is a bareback rider. To Jones, this is a graceful thought. It signifies audacity. It also means luck. Jones slips a twenty dollar bill in the pocket of his daughter's suitcase and drives her to the airport. The plane taxis down the runway and Jones waves, holding all their luck in his arms.

III

One afternoon, Jones had come home and found his wife sitting in the garden, weeping. She had been transplanting flowers, putting them in pots before the first frost came. There was dirt on her

1. Astrological terms.

forehead and around her mouth. Her light clothes felt so heavy. Their weight made her body ache. Each breath was a stone she had to swallow. She cried and cried in the weak autumn sunshine. Jones could see the veins throbbing in her neck. "I'm dying," she said. "It's taking me months to die." But after he had brought her inside, she insisted that she felt better and made them both a cup of tea while Jones potted the rest of the plants and carried them down cellar. She lay on the sofa and Jones sat beside her. They talked quietly with one another. Indeed, they were almost whispering, as though they were in a public place surrounded by strangers instead of in their own house with no one present but themselves. "It's the season," Jones said. "In fall everything slows down, retreats. I'm feeling tired myself. We need iron. I'll go to the druggist right now and buy some iron tablets." His wife agreed. She wanted to go with him, for the ride. Together they ride, through the towns, for miles and miles, even into the next state. She does not want to stop driving. They buy sandwiches and milkshakes and eat in the car. Jones drives. They have to buy more gasoline. His wife sits close to him, her eyes closed, her head tipped back against the seat. He can see the veins beating on in her neck. Somewhere there is a dreadful sound, almost audible. "First I thought it was my imagination," his wife said. "I couldn't sleep. All night I would stay awake, dreaming. But it's not in my head. It's in my ears, my eyes. They ache. Everything. My tongue. My hair. The tips of my fingers are dead." Jones pressed her cold hand to his lips. He thinks of something mad and loving better than he—running out of control, deeply in the darkness of his wife. "Just don't make me go to the hospital," she pleaded. Of course she will go there. The moment has already occurred.

IV

Jones is writing to his daughter. He received a brief letter from her this morning, telling him where she could be reached. The foreign postmark was so large that it almost obliterated Jones' address. She did not mention either her mother or the baby, which makes Jones feel peculiar. His life seems increated[2] as his God's life, perhaps even imaginary. His daughter tells him about the town in which she lives. She does not plan to stay there long. She wants to travel. She will find out exactly what she wants to do and then she will come home again. The town is poor but interesting and there are many Americans there her own age. There is a zoo right on the beach. Almost all the towns, no matter how small, have little zoos. There are primarily eagles and hawks in the cages. And what can Jones reply to that? He writes *Everything is fine here. We are burning wood from the old apple tree in the fire place and its smells*

2. Existing without having been created.

wonderful. Has the baby had her full series of polio shots? Take care. Jones uses this expression constantly, usually in totally unwarranted situations, as when he purchases pipe cleaners or drives through toll booths. Distracted, Jones writes off the edge of the paper and onto the blotter. He must begin again. He will mail this on the way to the hospital. They have been taking X-rays for three days now but the pictures are cloudy. They cannot read them. His wife is now in a real sickbed with high metal sides. He sits with her while she eats her dinner. She asks him to take her good nightgown home and wash it with a bar of Ivory. They won't let her do anything now, not even wash out a few things. *You must take care.*

v

Jones is driving down a country road. It is the first snowfall of the season and he wants to show it to the baby who rides beside him in a small foam-and-metal car seat all her own. Her head is almost on a level with his and she looks earnestly at the landscape, sometimes smiling. They follow the road that winds tightly between fields and deep pine woods. Everything is white and clean. It has been snowing all afternoon and is doing so still, but very very lightly. Fat snowflakes fall solitary against the windshield. Sometimes the baby reaches out for them. Sometimes she gives a brief kick and cry of joy. They have done their errands. Jones has bought milk and groceries and two yellow roses which lie wrapped in tissue and newspaper in the trunk, in the cold. He must buy two on Saturday as the florist is closed on Sunday. He does not like to do this but there is no alternative. The roses do not keep well. Tonight he will give one to his wife. The other he will pack in sugar water and store in the refrigerator. He can only hope that the bud will remain tight until Sunday when he brings it into the terrible heat of the hospital. The baby rocks against the straps of her small carrier. Her lips are pursed as she watches intently the fields, the gray stalks of crops growing out of the snow, the trees. She is warmly dressed and she wears a knitted orange cap. It is twenty-three years old, the age of her mother. Jones found it just the other day when he was looking for it. It has faded almost to pink on one side. At one time, it must have been stored in the sun. Jones, driving, feels almost gay. The snow is so beautiful. Everything is white, even the hood of the car. Jones is an educated man. He has read Melville, who says that white[3] is the colorless all-color of atheism from which we shrink. Jones does not believe this. He sees a holiness in snow, a promise. He hopes that his wife will know that it is snowing even though she

3. The reference is to Chapter 42 of *Moby-Dick* by Herman Melville. The entire chapter is an imaginative discourse on *whiteness*. A typical passage: "This elusive quality it is, which causes the thought of whitness, when divorced from its more kindly associations, and coupled with any object terrible in itself, to heighten that terror to its furthest bounds."

is separated from the window by a curtain. Jones sees something moving across the snow, a part of the snow itself, running. Although he is going slowly, he takes his foot completely off the accelerator. "Look, darling, a snowshoe rabbit." At the sound of his voice, the baby stretches open her mouth and narrows her eyes in soundless glee. The hare is splendid. So fast! It flows around invisible obstructions, something out of a kind dream. It flies across the ditch, its paws like paddles, faintly yellow, the color of raw wood. "Look, sweet," cries Jones, "how big he is!" But suddenly the hare is curved and falling, round as a ball, its feet and head tucked closely against its body. It strikes the road and skids upside down for several yards. The car passes around it, avoids it. Jones brakes and stops, amazed. He opens the door and trots back to the animal. The baby twists about in her seat as well as she can and peers after him. It is as though the animal had never been alive at all. Its head is broken in several places. Jones bends to touch its fur, but straightens again, not doing so. A man emerges from the woods, swinging a shotgun. He nods at Jones and picks the hare up by the ears. As he walks away, the hare's legs rub across the ground. There are small crystal stains on the snow. Jones returns to the car. He wants to apologize but he does not know to whom or for what. His life has been devoted to apologetics. It is his profession. He is concerned with both justification and remorse. He has always acted rightly, but nothing has ever come of it. He gets in the car, starts the engine. "Oh, sweet," he says to the baby. She smiles at him, exposing her tooth. At home that night, after the baby's supper, Jones reads a story to her. She is asleep, panting in her sleep, but Jones tells her the story of al-Boraq, the milkwhite steed of Mohammed, who could stride out of the sight of mankind with a single step.

VI

Jones sorts through a collection of records, none of which have been opened. They are still wrapped in cellophane. The jacket designs are subdued, epic. Names, instruments and orchestras are mentioned confidently. He would like to agree with their importance, for he knows that they have worth, but he is not familiar with the references. His daughter brought these records with her. They had been given to her by an older man, a professor she had been having an affair with. Naturally, this pains Jones. His daughter speaks about the men she has been involved with but no longer cares about. Where did these men come from? Where were they waiting and why have they gone? Jones remembers his daughter when she was a little girl, helping him rake leaves. What can he say? For years on April Fool's Day, she would take tobacco out of his humidor and fill it with Corn Flakes. Jones is full of remorse and astonishment. When he saw his daughter only a few weeks ago, she was thin and nervous. She had torn out almost all her eyebrows with her fingers from this nervousness. And her lashes. The roots of her eyes were white, like the bulbs of flowers. Her fingernails were crudely bitten, some bleeding below the quick. She was tough and remote, wanting only to go on a trip for which she had a ticket. What can he do? He seeks her in the face of the baby but she is not there. All is being both continued and resumed, but the dream is different. The dream cannot be revived. Jones breaks into one of the albums, blows the dust from the needle, plays a record. Outside it is dark. The parsonage is remote and the only buildings nearby are barns. The river cannot be seen. The music is Bruckner's *Te Deum.*[4] Very nice. Dedicated to God. He plays the other side. A woman, Kathleen Ferrier,[5] is singing in German. Jones cannot understand the words but the music stuns him. *Kindertotenlieder.*[6] It is devastating. In college he had studied only scientific German, the vocabulary of submarines, dirigibles and steam engines. Jones plays the record again and again, searching for his old grammar. At last he finds it. The wings of insects are between some of the pages. There are notes in pencil, written in his own young hand.

> *Render:*
> A. *Was the teacher satisfied with you today?*
> B. *No, he was not. My essay was good but it was not copied well.*
> C. *I am sorry you were not industrious this time for you generally are.*

These lessons are neither of life or death. Why was he instructed in them? In the hospital, his wife waits to be translated, no longer a woman, the woman whom he loves, but a situation. Her blood moves mysteriously as constellations. She is under scrutiny and attack and she has abandoned Jones. She is a swimmer waiting to get on with the drowning. Jones is on the shore. In Mexico, his daughter walks along the beach with two men. She is acting out a play that has become her life. Jones is on the mountaintop. The baby cries and Jones takes her from the crib to change her. The dog paws the door. Jones lets him out. He settles down with the baby and listens to the record. *Songs on the Deaths of Infants.* Controlled heartbreak. He still cannot make out many of the words. The baby wiggles restlessly on his lap. Her eyes are a foal's eyes, navy-blue. She has grown in a few weeks to expect everything from Jones. He props her on one edge of the couch and goes to her small toy box where he keeps a bear, a few rattles and balls. On the way, he opens the door and the dog immediately enters. His heavy coat is cold, fragrant with ice. He noses the baby and she squeals.

4. "Thou, Lord," by Anton Bruckner—Austrian composer (1824–1896). **5.** English contralto (1912–1953). **6.** *Songs of the Death of Children.*

Oft denk' ich, sie sind nur ausgegangen
Bald werden sie wieder nach Hause gelangen[7]

Jones selects a bright ball and pushes it gently in her direction.

VII

It is Sunday morning and Jones is in the pulpit. The church is very old but the walls of the sanctuary have recently been painted a pale blue. In the cemetery adjoining, some of the graves are three hundred years old. It has become a historical landmark and no one has been buried there since World War I. There is a new place, not far away, which the families now use. Plots are marked not with stones but with small tablets, and immediately after any burial, workmen roll grassed sod over the new graves so that there is no blemish on the grounds, not even for a little while. Present for today's service are seventy-eight adults, eleven children and the junior choir. Jones counts them as the offertory is received. The church rolls say that there are 350 members but as far as Jones can see, everyone is here today. This is the day he baptizes the baby. He has made arrangements with one of the ladies to hold her and bring her up to the font at the end of the first hymn. The baby looks charming in a lacy white dress. Jones has combed her fine hair carefully, slicking it in a curl with water, but now it has dried and it sticks up awkwardly like the crest of a kingfisher. Jones bought the dress in Mammoth Mart, an enormous store which has a large metal elephant dressed in overalls dancing on the roof. He feels foolish at buying it there but he had gone to several stores and that is where he saw the prettiest dress. He blesses the baby with water from the silver bowl. He says, *We are saved not because we are worthy. We are saved because we are loved.* It is a brief ceremony. The baby, looking curiously at Jones, is taken out to the nursery. Jones begins his sermon. He can't remember when he wrote it, but here it is, typed, in front of him. *There is nothing wrong in what one does but there is something wrong in what one becomes.* He finds this questionable but goes on speaking. He has been preaching for thirty-four years. He is gaunt with belief. But his wife has a red cell count of only 2.3 millions. It is not enough! She is not getting enough oxygen! Jones is giving his sermon. Somewhere he has lost what he was looking for. He must have known once, surely. The congregation sways, like the wings of a ray in water. It is Sunday and for patients it is a holiday. The doctors don't visit. There are no tests or diagnoses. Jones would like to leave, to walk down the aisle and out into the winter, where he would read his words into the ground. Why can't he remember his life! He finishes, sits down, stands up to present communion. Tiny cubes of bread lie in a slumped pyramid. They are offered and received. Jones takes his

7. "Often I think you have only gone out/ Soon you will come into the house again."

morsel, hacked earlier from a sliced enriched loaf with his own hand. It is so dry, almost wicked. The very thought now sickens him. He chews it over and over again, but it lies unconsumed, like a muscle in his mouth.

VIII

Jones is waiting in the lobby for the results of his wife's operation. Has there ever been a time before dread? He would be grateful even to have dread back, but it has been lost, for a long time, in rapid possibility, probability and fact. The baby sits on his knees and plays with his tie. She woke very early this morning for her orange juice and then gravely, immediately, spit it all up. She seems fine now, however, her fingers exploring Jones' tie. Whenever he looks at her, she gives him a dazzling smile. He has spent most of the day fiercely cleaning the house, changing the bedsheets and the pages of the many calendars that hang in the rooms, things he should have done a week ago. He has dusted and vacuumed and pressed all his shirts. He has laundered all the baby's clothes, soft small sacks and gowns and sleepers which froze in his hands the moment he stepped outside. And now he is waiting and watching his wristwatch. The tumor is precisely this size, they tell him, the size of his clock's face.

IX

Jones has the baby on his lap and he is feeding her. The evening meal is lengthy and complex. First he must give her vitamins, then, because she has a cold, a dropper of liquid aspirin. This is followed by a bottle of milk, eight ounces, and a portion of strained vegetables. He gives her a rest now so that the food can settle. On his hip, she rides through the rooms of the huge house as Jones turns lights off and on. He comes back to the table and gives her a little more milk, a half jar of strained chicken and a few spoonfuls of dessert, usually cobbler, buckle or pudding. The baby enjoys all equally. She is good. She eats rapidly and neatly. Sometimes she grasps the spoon, turns it around and thrusts the wrong end into her mouth. Of course there is nothing that cannot be done incorrectly. Jones adores the baby. He sniffs her warm head. Her birth is a deep error, an abstraction. Born in wedlock but out of love. He puts her in the playpen and tends to the dog. He fills one dish with water and one with horsemeat. He rinses out the empty can before putting it in the wastebasket. The dog eats with great civility. He eats a little meat and then takes some water, then meat, then water. When the dog has finished, the dishes are as clean as though they'd been washed. Jones now thinks about his own dinner. He opens the refrigerator. The ladies of the church have brought brownies, venison, cheese and apple sauce. There are turkey pies, pork chops, steak, haddock and sausage patties. A brilliant light exposes all this food. There is so much of it. It must be used. A crust has formed around the punctures in a can of Pet. There is a clear bag of chicken livers stapled shut. There are large brown eggs in a bowl. Jones stares unhappily at the beads of moisture on cartons and bottles, at the pearls of fat on the cold cooked stew. He sits down. The room is full of lamps and cords. He thinks of his wife, her breathing body deranged in tubes, and begins to shake. All objects here are perplexed by such grief.

X

Now it is almost Christmas and Jones is walking down by the river, around an abandoned house. The dog wades heavily through the snow, biting it. There are petals of ice on the tree limbs and when Jones lingers under them, the baby puts out her hand and her mouth starts working because she would like to have it, the ice, the branch, everything. His wife will be coming home in a few days, in time for Christmas. Jones has already put up the tree and brought the ornaments down from the attic. He will not trim it until she comes home. He wants very much to make a fine occasion out of opening the boxes of old decorations. The two of them have always enjoyed this greatly in the past. Jones will doubtlessly drop and smash a bauble, for he does every year. He tramps through the snow with his small voyager. She dangles in a shoulder sling, her legs wedged around his hip. They regard the rotting house seriously. Once it was a doctor's home and offices but long before Jones' time, the doctor, who was very respected, had been driven away because a town girl accused him of fathering her child. The story goes that all the doctor said was, "Is that so?" This incensed the town and the girl's parents, who insisted that he take the child as soon as it was born. He did and he cared for it very well even though his practice was ruined and no one had anything to do with him. A year later the girl told the truth—that the actual father was a young college boy who she was now going to marry. They wanted the child back, and the doctor willingly gave the infant to them, saying to their apology and confession only, "Is that so?" Of course it is a very old, important story. Jones has always appreciated it, but now he is annoyed at the man's passivity. His wife's sickness has changed everything for Jones. He will continue to accept but he will no longer surrender. Surely things are different for Jones now.

XI

For insurance purposes, Jones' wife is brought out to the car in a wheelchair. She is thin and beautiful. Jones is grateful and confused. He has a mad wish to tip the orderly. Have so many years really passed? Is this not his wife, his love, fresh from giving birth? Isn't everything about to begin? In Mexico, his daughter wanders disinterestedly through a jewelry shop where she picks up a small silver egg. It opens on a hinge and inside are two figures, a bride and groom. Jones puts the baby in his wife's arms. At first the baby is alarmed because she cannot remember this person very well and she reaches for Jones, whimpering. But soon she is soothed by his wife's soft voice and she falls asleep in her arms as they drive. Jones has readied everything carefully for his wife's homecoming. The house is clean and orderly. For days he has restricted himself to only one part of the house so that his clutter will be minimal. Jones helps his wife up the steps to the door. Together they enter the shining rooms.

TOBIAS WOLFF

In the Garden of the North American Martyrs

WHEN she was young, Mary saw a brilliant and original man lose his job because he had expressed ideas that were offensive to the trustees of the college where they both taught. She shared his views, but did not sign the protest petition. She was, after all, on trial herself—as a teacher, as a woman, as an interpreter of history.

Mary watched herself. Before giving a lecture she wrote it out in full, using the arguments and often the words of other, approved writers, so that she would not by chance say something scandalous. Her own thoughts she kept to herself, and the words for them grew faint as time went on; without quite disappearing they shrank to remote, nervous points, like birds flying away.

When the department turned into a hive of cliques, Mary went about her business and pretended not to know that people hated each other. To avoid seeming bland she let herself become eccentric in harmless ways. She took up bowling, which she learned to love, and founded the Brandon College chapter of a society dedicated to restoring the good name of Richard III.[1] She memorized comedy routines from records and jokes from books; people groaned when she rattled them off, but she did not let that stop her, and after a time the groans became the point of the jokes. They were a kind of tribute to Mary's willingness to expose herself.

In fact no one at the college was safer than Mary, for she was making herself into something institutional, like a custom, or a mascot—part of the college's idea of itself.

Now and then she wondered whether she had been too careful. The things she said and wrote seemed flat to her, pulpy, as though someone else had squeezed the juice out of them. And once, while talking with a senior professor, Mary saw herself reflected in a window: she was leaning toward him and had her head turned so

1. English king (1452–1485) generally regarded as ruthless and brutal.

that her ear was right in front of his moving mouth. The sight disgusted her. Years later, when she had to get a hearing aid, Mary suspected that her deafness was a result of always trying to catch everything everyone said.

In the second half of Mary's fifteenth year at Brandon the provost called a meeting of all faculty and students to announce that the college was bankrupt and would not open its gates again. He was every bit as much surprised as they; the report from the trustees had reached his desk only that morning. It seemed that Brandon's financial manager had speculated in some kind of futures and lost everything. The provost wanted to deliver the news in person before it reached the papers. He wept openly and so did the students and teachers, with only a few exceptions—some cynical upperclassmen who claimed to despise the education they had received.

Mary could not rid her mind of the word "speculate." It meant to guess, in terms of money to gamble. How could a man gamble a college? Why would he want to do that, and how could it be that no one stopped him? To Mary, it seemed to belong to another time; she thought of a drunken plantation owner gaming away his slaves.

She applied for jobs and got an offer from a new experimental college in Oregon. It was her only offer so she took it.

The college was in one building. Bells rang all the time, lockers lined the hallways, and at every corner stood a buzzing water fountain. The student newspaper came out twice a month on mimeograph paper which felt wet. The library, which was next to the band room, had no librarian and no books.

The countryside was beautiful, though, and Mary might have enjoyed it if the rain had not caused her so much trouble. There was something wrong with her lungs that the doctors couldn't agree on, and couldn't cure; whatever it was, the dampness made it worse. On rainy days condensation formed in Mary's hearing aid and shorted it out. She began to dread talking with people, never knowing when she would have to take out her control box and slap it against her leg.

It rained nearly every day. When it was not raining it was getting ready to rain, or clearing. The ground glinted under the grass, and the light had a yellow undertone that flared up during storms.

There was water in Mary's basement. Her walls sweated, and she had found toadstools growing behind the refrigerator. She felt as though she were rusting out, like one of those old cars people thereabouts kept in their front yards, on pieces of wood. Mary knew that everyone was dying, but it did seem to her that she was dying faster than most.

She continued to look for another job, without success. Then, in the fall of her third year in Oregon, she got a letter from a woman named Louise who'd once taught in Brandon. Louise had scored a great success with a book on Benedict Arnold[2] and was now on the faculty of a famous college in upstate New York. She said that one of her colleagues would be retiring at the end of the year and asked whether Mary would be interested in the position.

The letter surprised Mary. Louise thought of herself as a great historian and of almost everyone else as useless; Mary had not known that she felt differently about her. Moreover, enthusiasm for other people's causes did not come easily to Louise, who had a way of sucking in her breath when familiar names were mentioned, as though she knew things that friendship kept her from disclosing.

Mary expected nothing, but sent a résumé and copies of her two books. Shortly after that Louise called to say that the search committee, of which she was chairwoman, had decided to grant Mary an interview in early November. "Now don't get your hopes *too* high," Louise said.

"Oh, no," Mary said, but thought: Why shouldn't I hope? They would not go to the bother and expense of bringing her to the college if they weren't serious. And she was certain that the interview would go well. She would make them like her, or at least give them no cause to dislike her.

She read about the area with a strange sense of familiarity, as if the land and its history were already known to her. And when her plane left Portland and climbed easily into the clouds, Mary felt like she was going home. The feeling stayed with her, growing stronger when they landed. She tried to describe it to Louise as they left the airport at Syracuse and drove toward the college, an hour or so away. "It's like *déjà vu*," she said.

"*Déjà vu* is a hoax," Louise said. "It's just a chemical imbalance of some kind."

"Maybe so," Mary said, "but I still have this sensation."

"Don't get serious on me," Louise said. "That's not your long suit. Just be your funny, wisecracking old self. Tell me now—honestly—how do I look?"

It was night, too dark to see Louise's face well, but in the airport she had seemed gaunt and pale and intense. She reminded Mary of a description in the book she'd been reading, of how Iroquois[3] warriors gave themselves visions by fasting. She had that kind of look about her. But she wouldn't want to hear that. "You look wonderful," Mary said.

"There's a reason," Louise said. "I've taken a lover. My concentration has improved, my energy level is up, and I've lost ten pounds. I'm also getting some color in my cheeks, though that

2. U.S. general (1741–1801) in Revolutionary War, who became a traitor. 3. A tribe native to the lower Great Lakes region. War-loving by reputation.

could be the weather. I recommend the experience highly. But you probably disapprove."

Mary didn't know what to say. She said that she was sure Louise knew best, but that didn't seem to be enough. "Marriage is a great institution," she added, "but who wants to live in an institution?"

Louise groaned. "I know you," she said, "and I know that right now you're thinking 'But what about Ted? What about the children?' The fact is, Mary, they aren't taking it well at all. Ted has become a nag." She handed Mary her purse. "Be a good girl and light me a cigarette, will you? I know I told you I quit, but this whole thing has been very hard on me, very hard, and I'm afraid I've started again."

They were in the hills now, heading north on a narrow road. Tall trees arched above them. As they topped a rise Mary saw the forest all around, deep black under the plum-colored sky. There were a few lights and these made the darkness seem even greater.

"Ted has succeeded in completely alienating the children from me," Louise was saying. "There is no reasoning with any of them. In fact, they refuse to discuss the matter at all, which is very ironical because over the years I have tried to instill in them a willingness to see things from the other person's point of view. If they could just *meet* Jonathan I know they would feel differently. But they won't hear of it. Jonathan," she said, "is my lover."

"I see," Mary said, and nodded.

Coming around a curve they caught two deer in the headlights. Their eyes lit up and their hindquarters tensed; Mary could see them trembling as the car went by. "Deer," she said.

"I don't know," Louise said, "I just don't know. I do my best and it never seems to be enough. But that's enough about me—let's talk about you. What did you think of my latest book?" She squawked and beat her palms on the steering wheel. "God, I love that joke," she said. "Seriously, though, what about you? It must have been a real shockeroo when good old Brandon folded."

"It was hard. Things haven't been good but they'll be a lot better if I get this job."

"At least you have work," Louise said. "You should look at it from the bright side."

"I try."

"You seem so gloomy. I hope you're not worrying about the interview, or the class. Worrying won't do you a bit of good. Be happy."

"Class? What class?"

"The class you're supposed to give tomorrow, after the interview. Didn't I tell you? *Mea culpa,* hon, *mea maxima culpa.* I've been uncharacteristically forgetful lately."

"But what will I do?"

"Relax," Louise said. "Just pick a subject and wing it."

"Wing it?"

"You know, open your mouth and see what comes out. Extemporize."

"But I always work from a prepared lecture."

Louise sighed. "All right. I'll tell you what. Last year I wrote an article on the Marshall Plan[4] that I got bored with and never published. You can read that."

Parroting what Louise had written seemed wrong to Mary, at first; then it occurred to her that she had been doing the same kind of thing for many years, and that this was not the time to get scruples. "Thanks," she said. "I appreciate it."

"Here we are," Louise said, and pulled into a circular drive with several cabins grouped around it. In two of the cabins lights were on; smoke drifted straight up from the chimneys. "This is the visitors' center. The college is another two miles thataway." Louise pointed down the road. "I'd invite you to stay at my house, but I'm spending the night with Jonathan and Ted is not good company these days. You would hardly recognize him."

She took Mary's bags from the trunk and carried them up the steps of a darkened cabin. "Look," she said, "they've laid a fire for you. All you have to do is light it." She stood in the middle of the room with her arms crossed and watched as Mary held a match under the kindling. "There," she said. "You'll be snugaroo in no time. I'd love to stay and chew the fat but I can't. You just get a good night's sleep and I'll see you in the morning."

Mary stood in the doorway and waved as Louise pulled out of the drive, spraying gravel. She filled her lungs, to taste the air: it was tart and clear. She could see the stars in their figurations, and the vague streams of light that ran among the stars.

She still felt uneasy about reading Louise's work as her own. It would be her first complete act of plagiarism. It would change her. It would make her less—how much less, she did not know. But what else could she do? She certainly couldn't "wing it." Words might fail her, and then what? Mary had a dread of silence. When she thought of silence she thought of drowning, as if it were a kind of water she could not swim in.

"I want this job," she said, and settled deep into her coat. It was cashmere and Mary had not worn it since moving to Oregon, because people there thought you were pretentious if you had on anything but a Pendleton shirt or, of course, raingear. She rubbed her cheek against the upturned collar and thought of a silver moon

4. Plan for rehabilitating European economies devastated by WW II, formulated by George Catlett Marshall (1880–1959), U.S. chief of staff.

shining through bare black branches, a white house with green shutters, red leaves falling in a hard blue sky.

Louise woke her a few hours later. She was sitting on the edge of the bed, pushing at Mary's shoulder and snuffling loudly. When Mary asked her what was wrong she said, "I want your opinion on something. It's very important. Do you think I'm womanly?"

Mary sat up. "Louise, can this wait?"

"No."

"Womanly?"

Louise nodded.

"You are very beautiful," Mary said, "and you know how to present yourself."

Louise stood and paced the room. "That son of a bitch," she said. She came back and stood over Mary. "Let's suppose someone said I have no sense of humor. Would you agree or disagree?"

"In some things you do. I mean, yes, you have a good sense of humor."

"What do you mean, 'in some things?' What kind of things?"

"Well, if you heard that someone had been killed in an unusual way, like by an exploding cigar, you would think that was funny."

Louise laughed.

"That's what I mean," Mary said.

Louise went on laughing. "Oh, Lordy," she said. "Now it's my turn to say something about you." She sat down beside Mary.

"Please," Mary said.

"Just one thing," Louise said.

Mary waited.

"You're trembling," Louise said. "I was just going to say—oh, forget it. Listen, do you mind if I sleep on the couch? I'm all in."

"Go ahead."

"Sure it's okay? You've got a big day tomorrow." She fell back on the sofa and kicked off her shoes. "I was just going to say, you should use some liner on those eyebrows of yours. They sort of disappear and the effect is disconcerting."

Neither of them slept. Louise chain-smoked cigarettes and Mary watched the coals burn down. When it was light enough that they could see each other Louise got up. "I'll send a student for you," she said. "Good luck."

The college looked the way colleges are supposed to look. Roger, the student assigned to show Mary around, explained that it was an exact copy of a college in England, right down to the gargoyles and stained-glass windows. It looked so much like a college that moviemakers sometimes used it as a set. *Andy Hardy Goes to*

College[5] had been filmed there, and every fall they had an Andy Hardy Goes to College Day, with raccoon coats and goldfish-swallowing contests.

Above the door of the Founder's Building was a Latin motto which, roughly translated, meant "God helps those who help themselves." As Roger recited the names of illustrious graduates Mary was struck by the extent to which they had taken this precept to heart. They had helped themselves to railroads, mines, armies, states; to empires of finance with outposts all over the world.

Roger took Mary to the chapel and showed her a plaque bearing the names of alumni who had been killed in various wars, all the way back to the Civil War. There were not many names. Here too, apparently, the graduates had helped themselves. "Oh yes," Roger said as they were leaving, "I forgot to tell you. The communion rail comes from some church in Europe where Charlemagne[6] used to go."

They went to the gymnasium, and the three hockey rinks, and the library, where Mary inspected the card catalogue, as though she would turn down the job if they didn't have the right books. "We have a little more time," Roger said as they went outside. "Would you like to see the power plant?"

Mary wanted to keep busy until the last minute, so she agreed.

Roger led her into the depths of the service building, explaining things about the machine, which was the most advanced in the country. "People think the college is really old-fashioned," he said, "but it isn't. They let girls come here now, and some of the teachers are women. In fact, there's a statute that says they have to interview at least one woman for each opening. There it is."

They were standing on an iron catwalk above the biggest machine Mary had ever beheld. Roger, who was majoring in Earth Sciences, said that it had been built from a design pioneered by a professor in his department. Where before he had been gabby Roger now became reverent. It was clear that for him this machine was the soul of the college, that the purpose of the college was to provide outlets for the machine. Together they leaned against the railing and watched it hum.

Mary arrived at the committee room exactly on time for her interview, but the room was empty. Her two books were on the table, along with a water pitcher and some glasses. She sat down and picked up one of the books. The binding cracked as she opened it. The pages were smooth, clean, unread. Mary turned to

5. Before and during WW II the series of Hardy Family films was extremely popular in the U.S. Andy Hardy was played by film star Mickey Rooney. 6. King of the Franks (742–814) and emperor of the Holy Roman Empire.

the first chapter, which began, "It is generally believed that . . ." How dull, she thought.

Nearly twenty minutes later Louise came in with several men. "Sorry we're late," she said. "We don't have much time so we'd better get started." She introduced Mary to the men, but with one exception the names and faces did not stay together. The exception was Dr. Howells, the department chairman, who had a porous blue nose and terrible teeth.

A shiny-faced man to Dr. Howells's right spoke first. "So," he said, "I understand you once taught at Brandon College."

"It was a shame that Brandon had to close," said a young man with a pipe in his mouth. "There is a place for schools like Brandon." As he talked the pipe wagged up and down.

"Now you're in Oregon," Dr. Howells said. "I've never been there. How do you like it?"

"Not very much," Mary said.

"Is that right?" Dr. Howells leaned toward her. "I thought everyone liked Oregon. I hear it's very green."

"That's true," Mary said.

"I suppose it rains a lot," he said.

"Nearly every day."

"I wouldn't like that," he said, shaking his head. "I like it dry. Of course it snows here, and you have your rain now and then, but it's a *dry* rain. Have you ever been to Utah? There's a state for you. Bryce Canyon. The Mormon Tabernacle Choir."

"Dr. Howells was brought up in Utah," said the young man with the pipe.

"It was a different place altogether in those days," Dr. Howells said. "Mrs. Howells and I have always talked about going back when I retire, but now I'm not so sure."

"We're a little short on time," Louise said.

"And here I've been going on and on," Dr. Howells said. "Before we wind things up, is there anything you want to tell us?"

"Yes. I think you should give me the job." Mary laughed when she said this, but no one laughed back, or even looked at her. They all looked away. Mary understood then that they were not really considering her for the position. She had been brought here to satisfy a rule. She had no hope.

The men gathered their papers and shook hands with Mary and told her how much they were looking forward to her class. "I can't get enough of the Marshall Plan," Dr. Howells said.

"Sorry about that," Louise said when they were alone. "I didn't think it would be so bad. That was a real bitcheroo."

"Tell me something," Mary said. "You already know who you're going to hire, don't you?"

Louise nodded.

"Then why did you bring me here?"

Louise began to explain about the statute and Mary interrupted. "I know all that. But why me? Why did you pick *me*?"

Louise walked to the window. She spoke with her back to Mary. "Things haven't been going very well for old Louise," she said. "I've been unhappy and I thought you might cheer me up. You used to be so funny, and I was sure you would enjoy the trip—it didn't cost you anything, and it's pretty this time of year with the leaves and everything. Mary, you don't know the things my parents did to me. And Ted is no barrel of laughs either. Or Jonathan, the son of a bitch. I deserve some love and friendship but I don't get any." She turned and looked at her watch. "It's almost time for your class. We'd better go."

"I would rather not give it. After all, there's not much point, is there?"

"But you *have* to give it. That's part of the interview." Louise handed Mary a folder. "All you have to do is read this. It isn't much, considering all the money we've laid out to get you here."

Mary followed Louise down the hall to the lecture room. The professors were sitting in the front row with their legs crossed. They smiled and nodded at Mary. Behind them the room was full of students, some of whom had spilled over into the aisles. One of the professors adjusted the microphone to Mary's height, crouching down as he went to the podium and back as though he would prefer not to be seen.

Louise called the room to order. She introduced Mary and gave the subject of the lecture. But Mary had decided to wing it after all. Mary came to the podium unsure of what she would say; sure only that she would rather die than read Louise's article. The sun poured through the stained glass onto the people around her, painting their faces. Thick streams of smoke from the young professor's pipe drifted through a circle of red light at Mary's feet, turning crimson and twisting like flames.

"I wonder how many of you know," she began, "that we are in the Long House,[7] the ancient domain of the Five Nations of the Iroquois."

Two professors looked at each other.

"The Iroquois were without pity," Mary said. "They hunted people down with clubs and arrows and spears and nets, and blowguns made from elder stalks. They tortured their captives, sparing no one, not even the little children. They took scalps and practiced cannibalism and slavery. Because they had no pity they

7. Communal Indian dwelling, in actuality a wooden frame covered with bark.

became powerful, so powerful that no other tribe dared to oppose them. They made the other tribes pay tribute, and when they had nothing more to pay the Iroquois attacked them."

Several of the professors began to whisper. Dr. Howells was saying something to Louise, and Louise was shaking her head.

"In one of their raids," Mary said, "they captured two Jesuit priests, Jean de Brébeuf and Gabriel Lalement.[8] They covered Lalement with pitch and set him on fire in front of Brébeuf. When Brébeuf rebuked them they cut off his lips and put a burning iron down his throat. They hung a collar of red-hot hatchets around his neck, and poured boiling water over his head. When he continued to preach to them they cut strips of flesh from his body and ate them before his eyes. While he was still alive they scalped him and cut open his breast and drank his blood. Later, their chief tore out Brébeuf's heart and ate it, but just before he did this Brébeuf spoke to them one last time. He said—"

"That's enough!" yelled Dr. Howells, jumping to his feet.

Louise stopped shaking her head. Her eyes were perfectly round.

Mary had come to the end of her facts. She did not know what Brébeuf had said. Silence rose up around her; just when she thought she would go under and be lost in it she heard someone whistling in the hallway outside, trilling the notes like a bird, like many birds.

"Mend your lives," she said. "You have deceived yourselves in the pride of your hearts, and the strength of your arms. Though you soar aloft like the eagle, though your nest is set among the stars, thence I will bring you down, says the Lord.[9] Turn from power to love. Be kind. Do justice. Walk humbly."

Louise was waving her arms. "Mary!" she shouted.

But Mary had more to say, much more; she waved back at Louise, then turned off her hearing aid so that she would not be distracted again.

8. The two most famous martyrs among the Jesuit missionaries in North America. Tortured and killed by the Iroquois in 1649. **9.** Obadiah 1: 4.